PAROUSIA

DIAMONDS IN THE SKY – BOOK ONE

LANCE S A NIELSEN

For Jennifer Watson (Skinner)

Were it not for you, I would not be here typing this now. May angels be with you, always.

And Jason and Donal, you both know why.

CONTENTS

DIAMONDS IN THE SKY - PAROUSIA

FOREWORD

'The world has never been more divided...'

To summarise in a few short sentences the breadth and depth of my emotional motivations for writing this story is not an easy task. The phrase written above, those seven words, are something I would hear spoken time and again over the year of 2017, (and indeed more recently in 2018) not just among my friends but spoken among strangers in conversations that I would overhear in buses, on trains, on the underground (subway) and on the streets, bars and pubs of London.

You don't need to be on any particular side of politics to know that the chasm between the rich and poor in our society is bigger than it has ever been. You do not need to be an environmental scientist to know that the way humanity conducts itself and treats our planet is simply unsustainable. You don't need to understand the rule of law to know that the function of any national government should be to protect its people rather than serve the personal interests of its leaders and their associated business interests.

Divisions in humanity for reasons of religion, race, sexual orientation, ethnic backgrounds, culture and affluence are more keenly felt on the world stage than ever before. As a society we appear to be taking steps in the wrong direction. Instead of uniting us as a people to achieve great strides in the aim of a excelling all of humanity, world leaders often appear more concerned with funding wars and consolidating their personal assets because they know the planets resources are only decades away from exhaustion. These words are not Science Fiction. These are the words that describe the reality of our earth in a few, all be it somewhat broad, brush-strokes. It is within this storm of contemporary colliding human conflicts that I decided to write this book. I wanted to write something that would feel relatable and accessible to the widest audience possible but I also wanted it to be rich with humour and where possible believable. I wanted to put the reader in the shoes of this eclectic mix of culturally diverse characters and have them ask themselves what choices they would make. To that end I felt from the get go the story would be better served from a multi perspective of several different characters some of whom would be already connected or eventually destined to meet as the story unfolded.

Even though the indisputable arrival, worldwide of two hundred colossal alien ships formed the back bone of the story I didn't want to write some kind of post-apocalyptic or alien invasion narrative. I wanted the dilemmas of my characters to be something the reader could relate to. What if an alien presence did arrive on the earth that was so huge that it was impossible to ignore? What if the governments of the world had no answers to give us at all as to why they were here and none were immediately forthcoming? It is against this backdrop that I introduce the reader to seven different characters from all around the world. Each of these people will have things about them which I hope will both delight and annoy you in equal measure, much like most all of us. They're not perfect human beings although some have more redeemable qualities than others like 'Ryan' for example who at the beginning of our story has few, if any, positive traits at all. But the most horrid characters are always the most fun to write! Each character has been inspired in part, by at least one or two people I have met in my lifetime. This brings a degree truth to each of them that stems from a place of reality. You might not like them all, you might not be happy with some of the portrayals but I can assure people just like them do exist in the literal rather than just the literary world. You might even recognise something of yourself in someone you meet along the way.

You'll note this book is a fair length. I can assure you it was not my intention not to overwrite it, in fact it was edited down three times and cut down by some one hundred and fifty plus pages. It was however always intended to look and feel like an epic because that is what your about to start reading now, an epic story. You hold the first part in your hands (Or possibly on your kindle or other device) and it is a story that will not only determine the fate of all the characters that you're going to meet but the fate of the entire human race as well.

As I type this I am already well into the second volume of Diamonds in the Sky which I hope to complete some time in 2018. I hope you will join me on the entire journey to discover what fate awaits the characters you will come to know and some cases no doubt, hate.

I thank you in advance for purchasing (or borrowing) this book which has been the result of many months of tireless work, late nights of re-writes and more re-writes all done in the knowledge that I have no idea how many people will eventually read it or how it will be received or even of course, if it has any merit. But if you have enjoyed it then no writer can ask for more than that. Do then please spread the word, join my mailing list to receive unique updates and special offers and check out the website, Facebook and Twitter pages all listed below. I welcome correspondence from fans and am indebted to all those who spend their hard earned pennies to purchase this humble offering.

Finally I would like to say some words about my friend Jennifer Watson to whom I dedicate this book. Jennifer was an actress, singer, mother to her beautiful daughter Savannah and wife to her devoted husband Gregg. I cannot even begin to imagine their sense of loss. Jennifer and I had worked together on a couple of stage productions many years ago and despite the second of these being extremely stressful at the time, had remained good friends, even when she moved to New York. Jennifer was someone who personally intervened one evening on a night back in the year 2000 when I on the verge of doing something really stupid. She stayed on the phone with me for eight hours, talking with me until the sun came up, assuring me my life was worth living. Had it not been for her kindness, I would not be here now. There is no explanation for when the best are taken from us far to early and her passing left a huge hole in many people's lives, but I know she is still present, keeping an eye on all of us who knew her and urging us all to continue forward with our creative endeavours. To that, I have persisted with mine, as I always promised her I would.

Jennifer this one is for you.

Lance S A Nielsen November 2017

If you enjoyed this novel please do tell your friends about it and if you could review it on Amazon and if you can please write a comment on the books website, I would be most grateful. You can also vote for your favourite character on the site. Please do also subscribe to our mailing list at the website below for exclusive updates and promotions. If you enjoyed the novel, do take a picture of yourself with it and send it to us! We would love to hear from you.

www.diamondsintheskybookseries.com
facebook.com/diamondsintheskybookseries/
Follow me on twitter @LanceNielsenWD

ACKNOWLEDGMENTS

This book was written at a time in my life when both personal and professional pressures had never been more keenly felt upon me and consequently the journey has not been an easy one. A huge number of people supported me during this process, far too many to mention here, if I was not able to include you, you certainly know who you are.

First and foremost I must thank **Georgina Blackledge Leslie**, an actress friend of mine who offered to read my manuscript as I wrote it and unlike so many others didn't renege on that promise. No sooner had I sent her the first three chapters she had devoured them and her enthusiasm for the story and the characters continually spurned me along. Several other individuals provided me with invaluable insight both into the writing process and also the other aspects of this industry who included my fellow writers **Callie**, **Anthony Lowery**, **Mark Gardner** (Who also has given me countless tech support) and **Frank Tayell**, the latter two with their unwavering patience and constant advice was vital to bringing this book to publication. **Lelia Dewji** was also supportive in giving me a ton of advice and understood what I was trying to achieve with this series. The **Jake Francis** 9000 tech support system for his never ending assistance on various things including the website and his friendship.

Additional thanks to my friend **David Freedman** who works for Waterstones and my good friend **Zoey Dixon** who runs several Libraries in South London which are under constant threat of cuts or worse, closure. The two brothers at my local supermarket (Cheers guys) Others who gave me great emotional support and encouragement throughout the creative process (even if they did not realise it) include **Alyson Achieng, Sharon**

Sorrentino, Martin Hodgson, Matthew & Nadia Holmes, James Bushe, Patrick Ryder, Marc Zammit, Clare Hardy, Amber Blake, Alex Tabrizi, Christine Rivett, Alyson 'Wiggles' Stanford, Marcus 'Wingnut' Davies, Carly Houston, Neal Ward, Mike Beckingham, Danny Webb, Danny Rampling, Phil Davis, Rupert Penry Jones, Suzette Pluck, Shannon Cooke, John Kranz & family, Alison Bazaar and Alan & Linda Marques.

Another person who I met recently as I sprinted towards the finish line of this text was actor **Dennis Lawson** whose work I have admired for many years and he was most kind and encouraging about my efforts. I must also mention **Donal Logue** another fellow creative who is constantly supportive to both me and my work and always encouraging. This man has the kindest of hearts.

Then there is my frequent collaborator and good friend **Jason Flemyng**, a man who has literally more love in his heart than he has time to give it out. I have been fortunate enough to work with Jason five times now and I cannot say enough kind words about this individual who has been more supportive to me personally and given more time to assist my career, needlessly, than anyone else I know.

As a huge creative source of inspiration to create something epic I'll also mention film maker **Peter Jackson** and his collaborators **Fran Walsh** and **Philipa Boyens** none of whom sadly I have ever met. Of this trio I will simply just say their vision for a certain epic film trilogy gave me a light in my life during a time when all other lights had gone out. I shall be sending all of those above a physical copy of this book as soon as I am holding one.

The various colourful electric mix of characters and fellow writers I met and have still yet to meet at London's Science Fiction and Fantasy Club. Socials (And pub) meetings, especially those who have made me feel so welcome (Taz & Company) which has provided me with a much needed social circle away from the industry I normally populate and the writers I have met as a result which have included Science Fiction writers **Dave Hutchinson & James Swallow**.

I must also thank all of the cast and crew who worked on the two short films to promote the book series especially actors **Wil Johnson, Faith Knight, Dean Maskell, Ascandor Abbas, Angela Dixon & Tony Fadil**, the latter of whom effectively produced both shorts with me. **Richard 'The Walrus' Roberts**, **Christine Rivett** and others. Lastly I will thank **Jennifer Watson** and her friends and family. A truly special person, she will never be forgotten.

Proof Readers Elinor d. Perry-Smith, Alyson Achieng and Sharon Sorrentino

Cover - Design by Jeff Brown, graded by Richard Oakes – actress Angela Dixon portrays character Diana Morrow. Additional photography by Siobhan Doran, additional thanks to Eva & Erin Reynolds.

DIAMONDS IN THE SKY - PAROUSIA

PART ONE - THE FIRST DAY

CHAPTER I

If someone had said to me "I'm going to change the entire world in five years." – Well, I never would have believed them unless they were Jesus. I haven't met Jesus yet, but I do feel like the world has been touched by God. It was as though the world had been given another chance.

It was the day that everything changed for us, but if you ask me, the world has needed a big change for a very, very, long time.

From the diary of Blessing Amaka, Fife, Scotland, April 1st, entry made 5 years after the date of Parousia.

DIANA

U.S HIGHWAY 50, NEVADA, UNITED STATES OF
AMERICA – APRIL 2ND, 11AM

The day had begun with one act of kindness from a stranger, but now Diana found herself wishing for another. Clueless, she stared down at the engine, the acrid scent of burning metal and grease filling her nostrils. She was never good with cars; the landscape of her Toyota with its many connecting parts was entirely alien to her. Car mechanics was not her forte. She had only looked inside at an actual car engine on one previous occasion, and that was when Jackson Howard was mounting her from behind with all the finesse of an elephant, across the hood of his Dodge Charger. This had been the moment when Jules, her first-born, had been conceived. Her daughter now sat fidgeting with her phone on the backseat while Diana's youngest, Jack, was sleeping soundly alongside his sister, thankfully. Diana took a step back, the steam and smoke irritating her eyes.

"Can you fix it, Mom?" Jules asked, hanging her head out of the back window.

"I don't know. Do you have a signal?" Diana already knew the answer as her own phone also had zero reception. Jules shook her head. This was beginning to feel like a scene from a bad horror movie. There was a reason they called Highway 50 the loneliest road in America, because on some parts of it you could drive for hours without seeing a single soul. Perhaps some handsome mechanic would come along and save the day, fix the car and give them a ride. No. Handsome mechanics had been known to get her in trouble, the sort of trouble they would subsequently leave her to deal with later on her own. Diana Morrow cut an image that was pleasing to the eye for any man and, as it turned out, more than one woman, who knew? At a slim five-foot-seven, she'd always managed to turn heads back in high school. Her hair, which she had tied back in a ponytail for reasons of comfort over design, was just the right shade of light ginger to be considered strawberry blonde. It fell down past her shoulders and she would occasionally tuck it in the back of her denim shirt, until it tickled her neck and made her sweat. She was pleased she had at least had the foresight to pack the car full of food and supplies. Two large bottles of water sat next to a cooler box in the back and she had stocked up on some fruit and candy when they took a break at a small gas station at a place called Middlegate about five miles back. Less than an hour ago they had been sitting inside the small diner. The owner, Anita, a loud and imposing woman, all frantic hair and layers of makeup, had recommended ice cream for the kids and forewarned that her establishment was the last stop for quite a while.

"You're lucky the real heat of the season hasn't kicked in yet, otherwise you'd cook out there on the road for sure! You got good air conditioning? You have to have good air conditioning out here on these roads, yes ma'am! Rolling the windows down doesn't work in this place, no ma'am it don't. That just don't cut it! Does it now, Forest?"

"No Anita, it sure don't, not on these roads and not with this sun!" came a male voice from the diner's kitchen. Diana had strained to see him behind the old-school kitchen units and the vast block of a metal fridge that partly obscured his body. His arms had leathery skin that sagged between the joints and looked almost grey in colour.

"What y'all be taking two young children out on this road for anyway?" Anita said, without pausing for an answer. "Them poor critters gonna cook on that backseat if you're not careful! Is it a camping trip? I bet it's a camping trip. There be some right nice places to camp when you get nearer Lake Tahoe. Is that where you're going? I bet that's where you're going now! Forest, he goes fishing up there every fall, don't you Forest?"

"Yes Ma'am, I do...," came the reply from the leathery man in the kitchen. Diana gave up trying to respond to Anita's questions. They seemed to turn into rambling statements that went on as long as Highway 50 itself. Forest began to tell tales of mighty fish he had caught against the most insurmountable odds, but Anita cut him short.

They took a booth by the window and decided on fries, burgers and milkshakes all round. Anita came to take the order. Diana guessed she was nearly sixty years of age. She removed a sharp pencil from her hair bun in a well-rehearsed singular move and was ready with pad in hand. Her red painted fingernails glared with a life of their own; they matched the shade on her lips, which formed a warm, if slightly crooked smile.

In a heartbeat, the woman was away barking orders toward the kitchen, returning with sodas and a jug of nice cold water for the table. Diana had clasped the side of it with her hand and then swept the damp of the condensation from the glass through her hair. She could see her son, Jack, was tired and would soon sleep once they were back on the road. She had been blessed twice in this life and both of them sat across from her at the table. They were a reminder to be thankful whenever she felt life was overwhelming her and God, if it didn't just keep on trying. Jack, with his light tanned skin and short dark hair, was going to turn into a handsome young man. He had the looks of the father he was never going to meet, whereas Jules had Diana's features. As Diana observed her daughter gazing at the pictures of the ice creams on the menu, her heart cried out inside, wanting all the things for her children that she had been deprived of herself—a college education and a life with meaning. Not one like hers, which had felt like constantly moving deckchairs on *The Titanic* as it had slipped away beneath her. The food arrived and they all ate greedily in silence. A sign more of their hunger than good manners, yet despite being on the road for two days the kids had been remarkably well behaved, not complaining once about a thing. They had been so good when things had been so bad, it brought a tear to her eye just thinking about it.

She was completely lost in her own thoughts looking through the window, when Anita placed the cheque on the table. Two trucking rigs pulled up noisily outside, and their owners came in to occupy the bar stools up front with cries of "Hey Anita! Hey Forest!" and soon, familiar friendly banter filled the air.

Diana opened her purse to the paltry contents of half a dozen small bills and a handful of coins. Their lunch was twelve dollars fifty and she had already spent thirty dollars on supplies in the mini mart, plus another thirty on gas. Fallon Station was the next stop, and they were all good until then but she wasn't sure if they would make it all the way to Lake Tahoe today. She decided she had better call ahead.

"Be good and wait here for Mommy for a minute, okay?"

Jack and Jules nodded their heads.

"How's that shake, pretty good huh?" They nodded their heads again.

"I'll be right back, I'm just going to call Uncle Danny," Diana said almost apologetically in Anita's direction, looking for her to keep an eye momentarily on the children. Anita smiled back with a nod. Diana didn't know it, but all these years working in a diner had made Anita a very accurate judge of character. She waddled over to the table where the kids slurped away on the last remnants of their milkshakes.

"Aren't you just the best behaved children in the world? I think you've been so good I'm going to give you some extra candy. How would you like that?"

Jules abruptly spoke. "If Mommy says its okay, we will have to ask her first."

"Well I'll just do that for you then."

Diana stood outside in the warm air, phone in hand. Anita was right, it wasn't as hot as it could have been. She had that much to be thankful for. She scrolled through her list of contacts until she hit "Brother". The phone rang for what seemed like an eternity then finally a voicemail kicked in. "Hey this is Danny, you know what to do..."

"Hey Danny, it's me. We should hit Lake Tahoe by tonight, at least I hope so. I'm on the 50. It's beautiful here, peaceful, giving me a lot of time to think, which is what you said I needed so you were right about that. Anyway okay I'll...," The tone cut her off and gave her the option to re-record that message. She decided not to take it. Best to get what you want to say right the first time. If only her life had been like that. Diana came back inside to find the bill had gone from the table only to be replaced with a handwritten note on a napkin. She slid into the booth and noticed two packets of candies on the table.

"The lady said these were for the road. She said they were on the house. Does that mean they live on our house?" Jules asked.

Jack spoke for the first time in several hours. "We don't have a house."

Diana felt something inside her break and it took every ounce of mental strength she possessed not to show it. She could have just let the floods of tears come there and then, but she had already cried once in front of her children and had vowed not to do it again. Then she saw it written on the napkin. The words, written by Anita she assumed. Who else would it have been? Truckers were not famous for giving out kindness for free.

Sometimes we all need a fresh start hon, this one is on the house. Keep it to yourself now!

She looked up with gratitude but Anita was busy taking an order elsewhere and seemed, perhaps deliberately, not to notice her. She found a pen in her purse and scribbled a note of her own — *Thank you, this is the tip.* Leaving a five-dollar bill on the table, she got up and headed to the exit. She tried to catch Anita's eye but she was still busy. Anita had seen her but wasn't letting on. She smiled as she collected the tip, looking out at the single mother putting the kids in the car.

Diana had felt good leaving the truck stop at Middlegate; the act of kindness from a stranger one of those little surprises that humanity can occasionally throw your way. That good feeling had died along with the engine of her car. They were truly in the middle of nowhere and she knew she was entirely dependent on a stranger offering them a lift to the next town where she could find a tow truck. Not that she could afford the towing fee plus the costs of getting the car fixed. Of course, strangers giving you a lift on a lonely highway was generally never a good idea. It would have to be a family or an old couple but how long before someone suitable elected to stop? Ahead of her the road west stretched off endlessly into the valley. The horizon was cut across by a series of low-lying hills beyond which lay a second range of mountains, their tips capped with snow. It was a dramatic sight and one that she would have appreciated more if they weren't stuck here unintentionally.

It was at moments like this that she wished she hadn't quit smoking, but then smoking was a habit that the financially destitute could ill afford. A few miles back she had seen a turn off with sign for the *Pony Express Memorial*. She considered walking back there but quickly decided it was too far. It was, after all, exactly that—a memorial for the Pony Express and was unlikely to have a tow truck or gas station. She guessed she was about twelve miles east of Fallon. Too far to walk with the kids and she couldn't leave them alone in the car. Their only option was to wait. Someone was bound to come along soon, weren't they?

"Look Mom, a rabbit!" Jules cried, from the back seat. Diana saw the fleeting shape of the animal darting off in the scrubland to her left. Then a similar movement caught her eye to the right and then another and another.

"Lots of rabbits!" Jules got more excited. Her daughter had always wanted one. Assuming they got the car fixed it would be "When can we get a rabbit Mom?" all the way to Danny's. You could bet on that. If only she could bet on winning the Lottery. Hadn't some old couple in their eighties won seventy million dollars last month? What was an old couple in their eighties going to do with seventy million dollars? She couldn't really complain; she didn't, after all, play the Lottery and who was to say that an eighty-year-old couple was any less deserving of the money than she was. Her mother always said to her…

Her thoughts were interrupted by further signs of movement left and right of the road, more rabbits, and, she thought, one or two other animals. A screech from the sky made her look up to see flocks of birds heading east and disappearing over the low hills behind her.

"Why are there so many rabbits, Mom?" Jules asked, her head craning out of the passenger window.

"I don't know baby, maybe there's a fire up ahead?"

A thunderclap broke through the air announcing a military fighter jet, bolting across the sky heading west. Diana was trying to focus on its fleeting shape, when it was followed by two more in its wake. More rabbits bolted past her left and right. Diana was so busy staring up at the sky one minute and either side of the road the next, that she didn't see the snake crawling past her open-toe sandals until she felt its smooth scaled skin wriggling over her own. She screamed and jumped away before she even knew what it was.

"Mom, I think you should get back in the car," Jules said.

She looked at the tarmac on the road, and it was covered with moving shapes. Snakes, scorpions, spiders; three of the words that were the least favourite of Diana's on any episode of Animal Kingdom. She put the hood back down and took a deep breath.

"Yes baby, I think you're right."

Watching her step, she gingerly retreated back into the car, closing the door and checking the backseat. Jules was already winding her window up and Jack was wide awake, mesmerised by the exodus of creatures. The animals ran, scurried, slithered and flew, in the brush and on the road, totally oblivious of her and the children and it seemed, each other. Diana wondered what could be the cause of this spontaneous mass evacuation of creatures—it had to be a fire somewhere up ahead and now she was stuck here right in its path, without a moving vehicle.

"Damn, what is this? Is the rain coming, Noah?" she said.

"What do you mean, Mom?" asked Jules.

"It's from the bible, hon. Like Noah and the Ark that you learned at school!"

"Maybe that's the Ark then?" Jules pointed up between the seats past her face. Diana gave her daughter's hair a ruffle and looked for something to give the kids to occupy them. Hopefully someone would come along, and now with a fire up ahead she could plead with them for a lift, or perhaps the fire department would arrive... then she turned and saw it through the windshield, just hanging there in the air dominating the mountains below it to the west.

Like a diamond in the sky.

BLESSING

B lessing had been terrified of moving to Aberdeen. She had never liked the cold weather in England, and her previous stay in Birmingham was made up of more grey and rainy days than she could ever recall experiencing elsewhere. Her memories of Africa grew fewer over time but she treasured every one. Thinking back to those days as a child, playing by the river with the other children from her village and running up to the rare sight of an *Oyinbo* visiting the new clinic that had been set up back then by the United Nations. That was the first time she'd ever seen a white man, and to a child, they seemed to represent one thing; a man who brought sweets for them to eat. The world had seemed so small back then.

"Okay, you can get dressed," said Doctor Dutch as he put away his stethoscope; the cold metallic impression it had left on her back still sent little shivers across her skin. Everything in this country was always so cold! She went and got dressed behind the medical curtain as her doctor returned to his desk and began to scribble some notes.

"How are you getting on with your new medication?" he asked as she struggled to pull her jumper over her head. Blessing had recently had long braids put in her hair, they trailed right down to the small of her back and required some negotiation when getting dressed. There was a long mirror on the wall next to the examination bed and she took a moment to glance at her body. She had always been small, never growing above five foot one, unlike her four sisters—all of whom had towered above her back home, even when they were children. But what she lacked in height she made up for with an ample bust and behind, having what her friends would refer to as a traditional African shape, or, in at least one case, "A banging body."

Her father always told her, "Good things come in small packages." Her skin was dark, darker than any other African she had seen in Aberdeen, and she hadn't seen that many in the last six months of living here. The only one she had had a conversation with was her hairdresser Linda, the only other Nigerian woman she had met in the city. Linda was a talker, like most hairdressers in Blessing's experience, so she hadn't wanted to get too familiar with her. Aberdeen was not short on immigrants but they mostly appeared to come from Poland or Ireland. Her working hours as a cleaner did not lend themselves well to exploring such social circles, or indeed any socialising at all. People from different cultures mixing while not unheard of appeared to be uncommon in Aberdeen. How ridiculous that was, but she understood the need for people to congregate with what they felt was familiar and comfortable, and she was still finding her own feet in this vibrant, but cold, coastal city.

"Any problems? Did you miss any doses?" her Doctor asked.

"Just one, I think. I worked late and forgot to take it with me. I took it again the following morning!" That was silly but surely just missing one dose wouldn't make that much difference, would it?

"I'm sure that'll be fine. You can miss the odd one or two. Obviously don't make a habit of it. So, no side effects this time?'

"No, these are much better for me." Her last medication had been horrendous, giving her nightmares for months.

"All your counts look great, nothing to be concerned about there." He had a warm smile.

She pulled her jeans up over her best pair of underwear—the ones with the print of the butterfly on the back, which rode just above her bum, peering above her Levis. She got the idea from seeing someone wear them at the Notting Hill Carnival in London, when she and her best friend Susan had gone four years ago. He was a doctor, yes, and certainly he saw naked women all the time, but she wasn't going to turn up to the surgery and have a handsome man examine her in her granny pants. If this was the only man who was going to see her half-naked then she had to at least look good. Ah, Patrick, why aren't you single? As he studiously scribbled his notes into her folder, she saw the photograph of his two children, in the same place it always was when she came in for her check-ups, sitting next to the stuffed bear on the windowsill. There was no photograph of his wife but he still had his wedding ring on, and it was the first thing she took note of every time she came in. Yes, it was still there. Oh well. For a single Nigerian woman living in Aberdeen, meeting single men wasn't easy and she found it so hard to understand how the local people talked. Her English had always been good, but when she moved up here, it felt like a completely different language that everyone else was speaking. Patrick wasn't Scottish, he was from the South West, somewhere near Bristol. He did tell her where but she had forgotten and she didn't want to appear foolish by asking him again.

"How are your children doing?" she asked, trying to make the question sound casual. Was it right to be that personal? Of course it was, Patrick was a human being after all.

"Oh God, they're almost grown up now! Jamie has just started university down in Durham and George is in secondary school. Makes you wonder where all the time went, doesn't it?" He typed something into the computer and began to write out her prescription.

"It's not too late for you to have children you know. You're only thirty-two. Still plenty of time," he said.

"Perhaps you know someone you can introduce me to?" She sounded stupid and desperate. Patrick returned a meagre smile as she coyly bowed her head.

"Sadly, I am just a regular doctor, not a dating doctor. Doesn't everyone meet on the internet these days?"

"I did try that, and I found there weren't really many genuine people on there. I tried the other websites for people in my situation, but that was even worse!"

Dating sites in her experience were full of married men wanting sex. After three dates of men always turning the conversation to, "How much are you into anal?" she realised internet dating was probably not the place for her.

"Yes, a friend of mine said the same. Well, don't give up. Prince Charming or Miss Charming could be just around the corner. So I'll see you again in six months. Take this downstairs to the pharmacy and don't forget to book an appointment on the way out. You'd be surprised how fast they fill up."

Miss Charming. Did he think she was gay?

"I guess you're very popular here!" God, did she really say that? She was actually flirting with her doctor. Stop it now, Blessing! She couldn't help it. She'd always had a bit of a crush on him. The right age, and he had a good job—though, of course, she couldn't help wondering how many different pussies the man had seen. Of course he had seen plenty. That was his job.

"I am afraid it's more a case of our National Health Service bursting at the seams, but we struggle on!" Patrick closed her folder and tucked his pen back behind his ear. Their business together was done. A quick check in the mirror and she was out the door. He was right; it took three suggested dates to get an appointment.

In reception, she noticed how much busier the clinic had become since she had arrived earlier that morning. She was one of only three women there, and she was fairly confident that the other men attending that morning were gay. Straight men tended not to dress as well, nor sit with their legs crossed, nor had multiple ear piercings, and in her experience, gay men at the clinic normally had between one and three of those attributes. She had certainly talked to enough of them before she realised they were gay to avoid any further embarrassing romantic efforts in that regard. Her previous clinic in Birmingham had the same-looking men in the waiting room, only with different designer shirts. She thought the same company must employ several of them all over the country, as she saw that same logo *Alpha Industries* on so many different jackets. Occasionally, she would see another African woman at the clinic. Normally younger than her and doing the same thing she would always do: hide in a corner, avoiding eye contact with anyone, especially people who might be from the same country or, God forbid, the same tribe or, even worse, attend the same church. Connecting with people was hard in a country in which you had no roots. Connecting with someone in a Sexual Health Clinic was even harder, though it didn't seem to be such a problem for some of the gay men.

She walked outside to the sounds of city traffic and the dull grey tones of the surrounding towering architecture. Old Gothic buildings mixed with drab modern ones gave this part of the city an inconsistent feel. The cold wind whipping between the gaps in the buildings caused her to readjust the scarf on her neck as she turned on to Frederick Street. Even her extra layers never quite kept out that bitter chill from the North Sea. She crossed the road and turned onto Beach Boulevard, the busy two-lane carriageway that lived up to its name, leading to the Aberdeen seafront, but the beach there was like no beach she had ever seen, at least not before she had arrived in the UK. She spotted the number 15 bus coming up to the roundabout. The stop was just ahead of her and although she didn't even need to go that way, something impulsively made her run for it. She just decided she wanted to go anywhere but home today, where nothing but the most mundane of daily tasks awaited her. The weather wasn't the worst, the sky was just the standard perpetual state of grey that clung above the city threatening never to depart. Holding her woolly hat to her head with one hand and clutching her purse to her body with the other, she ran toward the bus, thinking she was going to miss it as there was no one at the stop to halt it. The bus sailed past then it abruptly braked to a halt just past the stop and the doors opened. She quickened her pace to reach it. Perhaps the driver—a man—had seen her, had felt a connection like in the movies and this would be the moment they would meet as she stepped up to use her pass. Their eyes would lock and he would know she was the one for him. He would take her for dinner, somewhere romantic, maybe a weekend in Edinburgh. She always wanted to go there and see the castle she kept hearing so much about. He might be Kenyan or Ghanaian—hell, he could even be a Tanzanian—as long as he was Christian. Forgive me, Lord. She arrived at the bus desperately out of breath, looking straight up into the eyes of a grey haired overweight pale pink Scotsman.

"Would ye hurry up noo, I'm running late as it is!" he barked.

Today would not be that day. She fumbled with her purse as she struggled to find her bus pass.

"Dinnae worry lass, this one is on me. Take ya seat noo." The driver shut the doors and began to pull away down the road, swearing at another vehicle who hadn't given way as he pulled out.

"Look where ye going you fookin' bampot!"

She took a seat normally reserved for older people a few feet back from the cabin, giving her a partial view of him. He looked in his mid-fifties, with his hair all slicked back by a heavy gel in the style of a film star. This man was no Leonardo DiCaprio though. His nose was like an overgrown vegetable from her father's gardening patch in their compound back home, his skin as red as a radish apart from his fingers, which were yellow with the stains of cigarette smoke. Ah, God no, she couldn't be with a man who smoked, not even one who went to church. She stared out of the window and thought about the rest of her day, which consisted of going home, reheating her stew for one and watching her soaps, before prayers and rising again at four a.m. to do her cleaning job. Her cramped one-room bedsit felt claustrophobic and was not a place of joy for her. She dreaded sharing the shower at the end of the hallway, the drain of which always seemed to be blocked with hair that was not her own. The bus trundled along and turned right on to the seafront past the Nobles Family Arcade and Amusement Park. The buildings here were unusually low prefabricated structures and nothing like the boastful structures she had seen during that day trip to Brighton on the south coast. They were grand regal affairs with white columns and rooms with balconies, swish hotels, sprinkled with bars and places of entertainment. The Aberdeen Esplanade was far less ambitious. Its low level concrete structures housing arcades and burger bars were occasionally interrupted by a bit of Sixties décor. The only thing to rise above these humble urban offerings was the Ferris wheel belonging to the same family-run arcade. Blessing had never graced the place with her presence. She didn't approve of gambling and it didn't seem to attract the nicest of people, at least not from what she could observe from the street. Further along, a few newer restaurant chains had moved in to capitalise on the summer's regional trade. The gaudy neon signage of *Frankie and Benny's* and *Bella Italia* rudely made their franchises known, but the seaside trade appeared very quiet at this time of year, though she couldn't imagine why anyone would choose to holiday here.

Small family run restaurants had become an endangered species in this country and she had yet to try a local dish. Everything seemed to be either from America or the Far East. Asian or Indian food and burgers. Where were the Scottish delicacies? She was not impressed with English food and even less impressed with ordinary Scottish cuisine. What was this Haggis she had heard about? Some people told her it was a pie, someone else said it was a wild beast that lived out in the Highlands, but that man had been drinking, accosting her in the street and then insisting on having a conversation with her about where she was from, and the United Kingdom's policy on immigration. She turned her head in the direction of the sea. How she missed the African coast with its warm breezes and the smell of fresh roasted chicken being cooked on the side of the road. Nothing here tasted or smelled the same as home.

Lying opposite to the arcades was the beach with its sand, a vague dirty shade of yellow, broken up by wooden breakers, dripping with seaweed that clung to the wood like a child holding onto a parent. At least the beach here had sand. Her previous trip to Brighton was her first experience of the coast in the United Kingdom. She had rushed down to the beach only to realise it was in fact made up of tiny razor sharp stones. Walking on it barefoot was an exercise in futility, making her wonder what the Lord's purpose for such a place was. As to her own purpose, that was a question she had been frequently asking but the Lord had given her no answers. As she dwelled on that thought the bus slammed to a halt. Blessing's head banged into the protective rail on the seat in front, and she fell back in a daze with the most excruciating pain. All the passengers had been similarly propelled and one fell into the aisle. A cacophony of swearing in Scottish accents erupted on the bus, the driver screaming back his defence.

"It's nae ma bloody fault. It was her in front of me. Braked just a few feet away from me she did! Cannae she see…"

Blessing's vision was cloudy for a moment, her head throbbing with pain. Instinctively she began to rub it and felt a bump already forming. One more insecurity to cover up from people on the street. She was retrieving her hat from the floor when she noticed that the voices were no longer just screaming on the inside of the bus but also from outside. The other passengers had all moved across to the windows facing the sea. A tiny dog being held in an elderly woman's arms barked up at the glass. What were they all looking at? The bus driver opened the doors and got out from his cabin. Blessing looked past the dirty stained glass and tried to focus, but too many people blocked her view. She grabbed her bag and made for the exit by the drivers door.

On the promenade, all the traffic had come to a standstill. Up ahead of the bus, a car had collided with another near the roundabout but it didn't look too serious and the drivers of both vehicles were standing upright and appeared to be okay. She thought to call 999 for a fleeting moment but it was then she noticed everyone appeared preoccupied with something else. Why was everyone staring out to sea? She reached into her bag to find her glasses. Her vanity made her briefly hesitate but her curiosity got the better of her, and with a quick glance to the left and right to make sure no potential suitors were in the immediate area—seriously, why would they be on the Aberdeen seafront on a windswept rainy day? She put them on. The bus driver had lit up a cigarette. He was definitely not on her list of *potentials*. The sound of screeching seagulls filled the air above her. She had never heard so many, flying inland as if protesting against the biting chill coming in from the sea. She couldn't blame them for that.

Peering through her spectacles and looking east across the sea she finally saw what had captivated everyone's attention so dramatically. It took her a moment to comprehend what she was looking at because she had never seen anything remotely like it before. Far out, and above the waves of the North Sea was a vast star-shaped object moving very slowly towards the Scottish coast. She found it difficult to estimate its size at this distance, but it dwarfed several oil platforms beneath it, and some of them must have been far closer to shore than it was. She estimated it to be at least three times the height of the big clock tower she had seen once in London. It was the colour of a pearl, which would have made it hard to distinguish against the overcast backdrop of clouds behind it were it not for a ring of soft blue lights which flickered continually towards the edge of its underside. The upper pointed structure of the vessel parted the lower hanging clouds as if it were Moses parting the Red Sea. Its shape reminded her of the plastic spinning toy she used to play with as a child. The lower part came down to a singular point that glided just above the white horses forming on the waves below it. The upper and lower towers formed from a central saucer section which extended outwards to form a wide circular disc that spanned some considerable distance from the spine of the object before folding back over on itself, its texture uninterrupted but for the underside ring of blue lights, then enveloping back towards the centre and ascending up sharply to a single pointed tower that sat topside of the object that reminded her of a spire of a church tower. Yes, essentially a spinning top, as though it were made for a giant to play with. It was both the most incredible and unusual thing she had ever seen, beautiful in its appearance and sleek in its design. She had heard of Unidentified Flying Objects before, but thought of them as only existing within the realms of film and television shows, not reality. She found herself rooted in awe at the sight, captivated completely. It loomed ever larger as it moved deliberately towards land, the saucer part extending its shadow across the dark waves of the North Sea below, like an oil slick, slowly creeping closer towards shore. All the fishing boats and cargo ships changed their course and rapidly turned away from it, fleeing in every possible direction. Inexplicably, Blessing did not feel threatened by it, but others did not share her sentiments and people on the seafront began to panic. Some attempted to get back in their cars and drive away, while others just ran from their vehicles, leaving the roads gridlocked. As the edge of the saucer drew closer to the beach, she could see that the surface of its lower tower had a sparkle as if were covered in glitter. The ring of flickering blue lights, like broken crazy paving, continued to slowly alternate as the vessel began to encroach its shadow upon the land. Apart from this one strange phenomenon it otherwise appeared completely smooth with no visible openings, windows, seams, or joints. The shadow from the saucer began to creep across the beach. It was close now. People screamed and fled in terror, but Blessing stood mesmerised by the object, finding herself unable to move. Soon the edges of the vast saucer section had passed over her with the central lower spire weaving gracefully past the tops of buildings of the sea front. The lower spire of the vessel appeared to deliberately avoid touching them. Blessing tried to guess the width of the saucer but she could not fathom it, certainly it was big enough to encompass the entire city of Aberdeen, for as the edge of it passed above her, the other side of the circumference was still far out to sea. As its shadow fell across the city, Blessing found herself almost alone on the seafront, staring in awe at the unearthly spectacle above her. As the city cried out behind her with the sounds of human chaos she found herself feeling unusually pragmatic.

Her thoughts turned to the Creator. Was this the Second Coming that she, a Christian, was privileged to be witnessing? Had He truly come to save humanity from all its evils, at last? Whatever it was, it certainly wasn't of man's creation. To her it was something quite alluring, majestic even, but somehow she did not feel endangered by it at all. If this was the end of mankind, she would not run but simply let it come. If it was something else she would embrace it, for something this magnificent could only truly come from God, couldn't it?

A Scottish voice accompanied by the stench of cigarettes bellowed into her ear, making her jump.

"Well, there's no need for me to fookin' give up noo, hey?" said the bus driver, as he lit up another cigarette. As he quaffed on his nicotine, they watched the vast glittering disk with its lower spire continue its journey over the rooftops of the city, completely filling the sky above them.

RYAN

"Where's the Prime Minister now?" the Commissioner asked.

Ryan entered the room as the question still hung in the air. He was quick to size up who had got there before him. The London Police Commissioner, Sir Derek Winston, was already seated at the far right end of the table. The acting Foreign Secretary, (the actual one being in Paris) Basil Badgers MP, was pouring himself a glass of water. Everyone called him "Brush" or "Bushy Brush" on account of his ridiculously unkempt blonde hair and Ryan felt it was only right that he should contribute to the man's ongoing buffoonery. Julie Compston, Deputy Director of British Intelligence at MI5 (filling in for her boss, who was in Paris), had come in just ahead of him along with the pint-sized Darren Fine, whom he had never liked, but who, unfortunately held the position of Director of Communications and Strategy and always had the ear of the Prime Minister, David Jackson. He, the Defence Secretary and the Secretary of State along with several other cabinet and military personnel were in Paris attending a conference on dealing with the escalation of terrorist extremism in mainland Europe. An anti-terrorist conference which, Ryan thought, was probably more of an excuse to speak with arms manufacturers and sample 5-star Michelin cuisine than it was too seriously talk about *extremism*, a word which had come to have any number of uses for the current serving Government. It was the current buzzword for the two thousand and twenties, what *WMD* were to the "noughties". Ryan had always hated his job. He had to contend with the position of Secretary of Health, which was a poisoned chalice if ever there was one. David knew he was good at making cuts and that was the reason he got the job, a job he never wanted. He got to attend lots of meetings with doctors who vented their anger at every policy he created and every decision he took, which in their view was always the wrong one. He would be lucky not to get spat at in the face by a nurse on his way to work because of the last round of cuts, which he wasn't personally responsible for but found himself having to enforce. Secretly, that act of defiance had turned him on, but he couldn't tell the nurses that. Normally he had to pay to get a woman to do that sort of thing for him; his arse was still tender from the whipping he got three days ago, and his cock was still sore from last night's physical exertions with two ladyboys from his contact at the escort agency. He had, of course, used a third party as always, to book them, and made sure his PA, Simon, removed their phones before he even met them. They didn't care, as long as they got paid, and that way he could concentrate solely on his favourite acts of sexual depravity, a list too long to be encompassed in a singular evening. It had been a long night, but shit, it had been worth it! Ryan prided himself on being a man of varied tastes. But more than anything he wanted to book the Brazilian transsexual, Candice, again. He knew that term, transexual, wasn't considered correct anymore and that everyone in the aforementioned demographic was transgender now but then Ryan hadn't exactly ever been afraid of offending people's sensibilities. He had to say she really was quite something and he had become quite fond of her.

Ryan hadn't slept much, but at thirty-two he still had the energy of a twenty-five-year-old, at least that was what he told himself every day. He was the youngest member of the cabinet and proud of it. He had always been destined for Government, but unlike his father, his work ethic was simple. Appear to be busy but, when possible, do nothing. Delegation was the key to this formula and he had it down to a fine art. He had had his meetings today rescheduled for the more congenial time of 11 a.m., so it was a most unpleasant awakening to get a phone call at 7 a.m. telling him there was to be an emergency meeting of Cobra at 9 a.m., which he was obliged to attend. It was now 9:30 a.m. It was apparent he wasn't the only one who had opted for a lie-in. Bags under eyes hung in abundance all around the room.

The Cobra meeting room was small but functional. They had to take a lift down into the bowels of Westminster to get here, and most of the light came from the bank of flickering television screens mounted along the left-hand wall. Currently they were displaying news reports from all over the world and every channel was running the same story. Vast objects of an unknown origin had appeared everywhere worldwide. Off the coast of Ireland and over Scotland, where the United Kingdom was concerned. Full blown panic taken hold of London just yet, but it was only a matter of time. When he first heard the news Ryan had seriously considered not coming into work at all. Perhaps this was the end, in which case surely his priority should be to get hold of his dealer, call the escort agency and go out with a bang. Or should he give Candice a call? He really enjoyed her company even though he hadn't known her very long. He did wonder if he was getting too emotionally attached to her. He was still hopeful the whole thing would turn out to be some sort of elaborate hoax. He took his seat towards the far end of the table near the door, noting that Darren Fine sat at the head of the table. Why? Ryan thought someone else more qualified should chair the meeting in the absence of his good friend, Prime Minister David Jackson. Fine had a thick head of curly hair, and was short, extremely short, and spoke with a voice that always reeked of condescension. He was of Oxford University stock, probably never did a hard day's work all his life, although Ryan was pretty close to achieving that goal himself. Ryan was sure the man had a cocaine habit; he knew a fellow drug user when he saw one and Fine had disappeared to the toilet once too many times at the last party conference only to emerge with a new found energy that little else could account for. They had never got on well and Ryan, who was considerably taller at six foot two, always felt Fine had it in for him because of his height, well that and all the other things Fine lacked, like his good lucks and charm. Fine was barely five foot three and Ryan was certain that he wore two-inch lifts in his shoes. As Fine stood up to speak, Ryan thought of offering him a box to stand on.

"Ah good, the Secretary of Health is here, we wouldn't want to start without you now, would we?"

Wanker. Ryan acknowledged Fine's sarcasm with nothing more than a nod as he sat down. Baroness Childs entered, providing him with a welcome distraction as she took the seat opposite him, apologising for her lateness. She was, as always, dressed immaculately in a well-fitted peach suit. She couldn't have been over forty-five years old and carried it well. Ryan pictured her over the desk, her skirt hitched up, his trousers down, banging her for all she was worth. She would probably love it. He'd seen her old man, twenty years her senior. She couldn't be getting much from him at home. He wondered whose cock she had to suck to get the job of Secretary of Culture, Media and Sport. What a cushy job that was, especially now the Olympics were out of the way. He imagined her having her free lunches in the Manchester United Club Box with all the suits sniffing around her like a bunch of dogs waiting for dinner.

The room was oddly quiet with no one making the usual small talk. Everyone looked even tenser than normal, which was a good thing; it would be harder for them to notice he was still struggling to contain his hangover. He had only been given the briefest of information on the way over and was simply told to tune into BBC News in the car on route. That was when he had first seen them, like some UFO hoax footage that you could see on YouTube, except that these images were live and all too real.

Like diamonds in the sky he'd thought. "Giant, glittering spinning tops" were how someone else had described them, but they weren't rapidly spinning, just moving execrably slowly toward their as yet unknown destination. Fine continued to speak and Ryan amused to himself about how even at full height the man was barely higher than the table.

"I'm guessing everyone has seen the news. These images behind me are on every major news network worldwide. The Prime Minister is already on his way to Charles De Gaulle Airport with the rest of those missing from the Cabinet and they should be in the air within the hour."

"Has anyone attempted to contact these… objects?" It was Percy Howells, the Secretary for Wales and he certainly sounded like he was Welsh, probably from the valleys, Ryan thought.

"If you would allow me to finish the briefing, I will tell you everything we know so far. Two hundred of these objects are presently being tracked all over the globe. To our knowledge, they all appear to have entered our atmosphere simultaneously and, as far as we can tell, appear to be heading towards areas of minimal population."

"So not the cities?" Ryan allowed himself to speak. He thought it a sensible fact to clarify there and then.

"Not as far as we can tell, no. May I continue? Thank you. All leave for members of the Emergency Services and Armed Forces has been cancelled. The Prime Minister wants to see a presence on the streets to calm the public and reassure them that we're doing everything we can to ensure their safety. I've asked General Spears to attend and he should be here shortly to discuss military options…"

"Military options?" Baroness Childs glared at Fine from down the table. "Isn't it a little premature to be thinking about an attack? We don't know what we're dealing with here!"

"That's right Baroness, we don't. We don't have any idea why they're here, where they originated from or what might be inside them. All we know is that they are here and the option of doing nothing simply cannot be on the table. The PM feels we have to prepare for the worst…"

"I understand that but surely…"

The door to the conference room flung open, cutting the Baroness off. Ryan turned to see the tall, greying figure of General Spears enter the room. Ryan recalled from his one previous encounter with the man that he always spoke in short sharp sentences and only said something when it needed saying, if he spoke at all. He wore his dark green dress uniform, nothing out of place, not a single crease. It looked as though it had been ironed in the lift and he had just put it on outside this very room. He sat promptly in the empty chair at one end of the long table facing Darren Fine at the other, placing a number of brown folders on the table.

"General Spears, it's good to see you, you made excellent time."

"Time is something we cannot afford to lose in this kind of situation. Please pass these around." The General pushed the folders over, which were rapidly passed along the table. Ryan opened his and a photograph of one of the objects fell onto the table. He noticed its scale next to the oil rig it was passing over in what he assumed was the North Sea. Several more shots from different angles were contained in the folder, along with two pages of what looked like technical information. Others began to read theirs, but he let his sit on the table—best to let the General do the work for him. He could tell he was about to take control of the room, no doubt much to the chagrin of Mr. Fine.

"We've had several objects examined both from up close and afar. According to our most recent data each one appears to be identical in shape but some appear to vary in their diameter and body mass. From the tip of the upper tower to the base of the lowest part they're twelve miles in height and at the widest part of the disk section, the one in Aberdeen is just over eight miles across in diameter."

"Good God, that's over twice the height of Everest..." Baroness Childs blurted out. The woman was more educated than he thought. Credit where credit is due.

"Have we attempted to communicate with it?" Fine asked the question without looking up from the folder, thumbing through its contents.

The General took a beat. Ryan could see the man resented Fine as much as he did. The trumped-up little pipsqueak sitting there as though he were the PM himself, chairing the meeting.

"I spoke with the Prime Minister on the way here and he was of the opinion, as am I, that we must call in the Territorials now and be ready to establish public order. I would also suggest an immediate redeployment of at least fifty percent of our troops stationed overseas if we're to protect our interests here at home."

Fine looked unhappy at being cut down mid-stride in his presentation by this far more imposing man. The General, whose age Ryan estimated was late fifties had a commanding voice, which he was confident would have got him considerable work on radio and television. Ryan found himself wondering if anyone still listened to *The Archers* anymore, a radio soap that had been broadcast for decades.

"Don't you think that is a little premature, General? We still don't know exactly what we're dealing with here!" Fine retorted. The general placed his hands on the table.

"I believe you made that same point just before I entered the room. I think it would be a prudent move as we may have to defend our sovereign nation in the next few hours, or even minutes. If this is a prelude to some kind of alien invasion, our ability to resist it would be severely impaired by the fact that over sixty-five percent of our total armed forces are committed to overseas locations. The nearest being Malta, Germany and Cyprus and I have already ordered a squadron of our aircraft from Akatori to return home immediately."

"I thought there were reports of an object approaching Cyprus?" The Under Secretary spoke up.

"Excuse me, General," Julie Compston added. "Northern Greece and Turkey both have objects approaching them.". Ryan searched his mind for something factual to add but came up with nothing. The General slowly rose from his seat, causing Fine to finally sit down. It was clear who had control of the meeting now.

"Can we have the computer image up of all the current locations of the approaching craft, please?"

The General's adjutant, whom Ryan hadn't even noticed until now, fired a remote at the monitors. The large screen on the furthest wall went from displaying global news reports to showing a single image with a map of the world in green graphics, over which several dozen red markers appeared, each one moving slowly.

If the General was afraid, he certainly didn't show it. It was good to have someone with real balls in the room. Ryan was certain it wasn't him and Fine might talk the talk, but he doubted he could cope with real pressure.

"If they were moving towards the main cities, which I would suggest would be the logical choice of targets for an invasion, they're certainly taking an unusual route." General Spears said.

"We've all seen Independence Day, Morris. Do you actually have a theory as to exactly what they are doing?" It was Metropolitan Police Commissioner Sir Derek Winston, one of the few people in the room who didn't have to refer to the man by his rank. Ryan suspected they were both members of the cabinet Golfing Club, something he had no desire to join. God, golf, what a boring game. It was true some of the best meetings were done on the green but an equal number were concluded at pole dancing clubs and Ryan knew which of those he would rather be a member of.

"No. But I've been in touch with SETI and some of our own scientists have some theories." General Spears gave a nod to his adjutant and the screens returned to the latest television reports. Every channel had an image of one of the objects.

"The closest one that came to a city was right here in the United Kingdom. The object now on display live on BBC1 has just flown over the City of Aberdeen, I believe."

"Where reports indicate that it did nothing hostile?" Another Minister asked.

"It set off a few car alarms, but no, Minister. No rays of light, no laser beams, no burning of buildings, no aggressive action of any kind. All of our attempts to raise communication with the craft have failed. We have, however, been able to draw a couple of conclusions…"

The phone rang on the table. Fine immediately answered the call, his face slit with a smile, which meant he could only be talking to the Prime Minister.

"Yes Prime Minister, putting you on now sir. Sorry to cut you off, General, it's the PM." Fine replaced the handset and looked back at the main screen.

The screen flickered into the image of Prime Minister David Jackson, who appeared to be seated on board an aircraft. As ever, he sported his crisp dark blue suit and neatly combed hair, and considering everything that was happening Ryan thought his mood to be surprisingly cheerful.

"Hello everyone, good to see you all. We're expecting priority take-off in the next ten minutes. We'll land at the City of London Airport and come straight to you at Cobra. Can I take it that the Met is ready to handle panic if it sets in?"

Ryan watched Sir Derek Winston lean in, adjusting his glasses. He knew the man was already covering his arse as soon as he spoke.

"Yes sir. We'll be ready, but you'll remember from the London riots, if we have something like that on a national scale, it will be extremely difficult to contain. I wouldn't advocate the army coming in right away to keep peace on the streets, but they should certainly be on standby."

"Glad to see you at the back there General. Will they be ready by the end of day?"

"Yes sir, we're mobilising now and I have taken the caution of calling up the Territorials to barracks. Just in case. As the one in Scotland is heading in the direction of the estate at Balmoral I ordered the Royal household there evacuated."

"Yes, very prudent. Still no idea of what we're dealing with?"

"Not really sir, but the objects appear to be ignoring areas of high population, so far at least. That is to say they've passed them without incident. I've taken the decision to redeploy one half of our Tornadoes from Cyprus back to the UK and Admiral Flemyng has already begun to redeploy part of our fleet from Gibraltar."

"What about our forces in the Middle East?" The PM asked.

"I've kept them as is for now, sir, as I expected you would still want a show of strength in the region."

"Quite right too. We can't be showing the ragheads we're weak at a time like this, can we?" Jackson smirked at his last comment.

Careless, Ryan thought. These communications were all recorded and there was always the risk that they could be made public one day. That remark the old PM made about the Nigerians and the Afghans never did her campaign any good. The General seemed unconcerned by it but he was certain he felt the Baroness give him a look of disgust. Darren Fine abruptly spoke up.

"Sir, are you sure you don't want to take the Tunnel? All the security measures have been taken. I know it would mean a greater delay in you returning to London but…"

"Thank you for your suggestion Darren, but I'm confident that these things, whatever their intentions, would have started shooting aircraft down by now if they were going to do so and Air Traffic Control assures us we can give them a wide berth. General, do we have any reports world-wide of any such aggressive action?"

The General looked around the room and back at the PM before he spoke. Ryan could see he was making sure no one had more up-to-date information than he did before he responded.

"No sir, not at present and we're in the process of grounding all civilian aircraft as are the United States, but Mr. Fine may nevertheless have a persuasive point. I think we still have to be cautious."

Covering his arse, Ryan thought. The General would have made a good politician, though perhaps the fact that he wasn't one was the reason why he was a better tactician.

"I can see one of the objects from here, but there's dozens of French fighters between us and it and so far it's shown no aggressive action of any kind. We might have to take a slightly different route and I've been informed the weather is a little rough coming into London, but otherwise the captain tells me he doesn't expect too many delays. Ryan Wallace, you with us?" The PM phrased the question almost as an afterthought.

Ryan thought he heard his own name echo inside his throbbing head. That was his name. The PM was singling him out. Shit.

"Yes Prime Minister, I am here. All off-duty nurses and doctors have been called in, well those that aren't on strike. But the general feeling is they'll come in on a day like this. Dunkirk spirit and all that…"

The Prime Minister cut him off.

"Yes, very good. I'm sure you've delegated well. Now look, I'm going to want you to run things there until I return."

There was a sudden stillness in the room. The colour drained from Fine's face as the statement hung in the air. Ryan felt the breath of the general almost on his neck.

"Run things, Prime Minister?" Ryan asked, trying not to betray the nervous tremble in his voice.

"Yes, you're among the youngest and the brightest of us. The Deputy PM is still on his good will trip to Uganda and under the circumstances we can't say when he'll get back. Travelling overland to Nairobi when we last spoke. I just want you to steer the ship until I return, just for a couple of hours or so, three at most. This is a very fluid situation and I think it's best that you're not all squabbling like a bunch of children over what to do until we land so I think it best that I officially delegate someone to run things…"

Fine seemed exasperated. "Prime Minister, are you really sure that…"

The Prime Minister cut Fine dead.

"I am sure that Darren Fine will assist you with everything you need. He knows our communications better than anyone and can deal with the press. The important thing is to keep everyone calm and make sure order is retained on the streets. With the Deputy PM being away I have to nominate someone. I don't want you lot turning into the Labour Party and cutting each other's throats. If the situation demands military intervention I'm sure you will defer to General Spears on all aspects of military deployment, but hopefully it won't come to that. Right, we're being told to buckle up now, so I will see you all shortly. Thanks Ryan, thank you ladies and gentlemen. Goodbye."

The screen flicked back to the world media footage and the room was plunged into silence with all heads turned towards Ryan.

'Goodbye, sir.' Ryan realised his friend hadn't even heard his farewell.

Fine sat back in his chair, arms folded, waiting for Ryan to speak. Ryan knew the next few words out of his mouth could well define his career. Few people in his position were given chances to prove greatness and truth be told he didn't want it. How did that saying go—some achieve greatness and some have greatness thrust upon them? Oh, he could feel it being thrust all right, right up his arse and not in a good way.

The General turned toward him.

"Mr. Wallace, perhaps you should take my seat at the head of the table." The General pulled out the chair and stood next to it, expectantly. Everyone waited on Ryan to speak. He took a beat and then got to his feet.

"Thank you, General. Let's get some good coffee and croissants in here for everyone shall we? It's going to be a long morning. I'll steer the ship, so to speak, until the PM gets back."

He took the chair opposite Fine at the end of the long table. Fine glared back at him. "Let's hope there's no icebergs before then!" he snarled, his face as cold as stone.

Obnoxious cunt! Ryan almost said it out loud. If this was the Titanic he was steering, then Fine was on it with him. No iceberg, just a potential alien invasion to deal with. He smiled back and put him to work. "So, Mr. Fine— what are your suggestions for this morning's first press release? I think the important thing is to make everyone feel safe."

CHAPTER II

"In what is sure to go down as the most momentous day in the history of the world, the question: 'Are we alone in the universe?' has finally been answered. They began entering the earth's atmosphere in the early hours of this morning. At first a few dozen, then over a hundred until finally two hundred alien objects, each the size of a city, arrived in our atmosphere and after moving very slowly, witnessed by millions, began landing all over the world. This was one UFO sighting that no one would debate the authenticity of. Within minutes, footage of the objects from all over the world flooded the world's Social Media. YouTube received so many uploads that it crashed for several hours. From the remote steppes of Russia to the highlands of Scotland, the coast of Southern Italy to the hills north of Rio de Janeiro they came, landing on both soil and sea, encompassing everything beneath them. Each object had the same diamond shape, with a spired tower that could be seen from dozens of miles away. Panic began to spread throughout the world. The military of every nation went on full alert. Naval forces from both North and South Korea clashed over the object that landed spanning both sides of their so-called 'Northern Limit Line'. China immediately declared war on the objects, with no less than four of the two hundred alien vessels landing on Chinese sovereign territory. Yet despite their arrival, as yet there is no sign of aggression from the invaders. Many people are asking if they really invading us at all? Australia's Prime Minister has called for calm from his nation. This dramatic event has

coincided with the third day of the Anti-Terrorist conference in Paris, which was immediately cancelled, with European leaders expected to immediately return home to deal with the crisis. Prime Minister David Jackson is already en route back to London. Government advice in the meantime is to stay inside and not to undertake un-necessary travel, adding to congestion on the roads. The hope is that they have come in peace but so far all attempts to communicate with and gain access to the crafts have met with failure. There are simply no answers to where they have come from or to the biggest question of all—why are they here? - From everyone at the BBC, our prayers are with you all."

Emergency News Bulletin from the British Broadcasting Company, April 2nd

TARIQ

Tariq unloaded the Stinger Missile carefully from its container and placed it in the back of the mini-van. The seats had been lowered to accommodate the device and allow for more space to conceal it. A cumbersome but effective weapon, it was five feet in length and once it had the missile inserted into the tube, weighed well over fifty pounds. This model, which he had been informed had gone missing a few years earlier in Turkey was the FIM 92 J, the most up-to-date variant of the *Surface to Air* missile launcher. Constructed with newer components, it had a far longer shelf life than its predecessors and had a more reliable Battery Coolant Unit (BCU), the older version of which would often leak gas and cause the weapon to misfire. Tariq had witnessed such an incident previously, which had resulted in the destruction of the laundry block at the ISIS training camp in Syria. People were not amused. The weapon's distinct advantage was that it could be fired from the shoulder pretty much anywhere with an effective range of up to eight kilometres. Their target would be at less than half that distance. Packed with an explosive warhead designed to bring down an aircraft of any size it was an extremely precise and deadly instrument. Such a weapon being in the hands of a group like his was every Western Government's worst nightmare and he was about to show them why. He checked his watch and knew they only had a matter of minutes. His two colleagues were both keeping lookout while he readied the weapon.

Tariq was the oldest of the three-man unit in the van at forty years of age. His grandfather had served in the Free French Army in World War Two, having answered the call to defend the homeland after the Germans came and conquered France in 1940. That year the world bore witness to the Nazis goose-stepping their way through the Arch of Triumph in Paris. It was a very different time and not one he had lived through personally, but the context of that war had felt a great deal simpler than the one they were fighting now. The public perception was that this war was about Christians against Muslim extremism, the West against some far-out fanatical religious ideal but for Tariq, personally it was a cause in which religion played no part. It was not religion that had finally made him to pick up a weapon, and unlike some of his brothers and sisters he vowed he would not deliberately target civilians. The attacks of previous years in Paris, London, Berlin, Istanbul, Nice and Manchester where the blood of innocent children had been spilled, had not helped their cause and had, in his view, done nothing but stiffen the determination of the West to act with more decisive measures. No, to him this was not the way forward and his argument wasn't with the civilian population, but with the people who governed them, who made the decisions, who sent young men off to fight their wars in the Middle East so they might control the forever dwindling resources that the world needed. He knew every military action or intervention in the Middle East was always about resources and never in the name of democracy, and to suggest otherwise was simply farcical.

His grandfather, on the other hand, had joined the Free French Army from Morocco in 1941 for a cause, which he believed France would later thank him for. He was wrong. He and many of his friends had taken part in the bitter battle for Monte Cassino in Italy, and then went to liberate Corsica before fighting in Southern France through to the borders of Nazi Germany. His Moroccan unit, along with others made up from the French Colonies of Tunisia and Algeria, would not be allowed to take part in the victory parade in Paris. Everyone in the Allied Command, all the way up to General Eisenhower, only wanted white faces marching in front of the cameras and those of other ethnicities found their units discreetly guided to other parts of the front. De Gaulle could have protested at this decision, but of course he did not, and soon the significant contribution made by the colonial soldiers to the allied war effort was all but forgotten. After the war, his grandfather decided to settle in Paris and struggled, like many of his former comrades, to make ends meet. In 1957, when Morocco gained its independence from France, he had his army pension suspended and spent the rest of his life trying to get it restored while living in a state of borderline poverty. It was a shameful existence for someone who had laid their life on the line for their beloved France!

He married a local girl, Claudette, and had three children, the oldest of which, Sami, was Tariq's father, who in turn found himself to be a father when he was just seventeen. Tariq's mother had died young, even before his grandfather. His father had only ever given him the vaguest of information, telling him she had passed just after Tariq was born. She came from a white French family and their relationship had met with mutual disapproval from all concerned. His father would give him no other information, nor had he even seen a picture of her, to remember her by. In contrast, Tariq remembered his grandfather quite clearly, sitting on the older man's knee and later playing cards with him when he was a teenager. He also remembered the arguments with his father. When Tariq was old enough to understand history, he had wanted to know what his grandfather had fought for and why, if they had won the war, was he and his father always so unhappy about it? His grandfather had told him, "I served this country with honour and would have given my life for it, as several of my friends did, but when it was done with me, it dishonoured me." Tariq never forgot the look on the old man's face, sadness hanging in every wrinkle, and the emptiness in his eyes. France could not get over its own pride and appeared to forget that the only reason it was able to take part in the liberation of its homeland from the Nazis in the first place, was because of the participation of the men from its African colonies, who had made up over two thirds of the Free French forces.

By the time the French government reviewed its policy on its soldiers' pensions in 2002, his grandfather had long since passed away. His father, Sami, tried to take the case of paying pensions in arrears to the European Court of Human Rights, but no one wanted to listen and the quest for justice seemed to consume and destroy him. He found it difficult to find work and soon turned to drink, eventually dying from liver failure looking twice his actual age at only fifty-seven. As a French National of Moroccan descent living in Paris, Tariq had experienced racism all his life—from the police, at school, on the street and at job interviews, when he was lucky enough to get one. In France, he always felt like a foreigner in a country that he didn't understand and which treated him like an adopted orphan that it didn't really want. He knew he had to work harder and be tougher than everyone else and that meant he had to learn how to fight. So he took up boxing. There was a club back then at a local gym, which had been given some Department funding and the rock of a man who ran it, Jafar, was second generation Tunisian and an ex-prizefighter with skin like leather. Jafar took the teenage Tariq under his wing and taught him how to fight which gave him a much-needed focus. Other kids his age born in similar circumstances would find themselves facing two career options—gangs or drugs. If they weren't taking drugs then they were soon selling them. Jafar had given him the escape he needed and he soon became a skilful opponent.

It was not hard to feel a little affinity for the West's number one enemy —*Islamic State*—in the neglected slums of Paris. Most people who lived there hated the police, and drug dealing was not just a means of survival for some, it was the only way of life they had ever known. Criminality in the ghettos had an uneasy and an unspoken alliance with those known to harbour strong anti-western opinions. Both existed side by side and were often neighbours. Neither wanted to know what the other was doing and neither wanted to get in the way of their respective goals. It was an unspoken treaty of sorts, bound by a mutual hate of authority. Jafar encouraged Tariq to start a boxing class at the gym for youngsters like himself, to get them off the streets. It met with some success and they even competed in a few junior tournaments, but this time of great potential was short-lived when a heart attack ended the life of Jafar very abruptly and his brother immediately sold the gym.

With no chance of continuing his boxing ambitions, Tariq found himself reaching his twenty-first birthday knowing the choices before him were few. He had been called a hypocrite by his friends from the estate, when he decide to join the French Army, but to choose between that or dealing drugs was an easy decision. The army taught him skills; skills that he knew he might need one day later in life. He learned to handle every weapon he could get his hands on and specialised in the infantry platoon anti-tank weapons section. He mastered the art to firing RPGs properly, and the more sophisticated weaponry available. After the second Iraq war officially ended, despite the fact that the French had not endorsed the invasion in the first place, the government used it as an excuse to make cuts in the military and he was given his marching papers. Those that were let go appeared to all have one thing in common; the same thing in common as the troops of the Free French Army who weren't allowed to take part in the victory parade in Paris in 1944—they were for the most part, not white. So it was in 2009 that Tariq found himself in a situation where history was repeating itself.

Tariq had noticed that the prospects for advancement through the ranks of the French military were extremely limited during his time of service. Almost all of his training instructors, except for those who taught lessons in undercover counter-insurgency, were from the white middle classes. They, like he, had families with a history in the military and all of their relatives had also served as career officers. It wasn't that they were all bad but among many there was a pervading air of entitlement that numerous officers possessed. In his judgment, these men made for appalling leaders, where as those few who had risen through the ranks were always of the finest quality and would treat everyone under them as equals. They would train and eat with their men, leading by example, not just by command.

At thirty-four, he found himself being offered private security work and took a contract with a company called *Executive Armor*. Run by an old instructor from his early army training days, Jean-Claude, it was a source of employment for many of his former colleagues who found themselves in the same situation. It was during his employment, both in Iraq and Libya that his eyes were really opened to what the western governments and their rebuilding firms were capable of, and the consequences to the Middle East of the actions sanctioned by the Bush-Blair administration. Once the second Iraq war was over, the western companies descended like a pack of locusts ready to seize the most lucrative contracts they could. *Executive Armor* would provide the security for those firms. Many of his colleagues at the company represented the worst of what humanity had to offer. But Tariq was biding his time, enhancing his skills and increasing his contacts to enable him to start his own little arms dealing business on the side. He knew there would be no shortage of customers in his old neighbourhood, wanting to increase their standing through a superior show of force. Selling firearms to gangs on the estates, plus a few weapons to old friends for protection, became very lucrative. His childhood friend and neighbour, Malik Masood, had begun to set up those lines of business for him, but he made sure he never attended the sales meetings himself, selling everything through Malik as his third party. At Executive Armor, they had offered training courses for their employees on everything that might be of use in the high-end security world. He took courses in Counter-Intelligence Training and made sure he knew how to use the internet safely. Hiding the tracks of his business interests had become second nature to him. Everything was in different accounts, under different companies, with different banks, addresses and names, all over the world. In two short years he became very successful and Tariq could provide better and more reliable weapons than many of his competitors, and often at a better price. But after a while his new line of work troubled him. He had become part of the machine he detested; contributing, in his own way, to fuelling the depravity that kept his own people in the ghettos. Arming them to kill each other. He wanted to make a real meaningful change.

Most of his associates invested heavily in property and Tariq saw the wisdom in doing the same, under a number of different shell corporations, none of which were connected to each other. Malik always had a good head for figures, so he became the de facto accountant for their business. The two of them had grown up in the ghettos of Paris together and always looked out for each other, but Tariq had always been reluctant to bring Malik into his political operations. It was enough they were both conducting extensive criminal activities but he didn't want to make him a terrorist as well. If Malik wanted to embrace a political armed struggle, that would be a decision he would have to come to on his own. So his friend knew nothing of the rapidly evolving plans that were being enacted on the outskirts of Paris that April.

A fourth member of the team was present in Charles De Gaulle Airport, they would text Tariq when the target was confirmed for departure. The target hadn't been due to leave until the following day, but earlier one of Tariq's contacts had informed him that the target's schedule had been moved up a day and they were expected to depart from the airport within the hour. Tariq had a vast network of contacts for such information; people in lowly jobs that no one else wanted to do, who had the best eyes and ears of any intelligence network. Cleaners and baggage handlers, porters, electricians, caterers and plumbers saw and heard things, as part of their routine, that no others could and Tariq had chains of informants everywhere, all of which he kept on a second phone and a different network. Only his four-man team, including Salim and Mutha (whose nickname was "Mud"), was privy to the operation. The fourth member of the team at the airport hadn't even met Salim and Mud, and they in turn hadn't met anyone else from Tariq's life. Compartmentalisation was always key. The only person outside the group who knew how to get hold of him was Malik. Yet despite specific instructions that he would not be available for the next forty-eight hours, and was not to be contacted, Malik kept calling him on his operational phone. When he checked, Tariq saw over a dozen missed calls from him. He knew Malik wouldn't normally call him from a registered phone, but now there was a tentative link that could be traced of someone making a call from the Parisian ghetto to this location near the airport, assuming Malik was calling him from that area. Tariq couldn't allow himself to be distracted with such thoughts. So for now the phone had to remain off. He would be disposing of it shortly in any case, and his third personal phone was located off-site. There could be no traceable evidence that he was present anywhere near the airport today. Contacting Malik would have to wait until he was very far from here. The mini-van was stolen and the plates replaced. Once the operation was complete, the cell members would go their separate ways and wait to be contacted via an email account with only the most basic of wording used. If they pulled this off successfully, everyone in the world would be looking for them, not just the French, and Tariq wouldn't attempt another operation for at least a year, perhaps longer. He would wait until things calmed down and then strike again. Why martyr yourself when you could fight another day?

The village of Le Mesnil-Amelot is located just east of Charles De Gaulle airport and was dissected through its centre by a pretty road that ran north and south called *Rue de Claye*. It was probably more attractive before the airport had been constructed, but the road retained much of its charm, with shuttered window-framed houses bursting with colourful flowerboxes and high stone walls that enclosed the street on both sides, making it very narrow in places and a tight place for an ambush. For all Tariq knew, his grandfather might have fought here because the most dominant pre-war structure, the Church, still had the scars of bullet impact points embedded in the stonework. They'd parked right next to it when they'd arrived an hour or so earlier. All three men donned high visibility work wear and carried tools, giving them the appearance of a street-cleaning team. The village was encompassed by developments either side, containing modern hotels and large storage units leased by companies based at the airport. It had been well chosen, offering a number of excellent escape routes. The village lay next to two motorways leading to and from the airport and another dozen main roads, the most important of which was only a couple of hundred yards away, the D212, which branched round the west of the village and ran parallel with the edge of the southern runway. From here a second access road called *Rue Perichet* ran within sight of the runway itself, with only a wire fence between the road and the aircraft taking off —a distance of barely two hundred metres. Though patrolled by the local Gendarmerie, Tariq was surprised to learn that this was otherwise a very poorly protected part of the airport. Planes taking off and landing would pass over the houses in the village at an extremely low altitude. Tariq had decided that being in position by the fence itself was too risky, and the chances of them coming across one of the local patrols too high, but they didn't need to be so close. The Stinger missile had a range of eight miles and could have even been fired from within the village itself. They had done a reconnaissance of the village many times and knew every single route in and out of it by every means of transport available, even the timetable for the local bus. Tariq took a last look at his operational map. Two major arteries lay on either side of the village. The A1 motorway headed directly north and the N2 to the north-east; these were the escape routes allocated to his team.

For Tariq's departure plan, he was going to take the minor roads and head east, then take a booked lunch at a restaurant he had visited before. He would then watch everything unfold on the news, and act as shocked as the rest of the people present. Tariq checked both his phones. He was waiting for the second and most important text. It was possible that the target might be redirected to a different runway, and he did not want to make the mistake of shooting down the wrong plane like those idiots did in Russia. The death of a party of schoolchildren was not something he wanted on his conscience. He checked on his team—Salim was looking through his binoculars at the planes taking off. Mud had gone to check on their second van containing the motorcycles, which was parked down a discreet side road away from the main thoroughfare. There were a couple of cameras on the main road at either end of the village and Tariq had them temporarily disabled by what he hoped would be mistaken as the work of graffiti artists. He came down and did a tag a couple of nights earlier near the motorway, and took the cameras out with his aerosol at the same time. He had a bet that the Department (The local French Council for the area) would take longer than two days to clean them up and sure enough, they were still painted over that morning.

The village had always been the intended strike point, but the plans had called for the operation to take place tomorrow, not today and Tariq's mind whizzed through every detail of the operation as he waited. Parking permits were dated incorrectly by one day, a small detail, but one they did not have time to correct. The team's second vehicle, also stolen, carried their departing transport, three light Suzuki motorcycles that had German plates; not unusual, but the bikes could easily have been spotted on close inspection through the window and he didn't like having to hang around. They were strangers here and he knew they would attract attention, so the high-viz work jackets were the best form of camouflage. Stand out for a legitimate reason. People of his ethnicity doing a lowly cleaning job were common and didn't attract much attention.

Once the operation was over, they would depart on their bikes each in a different direction, to a pre-designated place, where each member would change to a second vehicle. In Tariq's case, it would be a second bike. His main concern was that it might be stolen in his absence as such thefts were very common in France. The Stinger missile launcher lay across the folded seats in the back of the mini-van. Having checked the weapon carefully, Tariq pulled a sheet across it. The village wasn't exactly a hive of pedestrian activity, but he didn't want to take any chances. The sound of an incoming text went off in his pocket. He checked his phone—it was from a sender identified with the letter "A", and said simply one word—*Now*.

Tariq whistled and Salim came running over and got in the passenger side. "We're on, this is it—be ready."

Salim reached over to the back for a long sports bag and placed it between his legs as Tariq pulled out into the road. Mud came running around the corner and jumped in the side-door as the vehicle was moving.

"We nearly left without you." Tariq snapped, not even looking at him.

"Two gendarmes in the village were checking our other van." Mud was out of breath as he took an assault rifle passed over from Salim. He cocked the weapon immediately then put it down out of sight. Salim passed him a pistol and two grenades. Tariq turned down the side of the Church, an extremely narrow road called *De Bosnier* that ran between some more houses before finally being bracketed by bare fields on either side of it. It led towards the ring road, which curved round the east end of the runway, and from there they had a direct line of sight of the planes taking off. Tariq spoke, never taking his eyes off the road for a second.

"Salim, remember to confirm the make, model and courier of the plane as soon as we have it in sight. Do you understand? There must be no doubt."

Salim nodded. He was cocking his assault rifle and loading up his pockets with extra magazines. The three men all wore combat vests and body armour underneath their high visibility clothing. Tariq thought back to the previous evening where they had all discussed the possibility of being taken alive. All three had decided that was not an option. Ideally they would all live to fight another day, but either way they were committed, there was no turning back. Tariq pulled over on the verge. Ahead of them crossed the 212 ring road, which ran north to south along the eastern edge of the airport and was broken up by all manner of artery roads and tracks. From here, they were closest to the southern runways of the airport. They had only two minutes at most now, and this position offered a clear view of all craft departing from the south side of the airport. A queue of aircraft were taxiing for take-off, while another roared over him into the skies. Tariq's phone buzzed again. It was the operational cell phone and could only be "A" sending him a message, unless Malik was texting him again. He checked his phone immediately.

Taxiing to the northern runaway. Priority take off. ETA 3 minutes.

Tariq looked at the message then immediately removed the SIM card. He wouldn't be needing this phone again.

"Burn it. We're going to the northern side!" Tariq passed the SIM card to Salim who promptly produced a cigarette lighter and burnt it before passing the handset back to Tariq.

"Put it in my top pocket. In my shirt, Salim!" he snapped at the young man struggling to comply. Tariq gunned the engine and turned them onto the 212 heading north. Mud looked on in confusion.

"What happened?" he asked.

"The plane has been re-directed to the north runway. We have just over a minute. Get the missile ready. This will come down to a matter of seconds. Tell me about the Gendarmes back at the village!"

Mud pulled the sheet back off the weapon and began to load the missile from a second container. It was cramped in the back and he tried to do it with care, while the vehicle bounced around.

"Allah be merciful, keep the van slow, no sudden turns! There were two of them. They looked like traffic police, not airport security."

"Shit, the parking permit." Tariq knew it was the one thing they hadn't had time to correct, and with it being dated a day ahead of time, it could cause suspicion. They raced up ahead to the junction where the road connected to the main motorway and turned left onto a split road. From here, they could see straight through the fence to the northern runways and just over five hundred meters away, a row of planes could be seen lining up for take-off. Salim was already searching for the target through his pocket scope. He flinched and began spewing out the details.

"I have confirmation of the target. Grey Voyager, Airbus A330, Registration ZZ336. Distance to target on take off, I'm guessing to be one and one half kilometres. "

Tariq could tell Salim was trying to impress him, but it was good that he was precise. Nothing could be left to chance. He knew that at this part of the airport, cameras were far more frequent and their window of opportunity would be extremely limited.

"Masks on." Tariq ordered.

All three men pulled down black balaclavas. Mud took off his high visibility jacket, Salim had no room or time to do so in the front seat. Mud looked left and right out of the windows. He felt certain there would be more police traffic but he saw none, only civilians passing by.

"We're clear."

"Their getting in line for take-off now..." Salim cried, excited as the Airbus began to move into position on the runway. It could be seen turning in the distance through the fence ahead of them.

"Disembark!" Tariq ordered, as he pulled over the van to halt on the small patch of grass at the other side of the road, doing an illegal U-turn in the process so that the van would be facing the right way to make their escape. An oncoming vehicle swerved to miss him, blaring its horn as it passed. Salim tried to slide down in the front seat as he saw the French driver lock eyes with the masked figures of both him and Tariq in front. Mud slid the left-side door open, jumped out with his assault rifle tucked into his body. Tariq knew it was only a matter of seconds before they were spotted on the cameras.

"Here he goes..." Salim was still in the front passenger seat, his head twisted round looking back toward the airport, as Tariq came round to the side door, the engine still running, ready to take the Stinger.

The sounds of the planes' jet engines roared in the distance, it was just a matter of seconds now. Mud reached in and carefully lifted the weapon from the vehicle. Tariq did a final check, as the airbus roared down the runway and left the ground. It would travel almost directly over them. Tariq gauged his line of sight, then crouched next to the open passenger door, turning the weapon away from the direction of the runway just as the grey aircraft shot into the air overhead, climbing with every second. Tariq took one step to his right, took aim with the weapon, locking it onto the aircraft. Harsh sound blasted into Tariq's ear as Mud's assault rifle crackled to life with a long burst of automatic fire, the rounds impacting into something metallic. He had had the foresight to put in earplugs just before they set off, so Tariq's professional zeal allowed him to focus on one thing only: his target. He fired the weapon and released the missile. At once he discarded the Stinger and dropped to the ground, keeping close to the body of the mini-van. He now saw the source of the exchange of gunfire. A police car had pulled up about ten yards ahead of them on the other side of the road. Tariq hadn't seen who fired first but Mud had emptied a whole maga-zine into the vehicle, leaving them with a smouldering engine and shat-tered windscreen. A body lay motionless on the ground between the mini-van and the car, and a second officer was still shooting with a pistol from behind his vehicle. Tariq could not see him from his position. A cacophony of sirens could be heard converging on them from multiple directions. There was no time to delay. Salim dropped a weapon out of the vehicle next to Tariq on the ground. Mud was changing magazines and ducked inside the back of the van. Salim slid over to the driver's side as rounds from the officer's pistol shattered the front window of the mini-van. Just then a sound like a sharp crack of thunder filled the air; the missile had found its target, fully loaded with fuel for its return journey. The missile struck the aircraft just between the body and the right wing. A second explosion, bigger than the first, punched through the upper and lower compartments of the main fuselage and caused an eerie ripping sound: the body of the plane tearing itself apart. The death cries of the mechanical animal began to spiral downwards, with fragments of fuselage splitting off and hurtling towards the ground. The remaining police officer, though hidden behind the vehicle, was momentarily mesmerised by this gruesome sight, as the fragmenting aircraft fell to earth and stood up, making him an easy target. Tariq fired two well-aimed shots, striking him in the head and shoulder. He went down. Tariq put several more rounds into the vehicle, hitting the tyres and the engine to ensure its immobilisation. The barrel of his weapon smoked like a lit cigar.

"Let's go!" Salim shouted, pushing down the accelerator with Tariq barely making it back inside the van in time. He immediately reloaded his weapon, prompting Mud to do the same. Their vehicle had to dodge and weave around the numerous civilian cars that now littered the road ahead. Several road traffic accidents had occurred nearby, as people focused on the sky and not the road.

"Shit, we did it! We did it!" Salim shouted, rolling his mask up to his forehead.

Tariq shouted, "We're not out of this yet! Get us back to the village."

Mud checked his weapon and sank down in the back seat, as he spotted flashing lights pass them on an unmarked car. They were the airport police and were known to be far better-armed than their regular traffic counter-parts. Burning debris fragments fell around them, causing Salim to swerve the van, and the police vehicle passing them to do the same. Tariq watched for them to turn around in pursuit, but they didn't stop. He breathed a sigh of relief. Mud slapped him on the shoulder in congratulation, and soon they were turning on the road that headed back into the village. Another distant boom was heard off to the north-east.

'That must have been it hitting the ground!' Salim said.

"Fuck. Fuck..." Mud said. His head twisting in every direction looking for any other threat. They turned off the main road and were soon back on *Rue De Claye*, passing the Church. where they had parked their other van, in a small bay by a turn-off on the left side of the road. It had a *No Parking* sign and a ticket under the windscreen wiper.

"Shit, we've got a ticket! Doesn't matter now anyway." Mud jumped out the side door, still cradling his AK assault rifle. He checked the road in both directions but it was deserted. Salim, however, saw a twitching curtain from the windows on the other side of the road. "We're being watched..."

Mud still had his mask on, and Salim pulled his back down. Tariq slid over to the driver's side, as Salim got out. Underneath the seat, he found what he was looking for, a small black box with a small green button and switch. He flipped the switch and the green button lit up. He slid it back under the seat. Salim was already opening the back doors to their second van. It was blue and had a logo for a landscaping company on the side, complete with a fictional phone number and website address. Mud had decided to carry a pistol earlier that day; it had been spotted wedged under his jacket when he went back to check on the van, resulting in the local gendarmes being called. Things had moved very quickly since then, and now the whole of Charles De Gaulle was in lockdown and the air was filled with sirens. So, when one was heard coming down the street, the group kept calm.

Tariq removed his mask but made sure to avoid looking across the street. Mud got his bike and was already priming another black box, placing it in the gardening van. He put it back inside just under a small tool box. "Charges set."

With two bikes now out of the van, Tariq could have left there and then but Salim was young, and Tariq wanted to make sure that he got on the road. He was the last one to be brought into the group and as the youngest, Tariq felt an almost paternal responsibility for him. All three men had now removed their high visibility wear and replaced them with leather jackets. As the men were already wearing black jeans, boots, shooting gloves and now matching jackets and motorcycle helmets, it made them as nondescript as possible to the casual observer. Salim paused for a moment as he checked his motorcycle, Tariq knew why, he could smell it too. The breeze had brought with it the pervading odour of burnt metal, cordite and jet fuels, and there was something else, a foul stench which one could only associate with death. The smell of burning flesh wafted in the air around them.

"Stop fucking looking at us!" It was Mud. His angry shout brought Tariq's attention to the house opposite them. He was pointing at the ground floor window across the street. The curtain had moved again and an elderly woman could be seen behind the drapes, a phone held up to her face.

Tariq would have fired, but Mud got there first, bringing up his rifle and firing a short controlled burst through the window of the ground floor; the gunfire and sounds of breaking glass echoing down the narrow street. Mud crossed the road and looked in through the broken window. Tariq watched him peer inside, and heard a groan beyond. Mud fired two aimed shots in through the window and turned to come back across the street when the appearance of flashing lights up ahead made him duck into the frame of a doorway. Salim had just brought down the third bike from the van, when two cars came screeching to a halt, about thirty meters away from them. Four men disgorged from the vehicles, Tariq noting that the two in the front had the foresight to wear body armour. All four were armed with sub-machine guns and wore red armbands. They were part of a police unit. The nearest man was shouting something, but Mud wasn't going to let him finish the sentence. From the confines of the doorway, he took aim fired down the street, the sound of the gunfire bouncing off between the close-knitted buildings. Tariq saw movement from the left side of the road and a boy of no more than ten appeared in a gap between the houses, right between the two groups, before swiftly ducking back inside. Thinking he was another officer trying to outflank them, Mud almost took his head off with another burst.

The men in the cars hadn't chosen a good place to stop. The street here was especially narrow and they were overlooked by two level buildings on both sides. Salim was now on his bike and ready to go, but Mud was still trapped on the other side of the road. The exchange of fire became so ferocious that Mud dived into through the window while chunks of masonry fell off the corner of the building, smashing the front body of the mini-van. From behind it, Tariq fired a long burst and shouted to Mud, "Be ready!—Salim, Grenade!"

Salim threw him a grenade and Tariq gestured for him to go. Salim hesitated, but Tariq shouted, "Go!" Knowing that every second they delayed, the trap would soon be closing in with every police unit in the area converging on the village.

He pulled the pin on the grenade and rolled it down the street, ducking back under cover of the van, and reaching for a second one from his rucksack. An explosion ripped through the little French street, the sound bouncing back between the buildings like a continuous series of thunderclaps in a violent storm. Tariq pulled the pin on the second, but this time he snatched a glance around the van before he threw it. He judged the distance as best he could. In a heartbeat he saw the front of the first car had buckled upwards, and was aflame, its body work peppered with holes. The nearest man rolling on the ground behind it, screaming while another man audibly cursed to his comrades. Both had been terribly injured. The third man had pulled back and returned fire again. The fourth was nowhere to be seen. Tariq threw the grenade as high and long as he could. It spun up through the air as his quarry returned fire in the same moment, a bullet striking Tariq in the upper arm. Electric pain snapped through his body as the bullet tore into his flesh, but Tariq had been shot before and this didn't feel as bad as previous times. He ducked back in behind the van, and waited for his grenade to answer. The second explosion rocked the village even louder than the first, the sound reverberating between the buildings.

"Now, Mud! Now!" he screamed, and jumped on his bike.

Salim had already left. Tariq could hear the sound of his bike roaring off into the distance. Mud fired his rifle until the magazine was empty, then leapt across the road, immediately straddling his bike. No one fired back at them, but they didn't have the time or the inclination to check who had survived. Mud stared at the blood dripping from Tariq's right arm. Tariq wrapped a belt around it tight to stem the flow and pulled his leather jacket back on. The two men looked at each other, whatever would happen now, they had succeeded and shared something few others would ever experience: a sense of victory. They exchanged the briefest of smiles.

"God is great today, brother," Mud said. He turned his bike and immediately rode off. Tariq knew they had probably killed over one hundred people today and God was not involved.

They left in separate directions as agreed. Tariq winced in pain as he operated the bike controls. He had an army standard first-aid kit in the pannier, but there was no time to stop and use that now. He had to put as much distance between him and the airport as he could. His safe house was a few hours away, and with his wound he could not stop at the restaurant as planned, he had to travel directly to Belgium. He headed east out of the village, crossing the busy D401, which was littered with cars up on either side of the road, their drivers having abandoned their vehicles, standing and staring in the direction of the plane crash. On the side of the road lay two connected chairs from the aircraft, charred corpses still strapped into the smoking seats. The sight didn't phase him, he had seen worse. As he paused to turn at the junction, obeying all the traffic codes so as not to draw any attention, he heard the distinct clatter of automatic weapons fire. It was an AK assault rifle; he'd know that sound anywhere. It was followed by several more exchanges of gunfire but he didn't have the time to listen further. From the corner of his eye, he could see the main plume of smoke, north-east of the Airport, in the direction of the village of Moussy-le-Vieux. Several smaller black spirals of smoke rose over the area, the plane fuselage having impacted the ground in more than one location as it broke up. If he had turned his head just a fraction further he would have seen the large white object in the sky slowly moving east a few miles north of the airport.

But Tariq's focus was on his escape and he had not seen the news for twenty-four hours, so was blissfully unaware of global events unfolding across the world. He took the D401 as far as the next village and then turned off onto the back roads that went from village to village, on into the heart of the French countryside, leaving the sound of sirens and the stench of burnt fuselage and flesh behind him. It was for others to bear witness to the devastation he and his cell had created.

DIANA

Diana's first instinct had been to protect her children, but beyond putting them inside her broken down car there wasn't much else she could do. It had taken the object, whatever it was, thirty minutes to move towards them, during which time it appeared half the wildlife of Nevada had passed by, heading in the opposite direction, and she knew they should be doing the same. Animals were supposed to always instinctively run away from trouble, weren't they?

"What is it, Mommy? Is it going to hurt us?" Jules asked from the back seat, more out of inquisitiveness than fear, or at least so it appeared.

"I don't know, sweetie, we just have to stay in the car. Try not to be scared, okay?" She felt her words were futile, yet they seemed remarkably calm considering the circumstances. A shadow fell over the car as the edge of the saucer section began passing overhead, spreading out far and wide to both the north, south and the east. The cone shaped lower shaft of the vessel was still some way off, but appeared to be following the road toward them. The height and size of the object was simply astonishing and Diana thought it incredible that such a vast structure could stay airborne without any visible signs of propulsion. A ring of blue lights emanated from the underside, like scattered scales, each a different shape, formed a circular pattern towards the edge of the circumference of the vessel. Perhaps they were the source of its power?

She turned back to her kids, whose eyes were transfixed by the strange phenomenon. The alien object now reached out to touch every horizon around her. She felt confident it was alien, it must be and it certainly wasn't like anything she had ever seen. Still it moved on, the lower stalk that pointed down to the ground was traveling slowly but surely towards them. Diana hadn't noticed before but she realised it was slowly rotating as it moved, the downward stem of the object becoming more in focus as it got closer. The lower part of the vessel, reminded her of an ice cream cone. It was perfectly lined up with the road, almost touching the tarmac beneath it. It had changed its height from when it had first emerged over the low-lying hills to the west. It must have travelled over Lake Tahoe, unless it just appeared out of nowhere. She wondered if Danny would have seen it.

She checked her phone again but there was still no reception. No wonder, with her being right under this thing. Her children craned their heads between the seats to get a better look, apparently much less concerned for their safety than she was. Children could find things they didn't understand to be either very frightening or captivating, and she was grateful it was the latter in their case. They had been brought up on a diet of television shows, where man explored the stars and alien invasions of the earth were a weekly occurrence. Until fairly recently, Jules had believed some of these films were historical dramas and it took some explaining to make her understand they were works of fiction. Fiction no longer, apparently. They were here now and if this was the end of the world, at least she would be with the two people she loved the most, her children. If this was the beginning of an alien attack, best that she die in the first five minutes. She wasn't really up to fighting it out in the hills and foraging from the land. Diana remembered watching a TV series called *Project UFO* as a kid. It was rather tacky and cheap but still a childhood favourite of her brothers. There was almost always a logical explanation for each case that the two clean-cut men from the United States Air Force investigated, with all the show's encounters explained away by some natural phenomenon in the last five minutes. Well she would love to see them explain away this one. Yes, the government would sure have a harder time covering this up like they did with that other thing that was supposed to have happened at Roswell, New Mexico, back in 1947. Of course, that was supposed to be the aliens visiting us from the *Independence Day* movies. She had never really been interested in Science Fiction or spaceships, she left that to her brother, Danny, who was the big *Star Wars* fan. If she could manage to figure out a way to get out of this predicament, she guessed she might have more than a passing interest in such things in the future. She did her best to remain calm. Panicking would get her nowhere, and in the middle of nowhere was exactly where she was. If they tried to run on foot they would quickly become exhausted. She had two small children and she wouldn't be able to carry one, let alone both of them, in this heat. It was several miles back to the gas station in Middleton and that would have almost certainly been abandoned by now. If they took off across country, north or south, by the time they even got a mile, the vessel would still be above them. The total width of the saucer part was hard to gauge but she guessed it must be several miles in diameter. Its shadow began to cool the car down. A small blessing. There was literally nowhere to run or hide, so she reluctantly concluded all they could do was wait for the thing to pass over them.

"I'm going to need you both to be really brave, okay? We're going to have to sit here and wait for it to pass over us and then we're going to get some help and get to Uncle Danny's, okay?" Both children nodded their heads, still gazing up at the object, the car now became shrouded in darkness under the saucer. It completely filled the view through the front windshield. After what seemed like an eternity, the lower ice cream cone part of the vessel drew closer, its shimmering surface causing excited cries from her daughter in the back seat.

"It's so pretty Mom, look at all the Shinies!" – "Shinies" in the plural sense was Jules' word for all things associated with jewellery. Whenever they had gone to the mall and Jules had seen all the watches and rings glittering in the windows she would scream the word "Shinies!" and run over to them, her hands pressing on the glass. Diana had got her a few bits and pieces when she could—rhinestones, of course, and a pair of pearl earrings that had been handed down from her mother, on her tenth birthday. Jules was not yet old enough to know the difference in cost between fake diamonds and the real thing, but she soon would and that was when the real value of a dollar would be appreciated. With the distance narrowing between the car and lower shaft of the object, Diana noted that the surface was an off-white pearl colour. She tried to wind the windows up but, of course, the electronics were dead, not that she thought it would offer them any protection in any case. Radiation... Didn't these things have radiation? Wasn't that what happened to people after they saw UFOs? Their hair would fall out and then they would die or just disappear. Was she going to be visited by the *Men in Black* after this? Or was that just all in the movies?

"It's covered in Shinies, Mom!" Jules cried from between the seats, staring up through the glass.

She was right. The lower central stalk, looming ever nearer, almost like a solid tornado winding up the road, was covered in something that glittered and sparkled over the otherwise smooth surface. It reminded her of the white stones she would find as a child at the beach, that appeared to be covered in glitter and would sparkle in the sunlight. Diana checked her watch. They had been underneath the central disk for over twenty minutes now, the underside of the vessel moving continually overhead. It grew darker in the shadow of the behemoth, and soon it was hard to see the daylight between the gap of the edge of the saucer and the ground, yet total darkness had not encroached on them as she expected; there was still a light source emanating from somewhere... Diana searched frantically for a flashlight, before finally remembering it was actually next to her in a compartment in the car door. The lower central column of the ship had almost reached them and was now less than one hundred yards from the car. Diana could see that the tip of the cone was only a few feet from the ground and was not even the width of their car at its lowest point. At the base it looked to her as though it sharpened into a singular point, like the spire an old church tower. There still was no sign of any visible markings, openings, or a mechanism that would enable the vessel to move as it did. She had never been very good at science, but she didn't need to be a scientist to know that this thing defied all the laws of physics. She couldn't figure out how this thing moved, but she had to remind herself it was alien of course, so it wasn't likely to be using a means of propulsion that she could comprehend.

Now she had to make a choice. She realised that on its current course coming straight up the road, the lower spire of the object would come straight at the car and slice through it, potentially with them all in it. Staying inside the vehicle meant a real risk. At its lowest point, the end of the cone did not seem that wide, perhaps only a half foot across or even thinner. She could take the risk and stay, or she could grab the kids and leave the relative safety of the vehicle, standing a few feet away thus allowing the tip of the cone to pass them from a safe distance. Relative safety was right. She had only a minute or so before it reached them, perhaps less. She decided they had to get out.

"Jules, Jack—Listen to me very carefully, okay? You must do exactly what Mommy tells you. Do you understand? Uncle Danny and I will buy you some really cool presents if you manage to do this for Mommy, okay?" Bribing her kids with the promise of presents, which might never materialise, was not her normal route to try and elicit good behaviour from her children, but right now Diana didn't give a shit. She needed them to do exactly what she wanted with no questions asked, and she knew it was the best way. Besides, best to keep their minds distracted with thoughts of possible presents rather than potential kidnapping by aliens.

"Okay Mom. I'm not scared. This is so cool!" Jack said. He hadn't said much beyond "Wow!" since they first saw the ship and his first words put Diana at ease considerably. Jack's lack of a father figure had always made him quieter than other boys his age.

"I'm not scared either," added Jules. But Diana could see that she was, and had only spoken so her brother did not have the better of her.

"So now we're all going to get slowly out of the car, we're not going to run, okay? Jack, you're going to take your sister's hand and not let go. Then we're just going to cross the road and stand over there by that track. It's like a game and we're going to see who can do it the quietest and the slowest. Okay?" she whispered, gradually making her voice quieter all the time. As plans went it wasn't much, but it was all she had. The children nodded.

Diana wasn't sure why she thought if they moved stealthily it would make a difference, but at this stage they really didn't have anything to lose. She gave them a slow count of three and simultaneously they all unlocked and opened their doors to the left side of the road. Unlike earlier, now not a living thing could be seen in any direction. Jules, with Jack in hand moved gingerly out of the vehicle, closing the car door, but Diana stopped her with a deft movement of the hand and shook her head. Jules nodded, understanding. The kids had been so well behaved today she thought, what a funny story that would make when they got back to Danny's. "How were the kids?" Danny would ask. "Well you know, Danny," Diana would reply. "I have never seen them so well behaved during an alien invasion—I have to say I was impressed…"

She grabbed Jules' free hand and the trio tiptoed across the road and into the sparse scrubland beyond. Running parallel to the road, either side of it, were dusty worn tracks. Diana wasn't sure who used them, perhaps dirt bikers for fun, or farm vehicles maybe, but there was nothing to farm around here. North and south of the road was barren with nothing but small spiky shrubs and snakeholes that Diana was keen to avoid. On both sides of the road about five hundred yards in each direction, there was a gradual rise in the terrain up to a single hill. The one in the north was perhaps high enough to be classed as a mountain Diana thought, and even that still got nowhere near the underside of the vessel, which towered high above it. Scattered beneath its hulk were several small clouds almost as if they were balls of white cotton clinging to its underside. The sonic boom of jets filled the air once more, and Diana saw two Navy jets, mere distant specks, flying beyond the circumference of the vessel between it and the ground, buzzing in and out of view like angry flies circling a carcass. Great, that was all she needed—the might of the United States military springing into action, while they were underneath the middle of this damn thing. She heard several more planes take off to the south and thought there must be an air force base located in that direction. Briefly she heard the clatter of helicopter blades and hoped they might be rescued but their sound soon diminished quickly.

Looking east down Highway 50, she could see the underside of the vessel now extended all the way east past the hills behind them, which would mean it would have encompassed the truck stop at Middleton. Diana guessed the edges of the vessel must be reaching Anita's place at this very moment. Looking back west, the hills were much farther away but the saucer extended all the way to where the road rose and then dipped again behind them on the horizon. If the main body of the vessel had been lower, surely they would have been plunged into total darkness, yet two things prevented this from occurring. The first was that a thin strangled strip of light still existed between the edge of the vessel and the ground. Secondly, the soft glow from the ring of blue lights that slowly alternated towards the edge of the underside of the vessel. The shadow cast by the vessel as result was not dark or solid. Though the body of the object was opaque, it felt as if daylight was still being filtered through it somehow. Despite the sun being completely blocked by the craft, there was no noticeable drop in temperature. *Maybe that was just the radiation then!* Diana joked to herself, more to calm her nerves than anything else. She tried to estimate the size of the thing as it continued to move inexorably above them. From the base of the cone where it soared up and then spread into the saucer, must have been three, four, five or more miles high. She was frightened by the sight of something so powerful that made her feel so helpless, yet so far it had shown no hostile intentions of any kind. It was in its own way, very beautiful.

She had gone to the CN Tower once in Toronto, Canada when she was a child, and she remembered that was about half a kilometre in height. She'd seen a documentary more recently on the History Channel about the construction of the tower in Dubai that was over eight hundred metres, and this was certainly higher than that. Had it been a very cloudy day, she felt certain the saucer part of the object might well be sitting high above them and only the lower stalk of this giant spinning top would have been visible.

She felt Jules give a hard squeeze of her hand. Her daughter pointed down the road to where the lower tip of the cone was still moving towards their unoccupied car. Every few seconds she had the same thought—she must be dreaming. The pinch of Jules' fingers reminded her firmly of the fact that she was not. The tip of the cone was now barely twenty yards from their vehicle. She could see now that it did not reach a fine and sharp point at the end, after all, but was smooth and round at the base. The source of the sparkling glitter on the surface came from a number of phosphorescent stones that caught the light from above, as if diamonds encrusted its surface. Diana saw the tip was barely a few feet from the ground and certainly not high enough to miss the car. It continued its steady course along the road, then she saw the cone move upwards. A small subtle change in its height as the road dipped and lowered. It appeared to have the ability to change its mass to avoid contact with the surface or objects in its way. Diana recalled that when she'd first sighted the object, a second smaller cone-shaped structure rose from the centre of the topside of the vessel, being the polar opposite of the lower cone now before them. It continued to rotate ever-so-slowly, the surface shining back at them, tempting them to inspect it more closely, but Diana stayed rooted to the spot.

"Mommy, do you think ET will come out of a door?" Jules asked.

"Shhhh, don't talk," she said. Giving Jules a firm look that her daughter returned with an apologetic grimace. Diana had shown her ET one afternoon when she was six and she had loved it. Jules had thought the film was a true story and expected all aliens to look like ET. It would be good if it was ET, then he could phone home and go home, but there was no sign of any door or any opening for that matter, not even a window. The lower tip of the cone reached the car and stopped just a few feet from the hood. Diana saw the whole vessel had stopped. It still slowly rotated, but moved no further forward. Jack clung to his mother, wrapping his arms around her legs, while Jules gripped her hand even tighter.

"Sorry Mommy, I think it heard me," Jules whispered. Too late if it did now, Diana thought. The whole vessel from the lower tip to the upper top was slowly turning, revealing all three hundred and sixty degrees of the lower part of the cone, the small stones sparkling on the pearlescent surface. One thing that Diana noted was that it was emitting no sound at all, nothing, not even a low-level hum. Only the wind current, caused by the pressure in the air between the vessel and the ground gave cause for any noise. If she had been asleep outside in her backyard, it would have passed over her unnoticed. Well this was great, what the hell was she going to do now, stuck underneath this thing? A distant noise drew her attention; man-made sounds, the whoosh of jets roaring through the air followed by an echoing *crump crump crump*—then another sound, louder, an explosion? A rocket? She couldn't tell for sure. Oh great, yup, let's blow the thing up, that will work! Only then came a sound from the craft itself. A single pulsating hum, lasting only seconds, simultaneously accompanied the surface of the object glowing brighter, making it incandescent, sparkling momentarily with a greater radiance than before.

"Shinies!" screamed Jules, then abruptly shut her mouth. As the lower shaft of the vessel stood before them, Diana found herself putting on her shades to shield her eyes from the glowing light. She forced her children to look away, but Jules had already put on her own pink star-shaped sunglasses that she had picked up at some children's party or other a few months earlier. She looked hilarious. Jack simply covered his eyes with his hands, burying his face into her body. Diana allowed herself to smile. Here they were standing underneath an object that was obviously alien in origin, perhaps about to meet visitors from another world for the first time in the history of the earth and who was here to greet them? A single mother and her two children, one of whom was wearing pink star-shaped sunglasses. Perhaps they would pay her some money to tell this story on Oprah. Now there was an idea—if they ever got out of this. A distant explosion echoed around the hills, somewhere beyond the underside of the vessel. Diana strained to locate its origin but she saw nothing that offered an answer. Her view was limited to the narrow strip of light between the edges of the vessel and the ground, which was some miles from this position. God! It must have been the military. They must have been firing at it.

"Oh that's just wonderful! Great way to welcome you to earth!" She spontaneously found herself shouting.

"They don't represent us! They don't represent me!" she screamed at the daunting shape above her, to whoever might be listening. She was desperate now. Whoever they were (inside the cone-shaped vessel) or whatever they wanted, they obviously knew their ship was being fired upon, and she certainly couldn't allow the actions of the stupid people in government to be the only voice, especially when her children's lives were at stake.

"We're good people. Well, most of us are. We… want to welcome you. I am Diana and this is my daughter Jules and my son Jack!" She shouted. Both her children looked up and waved timidly at the ship, which did nothing in response except continue to slowly rotate the lower spire before them.

"We… aren't the best or the brightest of humanity. But we're good honest people." She momentarily thought back to when she had stolen some cheese from the supermarket a few weeks ago in desperation—that wouldn't count against them, would it?

"We're not religious or anything. I was born a Catholic. Not sure if that counts for anything. Actually the Catholic Church has a great deal to answer for, so forget I said that. If you've come to invade us then please…"

She looked down at her children, whose wide eyes were locked in awe on the vessel. Diana found herself moving towards the cone that was still positioned just in front of their car. At this stage, mercy seemed like the last refuge of the desperate and that's exactly what she was. Desperate.

"Please spare my children… and if you can't, then just make it quick. Make it painless. Don't make us suffer! Don't make them suffer! My children, they're only eleven and seven years old. They have their whole lives ahead of them. Mine is less… I…" Diana felt her voice tremble, it was as if this vessel had become her confessional, and once she crashed through that barrier, she could not stop.

"I… I did the best I could for them. I worked all the hours I could just to feed them, clothe them and put a roof over their heads but it wasn't… it wasn't enough. I wanted to give them so much more, and now we don't even have a home. I tried my best but I failed them. I failed them and I am so sorry. This is who we are. We're no one important. We're no threat to you…"

"You haven't failed us, Mommy!" Jules said, still gripping her hand.

"Yeah, you're a good Mom." Jack said, still gripping her legs.

"Kids, stay here, okay? Jules, look after Jack. I'm just going closer…" she snapped, defying any sense of reason or logic.

"Don't Mom! It might take you away!"

"If it does, it's better it takes me than you! Just stay here for two minutes." she added, fixing the children with a glare that meant they stayed rooted to the spot. She stared at the revolving craft.

"Please, if you must take anyone, take me, but spare my children! Spare them. They're innocent. Do you know that word? Innocent?"

Diana didn't know what made her do what she did next. Maybe she was feeling reckless, or maybe it was stupidity combined with a burning curiosity that consumed her like an itch that had to be scratched, but she had to see this thing close up, to touch it. Something made her want to connect with it. Even though her actions were contrary to every alien scenario she had witnessed on film or television, inside herself she somehow found a strange belief that nothing bad was going to happen to her. She somehow felt... safe. She unlaced her fingers from Jules' and crept towards the lower cone. As she slowly and deliberately took each step, she heard echoing thunder-cracks again, in the distance. Weapons firing. Probably the U.S. military, trying to bring the vessel down.

"We're not here to hurt you," she told the craft. "Not us personally. Those people, those men, showing you aggression. They're the worst of us. They're not who we are. Our leaders don't care about us, they don't care about much at all, actually! Um, so anyway... welcome to earth. We call this part America. Well, Nevada... not much to see here really... but Vegas is just down the road, if you want somewhere more exciting. Actually forget Vegas, I'm not sure that's the best place for you to start your tour..."

She edged closer, until the glittering surface was just a few feet away from her face, slowly turning, its surface twinkling with a thousand diamond-like objects that spread up the cone and into the beyond above until she lost focus, the distant haze of the underside of the saucer shimmering high above her. She stretched out her hand to touch the surface. She looked back at her daughter and son, then back at the object. Then it moved. The cone rose just a few inches in front of her so that the lowest point was now level with her face, just a mere few inches from the tip of her nose. She sensed that the rest of the craft had not raised with it but that just the base had changed to match her height. Was this a sign of intelligence? Was it alive somehow? Maybe it wasn't a ship at all, maybe it was organic. Every heartbeat was telling her not to be foolish and to step away, to run, to protect her children. Yet somehow there was a feeling of comfort, of protection and security that began to glow within her, as though she had just drunk a really expensive glass of champagne.

The ability to instantly change its mass would explain why the vessel was able to travel so close to the road, changing its height to move along with the terrain below it. For the first time she noticed a smell, it was familiar to her, something she recognised but she couldn't place. It was a sweet scent, like a flower, honeysuckle perhaps or fresh fruits. Only something about it was unusual, making it hard to define. The end of cone glowed once more, causing the surface to brighten momentarily. Diana's face glowed in turn, her children watching on in wonder.

"I think it likes you Mom." Jules said.

Diana turned and put her finger to her lips to shush her daughter, then turned back to face it. She felt an inexplicable desire to place her hand just beneath the end of the cone. She outstretched her hand just below it, almost touching it, when she felt a small object fall into the palm of her hand, followed by another, then another. She held them up as the rolled around in her palm, studying them with awe. They looked like diamonds, and they felt like diamonds. She cupped her hands together, holding them below the object's lowest point. Dozen's more of the precious-looking stones fell into her hands as if the surface was shedding them like dead scales from a skin. The largest was the same size as a small pebble from the beach, the smallest still larger than any rock she had seen on a wedding ring. Even Melania Trump's wasn't as big as one of these. There wasn't time for a closer examination now. She pushed them into the pockets of her jeans but the largest fell onto the ground. She dropped to her knees and quickly snatched it up in her fingers. This was too much for Jack and Jules who at once pelted over, each clutching her side.

"Please don't take our Mommy!" both the kids yelled in unison.

Again the object glowed brightly for a moment, before returning back to its usual pearly pigmentation. Nothing more fell from its surface. She knew she would need to find somewhere safer to store their gift than in the pockets of her jeans. She studied the one in her hand. It looked and felt like a diamond, that was the only way she could describe it, though she had never seen a stone this big before. It was smooth and when she held it up to her eye she saw a rainbow shimmering within its prism.

"Massive Shiny!" Jules shouted. Diana pondered its value, if it were real. Several thousand dollars for sure, perhaps more. She had thrown herself on the mercy of these... whoever, whatever they were and they had showered her, almost literally, with gifts. It didn't make sense. Why give her something?

"Thank you... I just need to add, this doesn't mean we're engaged or anything!" She laughed. What on earth were they going to do now? She immediately gave the largest stone to Jules and told her to hide it in her backpack.

"Jesus, lady—are you okay?"

The voice belonged to a man, shouting from behind her. She turned to see two young men standing just a few yards away, next to a parked-up four by four.

OMARI

H is three camels had noticed something was different that morning some time before he did. Omari was resting next to one of them, his makeshift shade propped up on poles next to the beast, his head resting on the blanket that had been draped over the creature's body. All three of his animals were sitting down on folded legs, resting from their long journey. Even for Chad, the heat that day had been relentless since dawn had broken across the desert. It was forty-nine degrees in the shade, Omari knew this because he had a small silver thermometer that he carried every-where in his belt.

The belt was a gift from his wife. It was made up of pockets and pouches and was probably the most practical thing she had ever given him. He hadn't liked it at first because it felt too modern and a break from the traditional garments of his tribe, but in the end he had to admit it was extremely useful and enabled him to keep all his money, tablets, compass, watch and a clip-on water bottle easily about his person. Since she had been taken by Allah, it had taken on a sentimental meaning and he never left home without it.

Omari normally travelled by night, when the temperature would plummet to such lows, an outsider would not have believed possible in such a hot part of the world, but today he had been forced to travel by daylight for as long as he could tolerate. His supplies were running low and his persistently bad toothache had been, making it very difficult to get any sleep. He knew it would probably have to be removed, bringing the number of teeth he had lost to a grand total of six. In his home town *Fada*, his final destination, there was a doctor at the small army barracks. Having

57

a dentist was a luxury in this part of the country and even now the local doctor would not claim to be an expert in teeth. If you had a painful tooth then this normally meant it was coming out, but having already lost so many he was now having trouble chewing his food! He just needed to rest for a few hours, then he could start off again. On this part of the trail, the dunes of the desert pitched and rolled like an ocean, interspersed by patches of burnt granite that rudely intruded through the waves of sand; scattered rocks the colour of charcoal. This part of the world was known for its unique rock formations that twisted and turned out of the desert like stalagmites would in caves, or extended themselves from mountain ranges as long graceful fingers that would form into unique arches of stone that could provide a valuable strip of shade from the unrelenting sun. The locations of many such places were known only to those few who could travel these remote trails and it was under one such rock that this trader had sought shelter.

Omari was dressed in traditional clothing for a man of his means and tribe. His loose-fitting, once-white cotton garments were a permanent shade of mustard, stained forever by the dust of his travels. His dirty white headscarf wrapped around down to his neck, the only thing poking through it was his dark wiry beard, the ends of which were beginning to turn grey. He produced a small glass bottle from his satchel and took a small swig of vodka, using it to wash around his mouth numbing the pain a little, before finally spitting it out, momentarily savouring the taste of the liquor, but not consuming any part of it. He took out a small piece of broken mirror, jagged down one side. Holding it up to his face he opened his mouth, trying to examine the source of his pain. Omari looked into his eyes for a moment and wondered how he had got so old and where all the time had gone.

Now in his fifties, he was a man with many sorrows. He had never concerned himself with the politics of his nation but was not a stranger to its history. He had always lived in the eastern regions, which were an especially remote and harsh part of the country, but were less troubled by its civil wars and military coups, which were always focused on the capital to the west and the more fertile lands to the south. Here the desert was sand and rock with little else and only those who had travelled the route many times could traverse its dangers without getting lost. Bandits here were rarer, because the areas of population were so sparse and concentrated to the south. These days little was to be gained for the considerable effort it would take to try and ambush someone in this part of the world. Omari had in the past carried a rifle for hunting, but it had recently rusted and fallen apart and he had not yet got around to replacing it. Another expense he really couldn't afford.

He had started his journey two months earlier from the town of *Mous-*

soro which lay just over 200 kilometres from the country's capital, *N'Dja-mena*. He had only been to the capital twice in his life, and the last time he was there fighting had broken out between the government and factions loyal to the one that had since taken its place. Omari had been with his late father and they had had to leave the city far earlier than expected. Those were golden days for the family, when they had run caravans with forty camels or more, bringing much needed rare supplies to the remote villages of the eastern region.

The whole family had moved in caravans back then, but he had always had relatives in the town of Fada and they would eventually always find themselves circling back there. The need for such trade was gradually being reduced by the modernisation and reduction of the country's corrup-tion under its current leader. The president, he knew, was a *Toubou* like himself, but beyond his knowledge of the man's tribe he could not even recall his name. Omari knew only what he heard on the rare occasions he listened to the radio or saw a television, and it was of little interest to him. "Take care of your family and the animals, the rest of the world can worry about itself." These were the words of his father and they had always remained with him; as though he had heard them only yesterday. Else-where his memory was failing him.

His family had always led a simple life and never asked for much, as was the way for most people in this region of his country. He wiped his brow and removed his most treasured possession from his pouch—A photograph of himself, with three women—A moment frozen in time that he always wanted to remember. In his twenties, Omari had married from within his clan to a local girl, Fatima, and she bore him two daughters. He was disappointed not to have had a son but he loved his girls all the same and brought them gifts on each return journey from his travels. The girls had often wanted to accompany him, especially his eldest, Nya, who always had such a burning curiosity to see more of the world that he suspected it would one day be her undoing. He had made his caravan routes shorter and shorter so he could spend more time with them. They had made their family home in Fada and there was, for the first time in his life, a sense of routine. He was a practising Muslim and prayed to Allah but had neither interest in doing more than was required, nor a desire to convert others to his religion. His life was simple, yet he knew many others who had far more material wealth than him, who were so unhappy. The recent years however had not been kind to him. His wife, Fatima, had died five years ago when he was away trading, and Omari found himself consumed with grief at her loss. Nya was now married to an officer in the army and had moved to the capital when her husband got promoted. He had not seen her in two years. She had sent a postcard and it had an email address on it, but he had no idea how to use email, he had never understood computers, which just confused him. His second daughter, Joy, now lived part-time with an uncle, his half-brother, back in Fada while he was away, and he had not seen her in several months. It was this reunion with his youngest that spurred his journey homeward. He knew Joy was not happy, and more than anything he wanted to see her heart fulfilled within his lifetime. It was his only prayer to Allah, but Allah was not with him on his most recent journey. His own caravan had been reduced from twelve to just three camels during this trip. He had lost two in a sandstorm and several others died of disease before he was able to help them. These recent events weighed heavily on his mind as he lay in the shade with his remaining three animals.

His living was dependent on a dying trade in a time where overland trading caravans were becoming obsolete. Even Fada now had an airport, which had reduced his trade, it was just a strip of sand large enough to land small aircraft, with barrels that were set alight at night for landing lights. Even so, not everything would always be brought in by airplane. Requests from the most remote villages for simple spices, dates, grains, oils and herbs for cooking were still there and it was by meeting these simple demands that Omari made his meagre living. Most men in his country didn't live past their fiftieth birthday and he was five years past that age already. His youngest daughter, Joy, was promised to marry a local man when she turned sixteen, but Omari knew she did not love him. He was a goat herder and almost twice her age and was known to have visited prostitutes when travelling away. This man had been married once before, but his wife had died mysteriously and Omari suspected she had not been well treated, but he also didn't trust his half-brother Attah, either and Joy needed her own man to look after her.

He turned this over in his mind again and again, and the negative thoughts added to his lethargy. He had never known the feeling of depression before; in his tribe there was no word for such a thing but today he was consumed by it. Negative thoughts had entered his head and they didn't want to leave. He just wanted to get home and see his daughter. Perhaps he could find some work in Fada to support them, because he knew somehow this caravan journey was to be his last. A movement beneath him made his head jerk, and he realised that his camel, Abu-Sir, was moving. (He had named all of his animals after characters from Arabian Nights, the tales of which his father would read to him as a child.) Abu-Kir, who lay nearby, also began to emit distressed high-pitched bleats and grunts. Something or someone was disturbing them; perhaps someone was coming out of Fada and taking the trail west. Omari pulled back his head scarf from his face and sat up, clearing his throat of dust. He reached for his water bottle and took a sip before standing up. The movement of Abu-Sir had caused his temporary shade tent to fall down as the camel stood. He approached the beast and did his best to calm it, as he had so many times before. Ali-Baba, his third camel, carried his supply packs, was roped to his foot and was tugging at him. Omari thought it wise to mount the creature in case it was going to bolt. He took the reins and tried to steady the animal, which he sensed felt as uneasy as the others.

"Come now, what is it, my friend? What frightens you?" he asked, leaning in to the head of the beast and patting it between the ears.

It was only then that Omari saw it moving across the landscape, parallel to him, perhaps five kilometres off to the north, travelling from east to west. Such a course would have taken it directly over the northern part of Fada already. It was the hugest object in the sky he had ever witnessed. The biggest construction he had ever seen was a tower in the capital city and that could have only been one tenth the size of this. The object, though a creamy white in colour had brown stains to its surface, Omari presumed from a sandstorm. Its shape was most unusual, like a large plate with two points coming from the middle, one down towards the ground, the other pointing skywards, as if it was a tower reaching to paradise. The lower part of the vessel sparkled, shimmering in the afternoon sun. Its shape actually reminded him of a child's toy, that one would spin on the ground in a market. The lower point of it could have almost been drawing in the sand below it. The widest part stretched out either side for miles and cast a huge soft shadow beneath it upon the rolling dunes below. Omari was quick to grab the reins of all three animals as they wailed, frightened by the object, but he held them together offering words of comfort.

"Easy. Easy. It is far from us and will do us no harm." That was his hope at least.

Then it just stopped.

The object just held itself there in the air, motionless, with nothing visible supporting it. He wondered if this was something the Americans or the Russians had created. He heard stories among other tribesmen of these faraway nations and their plans to dominate the world. They all used to laugh and say "Let them come, there's nothing here for them!"

Perhaps it was not of this world. When travelling with the caravans as a child with his father, they had seen many strange things. Balls of light in the sky would dance for them as he and his father watched. On one occasion one had come quite close as they sat outside their tent at night, a small fire burning before them. It was funny that he had forgotten all about that until this very moment. His father told him later that they had been visited by Allah and that it was a good omen for them. So it had been for that journey, no storms, no bandits, no animals getting sick. It was, Omari now recalled, a very uneventful caravan, apart from their glowing visitor. The small glowing orb had first appeared in the sky perhaps a mile or so from them before dancing freely, performing twists and turns, loops and dives that no man-made aircraft ever could. At least not any Omari knew of. Omari had approached it, breaking free from his father's grasp, but as he moved closer it toyed with him, moving always just a little further away. Finally after a final energetic display of movement, it took off into the night sky at a tremendous speed and was never seen again. Omari called them "The Sky Dancers". His father later showed him the secret caves east of Fada, with paintings on the walls from ancient tribesmen. One such painting depicted a similar orb in the sky, with the men seated around the camp fire before it, their camels resting nearby.

But the structure hovering before him now was not remotely the same as the dancing orb he had seen as a child. For one thing, its size was not even comparable. The circular spine of the craft pointed downwards, ever decreasing in its width until it came to a single fine point at the end. Omari could see a similar smaller structure rising from the top of the craft. His location was some way above ground level, he having climbed up a rocky outcrop that morning to seek a small ravine that he knew would provide him with more shade from the sun than just his makeshift shelter. From his current height and distance he could see the whole of the object from top to bottom quite clearly. Both cones sloped towards the wide disk at its centre, which then spanned some considerable distance across. The size of a city perhaps. It certainly would put all of Fada into the shade. Fada. His thoughts turned to his home and his daughter, Joy. He knew it was only a few miles further east and this thing, whatever it was, would have certainly passed very close to them. He glanced in that direction and there were no signs of attack, no spirals of black smoke, which he normally associated with conflict. Just the small dots of some of the outer dwellings along with the cluster of green palms that lay just beyond them could be seen on the shimmering horizon. He knew even if he travelled hard toward home now, in this heat, it would be risky.

But the child that still dwelled deep in Omari wanted to get closer to this strange sight. He wanted to know its origin and what purpose brought it to Chad. Was it a sign from Allah? Perhaps he had come finally to save the world from all its pain. Was this what Allah looked like? His God was said always to be present in all things but had never actually presented himself to Omari in a form that he could actually see. Could this truly be him? There was only one way to be certain. Convincing the animals to go any closer would be a problem, and if he lost them , it would be like losing everything. Then he noticed something about the object. It was slowly rotating and unless he was mistaken, it was descending, the lowest point pushing into the dunes below. Then dust and sand began to spew upward from the ground throwing up clouds that gradually fanned outwards. It made the most unusual sound as it began to push and twist into the ground, but not what he would have expected for such a sight. It was the sound he would have associated with the mass movement of earth rather than the drilling noise normally associated with tunnelling into solid rock, which Omari knew lay only a short distance beneath the sands. The sound of metallic drills hammering into rock was a sound he knew only too well. When he had visited the mines with his second uncle, Joseph, in the south, they had gone there for a holiday and Joseph demonstrated his use of the drill on a nearby quarry rock face. It was something of an adventure for the young Omari, and his uncle made him wear a heavy metal hat so he could watch safely. The sounds it made were so piercing. The shrill grinding noise would echo across the quarry and cause a ringing in his ears that would last for several days. His uncle had to wear ear protectors, but the boy was standing far away enough to be allowed to listen without, and the sound was indelible in his memory. This sound was different. Yes, there was noise, but it sounded more like the earth being rearranged than split apart. As though the earth was being blended.

Omari gazed at the incredible sight unfolding as the dust clouds expanded outwards and upwards, almost reaching the underside of the disk part of the object, and spreading out across the desert floor. Soon only the disk and the upper cone structure remained in view, but it wasn't long before this too was engulfed by the brown and yellow plumes of dirt.

Omari thought that even from this distance, with a cloud so vast in size everyone in Fada would be able to see this strange act of nature, if indeed it were that. His daughter, Joy, surely must have also been witness to its arrival. Joy. He longed to be reunited with her but this was something he needed to see. The sadness that had been his daily companion of late at once abandoned him to be replaced by a burning curiosity to examine the object. This sight before him was not of this earth. This was not of man. This could only be of Allah. He sat the animals back down. They had found a place of calm, their breathing having slowed down and were no longer fretting. He then re-erected his small shade tent so he had the best view of the events unfolding before him, facing away from the harsh glare of the sun. He could travel no further until the sun began to dip. He decided that on the last leg of his final journey he would make a small detour and see this wondrous gift from Allah for himself.

CHAPTER III

"This is not a time for panic; this is not a time for cowardice—nor is this a time for complacency. This is a time for bravery, a time for courage, a time for resolve, a time to show the world what the British people are made of. To lead the world by example, and say "We can survive this. We will meet the challenges that this event will bring to our lives, to humanity and to the world, head on." This will make us stronger, more resolute and more determined to protect the ones we love and to achieve great things in our brief time on this earth. We may feel smaller than we did yesterday, we may even feel insignificant but though we have been divided in the past, the human race must, for the first time in its history, feel truly united as a people; united in our curiosity to know more about our fellow travellers and where they have come from; united in our need for safety for our families, our culture and for our countries; united in our need to understand what this means for our future. For no longer are we individuals playing our parts on the world stage of history. Today, we have shaken hands with a universal destiny. Let us take those first steps carefully and cautiously but with open minds and open hearts. We should be open to the opportunities this will present for us all, whilst also being mindful of the dangers that may await us. What is not in doubt is that a united mankind will prevail. We may no longer be alone in the universe, but we're more united than ever before in the history of the world."

And if you believe I wrote that myself, you'll believe anything…

From the diary of British Prime Minister Ryan Wallace, April 2nd

BLESSING

EAST OF ABERDEEN, SCOTLAND, APRIL 2ND

"This is life changing, lassie, hey?"

Blessing had not imagined that the first adventurous thing she might ever do in her life would be to jump on a bus with a cigarette-smoking, foul-mouthed Scottish bus driver, whose name she still didn't even know, to go and look at an alien object that had first materialised over the North Sea. She and many others had watched the craft travel over Aberdeen and continue on a few miles west of the city before slowly coming to a halt, sitting over the areas known locally as *The Birks* and *The Tilly's* such was the size of the thing that its structural expanse entirely covered them both. Blessing had taken several pictures of the craft as it had travelled overhead earlier, the saucer part of the ship encompassing the entire city of Aberdeen. It was when she went to upload them on her Instagram and Snapchat accounts that she saw several missed calls on her phone from her friends back in Birmingham and London, along with texts from relatives in Nigeria. One rather pessimistic text from a cousin read, "Have you seen the news? They're all over the world. Over 200 of them! This is de end sista!"

She had tried to make some calls herself but couldn't get through to a single soul, every number she called was busy or currently unavailable. The networks must have been struggling to cope with the volume of calls. It was then that the bus driver announced he wanted to get a better look at the ship, or "sheep" as he called it and anyone who wanted to was welcome to come along.

"Any of you lot that wannae com to see that thing land, I'm gonnae go noo!"

People's reactions had surprised her. While many thought he was completely mad, several individuals jumped at the chance. A couple of young men, who, Blessing thought, must have been students, raced up to the front of the top deck shouting, "Let's go, Elvis!"

"Anyone else like?" The bus driver let the words hang in the air for the moment as he finished another cigarette. An elderly lady with bright white hair stepped forward, whom Blessing recalled had been on the bus earlier. "If they're going to take someone maybe they can take me and sort my arthritis out, and if they're going to invade and kill us all, well, I might as well get it over with quickly!"

"Aye that's the spirit Agatha, do or die, hey?" The man slicked back his hair causing his belly to stick out from beneath a white shirt that Blessing thought could do with a good iron. She spotted what appeared to be flakes of dried wax in his hair, either that or lots of dead skin. She often used oil herself to keep her roots healthy and stop them from getting too dry, but wax in a white man's hair, especially one whose hair was grey and trailing down the back of his neck while he was balding at the front was a new one on her.

"If we dinnae go noo, the polis are going to close it all off and that will be it! Once in a lifetime trip this lassie, hey?"

Blessing couldn't really understand a word the man was saying but she knew she wanted to know more about what they had just seen, not just hear about it on the news later. Her life was dull, uneventful and this was a chance to do something different. She contemplated the danger for a moment. True, they could be coming here to invade, but it had just flown over one of Scotland's largest cities and left it untouched. Why on earth would it just ignore it if it was going to attack? Perhaps there were men on board, blue men perhaps, but eligible men nonetheless. She made a quick sign of the cross and jumped back on the bus.

"That's the spirit, lassie, hey? Sit doon noo and hold on tight. We're gonna be breaking a few rules of the highway code today!" the driver shouted as he got into his cabin. The bus roared to life and shot off down the seafront, nudging (as the driver would put it to Blessing later) a few stationary cars out of the way.

Traffic in Aberdeen was at a standstill and at first they didn't get very far, despite the driver doing his best to avoid the town centre and get off the main roads as soon as possible. Blessing saw that people were panicking and cars had been trying to leave the city in all directions. Multiple collisions between vehicles, some more serious than others, had taken place. Some shops were in the process of closing while she witnessed scores of people queuing at others, mostly for food and other consumable supplies. Others ran through the streets with goods and clothing, the first sign to Blessing that law and order was breaking down. The driver cursed as he twisted and turned through the narrow streets, finally taking them out of the city centre. Blessing had opted to sit just to the left in the seats closest to the cabin, normally reserved for pensioners. Behind her sat Agatha, the elderly lady whose voice was soft and laced with a lighter, well spoken, soft Scottish accent.

"This is all very exciting, isn't it, dear? I never thought I would live to see the day. Aliens from another world! I might as well have a front row seat, don't you think?" She stared out of the window at the moving object, which they would glimpse between the houses and office blocks, filling the skyline to the west. They turned off Union Street onto Great Western Road with its neat two-storey grey-stone dwellings that were occasionally interspersed with the odd newsagent and charity shop. Blessing saw the spire of the familiar Mannofield Parish Church up at the far end of the street in the distance, and it made her wonder how full the church might be, and she momentarily contemplated seeking her answers in prayer. No, the good Lord would protect her wherever she was. Besides he might be getting off the ship in person and if that was the case, well, she didn't want to be late for the Second Coming. Maybe they were aliens from a dying world who needed to come and take women away to repopulate their planet. If that was the case then she would gladly go, as long as it was a planet that believed in the institution of marriage and not some massive alien sex orgy. Ideally it should have a male populace with good table manners and even better dress sense... She was getting ahead of herself. None of those scenarios was, after all, very likely. They might just be stopping and asking for directions. It could be as simple as that. Blessing saw people hailing the bus as it went past various stops on the route. The driver finally pulled up at one. The middle-aged woman standing there looked really confused.

"Have you been diverted?" she asked.

"Aye..." the driver replied. "Where are you going to now then?" said the woman.

"To the space ship, lassie. Wannae come?" The woman looked for a moment as if she was going to step on, then took a step back after clearly having second thoughts. "No thanks. I'll wait for the next one."

The driver wasted no time in shutting the doors and speeding off. "What's your name?" Blessing realised she had shouted the question at him without even thinking about it.

"Dinnae distract a man when he's drivin' noo!" the Scotsman yelled back at her without taking his eyes off the road. But Blessing could see him glancing at her in the wing mirror. She felt foolish for even asking him, but if she was being driven to her potential doom she might as well know who was taking her there. She sank back down in her seat.

"Dinnae worry noo, lassie, I was only jokin', like! Rules oot the window today, hey? It's Richard but my friends call me Elvis! What's yours?"

"Blessing!" She found herself shouting as the bus went over a speed bump, causing her underwear to ride right up her backside making her response somewhat higher-pitched than intended.

"Nice to meet you, Blessing. Never seen nowt like this in all mah life, wuid you just look at it! It looks like its slowing doon noo and we're going to be among the first ones to see it." He turned and smiled at her, showing his row of cigarette stained, dull yellow teeth. Blessing managed a weak smile back. "Aren't you nervous?"

Elvis, as Blessing would now call him, paused for a beat before he spoke more softly in reply. "Aye, I'm nervous, but since I lost my Jean, well, what's there to look forward to in life, hey? This is gonnae be special. This is gonnae be in the history books. I might as well be part of it, hey? You noo what I mean, lassie? Hang on tight now! We're going to be clocking up a few speeding tickets today, like!"

Blessing wondered who Jean was, then her thoughts turned back to the floating object that filled the sky all the way to the highlands in the west, blocking the horizon. It was as if it was standing on a single stalk. By the time they reached the edge of the city centre, it had passed well beyond the suburbs and the upper tower once again became visible.

"It looks like a spinning top, don't you think, dear?' Agatha said. *Yes, it was just like a giant spinning top*, Blessing thought, but far more beautiful. Either side of the street, people were packing their cars with belongings, but others just stood there mesmerised, many with phones in their hands, recording or taking pictures of it and sending them to their friends, or trying to. The level of panic was less than she would have expected. Maybe they had simply missed the worst of it, but Blessing noticed that every turn-off south that led towards Dundee and Edinburgh was clogged with cars fleeing the city. Heading west, they faced considerably less traffic. They passed the Mannofield Parish Church. Blessing could see the Pastor welcoming in a large crowd of people. She knew people who would not normally embrace the word of God would look to the church on a day like today, and no doubt they would see a swell in numbers all across the world. She had been having her own internal battles with her faith recently. Day after day the news on television and social media from around the world was always bad. Nothing joyful ever seemed to be reported anymore, apart from celebrity or royal marriages and the birth of the odd baby panda. It was always death, murder and misery. Maybe the news had always been like that, but the last few years seemed to have been especially relentless with bad news. For Blessing it had started when all those famous people had died in a single year, and their deaths were followed by a continual wave of bombings, killings and stabbings, not just in the United Kingdom, not even just in Europe, but all over the world. Such events had troubled her more than ever before. She despaired at the direction humanity was heading and could not help but think to herself if ever there was a time for the Lord to return to the earth, it was now. If he did so, even for the briefest of moments, she felt churches would fill up the very next day and the faith of all would be restored. Humanity needed that, now more than ever. So she had prayed every day for his return, for him to come and save mankind. Could this object be holy? Could it be here at the behest of God?

The sound of angry sirens drew her focus to the small fleet of police cars that quickly overtook them and sped on up the road.

"We're not the only ones in a hurry then! I expect they're going to try to block all the roads off leading towards it, don't you think?" Agatha said, leaning across the rail to talk into Blessing's right ear.

"Do you really think so?" she sounded as disappointed as she felt. Having made the commitment to go now, she really wanted to see this thing up close. She wanted to know what it was doing here, where it was from, and most of all who was inside it, and if it contained any eligible men, even if they were green and had strange genitalia. What on earth was she thinking about? So silly. She had been lonely and resolving that issue often preoccupied her mind. The world being invaded by aliens wasn't going to change that.

"Can they do that? Can they stop us from going to see it?" Blessing asked, entirely unsure of the legality of what they were doing.

"Aye! They can try. But not if we get there first. I'm gonnar be taking the back roads like, not the main road. Time for a few tunes then, hey?" Music instantly began to blare out in the bus, the driver singing along loudly as the lyrics played, matching them word for word, beat for beat. Sliding his dark glasses down his nose as the song began:

"A little less conversation
A little less conversation, a little more action please
All this aggravation ain't satisfactioning me
A little more bite and a little less bark
A little less fight and a little more spark
Close your mouth and open up your heart and baby satisfy me
Satisfy me baby
Baby close your eyes and listen to the music..."

Blessing thought the lyrics all sounded rather sexual, and concluded she had best ignore the song and keep her eyes open. She could hear the two boys on the deck upstairs enjoying themselves. One shouting "Yeah, we're going to see the aliens with *The King*!"

"Thank you very much..." Elvis said over the intercom, but in a strange slow American accent. He was impersonating someone, but Blessing had no idea who, though she remembered hearing the song once before in a supermarket. After passing the church, they turned onto the more residential Craigton Road, passing the grey stone walls of Springbank Cemetery which Blessing glimpsed off to her right. She hated the cemeteries in the UK. They were such morbid and gothic places. She had had to go to one once when her friend, Big Angie, had passed away in London. She'd had diabetes and a whole host of other health issues, but had been fine only a few weeks earlier, and was one of those people who would breathe life into any room with her smile and conversation. She missed their conversations. Blessing then realised it would be two years this week since she'd passed away. It was funny how she hadn't thought about her recently until this moment. She wondered what Angie would have made of all this. Never one to mince her words, Blessing expected she would have marched right up to the thing when it landed and said, "Right, whose party is it and where do I get a drink?"

Soon they were out of the suburbs of Aberdeen, and the road turned into a country lane. Several cars, many of them overloaded with numerous possessions on roof racks, passed them heading east. Blessing saw many drivers eyeing them with looks of dismay. Some honked their horns in warning, but looking out of the rear window, she could see that they were not alone. A small convoy of vehicles, presumably with other people keen to witness this historical event, had fallen in line behind them. The road was too narrow for them to attempt to overtake and other lane was filled with cars whizzing past in the other direction, escaping from the shadow of the ship. Soon the few remaining houses of the Aberdeen suburbs became interspersed with fields and woods, occasionally interrupted with a more modern housing estates that had been built in small patches outside this part of the city. Blessing felt Agatha tug at her arm as she pointed to a distant white building. "That's the Gordonian's Cricket Club over there. Harold, my husband, used to play there, oh, years ago now. Lovely little place on Sundays. They did delicious cream teas!"

"Perhaps we can go there some day? You can show me a game of Cricket. I have only ever seen it on television." Blessing replied.

Agatha looked surprised at the suggestion. "I haven't been there for years, love. I'd like to go again though. Maybe we can take our new friends there!"

As the bus turned into Friarsfield Road Agatha again pointed and reminisced about places from her past. "I remember coming here before, there's some lovely houses here, you know…"

Agatha was not wrong. Nicely spaced bungalows with generous gardens and small low-walled compounds, like those Blessing remembered from Nigeria as a child, sat proudly side by side along the leafy street. All had neatly kept gardens and large gates with ample parking space. These weren't mansions, just decent sized single houses, perfect for a small family, and Blessing thought, the sort of home that really every person should be entitled to regardless of their race, colour, creed or background. She dreamed of owning such a home one day, but such lofty financial goals were far out of her reach. Her memories of her life in Nigeria were few, but she recalled even the smallest home there was larger than her cramped bedsit in this city and all were free of the pervading damp found in the United Kingdom. Soon they were past the pretty dwellings, and the image of her desired home was replaced by more green fields. The bus arrived at a T-junction and the driver brought the cumbersome vehicle to a halt with a roaring hiss. Blessing could see he was thinking. Impatient drivers behind began to honk their horns, urging him forward. Between the gaps of the houses above and ahead of them the rim of the saucer filled the sky, the pearl white underside spreading back into the horizon and the central lower stalk coming down somewhere miles beyond. Blessing got up from her seat and pointed to it.

"That part is the centre! That is the piece that will touch the earth." It seemed an obvious conclusion to make, but she surprised herself by her impulsive comment. She was not normally so vocal but it was indeed a day for firsts. Elvis stroked his chin, trying to guess where that might be in geographical terms. He nodded and smiled back at her. He turned the bus left.

"To get under the middle we don't wannae go this way. We'll go via Petercutler and stay close to the river Dee then turn north. Sit back down lassie!" He turned left at the junction and sped off, barely giving Blessing time to take her seat. They were soon passing by houses again, rows and rows of them, with Agatha explaining that they were somewhere called *Bieldside*, which was at one time a separate town, but now was essentially on the outskirts of Aberdeen.

"Hi." The sudden voice from behind her made Blessing jump. It belonged to one of the students, aged in his early twenties with ginger hair and very pale skin, his face sporting a chewing grin. Blessing could see he was sweating and talking faster than normal.

"How you doing? I'm Ewen. Look at this, my friends just sent me these from London!"

Before Blessing even had a chance to introduce herself, Ewen was holding up his iPhone Elite and showing her and Agatha several images of the same alien object, but these pictures were not of the one in Scotland.

"There's more of them, all over the planet. There's one in Northern Ireland, apparently in the sea! Another in Southern Ireland next to the Giant's causeway! Maybe they were the ones who made it, huh? Several have landed in America. There's another north of Paris. This is going to change shit forever! I mean the government will never be able to cover this up, will they? You got any chewing gum?" he asked, finally downing a big swig of water from the bottle he was holding. Blessing thought she had some gum in her bag but she wasn't sure. This kid looked as though he was drunk. Instead, she shook his hand and answered his original question. "I'm Blessing. This is Agatha. Wow, so many of these things everywhere."

Her voice betrayed a tinge of disappointment, as if the uniqueness of their situation had been stolen out from under them by the confirmation that the phenomena that they were witnessing was not unique to Scotland, but in fact were a global phenomenon. Now she felt more determined than ever that they should reach the thing before anyone else.

"Yeah, but no one has sent me a picture of one really up close yet and that's what we're going to get!" Ewen stated, very definitely. His mission statement pleased her.

"Aye, we're gonnae get close alright... I'll see to that..." Elvis shouted back from the driver's cabin.

Getting through Bieldside took some negotiating, as its residents had decided they were too close to the object for their liking and were packing up and moving out. Fortunately the bus was mainly travelling east and its size and lack of manoeuvrability meant people had to give way to it or back up even when they didn't want to. Elvis said more than one unkind word out the window, some of which Blessing could not understand, while others she could comprehend all too clearly. After another ten minutes they were out of Bieldside and on to Deeside Road, heading west. Agatha's late husband had apparently also played golf at the Deeside golf club, but she couldn't tell Blessing what the tea was like there as lady members were not allowed, at least not in her day. Blessing had many desires in her life, and playing golf was not one of them. She made a mental note to find out if any potential suitors played golf because golf was normally played on a Sunday, and she didn't want her husband at the golf club on a Sunday—she wanted him sat right next to her in church. She was certain that the President of the United States would want to play golf with the aliens. He seemed to play a great deal of golf and would probably arrange to have them land on the golf course if he could.

She wondered if the aliens had ever heard of God. Perhaps she was destined to bring the word of God to the aliens! Maybe she had been chosen to do this... Yes! Now she thought about it she was certain of it, why else would she be here at this place and at this time? Her whole life was clearly leading to this moment. The Creator had planned it all along. She craned her head forwards to look out the front windscreen as the bus sped into the town of *Petercutler*. They went past the post office and small pharmacy, where queues of people were trying to pick up prescriptions. Blessing witnessed arguments, people wanting, no doubt, to get extra medications to make sure they had enough. She remembered her bag and checked inside it carefully. She had plenty of tablets on her and more back at the bedsit. Nothing to worry about. Now all she wanted to do was get there. The second youth came down from upstairs, who looked to be around the same age as Ewen, but he had thick, curly dark hair and wore blue jeans, a hoody and a warm-looking jacket that Blessing thought was making him hot, as he too appeared to be sweating.

"Hello ladies, hello driver. I'm Donny."

"Aye, hello, lad. Sit down noo and dinnae be bothering the lassies, otherwise you won't be coming on our little outing any further, like!" Blessing was touched. He wasn't exactly a knight jumping to her defence and the poor boy hadn't done anything to her but say hello, but she still had never had a man stick up for her before, this was the very first time. It felt like the act of a gentleman, even if that gentleman did stink of smoke, had really bad hair, and dubious taste in music. She'd take it.

"No relation to Donny Osmond, I suppose?" Agatha asked the young man politely. He shook his head. "You do look like him a bit with that curly hair. He was quite the pin-up back in my day! Every girl had a picture of Donny on their wall, you know!"

Blessing laughed to herself. The idea of a younger Agatha with Donny Osmand posters on her wall, staring at them longingly, was hilarious. She'd always thought it a little odd to pin a picture up of someone you didn't know and pine over them, hoping one day to marry them, but every girl had done it once. For Blessing it had been the English actor, Damian Lewis whom she previously thought to be an American. She had been subsequently corrected on that topic somewhat embarrassingly at a church group meeting.

"Don't worry, I'm just being friendly!" Donny said. "Did Ewen show you the pictures? Crazy isn't it! All over the world! These things are everywhere!"

The boy sat down in the cubby-hole seat behind the driver. Ewen had sat next to Agatha. The boys were harmless really, just a little happy, perhaps a bit too happy, Blessing thought. Ewen got up and rushed to the front of the bus, looking through the windscreen, holding on to the safety bar as though he was surfing, his body swaying as the vehicle weaved among the lanes. Blessing could see he was pointing up at the underside of the ship. The bus wasn't under it yet, they were still a couple of miles away, but they were getting close, to the extent that now they could no longer see above the rim of the saucer, more of the underside of the vessel was becoming visible with every passing moment.

"How many people do you think is on these things, then?" Ewen said, as he looked up in awe. His Scottish accent seemed very mild, probably as a result of being a student, and he clearly wasn't originally from Aberdeen, that Scottish accent to Blessing was very distinctive.

"Who says there's people on there at all, laddie? It might be animals or even fish!" Elvis retorted, as he twisted and turned the lumbering vehicle forever closer. Fish indeed! Blessing wondered why on earth fish would travel all this way.

"Fish? It won't be fish unless it's something like Admiral Ackbar!" Ewen replied.

"Two thirds of the earth is water, laddie. Stands to reason, it might be something that lives in the sea!" Elvis bellowed, as he turned into the next lane. The man had a point. A ship full of octopi? God, she prayed not.

They were soon out of Petercutler and onto the A93, which flowed between patches of woodland and low rolling fields that had not yet sprouted for spring. Here and there small white and grey stone cottages lay close to the roads, but the urban sprawl of Aberdeen was now well and truly behind them. Soon they approached the modern-looking village of *Drumoak*, an Eighties suburban development with its uniform Lego brick-looking, neatly arranged houses, one of which could have done Blessing very nicely, though she would have felt truly cut off from everyone in a place so remote, unless she had a car but she didn't even know how to drive.

"Look! We should turn off!" Ewen was pointing up ahead into the village where the oncoming traffic consisted of a series of dark green vehicles. Blessing had seen these types of convoys before and she always associated them with the army. Elvis didn't hesitate and turned the bus off at the next right turn, which Blessing caught the name of—*Sunnyside Drive*. An ironic name, she thought, for a part of the country so often devoid of sun.

They were now on a heading parallel with the edge of the widest part of the ship, which sat off to their left, towering above them, spreading across the sky in all its simple glory. The white pearlescent surface of the ship would occasionally reflect a glimpse of the peeping sun, and the bus would light up inside as if someone was shining a powerful torch into it. "Lucky I've got me binnaes on hey?" Elvis uttered pushing his glasses down on his nose again. "Not cheap these, mind. Proper Ray-Ban reflectors, the real thing."

Blessing wished she owned a pair, but since she had been in Scotland there were several things she hadn't needed. A swimsuit for the beach was one of them, and dark glasses were fairly close to the top of that same list. Blessing saw the Church of Drumoak pass them on their left. A small simple affair, the church did not even have a tower or a steeple, just a row of small spires along each side of the tiny white building. Even though it was not important to have a large church to be able to worship God, she had always hoped one day to see the grand cathedrals of Europe. They looked so beautiful, at least on the television. She wondered if this bus could make it that far. Maybe they could go on holiday in it to Europe. Only it didn't have a toilet. The middle column of the ship that plunged down towards the earth from the central underside still appeared extremely distant. Blessing could only just make it out from their location. They soon found themselves on a much narrower road with very deep green woods all along their right-hand side as they travelled in a northerly direction, parallel to the circumference of the ship to their left. Between them and the ship lay nothing but fields and the first low-lying hills of the highlands. Both Ewen and Donny had started referring to the object as "the ship" in their conversations, which Blessing thought seemed a reasonable assumption as it had obviously arrived from somewhere and that place was not here. The road abruptly ended at a small farm but then Elvis turned a sharp left onto another cramped muddy lane, that the bus struggled to negotiate.

Elvis announced over the speaker "Dinnae worry lads and lasses! I use to come up here with my bike. I know where I'm goin' noo. Those woods back behind us - that be the Drum Castle Estate. Ahead of us, this will lead to Coupers Road and that'll take us to the Birks which will get us under to the centre of the saucer!"

Blessing sure hoped so. It was coming up to four o'clock now and she knew it would get dark soon. Fear started to take hold when it occurred to her she was in the middle of nowhere with a bunch of strangers, on board a vehicle that she wasn't sure would get them to their destination and they had little in the way of food or supplies. That thought drew her attention to the fact that it seemed lighter outside than it would have normally been at this time of day. It felt warmer too. Certainly the two lads must have been hot, as they had both stripped down to their t-shirts. One of them had put on an iPod and was actually listening to music. Agatha pulled out one of his earpieces. "How can you put those on at a time like this? Don't you want to be part of history?"

"By giving this monumental occasion my own soundtrack to remember it by, I am creating my own moment in history." With that he replaced his earpiece and carried on staring out the front of the bus at the spectacle before them. The ship now spanned their entire view through the windscreen.

Blessing thought she noticed something. "Is it me or is it getting lower?" Donny joined Ewan standing at the front.

"It's rotating, but really slowly, but look, you can see it's descending." the student said, his teeth grinding as he talked. He took another swig of water. Blessing tried to focus on one part of the underside of the saucer just ahead of them. They weren't underneath the vessel yet, but she could see the underside stretching back towards the central column covering a distance that she thought must be around four or five miles. The underside of the ship sparkled as if covered in glitter, and a ring of odd-shaped segments towards the edge of the underside surface began flashing a series of alternating blue lights.

"He's right, the whole thing is turning and I'm sure it's lower," she said to Agatha, who strained to confirm the movement with her limited vision.

"Looks like it might be landing, then. I'll see if I can get closer but I don't think we should get under it noo…" The small tight country track, soon broke into Coupers Road, which crossed another lane that ran from north to south. Elvis seemed confident that he knew where he was going. "Up here we hit the B Road and can go west right towards the centre of the thing! Ah, shite!"

Blessing saw the cause of Elvis's profanity; a tractor coming the other way. There was absolutely no room for the vehicles to manoeuvre around each other and the driver of the tractor didn't look like he wanted to back up. Elvis leaned out the window and exchanged heated words with him. Blessing only overheard part of the conversation as she and the others were mesmerised by the sight of the ship, lowering itself to the ground.

"Why would ye bring a fookin' bus down here anyway? This isn't your route, is it pal? Where are ye goin'?" The man on the tractor yelled.

"In case you haven't noticed pal, there's an alien invasion going on here and I am trying to get these people tae fookin' safety! I have four lives I am responsible for here…"

Ewen and Donny turned to each other and went back upstairs. "We'll get a better look from the upper deck. I want to see what's going on." Ewen said almost apologetically, at leaving the two ladies alone.

"Dude, this is so amazeballs!" Donny's voice shouted from upstairs. Blessing was not familiar with this word but assumed it was some kind of youth slang suited to describe unworldly events. Agatha tapped her on the shoulder again. "Go on love, you go up and take a look. I'll be alright here. They're nice boys really, just a bit excitable,' she said.

Blessing looked at Agatha, she was such a small lady, but then she couldn't remember ever seeing any tall, old ladies. There was something very fragile about a person of that age but she was clearly enjoying every minute of their adventure together.

"It's warm isn't it, dear?" She struggled to take her duffle coat off and Blessing had to stand behind her to help. Underneath Agnes wore a strikingly loud lime green sweater. "Awful jumper, I know. A present from my grandchild, so I have to wear it. Makes a change though, doesn't it? Grandparents getting a gift from the grandkids for Christmas that they don't really like. That's normally our job!"

Blessing laughed. She liked this woman. Some of the older generation would totally lose their sense of humour, but not this lady. Blessing removed Agatha's coat and folded it up neatly, placing it on the seat next to her. "Go on dearie, you go upstairs and get a better look."

Blessing looked at her walking stick, propped up next to her. "Why don't you come up with me? I will help you."

"I'm not much good with stairs, I'm afraid. I took a bit of a fall on some not so long ago. I think if I do that again it might kill me."

Blessing offered her hand to Agatha. "I will make sure that doesn't happen. You're the oldest of us here and you need the best seat in the house." Agatha looked at her for a moment, then smiled, and took her hand. Blessing allowed herself to take all of Agatha's weight as she pulled herself up onto her feet, and then with one arm around Agatha's shoulders, and the second ready to support her, the two of them slowly took it one step at a time as they went up the stairs. Blessing called out to Elvis who was still arguing with his adversary. "Don't move the bus, I am taking Agatha upstairs."

Slowly they reached the top deck of the vehicle, where Donny and Ewen were already taking pictures with their phones from the front seats. Donny also had a larger camera he had wrestled from his rucksack and was snapping away, constantly changing his position. Blessing carefully sat Agatha down on a seat just behind the boys. It was noticeably warmer on the top deck, not uncomfortably so, but there certainly was no chance of them getting cold. Nevertheless, Blessing thought she would go back and get the lady's coat so to keep all her things together. As she went back down to the lower deck she could see the tractor reversing up the road. Elvis started up the engine. He looked round and smiled at her. "Our passengers alright then?"

"Yes, I think so. Do we have enough petrol to get back to town?" She asked.

Elvis looked at her and winked. "Aye, don't you worry noo! We dinnae wannae miss this, hey? Look at it!"

Blessing looked out. The ship was indeed lowering itself. Faster now. They couldn't be more than half a mile from the edge of the saucer but she could still see the underside quite clearly from this angle, the surface of it smooth and pearly white, just like all the rest. The central column that had been visible in the distance was now shrouded in a brown mist. Blessing assumed it must be digging into the ground and churning up earth, causing some kind of dust cloud. She thought about the people living here, caught underneath its descent. Wouldn't it crush them?

The bus started up again and headed down the lane, passing the owner of the tractor who gave Elvis a single-fingered salute which he returned in kind. Why anyone would want to drive a tractor with all this going on was beyond Blessing's comprehension, but the owner of the tractor probably thought the same about the occupants of the bus. They reached a small junction where five roads, some of them just farm tracks met. The western-most turning would lead them straight towards the ship, so Elvis made a sharp turn, narrowly missing an oncoming car that came screaming past them as he did so. The bus swerved hard, and for a moment Blessing thought it was going to topple over, already cursing herself for insisting Agatha go upstairs for a better view. As they turned onto the road Elvis spoke. "This is the B Road I told you about. It seems everyone is running away from the thing, lassie!"

He was right. A steady stream of vehicles; every type of transport that could move, was travelling in the other direction towards Aberdeen and, more importantly, well clear of the descending ship. Blessing noted that they had long since lost the small convoy of curious vehicle owners who had been heading west to see the ship for themselves. It was much lower now, perhaps five hundred metres above them and continually lowering all the time. The ring of blue lights on the underside towards the edge of its circumference still flickered as it did so. Fascinating, beautiful but also a little daunting to be so close to it. Yet despite being a little nervous, she could not say she was scared. She thought how lucky she was to be so close to something so wondrous. Few people around the world would be this close to one of these beautiful objects as it came to land on the earth. If it were some kind of invasion then surely she would be among the first to die, but such things didn't scare her. She was never afraid of death. It had stalked her for so long in her life that she had become immune to its intimidation and that was an advantage today. The bus continued on westward with Elvis noticeably reducing speed. He constantly arched his head upwards to make sure they were not going to travel underneath the ship, but he still wanted to get as close to it as he could. The ship continued its descent, all the while more vehicles sped past them heading away from it. They passed a couple of cyclists, frantically pedalling for all they were worth. There were even some people travelling on foot. A couple of hikers waved down Elvis and tried to convince him to turn around and take them with him, but he would not be deterred. They had not travelled much farther when Elvis pulled into a lay-by on the left side of the road next to what Blessing thought to be a small lake. The road stretched on ahead, rising up a little before curving slightly to the right and then on into the hills, the tops of which now were close to touching the underside of the ship. Just past the curve in the road, Blessing could see the tops of several white buildings that she felt certain would be crushed underneath as the ship landed. Elvis opened the doors, letting the clean air rush in to fill the bus, bringing with it a pervading sweet scent that reminded Blessing of honey. She had never been this far out of Aberdeen before, never into the countryside and hadn't expected it to smell so sweet. Elvis got out of his cab and stepped off the vehicle, proceeding immediately to light up a cigarette as he watched the ship landing less than three hundred yards away.

"This is close enough I think. Not too shabby a view, eh?" He said as he inhaled another drag, stretching out his arms and back. "I never thought I would live to see such a thing." He coughed and spluttered as he spoke. With his smoking, Blessing suspected that he probably wouldn't live much longer at the rate he was going. Donny and Ewen came down from upstairs and stepped outside, both with their cameras in their hands keenly filming every second of this historic event. Blessing looked to the upper deck to see Agatha waving back, who appeared quite content, giving everyone a thumbs-up, which Blessing gave back in return. All four of them now watched, their eyes locked on the vast ship that began to touch the land-scape below it. Blessing thought surely the craft would bend and break up, as the land around here was hardly flat, and she expected the highest peak underneath it would momentarily punch through and appear on the other side of the object but that didn't happen. Just before the ship reached the first point of contact with the highest point of ground, it glowed for a brief instant, the pearl white surface shining brightly and illuminating the surrounding landscape, casting shadows from the trees and farms below it. The terrain below the ship then simply appeared to be engulfed by it and the landing of the vessel was without interruption. The ship lowered itself further, with the surrounding landscape completely unaffected. It was truly a bizarre and an amazing sight, and one she knew she had been right to come and bear witness to. As the saucer part of the ship lowered itself onto the collection of nearest white cottages, the only structures that Blessing could see in its path from here, they simply disappeared beneath it and from her view it was as though they were absorbed without any discernible impact. She expected to hear the sound of falling masonry, but the whole scene played out before her with no such noise. The edge of the saucer part of the ship clamped down onto the ground about two hundred metres up the road from where they stood causing a cloud of thick dust and dirt to spew down the road towards them.

"Get back inside the bus!" Elvis shouted, jumping back into the footwell, waving at her and the two students to do likewise. Blessing didn't hesitate. The huge cloud of dirt, kicked up by the landing, expanded outward all around the saucer engulfing all in its path.

Ewen was hesitating to move, his camera still in hand. "I have to get this on film!"

Donny leapt onto the bus next to Blessing. Elvis stared at the approaching dark shroud heading straight towards them.

"Will you get on, laddie! I have to close the doors!"

Ewen kept filming for a few more seconds, before he bolted for the door and Elvis pulled it shut just as a film of dirt spread across the windscreen and enclosed the vehicle into darkness. Agatha squealed in delight from the top deck. "It's all very exciting, isn't it?"

"I think you're going to need to clean your bus!" Ewen remarked. Blessing could see Elvis was not amused, but it was hardly the young man's fault that the bus had got dirty. In her view, it was already in need of a good clean. Then they heard the sound of snapping electricity pylons, somewhere distant, but the sounds associated with the destruction of buildings and flattening of trees and walls did not fill the air. After a few minutes, the cloud of dust dissipated, leaving nothing more than a light film of dirt on everything it had touched. The air around them quickly cleared and then they all saw it. The upper surface of the saucer spread out endlessly before them, crossing the road up ahead from north to south and continuing its circumference in both directions until it was out of sight. The surface of the saucer extended flatly before gradually rising towards the distant cone-shaped tower at its centre, which rose to an impressive height above the rest of the structure and dominated the surrounding countryside with its presence. Blessing thought the tower beautiful, as though it were the pointed heart of a place of worship. She had never felt closer to God than in that moment. They were still so far away from the central structure that she guessed it would take several hours, perhaps even days, to walk across the surface to reach it.

"That cone thing in the middle looks like it might be the bridge," Donny said.

"Aye, could be at that, lad. I dinnae see noo windows though!" Elvis replied.

"It's miles away. You can't tell from here. How would we get there?' Ewen said.

Blessing's mind was filled with questions. What if the vessel itself was a great place of worship? Could it be that these were effectively churches, landing all over the planet? If so, she hoped the priests inside worshipped the same God as her own, because she knew there could be only one true Lord and she wasn't sure how she would deal with such a dilemma, especially if these new Gods were male, single and good-looking.

"Where's the door, like?" Elvis questioned. He was right, there were no openings, no doors, no piping or gaps in the structure, no bolts or rivets holding it together, no metallic plating of any kind. It was as if the entire thing was made of smooth pearlescent marble and the object was entirely solid. Ewen got off the bus and used the zoom on his camera to examine the surface of the saucer more closely.

"What happened to the hill? It must have crushed it. But how could it do that? Shouldn't it be damaged or something?" Donny said, asking no one in particular.

"But we didn't hear anything – It hardly made any noise at all. None of this makes any sense!" Ewen shouted from outside.

Blessing worried about the people who would not have had time to escape from beneath the thing as it came down. What had happened to them? Some must have been crushed to death, she thought. The edge of the craft spanned the horizon in front of them, and off to their left they could see the edge of the circumference begin curving back around towards the west. Off to their right, the edge had clamped itself across the fields and rolled around into the distance. The central cone of the vessel stood dominant, way off in the distance. It must have been visible for miles around for the top of it disappeared into the blanket of low-lying clouds above.

"How tall do you think that tower is?" Blessing found herself asking.

"Tall... Bloody tall! It must be four or five miles away from here at least, and over two miles in height, higher even," replied Donny.

Blessing noted the tower was not directly opposite them, but to their right by about half a mile. So despite the best efforts of Elvis, they were not lined up dead centre of the ship, but he had done pretty well all things considered. The topside of the object did not glitter in the same way the underside did, and Blessing wondered how far the lower part of the structure must have pierced the earth—she thought several miles at least. They all began to hear sirens in the distance, almost coinciding with the whirling engine of a helicopter that flew past overhead. It had civilian markings and probably belonged to a television news station, as there was a cameraman visible in the rear seat, filming everything below.

"I want to get closer!" It was Agatha shouting from the top of the bus, her head craned up towards one of the small windows, which she had pried open. Elvis looked around for the approval of his other passengers. Donny and Ewen were both nodding their heads. "Hell yes, if we don't go now this whole area will be closed off by the police and the army. That's probably them coming now. It could be our only chance!"

Blessing knew they were right. In her country, the army would be all over this and once that happened, no one would get anywhere near the thing. They had come this far, they might as well go the rest of the way. God was watching, whatever happened. "Yes, let's go," she said.

"Aye then, all aboard the skylark!" Elvis commanded, flicking away his cigarette and jumping back behind the steering wheel. Blessing who until then was not aware his bus had a name, raced upstairs *the skylark* to check on Agatha who was all giggles and smiles.

"Are we going to go and look, then?" The elderly woman asked with the excitement of a teenager.

"Yes we are," Blessing replied, taking a seat next to her. Instinctively the two women suddenly held hands. Agatha's hand was cold and bony, the skin loose in the folds of her fingers. It reminded Blessing of her Great Aunty Doris from back home who use to hold her hand and read her stories as a child. That all seemed so long ago now, almost a different reality to the one she was living at this moment. The bus roared to life as the sound of sirens drew closer. Ewen came up the stairs and ran to the back of the bus, shouting as he did so.

"I can see the police, lots of them, and army trucks, coming up the road behind us." Elvis once again flipped on this music, his voice coming across the speaker. "If we're going to meet beings from another world, best they get introduced to the King early on, hey?"

"It's now or never,
Come hold me tight
Kiss me my darling,
Be mine tonight.
Tomorrow will be too late,
It's now or never
My love won't wait."

Blessing listened to the tune, and recalled that she had heard it somewhere else as a child, but the lyrics and voice had been different and she was sure the song had been about ice cream. At least Elvis was romantic, she thought. Romance was always nice. No one had ever brought her flowers, in fact no man had ever brought her anything.

The bus screeched to a halt. Elvis got off, leaving the engine running, and picked up a discarded cigarette butt, then jumped back on board.

'I'm nae litter lout!' He shouted over the speaker as the bus tore out onto the road. They headed straight towards the edge of the vessel, the pearl-white surface of the structure beckoned to them just a short drive away, up the hill. Blessing hoped the aliens took a liking to Elvis, both his music and his bus. If they found him appealing then there was certainly hope for her.

RYAN

COBRA CONFERENCE ROOM, LONDON – APRIL
2ND 3PM GMT

"And you're sure they're all dead?" As he heard the question posed by General Spears, Ryan came to one conclusion about today; that he was living his worst nightmare, bit by vivid bit. The main screen in the conference room had crackled to life only minutes earlier with the image of Charles Gordon, the forty something, balding head of the British Embassy in Paris, who looked under terrible pressure, his voice not entirely composed as he spoke. The silence hung heavily in the room, no one moved, each person gripped to the monitors, the smaller ones displayed news reports showing the same piece of news footage again and again. Spirals of smoke just outside of Charles De Gaulle airport where the plane had hit into the ground, the fires of burning wreckage, and Ryan thought he saw at least one charred body caught hanging from a lamppost. Scores of French police, ambulances and armed response teams were on the ground, every report awash with their frantic activity, blended with a cacophony of shocked faces and tearful souls that looked on in disbelief at the latest loss of life, in another cataclysm of human tragedy. Ryan had seen so many of these over the last few years, but he knew this one was going to impact on him directly. David had been a personal friend of his, a guide and a mentor. All of those things were probably meaningless next to the times he had gotten Ryan out of the shit, for one indiscretion or another. He was going to miss the man, but his loss was going to mean far more than losing his *get out of jail free* card.

"Sir if I may…" It was Horace Saunders, the chief whip, who had only just arrived in the room moments earlier to alert the group of the news, whispered into Ryan's ear. Ryan just nodded in response. He knew it would be useful for him to view what the rest of the nation was witnessing in the media, and then he could think of how best to address it. Shit, what did this mean? His mind was racing with so many thoughts he could barely focus, and he felt his heart pounding. He had to face the room with confidence, and breathe, just breathe.

"Charles, I'm going to have to put you on hold for just a moment, please stay on the line." Ryan turned to the cabinet members, those who were left. "BBC News Twenty-Four everyone, probably best we have some insight into what the rest of the nation is being told." All present solemnly nodded their heads. Ryan could see Darren Fine sitting at the end of the table, his fingers interlocked pointing up to his face. No doubt he was wondering what move Ryan was going to make next and could not wait to witness his downfall. The drum beats of the news from BBC News 24 focused the room's attention elsewhere. Images flashed up before them as the announcements for the news of the day at three o'clock bellowed dramatically from the monitors. News days rarely came more dramatically than this, Ryan thought.

"This is the BBC News, I'm Fiona Bruce. *Boom Boom* – Terrorism in Paris, A British Government plane shot down in France, Prime Minister David Jackson is feared to be among the one hundred and forty-seven passengers thought to be dead. *Boom Boom* – Witnesses say a missile was fired from a nearby village close to Charles De Gaulle Airport just as the plane was taking off. French police are hunting several suspects. *Boom Boom* – Two hundred alien objects have now been confirmed to have landed worldwide, but seem to have avoided cities, many landing in isolated areas. Scientists speculate as to why they're here, but so far there's been no contact of any kind. *Boom Boom* – Panic buying in the shops...Tesco, Asda, Sainsbury's and Morrisons have found their shelves emptying as people rush to stock up on food in fear of alien invasion..."

The monologue suddenly cut to the brief interview of a man in his thirties outside a supermarket in Nottingham, where the scene behind him was a chaos of queues, and a number of private security men had been brought in to control things. "Well, if it's the end of the world then its best to be prepared, eh, duck?" Ryan noted some of the people round the room shaking their heads in dismay. He really did wonder if this was the best person the BBC could manage to put in front of the cameras at a time of such crisis, when they were trying to calm the nation.

"*Boom Boom* – Who is the UK's acting Prime Minister? As the remaining cabinet members meet to talk about the current crisis and the alien threat – we ask, who is making the decisions in Westminster?"

The stock image of the cabinet meeting suddenly cut to one of Darren Fine outside Parliament, talking to the cameras. The crafty bastard! He must have gone out and done the interview when they took the fifteen-minute break earlier so everyone could contact their relevant departments. Ryan had spent most of the time attempting to get a moment alone so he could snort a calming line in the toilet, but everyone, it seemed, wanted to talk to him and he didn't even get a moment to take a piss, let alone anything else. Fine almost squirmed with excitement at the sight of himself on the screen. The man was listening to the sound of his own voice and loving it, his crooked smile splitting his face at the end of the room.

"Obviously we still don't have confirmation of the death of Prime Minister Jackson from French authorities, but the public can be assured as we face the biggest challenge the world has ever seen, we will have the most suitable candidate steering the ship in his absence. We're meeting at this very moment to discuss this, and the current situation. This is not a time for leadership contests and old rivalries; this is a time for calm. On behalf of everyone in the government, and I am sure the entire nation, I would like to personally express my sincerest condolences to those friends and relatives who lost someone on the plane—Prime Minister David Jackson was an incredible man and will be terribly missed by all who knew and loved him…"

Ryan couldn't believe it. Fine actually had a tear welling up in his eye as he said those last words. This statement hadn't been cleared by anyone else in this room. He would have to address it or let the little pipsqueak run rampant up his arsehole. Something he was sure that Fine wouldn't object to.

"*Boom Boom* – House prices in towns, villages and cities near the alien crafts around the world have dropped dramatically…"

The screen cut once again to members of the public—A young couple in their late twenties.

"We were due to complete on our new home this weekend but its only seven miles away from one of those things; we just don't want to take the chance… I mean would you?"

General Spears stood up slowly. "Turn it off, please. We can see the highlights later." Horace looked to Ryan, who nodded. "Yes, can you give us Charles back?" Horace clicked the mouse and Charles Gordon appeared on the screen again, accompanied by an attractive young woman who was handing him a piece of paper. Ryan couldn't help wondering if Charles was boning her, but he put that thought to one side for now. As Charles read the contents of the note, his face drained of colour.

"Charles, we're back with you," Ryan said, doing his best to sound unshaken by the BBC summary of world events, which would have read like a list of potential reasons for suicide for any British politician. The Consul for Paris looked up and acknowledged everyone. Ryan went to speak, but Charles interrupted him.

"I have to tell you, I have to tell all of you, that the French have acted with great speed and efficiency in this matter and have already recovered forty-five bodies, including one that they believe is Prime Minister David Jackson's. I'm sorry, Ryan... the Foreign Secretary is thought to be among them as well."

"I see." Ryan could find no other words appropriate to the situation. The Foreign Secretary was certainly no loss to humanity, but David Jackson had always been a friend, one of convenience perhaps, but a friend nonetheless. Ryan felt all eyes upon him. How he responded in the next few minutes would determine who would be on his side and who would be asking for his resignation. In truth, right now the latter seemed like the best option, but this was not the moment to make that announcement. He hated responsibility, but here it was, well and truly thrust up to the hilt where he didn't want it.

"Charles, can you get down there with your people and get some boots on the ground and get a first account of what happened? Call all your staff in and have everyone work overnight. We'll arrange for some transport, probably a special train with Eurostar, to have the bodies brought back to the UK as soon as we can. Your staff will liaise with any relatives there of course, yes?"

Charles nodded. He looked at the screen and went to speak, but no words came. Ryan thought it best to get him to clear his mind, part of the grieving process. "You're doing a great job, Charles. I suggest we speak again at six pm our time. Is there anything else before we go?"

"The authorities tell me that the family of Prime Minister Jackson had not elected to stay on in Paris as originally planned. They... they were on the flight."

A second shockwave hit the room. Baroness Childs let out a small cry, which she immediately and unsuccessfully tried to suppress. It took the now head of MI5, Julie Compston, to speak up, breaking the heavy silence.

"You mean his wife, Bridget and their two children, Simon and Lucy, were on the plane as well?" she asked.

"It would appear so, madam. Yes." Charles uttered the words matter-of-factly, perhaps hoping they would turn out to be a falsehood if he did so.

Percy Howell, a half-finished donut still sitting before him, shouted, "Christ almighty! The bastards! We have to find who did this and bloody well kill them!"

Ryan's face drained of colour. He felt sick. He needed something, anything to get him through the next thirty minutes. He wanted to go to the toilet. He knew he had some coke in his suitcase. Candy had got it for him at their last meeting and it was the good stuff, but it did tend to have an immediate effect on his bowels and he wasn't sure this was the best time for such action. It was a small wrap of half a gram hidden in a little pouch on the inside of his carry-on case, which was always filled with packets of chewing gum. Handy for reducing the taste. But he couldn't excuse himself right now. More than anything, he wanted a smoke, but bloody regulations wouldn't allow for that either.

"Thank you, Charles. I'll get back to you at six pm." The screen switched back to News 24 but with the sound muted. The images of the burning aircraft wreckage filled the screen once more.

"Perhaps this would be a good time to talk about your position, Ryan?" Fine leaned in with his elbows on the table, letting the question hang in the air for everyone to digest. Ryan knew this was coming, sooner than even he expected. His friend's corpse wasn't even cold yet, but it was a discussion that needed to be had. He had to sound firm and took a deep breath; it was him or the wolves, and the wolves were hungry.

"My position, Darren? I thought our Prime Minister made it pretty clear in front of everyone here that I would be in charge until he got back."

"Yes, but he's not coming back is he? No offence, Ryan, but I don't think you're the most suitable person to run the country at this present time." Fine looked to the others around the room.

Percy Howells spoke up, "What is the legal precedent for the succession of leadership in a situation like this?"

Before Fine had the chance to answer, the London Police Commissioner Sir Derrick Winston was on it.

"There is no legal statute for such an event. Naturally, the Deputy Prime Minister would fill the role until such time as a leadership election could be called."

General Spears said, "The Deputy Prime Minister is currently in Africa and in view of the fact that we have just lost a government plane to a surface-to-air missile strike, combined with the fact that we have two hundred vessels of undetermined origin that have arrived on earth, I don't think it highly likely that anyone is going to do any flying any time soon. So, no offence everyone, but the leader of the United Kingdom for now has to be chosen from someone sitting in this very room, and that person needs to be chosen right now. Our nation is going to need assurances from someone who is used to going before the cameras, someone who looks good and can work a room. Clearly, no one here has the charisma of Tom Hardy, which is a crying shame as people would certainly listen to him. But this isn't a film and we don't need an actor, but we do need someone who can act calm, show some leadership and reassure the entire nation that we're in control."

"You mean lie, essentially?" Julie Compston said, cutting to the chase.

"Lying successfully to the public has always been an essential requisite for the job of Prime Minister. It's a simple case of who do we have who can do it? Until such a time occurs when we can follow the normal procedures and appoint someone else." General Spears waited for someone to disagree with him, but no one did.

Ryan could see which way the general was going and it was good to know he did actually have a sense of humour. He was marking Fine out for the job, and that was literally fine with him. He laughed inside at the irony of his last thought. He was going to have his hands full in any case. Certainly the hospitals were going to be pushed to the limit, he would have enough on his hands juggling the budget to work out how all the doctors' overtime was going to be paid, let alone dealing with running the country. If he stayed in this current position then his Under-Secretary would have to take on the temporary job of Health Minister. Ryan immediately discarded the notion. He wasn't qualified and he knew it. By all means let Fine or someone else take this poisoned chalice. Ryan had never had such grand aspirations himself, wining his place in Parliament with a very safe seat indeed, but something at the back of his mind gnawed away at him. This was a historic moment, there was no doubt about that, and he was part of it; how much though, was up to him. The general's voice broke into that thought.

"Now, I don't expect anyone here is going to suggest this is the right time to hold a leadership contest. Not at least until we have a handle on our nation's security and the current crisis, which the press is already calling, "The Alien Threat." His tone challenged the room to suggest otherwise.

"Not very helpful..." Fine interjected.

"No, indeed not." General Spears said. "Which is why, Mr. Fine, you need to get a handle on the PR for this thing. You need to be at the top of your game. Never before has our government needed someone with your experience at such a critical time. We're going to need you to meet with the heads of the BBC, SKY News and all the other main branches of the media, and make sure we can at least ensure their co-operation, not have them add to the nation's panic." Fine slumped in his seat, simply nodding his head. The General had set that up nicely, Ryan thought, underscoring the man's importance and making it impossible for him to change gears. Clever.

Sir Derrick Winston flicked through some notes in front of him.

"I've got reports of panic-buying from all over the country. People seem to think there's going to be a war. All the supermarket chains are reporting record sales. Our resources are already stretched to capacity dealing with public disorder, plus, the huge volume of RTAs when these things arrived. I also need to mention there have been reports of looting in a couple of cities in the Midlands. If that spreads across the entire UK, we'll be in real trouble."

The Commissioner left those in the room to ponder his comments. Ryan remembered the 2011 London Riots and how close they had come to total anarchy back then. Most of the United Kingdom had been unaware of it at the time, but the events of that summer had shown how unable they were to cope with social unrest on a national scale. Following the death of a young man in North London at the hands of the police, and failure of those involved to release statements to the public clarifying their actions, protests soon gave way to disorder that led to the worst rioting the UK had ever seen. Ryan had subsequently read a report drawn up by a panel whose job was to include plans for a more adequate response, should such a thing happen again. It was only upon reading it that he had the true picture of how pressed the entire country's emergency services had been over those three days. At one point, there was not a single spare police resource in the country, as they had juggled their meagre reserves to assist the counties most in need.

"I agree. We need to show the country our leadership is strong. Not least because the opposition will probably jump on this, and right now that's the last thing we need," Baroness Childs said, bringing Ryan's wandering mind back into the room. Fine stood at the end of the table, his fingers spreading out on the dark wood. Ryan decided to let him have his moment. Best way, he thought. Children get so easily upset when they don't get to speak. Fine looked rather pointedly at Ryan, grinning.

"What we need is someone to address the nation and we need them to do it now... A live broadcast, encouraging calm and order. If we don't show strong leadership now, we'll have anarchy right across the UK. Are you ready to do that, Ryan?"

All eyes were on Ryan in an instant. If he wanted to bail out, now was the time. He felt like he was facing the firing squad and no one had even asked him if wanted a last cigarette, and boy, he wanted a cigarette. He was either going to have to grow really big balls there and then, or step aside. He contemplated what this would mean for him, and what the alternatives were. Clearly there was no one else in the room that wanted the job, no one of course but Darren Fine.

"No, I'm not ready. No more than anyone else is in this room. I seem to recall when we first cracked open the documents presented to us by the Ministry of Defence for the *Alien Invasion Reaction Plans,* they were a tad thin on content. This is not something we could ever have planned for and to lose our leader, our friend, on the same day…"

He paused for a moment. To say it out loud made it all too real.

"Well, that is just utterly appalling and makes the difficulties facing us even more complex." Ryan was surprising himself, he was actually sounding quite convincing. "But there will be time for funerals and mourning, later. Our Mr. Fine could well be right, I might not be the best person in this room for this job, but it was the last wish of our right honourable friend that I should lead in his stead. What kind of man would I be if I just brushed those wishes aside? If I have to stand before the cameras, I'll do that. Get me the best writer to type up a speech to calm the nation and I will read it with conviction, because I know at a time like this it is the public that needs convincing that we are in control. Let's get a handle on the situation and keep public order, and then we can have a leadership contest, and those who feel more suited for the role can stake their claim. But for now, looking at those screens and those ships, whatever they are, we need to be seen as a united and functioning government who can handle a crisis, because a crisis, gentlemen…" Shit, he nearly forgot! "…and ladies… is what we're facing. Of that there can be absolutely no doubt." Ryan sat down, almost unaware that he had slowly risen to his feet as he had been speaking. He felt like a Catholic preacher in a pulpit asking for the blessing of his congregation to carry out an act of sanctified debauchery. Something that, Ryan reflected, hadn't ended well for many young Catholic altar boys all across the world. As he sat down, he thought he caught a nod of approval from the General in his tempered expression. With Morris Spears it was always hard to tell what he was thinking, but Ryan knew that the Prime Minister had always trusted his judgment, and this could turn into a military situation quickly, so he would certainly be needing his advice. Someone would need to help him write this speech. How had he gone from snorting really good quality white off a hooker's backside forty-eight hours ago, to being the leader of the United Kingdom? Shit, would one of them sell the story to the press? They didn't have any proof. It would be his word against theirs. He needed to call his PR girl, Jaynie but wasn't she in Gran Canaria this week? She had a degree in Social Studies and could always be trusted with his darkest secrets—probably. Fine sat opposite him with a look of profound surprise. Good. Ryan was pleased to have finally unnerved the man, and hoped the chance would come again soon. Ryan knew that he needed to back his words up with some substance. It couldn't be meaningless rhetoric.

'So what do you think we should do, Ryan?' Fine asked, sitting back.

"Our Police resources clearly are already stretched. There is no doubt we need to deploy the Army and Territorials. It would appear to make sense to have a local army presence in all the major town and city centres. This can be under the guise of protecting them from potential alien invasion, but in reality we're protecting our own infrastructure. We cannot allow rioting to take place in this country, nor allow vital food stocks to be pillaged. We should make plans for rationing in case it should become necessary. I'll need help with that speech and I should do a live televised address to the nation, within the hour. Leave for all emergency service and military personnel will be cancelled for the foreseeable future. How we act in the next twenty-four hours will not only define our party for the next decade, but also our nation." He was a good actor. Perhaps he could make a career of it. This new role as leader of the UK probably wouldn't last very long.

"What about the alien ships? What do we do about them?" Fine asked. The question was warranted, it was the elephant in the room.

"I suggest we secure the Aberdeen landing site and learn what we can. Put a qualified scientific team together and try and find out what they're doing here. I'm sure the Americans and Chinese will be doing the same. At the moment we only have two to contend with, I believe…'

'That's correct, one near Aberdeen and another off the coast of Galway. A third thought be landing in Northern Ireland landed in the middle of Atlantic.' Julie Compston read from a report in front of her.

'If we could have a chart showing the whereabouts of all the vessels worldwide when we reconvene, I am sure that would be useful." Ryan added.

"I'll see to that and I'll get someone working on that speech for you," said Horace Saunders, immediately leaving the room barely giving Ryan a chance to utter a thank you in acknowledgement. As Saunders departed, the priority phone rang. General Spears took the initiative and answered it promptly. "Cobra. I see, yes, thank you." Spears covered the receiver with his hand. "The President of the United States called to offer their condolences on the death of our prime minister."

"Nothing else?" Ryan asked..

"They suggested a teleconference at our convenience to discuss the alien threat," the General added.

"Good to know they're calling it a threat already… We come in peace, shoot to kill," Percy Howells joked, which led to a few restrained titters around the room. At least they could still laugh, even on a day like today.

"They want to know what we know, which means they know nothing more than we do about our alien friends," Julie Compston said, with authority. "I've dealt with them long enough to know, Ryan."

"Can you speak to their intelligence agencies and verify that?" he replied.

"I can as soon as we're done here. They'll be fishing to see what we know in return but seeing as what we know is very little there isn't much I can tell them, is there?" Sarcasm didn't suit Compston, who was always all business and thoroughly professional. Ryan had heard she was a lesbian, despite being married to some retired banker or other. No doubt she had some hot young femme stashed away somewhere in a swanky apartment overlooking the Thames.

"Okay everyone, let's meet back here in thirty minutes. I'll need to be before the cameras within the hour. We can't afford to leave it any longer than that." Ryan wished that they could but he knew the nation would want answers to a great many questions, none of which he would be able to provide. All he could do at this stage was try to reassure them and hope to get some answers himself, in the meantime. Ryan excused himself and finally dashed to the toilet leaving the mutterings of Fine and his cronies behind him. Even world leaders had to use the loo, apart from the Queen, of course. Her Majesty it was universally agreed, would never have to take a shit, because she was, well, the Queen.

Ryan wasted no time. Just along from the corridor of the Cobra meeting room there were executive washrooms. Ryan had only been in the spacious gents once before. It contained five cubicles, a row of state-of-the-art wash-basins and hand driers, all overly elaborate in their design, along with a stack of snowy-white, fresh towels. Everything else was in black, white and grey marble, reminding him of the bathrooms at *The Ivy*. All that was missing, Ryan thought, was an immigrant selling a selection of perfume, lollipops and deodorants.

He quickly inspected all the toilets and found himself to be alone. He opted for the last cubicle, farthest away from the door and quickly dug into his bag to find the wrap of coke. It was still there, thank God. Ryan pulled out his wallet and expertly rolled up a twenty pound note to act as conduit from the drug to his nostrils. Now all he lacked was a smooth surface from which to snort it, but he remembered he had a soft cover book in the other compartment of his bag. He retrieved it, rested it on the top of the toilet and emptied the cocaine on to the back of the book, which was still perfectly flat, as Ryan had yet to find the time or the incli-nation to actually read it. He had kept it because Candice had given it to him as a present and Ryan was not used to receiving gifts of a sentimental value, especially not from a transexual woman he was beginning to harbour strong feelings towards. It was a novel, a work of fiction that he had a vague recollection of being a source of inspiration for her in some past dark times. Candice was the one person he had opened up to about some of his demons, and recently their clandestine meetings had come to mean more than just a source of brief sexual gratification. He hadn't told her that of course, not wishing to alienate her, knowing such members of her profession were probably unique and he didn't want to spoil what they had. He knew if he expressed the desire for anything more perma-nent she would run a mile. Besides, openly dating a transsexual woman would be political suicide, especially now. His thoughts were brushed aside by the sound of the washroom's door opening followed by slow, purposeful footsteps crossing the room. They stopped right outside the door of his cubicle. Ryan froze, half-hunched over the small mound of powder, a rolled note in one hand and the remains of the wrap in the other.

"Mr. Prime Minister?"

It was General Spears; the man who had only moments earlier appeared to be his only ally in the briefing room. His tone weighted with authority.

"I'm just finishing up. Tell the others I am just coming." He had to get him out of the room. As soon as he snorted, Spears would either think he had a terrible cold (which he obviously didn't) or he was consuming class A drugs (which he obviously was). The General's reply was a little unexpected and caught him somewhat off guard.

"Leave whatever it is that you're going to shove up your nose and come out here, NOW!" he shouted. Ryan had no choice. Ryan looked up at the ceiling and wondered if Spears was like that American President, who used to bug all of his own offices and listen in on everyone. He searched for a place that could hold a hidden camera, but saw none. Installing one here would involve a rather large expenditure just to make a recording of a minister taking a shit. Ryan left the cocaine and the book where they were and slid back the bolt on the door, and left the cubicle. He tried to close the door but as soon as his hand left the handle, it swung back open behind him. Bollocks, he thought. Nothing to be said now. Like a lion, who had smelled blood, The general leapt toward Ryan, picked him up by both shoulders and slammed him into the wall.

"I'm not sure if you're aware, sir, but we're facing the biggest, probably most dangerous crisis this country has ever seen and you're getting high?"

"I needed something…" Ryan tried to formulate a sentence but it didn't go anywhere. Ryan felt his face flush with embarrassment as he was pushed up against the wall so hard that he could feel his feet leaving the floor. At any moment, he was expecting to be asked about the location for the Death Star plans, when the general released his grip from Ryan's suit, almost dropping him to the floor. Ryan only managed to stay standing upright because of the wall behind him.

The tone of Spears words left no room for ambiguity. "I'm sure you did, but for the next few days, or weeks if need be, depending on how long you actually stay in office, you're going to be stone—cold—sober! No drinks. No Drugs. No women. No men."

Ryan had to take issue with him on the last comment. "I'm not gay." The General leaned so close to his face that he could smell the man's breath, which had a scent that was surprisingly appealing. Ryan had expected quite the opposite.

"What you are outside of these walls is no concern of mine, but who you are perceived to be by the general public could mean the difference between life and death for people in this country, perhaps even the world." The General finally backed away giving him space to move.

"I think that's overstating it a bit…" Ryan retorted, yet he wondered if it really was.

"I think it's the understatement of the year," the General countered. "But we don't have much of a choice. David Jackson was a fine man, a natural leader, he knew when to keep it in his pants and focus on his job. Get your phone out."

Who on earth did he want Ryan to call? Surely he had everyone's number himself and could certainly get to higher powers on any level, faster than he could. Ryan got his mobile from his pocket. While he did so, the General slid around him and lifted the book off the toilet seat carefully with one hand, while lifting the lid with the other. Ryan wasn't going to get to do his line; in fact he wasn't going to do any lines soon if this bullish man had anything to do with it. The General tipped the coke down into the bowl and swept the cover clean. He flushed the toilet. Ryan could go back in to Cobra right now and resign, say he didn't feel he was up to the job and someone of more experience should be appointed. Preferably someone who actually cared. His political career would be over, but maybe that was the best thing. He would find something else to do. He could run courses on how to avoid paying tax, or maybe open an escort agency. He had plenty of experience with both of those.

"Why don't you just suggest Darren Fine should take over? I'll happily go along with it. He's handled the press before on a daily basis, he can even write his own speeches. He's more qualified than me for the position and you know it." Ryan knew he was throwing himself to the wolves, but this way he could absolve himself of all responsibility and take a plane to Fiji or somewhere and wait this thing out. Ryan could see from the expression on the General's face that he didn't like the idea.

"Fine can't stand in for you! He's good at his job, yes, but he's not a leader. Besides, he has even more skeletons in his closet than you. I expect some of those will surface soon, and that would be all this country needs." Ryan had no idea what he meant. Fine wasn't married and he was fairly certain he was gay, but that was hardly a big deal these days and could in many ways be a positive thing. Besides, maybe the aliens were of of an equal persuasion and friendly contact would be established once both sides had sung the chorus of *YMCA* by the Village People. Candice had told him it was fairly common knowledge among the rent boys in London that Fine had a thing for young Spanish and Brazilian boys but homosexuality was no bar to leadership these days; if anything it might be seen as a political badge of honour. The General clearly did not share this view, unless he knew something else about Fine? He hoped the General wasn't going to do something overtly dramatic like tread on his expensive Samsung. He had spent ages getting his favourite games and music on the thing and hadn't backed up his choices on any other device. He made a *note to self* to do it later.

"So, who should I be calling, or am I not allowed to have a phone now?" *Careful*, Ryan thought, *do not provoke him.*

"Not that phone, the other one, please. The one with the numbers of all your little whores. There's someone on that list you're going to have to call before we go back in that room and you're going to tell her you cannot see her anymore, not for the foreseeable future."

Ryan knew at once who he meant, but he had no idea how the General knew about her. He had been so careful where she was concerned. So, so careful. The General cocked an eyebrow in expectation. Ryan removed the smaller, older Nokia from his bag and made the call.

CANDICE

"You bastard!" It was useless. Ryan had already hung up. She tried calling back the number straight away, but the phone was already switched off and she knew she couldn't leave a voicemail—not that there would have been any point. Candice looked in the mirror and could see her mascara was running from the stream of tears that fell down her cheeks. She looked pitiful, and hell, pity was one thing she did not do or endorse in any one else! She took a wet-wipe from the box on her dresser and removed the running makeup from her face, staining the tissue with pink and brown. She would have to start again. Candice had only woken ten minutes earlier, and was sitting at the dresser wearing her white lace camisole. Staring into the mirror, her dark brown eyes glared back at her, as if her conscience was taunting her with a look of, "I told you so." She had been applying her lipstick when he called; testing a possible look for the day before she woke up fully. It had been all so sudden and abrupt and her head was still spinning with his hurtful words. Her own face looked back at her unsympathetically, "You've only yourself to blame." If a mirror could talk, she was certain that would be its wise fact of the day.

"Mirror, mirror on the wall. Who is the stupidest one of all?" her Brazilian accent purred. She blew her nose and tossed the used tissue aside. She glanced once more at her phone, displaying the name *Ryan* and debated deleting his number. She had broken her own rules and now she was regretting that decision, angry at her own stupidity which had, in turn, led to vulnerability.

"Never get emotionally involved with the clients."

That was the golden rule in her business, never to be broken. But Ryan had always been different with her, from his very first visit. He had a certain presence that few men possessed. Like many, he behaved like a frightened schoolboy the first time he came to see her, but gradually over time his visits became less sexual and more conversational. That was normal, it had happened with many of her regulars before, but Ryan began bringing her gifts and would take her out to places that felt more like an actual date, and less like work. He wanted to know more about her, what her life was like growing up in Brazil, and how she overcame challenges as a transgender woman in today's society. He wasn't the first person to ask her those questions, nor was he the first to take a genuine interest in her but there was something undefinable about him that set him apart from the rest. He was charming and funny, a side of him, he informed her, that few ever got to see. He told her his day job was always so serious, but with her he could let go and just be himself. She still charged him the same rates, always keeping it professional, never giving him a discount regardless of how the night ended, but then he never asked for one. As with all her clients, Candice never asked him what he did and what little she knew he had volunteered himself, and that wasn't much. He said he worked in public relations and management for a local authority, which was appropriately vague. She didn't discuss her personal background with people either, so they had always talked about art, music, films, theatre and her greatest love, ballet. It had been a passion of hers when she was younger; studying the body's elegant movements had led to so many other awakenings in her. He had been to see performances all over the world and when she had made a passing comment, "If only I could be so lucky and someone would take me to see The Royal National Ballet company perform one day." He had made that happen. It took effort in London to go and see something on your own – the theatre, a show, a film, a performance of any kind. A solitary visitor would have to sit there among all the couples and groups, pretending to be fiddling with their phone or writing a review until the thing actually started. She hated going alone. She enjoyed having someone to talk to about the experience afterwards, and she didn't want such memories to be so internal. She could remember the first time she realised she had feelings for him; the exact moment she knew her heart was leaping across the boundaries that she had built around herself. He surprised her one evening with two tickets to see the Ballet Rambert Theatre Company which was on tour in London from New York. She had tried to see them once before in their home city, but an all-night bender with another girl and two clients had put paid to that idea. It had been a wonderful evening (the one with Ryan, not the weekend bender with her friend), he told her that she brought out a side of him that others rarely saw. He had revealed that he had married young, but the marriage had broken down early on, because of his compulsion for sex and drugs, which with his wealthy background, he had no problem affording. A quick divorce had followed and he had little desire ever to marry again. It was actually through the drugs, not the sex, that they had been first introduced to each other. Candice was a dealer on the side, mainly to her clients and friends, never total strangers. A *bona fide* recommendation was everything. It had always been cocaine that everyone wanted up until a couple of years ago, but now crystal meth was equally in demand in London but she refused to sell the latter. She was shocked at what it would reduce people to. Fit, healthy young boys she had known on London's gay scene a year earlier were now reduced to ghostly skeletal figures with vacant eyes. They became moody, paranoid addicts who would quickly lose their temper when she didn't have what they wanted, at a price they could afford. Worse still was that some of her regular escort clients were taking it too. She had lost count of the number of times she'd received a call at three in the morning to go to some flat in Chelsea to party with someone who had been "playing" since Friday night. Candice would arrive to find men with trembling hands who couldn't sit still for longer than a few seconds, sweating profusely, their eyes rolling around the room. They weren't just on another planet; they might as well have been in another universe. "Tina" had been their mistress and after one turned violent, she vowed never to take such a booking again. It was becoming almost impossible to avoid clashing with this drug on London's gay scene and it had, of course, slowly seeped into the transgender community where sex and drugs would often go hand in hand.

Her clash with Ryan on the phone could not be allowed to upset her, she decided. She had a busy day ahead and had already got up late as it was. Sunday night had been a flurry of last minute deliveries and requests for quick liaisons, and she hadn't got in until the early hours of Monday morning. She had at once switched off her work phone, taken her regimen of tablets, and had gone straight to bed, falling at once into a deep and heavy sleep.

Now she sat at her dresser and worked her moisturiser furiously into her light almond-coloured skin and rapidly re-applied her makeup. Candice never got more than a few feet from her bed without doing her lipstick, eye shadow and mascara. To look this good you had to put the time in, and she knew she had to make an effort to stand out from the other girls. This was the year she hit thirty, but she was determined to stay twenty-eight for as long as she could manage to get away with it, and that required patience, effort and a wide selection of makeup and skin-care products. People of her gender and attributes were at one time rare creatures in London, but a continual influx of new girls every year had long since put that out to pasture. She ran her hands down from her silicone breasts to between her legs, feeling the piece of flesh that loosely hung there. She was blessed in that respect, but she knew she was no longer a unicorn on the transgender scene. Competition in her world was fierce and persistent, and she wasn't the only well-endowed girl in town. She ran her hands back up across her body, a ritual she did every morning to remind herself how hard she had fought to get here, to become the woman she was. Yet she knew people wanted her because of the part of her that remained a man. She couldn't help but wonder if Ryan ever would have been interested in her at all without it.

What the fuck was that phone call about, anyway? It didn't make sense, only last week, he had been talking about taking time off to go on holiday with her, now that she was able to travel freely again. She had outstayed her welcome in the United Kingdom some time ago, and it was only when Ryan became aware of this problem that he had used his contacts within the Foreign Office to get her a permanent work visa. She suspected he worked for immigration to have got her the papers so quickly. When she had asked how he had managed to do it, he simply replied, "Friends in high places." She knew better than to press him on the issue. He had discussed taking her to the Seychelles, and they had even looked at some resorts on line. Ryan said they would feel truly free there away from the eyes of the world. She had been looking forward to a break from London and its craziness. It was an exciting, vibrant, and at times incredible city full of weird, wonderful and exotic people just like her, but it could also be a city full of users and takers, a place that ultimately was very unsympathetic to the lonely. As she held her fingers up to the mirror and pondered which colour to paint her nails that day, she knew she could count her dependable friends in the city on a single hand—Pearl, Joanne, Steve her driver, and until today, she would have included Ryan. There were some other people she knew through work or from the transgender clubbing scene, but these were not people who would stick their neck out for her if she was in trouble. Her head was throbbing and her throat was dry. She downed a couple of Nurofen with a pint of water. She had always stayed away from the harder drugs and she couldn't deny that she enjoyed a bit of Charlie, but it was getting to a time when she was going to have to stop. She and Ryan had been doing cocaine together this past weekend. It had become part of their sexual ritual, another rule that Candice had broken. He had suggested they made their meetings during the week more social and their weekends more sexual. Ryan did love sex, but he also loved his coke. Ryan, like her, had a greedy and compulsive personality that became amplified when drugs were involved. It was a side of him that Candice recognised in herself, and she knew together they might make for a toxic combination. She found herself in the role of big sister when they took their chemicals, always having to remain just one notch below Ryan's level to ensure the two of them were never in danger. Ryan always wanted more—more sex, more cock, more drugs and she knew his proposed holiday would have given them time to take a respite from all that. The trip would have just been about them, alone, no work. Sure there would be sex, but not chemical sex, and there would be conversation and cuddles, dinners and romantic walks on white sandy beaches. The sort of thing every girl wanted. Ryan was one of her younger clients and someone she wouldn't be ashamed to be seen with. He took care of himself for one thing, and always had well-manicured nails, even his feet, which for any man, as she well knew, was a rare thing indeed. He smelled good too. Always clean and fresh, though by the time they finished playing together they would both be drenched with sweat in a room smelling of used condoms. Candice didn't mind, these were things she associated with real sex rather than mechanical sex that she would normally perform at least once a day with someone else.

She lit a cigarette, her first of the day. Today was normally her quietest day of the week and her routine would have been a lie-in, get up just after lunch, then transforming herself from looking like she had just been hit by a truck to beautiful. Eat a light salad. Strap herself in. Choose her outfit and then go and meet her supplier, Pearl, who lived in Walthamstow Village with her girlfriend, Joanne. Pearl worked as a DJ in bars and clubs in hipster Shoreditch. Pearl had incredibly short hair, petite breasts and despite her boyish appearance, up close there was something definitely feminine about her. Not quite a girl, not quite a boy. She was unique and Candice decided upon first meeting her that there and then they had to become friends. It was while she had been loitering near the DJ booth that they had first met, with Pearl elaborating why she didn't work in the lesbian clubbing scene anymore.

"Too many girls hitting on me every night. It's not that I can't handle it; it's just that it gets so tiring after a while, especially when they come with their girlfriends and they choose to hit on me while their other half is in the toilet. I mean, really?" Pearl had shouted this to her one night from the DJ box, followed by the abrupt question, "You're not hitting on me are you?"

"Honey, not unless you're interested in the twelve inches between my legs…" had been her come-back.

Pearl's eyes went wide at the revelation, followed by a smile. She had decided they were going to be best friends too. Candice ended up back at a social gathering in their ground floor flat, joined by a lovely gay couple from upstairs, whom they had befriended shortly after moving in. An abundance of cocaine appeared on the table and everyone was doing lines, except for Ross who was the self-coined "sensible one" in their relationship. Ross and Andy, the gay couple, were both in their late forties, slim skin-head types who had been together for twelve years and were still proud to boast of the very active sex life they still had together.

"So many of our friends don't. We can't understand it. I know they stay together because they love each other, and seek sexual gratification elsewhere, but I can't imagine never wanting the man I love more than anything," Andy said, harping on as though he were writing a book on the subject. Ross, who was the more camp of the two, just gave a naughty smile and said, "Our monthly sex parties probably help."

Joanne was shorter than Pearl but no less attractive, with big brown eyes and breasts that would make Candice stare at her own implants with a tinge of disappointment. Conversation and wine had freely flowed, and she had a vague recollection of grabbing an Uber back to Waterloo in the early hours of the morning, as the first crack of a cold grey dawn began to rise between the buildings on the South Bank. That encounter had been over a year ago and Candice was now lucky to call Pearl a true friend, plus she also did her a great rate on bulk purchases of coke, which she could sell for fifty percent profit on the gay scene. That was how she fell into dealing. It was never intentional; people wanted it and she could get it. Pearl only sold her supply on the straight clubbing scene or direct to her friends by delivery, so their stomping grounds were mutually exclusive. She avoided selling anything at her regular haunt.

The most popular London transgender club was aptly named *Here Come the Girls* and was run by a real old-school trans woman called Becca. Becca was in many ways the type of person their community had always needed. She had dedicated her life to making the world more accepting for people like Candice, and to provide a place where they could feel completely comfortable. All sorts would come through its doors on a Saturday night. Girls from Thailand, fetish couples, straight men, cross-dressers, sometimes alone and sometimes with their partners, and some of the most feminine transgender individuals London had to offer, would all come seeking something or someone. All the transsexual escorts that didn't have something better to do on a Saturday night would often congregate here to dance, pick up, and in some cases, do drugs in the bathroom. It sounded so stereotypical when said out loud, but those three things put together were no different from any gay or straight club in London on a Saturday night, so Candice was always ready to confront anyone who waded in with that argument to her face. Dancing, sex and drugs were not something unique to the transsexual scene; they were as rampant here as they were everywhere else.

Here Come the Girls was her semi-regular Saturday night venue. It was fun but it had all become very competitive; who could look the best in the club, as if they were all being judged in some kind of pageant. It was a human frailty, not unique to the transgender community, to make yourself feel better by putting others down. Not everyone did it of course, just those who were utterly insecure about themselves. One time she witnessed an individual crying in the toilets. It was a cross-dressing man in his fifties who was weeping at the mirror, his makeup streaking down his face.

Candice had asked him what was wrong and he had blurted out that he realised he would, "never fit in anywhere. All the girls here are so pretty and look at me, I'm just a guy in a dress." Despite the fact that she had a potential client outside, who had already brought two magnums of champagne to their table, she spent twenty minutes with this lost soul, helping him reapply his eye-liner, giving him a hug and saying, "There, now you look great!" before going back to her table.

To help strangers was, admittedly, not in her nature and she was becoming scared that she too, somehow, was going to end up like the worst of them. Capable only of self-appraisal and self-interest and incapable of connecting emotionally with anyone during sex, paid for or otherwise. So many others around her were so self-absorbed, she didn't want to make that mistake. She made a conscious decision to do one act of kindness, ideally to a stranger, every day. Give some spare change to a busker or a homeless person. Hold the door open for someone, well not a man, but maybe an elderly lady at the supermarket or just even smile at a stranger, though sometimes that brought the wrong kind of attention in return.

She was wondering if it was worth the effort. Everywhere around the apartment there was something that reminded her of Ryan. A Valentines card sitting on her makeup table, a favourite set of earrings he had purchased. It seemed every time they met he would do one little thing differently from the last time; a surprise outing or a little gift. Sometimes these would take the form of little notes or friendship cards with a hand-written message inside, which he would always sign with just a large capital "R" followed by a few kisses. Candice did not kiss her clients, but she had kissed Ryan, the night after he took her to see the ballet company in Angel. It had happened under the wings of the metallic angel sculpture in the aptly named Angel part of London. He had never wanted to walk anywhere with her in public before, and Angel was quite a lively place on a Friday evening, its bars and clubs packed to the hilt with revellers of all ages, who would spill onto the streets to smoke their cigarettes or puff on their vapes in the night air. They were walking just under the sculpture when he just pulled her towards him, almost causing them both to fall over. The kiss then just seemed to happen in the shadow of the angelic art. His lips were soft, fresh, and attached to someone she actually cared about. She felt like a schoolgirl getting that all-important first kiss on her very first date. Something of the child was awoken in her. That child had of course been a boy, who wanted to dress like a girl, but hang out with other boys, as her older sisters had done. The kiss brought a stirring of unique feelings flooding back into her body. The memory of that moment could never be taken from her, not even by him.

Candice had learned to become tough before she ever set foot in the United Kingdom. She had been sleeping with men for money long before she ever came to London. Gay men, straight men and everything in between had always been at her beck and call back home. Her early twenties back among the clubs and bars of Rio had been a hedonistic time of parties, drinking and fucking. When the beautiful, young, passive gay boys turned up at her door wanting to be screwed silly, those days had seemed like Christmas. Gradually older married men began to hit on her and money was offered if she did not show interest. Soon it was easy. Sex ceased to become about recreational fun, it became a service for money and one that she was very good at providing. Tales of high paying clients in Europe soon began to filter back to her. Barcelona, London—these were the places she had dreamed of visiting, and her friends told incredible tales of men who would pay for everything. The trip, if planned well, would pay for itself and sure enough her expectations were not disappointed. London did have an abundance of men wanting to sleep with her, and some were beautiful sculpted creatures from Italy, France, Holland and Denmark. Polite, well-spoken, clean men who took care of themselves. These were ideal clients and it made the work bearable, sometimes even enjoyable but never quite a reality that she could completely let herself fall into. Not all of her clients were like that though, and now she vetted them incredibly carefully. Many were fat and old with dubious hygiene, who thought they could just turn up in a t-shirt that hadn't been washed in weeks and jogging bottoms held up by an old piece of string. She would show them the door. She learnt very quickly to only take callouts to up-market London hotels; being alone in someone's home could be dangerous. There was no shortage of clients with repressed homosexual self-hating issues who could snap in the middle of a session, and it had happened to Candice on more than one occasion. Once with a man from Turkey and the second time with an Eastern European. She handled it and both men left with very sore genitals, their voices two octaves higher than when they'd arrived. Most of her clients though, were harmless. Nothing more than sexually frustrated Mummy's boys wanting to get fucked by a really big dick—just one attached to a she-male, not a male. A compromise for their repressed feelings of homosexuality? She didn't care, she wasn't here to analyse their inner child, just to get paid for her time, if she chose to give it to them. Selling drugs came later. Clients had, on more than one occasion, requested her to get "chems" for a session. In the end, Candice decided to sell only to those with whom she had already an existing professional relationship, and to avoid selling or even taking drugs at any clubs. Ryan, of course, had been into his cocaine a long time before they ever met, it was just that she provided him with a better quality of chemicals than his previous supplier. Perhaps at first that was why he kept coming back, but for the last six months drugs had been less and less of a priority during their time together, which is why his phone call to her this afternoon made no sense at all. When he called that day, she knew immediately something was wrong. His tone, his breathing, everything was different. He was abrupt, cold and blunt. The conversation was as short as he could have possibly made it, and straight to the point. He couldn't see her for the foreseeable future; with everything going on, the dynamics of his job were about to radically change. It wasn't what he wanted but she would be well taken care of and she would understand when she saw the news. Well taken care of? Fuck you Ryan. She had never needed anyone to take care of her before. He obviously didn't have the balls to do it... what did he mean about the news? What news? She looked at her phone; it was coming up to 3.30 p.m. She really had overslept today. She left the bedroom and walked into her open plan kitchen and lounge; it was small but modern, and well-finished with sleek and slender lines. She had kept the place in pristine condition. Two white bar stools were in the kitchen where she had left her propped-up iPad. She flipped the images across until the logo for BBC News 24 came up, and hit play. At least this would tell her what was going on in the world. Had there been another terrorist attack? Wait, yes there had been. The image on the screen and the accompanying text, cut with images of a burning building could mean only that.

A man in a crisp new suit was talking to camera surrounded by a number of microphones. Judging by the number, half the world's media was present... she saw words scrolling at the bottom of the screen and read: *Paris Charles De Gaulle Airport Terror Attack—129 feared dead.*

Another caption just below the man read, *Live from Paris.* He was just taking questions from reporters, when Candice flipped on the sound.

"Can you confirm that British Prime Minister David Jackson is among the dead?" The man visibly flinched at the question, his voice breaking as he answered.

"I can. I can also confirm his wife and two children were also on board. They were to have remained in Paris for a short holiday, unfortunately they decided to accompany him to ensure they were in the UK at the time of the current crisis.'

Someone else immediately announced they were from Sky News and fired another question.

"Is the attack anyway connected to the object that landed in Northern France?"

The man, whose name she could now see was captioned as *Charles Gordon* was obviously uneasy as he answered the question. Candice wondered what object were they talking about.

"You will have to understand that it is too early to make definitive statements about the origins of the attack on the Prime Minister's plane and any correlation this might have had with other world events. The investigation in France and the UK is very fluid and moving rapidly forward. My present understanding, however, is that the two events are not related, and the weapon fired at the plane came from the ground close to the airport."

Candice was still trying to process what she was hearing. The British Prime Minister killed? What object in France? Who was responsible? This was like another 9/11. Candice instinctively reached for her vape dispenser and took a heavy drag on it, her eyes not leaving the screen as another voice fired a question.

"Mr. Gordon, we're getting reports of a fire-fight having taken place between French police and a number of unknown assailants just before the plane was shot down. Can you confirm any of these details?"

Another question, from someone with an Australian accent. A bit far from home aren't you darling? Candice thought, but then she remembered there was some sort of anti-terrorist summit occurring in Paris this weekend. So, the world's press would have been there to cover that no doubt, for all the good it seemed to have done.

"I am informed by the French authorities that there was an exchange of gunfire between a group of individuals and French airport police on the eastern edge of the village of Le Mesnil-Amelot, where there's unconfirmed reports that at least three French police have been killed and several more wounded. One terrorist is believed to have been killed. I am expecting there to be a statement from the Paris Chief of Police some time later today."

This was just too depressing. The world was a terrible place, people died every day and she tended not to listen to the news anymore. If she had watched the screen for another second, she would have seen the news report flip to London and an emergency meeting of Parliament where a familiar face was about to speak to the nation. She muted the sound turned away to grab her Levi's when she heard the phone beep, back in the bedroom. Someone had sent her a text. It could wait. It was her business phone, not her personal phone, though almost no one had the number for her personal phone, not even Ryan. She had been on the verge of giving it to him, as there had been a growing desire to set him aside from the other clients in her directory, to elevate his status to something else.

Candice took a shower. She removed her wig and what little makeup she had applied and walked through to the wetroom that had been built on the other side of her bedroom. She had been lucky to get this flat. It was brand spanking new when she'd moved in, and owned by one of the first clients she had met in London; all she'd had to do was fuck him once a week and the rent was free. Oliver was in his sixties, married and undemanding in bed, which for her was the perfect arrangement. Occasionally, he would come and stay and she would sleep on the couch, but his job kept him mainly overseas, which suited her just fine. Before this, she had been sharing a two bedroom flat with two other girls, in ironically, Queensway. It was above a shop and looked like it hadn't been decorated since the eighties. None of the furniture matched and her bedroom was the size of a box, containing no more than a dirty mattress and a stack of plastic tubs, where she would store her clothes. The fights to get to the single mirror in the bathroom were legendary. The owner, a horrid little Indian man named Rajesh lived in another flat two doors down. There was an unoccupied damp bedsit two flights above their apartment, which wasn't fit for the cockroaches that lived there, but if you climbed those narrow stairs on rent day and let Rajesh suck your cock, you would find your rent reduced by one hundred pounds. Candice got out of there the first chance she could. That was three years ago. She found it hard to believe that time had flown by so fast already. It was only April now, but last Christmas felt like it was only yesterday and soon the summer would be beckoning…

She let the beats of warm water hit her skin as she thought about the day ahead. First, she needed to go and see Pearl and re-stock with supplies, then do her East London deliveries on the way back with her driver, Steve. He had been her driver several times from *Here Come the Girls* on a Saturday night, and was well known to all the staff there. When collecting money, she knew it wasn't safe to trust some random Uber driver, so she offered to pay Steve one hundred pounds, plus petrol, to take her around London twice a week. She would deliver to all of her East London-based customers first, leaving anyone who wanted a date for last, and then she could let Steve go and take an Uber home, but he always offered to wait, even if it was until the following morning. This was rare, because Candice didn't like to do bookings on a Tuesday, she was normally too tired from her antics on the weekend and Tuesday was normally her week night with Ryan, because by then she felt able to do something civilised, and would have all day on Tuesday to get ready or go shopping for new outfits. Steve had been her driver for over a year now, and was one of the few people in her very small social circle that knew anything personal about her, but even that wasn't much. He was an older man in his sixties from St Vincent's and spoke with a lovely warm Caribbean accent and must have been something of a looker back in his day, no doubt. He didn't speak much, he didn't ask questions, but when he did he was polite and kind. These qualities made him her go-to guy whenever she needed a trusted driver and in her experience, there weren't many people you could trust in London. He was one of the few people whose number she had on both of her phones.

The warm jets of water permeated every part of her body as she turned towards the showerhead and back again. The warm liquid wrapped around her like a blanket. Soothing. Safe. She covered herself in shower gel and worked up a lather of soap across her body, looking down at the soft, dark meat that hung between her legs. When she had been young, it was a source of much embarrassment and she hated sharing showers with the other boys. Now it was a source of pleasure and money, though having such an attribute could at times be really tiresome. If she hadn't been so blessed she knew half the people it her life wouldn't give her the time of day. She stopped the flow of water and grabbed the dark brown towels she had just bought from Marks and Spencer's. She loved this apartment, but she knew she was staying here on borrowed time. That was the dream, to own a flat like this, bigger than this, only as Carrie Bradshaw put it, with a really big closet. Every penny she could save was being kept for that purpose. She had a long way to go. Any decent two-bedroom flat in London now seemed to cost nothing short of a million pounds. It had been a huge political issue recently, constantly in the news, with thousands of buyers being forced to buy out of London, some of them even giving up their jobs to simply live elsewhere. She had considered Manchester but it was too cold. No, eventually she would return to her native Brazil and buy an apartment in a secure high-rise protected by a compound. She'd had hoped Ryan might be the one to come with her and they could grow old together. You didn't hear many transgender people talking about their plans of growing old with their partners, because most of them didn't expect to live that long. Long-term relationships for them were often complex. Another human fragility that was not unique to the transgender community. Perhaps their relationships just came with more complications. Who could really say? She threw the towel on the bed and looked for something to wear. Her phone beeped again. It was her client phone, but the message on it was not from a client and sadly, not from Ryan; it was from Pearl. Pearl was one of the few people who had actually seen Ryan. Not in person, but she had seen a picture of him, one that Candice had taken sneakily with her phone when he was sleeping. She took some erotic pictures too, with her naked, lying next to him, even one with her soft cock draped across his cheek like a slug. So childish. Pearl and Joanne thought them hysterical. Candice knew it was a little infantile and she wasn't sure why she did it at the time, but concluded she was probably flying a little from the night before and you did silly things when you were in love (And even more silly things when you were high). God, was she really in love with him? They had never said it to each other but she knew her feelings for him had grown beyond their professional friendship. She had intended to show him the pictures, then delete them the following day but then he had had a call from work and had to leave earlier than normal. Pearl had said then that she thought she recognised him but couldn't think where from. As she reached for the phone, it beeped again. She scanned the screen and could see her inbox was full of unopened texts, several of which were from Pearl. They had started not long after Candice had come home from partying, taken some sleeping tablets and gone to sleep. There was a series of text messages that were a running commentary of something happening on the news. At first Candice thought she must be referring to the attack on the plane in France, but she soon realised the content of each message did not tally with those events. She read Pearl's texts properly, one after the other.

"Have you seen the news from America?"

"Wow, they're everywhere. France, Italy, Spain, there's even one in Brazil."

"They're saying two in Brazil now! I think they look beautiful. Joanne is a little scared. What do you think?"

"Have you spoken with your Mum?"

What on earth was she on about? Candice quickly chose a wig for the day from her selection. Twenty of them, all colours, shades and types adorned the top of a mounted shelf that ran along one wall of the bedroom. Some people had books on their shelves; some had CDs or DVDs or a Blu-ray collection. Candice had wigs and she didn't own a Blu-ray player, let alone any Blu-rays. She scooped down her choice and fitted it onto her scalp. It was dark brown, with a long cascade of curly locks that fell about her shoulders. She stretched out her legs, put on a matching set of blue underwear followed quickly by her jeans and a tight, light blue crop-top, which her augmented breasts protested at, struggling to get underneath the limited material available. She sat at her makeup desk and prepared to do her face, scrolling through more of the messages on her phone.

"You must be asleep; I cannot believe you're missing this."

"Wow, did you see the footage of the one in Aberdeen? The news says there's 200 of them all over the world!"

Candice flipped open the older laptop she had in the bedroom. She normally used it for watching Wendy Williams' shows before bedtime or, if she was really bored, a bit of Oprah, but now she typed into Google. "World News in the last twenty four hours." Then she added the words, "Two Hundred". That, she felt, would cover whatever it was Pearl was rattling on about.

She saw it—the headline reading like something from a bad Michael Bay movie. "Two hundred alien vessels land all around the world. No communication say Scientists."

Two hundred what? This had to be bullshit. Wasn't it April Fools' Day, today? No, she remembered that was yesterday. She clicked on images and there they were, pictures of several dozen of them, all over the world. They were an extremely odd shape. They had a saucer section in the middle of the design, but with long towers on the top and underside which formed into points at their ends. Not quite white in colour, perhaps cream with a slight shine to them, and the underside seemed to sparkle in some of the images. She flipped through the Internet on a multitude of links and saw one vessel passing behind the Eiffel Tower in Paris, though it was some distance outside of the city itself. From what she saw, they all appeared to be the same colour, shape and size. She went to YouTube and typed in, "Alien ships arrive..." and sure enough there were so many clips uploaded that not a single other unrelated clip of some phony UFO footage was anywhere to be seen, even in the suggestion column on the right. People had been filming these things all over the world since this morning and a quick search showed one passing right over her home city of Rio. She could tell the footage had been taken from someone with a phone high up in one of the *favelas*. It had moved gently above the city as though it were drifting, coming in from the sea to the south and moving across *Guanabara Bay*. The lower point of the object barely missed the top of the 101 highway—the man-made bridge that spanned the two sides of the bay—by just a few feet. One of the clips had been taken by a driver from directly underneath it, Candice could see the bottom of the lower structure very clearly; its lower surface sparkled as though covered in diamonds, which she thought was exquisitely beautiful. How amazing it would be to see one of these things so close! The footage of the vessel, if that was what it was, was simply astounding and she knew she was witnessing a moment of world history. She re-typed, "Alien ship landing in Rio" and there were over a hundred clips, all taken by phones that had been uploaded to YouTube, showing the object slowly landing in the mountains north of the town of *Majo*. The lower point of the ship vanished into the ground and this was the first time she realised the ship had been rotating. It began to disappear behind the forested mountains but then it stopped, the upper part of the object still completely visible, and remained there, like a huge white church sitting in the distance. Religion coming to earth from another planet? She certainly hoped not. That would only cause one thing—more wars. Most of the images were taken from quite a distance but its location was easy for her to place; Candice recognised the location of Rio's largest prison in the fore-ground of one of the more distant shots that had been filmed. This was somewhere she had visited frequently when she was younger. The ship had gone north from there, before landing somewhere just south of the town of *Juiz de Fora*, according to some of the comments she could hear on camera. Other footage in the town of Juiz had also been uploaded and confirmed its location. She knew this part of Brazil well, so it wasn't too much of a chal-lenge to identify the towns, hills and landmarks. She skipped through several other clips from all over the world. Australia, Thailand, Chad, Sudan, where one of these vessels had landed within a stone's throw of the largest refugee camps in the world. The soldiers of the UN had panicked and left the refugees to their fate, but there was no report of any deaths. In fact, she could find no reports of any deaths anywhere, though several people did appear to be missing, and there were people complaining about property damage and a slump in property prices near where various vessels had descended. She watched one clip of a man being filmed as he watched in awe at the sight of one of the objects moving through the night sky which according to the graphic written below the footage was recorded from the town of *Parkes*, Australia. She'd never heard of it. The man looked to be in his forties, sporting a wiry ginger beard and was jumping up and down in excitement at the sight of the alien craft. His name, again according to the graphic, was *Rafferty James, Ufologist, Project Listen*. But his accent sounded more Kiwi than Aussie. Candice had met enough of both to tell the difference. He certainly appeared more elated, than scared. Others were calling the day *Parousia* - which she heard someone mention was an ancient word for *Arrival*. They'd certainly arrived all right.Then Youtube crashed. She thought it must have reached its data storage limit.

Candice returned to her phone and scrolled through more messages. There were several cancellations from her escorting clients for the week. Tomorrow's appointments, daytime, cancelled; all of Wednesday's, cancelled. People stating it could be the end of the world and they needed to be with their families. There were those, however, with alternative suggestions, "How about we drop some pills and fuck until the end of the world?" Yeah, no thanks.

If this was the end of the world, she certainly wasn't going to spend it with one of her clients. Could this explain Ryan's phone call? Had he lied to her all along? Maybe he had a family after all... She focused on the messages from Pearl, then she remembered her other phone. Her mother! She must be worried sick... She ran and snatched it from the bedroom, only to discover it was dead; in her rush to get to bed last night she hadn't plugged the charger in properly. She immediately did so, knowing she would be able to give home a call in a couple of minutes if her mother wasn't already on Skype. She logged into Skype on the laptop while she waited for it to charge up, she kept reading the messages from Pearl.

"Let us know if you want to come here tomorrow. Whatever's going to happen, we can all be together here and see out the end in style."

Was it the end of the world? She wanted to know more. Searching through the multitude of clips online, she wondered in some cases how they were able to land on such unforgiving terrain without any difficulty. There were even shots of some landing in the oceans, with multiple footage taken of one entering the water just off the coast of Southern Italy, between the heel and the foot, taking up almost the entire span of water between them. Perhaps they weren't all the same size? Candice tried to get her head around so many bizarre images. This was just all too much to take in. Skype was unobtainable, overloaded probably. Her work phone beeped again. She skipped ahead to the latest unopened messages and saw that the last three were all from Pearl, and had come in the last three minutes.

"Are you awake yet? If u r turn on BBC 1!"

"Candice get up. I am sure that's him on the TV."

"Candice, I'm sure that's him!!!!!!"

The last message was from sixty seconds ago. She poured herself a vodka and apple juice to steady her nerves. This was too much to take in! Now she desperately wanted to talk to her mother, but she knew she would have to wait a little longer for her phone to charge. She could call her mother from her work phone but she didn't want her mother to have that number. It would cause immediate suspicion and her mother was no idiot. She voice activated the wall-mounted TV in the open plan living space and at once she saw him. All forty-two inches of him across. She didn't remember losing her grip on her glass but just heard it smash on the tiled floor below.

It was Ryan, on the television. She read the scrolling caption below the image, even though she couldn't hear what he was saying.

British Cabinet elects Ryan Wallace to serve as temporary Prime Minister in this time of crisis...

"Oh shit," she said. The man who was now running the United Kingdom only thirty-six hours earlier, had been doing lines of coke in her flat and had her cock up his arse. She didn't need to be a clairvoyant to know this was not good news for her, not good at all.

CHAPTER IV

'I think everyone was surprised when they didn't attack. I know I was. I guess that was what we've all been led to expect because of the kind of things we've all seen on films and television. So it didn't surprise me when all the UN Troops turned and ran when one of the ships began landing right next to our refugee camp. I could have gone with them and most of the medical personnel and volunteers from the charities did exactly that. They took all the transport and they fled, abandoning those they left behind to their fate. I couldn't blame them really, the sight of something so alien landing so close was truly terrifying but I took an oath in my job and I believed in it. Many of the refugee's fled on foot but many of them were too weak to go anywhere. We had hundreds of people we were caring for who were close to death from starvation and couldn't be moved, so I and a few of my team elected to stay and see things through. I'm so glad we made that choice. Those who ran, well, that's something they will just have to live with.'

Doctor Henry Parnell, United Nations Refugee Camp, Sudan, Africa - Date unknown

DIANA

U.S HIGHWAY 50, NEVADA, UNITED STATES OF
AMERICA – MONDAY APRIL 2ND

"It's coming down, we have to go!" the older of the two men shouted as he ran towards her. He was the tallest, dressed in jeans with a short-sleeved check shirt, over which he wore a brown waistcoat, which had pockets filled with what appeared to be photographic accessories, giving the impression he was some kind of war correspondent. In contrast, his shorter friend with baseball cap and unkempt hair looked like he'd come from a comic book convention. Maybe they were UFO bloggers, come to get a first-hand look. This seemed a reasonable assumption considering the one running towards her was holding a very professional-looking camcorder. He had thick, dark curly hair and reminded her of an actor she had once had a teen crush on - Lance Guest in The Last Starfighter, only older and with spectacles. When was that released? Early eighties? She must have been only seven when she saw that movie.

"Lady, we have to go!" He repeated, holding out his hand.

Diane felt her children gripping her tightly, looking up to her for a response as her mind was racing. She was stuck here with no other way out and her options were limited. Behind her, the lower cone of the ship was beginning to extend itself down into the ground. Glancing up, Diana could see the man was right – The saucer of the ship was closer to the ground than it had been before.

"My car won't start!" She glanced round at her ride, knowing if she lost her car, it wouldn't bode well for her and her children. "Can you tow it?" Such a request was very optimistic. Their vehicle was similar in size to her own, only with an extended hatchback. It might have been able to manage it, if there was time, which there wasn't.

"Tow it? Lady, if we don't get out from under this thing right now, we're all going to die! Haven't you seen the news? These things are arriving all over the planet and this one is landing here right now!" the man shouted in exasperation.

All over the planet? The second man was by the passenger door, frantically beckoning them over to the vehicle. "Guys, can you just skip the goddamn introductions and get into the goddamn car!" he shouted. Perhaps they were brothers. They didn't look alike. Diana didn't know what *Chunk* from The Goonies looked like now, but she thought he might look like this guy.

"Please!" The man stretched his hand out to her and she took it, dragging her kids with the other as they ran towards the vehicle.

"I thought you told us never to get into cars with strangers, Mommy!" Jules said. Diana couldn't help but smile.

"When a spaceship is about to land on you, honey, sometimes you might have to break those rules!" Jules just nodded, looking up at the descending ship above them all. The first man opened the back door for them, and the kids jumped in. Diana remembered that her phone, her driving license, their bags, what little money she had, were all back in her car. The two men had already got in the front of the vehicle. Wind and dirt began to kick up around them as a torrent of air pressured downward from the object's descent. Diana screamed to the man in the passenger seat, the one who looked like (a young) Lance Guest. "Wait one minute!" Without even waiting for his response, she bolted back towards her vehicle hearing her children screaming her name behind her.

"Where the hell are you going?" The car behind her had already started up and was revving the engine when she sprinted back to her own car, adrenaline and fear surging through her body in equal measure. Diana saw the base of the cone of the ship had reached the ground and was beginning to push into the dirt, but unlike a conventional drill, it was as if the end of the vessel became liquid, seeping into the desert floor below it. She furtively looked up and estimated that the underside of the ship must have been over a mile above her. She reached her car and wrenched open the door so hard it bounced back and banged her on the leg, catching her jeans.

"Sonofabitch!" She hoped her kids had not heard her profanity.

The wheels of the other car screeched, as it pulled up alongside her own vehicle. She wrenched out her rucksack and handbag from the front seat followed by her kids' bags from the back, throwing them in through the rear window of the neighbouring car.

"Lady – what on earth are you doing?" It was Lance Guest again.

"I have a car full of food and supplies for me and my children. Don't you think we might be needing them? Besides my driving license is the only ID I have! Help me unload the trunk, you can have half of everything!"

Much to the total dismay of his companion, *Lance* got out of the front seat and ran round to the back of her car, as she popped the trunk open. He grabbed the two large bottles of drinking water she had packed for the journey, while his friend came around from the other side to assist, shaking his head in anger and dismay.

"Lady, we don't need half. Let's just get this and go, we don't have time for a tow or to jump start your car, this thing is coming down right now and we need to get out from under it real fast! – Owen grab as much as you can!'

"Mum, do you want us to come and help?" Jules shouted, her voice barely audible above the sound of the air whirling around them.

"No! Stay in the car, honey, hold on to your brother!" Her daughter nodded through the window, holding onto her brother in a mutual embrace of comfort. Cute. Time to admire their emotional support for each other during extraterrestrial encounters later, if that was what this was.

"That's everything!" she shouted, remembering to grab her car keys at the last moment.

"Great, can we go now?" Cried Owen. Diana jumped in the back with her kids, causing Jules and Jack to promptly shift up. She ruffled their hair and put her arms around them, partly to comfort and partly in relief.

"We're okay. We're okay." She was almost breathless.

"Not yet we ain't! Go Craig, go!" Ah! So Craig was Lance Guest's real name. He slammed on the accelerator and the car rocketed down the straight flat road ahead, which was covered in the shadow of the saucer which spread all the way to the hills on the horizon.

"God, we're not going to make it! Go faster!" Owen shouted, his voice was full of panic.

"I'm at the maximum speed limit!" Craig yelled back. Diana could see ahead in the distance the lower edges of the underside of the saucer slowly creep in at the top of the car windscreen. The gap between the ship and the ground was narrowing all the time, and a darkness began to fill the car. Diana could tell Craig wasn't driving as fast as he could. She found herself leaning in the front between the seats of the two men. "Don't you think this might be a good time to break the speed limit?" she said sarcastically.

"I have a clean license. I don't want to get a ticket!"'Craig replied. Was he fucking kidding? Were there more appropriate circumstances than this to be breaking the speed limit? If there were she couldn't think of them.

"Who do you think is going to be hanging around to give you a ticket while this thing is coming down? Rosco P. Coltrane? Hit that accelerator boy, before this thing turns us all into cheese!"

"Boy?" Craig managed a quick glance back at her. "I'm thirty six years old ma'am!" Shit – really? He looked pretty good for thirty-six. Owen just glared back at Diana in confusion. Beads of sweat broke out all over Craig's forehead, but Diana could tell from his scent that he had good hygiene skills, though she was not sure if that was going to help the car go any faster.

"Who's Rosco P. Coltrane?" Owen asked.

"Never mind! Just floor it, Craig!" Diana shouted. She could see he was still being way too cautious, yet all the while they could see more and more of the saucer dipping down into the windscreen. Craig slowly increased the pressure on the accelerator and the car picked up speed to 70.

"Didn't you ever own Grand Theft Auto? Pretend you're playing a game of that!" She thought maybe that would get through to him. He must own a games console of some kind!

"I was always more of an RPG guy..." Craig said, his hands gripping so tightly to the wheel she thought it might break in half. Owen looked at both of them in disbelief, still filming everything on his camcorder.

"Can we discuss gaming preferences once we get out of here please?"

"Just pretend you're in The Fast and the Furious!" Diana yelled into his ear. They were still only going at 70, when finally he seemed to find his balls.

"Got it!" Craig slammed his foot down and the car promptly picked up speed, throwing Diana on to the back seat. She looked at her children. Christ! They weren't wearing their seat belts!

"Jack, Jules – belt up. Now!" Her children obeyed her without question. They knew that tone and it was never to be crossed without consequences. With a spaceship about to come down on top of them, Diana saw she need not reinforce the point. She fumbled around trying to connect her own seat belt but it would only come out so far. She realised she had trapped it in the door getting in the car. Shit.

"Don't lose control, don't lose control! Wow, I just have to get this!" Owen was filming up at the descending underside of the ship. It couldn't have been more than 500 feet above them now, the white glittering structure coming ever closer and the gap between the edge and the landscape ahead of them rapidly diminishing in the distance. Diana contemplated opening the door but they were now going at 105 and still increasing in speed. The smell of burning rubber began to fill the car and she became acutely aware the driver was not confident at travelling at such a velocity. Sweat poured down off his forehead causing him to blink. She grabbed a small flannel from her larger bag and wiped the drips from his brow and nose.

"Thanks," Craig said, without taking his eyes off the road. He stole a quick glance at the speedometer and then focused on the road ahead.

"You looked like you wanted to scratch your nose," Diana said. Well, it was true, he did.

"You're right there. I'm Craig, this is Owen," he said, his eyes still staying on the road. Diana thought the scene outside the car window vaguely reminiscent of a seventies cartoon, where the background would constantly stream past the characters. The sparse vegetation passing them was certainly reaching the point where it was almost just a blur on the side of the road, and seemed to be repeating itself. Diana kept a reassuring hand on Craig's shoulder.

"Keep steady, you're doing fine. Eyes on the road. I'm Diana and these are my kids, Jack and Jules."

"Nice to meet you kids, but Uncle Craig is a little busy right now, so he won't shake your hand. Y'all strapped in back there?' he asked. Uncle Craig? Was that him being cute, trying to reassure the kids or too familiar, too fast and a little creepy? Right now, under the present circumstances she decided to give him the benefit of the doubt and go with cute.

"Shit, we're not going to make it!" Owen pointed ahead as the underside of the saucer still stretched out endlessly in front of them. Diana could see the highway rising slightly up ahead and then dipping behind the hills. The gap between the edge of the saucer and the ground was now no more than a thin strip of white light. Its underside was already touching the hill tops that flanked the road. Diana stole a glance out of the back window and saw the central cone of the ship had completely penetrated the ground, yet it had caused only a little dust and dirt by doing so. Sure there was some, but not as much as she would have thought from such an event. Air and wind raced past the car, causing a terrific roar that made the whole vehicle shake. Either side of them, Diana could barely make out the gap between the saucer and the ground in the distance. The speedometer read 120 now.

"Shit, she might flip…" Diana could see Craig was losing confidence. If he didn't stay steady on the wheel they were either going to crash or not make it out in time. The highway had a slight curve to it as it weaved into the hills and then down again. The underneath of the saucer was now engulfing the tops of the hills all around them, forcing Craig to switch on the headlights. Owen watched in confused awe as the pearly surface of the vessel came ever closer.

"The hills aren't stopping it! It's just flowing around them, like it's swallowing them up or something. Shit, we need to get out from under this thing!"

The fear in Owen's voice made Diana increase her grip on Craig's shoulder, knowing full well the lives of all them were in his hands.

"You can do it! Steady, steady..." she whispered into his ears. "Anyone ever tell you, you look like the actor Lance Guest?"

"Lance Guest?' came Craig's confused reply. "You mean Alex Rogan, from *The Last Starfighter*?" Well, look at that, the kid knew his Science Fiction. "I saw that one on DVD when I was kid. Classic film. Thanks, I think. That's a compliment, right?"

"It is." She had to get him to just focus on the road and her voice, not to look up. If he looked up, he would come off the road and right now there were a lot of reasons to look up. Craig's voice was shaking as he replied, "No offence, but you don't really seem the Sci-Fi fan type." Diana wasn't offended by the comment. He was right, she wasn't really, but she had watched a great many movies with Danny in the eighties during those many long weeks when her father was away.

"I'm not, but I always loved that movie. The trailer park..." That was why she always remembered the film. The trailer park. It was a mirror image of her youth.

A smile broke across Craig's face. "Starlight, Starbright! Alex Rogan was the handyman everyone needed, but all he wanted to do was play the video game and get his girl out of town."

Craig remembered the name of it from the movie, how funny was that. She was touched, though she wasn't really sure why. He wasn't wearing a wedding ring. She definitely would not have noticed that, had his hands not been placed so steadfastly in front of her, gripping the wheel. Yes, definitely not. Still, good to know, though not really relevant right now.

"Yeah… that was like my home growing up. Things always needed fixing, that was for sure." Diana regretted saying that immediately. He didn't need to know she had once lived in a trailer park. The ship was filling more and more of their view ahead, the gap between it and the ground getting ever smaller but they were closing the distance.

"Did it have an Alex Rogan fixer-upper type living there?" he asked, his voice now trembling. It certainly didn't. It did have plenty of boys trying to get her up to the lake and get inside her pants. She seemed to recall that was also part of the movie's storyline, if her memory served her well.

"No," came her flat reply. "So just keep looking straight, hold that wheel, you're doing real well, real well. We can talk favourite movies when we get out of this."

"I've never driven this fast before!" His voice betrayed his fear and perhaps, Diana thought, he was a little thrilled at the same time.

"I've never been in a car going this fast before." That was a lie, but it was all she could come up with in the moment.

"So you're the trailer trash girl my Mom had always warned me to stay away from?' Had she now? She'd like to meet Craig's Mum and give the woman a piece of her mind for being so judgmental… From Craig's tone she could tell it was a comment born of nervous humour, with no malice, so no offence on her part was taken. This was a very odd conversation to be having in very odd circumstances. Still, she hadn't done much to break that stereotype, being a single mother with two kids.

"Yeah, that would be me," she said unapologetically, with a certain dryness. She thought she saw a smile on Craig's face in the mirror when he said, "Well, I was never very good at listening to my Mom...'

Was he flirting with her? Really? People did strange things when facing death. No time to think about that now. She thought back to all those animals running. It must have been instinct. Like when beasts flee from fire.

"There's the edge!" Owen shouted.

"I see it too, Mom!" Jules and Jack screamed from the back.

The distinctive curve of the structure above them was far more notice-able this close to the object. There were no sharp edges, the sides curving upwards into the saucer as if made from smooth white marble. For the first time, she noticed faint lines beneath its surface. They spread out in all directions on the underside of the ship forming a faint spider-web-like pattern just underneath the hull. They reminded her of veins under the skin. Diana saw the small gap up ahead, now perhaps a mile in front of them, the last finger of light peeking through between the object and the ground. The road was straight and level again. She felt Craig relax just a little.

"It's getting closer, Mom!" Jules had leaned across her brother and was straining to look up through the window. The underneath of the ship now filled every space outside between the ground and the sky. Only the singular slither of light up ahead on the road conveyed the last remaining trace of the day.

"It should be darker under here, shouldn't it?' Owen said, looking up. "There must be a light source coming from inside it somewhere."

Diana had thought that before, it was darker than day but not anything like night. Somehow the ship itself had an illumination coming from beneath its surface, almost like a glow. Yet the light itself was almost unob-trusive, as though it were bathing them in a softer form of daylight.

"Just keep filming, we can debate all that later." Craig snapped.

"Shit! I have to change cards." Owen struggled with the camera and quickly removed the SD card.

"Do it then, top right pocket." Craig gestured with his head towards the top pocket on his vest. Owen quickly retrieved it.

"Got it."

"Put the other one where no one will find it," Craig shouted. The gap between the ship and the road seemed to have almost vanished ahead of them now.

"Like where?" Owen asked.

"I don't know, be creative..."

Diana tapped Owen on the shoulder.

"Put it in the inside lining of your baseball cap." An ex of Diana's had been partial to taking illegal substances, and had always hid his wraps in there. Owen took off his San Diego baseball Cap and put the 64GB card in between the lining of the elastic. It slotted in perfectly.

Ahead, the edge of the craft could not be more than a dozen metres above the road. Diana could see something distant on the highway beyond the circumference of the craft, but it was too far away to make out clearly. Shapes lining the road. Possibly a group of vehicles. The press and their camera trucks maybe? They would want to be filming this event for certain. It was the biggest thing to happen in America since 9/11, and if these things were all over the world then there would be no hiding it from the world's media, not this time. Just thinking about the global ramifications of this were mind-boggling, and not something she could dwell on at this precise moment. At the alien vessel's current rate of descent, and judging from the distance they still had to travel to get out from underneath the thing, she could see their chances of escaping were slim. God, why didn't she just leave their things in the car? Material goods could be replaced, her children's lives could not and now she cursed herself for gambling with them so foolishly – an extra second or two could have made all the difference. The underside of the ship now came down ahead of them, and in full view. Diana knew it could only be mere feet from touching the car roof.

"Keep going... keep going!" Owen gripped the door handle, tensing his whole body as the vehicle bolted towards the small gap ahead.

"Shit, I'm going to lose control of her..." The vehicle shook furiously as they sped towards their intended finish line, now just a hundred metres away. Diana glanced again at her children; both were clinging on to each other and had their eyes firmly shut. Blue sky abruptly filled the windscreen and stretched out before them. The low rolling distant hills and mountains once again broke into view. Craig and Owen looked at each other and broke into fits of nervous laughter.

"We made it, we fucking made it! Shit, sorry ma'am!" Craig added apologetically. He began to decelerate. Diana looked back and saw the body of the saucer touch the ground behind them. It felt as though the impact of the ship on the flat, uneven landscape should have been more dramatic in some way. But it wasn't. There were no explosions or sounds of destruction, just the sound of the wind and air being pushed out from under the object. The car shook. They were down to 70 but the momentum carried the car toward a wire barricade that had been placed across the road. Diana could just make out a group of green camouflage-clad figures standing next to a cluster of vehicles that flanked the highway on either side. It was a military road-block.

"Jesus, it's the army – stop the car, Craig!" Owen yelled at him from the passenger seat. Diana felt something push the car from the rear, but she could see there was nothing behind them. Jules gripped her hand tightly.

"Brake, brake!" She screamed, as she felt the back of the car lift from the road. Diana grabbed on to the door rail with one hand and held her children with the other. There was no time to retrieve that trapped seatbelt from the car door. Something had lifted the back wheels from the ground and was now propelling them forwards.

"What the fuck is happening? Why aren't you braking?" Owen screamed at Craig.

"I am! It's not working, man!" Just as Craig spoke, the car collided with the barrier. Diana saw a mass of running figures bearing weapons. Wire became impaled on the car windscreen as Craig lost control of the vehicle. It rolled, tumbling over for an eternity.

As Diana came to, she tasted blood on her lips and the feeling of a hot sticky liquid running down the side of her face. She couldn't tell how long she had been out for, but her head pounded worse than any migraine she had ever experienced. She opened her eyes and felt a stinging sensation from the light. Voices shouted but she couldn't make out the words. Her children. She struggled to bring her surroundings into focus. There was a smell of burnt metal, leaking oils and petrol fumes. Then she could just make out the unmistakable form of her daughter. Jules was being carried from the car by a man in combat fatigues. Her arms were hanging loosely by her sides like a doll. God, was she hurt? She had to get to her but found she could not move. She tried to call Jules' name but no words came from her throat, only the taste of more blood in her mouth. Voices called. She thought she saw Lance Guest again. Maybe there was a Starfighter left, was that the line from a movie? Was she dreaming? Then the world turned to darkness.

OMARI

He had worked out that the object was probably an hour's ride away, if he could convince his lead camel, Ali-Baba, to head in that direction, he could cover the distance relatively quickly. Since Omari had first witnessed its dramatic landing things had been, well, rather uneventful and he had subsequently felt a little disappointed that nothing else had happened. Yes, it was remarkable, this object that had appeared and landed in the desert a mere few miles north of him, but after its arrival he had expected more to transpire. Nothing emerged from the object, which having landed, now just sat there, the circumference stretched out for some miles across the horizon before him. It was colossal in its dimensions, easily the size of a city, he thought. The surface of the object gradually sloped upward forming into a tower that ascended into a thin circular pointed structure so high that its tip almost tickled the clouds above it. He wondered if it had any kind of religious significance. It reminded him of Christian churches he had seen pictures of from faraway places, but this structure had no cross on the top of it. It looked to be as high as the highest mountain he had seen, but from this distance it was hard to judge for certain.

Omari weighed up the dangers. Joy would be safe in Fada for now, and although he really did need to get home, his curiosity would not abate. If it was made by men, why would it come to such a remote place? There was nothing of value here and nothing to conquer. He concluded it must be from elsewhere, perhaps not of this earth at all and it was Allah's will that he had witnessed its arrival, so therefore he must investigate this strange craft and discover its purpose. The pain in his tooth was his only nagging doubt, but he would tolerate it a little longer to see this strange miracle.

As the sun began to set, he saw the distant fires lighting up among the homes of his people in Fada to the east. Then he saw some distant car head-lights approaching the object, but they stopped, turned around and went back towards the town, not reaching even half as close as he was now. Sunset - this had always been his favourite time of day. It was as if the hand of Allah painted the skies, turning this harsh land he called home into a thing of dazzling beauty. The sands beneath his feet would finally began to cool and the warm air would feel fresh upon his face as the temperature dropped. He removed a second wrap of clothing from his satchel and wound it around his body, for he knew it would soon become bitterly cold. His country had always been a place of such extremes of temperature. He studied the object once again, looking for signs of change but could see none beyond it catching the dropping sun, causing its surface to glow brightly in the dimming light, as if Allah himself was continuing to beckon him forwards. He had tethered all three of his camels together and mounting Ali-Baba at the head of his small column, he proceeded to gently steer them towards the capacious white disk that lured him ever closer. The sky became awash with its habitual display of rich purples and reds, as the last drops of daylight finally drained off to the west. Omari noticed that the object appeared to glow most softly in the encroaching night sky. It was unlike any kind of light source he had ever seen. He could not tell if it was caused by the reflection of the rising moon, or was in fact coming from within. It was not bright enough to cause discomfort to look at, but strong enough to reflect soft shadows off the surrounding rock formations that were grouped at intervals around the landing site. Ali-Baba and his brethren seemed undeterred as Omari gently trotted the three animals in the direction of the glowing expanse ahead of them. His tooth however, was not being so co-operative. It had been paining him all day and even the little swigs of vodka were no longer giving him any respite. Sharp stabbing pains had become more frequent in his mouth, and were now becoming a major source of discomfort. He was going to have to have it removed, and now regretted not going back to the village, but he knew this was his only chance to investigate this divine occurrence totally unmolested.

As he got about 500 yards from the edge of the object, he saw a trickle of moving lights emerging from the east track to Fada, heading in his direc-tion. Transport of some kind that in such a number could only belong to the Chadian military. The object was obviously their destination. The time for subtlety was over. He knew once the army got to this thing they wouldn't let anyone near it, at least not without having to pay them a substantial bribe. Something he certainly could not afford and even if he could, it would not be money he would wish to part with. This would not be the will of Allah; for the closer he got towards the unearthly structure, the more certain he was that he was supposed to be there. Fortunately, it appeared his animals were in agreement for as he spurred Ali-Baba on, the animal did not resist and all three of the creatures happily increased their speed toward the vessel, even more determined to reach the base of the craft than he was. Omari was soon to discover why. As he drew closer, he decided it would be best to dismount and proceed on foot. As he got down from Ali-Baba, he jumped in shock at the unexpected sensation of cold liquid on his feet. He was standing in water that came just past his ankles. How could this be? The nearest source of water was in the town of Fada, and this was a relatively dry time of year. He knew every single well in this region, even those well-hidden and kept secret for many generations. It was unmistakable; he was standing just past his ankles in water and it was not a puddle, it was as if a ring of liquid had formed around the object, perhaps eighty paces in width, that followed the edge of the vessel in both directions. His camels were overjoyed at its presence, bending their necks to lap greedily, quenching their thirst. It was their first drink in forty-eight hours. Omari knew his animals well and could always tell their mood – they would not drink water they knew to be bad. The water was not the only thing that had changed near the object. The ground beneath his feet was hard rock. A level basin had formed, only just below knee deep. He removed his sandals and felt the water run between his toes, soothing the weary soles of his feet. The dirt and sand freed itself from his skin. It was all most unusual. Where the rocks protruded in this part of the desert, they were always rough and jagged, but here the ground was smooth beneath his feet. It was as if this strange object had created its own source of water in a place where such a thing was impossible. He looked back at his camels to see that all three of them had now sat down at the water's edge together, lapping up a few more mouthfuls of the cool, inviting water. He thought Abu-Sir actually smiled at him. He knew his creatures had a sense of humour, and he knew their differing temperaments. Right now, they were as content as he could ever recall. He looked across the water with many questions forming in his mind. What had brought this magical sight to the deserts of Chad? Was this unearthly happening the will of Allah? Perhaps Omari had been chosen by Him, chosen for something important! Chosen to be the first one to greet Him on His return? Possibly. He at once began to regret not taking his religious vows more seriously. He always did the least that was required of him. What was it then that Allah required of him now? He knelt at the edge of the water and cupped his hands, trapping a small amount between his locked fingers. After a moment's hesitation, he brought his hands to his dry lips and let the cool liquid fall into his mouth. It was refreshing and tasted sweet. He immediately refilled his water bottle, before drinking several more handfuls. At once, he felt invigorated.

"Now I see why you're all smiling! It tastes good, no?" He laughed, and the camels all bleated back as though laughing with him. Perhaps they were laughing at him, the crazy old man drinking the water from the desert where there should have been none. He did ponder if the whole thing was a hallucination, but the eastward convoy headlights loomed ever larger, and quickly convinced him otherwise. The sound of their engines indicated it would only be a matter of minutes before they arrived, close to where he stood. Feeling refreshed, he refilled all his water bottles and gathered as many of his personal belongings as he could manage, then tethered his camels to the ground.

"I'll be back soon. Don't worry," he said to Ali Baba, kissing the creature's head before striding towards the edge of the vessel, the water cool around his calves. His body felt strong and revitalised with energy. The water depth remained constant, which surprised him. He thought it might be some kind of defensive barrier and he expected it to get deeper closer to the object, but it did not. Looking back, he could see the convoy consisted of army two trucks and two Land Rovers. He wondered if Doctor Aziz might be with them. He was one of the few people who owned a Land Rover, and the only man who could resolve his toothache, which still throbbed in his mouth. Omari pulled his pocket torch out from his belt. Another gift, but this time from his older daughter, Nya. She had told him he could use it to read books when he was travelling, to help improve his literary skills. Omari had never had much use for reading. Maths was his strongest subject, to ensure he was not cheated on by other traders. The small black penlight had a powerful beam on it, but Omari saw that he didn't need it and soon put it back for fear of attracting attention. The surface of the water glittered not only with the moonlight, but from the soft glow that emitted from beneath the alien surface. As he reached the edge, he saw it met perfectly with the ground, the same way an upturned plate would sit upon a flat table. He could see he would be able to simply step from the water onto the upper part of the surface, with little difficulty. He stood staring for a moment at its strange pearl-coloured exterior, uncertain if he should tread upon it. He saw that it had a texture of marble-like material, noting it was not in fact entirely one colour. Under the surface, he could see a series of connected faint dark lines that ran in numerous directions and bisected each other at different intervals. It was, he thought, like looking at the veins under his own skin. He listened for sound, but all around him was quiet, except for the sound of the water lapping against the edge of the object, the occasional grunt from his animals and the distant sounds of the approaching vehicles. Omari looked back on his three friends. Across the water, they sat content, each occasionally craning their heads down to take another drink. Beyond them, the vehicle lights were edging closer but Omari could see they were struggling with the terrain, and they had only got marginally nearer. They would be here in perhaps thirty minutes, more than enough time for him to walk onto the surface and look around, but not enough time to reach the tower that rose slowly up from the middle; at least half a day's travel from where he stood. Omari wondered if the water around the object had some sort of religious significance. Was he perhaps supposed to bathe in it as one washed one's feet before entering Mosque? He decided not to take the chance, removing his sandals and placing them in his bag then and recited a short prayer to Allah. The ground beneath him felt so smooth, as if the sand had been turned into glass. Drawing a heavy breath, he cautiously rose one foot, stretching it out above the gentle sloping rim of the object. He had heard stories of men walking on the moon in the past, though he had never personally seen any proof of it. People said they had travelled up there by rocket ship and walked upon it. His father had said that this was a fantasy story told by the Americans to make themselves seem like Gods to the rest of the world.

"No one could ever walk on the moon!" his father had said, laughing. Omari was surprised he could remember now that conversation from so long ago. This might not be the moon, but it certainly felt like he was about to take a big step. His right foot touched down carefully, with Omari trying to put as little weight on it as he could manage without falling over. He didn't know how fragile the surface might be, and he was worried he might simply step through it as though stepping upon a giant eggshell. It felt cool but not cold. It was completely stable. He took a second step and found the surface to be completely solid. He tapped it with his walking stick but it made no noise, giving no indication of being hollow inside. He quickly stole a glance back at his camels. All three of them were transfixed on his actions, following his every move. He smiled at them and spontaneously did a little jump. He wasn't sure if it was for joy, or he was just excited at having been the first person to reach the object. Maybe he wanted to test his weight upon it. All three of the beasts grunted back at him, bemused by his actions, which were a little out of character for a man normally so reserved. The surface of the object spread out ahead of him, like a vast white desert plain of its own, before it began in the far distance, a very slow curve upward towards the central structure, standing aloof, like a tall, alluring white finger. From where he stood, it would be a considerable journey to reach it and not something he could do in a couple of hours, unless he used his camels, but with the surface being so hard, he knew he couldn't risk it causing serious injury to their legs. To reach it travelling on foot before the occupants of the convoy caught up with him was unlikely, but something within him was determined to try and do so. He bent down at the saucer's edge and took out another two water bottles from his backpack, refilling them before drinking the entire contents of the third one that was attached to his belt. He drank over two pints before finally refilling the flask. He knew he would need to stay fully hydrated, even though he wanted to return to his camels as soon as possible and be underway again to Fada well before dawn.

He walked at a fast pace towards what he assumed to be the centre of the vessel, occasionally stealing a glance behind him to check on the approach of the convoy. His running days were long since over, and even walking at this rapid pace caused him some discomfort. It was not long before pains stabbed at his chest and he begun to cough uncontrollably. He took a brief rest. He had been walking for perhaps four hundred paces when he stopped to take a swig of water and some dried meat strips from his pouch. He was hungry and knew he had to try and eat something or he feared becoming faint, so he sat down facing the way he had come so he could watch the approaching convoy's movements as he ate. It had come to a halt. He struggled to chew on the food because of the pain in his tooth, which had now reached excruciating levels. He restricted himself to eating on one side and to chewing extremely slowly. Omari had always been a patient man and it had served him well. He wasn't going to change this habit now, even in the face of Allah's wonderful blessing to his people. The convoy halted some way back from the water's edge and a chain of torch-lights appeared, soon fanning out into a line, walking cautiously in his direction. They could only be 200 paces away from the edge now, perhaps over 600 paces or so from him. Omari was pretty good at judging distances, a skill he had naturally picked up through his travels. He could no longer make out the shape of his camels and debated going back. If it was the military, they would ask him to leave, probably asking for a bribe to stop him from being fined, which amounted to the same thing. He had made so little on this trip already, that he knew he couldn't afford to give them anything. No, he could not give up now. He finished his small meal and continued in the direction of the aloof tower on the horizon. Soon he became aware that he was walking on a very subtle and gradual incline that rose ever so gently. He increased his pace and did not look back for another ten minutes. Omari finally became out of breath and stopped again. The last gasps of the dimming red skies were fading and the dark blue heavens above him began to wink with stars. He wondered from which star the vessel might have travelled from to come to Chad, and how long it had taken them to do so. He took his last swig of vodka to try and numb the pain of his tooth but it did no good. As he swirled the bitter liquid around his mouth, sucking it from left to right between his teeth, he realised he didn't want to spit it out. If this thing, this object, this ship, was indeed a vessel of Allah, such an act would be shameful. He could not do it, but he also could not drink it. He shook his water bottle, and realised the one attached to his belt was already a third empty. He unscrewed the lid and spat the contents of his mouth back in the bottle. He would drink from that bottle last, if he had to. Behind him, the ring of torchlights had reached the edge of the water, where they stopped. Omari heard faraway snatches of frantic conversation and confused dialogue between the men. They must have been as surprised as he was to see the ring of water. He knew they must have been able to see him but they were too preoccupied to act. There were shouts, perhaps an argument, but he was too far away to distinguish the words. He kept moving forwards even though he had no real idea of his destination, other than the distant white tower. Still he could see no openings, doors or windows—how would he get inside? Then, just ahead of him, a rectangular patch on the surface briefly glowed brighter, drawing his attention to something he had missed; a depression just twenty paces away to his right, sloping down into the surface. Hurrying towards it, he saw it ran downward for about sixty paces before ending in a blank wall that was about the height of a man. Was it even there a minute ago? He was sure it was not. He looked back again and could see the ring of torchlight at the edge of the object, hesitating. He suspected some of the men did not wish to walk upon this holy object for fear of offending Allah, or maybe just for fear. He could not afford to delay. They would be fit young men with training, and if they overcame their fear they would be able to cover the ground in half the time that he had taken. He walked down the slope towards the blank wall ahead of him. The slope descended steadily at an angle, until he was no longer visible from the surface. The walls were identical in appearance to the surface he was walking on. There were no edges, openings or lines, it was simply a smooth depression that had been gouged into the surface that appeared to go nowhere. He was comforted by knowing that while in this depression at least he would be hidden from view. He studied the blank wall in front of him, looking for symbols or buttons but there were none that he could see. Was it some kind of test? Perhaps it was as simple as knocking on the door… He smiled to himself as he rapped on it with his stick, taking a step back and dropping to his knees in case Allah himself was about to open it, but nothing happened. Nothing opened. There was no Allah, no aliens, no one at all. Perhaps he was not chosen, perhaps he was just here in the wrong place at the wrong time, as the saying went. Maybe this was not a vessel of Allah at all. He placed his hand on the wall to steady himself as he rose, contemplating his pending return to Fada. There was, it seemed, very little to see here, wondrous though the place was. When questioned by the army, he would say the rest of his animals had become separated from him, he thought them trapped beneath the vessel and he had come to look for them. That was reasonable enough, and if it was the local Commander of Fada out there with his men, he knew Omari and was unlikely to be angry with him because they had traded in the past. His hand felt warm. Omari turned to see the surface of the wall around his hand beginning to glow. He snatched his hand away, stepping back from the wall as he did so. His hand was sticky and felt as though it had become glued to the surface, yet he had had no trouble removing it. He rubbed his fingers and felt the ridges of his skin, but could find no trace of a substance of any kind. Nothing here made any sense to him until he looked back at the wall. There was a print of his hand where he had placed it, on a protruding transparent square, back-lit by a soft, white light from within the wall. He examined it closely, noting that part of the wall had changed to a small square shaped glass-like protruding plate, and on that plate was the print of his hand, fitting neatly in the middle of the square. *How odd,* he thought.

For the first time he was a little scared. He edged slowly back up the slope only to peer above it and saw the mingling chain of lights now on the surface, heading straight toward him. Several men in combat fatigues were now hurrying forward in a line, sweeping torches across the surface. There were shouts and cries, and the pace of the men appeared to quicken. He instantly ducked, shuffling down the slope, uncertain if they had seen him. The sky had grown completely dark, but the illumination from the surface of the vessel radiated even stronger than ever in the moonlight. If he emerged from the depression there was no doubt they would see him. Then Omari heard it. The unmistakable sound of gunfire. Several bursts in the distance. He raised his head again as much as he dared, his body now lying prone, and witnessed flashes of gunfire coming from around the edge of the object; not from those men moving toward him. The group of vehicles that had brought the men from Fada had been joined by others, there were torches approaching the object in clusters, indicating that others, probably villagers like himself, had come to investigate for themselves but the military had other ideas, and some fighting had broken out. The men on the surface paused and crouched, facing back the way they came. Almost everyone in Fada owned a firearm of some sort. He feared for his camels. If there were gunshots they would certainly try to run away. His herbs and spices were still packed on their saddles, so his curiosity to see this thing might have cost him his delivery. If they fled, they might eventually come back to the nearest source of water, which meant he would have to wait for them here. It was more likely they would be stolen, so he cursed himself for being so stupid. He had taken a huge risk and there was nothing here. Perhaps this was some kind of thing made by the government or even the Americans for generating water in the desert. Now he thought about it, that sounded like the sort of thing they would do. His father was always telling him how foreign powers were always testing things out in Africa, to see if they worked or not. If many Africans died no one would care, he always told him. But if this was something made by man, why did it repli-cate the print of his palm? He knew it was his own, because he had a very distinct scar on his right hand that had once led a local witch doctor to reveal to him that one day he would be a very rich man. That day had yet to happen and he dismissed her ramblings as that of an insane old woman.

He retraced his steps to the wall once again, but his palm print on the small square of glass was nowhere to be seen. The wall at the end of the slope was as it has been before. He heard more shots. There was no more time for internal debate, he had to try something. He touched the surface again with his right hand, and as soon as he reached for it the wall changed again and the plate with his handprint emerged, exactly where it had been before. He placed his hand on the warm glass, and again the pearl surface glowed all round him for just a second. Then the wall in front of him just peeled back in on itself, taking the glass plate with it and creating an opening. There was no door as such, it was as if the wall ahead of him just folded inwards to reveal a long white corridor, fully lit with the same soft glow as the surface, its smooth walls identical in every respect. Omari cautiously put one foot in, and then another before finally taking several large strides inside. The opening sealed behind him as quickly it had opened, trapping him inside.

BLESSING

B lessing and her small group had been walking on the surface of the ship for some considerable time. When they had driven to the edge of it some hours earlier, there was some debate as to how they should proceed. The two students wanted to make sure they filmed everything, but they were both talking so fast and kept switching to random topics, before declaring how much they loved Blessing, Elvis and Agatha and how great it was that they were all friends. She was sure they were drunk. Agatha just laughed and gave her a wink. Agatha wanted to push on as fast as possible and find a way inside. As far as the old lady was concerned, it seemed unlikely she was going to see something this remarkable again like this in her lifetime. She wanted to make sure she got to see as much of it as possible. Having found no obvious way to access the object, the general consensus was that if there was a way in, it would be located towards the mysterious tower that lay at its apex, but Elvis had estimated that this was several miles away from where they were standing. Everyone agreed there was no way that Agatha could walk that far. Agatha reluctantly concurred that it would be difficult to walk such a distance at her age. Donny speculated that the object might in fact be a large alien egg, and there was every possibility that stepping on it might cause it to break. Ewen had decided he was going to test this theory: much to everyone's horror he jumped up and down on the surface of the object.

"Nope, it's not an egg!" he stated, as if it were a definitive fact. Blessing wasn't sure his methods were very scientific, and Agatha's scowling expression reflected her disapproval. Having found the surface of the ship to be quite solid, Ewen and Donny spent several minutes lying down upon it, and stroking it, after which they concluded that the surface did not sound hollow and should be able to take everyone's weight. As Blessing witnessed this discussion reaching its pointless climax, the sound of two fighter jets roaring past overhead filled the air. They banked over the saucer several times and then headed west, dropping out of sight. There followed a quick examination by the group of their provisions. Between them they had plenty of water, as the two young men had a rucksack each completely full of small water bottles which Agatha commented was most ingenious of them. Blessing observed that the two young men were singing one minute, then laughing the next, barely able to string a coherent sentence together.

"If we are to be among the first people from earth to greet our visitor friends, I don't think some of us should be so, well, intoxicated." Blessing said, giving a nod to Elvis in the direction of Donny and Ewen.

"I dunno, it might be better for any visitors to see the greatest disappointments of the human race up front. That way things between us and them could only improve later like." Elvis replied.

Blessing was not sure she saw the logic of this argument. Looking at the far-flung tower, she wondered if it held a religious significance. It was not unlike a spire of a cathedral, after all. Could it be that Our Lord had finally come back? If all they had to offer in the way of a reception committee were sinners and well, inebriated singers, He might well get back in His ship and go back to Heaven. No, she couldn't be sure this was a vessel of God. This wasn't the only ship that had arrived, there were many more after all. All she could be certain about was that it wasn't from Earth, but she wanted to be among the first to find out its origin. People would want to interview her; the newspapers, the local radio, perhaps even the television! She would need to get a new weave if she was going to be seen by millions of people... Maybe she would get to go on that chat show that she liked, with the nice man who always reasoned his arguments so well. That must have been why his surname was Wright. Sadly, he wasn't single. She had already checked. If this had been the only ship she felt certain she would have been a guest on Wendy Williams or even Oprah! If they could be the first to get inside it maybe that could still happen. Elvis had taken charge of checking the group's provisions. It was already late and he had made the very valid point that if they were going to travel any further they would need to see what supplies they had between them.

"Right then, noo. This be everything we have. Two Mars Bars, like. Agatha's sandwiches. Thanks very much for those. Five cans of Boost from our young friends, here. Ten bottles of water. What kind of party's that then, eh lads? Some Polos from myself, and some chewing gum from young Blessed here."

"Blessing," she promptly corrected him.

"Blessing, Aye. Oh aye, and some Fisherman's Friends." Blessing had never seen them before. They looked like a dark medication tablet and extremely unappealing. She wondered what situation would cause a fisherman to take them. Elvis had been quick to assess their best course of action. He said *The King* would never go anywhere without a plan. She wasn't sure who The King was. She thought the UK only had a Queen, but thought it best not to complicate the discussion further. It was already beginning to grow dark, and the realities of their situation were already beginning to dawn on them. Blessing knew they all had homes and probably jobs to go to, or in the case of the two students, classes to attend the next day. Everyone expressed their concern for Agatha, but she was relentless in her demand not be the decisive factor in the group turning back.

"I'm perfectly capable of making my own decisions, thank you very much. I've got my pills, and half of these ham and cheese butties will do me right until tomorrow. You young 'uns can have the rest of them. I'll be fine. I want to go on. I want to see the middle and go up in that tower thing! Maybe my Charlie's in there!"

"Charlie? Your dead husband?" Ewen asked. Blessing thought that rather rather insensitive.

"Dead budgie," Agatha said, winking at Blessing. Blessing could only admire the plucky determination that a woman of her years possessed. She certainly hoped she would have as much gusto and energy when she was Agatha's age. As for going on, she felt the same. She had never done anything dangerous in her life before, just to satisfy her own curiosity. Impulsively coming here had changed all that, and it felt good to have done so. She always felt she should be more daring in her life. Men liked daring women. She often wondered if that was what Brad Pitt was thinking when he went off with Angelina and left Jennifer. She always preferred Jennifer. She always had such lovely hair. Everyone had a quick bite to eat and a drink. Elvis suggested he drive the bus onto the object itself. He told everyone to wait, while he tried getting it up onto the surface to see if it could take the weight. The surface itself had felt like walking on cool stone so everyone agreed it was practical, but Blessing was more concerned about leaving tyre marks all over what was essentially an alien artefact. As Elvis gunned the bus up the slope and onto the surface with little difficulty, Blessing's attention was drawn to the sound of several motorbikes off to the north. A small group of a dozen or so were already on the surface of the ship, and were racing ahead towards the central column. Elvis stepped off the bus and waved everyone back on board.

"See, its nae problem. Let's get going then. Someone else is already racing us to the finish line!"

At least he hadn't lit up another cigarette, not yet anyway. Blessing wasn't happy though. They couldn't be driving this dirty old bus all over the lovely white surface of this beautiful ship. Supposing it was a vessel of

God, or some even aliens visiting? She would be most unhappy if someone drove all over her car, not that she actually owned one.

"If you brought your nice new car to visit a planet and then some dwarf decided to drive all over it, don't you think you would be a little upset?" she had said, surprising herself at her ability to challenge the man. He looked a little hurt by the comment. Agatha simply looked confused as she got back on the bus with Elvis's assistance.

"Who's the dwarf in this scenario?" the elderly lady asked.

"Me apparently, lassie," Elvis replied.

"You can't say dwarf, that's disablist,' Owen added.

"No one is a dwarf!' Blessing said apologetically, as she struggled to make sense of her own comment. "I meant we might look, well, small to these people perhaps, so it might be like a small person with a small car, driving over your nice new big clean car."

"But lassy, this ain't no car noo. It's a spaceship from space. I'm sure they have a car wash up there. You know, like a space wash." Even Elvis didn't look like he actually believed what he was saying, but the decision had been made and everyone was back on board again. Donny and Ewen were at once again preoccupied with taking selfies, and loading them up to Facebook. The pair sat opposite each other downstairs at the back of the bus, which Blessing found a relief because she was certain they couldn't have made it back up the stairs in their current state. She watched their conversation in amusement. Donny had his phone pointed at Ewen as he began to speak. They were on *Facebook Live*.

"Hey guys, so guess where we are? On a bus driven by a man named Elvis..." The boy could barely contain his laughter. "And we're riding around on a ship that just landed from outer space. Yeah that's right, you heard! On a bus, on top of a spaceship and now we're going to look at the tower bit in the middle and see if we can get inside! You just couldn't make this up!"

A voice on a loudspeaker boomed from outside, as the sound of helicopters buzzed overhead. Blessing and Agatha both looked out the side window and could see a dark green 'copter hovering just ahead of them. She thought it might belong to the military.

"You in the bus. Turn your vehicle around immediately and go back to the road. This area is now restricted by order of the Government of the United Kingdom. Turn around or we will be forced to take action," the 'copter broadcast its demands over the din of its whirring blades.

Ewen shouted to Donny, "Keep filming me, keep filming me! Take my phone, Blessing!" Ewen threw his phone towards her. She lunged to make the catch, feeling a muscle stretch under her arm, causing her to wince in pain. The phone fell through her fingers only to be caught by Agatha in the seat next to her.

"I got it! What do I win?" the elderly lady screamed in excitement, not the least bit deterred by the presence of the British Military hotly pursuing the groaning vehicle. The stench of burnt rubber came in through the windows.

"Hold on noo, everyone!" Elvis shouted from the driver's cabin, as the bus began to speed up. Blessing wasn't sure how fast these things could go but safety was never a concern of any of the bus drivers back in Nigeria, so it was hardly her first scary experience on public transport. Blessing could see the rising tower ahead of them and felt the bus was on a slight gradient, as though they were driving up an ever-so-gentle hill.

"How close are you going to get?" she shouted at Elvis.

"As close as I can, lassie! We're not having them bampots from the government tell us what we can see or do, eh?' She caught his smile in the mirror. It was the first time a man had smiled at her in as long as she could remember. Elvis would have had a nice smile but for his yellow-stained teeth, which she found repulsive at even this distance.

"This is your final warning. Turn your vehicle around immediately. This is for your own safety. You may have been exposed to harmful radiation. You must return to the edge of the object before you cause yourself or anyone else any further harm," the voice bellowed out above them.

That didn't sound right to her. She hadn't felt any side effects at all. In fact, if anything she felt better than she had in ages. She thought she should have been more tired by now but she wasn't, she felt fully awake and alert. Something else was different, too. Her sense of smell, it seemed, was more acute. The only thing that appeared to be a threat to her here were the actions of the British Army. Elvis responded his own way by flipping a two-fingered salute out of the window. Blessing thought this was a bad move, and besides, what would their visitors make of such a thing? Two 'copters now buzzed the bus. The smaller one had weapons mounted on the sides; the second was much larger with two rotor blades, one at the front and one at the back. Blessing thought it was effectively a flying bus. While it didn't have weapons, it looked equally menacing and the deafening rotor blades drowned out Elvis's song on the radio. With its nose angling downwards, the larger one sped past above them and then hovered about a mile ahead. A number of dark-clad figures descended from the machine on ropes until around twenty of them had assembled on the surface some way ahead of the bus. She was certain the men were carrying guns. Having deposited its passengers, the larger helicopter immediately flew off to the west, leaving the group of figures on the surface to fan out into a line, moving towards the bus. Elvis swerved the bus and changed direction, while still trying to maintain a course towards the tower. The second, smaller helicopter kept pace with him and was trying to block his path by swooping in low, but Elvis would not be deterred. He swerved the cumbersome vehicle first left, then right, then left again causing Agatha to scream with delight as she gripped the handlebars mounted above the seat.

"This is so exciting isn't it, dear? Reminds me of the rollercoaster at Blackpool!" Blessing hated rollercoasters. She hadn't been on a big one, only a small one at a funfair in Birmingham and that had put her off them for life. She couldn't understand why people would pay money to be scared. Life was already full of horrors. Agatha was grinning as Blessing sat terrified next to her. The students seemed totally unfazed by the ongoing dramatic events.

"So Donny, you getting this?" Ewen asked. "That's a military helicopter that has been trying to stop us from getting towards the centre of the ship, people! We're maybe two miles in from the edge, and if you look out of the window, you can see the surface of the object we're on in every direction. I mean this thing is really big, guys! I don't know how big, but bigger than that big stupid tent thing down in London!'

"You're talking about the O2!" Donny said.

"Yeah, it's way bigger than the O2!" Ewen said. Blessing had no idea what the O2 was so she couldn't agree or disagree with them. Certainly the surface of the ship was vast, the size of a city and not something they could travel over quickly. The bus skidded as Elvis spun the wheel and swerved to avoid the angry, swooping helicopter. Blessing looked at Agatha for some support, but she seemed to be taking it all in her stride. Agatha just smiled back at her and laughed as the bus continued to slide wildly. Blessing was certain they were spinning 360 degrees around at one point, forcing her to close her eyes. When she opened them again she saw the ivory spire looming larger ahead of them.

"If you do not stop the vehicle we will be forced to disable it," came the booming command from the smaller helicopter. A short distance ahead Blessing saw the line of armed men dressed in black all levelling their weapons at the bus. Just then, she noticed two people on what appeared to be a large motorbike with three wheels travelling parallel to them, its occupants waving.

"Hey look Donny! It's a trike!" Ewen shouted, as if it was the first time he'd ever seen such a thing. It was certainly the first time Blessing had laid eyes on this particular mode of transport. The passenger of the unusual-looking three wheeled contraption had a video camera in one hand. Blessing thought that they might be members of the press, but this was dispelled when a dozen other motorbikes joined the first, and she observed that the group had matching insignia on the back of their jackets; they were some sort of gang.

"We're not alone in this. Yeahhhhhhhhh. Here's the fucking cavalry!" shouted Ewen, waving back at the group.

It was then that the first gunshot rang out, and a metallic thud hit the side of the bus. Blessing had heard gunfire before in Nigeria, when she was a little child and it was a sound she would never forget.

"Someone's firing at us!' Donny yelled, as he ducked down in the back seats. Ewen tried to keep filming but Donny grabbed him and pulled him away from the windows. A second burst of gunfire shattered the back window of the bus, causing the two young men to scream as shards of glass fell on them. It was then Blessing saw it; a large opening in the ground, a slope descending into the structure of the vessel off to their right. It reminded Blessing of the ramps that went down into large underground car parks in the city. For a moment it had glowed brighter than the rest of the surface, drawing her attention to it. She couldn't tell how deep it went, but it was clearly there.

"Elvis I think I see a way in! Stop the bus!'" she shouted. Elvis slammed the brakes on, causing the tyres to squeal in protest. Blessing and the others held on tight. The back of the bus swung around bringing the vehicle to a stop, presenting itself side on to the approaching men in black. Blessing held Agatha in her arms, making sure the old lady did not bang her head. Agatha's previous jolly composure had stopped at the sound of gunfire. Blessing could see she was in a state of shock, as if the danger of their situation was finally dawning upon her. Donny came tumbling down the aisle, ending up on the floor next to them. Blessing could see he had a small cut on his cheek, probably caused by the breaking glass. Elvis had managed to put some distance between themselves and the men from the larger helicopter, but they were fast and agile, covering the ground between them quickly. The smaller helicopter swung around and hovered buzzing angrily like a giant wasp above them. Now it had a whole host of targets to contain as the thunder of motorcycles filled the air. Elvis left his cabin, crouching low in the bus and pulling Donny up from the floor.

"Up you get, lad! Where did you see it, lassie?" he asked Blessing.

Blessing looked around and saw the slope just a short distance from the bus behind them and to their right.

"There!" She pointed. "Agatha, can you make it?"

"I'm all right dearie, don't you worry. Pass me my stick!" Ewen, still filming, opened the side doors with the emergency handle.

"Guys, we have to get off this now. They're coming!" Ewen jumped off the bus with Donny following him, and the two of them broke immediately into a run. Blessing and Elvis patiently assisted Agatha to step down as the sounds of helicopter blades mixed with motorcycle engines filled the air around them. The loudspeaker from the helicopter boomed out once more:

"All of you on the bikes leave the area immediately. This area is now under control of Her Majesty's Armed Forces and is under quarantine. You will turn around and leave the area at once, or face arrest and detention."

As Blessing helped Agatha down from the bus, the bikers had

converged on them, coming to a halt around their side of the bus. It was an unusual group of occupants who sat astride their roaring machines. There must have been about twenty of them, male and female. Each wore a cut-off denim jacket over their black leathers with an emblem patch on the back. Blessing assumed this must be some sort of criminal biker gang who had come here for their own illegal purposes. Perhaps to see what they could steal from the ship... How embarrassing would that be? It would certainly give the wrong impression to the aliens. They certainly did not look like people who went to church. Many wore helmets, but several of them did not. At least two of the group were women, one was white, maybe in her forties with long dark thick hair and quite pretty in her own way. The other had pulled up right in front of her and was mixed-race, sporting short spiky, dyed-pink hair, which was shaved at the sides. She had a tattoo of a rose on a vine creeping up her neck from under the collar of her leather jacket. Blessing guessed she was in her late twenties. She had a face that was very striking and one that she would not forget. She wondered what her ethnic mix had been. Perhaps an African father and a Chinese mother? The girl glared back at her. Many of the men sported large beards to match their even larger bellies and must have been all over forty, while others were younger but seemed slight in build, and unimposing. Nope, not much in the way of potential dating material here, she'd be better off waiting to see what the aliens had to offer. Blessing took a moment to peer back around the bus. She saw the gradient of the descending slope less than one hundred meters away. It was hard to make out but also it was too far for Agatha to walk unassisted. For a moment she thought she saw the surface glowed a little brighter in the area around the depression, as if it were beckoning them to investigate. She saw the men from the helicopter were less than three hundred meters away in the other direction. In a matter of minutes they would be upon them. Blessing saw that Donny and Ewen had taken off in completely the opposite direction away from the depression, Ewen still filming as they did so. The remaining helicopter turned to pursue them along with several of the bikers. Her view became blocked as one of the bikes pulled up in front of her with its rider dismounting and removing his helmet in a singular motion. He had a short goatee and was probably no more than twenty-five with quite a thin face. He didn't look anywhere close to the heavy set hard criminal biker types Blessing had seen depicted in television drama shows. This kid looked barely old enough to have a driving license. He and the pink spiky-haired woman approached her. The woman looked Blessing over as her male companion spoke.

"Hey, I'm Khai. They put a round in your fuel tank. These guys are seri-ous. We've been looking to see if there's a way in but we can't find one and no one wants to get arrested, so we're going to make a break for it. Do you guys want a lift back to Aberdeen?"

Upon hearing of the damage to his precious bus, Elvis ran around the side to check. The young man was well spoken, his voice soft like velvet which made Blessing feel creamy inside. Now she understood why he was the group's leader; he had a certain charm and he held her gaze when he spoke to her, a quality that so many men lacked. He had a small patch on his denim waistcoat which read *Club President*. Yet, so many more of the group were so much older and larger than him. Blessing saw the man also had a smaller patch, which had the abbreviation, S.S.U.K.S.O.B – Below this there was an emblem of something white. It looked to her like a spaceship of some kind. It was familiar but she couldn't place where from. The jackets of the group were decorated with similar emblems, some it would seem, from all over the world. One read *Destination San Diego* and others referred to Manchester and Birmingham. Blessing was not sure why anyone would want to go to a biker event in Birmingham but then her knowledge of biker gangs was extremely limited. Agatha looked the young man up and down, her tone indicating she was not impressed.

"Young man, we have just seen a way in right over there, so why don't you give me a lift over to it before those angry men get here from the army?" She pointed at the black-clad figures who were steadily moving towards them. One of them was kneeling down and appeared to be looking at them through a long object. The bus acted as a shield between the approaching soldiers and the group as they talked, but the biker leader was growing impatient.

"I'm not hanging around here. This is going to be a government cover-up and I don't want to be some statistic lost in the middle of it." Kai blurted with little enthusiasm.

"God, grow some balls Khai! How can they cover up 200 of these things? They're all over the world, for Christ's sake!' It was the voice of the spiky-haired girl with the rose tattoo. Now she was closer, Blessing could see she had light caramel-coloured skin and had an American tinge to her accent. Blessing couldn't help wondering where she was from. There was something almost oriental about her facial features, yet she wasn't quite that ethnicity. She had those beautiful sloping eyes that often appeared in the mix of so many women of her own country. Blessing's own eyes were more like saucers, like a character from a Disney film. She had often wished they were smaller. She had never seen such a unique woman and it took a moment before she realised she was, in fact, staring at her.

"What on earth made you guys drive a bus up on to this thing with a pensioner on board? Have you all been taking drugs or something?" the girl asked.

Agatha pointed to the distant figures of Donny and Ewen who were still being chased by the helicopter.

"Just those two," she said, drily.

"We were giving Agatha a lift," Blessing added, which was partly true.

"That's right. I wanted to see it up close! I demanded they bring me here! So this lovely young lady and this helpful man decided to take me." She pointed at Elvis who had returned from his investigations, his hands covered in oil, looking extremely displeased.

"They've shot me legs oot from under me! I'll be fired from me job for sure noo!" Blessing tried to think of something to say to cheer him up, but the spiky-haired girl beat her to it.

"Don't worry about it man. From where we're sitting I doubt anyone is going to worry much about firing people. They'll be lucky if they have any drivers reporting in at all tomorrow. Get on, old lady, I'll take you where you want to go." The girl gave Agatha a smile. Agatha grabbed her stick and struggled to straddle the machine.

"Just sit side-saddle. Rest your feet on the pannier on the back." The girl suggested.

"Good idea love. Especially with my waterworks! I'll try not to pee on the seat," Agatha said as she sat, causing the girl to give a brief look of regret at making her offer.

"I'd appreciate that. You coming too, beautiful?" It took a moment before Blessing understood the question was being directed at her. It was the first time anyone had ever called her beautiful and she was not used to hearing it, especially from a woman. Elvis seemed wounded by the compliment and immediately stepped in between the two of them.

"I'm responsible for these passengers noo. So anywhere they go, I go too."

"Fine with us, get on the back, old man," Kai said, his patience obviously wearing thin.

"The name's Elvis, like the King," Elvis said, with the same deeper voice he put on while singing his songs. Blessing was not sure why he referred to himself as King Elvis. Maybe Elvis was part of the Scottish Royal Family. Was there a Scottish Royal Family? She wasn't sure.

"Whatever, your majesty. You coming or not?' Kai said, unimpressed.

A single gunshot echoed across the valley and punched into the right front tyre of the bus. It exploded with a startling bang. Blessing jumped, as did Agatha, who by now had her arms wrapped around the spiky-haired female biker.

"Get on the back of Tommy's bike then, your majesty, otherwise you're likely to have your crown shot off!"

Khai turned his bike so that the back was facing Blessing. He nodded for her to get on. She sat on the back the same way as Agatha had, with her feet sticking out at one side.

"What are you doing?" Khai asked.

"Sitting on the bike." Blessing had always sat side-saddle on motorbikes in Nigeria.

"Not like that. You're not an old woman, are you? Straddle the beast!" Blessing reluctantly did as she was told and straddled the machine, which sent her underwear riding up her backside and the vibrations of the machine rippling across her pelvis. The letters S.S.U.K.S.O.B. stared back at her from the cut-off denim jacket. She wondered what they meant, but there would be another time for such questions. She gripped the man's waist. It felt nice to do so, even if he was a little young. It was just a shame it had taken an alien invasion for such an occurrence to take place.

"I'm going to go to warp factor seven on this motherfucker!" Khai shouted, ruining the moment for Blessing with his bad language.

"Don't swear, Khai, it really doesn't suit you. Nice butterfly, by the way." The spiky-haired girl shouted over as she began to rev up her engine, giving Blessing a wink as she did so. No one had ever winked at her before, nor called her beautiful, nor complimented on her underwear which she realised must have been visible and the source of the compliment.

"So are you all in a gang, like?" Elvis asked as he got on the back of Tommy's bike. Tommy handed over a spare helmet to the spiky-haired rider who handed it to Agatha who put it on, giving the girl a thumbs-up.

"Society," Tommy answered flatly. "Sorry mate, no spare for you I'm afraid." Elvis grinned, uncaring.

"Nae bother, man. Blessing, where was it, like, the depression?" asked Elvis. Blessing pointed to where she had seen the incline; it was becoming increasingly difficult to make out. She strained her eyes scanning the white surface of the ship when it briefly glowed again enabling her to make out the area of descent.

"There, there! Just ahead!" She pointed.

"Okay, let's go!" the spiky-haired girl yelled. The trio sped away from the bus in unison, the trike and several other bikes accompanying them. In only a matter of seconds they were at the top of the depression that sloped down to a blank wall some twenty metres down into the surface. Khai reached it first, followed by Tommy, then the spiky-haired girl, whose name Blessing still had not yet learned, followed by the rest of the group apart from those who had gone after Donny and Ewen.

"It doesn't go anywhere. It just goes to a blank wall!" Khai said. Everyone looked unimpressed, except for Agatha who removed her helmet and handed it back to the girl. The slope descended at quite a steep gradient downwards before levelling out for a few metres and coming to a dead end. Blessing could not see any openings or lines and where the floor joined the wall there was simply a continuous smooth flow of the white surface. Agatha slid off her bike and at once began to hobble down the gradient.

"He's right. I don't see any way in. Maybe it's some kind of vent or design to help it fly?" The biker girl said. Blessing thought she might be right, but she still wanted to get closer and see for herself. Besides, Agatha was certainly not going to be deterred. Blessing dismounted, and rushed to take Agatha's arm but not before readjusting her underwear. Agatha was determined to get to the bottom of the slope, assisted or not.

"Where you going?" Khai shouted.

"To help her!" Blessing did not like people to shout at her. Elvis watched on in dismay, but then he too dismounted and ran down to them, taking Agatha's other arm.

"I want to touch the wall at the end!" Agatha said, resolute.

"Guys! I don't want to piss on your little scientific experiment but our friends in the black with the combat gear and rifles will be on us real soon!" Tommy shouted, sounding afraid. Blessing thought that, for bikers, these guys certainly weren't very tough. The spiky-haired girl dismounted and came down the slope to assist them.

"If you get to touch the wall at the end will you be happy?" she asked, looking Agatha straight in the eye.

"Oh yes, very happy," Agatha replied.

"You, what's your name?" the girl asked, turning to look straight at Blessing.

"Blessing," she replied, finding her stare a little intimidating.

"Of course it is. Suits you. Take her weight on your side, we're going to lift her." The girl took Agatha's arm and put it around her shoulder and then placed her own left hand over to Blessing. She completely ignored Elvis, whom Blessing sensed felt a little offended.

"Take my hand, we're going to make a seat."

"I don't want to hurt you both," Agatha said, with a worried look.

"Don't worry honey, I think we can take your weight," the girl said, with a wink. Blessing wasn't sure if it was meant for her or Elvis, but the biker barely even acknowledged the presence of the bus driver. Together, the two women carefully locked their hands, fingers intertwining as Agatha gripped their shoulders for support. Elvis stood there, watching. He coughed, uncertain of what else to do.

"Okay great, let's get to this wall!" Blessing and the girl hurried forward carrying the pensioner, Elvis jogging behind them, holding onto Agatha's walking stick and bag. At the bottom of the slope, the gradient of the floor became flat and levelled out for about four metres, ending at the wall which rose up in front of them about three metres in height, but on closer inspection there was little else to see. The white walls just flowed and curved naturally with no lines or edges. The trio reached the wall and let Agatha slide off their arms down to her feet. Blessing could see that the texture of the surface in front of her was not, in fact, completely white. There appeared to be black lines like thin vines, growing just beneath the surface. She realised their fingers were still locked together, the girl stared at Blessing for a moment before releasing her grip. Her hands had felt smooth and well-manicured and had a faint scent of cocoa butter. Perhaps she was a church-going girl? All the women at her church always looked after their nails, some of them going to great lengths to outdo each other every Sunday: the ladies comparing each other's hair, nails and shoes was as much of a ritual as the act of going to church itself. None of the congregation had pink hair or tattoos though, and she was fairly sure none them rode a motorbike either.

"What's your name?" Blessing thought she ought to know how to address this girl.

"Rain," she replied, examining the wall herself. "I normally like to be taken out for dinner first before I hold hands, though…" she said, without even looking back at her. Blessing was not sure if she was joking. Dinner? What on earth did she mean? Blessing wondered if she was talking to a very feminine-looking boy for a moment. Maybe she was a he?

"There's no mechanism that would open anything that I can see," Rain said, as she studied the surface in front of her. Blessing could see Rain was about five-foot-eight, with a slender but curvy build. She seemed to have the perfect physical attributes that most women spend much of their life trying to obtain. Blessing felt positively short in comparison. Agatha touched the wall in front of her and an instant change in its appearance caused everyone to gasp in unison. For the briefest of moments, the wall glowed and the area beneath Agatha fingers appeared to move. Even the bikers collected at the top of the ramp had seen it.

"Did you touch it? Try it again!" Tommy called down to them.

Agatha had not yet removed her hand from the surface which now began to form something around Agatha's hand…

"The Wall… it's moving like!" Elvis shouted. A handprint appeared on a small square transparent plate that swelled from the wall beneath her fingers.

"How peculiar," Agatha said, placing her hand firmly on the palm print on the square, before anyone else had even had a chance to stop her. The wall then peeled back upon itself like the skin from an orange, revealing a smooth white corridor beyond it. The corridor went ahead for some considerable distance and then curved out of sight. Blessing was expecting someone or something to greet them; perhaps a voice or some kind of floating orb. Science fiction shows had never been her thing, but when flicking through the channels, she had caught enough glimpses of scenes of aliens from older movies to have some level of expectation. But there was nothing of the kind and no one to be seen. Elvis peered in.

"The air in there, it's different somehow..." he said. Blessing inhaled and knew at once he was right. It felt cleaner, which was unusual because the air in this part of Scotland was noted for being relatively pollution-free; the one notable positive difference she had liked about Aberdeen compared to Birmingham.

Shots fired in the air, startling the group. "Shit guys, we have to go!" Tommy shouted from above them.

Agatha took the warning as her cue and grabbing her stick from Elvis, took a single step inside the corridor, and then another. Blessing, Rain and Elvis just stood there. None of them was sure of what to do next. Blessing heard the revving of bikes from above and turned to see members of Rain's gang race off out of her line of sight. They were making a run for it.

"Shit! Wait guys!" Rain shouted. Another shot rang out as Rain and Elvis ran back up the slope. Blessing did not want Rain to leave their little group. Something about holding her hand for the briefest of moments had made her feel safe and protected. Agatha was frail and old, Elvis coughed if he ran more than a few feet, but Rain was young and energetic, headstrong and certain in her actions. She was decisive and impulsive. Everything Blessing found appealing in a man. But she wasn't a man, was she? She had not yet had time to ask, and this was certainly not the moment for such intimate questions.

"Rain! Wait! We can't let Agatha go inside alone!" She felt a sudden rush of air blow across her legs. Rain stopped and turned around. Blessing could see her full body shape now, silhouetted against the white glow that came from the surface all around her. She was a girl. Maybe she had a brother with all the same qualities?

"Honey, I'm not going in there. Not even with someone as hot as you!"

Elvis turned and came running back towards the opening, when a second round of gunfire, much closer this time, forced both he and Rain to drop down and hug the sides of the slope, which sent Elvis sprawling forward clumsily. He regained his footing and ran towards Blessing, almost knocking her over. Blessing turned back around only to discover the opening had vanished and Agatha along with it. She and Elvis both ran their hands over the surface of the wall, but it was as solid, as if the opening had never been.

"What happened? Where's Agatha?" she asked.

"The hole just closed in, like! I didnae touch a thing!"

Blessing was certain Elvis must have leaned on something when he ducked down from the gunfire. That always happened in the movies; people leaned on a wall and a trap would come down and capture them, or even worse, kill them. She worried about the poor defenceless pensioner on the other side, alone and imprisoned. She scowled at Elvis.

"I promise. I touched nowt!" he cried, feeling the wall.

"You're touching it now!" Blessing shouted. Elvis pulled his hands away from the surface and stared back at her despondently.

"Shite, what have we done? We made a pensioner disappear, like! She's been kidnapped by the aliens!" All the enthusiasm Elvis previously had for their adventure seemed at once to desert him. More gunshots rang out. Rain came running back down to the wall.

"Everyone's left us! Those guys are really close. Can we get inside?"

Blessing looked at the spiky-haired woman and the greasy-haired middle-aged man standing before her. In her wildest dreams she could never have predicted the events of this day, and now these two people, neither of whom she really knew were looking to her for answers. She remembered what Agatha had done with her hand and decided it was best to follow suit, placing her hand upon the surface. It was cool to the touch. She ran her hand over it for several moments, there was a surge of light and for the briefest of moments the wall lit up before them. Blessing noticed it made the others around her glow and saw Rain was impressed.

"How did you make it do that?" she asked.

"I don't know. I just touched it." Blessing said.

"Honey, people have touched me with their hands but no one has ever made me glow!" Rain laughed. Elvis pointed to a section of the surface that was changing. A transparent square plate formed at Blessing's head height, protruding outwards slightly, a hand print visible upon it. Blessing thought the print and size of the palm matched her own. She was about to place her hand on the plate when above her came the metallic click of a rifle.

"Step back please and walk slowly back up towards us."

The three of them looked up to see four men, clad in black, all with weapons pointing down towards them. The man speaking was actually behind them. They turned to see a second group of men at the top of the slope, weapons raised, all pointing at them. Trying to run was pointless. Even if they could get to the open surface again, Blessing knew they would never outrun the men on foot.

"Raise your hands, please."

Elvis complied with a look of contempt. Rain, however, was having none of it.

"You've no right to stop us from being here. We're not trespassing and we've broken no laws!" she said, angrily.

"Step towards me and walk slowly up the slope, I won't ask again."

Blessing gave Rain a nudge; she could tell the man was serious. Glancing back at the wall, the small square plate had already vanished. All around the top of depression, she saw more armed men, their weapons ready. There was a sudden downdraft of air as another helicopter swooped in low above them.

"You've put yourselves in danger and behaved extremely stupidly," came another voice. Someone in charge, judging from his tone, which came from above and behind them. She turned to see it belonged to a tall grey-haired man whom Blessing thought was in his late fifties. He wore a dark suit under his heavy overcoat, and held a phone in his hand. Blessing was quick to spot he wore a wedding ring.

He nodded to his men. "Get them out of there."

Several of the black-clad figures dropped down into the depression, one slipping on the smooth surface, falling straight on his back. The man in charge noticeably winced at this ill-performed manoeuvre. Blessing and Rain both laughed, only to find weapons pointed in their stomachs.

"We'd better do as they say, lassies,' Elvis said, as he complied.

The trio were escorted reluctantly back up to the slope to await their fate. The man in the heavy overcoat was approached by a second man in military combat fatigues. They exchanged a few brief words. Blessing tried to hear but they kept their voices deliberately low. Her braids fluttered in the downdraft of the helicopter, which was landing some fifty metres away from them. It was the same one with double rotor blades that they had seen earlier—she had remembered the number on the side. This time it landed on the actual surface of the saucer, and from a ramp at the rear unloaded a second group of people all of whom were dressed in blue rubber suits, encased with matching helmets. They began to unload crates, the contents of which Blessing could not begin to fathom.

"Why aren't yous wearing radiation suits if this area is dangerous then?" Elvis asked the nearest man clad in black.

"You didn't give us much choice, did you? We're paid to put our lives in danger, you're not," came the rather unconvincing reply. All three of them were immediately and thoroughly searched, leaving Blessing feeling she had been personally violated. Whoever's hands went up and down her thighs and cupped the undersides of her bottom certainly were leaving nothing to chance, and in her view lingered a little bit too long. Phones were removed. Blessing noted Rain had a small camera that was taken from one of the pockets in her leathers, despite her making vociferous protests about its removal. The previously unoccupied expanse of the surface was now teeming with activity. Several more army vehicles had arrived next to the bus, disgorging military personnel. Small chains of lights were being erected on yellow-coloured metal stands, though Blessing could not see the need for them. Below the surface of the ship something, somewhere was giving off its own unending glow of light. The man she assumed to be in command stepped forward, and looked to be about to speak when there was a cry from behind them. Four of the men in the black combat fatigues found themselves rolling on the floor as the ground beneath their feet rose upward. They had gone down the depression to investigate the wall when, the surface reformed to its original state. Where they had descended to the opening had simply vanished, replaced by the surface as it was before. The men in combat fatigues looked on in bewilderment, uncertain of what to do next. The tall man in the overcoat came over.

"How did you create that opening?" the man angrily demanded. He stepped up so close that Blessing could smell his breath; Airwaves, she could recognise the scent of that chewing gum anywhere. Her Pastor's mouth had tasted of it when he rammed his tongue down her throat. Blessing was thinking of how to respond, when Rain spoke up, her voice full of a fearless tone.

"We didn't. We're guests here, same as you."

"Take them away to decontamination and questioning," the man said, dismissed them from his sight. The trio was ushered at once towards the helicopter, where two more of the men in black combat fatigues were waiting. Blessing stole a look back and realised she would never be able to tell exactly where she had stood, should she ever return here. She tried to take note of their position in relation to landmarks around them; the outline of the low hills and distant mountains, but it was useless. It was now too dark. The illumination from the vessel did extend to some of the surrounding countryside, but everything was so far away at this distance, the Scottish landscape had become one of shadows and silhouettes. The only thing that marked where the depression had been was the lone motorcycle that she presumed was Rain's. Of the rest of her group and Ewen and Donny there was no sign, though the sound of roaring engines and police sirens could be heard far off in the distance. Blessing looked at the white tower in the distance. As the last of the daylight began to drain away beyond the peaks in the west, Blessing's mind raced through everything that had happened. She had seen her palm print on the wall and felt like Agatha; she was obviously supposed to come here and go inside the ship. Why hadn't she stepped inside when she had the chance? Had it been a test from God? Had she failed it? She cursed these bloody military men for stopping her. It was they who made her hesitate. She clearly had been chosen to enter the vessel, perhaps by Our Lord Jesus Christ himself! Who could say? Maybe they were aliens and they needed women to repopulate their dying planet, so perhaps it was only women who were allowed to enter? Of course! That must have been it! Elvis had touched the wall, or he said he did, but nothing happened. Yet when she and Agatha had touched it a plate had appeared that would allow them access. Blessing noticed Elvis did not have Agatha's bag, so she prayed he had given it to her. She was about to ask about it, when Rain was brutally struck in the stomach by the rifle of one of the men in front of her. Elvis reacted by stepping towards the man, raising his fist but found himself with a rifle thrust in his face by another soldier.

"Don't."

Elvis stepped back. Rain got herself to her feet, somehow still smiling. She had refused to leave her bike behind. It sat near the bus. Rain had become increasingly vocal about her displeasure in being forced to abandon it.

"We need to take you away from here for your own safety. You're putting yourselves in danger just by being here!" The man in charge of marshalling them shouted.

Blessing knew that was not true, but she decided against speaking out. She could have said about the door, about Agatha and about her being in the ship, yet she was more worried about the danger these men presented to them, than she was about the danger the ship presented to Agatha. Somehow she knew in her heart, Agatha would be okay. Elvis exchanged a look with her as they were all forcibly herded to the waiting helicopter. It was as if he was seeking her permission to say something. Blessing simply shook her head gently making it clear this would be unwise. Rain said nothing either. One of the men dressed in the blue suits stopped to speak briefly to the man leading them, before nodding and letting them continue. Blessing did not relish the prospect of travelling on such a mode of transportation. She had only flown once and that was to travel to the United Kingdom and that had not been a pleasant experience. They had hit an especially rough patch of turbulence which made the entire aircraft drop. Her drink ended up in her lap, which would have been fine if it hadn't have been a hot coffee. She had arrived in England wearing damp underwear. The whole thing had been highly undignified. Standing by the ramp was another man dressed in camouflage military fatigues who addressed all three of them as they were lined up in front of him.

"Inside the Chinook you will sit down and buckle up. The flight will be very short, we're taking you to an area just beyond the perimeter of the ship. There will be showers, hot food and drink and you will have to be examined and answer some questions. After that a second mode of transportation will take you back to Aberdeen. Enjoy the flight."

The group was ushered on board up a ramp, with two other soldiers. As Rain went ahead, Blessing saw Elvis studying her denim cut-off and the strange logo and lettering on the back. Two more men awaited them inside, and motioned for them sit down on the rows of seats that ran along the inside of the transport. Rain ended up opposite Elvis and herself. The sound of rotors turning filled the compartment, and Blessing felt her stomach doing somersaults, as her nerves began to fray. She tried to slow her breathing, something else she had seen people do on television. Elvis tapped her.

"Dinnae worry, lassie. You'll be fine in one of these. Built to last they are." He gripped her hand. It was rough, and she could smell the cigarettes on his fingers, but right now she needed to hold onto something as the craft began to vibrate in preparation for take-off. Rain smiled over at them.

"So are you two a couple?" she asked as if the question held little importance.

"No!" Blessing said at once.

Elvis gave her a weak smile and tried to laugh it off.

"I only met the lassie on my bus this morning. She's just nervous, like. She's nae been in a chopper before!" He smiled at her again. Blessing noticed his teeth, they were different. They were white. The yellow staining from before had completely vanished. She had to look again to be sure, but she was certain of it, his teeth had completely changed colour.

"It will be all right," Rain shouted over to them.

"So lassie! I'd been meaning to ask you... What kinda bikers' club is S.S.U.K.S.O.B. anyway?

Rain looked at them both and laughed.

"The Star Trek UK Society of Bikers," she replied.

Blessing had watched a lot of television shows, but Star Trek was not among them. However, in her present circumstances she, found herself beginning to wish she had.

CHAPTER V

"I don't know when the western media first became conscious that people were going missing in large numbers. You have to understand the news at the time was just overloaded. There was so many extraordinary things happening everywhere that the sheer volume of information was hard for the public to absorb, let alone individual journalists. The first week was really confusing. Everyone expected some kind of 'end of the world' scenario and many people fled their posts of work to spend their final hours with their families. It was at least a week before that panic subsided. Then you also have to think about the animosity that this caused across the world socially; between those who were rich enough to jump into private jets and flee to their hideaways and those of us who were left to face the music. I think that really underscored to all of us which leaders cared about humanity, and which just wanted to save their own skins. That one was one of the things that the British Prime Minister got right over our President who fled the Whitehouse to NORAD.

There were reports early on about large numbers of people missing at the Mexican/US Laredo landing site. These were dismissed as false, until those same people started posting videos online from inside the ship. The American government couldn't get them taken down fast enough. I guess it was pretty embarrassing that after a month the top minds within the global scientific community hadn't been able to work out how to access the ships, yet you had a collection of seemingly random people from all over the world who not only appeared to have done so, but were also posting blogs about it online. That was when the cat was really out of the *bag. I think that was the beginning of the divide that would come later. That, of course, was when the problems for the world really started."*

Wendy Wiseman, day time television personality and journalist, speaking one year after Parousia

TARIQ

"I heard the British Prime Minister is dead. His wife and children too. Can you believe it? On a day like today with everything going on!" Speaking in her native French, the woman clutched her daughter tightly, as if they were in immediate danger. Tariq had to sympathise with her, at least in this respect. She was expressing her fears to another man in the queue just ahead of him. Good. This is what he wanted.

Tariq stood in the queue waiting to pay at the *Total* petrol station and was extremely conscious of where the cameras were, before taking off his motorcycle helmet. To not have done so would raise suspicion, but still he had put on his shades and wrapped his scarf high around his neck, so that any visible facial features were minimal. It had not been in his plan to have to refuel his bike so quickly, and it frustrated him to have to change his movements accordingly. His second bike, well secured by two strong chain padlocks and two U-Locks through the wheels was still where he had left it, but someone had decided to have a go at siphoning off his petrol. He had left the bike at the location three days earlier, and he knew there was a risk of such a thing happening. Theft of petrol was more and more common these days and annoyingly, someone had stolen at least half of his. He had stuck to the plan as best he could. Once he switched bikes, he took the B-roads and kept away from the toll roads and their cameras. It took longer, but he could already see on the news that there were numerous roadblocks on all the eastern and north eastern arteries going in and out of Paris, and the area around Charles De Gaulle Airport. People everywhere in the service station were going about their business that bit slower as they stopped to watch the television monitors in the café, which he could see had all been tuned to the world's number one news story. It was all there - The fires, the burning wreckage, weeping relatives and politicians spouting rhetoric and condemnation of those who had committed this terrible atrocity. All European flights had been grounded. The French President had appealed for calm, and the British were said to be putting the Health Minister in charge until the Deputy Prime Minister could travel back from Kenya. But with the flight ban people had no idea how long that would be. Really? A complete international ban on air travel? Had their one attack really struck such fear into them that all planes had been grounded? If so, that was an incredible achievement. Then came an additional headline – *Prime Minister's wife and two children thought to be among those on board*. The news about the children was a shock. The death of innocent children should always be avoided. He was very clear on this. He knew the Prime Minister had his family with him in France, but his contact had told him they were due to travel to the south of France for a holiday, where he would join them after answering Prime Minister's questions in London. Had this information been inaccurate? Why would they have been on the plane travelling back with him? In fact he still hadn't established what had made the target package change schedule to departing a day earlier than planned. Why had the Paris terrorist summit ended early? The plane was originally not supposed to take off until tomorrow. They had been prudent enough to be in the area early, and so had been able to counter such an eventuality. So far everything had gone more or less to plan, despite this setback but the death of children was something he hadn't wanted on his conscience. When the plan had first been conceived, it had been the first question he had asked on his last visit to Brussels. He was reassured that no one on this plane would ever take their families with them to such a conference, it would be too much of a distraction to the mindset of the working politician, and besides many of these men had mistresses, especially in a city so close to London, like Paris. They were more likely to be wanting to take advantage of the local élite escort service than they were to be bringing the baggage of wives and children along. So what had gone wrong here?

"Just Petrol?" the cashier asked, her head craning to look at the television. She wasn't paying any attention to Tariq at all. So much the better. Tariq grabbed some chewing gum with his good arm. He visibly winced and knew he was noticeably sweating, but the cashier didn't seem to notice.

"Pump 5, and this please." He had managed to take some strong painkillers that he had the foresight to bring with him. He had downed triple the normal amount only thirty minutes earlier, when he pulled into a lay-by to inspect his wound. He cleaned it and changed the bandage, but it still hurt and he knew he would need to tend to it properly and soon. The pain began to numb a little, but no doubt would soon return and having to ride a motorbike certainly wasn't helping. The one place he knew he could go to get it sorted was his old stomping ground back in *Clichy-sous-Bois* in Paris. Malik and he both had plenty of doctors and nurses on his payroll who would tend to gunshot wounds for the right price.

"That will be forty-five euros please."

Tariq kept his movements slow as he reached for his wallet. He had to do everything with his left hand as moving his right caused pain that would be hard to conceal, even to the most casual of observers. He placed the exact money on the counter, the cashier still barely acknowledging him. He waited for a receipt so not to arouse suspicion, and attempted to keep his gaze down, pretending to take a passing interest in the magazines. It was only then that he caught the front page of several late edition newspapers. The images that adorned them were not what he expected, nor were the headlines. His attack appeared not to warrant a front page but perhaps it was too soon. *We are no longer alone...* read the cover of *L'Humanité*. *Where are they from?* Was the question posed by the cover of *Liberation*. Both headlines had accompanying images that Tariq could not make a mental connection with. What was he looking at? Both newspapers had a similar image on the front - that of a large object in the sky. A U.F.O he would have called it. Diamond-shaped, and vast in size if the perspective of one photograph was anything to go by. The silhouettes of military jets had been caught in the foreground of one such picture. Compared to the size of the object behind them, they were mere dots. Tariq could not quite absorb what he was looking at. When had this happened and how had he missed it? His cell had been essentially on a media blackout for the last forty-eight hours, but one of his contacts certainly would have mentioned something of this magnitude. Then he remembered: the dozens of missed calls from Malik on his second phone. Malik would have concluded this was something he should have known about. Now the reasons for the target's change of plans became clear. This must have been the reason the plane was heading back to England one day ahead of schedule. Yet his team still had succeeded in shooting it down. When the world was facing a global crisis, he had robbed one of the major powers of its leader, along with many of his cabinet into the bargain. He scanned the headlines of the other papers. He didn't want to go back to the counter to pay for one, not here, there were too many cameras and he didn't want to pick one up either. That would leave fingerprints that might be traced later. Not worth the risk. *La Croix*, the paper of the Catholic establishment ran the same story, only with a more religious slant. *Are these vessels of God?* questioned their headlines while the economical *Les Echos* was more concerned with the financial impact – *House prices plummet near landing sites...* was its byline, while their headline was surprisingly more upbeat reading *A slow day at the markets as the world braces for third contact*. *Le Figaro* was somewhat more militaristic in their stance. *Inva-*

sion! was their headline and the front page was a collage of ships, presumably from all over the world, the most spectacular of which was a photograph of one passing above the statue of Christ looking over Rio De Janeiro. Tariq was not alone gazing at the papers.

"Terrible isn't it? So much bad news on one day! People say it might be the end of the world!" The voice came from a short, middle-aged French woman standing next to him. She was holding her car keys in one hand and had a shopping basket in the other that was filled with two types of bottles – shampoo and wine.

"You look like you only just found out!" She said. Tariq realised the expression of blank shock on his face must have been quite telling.

"I have. I haven't watched the television for days. When did this start?"

The woman, who he thought was wearing too much makeup for her age, and a yellow sweater that was far tighter than it needed to be, looked surprised by his response. He knew he could have just ignored her and walked away, but sometimes that could attract more attention and he knew it was better to be polite. Besides, she was not wrong; he was shocked and had only just found about this. Had he known, he wondered for a brief moment if they still would have carried out their operation.

"So this is happening all over the world?" he asked.

She picked up the paper and actually opened the pages for him to see the inside story.

"Oui Monsieur. Two hundred of them! Everywhere! All over the world! There is one just north east of Paris. One in Spain, Germany. They say there's several in Russia and Eastern Europe. There's even one in the sea off the coast of Southern Italy. Do you think it's the end of the world?"

She asked him the question quite sincerely, but he was still trying absorb this information, the pictures of the objects. They were as wide in the middle as they were tall, coloured white, smooth and quite elegant in their design.

"They say they're the size of cities!" Tariq barely acknowledged her as he absorbed the information. There was something almost mystical about them, perhaps even magical. Tariq was not someone who believed in magic, but he also didn't believe in UFOs either. He had watched so many shows about such things on the History Channel on Sky, and even French stories on the subject, but he was always convinced such sightings were almost certainly something to do with the military of one country or another. The rest were always hoaxes of the bored and deluded. This was clearly something different and on such a global scale that it could not be denied. Yes, this was a game-changer for the world, he thought, finding himself nodding.

Le Monde had its own cut-and-dried take on the situation with their head line reading, *Salvation or Annilation?* He wondered the same thing. He bid the woman farewell and made his way back out to the garage forecourt, and mounted his bike. A myriad of thoughts raced through his head. The woman hadn't even mentioned the attack on the British Prime Minister's plane and although it was still a front-running story on the news, he must have just caught that part on the television when he arrived at the garage. He had carried out one of the most successful terrorist strikes in the history of the world and it was to be eclipsed by the arrival of ships from who knew where? Two hundred, had she said? Each of them the size of a city… What would this mean for the world? For him and his brothers and sisters? Too many questions. One thing was certain; the authorities were not going to stop looking for him. He would phone Malik and soon, but first he needed to get to a place of safety.

Tariq's destination was the small city of *Namur*, just over the Belgian border in the province of Wallonia. He had property there, a small house overlooking the river and a second house that he rented under one of his fronted companies, that provided low-rent housing to low-income tenants, almost all of whom were descended from citizens of the French-African colonies. This had proved a useful recruiting tool when it came to forming his cells for operations. Tariq, in his position as landlord, could have his company carry out detailed background checks on all his potential tenants, which helped him to identify possible recruits for his cause. This also kept such recruits in a completely different social circle to his other business activities, enabling him to isolate Malik from such activities. He could also avoid delving into the more fertile slums of Paris, a more obvious recruiting ground but far easier to trace back to him and riddled with informants. Salim had come to him via one such property but he was already beginning to regret recruiting the youth. He wondered if the young man had made good his escape. He remembered those distant gunshots. If either Salim or Mud had got into another firefight there was no mention of it in the brief newsclip he had seen back at the petrol station. They would contact him via the email account if they'd made it to their own respective destinations. They had set up their safety networks independently of his own. He had given them the means and the money to do so, but nothing would be traced back to him directly. If they were caught, the only thing that would bring the police to his door were the words of the men themselves, and Tariq was confident, even under torture, neither man would name him. It was doubtful either would be captured alive. If they were cornered, he knew they would go down fighting.

Tariq continued on his journey, keeping his speed below forty so as to not attract any unwanted attention. He wanted to get to Namur before it was too dark. He was tired, in pain and also hungry, immediately regretting not purchasing some chocolate to keep him going, but he knew there were plenty of towns where he could stop on route. He would find a late night tobacconist or café and get himself something to eat. There were certainly enough of those around, but so much of northern France was so rigid about opening and closing everything between certain times that going for a meal would take some planning. It was not like the south with its laid back and more liberal approach, where you could find late night eating on the piazzas of Antibes and still buy sushi at midnight on the paved streets of Nice.

Tariq knew the A34 would be the faster route, but at the roundabout just up from the service station he took the D951, which he had been paralleling for the last hour. Tariq noticed the traffic was busier in this area than it should have been. Several cars passed him, loaded up to the hilt with boxes of belongings and supplies. People were on the move, and the general direction of that movement was to the south. With the French UFO reported to be landing somewhere north-east of Paris, that decision made some sense. It occurred to Tariq that it would not be too far from the crash site of the plane. The roads in all of that part of France must be in chaos. In every village he passed, there was unusually frenetic activity. In every residential street he rode through, there was a buzz of activity. People were transporting families and elderly relatives. Everyone, it seemed, was taking someone somewhere. Tariq pulled over on the side of the road and took a long swig of water. The sky was turning grey with the coming of the night, and the countryside was twinkling with the lights of the houses and highways. Tariq sped along the small country road as it twisted and turned through the endless small towns and villages. He turned on to the D3, which led him in a more north-easterly direction and better served his final destination. The traffic immediately decreased, much to his relief. The road weaved through a sparsely populated area, and for a while all he drove past were pretty cottages and isolated farms. He sped across a railway crossing and turned left into the small village of *Launois-Sur-Vence*. There was a hotel where he could have stopped but he wanted to keep human interaction to an absolute minimum and decided it was best to continue. Here too, he passed more than one family loading their car and preparing for departure. He thought this decision stupid. If there were 200 of these things and they had landed all over the world where would you actually hide? The pain from his wound was beginning to intensify but he knew he needed to keep going and wait until he could assess it properly. He had been lucky, the bullet had not given him a major shoulder wound but it still had to be cleaned. The bleeding had nearly stopped but his arm was getting stiffer by the minute, and riding the bike was becoming uncomfortable. He had considered dumping the vehicle and stealing a car, but the latter action had too high a chance of being picked up by the police, and would only lead to him directly. It was too risky. He had to carry on.

As he came out of the village, he turned left onto a road that connected to the D20. Tariq had done this route a dozen times, and knew these back-road networks and turnings even at night, but he was exhausted, injured and not as focused as he might have been. He needed to make sure he got as far as he could before total darkness enveloped the countryside around him, because the one thing these back roads did not have going for them was good lighting. Most of them didn't have street lights at all, and to negotiate them safely as he dodged and weaved among the tree-lined lanes and hedgerows required a level of concentration that was beginning to desert him. He passed through the village of *Thin-Le-Moutier* and into the heavily forested roads beyond as they closed on the border of the Ardennes region. He knew this road followed the river Meuse practically all the way to Namur, taking him next through the pretty town of *Revin*. Tariq was going to have to stop somewhere soon. He had to get some sugar, or a coffee, anything to keep him alert and focused or he knew he wouldn't make it. Operating the bike with his arms outstretched was already inflicting untold agony upon him. It felt like fire as soon as he relaxed them from the handlebars, whenever he came to a stop.

He reached the centre of Revin: a small congregation of shops but nothing appeared to be open. He continued past and headed over the first bridge that led to the upper part of the town, passing a small kebab and hotdog vendor who was serving a young couple. He considered stopping there, then he recalled there was a café bar just ahead. Sure enough, just another hundred yards up the road there it was – *Café De Jeunesse*. With a scattering of silver metallic chairs outside, the café was nestled at the T-junction where all of the other exit roads headed off towards the forested hills of the Ardennes. The pain and stiffness was now relentless and unforgiving. Feeling faint, he pulled across the road and nearly collided with an oncoming car that had to swerve to miss him, the driver blaring his horn at Tariq in anger. He drove onto the tarmac right in front of the café and pulled up his bike next to one of the empty tables. As soon as he took his hands from the bike, pain shot through his right arm, which was now so stiff he could barely bend it. He carefully dismounted and composing himself for a moment, headed inside. Behind the counter was an over-weight middle-aged Frenchman with greying hair and nicotine-stained fingers who barely nodded as Tariq entered. Otherwise the place lay empty. A television set played in the top corner, just above the door, and once again Tariq saw the unearthly objects filling the screen. Tariq chose a seat where he had his back to the wall, so he could watch the television and see the door, wincing in pain as he slowly sat down. Someone had shot footage from the Eiffel Tower, capturing the ship north-east of Paris, the title below ran *Alien vessel lands ten miles outside of Paris – Immigrants travel to the south of the city – Chaos on the metro.* There was a montage of images showing blocked roads and human traffic streaming southwards out of the city, laden with suitcases, bundles and boxes, over-stretched roof racks spilling over with possessions. The mass exodus of people highlighted how little the power of financial wealth mattered in the chaos caused by such fear. Charles De Gaulle Airport was closed because of his attack, and was only a few miles from the ship, which now had since landed. The perspective changed. Eye witnesses who lived below the descending ship had shot footage of the smooth underside, which glittered back at the camera. The Government had evacuated as many people as it could from the area and advised the population to stay in their homes, but this advice had evidently gone unheeded. People wanted out and were travelling either west or south; east was not far enough away from the object, and explained the lack of traffic going in the direction he had been travelling. The news reports showed endless images of human chaos. The arrival of the objects world-wide had caused more confusion and panic among the population than his terrorist cell could have ever achieved. Wealthy men and women in designer clothes rubbed shoulders with street sellers and beggars all of whom tried to flee the city by any means they could get their hands on. All police leave had been cancelled and the French army was on the streets in force. He had expected such an occurrence after what they had achieved, but what he saw unfolding on the television angered him even further. Immigrants were shown being rounded up and returned to their homes. Many were not permitted to travel on the metro. The authorities seemed determined that the lower classes of Paris should not inconvenience the escape of the rich and powerful to a safer destination. After a brief montage of other landing sites around the world, news moved onto the plane crash: "137 people are now confirmed dead," stated the reporter. The café owner approached him to take his order. He asked for a strong coffee and a choco-late croissant, deliberately avoiding eye contact with him, focusing his attention on the television, which considering the events unfolding on the news would have been natural behaviour for anyone. He took out his phone and placed it on the table. If he could get a little rest for ten minutes, he still might be able to make it back tonight, then he could see to his wound. A group of five, tanned, noisy middle-aged men entered the café and immediately ordered a round of strong coffees, taking the table by the door. One, the oldest, an animated short, stumpy man with thinning grey hair talked to the owner. Tariq thought he heard the man call the café owner 'Brother' at one point, and there was a debate over leaving the town and where to go if they did so. The men seated were all of a similar age and talked in rapid nervous exchanges about the day's events, many taking to adding a shot of brandy to his drink. "An act of terrorism and an alien invasion on the same day, it's unbelievable!" one said. "Run? Where would I run to? To become a refugee in my own country? Why? What for?" said another. The argument between them went back and forth, escalating a little, which Tariq could see was only delaying the arrival of his croissant and coffee, as the owner was dragged unwillingly into the conversation. "My wife thinks we should drive south. We have friends in Avignon!" Tariq could see the appeal for the man, Avignon was a beautiful city. He had stopped there only once to check on some properties, but the prices had been a little too high for his tastes. "Where is safe? They're saying these things are everywhere! My cousin says they land and drill into the ground," another said, checking his phone as he did so. "They have landed, so why don't they speak to us? There's been no attack – perhaps they're friendly!" The owner finally came over to him, placing the croissant and coffee in front of Tariq. "Sorry my friend, distracting times!"

Tariq winced as he smiled but did his best not to show it. "I understand. It has been a day filled with bad news." He tucked into the croissant at once. It tasted good, dropping down into an empty stomach. "Get me another one of these please. I haven't had a chance to eat all day." The owner nodded and went back to the counter to get a second one. The "brother" sat down at the table with his friends, who were focused on the endless reports on the television. The American President had called for "World calm". The Russian Premier had been less forgiving, calling the landings a direct attack on their nation, stating they would do whatever it took to get them to leave, by force if necessary. It was, Tariq thought, a typical one-dimensional response, backed no doubt by the high ranking and influential Russian military. The rhetoric from China was much the same.

"Look! They're showing a map of where they've landed!" one of the men cried, as the newsreader switched to a world graphic. It zoomed in on the different continents. Everyone, Tariq included, watched the report with fascination. North America was first, the continent littered with red dots all across it. It looked to Tariq as though more were in Canada than America, perhaps six or more north of the American border. There was even one in Greenland. Who would ever want to invade Greenland? America itself seemed to have comparatively fewer than the countries around it. One had landed just outside of the city of Michigan in Saginaw Bay and had caused chaos among the population there, with the police being completely unable to handle the situation. There was another one in Nevada that had landed in the middle of nowhere, and a third just off the coast of Southern California but most dramatically, one had come down halfway between the border of Mexico and the state of Texas, just south of the town of Laredo, east of Highway 35. Shots of this vessel were most spectacular. It had fully landed, and the lower part of the vessel must have drilled well below the ground, while the vessel's circular body sat sprawled across the border. Excited Mexican civilians had been filmed walking on it, apparently searching for a way inside. Tariq had to smile to himself, knowing the problems this would cause for American Border Control. There was another in Northern Cuba, one just south of Panama that had landed in the bay, another off the coast of Haiti, three more across Mexico itself, not including the one that was straddling its border with America. A similar event had taken place between the borders of Honduras, Guatemala and El Salvador. A vessel was reported to have landed where the borders of the three countries were joined, presenting all of them with something of a mutual dilemma. The vessel that landed there was so large that it had covered the entire National Park of Monte Cristo, a mountainous nature reserve that was protected by all three countries. Upon landing, the edges of the vessel had touched the outskirts of the three nearest towns, each in different countries. The graphic zoomed in to show the area, and estimated the size of the vessel to be over twenty kilometres across at its widest part. The eastern edge of the saucer touched the outskirts of the town of *Metapan* in El Salvador while in the north it edged towards the town of *Esquipulas* in Guatemala. East it sat on the edge of the river just before the town of *Ocotepeque* that was just over the border in Honduras. The news report claimed this situation was unique of all the landings in the world, and the Governments of all three countries were working closely with each other to resolve the issue. Tariq had to laugh – what were they going to do? Ask it to move? The newsreader droned on, the graphic zoomed out and moved to South America, which the French news agency couldn't have considered that important as it only warranted thirty seconds more of discussion. Tariq sipped on his coffee. Thirty-five ships had landed across the South American continent, he said, many in extremely remote and almost unreachable places, while others were closer to several cities. If there was a pattern to the landings he couldn't decipher it. Next a graphic of Europe followed, causing everyone to lean closer to the television. The owner grabbed the remote and turned the sound up loud. *Did we need more dramatic emphasis for Europe?* Tariq wondered. Apparently the café owner thought so. Twenty-four had landed in Europe. One in Scotland, one in Ireland, one in Norway, or relatively close to Norway (It was just off the coast) there was one in Spain, right in the middle of the country over somewhere called *Campo De Criptana*. The country was calling it a national disaster. The ship had engulfed the entire town and several hundred people were missing. All attempts to gain access to the ship had failed, and the Spanish authorities were making plans to burrow a tunnel underneath it, and locate survivors. The landing in France was covered next, and naturally received a more detailed analysis. Events in Paris were covered exhaustively. There were discussions around the possible connection between the landings and the crash of the British plane. French police were not ruling anything out at this stage. People were advised again to stay indoors and not to panic. French military and police were forming a cordon around the ship and the area of the crash was completely sealed off. Tariq's phone vibrated on the table. It was a text from Malik. "Where are you? Have you seen the news?"

Tariq typed back quickly. "I have. Terrible. I will call you later, still travelling at the moment."

His phone buzzed again. "Okay. Glad you're safe. Speak later." Malik knew to never say more than was needed.

"What are you going to do?" It took a second before Tariq understood the question was directed at him.

"What are you going to do? Are you going to run as well?" Tariq looked up to see all the men were staring at him. The café owner placed the second croissant in front of him. To not respond would be misinterpreted as rudeness. The irony of the question was not lost on him, considering he was on the run already.

"I'm travelling to my brother's to wait it out. See what happens." He took a large bite of his second croissant, making sure to fill his mouth with the pastry, so answering a second question was not possible. The men's stare lingered on him, then they turned back to the television where the graphic on the landings of the world had turned to Australia and New Zealand. Fourteen ships had landed there, thirteen of them across Australia, most of which (from what Tariq could see) were in quite remote locations. Tariq asked the owner if he had wi-fi. He did, under the name of the café. Tariq logged on to his gmail account. It was used only for the purpose of communicating with the other members of his team. There was one message from S, the fourth member who had been stationed at the airport. Their email read "My new number is 07788 414888." Tariq saved the number in his phone then, leaving some euros on the table, thanked the owner and gave the men a nod of acknowledgement as he left. If questioned later, he knew they would remember him but hopefully they would be too preoccupied with world events to recollect any details. His group's identity was, it seemed, still not known to the authorities. He needed to move on as fast as possible. In considerable pain, he straddled his bike outside the café, and dialled the new number on his phone. A female answered, speaking in perfect French. Her tone was soft and her voice sounded young. Being able to hear her voice again made Tariq smile with relief. He was pleased she was safe and well.

"Are you back?" she asked.

"No. Not yet. I was delayed." He began to check for traffic, getting ready to pull out into the road.

"Are you okay?" she pressed. Tariq knew at this stage it was better to tell her very little. "I'm fine. Can you tell me what the status is of the others?"

"You haven't heard?" Tariq knew then it had to be the boy. Salim was bound to have made a mistake. "Mud is dead." Tariq was wrong in his assumption. He and Mudutha had known each other for three years. It was a friendship bred from commitment to a common cause, but there was little else to it beyond that. He would now be in Paradise. "I will call you again when I reach home. I should be there within an hour." He hung up the phone and put it back in his pocket. Even the simple act of putting on his helmet was causing him jabs of pain. Had Salim made it out alive? How had Mud died? He started up his bike and headed out into the night, unaware that the café owner had made a note of his number plate as he departed.

OMARI

What on earth was this place? Omari almost said the words aloud. He caught himself, mid-thought, remembering that where he stood was not a place of this earth. In all the years of his life, Omari had seen many things in his time in the desert, experiencing many great wonders of nature. The lethal brilliance and beauty of the dawning sun would turn the colour of the dark, twisting rocks to wondrous shades of red. The fantastic palette of the last moments of the day that would paint the desert skies with the most unique wash of tones. He had survived brutal sandstorms and thieves, snakes and scorpions, hunger and disease and the occasional brawl in remote bars, that attracted the most savage of men who took pleasure in preying on the weak. All this he had experienced and more, but how he would ever even begin to describe to his daughters the things he was seeing now, eluded him. Perhaps the desert had killed him. At this very moment he was walking towards the gates of Paradise. Could he have died already? Was this the beginning of his journey to Allah?

Upon entering the vessel, the opening had closed promptly behind him. Nervous that he might be trapped, he turned around and approached the wall, placing his hand on the surface where, only moments ago, there had been a doorway. Once again, his handprint appeared on the neat, transparent square in front of him. He thought about leaving, but remembered the approaching soldiers. If he was indeed still alive, then at best they would force him to leave the area immediately. At worst they might shoot him straight away just for being here. If all they had to do to access this place was the same thing as him, it wouldn't take them long to figure out how to get inside and follow him. If he was still alive, then his window of opportunity to investigate the interior of this holy place was certainly limited. He would place his trust in Allah.

He was in a passageway that simply ran in two directions: ahead or back, which would lead to the opening from where he came. He chose ahead. The interior walls matched the exterior of the ship, in both their colour and texture. Like the outside, it had a soft light that glowed from within, ensuring he was not plunged into total darkness. Omari found the surface cool to the touch, like marble. It was completely smooth with no visible rough edges that he could see. Where the walls met the floor and the ceiling, there were no visible joins or links of any kind. The floor simply curved into the wall and the wall arched into the ceiling. It reminded Omari of something he had seen in a village once, in the south. Several connected dwellings had been made of clay and mud, but with such care and good craftsmanship that all the connections to each room were seamless and the house, which belonged to a fellow trader, was connected by a series of short tunnels which all flowed together. The vessel reminded him of that. Only here the walls had their own light source, and were not full of rats and spiders. It was all so alien to him. He paused to take it in before exploring further. The passageway was exactly the same for as far as he could see, and he wasn't sure how much further he wanted to go. But he was here now, and he was curious. He wondered again about the afterlife. Maybe he had died when the rest of his camels had been poisoned at the well they had drunk from several days ago… He looked at his hands for a moment. The skin was still rough and worn, his lower arms covered with old cuts and scars from his many travels. If he was to meet his wife again and hold her in his arms, he wanted to be the young man he once was. That was how he imagined Paradise to be, but his hands still looked aged and fragile, his youth long since drained from his skin. Women of his tribe moisturised their skin with peanut oil, but the men in his tribe did so very rarely. To touch the hands of a man who spent his life travelling the desert was to touch the desert itself. As he walked on, he noticed the walls were the same colour of the necklace he had once given to his wife. A family heirloom from his mother, long since lost. After her death, Omari had suspected his eldest daughter of stealing it for herself. An act, which if she had been guilty, was entirely unnecessary, for she would have inherited it anyway. It was a series of connected pearls with tribal beads hanging in-between. Nya had sworn she knew nothing of its whereabouts. Now, standing here, in the strangest of places, Omari could not help but think the walls were made of pearl. Yet upon closer inspection, he realised they were not entirely composed of a single colour. Under the surface could be seen a faint array of dark vines that spread and connected with each other in all directions. Their presence was so unobtrusive, that Omari had almost missed them. He wondered if they were perhaps part of the structure, a network of inner materials supporting the design of the vessel, in the same way that steel rods would support the construction of some of the more luxurious dwellings in Fada. The atmosphere was cool, yet he was not cold. It was now two hours since the sun had set. Omari knew the temperature outside would have dropped rapidly since he had entered, but he wasn't feeling the effects of it here. The air inside was crisp and fresh, like that in the moments before dawn, when travelling the more fertile southern region. Each breath he took felt clean and sweet, filling his lungs with joy but after taking several deep breaths, he began to cough uncontrollably. He felt something in his throat. Bile, thick and heavy, snaked its way up into his mouth. He coughed again hard, accompanied by a sharp pain stabbing in his chest. He fell to his knees in agony, coughing a third time, retching as he did so, vomiting onto the vessel floor. It tasted vile. He saw there was blood among the congealed mess, but his body was not finished with him. He vomited again. A second mass of sputum, larger than the first, leapt from his throat, splashing across the floor. Breathless for a moment, he leaned on the nearest wall and gasped for air, drinking it into his lungs as if it were water. As he exhaled, something felt different. The pain in his chest had abated. The taste of blood and bile in his mouth disappeared as he exhaled. He took a second deep breath, in and out, as though doing so during one of his rare visits to the town doctor. Breathing had been something of an effort for him of late and he would often feel laboured, weak, even exhausted. Omari stood up and drank in the air. The air tasted different. It tasted incredible! It flowed in and out of his lungs as though they had been purged of an unforgiving ailment. With each breath he took, the air rushed into his body as though he were taking it in for the very first time. He felt energetic, his fatigue having left him completely. It was as if all the dust and dirt from his lungs had been purified from his innards. He could not remember when last he was able to breathe in such a manner. Looking down, the pools of bile that he had so vociferously expunged from his body had vanished from the ground before his eyes. He could not have looked away from them for more than a second or two, three at most but it had completely gone from the floor, without leaving so much as a stain.

A scent reminding him of honeysuckle filled his nostrils. It was there before but now he could really smell it, even taste it. He took another sip of water from his bottle and washed his mouth out, but decided he could not spit it out. He felt that this truly was a holy place and to do so would only add to the disrespect he had just shown by vomiting the contents of his chest all over the floor. He tasted the water and let it swirl in his mouth before he swallowed it, feeling it drop down into his stomach. It tasted different somehow, far cleaner than the water he was used to drinking from the local wells.

Ahead, the passageway carried on for some way before gradually rising up and disappearing from view. If he wasn't dead, he was concerned for his camels but he knew if anything had happened to them there was little he could do for them now. His best choice was to continue. He took two more big swigs of water and walked at a brisk pace further along the passageway, heading towards what he hoped would be the central part of the vessel. He had only walked perhaps another hundred paces or so, when a brightly illuminated opening appeared on the right. Upon investigating, he could see ended in a blank wall only twenty paces away. Omari thought it must be there for a reason and took the turning, cautiously approaching the wall. Part of it began to change shape and he found himself once again staring at the depiction of a handprint on a square. This time he had not even touched the wall. Studying it, he could see it was entirely identical to the panel that had appeared at the entrance. Omari concluded he was looking at an outline of his own hand. He felt excited for a moment at what this could mean. Allah was truly merciful and great to grant him a personal entrance to Paradise. For truly this must be that place, how could it not be? There was only one way to find the answers. He placed his palm on the small square as he had done at the entrance. Like the walls, it was cool to touch. Immediately the passageway opened up, the walls once again retracting in upon themselves and forming an opening for him to pass through. His caution forgotten, he entered and found a space lighting up before him. He stepped down into a large room that was oval in shape, with walls that formed naturally up into an arched ceiling some dozen or so metres high above him. The size reminded him of the space back home, where clan leaders would hold their meetings. The light source emanated from a number of small alcoves that formed naturally at intervals along the floor and walls. It was unusually spacious, and though devoid of any furniture, it flowed and weaved to form a number of depressions, where one could sit or lie down. There were no other trappings that Omari would associate with a home, yet somehow it felt like a dwelling. His ears detected a sound that he had not heard in a long while. He knew it at once, it was unmistakable; running water. A stream? In here? Was this his entrance into Paradise or part of some test he had yet to pass? He stepped further into the room, noting that on either side of him were smaller alcoves just above the floor, which gave the appearance of being a comfortable space one might sleep in. Directly ahead, the room descended into an oval shaped pit that formed a horseshoe-shaped seating area. It surrounded a small plinth that rose to form a natural table from the floor. The room had a circular feeling to its overall shape, and the walls flowed out from the entrance naturally adjoining into ceiling and floor. Omari ran his hand along the walls. They felt as cool as the interior passageway. Cool and smooth, but not cold. Omari searched the memories of his previous travels to recall anywhere similar from his past that matched the sight before him. His Father had certainly taken him to see some wonderful places on their travels, and he had visited the cave dwellings of many tribes during his journeys as a trader, but nothing could compare to this. The walls in such places were always cold to the touch, often with little or no light and had a pervading smell of damp about them. They were fascinating places, full of the secret history that his country had long since forgotten. Here, the air felt cleaner than it had in the passageway, but maybe that was because he had cleared his lungs of all that sputum. He could not be sure. He smelled fresh water.

Past the sunken seating area, he saw a second opening leading to another chamber. Through a high arch on the far side of the room came the sound of the falling water originated. He walked through to it and found himself standing atop a staircase that extended out from the wall, curving with it down to a lower level. The dwelling, if that was what it was, was effectively split into two large spaces, one above the other with the staircase connecting the two. From the small landing he looked down into the room below, beholding the sight of sparkling water which came from two overlapping circular pools of water, one larger sunken into the floor below him. The smaller pool occupied part of the open space of the lower chamber, just along from the base of the stairs. Its design was almost like an old hammam that he had seen once before in the city baths, but that had been dirty, this was clean. The larger pool which overlapped it ran through another arch into an alcove space, creating a cave in the lower level that offered some privacy from the landing. The source of the falling water came from a circular opening above and across from him on the opposite wall. From it, a steady flow of water fell down into a third much smaller pool that was raised just above the others, about halfway down the staircase. This created a small waterfall between them. Off to one side, a small ledge shaped like a half-open pipe conducted the flow of water along one side of the room into another opening close to the floor allowing it to exit. A small, flat surface big enough to allow two men to walk side by side followed the circumference of the larger pool. It would allow space for a person to sit on the edge or position themselves beneath the falling water, if they wished. The sight before him confirmed his previous thoughts. This was a truly place for *Ghusl*, the act of bathing before prayer. It might even be a requirement of him before travelling further. Now Omari found himself giving serious weight to the possibility that he had indeed perished in the desert along with the last of his animals, and that everything else had simply been a test of faith at the gates of Paradise. Nothing else made any sense at this stage. Impulsively, Omari began to undress and drape his garments over the wall at the top of the steps. He folded his clothes neatly. His skin was coated with the sand and dirt of many days of travel, and the cuts and bruises of his toil had gone unwashed for longer than a week. He took off his underwear and stood at the top of the stairs, completely naked. He felt a slight chill but then he sensed the room was getting warmer. He descended the stairs with care, placing one hand on the wall only to find himself jumping back in shock when something moved beneath his hand. He almost fell off the stairs, but quickly managed to regain his balance. He stared intently at the curved wall that descended with the steps. Something had changed. A singular shape had formed, curving with the steps in the form of a solid handrail. What sort of miracle was this? Allah himself must be behind such magic, if the wall could change shape, simply to aid him in walking down a staircase! He took hold of the newly formed rail, steadying himself and began his descent. The lower area glowed more prominently than the rest of his surroundings, bathing the water below in a cool wash of soft light that caused the rippling surface below to flicker magically. The light seemed to dim a little when he squinted. The sound of the falling water echoed around the room, a soothing accompaniment to his slow and deliberate steps to the lower level. Upon reaching the pool, he sat at the water's edge like a child at his first swimming lesson, waiting for the teacher to give him permission to enter the water. After a moment's hesitation, he placed his right foot slowly beneath the surface expecting to recoil at its cold temperature, but it was warm like the water in an oasis in the midday sun. He put both his legs together and let them sink beneath the surface, his feet touching a shelf just a few feet underneath. Its presence meant he would be able to sit in the water comfortably, so he slowly slid himself down onto it. The warm water rushed up to just below his chin, before his buttocks found themselves touching the shelf below him. It was just the right height to allow him to sit with his head above the surface. The warm water seeped into every pore in his skin, the dirt and sand of many weeks lifting itself away. For a moment, the water went dark and dirty but in an instant it was clear again. This was indeed a magical place.

"Allah be praised!" Omari said, glad to say the words aloud simply because he felt he should give thanks for experiencing something so wonderful. He held his breath, dipping his head under the water, covering his ears with his hands to prevent water from running into them. For a moment, he stayed submerged, alone with his thoughts. The sound of his steady heartbeat and the cascade of water hitting the surface above him the only things he was aware of. A rare moment of pure peace. After he could no longer hold his breath, he rose above the water and exhaled slowly. He ran his hands over his skin, feeling the scars his journeys had left him with. Each one attached to a memory of a moment where he had stumbled upon rock or had an unwelcome bite from a disgruntled animal or feeding insect. He knew each one intimately; every wound, every scar. He wanted to check they were clean. Yet when he felt for them, there were none. He checked again for the biggest scar, a knife wound on the upper calf, which had occurred as a result of an accident at home for which his late wife had joked, "You now have your own knife story. You can say you got it fighting off bandits!" It was not there. He pulled himself out of the water, to check his body again. He sat upright on the shelf and held his arms up, watching the beads of water trickle down and fall from his limbs as he twisted them around, inspecting them. Of his scars, even the latest cut on his finger that had occurred just two days ago he could see no trace. It was only then that Omari noticed his toothache. The pain that had been bothering him for so long had simply abated. In fact, the last time he remembered it hurting him was when he was on the surface of the the object, but after that he wasn't so sure. He felt inside his mouth, prodding the molar that had been the source of so much pain. He felt no sensation at all. When he sucked on it previously, he would taste blood and pus all mixed in with his spit, but trying it now there was nothing; no blood just his tasteless spittle.

Omari stood up and walked along the shelf of the pool until he stood underneath the waterfall, letting it cascade over his back, cleaning his hair and beard until wet, they clung heavily to his head and face. He closed his eyes, enjoying the feeling of the warm water as it pounded his skin and ran through his hair. He felt so clean and refreshed, recalling moments from his youth as his mind wandered to the past. He saw images of people and places, long forgotten. His memory felt sharper. He saw his family; visualising his father with incredible clarity. He could see his face, his smile and hear his gentle voice as though he was speaking to him now. The sounds and images were so vivid. Events from his past that had been distant fragments, now came into instant focus one after the other. He could summon a specific moment from his life and he would see it as if it had only happened yesterday, playing out before him. He saw his mother, so young, his first moments with her as child. Things long since forgotten were now so visceral in his mind: the first kiss with his wife, their first home, the first time he laid his eyes on his firstborn, their second baby, everything, all so clearly recalled. It was as if he could smell and taste very part of it as he relived it in the present. It was overwhelming. He opened his eyes, feeling the water running causing him to squint. As he stepped from beneath the waterfall and back into the pool, he waded across to the seating shelf and sat, his body half-submerged in the water, the rest of him leaning against the wall behind him. It was then, as he was lost in a myriad of memories that he realised that the edge of the pool behind him was soft against his back. He turned around and touched the white surface with his hand. He could feel it beginning to harden again, like the rest of the floor. This was incredible. It was as if the room could mould itself to his contours. This was indeed Paradise. He could conclude nothing else. But should he stay here, alone, and never leave? That didn't make sense. If his life in this wondrous place was to be a solitary one, he couldn't imagine a more lonely existence. Even if it gave him the ability to access every day of his life, they were still just memories. He thought this must be one of many such rooms, so many people could live here. How many would this vessel carry? Thousands perhaps... This blessing of a new Paradise was not for him alone, it was clearly intended for others. He thought about his tribe and the harsh living conditions they endured all year round. It was something they accepted yet few of them would trade it in for a life in the big city. You couldn't miss what you'd never had – it was true. Coming here would present them with such a drastic change, he was sure many would not accept it. Perhaps it was something he should consider only as a place of worship. A place of rebirth. Was he dead? It was still possible. He certainly felt healthier than he could ever remember; his mind was sharp and full of thoughts, facts, figures and so many memories, accessed in an instant. It was as if he could re-live any moment from his life by simply shutting his mind off to other thoughts and running back through his life until he found the memory he wanted to see. Incredible. He ran his fingers once again across his body, searching for those old familiar wounds but there was not a single one left. This place had the power to heal the sick, of that he was certain. It was a miracle of Allah that this vessel had come and landed here of all places. Fada, one of the most remote towns in his country, probably even the world, though Omari was no expert on Geography, and could not be certain of this. He pulled himself up and out of the cooling water, surprised by the strength in his arms. As a child, he could vault a fence and quite nimbly too. Such were the skills of youth that he thought had long since abandoned him, but here he felt such strength again. He bounded up the stairs in long strides, almost bouncing as he did so. He fetched his clothes and began to get dressed on the landing, his thoughts turning to getting back to Fada.

"Well, that is odd!" he said aloud, as he looked down and noticed for the first time he had an erection. Omari stared as his hand greeted a friend he had not seen in some time. He was puzzled even further by its appearance, for he was not feeling sexually inclined in any way, nor had he had any sexual thoughts. To do so would be a dishonour to the memory of his beloved wife. Yet there stood his penis, as solid as could be, reaching up from a mass of pubic hair, which he had not trimmed in many years. He felt embarrassed, looking around to check no one was observing him as he continued to dress himself. He knew this thought was absurd, because he was certain he was still alone. Omari had to laugh; he did look ridiculous with his member protruding out from under his clothes. He did everything he could to empty his mind of any thoughts that would encourage it to remain erect, but it was obviously making up for lost time.

He focused on his plans to get back to his daughter, knowing he must make preparations to do so at once. Omari re-entered the upper part of the dwelling again, with its sunken seating area and curved smooth lines. It had not changed. He sat in the sunken oval area and reached into his satchel, eating some dried beef before removing the small broken mirror he kept wrapped in an old cloth. He held it up to his face, seeing he looked markedly different. He wasn't younger perhaps, but something about him was certainly more relaxed. The lines in his face had vanished, as had the tired bags that always hung so heavily beneath his eyes. His skin, so worn and leathery from many travels under a relentless sun was now soft and smooth. He held the mirror above him in many directions, so he could examine his body from different angles. His moles and birthmarks were all still there, but nothing else that a history of living in the remote deserts had given him remained. He stretched his limbs and spun his arms, kicking his legs, feeling the energy of youth imbued again in his very being. It was as if he was in his late twenties. He stood and went over to the landing, staring back down at the pool below him. The dirt and grime he had left behind was diminishing. In a moment, the water was as clear and clean as it had been when he first entered it. This was truly a blessed place but now he knew he faced a dilemma - Who could he tell about it and what would he say to them? If he left now and was caught by the soldiers they would want to know how he got inside. He knew they were more than capable of torturing him in order to find out the answers. Men of violence could not be allowed to enter such a sacred place. What should he do? There were so many questions and he cried out for Allah to come before him and provide him with some answers, kneeling as he did so. Allah's name echoed around the room, along with his pleas, but after many minutes of vigorous vocal prayer no one came to answer him. The only sound was that of the water falling into the pools below.

There was only one thing of which he was certain. He had to get back to his daughter. He wasn't sure if it was as a result of his dip into the pool, but his mind had become sharply focused. Any thoughts of remaining in this place of Paradise were dismissed. Joy was his family and he had been gone too long. His focus turned immediately to her uncle, Attah, Omari's half-brother. He was older than Omari by several years and when he had offered to pay Joy to cook and clean around his compound until her suitor could find the dowry to pay Omari for her hand in marriage, he had readily agreed. Back then it made sense. Joy hated being alone when he travelled, especially since Nya had left for the capital, and had begged him not to leave. Omari recalled that conversation with so much more clarity now. It played out before him with small details filling his mind. He recollected things he had not even noticed before. The brief touch of Attah's hand on her shoulder, when he had greeted them that day, the look in his eyes when he took Joy inside his house as Omari left. He felt uncomfortable. It was time to go home. He ate the remainder of his food and drank again from his water bottle, before re-filling all three of them from the pool. He returned to stand before the wall, where he had entered. The wall retracted in the same way it had before, leading to the short corridor from where he'd come. He stepped through and the opening closed up immediately behind him. He took a few steps forwards then hesitated - A quick test. Could he come back? He faced the wall and as before, the transparent square with his handprint appeared again before him. No further reassurance was needed. He would clearly be able to come back and re-enter this place anytime. He thanked Allah and returned to the corridor. Everything was as before. He felt an urgency to run and did so, the clean air rushing into his lungs and filling his body with all the energy required. It was almost effortless. His strides were that of an Olympian and in a short while he had reached the wall where he had entered the vessel. Though the ship had not required him to use his hand to exit the dwelling space with the water, here the palm print device appeared once again in front of him, indicating that to leave the vessel he would be required to press his hand upon it. Good. He thought that most wise. His mind turned again to the soldiers. How long had he been gone? Perhaps an hour... Would they still be outside? What if they captured and detained him, preventing him from reaching Joy? He pictured Attah's face again. The urgent need to return home began to nag and at him. He had no choice, he must leave this holy place for now, no matter the risk. He placed his hand where required and as expected, the wall in front of him parted, the cold night air rushing to greet him.

It was an unusual experience to go from somewhere inside, that under any other circumstance would probably feel stuffy and humid, usually a step outside brought the welcome relief of fresh air. Here the opposite was true. The cold night air smelled and tasted as it always had in the desert, but it was not as clean and fresh as that inside the ship. The difference was at once very palatable, if not uncomfortable. Omari stepped outside the vessel and into the short depression that led to the surface. Crouching, he moved slowly upward, leaving the entrance to seal silently behind him. He peered cautiously above the rim, looking towards the town, where he could see a sprinkling of lights, torches and fires dotted among the distant buildings of Fada. Evidently, few people had gone to bed that night. Between him and the edge of the vessel he could see no sign of any activity. He looked around, towards the central part of the ship, at the tower that loomed above him, glowing in the night sky. There he saw them, a sporadic line of torches that were now mere dots at this distance. They had long since passed him by, and were investigating the area around the tower. There was no sign of any other activity. Omari could see they were far too preoccupied to notice him, so he bolted from the relative safety of the depression back towards the edge of the ship. He had not run this fast since he was a young man, yet the bounding strides he found himself achieving required little effort from him. He had soon covered a distance of some five hundred paces in barely a minute. Finally feeling a little breathless, he halted briefly before jogging on gently until he reached the edge of the surface. The soft illumination coming from within the ship still cast a gentle light on the surface of the water surrounding it. Omari saw the moat of water had expanded further out and he saw something else - several small clumps of vegetation nestling among the rocks at its edge. They were plants of a type he did not recognise from the region. They hadn't been there before, had they? No. Nothing ever grew around here, at least not before today. The water felt cold from the night air, sending a chill through his body as he stepped down into it. He broke into a run immediately, realising this was perhaps not the stealthiest of methods available to him, but it appeared the patrol from the barracks had left no one behind at the water's edge. Omari wondered if they would find a way inside as he had. He hoped they would not. He knew any number of enterprising individuals back in Fada who, given the chance, would stand outside charging an entrance fee for the townsfolk to take a look. Such a holy place could not be allowed to be tainted with such activities. As he reached the edge of the water, he glanced back and saw the continual movement of torchlight in the distance upon the vessel's surface. Small bright dots that stood out on the pearl-white landscape, as he too must have done when they were searching for him earlier. There were perhaps two dozen figures walking on the vessel, still heading towards its central structure. If they had spotted him they gave no indication to show it, and he felt relieved. He had not walked much further when he was alerted by raised voices just ahead of him. A group of men were arguing off to his left, about one hundred yards away. He crouched by an outcrop of rocks at the water's edge and observed them. The cluster of half a dozen men were partially lit up by the glow coming from the vessel. He caught a glimpse of someone who had flashes on his clothing; insignia of some kind. An officer from the army probably, but it was hard to tell from this distance and he was thankful it was still dark. The group became very animated and their verbal exchanges grew louder with each passing second. He could only make out parts of the conversation, but the gist was an argument between a group of villagers who wanted to inspect the vessel for themselves, and the men from the army who were refusing to let them pass. The villagers were refusing to move and the soldiers were too few to contain them. Omari didn't see how the army could secure such a place. The perimeter of the vessel was so colossal he couldn't see how it could be guarded properly. He was using the argument as his chance to move further away from the group, when a sound and a blur of movement to his right startled him. Omari thought he had been discovered but then he recognised the shape. It was Abu-Kir along with his two brothers, Abu-Sir and Ali-Baba. All three were sitting quietly where he had left them, along with Omari's spice packs and other belongings. He had been lucky. The group from the army barracks had arrived some distance from his own animals and they had remained undiscovered. He was so pleased to see the animals he almost hugged them. Their bleats and grunts back at him indicated they felt the same.

"Okay my friends, I am pleased to see you too. But we must be quiet! It is time for us to return home," he whispered as he took the reins and led them slowly away from the water and Allah's gift from the heavens. His sole focus was now his daughter, Joy.

RYAN

"I am going. This is not up for discussion. If we're going to show the people of the United Kingdom that they must not panic then the sooner the media see me near one of these things, the better."

Ryan stood facing the Cobra Committee, hands spread on the table. He had been arguing this point for the last thirty minutes. Several things had come to his mind when he returned to the room hours earlier. Firstly, that he had no idea how to run a country. Whatever decisions he made, he would effectively be making it up as he went along. Secondly, General Spears wanted him to remain in the role, quite why he wasn't sure, but if Spears was going to fuck with him then he was determined to cause the man as much grief as possible. Thirdly, because he didn't want this job and had no ambition to remain in power, he could afford to take ballsy decisions without worrying about the long-term repercussions, this being one of them. He could in fact be the best kind of politician; one who didn't worry about the effect his decisions had on his own political career, because he really didn't give a fuck. For better or worse, this would be the highest peak of his time in office, and it was a pinnacle he would be quite happy to see the back of as soon as possible. If he did a reasonably good job and these things from outer space fucked off sharpish, then he could look forward to a career of appearing on chat shows, and maybe even get a book deal out of it... Not long after his encounter with General Spears in the toilet, he had had to make a live broadcast to the United Kingdom addressing not only the alien threat, but also the death of Prime Minister David Jackson and his family, killed in a terrorist attack. Then he had had to inform everyone that he, The Minister of Health, was going to be running the country, their new and temporary unelected leader. In the last hour alone, various personnel—including a new PA—had been assigned to him. The PA was a lovely-looking creature who went by the name of Jennifer Brewster-Smith. Ryan liked to think of all women as beautiful creatures, at least the ones he wanted to shag and she was no exception. She stood an elegant five foot seven, without her boots, which when added into the equation, made her the same height as himself. She wore her dark brown hair straight, and her makeup, even on the day of an alien invasion was immaculately precise in its moderation. She was so perfectly tall and slender that Ryan wondered if she actually ever ate anything. She wore a dark blue ladies' suit that had been perfectly tailored to fit her lean figure. Ryan had just thirty seconds to glance at her CV before approving her for the job. At a time of crisis, thirty seconds was considered a luxury, or so he had been told by the Chief Whip. Her parents were of West Indian origin and she was the third generation of her family to be born in the UK. Her skin was the colour of cocoa butter and Ryan found her exotic looks appealing. Something of her reminded him of Candice, though he personally doubted she had a massive cock between her legs. He wouldn't mind finding out, either way. She'd been educated in Cambridge, studying Political Science, graduated with honours and was also training to be a lawyer, part-time. Jennifer was to deal with his daily appointments diary from here on in, but she had already proved to him that she was capable of so much more. Earlier she had handed him a speech she had written, as he was having his makeup done to go before the cameras. "Just to take the shine off…" they'd told him, as he found his face being doused in far more powder than he thought necessary.

As he'd begun to read it, the words leapt off the page at him. It had something of the guts of Winston Churchill about it. Not so much "We will fight them on the beaches…" but more of the "We will show the world what the UK is made of…" It was exceptionally good. He substituted it for the one Darren Fine had given him and took great pleasure in seeing Fine's face go pale, as he read out the unsanctioned text live on national television. Everyone else seemed extremely pleased with it. It appealed for calm among the population, though how long that would last was anyone's guess and this was the reason he felt he had to do something personally to ensure that his rhetoric was backed up by action, not just words. It had been a hell of a first day on the job and his decisions were not going to get any easier. No one in his cabinet wanted him to go anywhere near the landing site in Scotland, stating unanimously that it was "Far too dangerous". They were right, of course. Such a show of bravado bordered on stupidity, but Ryan actually didn't care and if such a thing added to a vote of no confidence in him, and got him booted out, so much the better. He had to admit to himself however, that he did have a burning curiosity to see one of these extraordinary vessels up close.

"Prime Minister, when Maggie faced the Falklands' Crisis she didn't head down to Stanley with the Task Force! It's just not the done thing," said Basil Badgers, who now assumed the post Foreign Secretary, no doubt thinking about himself. If anything was to happen to Ryan he would almost certainly be thrust into the Prime Minister's position, a prospect he clearly did not relish. Julie Compston, now acting Head of British Intelligence was also quick to jump in.

"I have to agree with the Foreign Secretary on this, Prime Minister. Apart from the security implications, that General Spears has himself just outlined, there's other things to consider. You're leading a country, which only hours ago found itself leaderless. We need to lick our wounds first. You've just made a great speech, I'm sure everyone agrees with me on that..." Compston looked around the room for agreement and got a series of approving mutters. "But we cannot afford to lose anyone else at such a vital time. As you said yourself, this is a time for calm." Then Ryan got a lone voice of support from the last place he expected.

"I think it's an idea with a great deal of merit," Darren Fine said, speaking from his throne at the table's opposite end. Ryan and he locked eyes for a moment, each trying to gauge the other. Ryan got nothing. Reading people for their motives was not his strongest suit. Candice was so much better at that than he was. If only she could be here, she would have his back. A transsexual facing Cobra down. That would be a first, for sure. Fine had such great projection, Ryan noticed - He'd probably been an actor in a past life or a member of *Footlights* at the very least.

"Why would you think that?" asked General Spears.

"Our country is facing a truly unique crisis. I don't think one good speech is going to be enough. Showing the country, and indeed the world, that our new leader is not afraid and is, in fact, willing to go to meet... whoever or whatever this is in the field would not only send a message of calm, but it would be the PR coup of the century. The American President couldn't have left Washington for NORAD any faster if he tried. Ryan would be the focus of the media on the world stage, and it would show Britain taking the lead in this international crisis. No other world leader has been so bold. Not yet anyway.'

Ryan suspected the man was hoping this trip would be one from which he might not return. No wonder he made such a good argument.

"Nor have they been so stupid," Julie Compston retorted, staring Fine down. He held his poise, waiting for Ryan to give a reply. Perhaps this wasn't such a good idea, after all. Ryan wanted to be in and out of this job quickly, not become the world's favourite television personality in a time of crisis, nor its sacrificial lamb.

"It will be a PR disaster, and send panic throughout the world if he's killed on live television," the General countered.

"We don't even know why these things are here yet, or even if it's safe to approach them!' Police Commissioner Winston said, causing a wave of nodding heads around the table.

"If I could turn everyone's attention to the monitors for a second," Fine interjected, with the remote in his hand.

"This footage was taken by one of our own helicopters only an hour ago, over the vessel in Aberdeen," he added.

The image on screen was something of a surprise. A beige-coloured double-decker bus was driving on the surface of the saucer shaped structure, dodging and weaving below the helicopter.

"What on earth is that?" Heather Childs asked, sitting up in her seat.

'That Minister, is a double-decker bus, the number twelve I believe, from Aberdeen. It was known to have five occupants on board at the time this footage was shot. Two young men, both students, who have been identified, a young black woman, a second woman whom we believe to be a pensioner, and the driver. This footage was also broadcast on Youtube and Facebook Live." Fine pointed the remote at the larger monitor, and the face of a young man appeared. He was inside the back of the bus, talking directly to camera. The voice of a second man exchanged commentary with him as he pointed the camera out of the windows at the pursuing helicopter, and the surface of the ship before speaking to camera again. The vloggers, whoever they were, revelled in chase from the army. Ryan could tell they were off their tits on something. God, this was all he fucking needed.

"By now, the whole world will have seen this. So if Ryan… sorry, if our Prime Minister does not go and take a look at the site of the vessel for himself, we're saying to the nation he will not go where old ladies, students and bus drivers had no fear of treading.'

"We've identified the two young men in the video, both second year students from Aberdeen University with their own Youtube channel. This footage has had over 3 million views already. We've also identified the bus driver, but nothing so far on the black female passenger or the pensioner.' Spears tone betrayed no surprise at Fine's news.

"Are you telling us, General, that a bus driver decided to take a day trip and drove around on this thing before we were able to seal it off?" Compston asked. If the General was shaken by this, he did not show it, delivering his response in his usual non-committal fashion.

"That would seem to be the case, yes."

Silence fell on the room. The footage was repeated. Ryan thought the old woman on the bus looked familiar for a moment. It looked a bit like… but it couldn't be, could it? God. He needed to make a phone call. The

General must have known about this. He hadn't said a thing when Ryan had come in from addressing the nation.

"General Spears, when were you going to inform us all about this?" Ryan's anger gave his words extra weight. He looked hard at the General who this time was seated. The General did not even flinch.

"Most of the people shown in this footage are now in our custody. The vehicle was able to reach the ship only minutes before the local authorities had a chance to close off the roads leading to the landing site. Our helicopters had only just arrived on the scene when this footage was taken."

"I'm sorry, did you say most of the people? What does that mean, exactly?" Ryan asked.

"Two escaped the perimeter. A group of bikers also reached the ship, again before the approach roads could be closed."

"Bikers?"

"Yes, Prime Minister. We have one of them in custody."

"These people haven't actually broken any laws, have they? I mean they can't be the only people that decided to throw caution to the wind and came to take a look," Ryan said.

"They weren't. They were the only ones who got to it before we closed the roads off. I might remind everyone this is an extremely fluid situation. We weren't even sure where the object was going to come down until a few hours ago,'" General Spears said. "The landing site is now completely secure."

"Can we get the footage removed?' Ryan asked, knowing by now that it would probably be pointless.

"That would be like closing the barn door after the horse has bolted, Prime Minister. It's already had several million views and that figure is going up by tens of thousands every ten minutes," Fine said. Ryan could tell he'd been keeping abreast of the numbers. He must have known about this footage within moments of it going live. Probably even before General Spears found out. If Spears was seeing it now for the first time, he certainly wasn't letting on.

"It's also not the only footage online of civilians reaching the objects. A group of Italian fishermen went on the surface of the one that landed in the sea south of Taranto. That was on CNN," the Police Commissioner added.

"Has anyone actually got inside one of these things?" It seemed an obvious question, but in politics, Ryan found it always paid never to assume the obvious.

"Not to our current knowledge, Prime Minister," Julie Compston replied, her face blank. Ryan didn't trust people with blank expressions. The less people gave away in their facial expressions, the less he trusted them. It meant they were good at hiding something.

"Not to your current knowledge? I notice you phrased that very carefully Ms Compston," he fired back.

"We're certainly not aware of it, but it doesn't mean it hasn't happened," she replied with equal care. Ryan thought for a moment, studying the images on the screen.

"What is the fastest way for me to get to Aberdeen?"

"By air to Aberdeen International Airport from London," Compston said.

"Aberdeen has an airport? I never knew that." God - He already wished he hadn't said that out loud. He hadn't been back to Scotland since his childhood. He couldn't think of more extraordinary circumstances under which to be returning.

"I doubt most of us did, Prime Minister. It's just north of the city. By my calculations, it will put you less than 20 kilometres east of the object." General Spears was clearly well informed.

"Look everyone, I'm going to see this thing for myself. If anyone disagrees then you can take my job here and now."

No one said anything, not even Darren Fine.

"Right then. General Spears, can you arrange to have a helicopter pick me up from here and take us to RAF Northholt? Then we can fly directly to Scotland from there. I think in light of what happened in France, it's best we avoid public transport hubs for the moment." Ryan still didn't know who was responsible for what had happened in France. He was less worried about the alien ships, than he was about those who had shot down the plane outside Paris.

"That's standard procedure, Prime Minister. I will make sure the pilots know to chart a course that doesn't take you too close to the object itself." Ryan thought the General's tone reeked of condescension.

"Okay. Can we just call this thing *The Spaceship*. I mean it is a ship and it did come from space and it landed, so let's not call it the object, it's not a meteor, is it? I think it's safe to assume that it's been piloted here by sentient life of some kind."

The room did not disagree with his assessment. Darren Fine whispered something to the person on his left. Ryan was sure he had said "he's using big words today..." or something along those lines.

"Fine, I think you had better come along with me. The press up there are bound to be all over this already. Your expertise will be invaluable, wouldn't you agree, General?"

"Oh yes. Most invaluable," the General said, almost smiling.

Fine did not look happy, but he just nodded. There weren't many small pleasures to be had in this new job, so Ryan would take those he could get.

In less than twenty minutes after the meeting was adjourned, they were airborne. The inside of the helicopter rattled intensely. Ryan had never travelled on a Chinook before, and judging from the green face opposite him, neither had Darren Fine. General Spears had accompanied them, along with Jennifer, the new PA, whom Ryan had given the choice of staying behind or accompanying them. She had readily agreed to the latter. She informed him she had other speeches prepared that they could discuss on the plane, which sounded good to Ryan because he certainly needed more good speeches. After the last one, he would have a standard to maintain. There was a sudden drop in altitude as the aircraft hit an air pocket. Everyone lurched forwards. Fine vomited spectacularly across the cabin. They sat in two rows facing each other, so virtually no one was spared the contents of Fine's stomach, which Ryan judged to be Italian. There was a brief flurry of activity as everyone sought something with which to remove Fine's lunch from their person. Additional personnel had been allocated to travel with them, whom Ryan assumed to be of a scientific background, bolstering the numbers of the team already on the ground. A happy coincidence, as fortunately they bore the brunt of Fine's vomitus. Their numbers filled the rows of red-coloured cargo seats that hung from straps, running down both sides of the 'copter. Apparently the Chinook that had the more plush interior had some maintenance issues so they had been forced to travel in a standard army one to avoid any further delay. General Spears had been talking to the pilots, and came back to find his seat covered in Fine's vomit. The flight was full and there was nowhere else to sit down. Undeterred, Spears produced a handkerchief (did anyone really carry those anymore?) and tried to clean the worst off. The smell reminded Ryan of leaving a cheap nightclub in his university days. It filled the cabin and the others began to look rather queasy - either that, or they were suppressing their laughter, Ryan wasn't sure which. Jennifer passed Fine some tissues, which he took gratefully, clamping them to his mouth. For Ryan, the jolts and bumps of the journey were uncomfortable but not unbearable. He had flown in smaller helicopters before. He had even taken one to the top of a hospital in Manchester. It had saved time during one of his visits there, to meet with the senior managers. He had been most disappointed to find he could not travel back the same way, as an air ambulance was due to land and the pad had to be cleared as a priority. Having not anticipated such an eventuality, he caught a far less glamorous black cab back to the airport that was subsequently stuck in traffic. For over an hour, that cab driver had talked to him about everything from the Middle East to the complete history of his bowel troubles. Ryan promised to see what he could do about getting the man an early appointment for his next colorectal surgery. Ryan wasn't sure why he had remembered that particular detail, but he would take a helicopter over a black cab any time. The pilots couldn't turn to have a casual chat with him for one thing. He turned to General Spears who was sitting to his left, directly over from Fine.

"So General. What else do we know about these things?"

General Spears had just pulled out his iPad, when the helicopter abruptly dropped a few feet causing Fine to vomit again, most of which General Spears avoided with a prompt lean to his right. Jennifer passed Fine a sickbag, which he quickly filled. The sound of laughter joined the stench in the air. Ryan noted that some of the sick had been deposited on the General's iPad screen, along with a second splash on the lapel of his jacket. General Spears did not bat an eyelid. He whipped away the undigested sediment from the screen of his device, opening a collection of folders and emails where different information had been summarised.

"We know very little. I'm told each ship was the same size and shape when they entered the Earth's atmosphere, but several appear to have changed their configuration since landing. From these satellite images, we can see the width and circumference of the saucer section at these landing sites varies considerably: from six to ten miles across, while some of the larger ones appear to be upwards of twenty miles across or even larger. Doctor Jacobs will have all the latest information on that, she's heading the scientific team based in the village of Garlogie, on the eastern perimeter of the ship in Aberdeen. They've set up in a farm just across from the edge of the saucer. You can literally walk straight on to it from there. This is the image of our one. Down here below it in the south is the town of Banchory. We've deployed a small military presence there and evacuated the town."

Ryan studied the device, with the General swiping several images past his eyes. The ship appeared to have landed avoiding large populated areas, but nevertheless consuming several small villages and farms somewhere beneath its mass. Ryan wondered what had become of their inhabitants.

"What about casualties so far?" he asked.

"Curiously few. The reports indicate when the ship began to descend, it came down so slowly that there was adequate time for people to escape from beneath it. It's not confirmed yet but something else struck me as odd about the pattern in which they all arrived."

"Go on..." Ryan prompted.

"Even though the ships arrived all across the world, with the one exception of Australia, the actual time of arrival of each vessel coincided with daylight in that country. Each arrived either just before dawn, in the morning or afternoon, but none after dark. Many of them also took a flight path over a large populated area but then landed somewhere much further away, in largely unpopulated terrain. What does that suggest to you?"

Ryan wondered what was unique about Australia. It seemed an odd military tactic. To play your hand so early in plain sight of your enemy. If indeed this was an invasion.

"They wanted to be seen?" It seemed logical. Why else would you fly so close to a populated area and then land so far away? General Spears nodded.

"I concur with you, Prime Minister. It's as if they arrived intending maximum exposure." It was the first time the General had addressed him formally.

"I like the way you said that, General Spears," Ryan said, with a smile.

"Don't get used to it, Prime Minister Wallace," the General said flatly. He man was a bastard, but for now he was his bastard. Ryan would have to be careful with him. He was a powerful individual, holding the other title of Chief of Defence staff, which meant he oversaw the small committee of high-ranking military officers that would sit in on the COBRA meetings. Ryan hadn't yet had the chance to meet them all. The First Sea Lord, Admiral Alun Flemyng was on his way back from Malta, on board HMS Horizon and was expected to arrive in Southampton early tomorrow morning. Air Chief Marshall Henry Davies was expected to greet them at RAF Northholt, and brief them with any updates. He would then return to COBRA, which would reconvene tomorrow isafter lunch. That morning, Ryan had been assigned two personal bodyguards, Willis and Dilks. He wasn't keen on their names, so had already taken to calling them Crockett and Tubbs, both of whom now accompanied him on the helicopter. He leaned over to Crocket (Dilks)

"I don't suppose there's any *Redbull* on board?"

Crockett said nothing in response. It wasn't hard to tell if he had the respect of his security guards or not; he clearly didn't.

"So Dilks, is it? What did you do before this?"

"I worked the security detail for Prime Minister David Jackson."

That was a conversation killer right there and then. Obviously, Dilks hadn't been with Jackson in France, otherwise he would be dead. Ryan certainly hoped he had more success in the role.

"He's given me some very big shoes to fill," Ryan said. He couldn't think of anything else to say, feeling anything wittier wouldn't go down very well.

"That he has, Prime Minister," Dilks said, as a voice came over the loud speaker.

"Touching down at RAF Northholt in two minutes."

It felt like even less time than that, when Ryan felt the helicopter touchdown with a bump. As the ramp came down from the rear of the Chinook,

Ryan could see there was a group of men in blue Royal Airforce uniforms waiting to meet them. The last shreds of daylight were already beginning to disappear far off to the west. The tarmac was illuminated by bright floodlights from either side. Ryan left the helicopter flanked on either side by his vigilant security duo, their eyes darting in all directions. He was instantly greeted by the tall figure of Air Chief Marshall Davies. The Air Marshall had a firm handshake, not unlike the General's and was extremely well-spoken. Ryan couldn't help but notice that his clean, pressed blue uniform, adorned with epaulettes and badges had not a single crease out of place. He could have almost been a model, but not runway, more like the Kay's Catalogue type of old. He could see this man advertising men's sportswear.

"Good evening, Prime Minister. I wish we were meeting in better circumstances." Definitely a private education, Ryan noted immediately.

"So do I, Air Chief Marshall. Is there anything pressing that myself or General Spears need to be updated on before we carry on?" As he asked the question, the group was being steered towards a black jet. Ryan wasn't sure of the type, but it was similar to the private jets he had seen lining the runaways at Nice Airport, the one time he had managed to get to the Cannes Film Festival. Yeah, that had been a good time. Nothing but drugs and a wide variety of sexual encounters all week long. He never did manage to see any of the films.

"We've designated the airspace *Red* from here to Scotland, Prime Minister. This will give you an unrestricted purview to Aberdeen as fast as possible. Not all civilian air traffic is down yet, we've still several international flights coming into land but you should reach Aberdeen in just over one hour after take-off. Two Harriers will accompany you on the trip, a precaution we thought wise in light of recent events."

Ryan felt a little more secure. At least there would be three targets, for someone to shoot at instead of just the one.

"Very good. Any updates from Scotland?" he asked.

"No sir. We'll be in contact with the pilot the whole way. He's a civilian, but ex-RAF and an old colleague of mine so you will be in very good hands, I promise you," the Air Chief said, firmly.

"I trust your judgement," Ryan said, not trusting it at all. It was to be a day of extremely limited choices, and it was his idea to fly up there, after all.

The Air Chief Marshall pointed towards the steps leading up to the door of the jet, where a pilot and a young male air steward were waiting. Ryan's entourage began to board with Darren Fine trailing at the back, still holding his sickbag. He had thrown up once more as soon as he left the Chinook. Someone had passed him some water to rinse out his mouth before he came on board. The Captain smiled at Ryan, as he boarded the aircraft. Another firm handshake, but by the time the steward had shown Ryan to his seat, he had already forgotten their names. The seats in the small craft were luxurious white leather with ample leg room. Ryan felt himself sink down into his. He hadn't got much sleep the night before. It was now seven o'clock in the evening and fatigue was beginning to kick in. The rest of his party, including General Spears, Fine, the two security men and some other odds and sods who were hitching what available space was left, came on board. The plane was soon taxiing for take-off. By then, Ryan's eyes were already drooping.

"You look exhausted." It was Jennifer, his PA. She had taken the seat opposite him and, as before, she looked absolutely pristine, nothing out of place, and she even smelled good; probably the only person impervious to the odour of Fine's vomit, he thought, though some others had carried it with them onto the plane. How could she look this good, when he must give the appearance of someone who had been dragged all the way here from Whitehall under a truck?

"It's probably because I am. I didn't sleep much last night. I had some friends over who I hadn't seen in a while…"

Right. Yeah, that was true. Kind of. What he had had was two tranny cocks up his arse and a ton of Class A White up his nose, which had come as part of the evening's entertainment.

"I see," she replied. Ryan was trying to read her brief response, which only confirmed what he already knew. He was shit at reading people's thoughts and she didn't give anything away. She wore a light-coloured lipstick, a shade which he thought would look good on Candice. He made a mental note to ask her what brand it was at a more appropriate time. Candice was still on his mind. He knew he had hurt her, just when what they had was growing into something real. The sex was great, sure. But it was the conversations with her that he had begun to look forward to the most. He had to find a way to explain. He had to see her, somehow, and apologise. Still, he couldn't deal with all that now.

"Why don't you try and get a power nap? If there's anything you need to know between here and Scotland I can always wake you."

He couldn't argue with that logic. An hour's nap sounded good. He set the chair back, hoping the steward wouldn't ask him to reset it before take-off. He never got the answer to his last question. He was asleep before the plane even left the runaway.

Candice looked good in her lime-green bikini, as they held hands. They were walking along a sandy white beach that felt soft beneath his feet, crumbling between his toes. Ryan had always wanted to take a long walk at such a picture-postcard location. They had rented one of the huts that extended out into the sea; the type that had a glass window next to the bed where you could look at the fish swimming. Outside, there was a deck sporting a jacuzzi where they could make love as the sun sank on the clear blue water horizon. He felt her hands run along his legs, there was a jolt and then he was awake.

It took Ryan a few moments to realise he had been dreaming, and the hand he felt tapping on his leg was that of his PA, Jennifer. "Sorry to wake you, Prime Minister. The Captain thought you might want to see this."

"You can call me Ryan. You're my assistant, after all. We shouldn't be so formal." His mouth felt dry. He grabbed a water bottle that had been placed next to him, downing the entire thing. He checked his watch and saw he had been asleep for well over an hour.

"I don't think that would be appropriate, Prime Minister," Jennifer replied.

"No, it wouldn't," Came the unmistakable voice of General Spears from above him. Ryan turned to see the man was standing in the aisle behind his seat. He had changed from his dress uniform into actual combat fatigues, presumably in the toilet. He was even wearing a peaked cammo cap.

"That's definitely your colour, General, you should wear it more often," he said, dryly. The General did not flinch at his sarcasm. "Where are we?"

"Look out of the window," the General replied, lifting a blind. Ryan peered out and at once he saw it. He couldn't miss it. To the left and below them was the saucer part of the ship. The circumference of it was so large the edge was only partly visible. He could not help but marvel at the alien structure beneath him. The images on the television had not prepared him for a close bird's eye view of Scotland's ship. The central ascending spire almost matched their own height; the top part of it was some way off to the side like a bright icicle pointing skyward. From this vantage point, he could see that the structure of the craft appeared completely smooth with no other markings. And it was glowing.

"Is it me, or is it glowing?" he said. Ryan noticed that the soft illumination coming from within the craft lit up the land around it for some distance. The General leaned in next to him to get a better look himself.

"There is some kind of light source that comes from within the ship, we think to time with the sun going down. Its glow can be seen from a considerable distance away.'

"How tall is the tower in the middle?" Ryan asked, looking at the central spire.

"Ours is estimated to be over two miles in height. We're at 15,000 feet now, so we're about 5000 feet above it."

Ryan couldn't even guess how wide the saucer part of the object was, but it was several miles. He noticed a number of tiny black shapes on the surface of the ship, moving around like frantic ants. He thought them to be jeeps, but at this distance, he really couldn't say. Several helicopters below them buzzed back and forth, including another Chinook, which was in the process of removing the double-decker bus from the surface of the ship.

"This is the captain, we're 2 minutes out from Aberdeen. Would you like me to circle round one more time for a second look, Prime Minister? I will, of course, maintain this distance." Ryan nodded at the General, who stood back in the aisle and gave a thumbs-up towards the cockpit. The jet banked around again, reducing speed and angling slightly to give everyone on board the best view possible. Ryan spotted the large military camp that had been set up to the south of the vessel, and just north of the River Dee. Groupings of tents, both small and large had been erected in field after field as though someone was putting on a music festival, only here, the theme of the festival was khaki green. Makeshift helicopter landing areas had been set up in the encampments to the south and east of the ship. The plane turned to afford them a view of the second one. The eastern camp was a far smaller grouping of structures and was lit up by clusters of powerful portable floodlights. Several large white and green tents had been erected in fields adjacent to a small collection of grey stone cottages and a farm, which seemed from the air, to Ryan at least, to be very Napoleonic in its design. It had a square courtyard in the middle and paddocks on all sides. Vehicles of all types were coming and going from the area and Ryan could see well-lit checkpoints further along the road to the east, in the direction of the city. This had all been set up incredibly fast, making him wonder when the ships had first actually been detected. A question for later on.

"That's where the science team are based. Doctor Jacobs and her team," the General said, pointing to the collection of tents around the farmhouse.

A string of lights had been erected on the surface of the vessel, forming two columns. One heading up from the camp in the south to the central part of the vessel, and another from the eastern encampment doing the same. These acted as a guide for the small vehicles travelling back and forth to the central part of the ship, where the activity on the surface was focused. A Chinook rose into the air below them and began to fly east, the distinctive city bus swinging from cables underneath it.

"What are they going to do with the bus?" Ryan wasn't sure why he asked, but it had occurred to him that flying it over Aberdeen City Centre might raise more questions than they had time to answer right now.

"It's going to the science team for analysis and a clean-up check. Seen enough?" asked the General. Ryan nodded.

"Once we land at Aberdeen, we have a helicopter assigned to take us straight to the camp to meet Doctor Jacobs."

"What's she like?" Ryan asked.

"You'll see." The General returned to his seat. The helicopter would save a drive at least, though Ryan suspected Fine would probably want to take a car. His stomach growled loudly. Apart from coffee and biscuits, he hadn't eaten a thing all day. He sat up in his seat and wondered if he might be able to charm the cabin crew into getting him some food. He remembered that the steward was male, almost certainly gay, which may well have worked in his favour, but he was unable to explore this further because the captain announced they were doing final checks before landing. He took a final glance at the alien ship. Its central structure was almost royal in appearance, conveying the sense of a regal palace, a magical tower like you'd find in fairy tales. Though he could see the texture of the entire surface had a cream marble-like quality, there appeared to be a second set of fainter marks underneath the surface, which Ryan thought was odd. They could have almost been veins, yet there was nothing else organic about the ship at all. It could have almost been carved out of stone.

A voice came over the tannoy. "Okay, I am going to take us into Aberdeen International now. Would everyone please strap in and buckle up? The time is just coming up to 8.20 p.m. I just want to take the chance to wish our new Prime Minister, Ryan Wallace, good luck, we're all behind you, sir."

Ryan hadn't expected that. It was good to be well thought of by the pilot, seeing as his life was entirely in the man's hands until they landed. He smiled over at Jennifer, expecting her to acknowledge the compliment he had been given but she folded her arms and looked out of the window. Probably a lot on her mind, Ryan thought. The Air Chief Marshall had been right about the pilot, it was the smoothest landing of a plane Ryan could ever recall. As they disembarked, Ryan noticed the prominent glow emanating from west. The saucer section of the ship was not visible from the top of the gantry steps, but the white tower of the alien ship still completely dominated the skyline, visible even from this distance. Ryan made sure to shake the pilot's hand as he left, and also thanked the steward, forgetting both of their names instantly. Treat the little people right, at all times, even if you cannot remember who they are. A valuable lesson that many were not good at embracing, but it was something his mother had drilled into him from an early age. He was rude to their cleaner once, and she had given him a hiding he had never forgotten. Awaiting their arrival was a man dressed in combat fatigues who exchanged salutes with General Spears. Ryan then caught part of their conversation as he descended from the plane.

"So far there is no report of radiation of any kind, and, as far as we can tell, no communication from the ship, nor, as far as we know, from any of the others from around the world. There is still no sign of a way inside, though one of our pilots swore he saw an opening during the incident with the bus. Doctor Jacobs can give you the most up to date information."

A small convoy of black 4 x 4s was waiting and everyone in their group quickly entered the car assigned to them. Aberdeen International was a small airport and the vehicles did not need to travel very far, but he was glad they didn't have to walk it. Ryan found the place to be similar in size to the airport at Nice, but it was hard to tell at this time of night. The glow from the alien tower reflected off the white walls of the main terminal building, giving the structure an eerie appearance in the cold night air. A small number of private jets littered the side of the main runaway, but most of the parking bays for commercial planes were empty. The traffic that had been due to land here had been diverted elsewhere. He overheard someone saying the airport closed soon after the spaceship had been sighted coming in from the North Sea. The small group of cars drove across to the adjacent heliport, where a number of military and civilian helicopters were landing and taking off. Nearby, two large silver Hercules transport planes were unloading their cargo and already refuelling.

"This is where we are supplying our forward-operating bases from. Everything you see here is connected to the security operation around the ship," said General Spears. Ryan nodded, imagining that anyone flying from here with Easyjet who had holiday plans tomorrow, was going to be sorely disappointed. Jennifer offered Ryan a polo mint. He snatched the packet from her, shovelling the whole packet in his mouth. He'd eaten them all by the time the cars came to a halt in front of one of the hangers.

"I think the Prime Minister may need to eat," Jennifer said. She was sitting in the back of the car with him. Spears had elected to sit in the front. He dismissed the idea. "There will be time to eat later.'" Jennifer took a look at Ryan, pale and tense, and leaned into the gap between the front seats.

"He hasn't eaten a proper meal all day. Now, if you do not get him some food he will suffer from exhaustion and then he will not be able to function properly. Do you want him making important decisions in that kind of state? Because I don't." Jennifer sat back and folded her arms. *Way to go Jennifer*, thought Ryan. He liked this new PA of his. He might have to give her a raise.

"There's a mess hall set up over there. I'll see what they have but we'll have to be quick,' the General said, through gritted teeth.

"They say an army marches on its stomach," Ryan said, thinking the remark appropriate, because it was true. The General stopped the car and waved everyone out. The dark night was now fully upon them, but the tarmac and hangers of the airport were lit by multiple sources. Total darkness would only come to this corner of the world if there was a power cut. Darren Fine excused himself and headed off to a row of portaloos that stood by the entrance to a large marquee, from which drifted the smell of cooked food. The General led the small group inside the spacious tent. Ryan sat down at the end of a long, empty, wooden table. The marquee was huge. It had the capacity to seat up to two hundred people and Ryan was again impressed by how quickly such facilities had been erected and organised. Sitting in one corner eating a late meal, was a motley collection of ground crew and maintenance men. No doubt like him, they just grabbed their food when they could. Otherwise, the place was empty, except for two cooks with white aprons over their camouflage fatigues.

"This seems to have been set up very efficiently, General," Almost too efficiently, Ryan thought.

"I believe very strongly in the six *Ps*, Prime Minister. *Proper preparation prevents piss poor performance.* We simply adapted plans from similar scenarios."

Ryan couldn't help but wonder how many similar scenarios there were to two hundred alien ships landing worldwide. He sat down with Jennifer, while General Spears went to speak to the two cooks about getting some food. Ryan noticed that his new security duo Dilks and Willis did not sit down, but just stood, surveying the area.

"When are you guys going to eat?" Ryan asked, wondering when they'd had their last meal.

"Don't worry about us, Prime Minister. We'll be fine."

Ryan wasn't going to leave it there. "General Spears, can you have two additional armed men come and stand guard, in the unlikely event that there is going to be a terrorist assault on the mess tent in the next fifteen minutes, so that my security detail can have a quick bite to eat? Crockett and Tubbs here are hungry."

Willis, the younger of the two men, stepped forward. He was well-spoken, unlike Dilks, who sounded a little more *Albert Square.*

"That really isn't necessary, Prime Minister..." Ryan cut him off.

"I will decide what is necessary. You'll be able to function better if you've eaten something, won't you? General Spears, the soldiers if you please. If it's not too much trouble."

Spears glared back at him, abruptly turned and left the tent in search of two spare men. Jennifer let out a little chuckle.

"You're going to have to be careful with him," she whispered to him. Ryan turned to Willis and Dilks, pointing over to the row of steaming metal containers, where the cooks stood waiting. "Off you go then, grab some chow and sit down."

Dilks signalled for Willis to go, while he remained on guard until a minute later when two soldiers appeared at the mess tent door. One stood by the entrance with a rifle, and the second came and stood by the table.

"Excellent, now we have someone who can pass us the salt," said Ryan.

The soldier didn't even blink, simply standing on guard reminding him of those who stood outside Buckingham Palace resisting all attempts to laugh as annoying tourists took even more annoying photographs. General Spears had not returned with the men, and Ryan wondered what he was getting up to. A woman dressed in combat fatigues came over and put two plates down in front of them. It was a meat stew, potatoes and veg and was still steaming hot. To Ryan it looked like the best thing he had seen all day. It tasted good and every piece of food dropped into his stomach as though it were entering a bottomless pit. Jennifer looked down at hers and pushed it away. He was going to ask why, when his attention was drawn to the group of ground crewmen eating in the far corner, talking in hushed whispers while occasionally stealing a glance in their direction. As he greedily ate his meal he wondered what they made of him, the country's new Prime Minister, eating dinner in a RAF mess tent.

"Is there a vegetarian option?" Jennifer asked the female soldier.

"Yes. Don't eat the meat," came the curt reply from the woman.

"Excuse me!" Ryan said the words so loudly, that both the cooks and the table of seven ground crew all looked up simultaneously. Ryan had directed the comment at the female soldier as she'd turned. She did an about face and came and stood in front of Ryan, standing to attention.

"Sir?"

"You don't have to refer me as sir, Private. I don't hold a rank in the army. Just Prime Minister will suffice."

"Can I help you with something, Prime Minister?" The Private asked.

"My assistant has had a really long journey and an extremely busy day, as I am sure you can imagine. No doubt you have had one yourself. So if it's not too much trouble, perhaps you could just get us another plate of vegetables, no meat. Thank you."

Jennifer looked as though she was going to interrupt him, but then clearly thought better of it. The Private did an about face and returned to the cooks, who produced another plate. She came back to the table and banged the plate down. Ryan stared at her a moment. Jennifer said nothing.

"Anything else, sir?" the Private asked.

"No, thank you. Keep up the good work."

The woman glared at both him and Jennifer before turning around and leaving the tent.

"Clearly she wasn't one for a bit of female solidarity." Ryan said with his mouthful.

"I don't need you to fight my battles, thank you, Prime Minister. You're going to have enough of your own to deal with," Jennifer said, taking her first mouthful of food.

"You got me my food, I got you yours." Ryan replied.

Having finished his own meal, Ryan got up and decided to go over to the cooks and introduce himself. The soldier assigned to him went with him. Ryan was a Prime Minister now and that meant shaking people's hands and smiling, whenever and wherever possible, a role not entirely dissimilar to that of the Queen. He introduced himself to the two cooks, asked them where they were from, forgetting immediately, thanked them for a wonderful meal and then went over to the table containing the ground crew. Dilks and Willis were watching his every move as they quickly ate their food. The soldier assigned to him diligently stood close by. Jennifer observed Ryan moving around the room with curiosity, as General Spears came back into the marquee. He had a plate in his hand. His food looked as though it had been specially prepared. He sat opposite Jennifer and dug into his meal.

"What's that?" Jennifer gestured towards his plate with her fork as she ate the last of her potatoes.

"I have lactose intolerance and some allergy issues. They always prepare my food separately," he said, calmly tucking into his dinner. He observed Ryan's actions.

"What is he doing?" the General asked.

"Introducing himself to the troops," Jennifer replied and turned her attention to the remaining carrots on her plate.

Ryan approached the group of seven men with a smile, handshake at the ready. They all looked to be under the age of thirty, with bright, fresh handsome faces. Most were Royal Air Force personnel, but two were regular Army Privates. Ryan presumed they had been asked by the others to join them for dinner.

"Good evening, gentlemen. Ryan Wallace. I just wanted to thank you for working so hard and keeping a cool head in such unusual times." He stretched his hand out to the first man, who looked to be one of the youngest, and Ryan hoped, least cynical. After a brief pause he took it and shook hands with him. Everyone in the military, it seemed, had an extremely firm grip.

"I saw your speech today. About what it means to be British and giving an example to the world…" the young man said.

The heads around the table nodded, indicating to Ryan that they had all watched it.

"Great. Glad you got to see it. Was it okay?"

"It was pretty good, Prime Minister, considering you were thrown into this job only a few hours ago."

Everyone murmured in agreement. Ryan shook the hands of the other men, the last one posing a question to him as he did so.

"It was very inspiring what you said. Did you write that yourself?"

Ryan caught Jennifer's eye looking over at him just as Darren Fine entered the mess tent, looking a little better. He went straight over to the cooks to get some food.

"I had a little help," Ryan said. "But I certainly meant every word of it."

The youngest man looked up at him, speaking with a most sincere tone.

"Why do you think they're here, sir? I mean, what do they want?"

What, indeed? Ryan would have liked to know the answers to those questions himself, but at the moment he probably knew less than the crewman did.

"That's what I'm here to find out, if I can. I know you're doing a dangerous job up here, in the eye of the storm as it were. I thought it was important that I showed you I was willing to come here myself and if possible, speak to them in person."

The men seemed impressed by his answer, but the only problem was at the moment there wasn't a *them* to speak to. Just an object the size of a city, with no apparent way inside.

"Anyway, gentlemen, I had better go. I just wanted to thank you personally. You must be working around the clock with all the comings and goings here."

"That we are, Prime Minister. This is the first break we've had all day."

"I had best let you get some dessert, then." Ryan shook the hand of the youngest man a second time and patted him on the shoulder, instantly feeling it was perhaps a little patronising. He returned to the table where Dilks and Willis, having bolted their food down, were now standing. General Spears waved away the additional guards he had assigned with the words, "Get some scran, lads."

"Your men here have been working flat out, General." Ryan remarked / Jennifer nodded in agreement. "But considering the crisis only started this afternoon, I'm very impressed by how fast this has all come together."

General Spears sipped some water to wash down his food, then took up a napkin, dabbing at his mouth. He took out a map from his top pocket, which already had the circular outline of the vessel drawn on it with a black marker pen. Around it were various other markings and crosses, indicating what Ryan assumed were military deployments in the area. The General spread the map out on the table, as he spoke. Jennifer leaned in with fascination. "We simply implemented an emergency action response plan, not dissimilar to the kind of thing we would implement in London, for a terrorist attack. It is a somewhat different scenario, of course. The GCHQ is set up here, so any time you want to talk to Cobra, you can do so in the building just across from the hangar, outside. At the moment, we have two FOBs at the perimeter of the ship, with several more checkpoints around the entire thing…'

Ryan put a hand up to stop him.

"Sorry General, I'm not a military expert. I know GCHQ, but FOB?'

"Right, yes. I must remember you're not a tactical man. Forward Operating Base. We have two. One in the south with a large ground force deployed there, currently two battalions of marines from 3 Commando. They're deploying around the southern perimeter of the ship. They're reinforced by 7th Armoured Brigade, some of whom arrived this evening, and the rest will be arriving tomorrow. Together they will secure the landing site and provide security and protection, should we need it.'

"Is it your opinion that they're going to attack? That this is a prelude to invasion?" It was a question Ryan had constantly turned over in his mind on the journey up to Scotland.

"It is possible, and until we know otherwise it is my job to assume they might, and make our depositions accordingly. We still don't know what's inside it, for one thing. The Science Team will be able to tell you more about that. I'll be taking you there as soon as you're ready. They're located here on at the second FOB, just east of the ship.'

Fine had said nothing since sitting down with his plate of food in front of him, eating it slowly in small mouthfuls.

"How are you feeling Mr Fine?" Ryan asked, trying to sound as sincere as possible.

"I'll be alright, as long as we don't have to get in another helicopter."

"We're about to board a second one to the landing site," General Spears said.

"Would you mind if I took a car and met you there, Prime Minister?" Fine asked weakly, his face still looking a little green.

"Take your time." *You have to enjoy the small pleasures in life*, Ryan thought.

Moments later, their small party, consisting of himself, Willis, Dilks, Jennifer, General Spears and his aide boarded a smaller helicopter bound for the east FOB. Ryan noted a hastily painted sign had been placed near the hangars, inscribed with the words *Camp ET*. It felt appropriate.

The helicopter took off and headed east over the Kirkhill Industrial Estate, which sat next to the airport. Ryan could see that more transport planes were arriving as they left. The landscape below them had a strange light to it with the rows of trees and houses all throwing shadows around them, as if lit by a low hanging sun. Ryan knew the shadows could only be caused by one thing; the light source coming from the tower of the ship. The helicopter followed the line of the A road which ran all the way from the city centre towards the landing site. The dual carriageway was joined by a B road from the south, which twisted and turned west through the

Scottish countryside. Their helicopter turned to follow it. Wherever there was a road heading west towards the landing site, Ryan saw another well-lit military roadblock; normally, four men with a vehicle next to a barricade, sometimes accompanied by the flashing lights of the boys in blue. Just as well, they couldn't have more people coming out to see this thing for a Sunday jaunt. He wondered how the local Police were coping. His thoughts turned back to London.

"Jennifer, call Cobra and ask them to put me through on a conference call."

Jennifer duly complied and passed him the phone. "Ryan Wallace here, who I am on with?"

"It's Julie Compston here, Prime Minister. I'm here with Commissioner Winston…" Ryan thought he heard a male voice correcting her in the background. "That's Sir Winston…" Yes, that was him all right.

"Right… we have the Deputy Prime Minister on the line with us from Kenya…"

The conversation was short. Ryan wanted an update on what the population of London was doing. Several thousand people had fled the city, resulting in the motorways leading to the West Country being clogged with traffic. But many, it seemed, had elected to stay. All public services were running at 80 percent or higher efficiency, while the NHS was running at 95% capacity. The Emergency Services were coping, just. There had been an alarming number of suicides, but as yet, rioting and looting had not yet broken out. As Baroness Childs put it with her one contribution to the conversation: "An uneasy calm is hovering over the city, but how long it would last was anyone's guess."

The Army Reserve had all been called up, and were ready to deploy, if needed. The Fire Brigade were at full strength, manned and ready. London stood firm, waiting to see what the next day would bring. The Deputy Prime Minister had little to offer. The Kenyans did not want anything to fly in their airspace until they had determined it was safe for to do so. The combination of the arrival of several ships in Africa, and events in Paris had made them extremely reluctant to let him go anywhere. He was, in any case, out of action, with both his legs broken following the car crash that occurred shortly after one of the ships landed just north of the capital, Nairobi. Offers had been made to get him out of the country by sea or overland, but with his current injuries neither journey appealed. It was agreed for the moment he should remain where he was. Ryan would stay in charge for now. Ryan sensed the man honestly didn't want the job, and frankly he couldn't blame him. He ended the call by suggesting they should all get some sleep, and that Cobra would reconvene at daybreak, 6am, should nothing else happen in the meantime. He would try and get some rest himself before coming back to London. Fat chance of that.

The helicopter passed over the small town of Elric, which was in the process of being evacuated. As Ryan had been on his call he caught sight of several families and the elderly being loaded up onto convoys of trucks that were heading east, back to Aberdeen. He wondered where people would stay, making a mental note to ask what the legality would be for taking control of hotels in a time of a national emergency.

The helicopter proceeded to land in a field marked with portable rotating lights, behind what turned out to be a rather quaint-looking Scottish country pub, The Garlogie Inn; a small unimposing white two-storey building that had the second level built into the attic as an extension. Outside the pub, a number of soldiers sat drinking steaming coffee on wooden tables. Upon leaving the helicopter, General Spears was greeted by a younger officer. Some words were exchanged between them, before he saluted and went elsewhere. A series of khaki tents had been erected in the adjacent fields, on both sides of the road. Ryan wondered if the pub served food and what its review rating was on Tripadvisor. Perhaps he could have his meeting with Doctor Jacobs there, and get a decent shot of local whisky. Shortly after disembarking, both he and Jennifer were handed padded camouflage jackets by another soldier who advised them to wear them for their own comfort. Ryan immediately put it on. The night was chilly, and it was a relief for Ryan to inhale air that was not filled with the odour of jet fuels. The air in this part of the country was noticeably different from London. It was, Ryan thought, remarkably different from anywhere he had travelled in the world. As he breathed it in, he couldn't help but notice how clean it was.

"Is the air always as clean as this in Scotland?" he asked.

The General was out of earshot. Jennifer gave him an odd look.

"We're not in London any more, Prime Minister."

The General returned with a high-ranking officer who was introduced as Colonel Saunders. Ryan thought that was the name of the guy behind the Kentucky Fried Chicken franchise, but decided it was best not to mention that. All of the group were handed a pair of Raybans and issued passes by the aide, who accompanied the general. Ryan wondered why they needed dark glasses at night. He wanted to ask the aide, but couldn't remember his name. The Colonel informed them he was going to drive them personally to their next destination. The group jumped into a 4 x 4 jeep and drove a short distance towards the ship. It was only one hundred metres or so, a distance Ryan thought they probably could have walked, but the road ahead was so brightly lit, it was painful to look at. The body of the ship cut right across the road in front of them, filling the gap between two hills. Ryan noticed it would have been possible to drive across the lip of the saucer and onto its surface directly from the road without much difficulty. The glowing tower dominated the sky, posing so many questions.

Two grey stone farmhouses occupied the fields just to the east of the saucer's perimeter. The jeep turned into the drive of the second of these, a private cottage that had been requisitioned by the army, no doubt, Ryan suspected, in the face of considerable protest by the owners. The area was swarming with activity. White tents had been erected in the fields and gardens behind the buildings. There was a hospital tent with a red cross marked on it. For the first time, Ryan saw a number of civilian personnel, all with visible security passes hanging from lanyards around their necks. Colonel Saunders pulled the jeep to a halt outside the front of the cottage. It was a two-storey building, typical of many in the area but this one had been fully renovated and extended, expanding it to twice its original size.

"The briefing room the civvies have set up is out back, sir," the Colonel said, pointing to a path that went around the side of the house.

The men exchanged salutes and Colonel Saunders jumped back in the jeep and headed back the way they'd come. A second jeep pulled up, bringing Dilks and Willis, who quickly rejoined the party. Ryan noticed their eyes darting in every direction as they surveyed the busy scene around them.

"What are you checking for now?" Ryan asked.

"Everything and anything, sir," Willis replied, without making eye contact.

"But we're inside the army perimeter now. Surely the risk is minimal?"

"Don't tell us how to do our job, Prime Minister and I won't tell you how to do yours. Is that a deal?" Willis's eyes had now locked with Ryan's. He could see the man was deadly serious.

"Deal." Ryan needed a piss and it wouldn't wait.

"This way, Prime Minister," the General said, already leading them away round the back of the house.

"Hang on a moment." Ryan strolled over to the trees at the side of the garden and whipped his cock out, almost crying in relief as he unleashed probably the biggest and longest stream of urine he had ever deposited in the world. It was dark, so he couldn't see the flowerbed below his feet, nor did he notice the soldier standing by the entrance to the house who thought this might be an interesting time to get his phone out. He returned to his group with a visible expression of relief on his face.

"That's better. Shall we?"

General Spears shot him a look of disapproval. .

"You're aware there's a row of portaloos at the front of the house, Prime Minister?' Jennifer said, pointing them out to him. Ryan hadn't seen them. Oh well. Now that he'd had a piss he could actually think properly. The group walked along the track past the first cottage, and came into a small courtyard with two more similar-looking dwellings. Evidently, people had been billeted in the cottages and he thought of the dirty army boots that must be trudging up and down on someone's clean carpets and nicely tiled floors at that very moment. Someone, somewhere where would be very upset when they came home, but this was a National Emergency. Besides, the owners should be grateful the aliens hadn't razed the entire farm to the ground with a ray gun. A number of Land Rovers filled up the parking bays, while small groups of soldiers and civilians were moving purposefully back and forth between the buildings. A starlight truck was parked up next to the largest house and the buzz of several large portable generators hummed close by.

"Where are the owners?" Jennifer asked.

"In London at the moment, I believe. We've been in touch with them, they're going to stay down there. No one wants to be within one hundred miles of this thing. It's about one hundred metres from the rear of that cottage, to the edge of the saucer from here. We have a path of lights set up on the surface going all the way to the centre, a distance of just under three kilometres.'

"Hell of an electric bill," Ryan joked.

"As you can see, we brought our own power. So this is officially known as Camp Heart, or the FOB with the scientific emphasis. All the scientific personnel are based here, either in tents or billeted in these buildings. We also occupy the next farm along from this one."

Behind the neat collection of dwellings sat a low, sloping field that was occupied by two large marquee-sized tents. The area was well-illuminated, primarily by the saucer. Several light towers had been erected, and tape marked a path where metallic steps had been erected over a low stone wall, to allow access to the field from the cottages with ease. It reminded Ryan of the bridge that allowed contestants to enter *The Big Brother House*. A man swore loudly at the arrival of a blue Land Rover. Ryan noted the uniformed officer. He wore the red cap and MP armband of the Military Police. He was in the process of bollocking the female driver as she disembarked from the vehicle. She completely ignored the torrent of expletives he hurled at her. She was followed by three other civilians, all of them wearing what Ryan could only describe politely as white sperm suits. The sort you would see on an episode of CSI. Upon seeing the identity of the driver, the Red-cap offered an immediate apology.

"Sorry Doctor Jacobs, I didn't know it was you. Can you have someone park it just outside please? The Prime Minister is expected to arrive at any moment."

The Red-cap seemed oblivious to the fact that he, the Prime Minister was already here. Camp inter-communication was not quite up to scratch yet, then. Ryan eyed Doctor Jacobs. She was in her forties, with a short, dirty blonde bob and glasses, which Ryan thought had always been a mandatory accessory where scientists were concerned. She was incredibly petite in stature, but her voice had a natural projection and her words could be distinguished quite easily from all the bustle around her.

"Great, when that young fucker gets here he can find his own fucking parking spot! I have work to do!"

Ryan had always thought of himself as a young fucker, in a quite literal sense, so it was nice to hear someone of such high intellectual stock refer to him as such. The Doctor was already on her way to the metallic steps that bridged the wall from the courtyard to the field, when General Spears saved him the trouble and called over to her.

"Doctor Jacobs, this is Prime Minister Wallace." the General gestured to Ryan, who stood just behind him. Ryan stepped forwards and offered his hand, which she shook, very quickly.

"Ah, so you came up then! I thought they were joking. Follow me, Prime Minister. If you want an update, my team and I are about to do a briefing. I don't have time to mess about!" She pushed her glasses back on her nose and strode up over the wall and towards the larger of the two tents on the sloping field. Ryan realised a second too late that his hand was still wet with his own urine. Oh well, she was a scientist, after all, she should be able to take urine samples in her stride.

"Lead the way." He followed her over the temporary metal steps.

"I guess this is what it feels like to enter the Big Brother house, then?" Ryan said.

"It's actually called Garlogie Hall," said Jennifer.

"How do you know that? You're not from round here are you?" Ryan asked.

"No, there was a sign by the road on the way in," she replied flatly.

"Really? Couldn't we have all met in the hall then, or would that be too logical?"

Ryan supposed that perhaps the scientists liked the great outdoors. His foot hit something as they walked across the wet grass. He looked down and noticed he had clipped what appeared to be the top of a pineapple. *What an odd place to leave discarded tropical fruit,* he thought. Before he entered the tent he turned once more to look at the ship. The single pointed shaft of its central tower looked almost magical in the night sky. It was time to find out what it was doing here.

Inside the tent, the layout was unusual, as it had been erected on uneven ground. Three dozen foldable chairs had been laid out in rows, all facing the door. A second opening on the side of the room provided access for a number of cables, where a large screen had been erected just to the left of the entrance. Ryan noticed the room was full of people wearing lab attire, but others were just dressed in duffle coats and puffa jackets. No one here was going to win any awards for fashion or hygiene, with Ryan spotting at least one man with crisp fragments nestled in his beard. Beyond the screen and the chairs, the room was bare, apart from two laptop worksta-tions sitting off to one side on a rickety foldout table. The men and women in the room were all between twenty-five and fifty years old. They could have been on a night out in Shoreditch, with the men all sporting their oversized beards and the women in designer glasses. Underneath the open lab coats were check shirts, sweaters and cardigans. Footwear appeared to be everything from pink trainers to flip-flops and Caterpillar boots. It was an odd mix of people, and reminded him of the members of the old televi-sion show *Castaway*, where a bunch of social misfits and media whores were stuck on an island in Scotland somewhere for a year. Ryan only remembered it because it was so fucking boring and trounced in the ratings by the first season of Channel 4's Big Brother. Any idea that they knew the Prime Minister was dropping in was quickly dispelled. The group barely reacted to his presence and continued to talk among themselves. Someone, somewhere was eating a wonderful-smelling bacon sandwich. Ryan could see Jennifer's face react in disgust to the smell of the roasted pork, but he was licking his lips. That was her crossed off his soulmate list. He loved bacon. With a loud clap of the hands, Doctor Jacobs brought the room to attention in an almost teacher-like manner, causing Ryan to wonder what her previous occupation had been. Chemistry teacher perhaps?

"Right then boys and girls, all the teams are back in from tonight's little jaunt to the surface of our new-found friends up the road. So, what do we know and what can we prove? Lights off please."

Ryan noticed several military personnel slip into the tent at the last minute to join the briefing. Ryan and Jennifer stood at the back with General Spears. Just as the last group came into the tent, Darren Fine arrived behind them looking lost and still somewhat pale. Jennifer waved him over to their group.

"We've been joined by some of our friends from the military, who have informed me that you will not be getting past any of the checkpoints from here on in without your passes!" Jacobs held up the card she was wearing on a red lanyard around her neck. "So please, keep them with you at all times. We also have some special guests with us from the government. As we're pushed for time, I'll skip the introductions."

Ryan was relieved. Fine fumbled his way to the back of the room and came to sit down just in front of Dilks and Willis, whose eyes scanned the room. Doctor Jacobs waited for Fine to sit down before switching on the screen. A bird's-eye satellight image view of the landing site appeared.

"Everyone sitting comfortably? Good. So far, what we know is our ship, which has been designated with the call sign *UKS1* – is seven kilometres in diameter at its widest point. At about two kilometres in from the centre, it forms a gradual upward gradient towards the central tower, which itself is just over two kilometres in height. We can see here from the satellite image that it covers the entire area known as The Birks and several of the outlying villages. Seismic tests into the soil surrounding the ship suggest it's penetrated at least two kilometres into the earth at its deepest point, though we're still waiting more confirmation on that. Our walk around the vessel has provided us with pretty much nothing that we don't already know. There is no visible way in. Not just on the saucer section surface but on the central tower too. Jane, however, has discovered something interesting. Jane?"

A short oriental woman stood up who was even smaller than Doctor Jacobs. *Were all female Doctors this short?* Ryan couldn't help but wonder. Jane sounded as though she was educated in England but she still had a soft oriental accent that Ryan thought had a trace of Japanese. "She went to Cambridge..." Jennifer whispered into his ear. Damn she smelled good, and she could read his mind. He tried to remain stoic.

"These pictures are of the same ship designated UKS1, coming in over the North Sea earlier today. This is a satellite photograph of the same object, taken around the same time. You can see if we compare the earlier images to the one taken this evening, the ship is not the same size in circumference as it appeared to be in the earlier image. Here we guess the distance of the widest part of the circumference to be eighteen kilometres."

"That can't be right, that's wider than London!" Fine whispered. Ryan was confused. He needed to clarify this. He stood up as he spoke.

"Sorry, Jane is it? Are you trying to tell us that the craft has changed shape since it landed?"

"Shape? No, the shape is still basically the same, but it has changed size and reduced its diameter. Since landing, its mass has decreased and the circumference of the object at its widest is now less than half the width it was when it arrived in the Earth's atmosphere."

"How is that possible?" Ryan pressed. Jacobs was not pleased to hear him interrupting her presentation.

"This is a scientific presentation, not a Q and A at the Odeon on a Wednesday. Please carry on, Jane." Ryan felt Jennifer tug at his jacket, and sat down. A few people in the room had now noticed him and there were more than a few turning heads accompanied by murmurs in his direction.

"We have confirmation that the same thing has happened with several other ships. This one..."

Jane changed the picture and zoomed in on a satellite image showing the lower boot of Italy where a large circular object could be seen clearly from a vast distance away, bestriding the sea with ease touching the land masses either side of it.

"This one was the same shape and size as our own ship UKS1. The vessel, which we shall call ITEU1 - I didn't make up the designations, that was all Susan... sorry... this one is now fifty kilometres in diameter. It is so large that the edge of the saucer sits upon one part of the coast of Italy in the east, and touches another beach here in the west. For it to have occupied this much space, we estimate it would have had to increase its mass by at least three times since it first arrived."

The woman stepped aside, and Jacobs once again had the floor.

"Thank you Jane. So they can change size. I know what you're thinking. Are they organic? Are they draining something from the Earth, somehow? Perhaps they've come here to consume the water... So far, having consulted with my colleagues from around the world, there is nothing which would bring me to any of those conclusions, but it is of course very early days. So what are they made of? Simply put, we do not know. It appears to be some kind of solid alloy, but every attempt we have made to try and get a sample, even scrape the smallest fragment from this thing has met with no success. Drill bits have been broken as have blades. Everything we've tried has had absolutely no effect. Then earlier today, this happened...."

Doctor Jacobs loaded up a clip marked *UKS1 Diary 70 Group 3 – Doctor Hesketh-Gardener*. Ryan could see that the clip had been shot earlier that day and showed several scientists milling around a small drill bit on the surface of the object. People were losing their patience, when one of the security detail whose face Ryan could not see pulled out a pistol and fired it into the surface in frustration. The bullet ricocheted straight into the leg of the team leader, who began to swear and cry like a child. *Shit* - thought Ryan *that had to bloody hurt!* Jacobs paused the video. The expression of said scientist was caught in close-up, with the most intense look of pain someone could have possibly experienced.

"Yeah, so if anyone is wondering where Clive is, he's in the medical tent right now having a bullet removed from his leg by an army surgeon..."

This caused a massive grumble of discontent from all those present. Ryan watched in disbelief. Comments about the military and their *shoot first ask questions later* tendencies abounded. Someone remarked loudly, within deliberate earshot of General Spears, that they shouldn't even be here and their presence would only increase the likelihood of something going wrong.

"Who was the bloody idiot that fired the gun?" shouted Jane angrily.

"We're trying to deal with *First Contact* here and your men are behaving like bloody idiots!' said another man.

"Okay, that's it, settle down everyone," said Doctor Jacobs. "I've asked all the senior army officers operating out of the southern FOB here to see this. So they can see just how dangerous such actions can be. Moments later, this is what happened..."

Jacobs resumed the clip and the wounded doctor continued to scream, his blood spilling onto the surface of the ship. Then, off-camera, someone else could be heard screaming. The person operating the camera turned to show a member of the security team, dressed in black combat fatigues, who had dropped his weapon. Someone called out, "What happened?" He cried out, "Look at my hands!" The camera showed his gloves had been burnt through and his charred flesh could be glimpsed through the holes. The soldier began to shed his weapons. A second rifle was thrown down on the surface and he doubled over, throwing up. The other men in the unit also dropped their weapons, falling about in agony. Jacobs paused the image.

"Something from within the ship saw this man as a threat, which he was, and made his weapons burn him."

One of the army officers whom Ryan had noticed was a late arrival, was lingering by the door.

"How can you be sure that it wasn't a misfire or weapons jam that burned his hand? What actual proof do you have that this ship was somehow responsible? Who is to say that it wasn't your team drilling into the skin of this thing that was perceived as the actual act of aggression?" Ryan wondered if the soldier who had fired the weapon served under his command, and he was looking to place the blame on someone else for his failings. It certainly sounded like it. It was exactly what Ryan would do.

Doctor Jacobs wasn't having any of it.

"Well, there is a very easy way to find out if the ship is behind this or not, Captain. Why don't you have ten of your men take a cow, or other animal that's going to be butchered anyway, as I don't want to offend any of the vegetarians present in the room, out onto the surface and have them fire at it and see what happens. I'd certainly be keen to know the result!"

Ryan decided this was a good time to cut in. "That sounds like a very sensible suggestion to me. What else do you know, Doctor? My time here is rather limited." He wanted to go and see this thing for himself, so he thought it was best to cut through the bullshit.

"Sorry everyone, just for clarity, the man asking all the questions at the back is the newly appointed Prime Minister, Ryan Wallace."

This drew gasps from those inside the tent who had not yet caught on to his presence. Someone flicked on the lights. All eyes in the room were upon him. Ryan decided it was time to go on a charm offensive. Once again, he got to his feet.

"I came here because I wanted to see what was going on first-hand, but also because I wanted to assure the public that we are doing everything humanly possible to ensure their safety. So I just wanted to ask you, Doctor, so far, have you seen anything at all that would lead you to suspect that the intention of these ships is hostile?"

There was a moment's hesitation before she answered the question. "No, I haven't, I believe what you witnessed was an act of self-defence but there is so much we don't know and it hasn't even been twenty-four hours yet."

"I want to see this thing for myself. It doesn't seem as if it's dangerous. Will you take me up there?"

"I can't vouch for your safety," she stated. Ryan respected her lack of ambiguity.

"Don't worry, that's what I have these two guys for." Ryan gestured to the two men behind him. "Look, Helen - can I call you Helen?" Doctor Jacobs stood rooted, her expression unchanged. He already knew that sounded way too informal.

" I prefer Doctor Jacobs."

"Right, Doctor Jacobs. Basically, if I have this summed up, the one thing you know for certain is that these things have changed size, or the saucer bit has got larger or smaller, depending on which ship we're talking about around the world, smaller in the case of our one here. Now I have to address the nation again tomorrow, and there's a lot of people out there who are very scared. I'm not going to go on television and tell them, it changes size a bit. So if that's all you have for me, then I think I would like to take a walk on the surface of this thing for myself, because that may be the only course of action I can take in order to calm the nation."

"There could be radiation effects or other unknown effects to being this close to the object that we have yet to see or feel," she countered.

"What do your Geiger counters say?" Ryan asked.

"So far we haven't been able to detect any radiation at all."

"Does anyone on your team feel unwell?"

"No."

"And those people we took off the bus, I assume they're being held somewhere nearby?"

"Yes, we have them. Well, the army has them secured in a detention area. It's more like a free-standing cage really, with some cots in it, in the barn."

Basically imprisoned. This was going to be a public relations nightmare. Ryan would have something to keep Darren Fine busy after all.

"Sounds lovely. And are any of them showing any signs of being unwell?"

"No, in fact, we've spent most of the evening testing them in quarantine, we've only just put them back to the holding area."

"How did they check out?"

"Absolutely fine so far, Prime Minister. In fact, all three of them were in excellent health."

"Right... wait, did you say three of them?"

"Yes, the army detained three. Two escaped with a motorcycle gang I believe. One of the three in detention is a member of the same motorcycle club."

Ryan thought back to the video they had seen on Youtube for a moment.

"General, weren't there five people on the bus? The driver, these two students, a young black woman and a female pensioner.'

"I believe that is correct…"

Ryan hadn't seen General Spears face turn white before, but it did in an instant. He got up and immediately headed for the exit. Fine looked on in confusion.

"I don't understand sir, what's your point?" Fine asked.

"Who do you have in detention, Doctor Jacobs?" Ryan said, ignoring Fine.

"The bus driver, one Richard Simpson, or Elvis as he likes to be called, two females in their twenties, a Blessing Amoya and Rain Cameron. We're still checking on their backgrounds."

"Can you get the clip from YouTube up on the screen that was taken on the bus, or do we not have good internet here?"

Jacobs was losing patience.

"Prime Minister, we have a scientific briefing to finish and as much as we're grateful for your interest in what is happening, we know you have a country to run…"

"I suggest you put the clip up. I am about to demonstrate its scientific value," Ryan cut in, making his way down to the front of the room.

"Do we have it on here? Okay, get it up for me please."

Jane sat working on the laptop. On the big screen the mouse could be seen opening and closing folders, one of which was marked *YouTube clips*. Then a second folder within that, which was marked *Aberdeen, Scotland*. Inside that there were over one hundred clips. Each had been labelled. Ryan knew what he wanted to see.

"Can you open the one marked *Aberdeen Bus Facebook Live Broadcast* please?'

Jane did so and it began play on the big screen. Ryan was pleased someone had had the foresight to download and organise the footage otherwise they could have been looking for it all day. The clip showed the two young men, eyes wide and pupils even wider, talking fast as though they were coming up at a rave. They were, Ryan could see, clearly off their tits but there was no doubting their location. They were inside the bus on top of the craft at the Aberdeen landing site, acting as if they were on some kind of joyride. Ryan couldn't blame them. It would be one hell of a way to come up on a high. One of them spoke into the camera while the other held it, but occasionally he would turn it on himself and comment into the lens. They grew excited at the presence of the helicopters chasing them, but didn't seem the least bit scared. They treated the whole thing as some kind of game. Then Ryan saw it: the shot he wanted to show everyone. It had stuck in his head from before, because the person in it, who he had seen only very briefly, had reminded him of someone. As the bus swerved and the camera operator fell forwards, staggering to get up again, he caught her dead centre in the screen.

"Pause it there!" Ryan shouted. There she was, smiling away, looking sweet and innocent in one of the chairs at the front, turning towards the camera asking if the young man was alright. He was hoping he had been wrong, but there was no mistaking it; the woman he was looking at was Agatha Davey, or to put it another way, his grandmother on his mother's side.

"If the two young men escaped on the bikes, and you're holding the other three here, two of whom were on the bus - Can someone tell me where exactly this woman is now, please?"

It appeared that even Doctor Jacobs did not have an answer for that.

CHAPTER VI

"*As you know, I've seen a great many things during my travels in America, but one thing I never thought I would live to see in my lifetime is ships from another world. Now I wanted to say 'aliens', but as you can see from the image behind me, which is as close as the military will allow us to get to this object, so far there are no aliens to see. This landing site, which local people are referring to as 'The Mount Augusta Landing' is believed to cover an area almost 30 kilometres wide in diameter at any given point. Now we were able to get closer earlier, before the United States Airforce closed down the airspace, to bring you these pictures. As far as we can tell this ship, like the rest all over the world, are all identical in shape, though not necessarily in size. I understand from the reports coming in, that some in Europe for example are smaller, while the one in Brazil north of Rio is considerably larger. The area within the ship's perimeter behind me just east out of Fallon on Highway 50 has covered a number of very small populated areas including covering an entire Naval Reserve Station, which we believe has been out of contact ever since the craft arrived. So far however there's no confirmed casualties but I understand a number of personnel and civilians are still unaccounted for. So, is this an attack? We still don't know. The military, as you can see, are certainly not taking any chances and have been arriving here all day and continue to cordon off the landing site. One question is still being asked by everyone around the world – why are they here? So far, to our knowledge, unless someone, somewhere, isn't telling us anything, there has been no communication of any kind from any of the ships. So the answer still continues to elude humanity. This is Steve Holloway, literally on the road, outside Fallon Nevada, back to you Diane, in the studio."*

Steven Holloway, CBS news, April 2nd

BLESSING

She was grateful for the food. Blessing, Elvis and Rain had been sitting in the plastic bubble for several hours now. She thanked the Lord they had finally been given something to eat through the serving hatch. Earlier, they been taken by helicopter somewhere east of the ship. Blessing could tell the direction because she spotted the lights of Aberdeen in the distance, just before they touched down in a muddy field surrounded by rotating portable yellow lights. Blessing observed that a row of similar landing sites had been set up across the field to accommodate the helicopter traffic, which was facilitated by a pair of men waving light sticks to guide them in and out. They were met by a group of four people as they disembarked, all of whom were dressed in what appeared to her to be some kind of space suit. She thought this attire pointless, as the soldiers who had boarded the helicopter with them were not wearing any kind of protective gear beyond their body armour. A muffled voice instructed them to follow and led the small group towards a cluster of tents near some grey stone cottages. A large green truck with a radar dish on the roof sat nearby. The adjacent field was full of men in military fatigues constructing what looked like a guard tower. The presence of so many men with guns sent a chill down her back. She didn't like guns.

"Look at all this, noo!" Elvis said in wonder, taking in the hive activity all around them.

"No talking." The words came from one of the soldiers escorting them, his tone leaving little room for doubt. Then they were led into a long, plastic tunnel that reminded Blessing of an entrance to a circus she had once visited. But here, the door had to be unzipped and once inside they went through a second door, which was zipped back up behind them. Two men dressed in blue plastic suits, with some kind of breathing apparatus mounted on their backs, asked them to undress. Blessing did not want to take her clothes off in front of Elvis. She didn't mind doing it in front of Rain so much, as she had undressed in front of her sisters back home all the time. Fortunately, Elvis voluntarily turned his back as he undressed himself in the corner. He looked embarrassed and when she saw his underwear, it was easy to see why. Who would wear underpants with *Wally World* written on them?

The men distributed small black plastic bags, which they demanded everything be put into. Blessing complied. She wanted this ordeal to be over as soon as possible. She thought it best to just do as she was told. Rain did not agree so easily however, spouting on about their "Human rights being violated!"

Blessing changed as slowly as she could, picking a separate corner of the tent from Elvis. Rain finally relented and began to undress right in the middle of the room, facing the two blue-suited men. Blessing thought she was deliberately teasing them as she began to undress in an overly provocative fashion, as though she were performing some kind of strip-tease. Blessing realised she was staring, and promptly turned away.

"Seen enough, have you?" Rain said to their captors, causing the two figures in the blue suits to turn around. Blessing folded her clothes neatly and then turned to see another exit had been revealed. The men were already waving Elvis through the door into the next part of the passage ahead. Elvis had politely stood in front so he did not offer himself the chance to look at either Rain's or her own naked body. Facing forward, he stepped into the next room. Blessing however, got to see both him and Rain from head to foot, or at least their rear views. Elvis had a tattoo covering almost his entire back, of a man holding a guitar, craning over a micro-phone stand, his legs apart, sporting some kind of pointed-collar shirt, which was open and showing his chest. The man was singing. The design was quite intricate, and she guessed it might have a connection to the music that had been playing on the bus.

"Nice tat, man." It was the first time Rain had said anything to Elvis, at least anything complimentary anyway, Blessing thought.

Elvis was quite tall, taller certainly than herself and Rain. He must have been six-foot-two. Rain was perhaps five-foot-six without her shoes, making Blessing feel positively petite. Rain's light, caramel-coloured skin also sported several tattoos, the first of which was curving round her right arm. Blessing couldn't see it all clearly, but it must have been part of the rose she had noticed before. The second was much larger and had been inked just above her buttocks on the small of her back. It too was quite an intricate design, that curved with her body and then flowed down her thighs. Elvis's upper back was covered in dark body hair, but there wasn't a single hair on Rain anywhere except her head. Her hair, dyed bright pink, had a thin ponytail tied in a knot that hung ten inches down her back. Blessing hadn't noticed it before, the rest of her hair being so short. It must have been tucked in the back of her top. She was staring again, but it was hard not to. Beyond her family, this was the first time she had ever seen anyone naked in a very long time. She felt ashamed and made herself look at the floor.

"You'll get your property back later, once it's been through decontamination," one of the men said as they stepped into the next room. The suited figures gestured for them to pass through the next door. Blessing did her best to cover her modesty. The man closed up the door, leaving the three of them in the small passage way. Then they were hit with water, the cold beats on their skin causing all three of them to scream. A series of nozzles hung from the ceiling spraying them all completely. A voice boomed out from somewhere unseen.

"Please use the cleaning lotion available and have a good and thorough wash. A change of clothes awaits you in the next room."

Everyone did as they were told. Blessing found she actually enjoyed the shower. She always washed daily and was beginning to feel she smelled. They got changed into bright orange overalls and proceeded down a second corridor that led to a large, white metal door, where another blue-suited figure awaited them. He punched in a code to a keypad on the door itself, which emitted a popping sound as it opened. It reminded Blessing a little of the noise that came from her fridge at home sometimes, which could take forever to open. Once inside, Elvis and Rain protested at their detention but it didn't seem to get them anywhere. Someone arrived and took everyone's blood pressure and they left, then someone else came and listened to their chests and then they left failing to answer any questions. Soon a sullen silence had fallen over the group. It was an hour later when a woman's voice spoke from behind them. Blessing turned to see a short blue-suited figure standing in the doorway.

"I'm Doctor Jacobs. I'm sorry you have been detained in this way but as you have been close to the object, we need to make sure you're all okay." Blessing thought she was a redhead but it was hard to tell through the visor of the mask.

"We'll be coming to take blood samples from you all momentarily and as long as there's nothing abnormal, you should be released shortly. The police may have a few questions for you afterwards."

A nurse in identical dress entered, wheeling in a metal trolley on top of which sat a series of syringes. All three of them complied without fuss. When Blessing pulled up the sleeves of her new overalls, the nurse noticed the plaster on her arm from her recent visit to the clinic.

"You've had yours taken recently?' Doctor Jacobs asked. Elvis and Rain immediately looked up. Blessing did not want to reply.

"Did you visit the doctor today?' the Doctor said.

"Yes. I did. It was nothing serious. Just a regular appointment," Blessing replied, feeling at once she had already overstated her answer.

"Are you pregnant?"

She was offended by the question. Who was this woman to ask her about her sex life? Even if it had been non-existent for some time, it was not something she wanted to be asked in front of virtual strangers.

"Why don't you mind you own business, like? I'm sure the wee lassie disnae want to be asked such questions in front of us," said Elvis.

The nurse swabbed her skin and took out a needle. Blessing hated needles at the best of times, and now she had to be jabbed by one twice in twenty-four hours. Blessing felt the scratch of the needle penetrate her skin as the Doctor replied.

"I'm sure she doesn't, but I am afraid this is the only holding area we have. So there isn't much room for privacy. How long were you all on top of the object for?" The Doctor threw the question out to the room as she moved on to Rain.

"I'm sure you know the answer to that question already. You had helicopters up there. Probably filmed us the entire time anyway," Rain responded angrily.

"I don't actually. Those were part of the army unit sent to cordon off the ship. I'm a scientist, I'm not with them." The Doctor tried to sound sympathetic in her response, but Blessing could see that Rain was not buying it.

"Unfortunately they took my watch, so I can't really answer that question." Rain did not bother to hide her sarcasm. The Doctor moved on to Elvis.

"Did you find a way inside?" she asked, with a veil of unconvincing nonchalance.

Elvis looked as though he were about to speak, but immediately Blessing found herself cutting in.

"No, there was no way in."

"Yeah, we looked for ages, there was nothing - it was all a bit disappointing, you know, like your sex life," added Rain, folding her arms and awaiting the woman's rebuttal. Blessing thought such a rude remark was uncalled-for, but the Doctor seemed unfazed by the comment. Elvis said nothing, and let the Doctor extract his blood. Blessing noticed Elvis had additional tattoos on the inside of each arm. One read *Jailhouse Rock*, the other, *All Shook Up*, which Blessing couldn't help think was the way she feeling right now. She was shook up and basically in Jail – ironic. Blessing thought they all looked like extras from an American prison television drama in their orange overalls. She hated it. This colour was definitely not the new black, and who was to say one of the many men she had met today wasn't single? She needed to look her best. The room they had been placed in was bare, except for several small army issue cots placed on the floor and a small portable toilet in the corner. Blessing could tell immediately that she would get no sleep at all on one of those things. She slept badly at the best of times, and this was certainly not the best of times.

"I'll be back to see you again soon, and I'll see what I can do about getting you all some food as soon as possible. I know this is really inconvenient for you all but you undertook a very foolish enterprise so just be grateful that the consequences were not more serious. Please don't try and leave."

With that, Doctor Jacobs stepped out through the door, shutting it behind her. The bubble they had been left in was about twenty feet by twenty feet and had only one way in or out, other than a small serving hatch of similar design. The walls were transparent, but the room around them was blurred by the thickness of the material. Two large window portals adorned the wall either side of the door. Here the material was clearer, and afforded a view into the larger room that surrounded the bubble chamber. She saw two men armed with rifles, one in each corner of the larger room beyond the bubble window.

Rain did not contain her feelings on the matter. "You can't keep us locked up in here! This isn't legal!" she screamed.

The men standing outside cocked their weapons in response, making it very clear they were not there to debate the issue. Only to shoot them if they tried to leave their confinement. Blessing found herself wondering why the guards also had to wear breathing suits. Had they been infected with something? She didn't feel unwell. In fact, she felt better than she had in ages. Elvis lay down on one of the cots. He tried to sleep, but the lighting was intrusive and made getting any real rest problematic. After what seemed like an intolerable wait, some blankets were brought in followed by some food, passed through the small hatch on the far side of the wall. The food was a meat stew. It was hot, at least. They were all hungry and devoured it quickly, with Rain mumbling something about being a vegetarian, but knowing it was pointless to complain. Blessing found the whole thing to be so extreme. Armed guards and breathing suits? Did they think they had Ebola? They were only doing their jobs, she supposed. Certainly there was no one willing to listen to their complaints. Her mind turned to Agatha. She wondered how the old lady was doing. She felt guilty for leaving her inside the ship, but the timing and circumstances of that moment had afforded them little other choice. The fate of the elderly woman in that strange place all alone concerned her.

"How do you think Agatha is doing?" she asked the others.

"Be careful what you say in here," replied Rain, softly.

"Why?"

"The room is bound to be bugged. I bet they're listening to us now." Rain sounded very certain, but Blessing couldn't see any bugs although that presumably was the point. You weren't supposed to be able to see them. Elvis was also losing patience.

"I wonder what the time is noo? Those bastards even took me watch!"

Blessing had no idea. The only contact they'd had from anyone since they were given their clothes and had their blood samples taken, was with a young man who'd appeared on the other side of the hatch a few minutes earlier, pushing a trolley with three trays of food on it. Elvis lay down and was soon asleep, snoring loudly, causing Rain and Blessing to smile at each other.

"So where are you from, Rain?" Blessing asked, trying to make conversation.

"I'm from here but I was living in the U.S. for quite a while."

Blessing thought she had heard a hint of American in the woman's accent.

"What about you? You're not from Scotland," Rain asked.

"No, I have lived here for a few months, before that Birmingham, before that London…" She trailed off.

"And before that?" Rain pressed.

"Nigeria…"

"Africa. Nice. I always wanted to go there."

"Really? Why?" She couldn't imagine what someone from America would see in her country.

"Get back to my roots. Taste the food, I hear it's great."

This was true. English food could be so bland. Though in London you were never short of spicy options on any high street.

"So, boyfriend?" Rain asked very bluntly. The question caught Blessing off-guard.

"No. Not at the moment. I don't have time for that sort of thing," she spluttered, trying desperately not to sound like some kind of lonely spinster.

"Girlfriend?" Was Rain actually asking if she was a lesbian? What on earth would give her that idea? Perhaps it was the fact that they were both now in orange boiler suits. Everyone on *Orange is the New Black* seemed to be a lesbian.

"No!" she said, very definitively.

"Ever?" Rain did not seem to want to stop with the questions.

"Of course not!"

"Honey, you don't know what you're missing," Rain smiled.

Blessing did not want to take the conversation any further, so lying down seemed the best way to end it. Elvis was still snoring. Sleep would be challenging for either of them.

"I am going to try and rest for a bit," Blessing said, pulling up the blanket around her she wondered if the bizarre events of the day had all been a dream. If so, then she could go back to her mundane but functional life. On reflection however, she hoped it was not a dream. A functional life was not as interesting as this.

Some hours later, she was on her seventh attempt at trying to discover the most comfortable position in the army cot to sleep in, when she heard voices talking on the other side of the bubble. Elvis and Rain were already standing at one of the portals, looking through the window. Staring back were a group of four people, in the same blue suits as before. One of them pressed the button on an intercom system.

"Hello, it's Doctor Jacobs. How are you all feeling?"

"Doctor Jacobs, is it? When you going to let us oot of here?" Elvis asked marching over to the door, the anger in his voice completely evident.

"You can stay by the window, wherever you speak in the room we can hear you," the Doctor responded calmly.

Rain looked at Blessing, her eyebrows raised.

"I told you they could hear everything."

"Yes we can," came a new voice. It was that of a man's whom Blessing thought sounded familiar, but she couldn't place where from.

"When are you going to let us out of here? This isn't legal and my sister is a lawyer," Rain shouted.

"I am extremely sorry that you have to be detained in this way. If all the tests come back normal, then I see no reason why you should not be released tomorrow morning," came the male voice again.

"And who might you be, pal?" Elvis asked.

"I'm Ryan Wallace, MP."

"Nope. I don't follow politics much, pal. Still none the wiser," Elvis said.

But Blessing did know the name. She had heard it in conversation more than once down at the clinic, and never in a positive context.

"You're the Minister of Health," Blessing said. Rain looked impressed by her political knowledge, but she was not long in being corrected.

"Was... I was the Minister of Health," The male voice replied.

"What happened? Did you get fired then, pal? I'm not surprised, because to be honest you were doing a pretty shite job, like. Closing everything down an' that!" Elvis laughed, smiling at both women. It was the first time he and Rain had smiled at each other. Through the window they could see the group of four figures consult for a moment then the voice came again.

"When was the last time you saw the news? Any of you?" Wallace asked.

"I don't watch the news, it's just too depressing," Rain replied. Elvis shook his head.

"I've been working all day, pal, until I came here. So not much time for the TV!"

Blessing herself hadn't seen the news since yesterday, but it occurred to them that they themselves must be all over it. Wasn't Ewen broadcasting on Facebook live at one stage? He must have been. Were they all famous now? Had they been on the news? God, all manner of eligible men may well have seen her! Blessing tried to recall how her hair had looked earlier.

"None of us have seen the news today. Have we been on it?" she asked. There was a long moment of silence before the voice of the ex-Minister of Health responded.

"Yes, you have been on the news but if you haven't watched it today you wouldn't be aware that our Prime Minister, David Jackson, was killed in a terrorist attack in France earlier this afternoon."

The words were said to them very coldly. It was a clear statement of fact, not a joke. *Good God*, were the first words that came into Blessing's head. Elvis response was more colourful.

"You have to be fuckin' kiddin', like! How?"

"Good riddance," Rain muttered. Blessing frowned and shook her head at her, a warning to try and be more diplomatic in her response, especially in light of their current circumstances.

"We're not sure yet. It's believed to be ISIS. I am running the country until such time when we can properly elect a new Prime Minister."

He sounded detached, yet Blessing could sense something else in his voice. Sadness? Regret? A little of each perhaps.

"I'm very sorry Prime Minister. Mr Jackson was a good man. He will be in God's arms now and you will have to trust in the Lord to look after him." She said the words with such conviction, that they produced a shake of dismay in Rain who turned away muttering, "God had nothing to do with it…"

"Thank you, Miss…?"

"Blessing Amoya. I will pray for him tonight and I will pray for you too, Mr Wallace."

Through the plastic, she could see the man standing staring back at her. Encased in his blue body-suit she couldn't see his face. He must have had some kind of radio to be able to talk to her, as he brought his gloved hand up to his visor every time he did so.

"Thank you. I am sorry you have to be detained in this way, but I am certain you will be released as soon as possible. I will see what I can do about the police. You... your zealous attempts to see the ship are to some degree understandable..."

He sounded genuine. This did not sound like the man she had heard others comment on in his role as the Minister of Health. Rain was less convinced. She sat back down on one of the cots, her head in her hands.

"He's a politician, you cannot trust him," she said.

"The lassie is right. He was bloody useless bag o' bones as Minister of Health and he'll make an even bigger bampot of a Prime Minister..." Elvis said, still staring back out through the window at the group. Wallace stepped closer to their enclosure as he responded.

"He's not wrong. I wasn't a very good Minister of Health. Not much point saying otherwise. She's right too, generally you can't trust a politician. I certainly wouldn't. I had no plans to be in this job, but I am. You probably didn't have any plans to be here this evening either, but here we all are..." Blessing saw someone in the group take his arm, wanting to stop the man from talking to them. There was a brief argument before the speaker crackled to life again.

"I will do what I can to make the charges go away and have you all home as soon as possible. I just need to know the answer to one question in return."

Rain looked at Blessing. Blessing looked at Elvis, who turned from the window and looked back at both of them. Blessing felt they were all connected in that moment, because they all knew what question was coming.

"What happened to the elderly woman you were with, on the bus? Her name is Agatha Davey and her relatives, well, they're understandably very worried about her. If anything happened to her and you were all party to her travelling to that ship against her will, well then, things with the police might be a tad more difficult."

Elvis backed away from the screen, and sat next to Rain causing Blessing to feel she should do the same. All three looked at each other, no one wanting to be the first to speak. The speaker crackled to life again.

"We know she was on the bus, we've seen her in your student friends' YouTube video, and so has half the nation. Probably half the planet by now."

The group stared at each other, not sure of what to say. Elvis looked the most worried. It was his bus, after all. Rain didn't need to be concerned, but Blessing could see the young woman understood the gravity of the situation perfectly. She grabbed Elvis's hand and wrapped her slender fingers around his. Elvis grinned at them both. Blessing's attention was immediately drawn to his mouth. She was right! His teeth had changed colour from when they first met. When she'd boarded the bus, they were a dirty faded yellow, and his breath had reeked of cigarette smoke. Now his teeth were bright white, the brightest she had ever seen on a white man. There was no point mentioning this right now, but she had to get him to look in a mirror at the first opportunity. What could have done such a thing? Was it something to do with the ship? It couldn't have been anything else. That would explain why she felt so fit. Normally by this time of day she would be asleep, yet she wasn't tired. It must be getting on for midnight, for certain.

"If you can't help us, I will not be able to help you with the police."

Blessing snapped.

"Agatha was the one who wanted to go and see the ship! She told us she was going to go anyway. We didn't want her to go alone, so we all agreed to go with her."

"Aye, that's right," Elvis said, nodding.

"So what happened to her?" the Prime Minister asked. Blessing looked at the other two, who looked back at her for answers.

"Shit, I wish I hadn't stopped to help you guys out, now," Rain said.

"We'd best tell them lassie. It was her choice."

Blessing didn't really want the final decision to rest with her, but it appeared the others were passing her the leadership baton and she was going to have to take it. A leader was one thing she was not, she felt.

"She found a door, but when we looked back, she'd gone."

"Aye, and so had the door," Elvis added.

"Gone where?" asked the Prime Minister.

The group was silent a moment, before Blessing stood and walked over to the window, so the group could see her more clearly through the plastic. The four figures in suits waited impassively for an answer.

"Inside. She went inside," Blessing said, pressing her hand on the window. "Can we go home now please?"

CANDICE

C andice had never seen the carriages of the London Underground so devoid of people. She had not been able to get hold of her driver, Steve, which in light of recent global events was not all that surprising. His phone was off, which could have been as a result of an overloaded network, or simply that with spaceships landing all over the Earth, he had better things to do than drive her around. Evidently not everyone's phone was affected, as her inbox was continuously buzzing with messages. People were still expecting their deliveries, and some of her clients had even messaged her to say they were having End of the World parties and wanted her to up their orders.

The day was turning out to have something of a silver lining. On the one hand, this could be a really great time to make some extra money. If people really thought this was the end of everything, then she would be cleaned out within a couple of days, along with every dealer in London. There would be a massive demand for product in a very short period of time. Certainly there would not be enough supply to meet that demand, meaning that she could put the price up. But there was an obvious draw-back to this plan. What was the point in spending the next two days trying to make a ton of money if this really was the end of the world? She needed to think with a level head here. Travelling around doing her deliveries on the tube was usually a massive no-no. London Underground employed plain-clothes police who worked alongside uniformed officers. Random stops at stations were not uncommon. Even though she knew these were to catch people out who were travelling without a ticket, or with someone else's travel pass, they were also for drug and weapon searches. Sometimes, the teams were accompanied by sniffer dogs. Never good. If these were indeed the end times, then she wanted to spend them like it was Sodom and Gomorrah; having great sex and great food with someone she loved. Or if she were to spend it with her mother, then just great food. But her mother was back in Brazil and all attempts to communicate with her had failed. Overseas calls didn't appear to be working. She was not on Facebook, Skype was down and even getting her friend Raquel on the phone had been something of a challenge. Raquel was her go-to girl for any clients wanting a threesome and to be fair, Raquel had told her that this was going to be her day off and she was probably still asleep. Candice tried Steve again before resigning herself to the fact that she was going to have to use an Uber. She had used them before, but the drivers could be a mixed bunch and many were not transgender-friendly. Looking in the mirror at her third change of outfit that morning, she knew she was more than passable to anyone in the street, but she always wore scarves to hide her Adam's apple. There wasn't any other way to conceal it, short of having some surgeon in Thailand remove it. That was an absolute no-no. There were parts of her body that she always wanted to remain male, and that was the second one.

The alien invasion was all over the news on every television channel, and every part of the internet. Some regular programming was still being broadcast according to schedule, but most were broadcasting constant news updates. No doubt many people would find this world event fascinating or frightening, but she really didn't give a shit. If they were aliens then either come out and say hello, or get on with your invasion, that was *Wendy Williams* take on it. But if they could let us know by the end of the day that would be great... Her schedule was being turned upside-down, and she certainly didn't want to miss the latest episode of *Modern Family*, a programme which, if on, she would make clients watch with her. Few complained, because the show was so funny. Scanning her phone, she ordered the Uber, which annoyingly had a wait of over twenty minutes. Who waited twenty minutes for an Uber in London? Oh yes, people who were being invaded by aliens. No doubt many drivers had decided in a time of crisis that they had something better to do than drive strangers around to their respective destinations. Understandable, but a total pain in the ass. At least Uber got its legal issues sorted out last year.

Candice checked herself over in the mirror. Her lipstick was a dark, subtle red. Her blusher and foundation was kept to a minimum. She would never go anywhere without her lashes, and had made certain she stayed away from the cheaper brands. Hers were the best and the biggest, and they didn't come off until she was ready to take them off. She batted them in the mirror. She felt she could have been a Disney cartoon character pitching for votes with these eyes.

"Jessica Rabbit, you ain't got nothing on me, honey." She packed her heels in her bag and put on her flats then lit a cigarette and carried on watching the news until the Uber arrived. It was the most information she had ever had to take in from a single news broadcast. These things, whatever they were, had landed almost everywhere. As she flicked through the channels, she caught a different image on CNN of the one from Brazil, north of Rio. A cameraman had caught a shot of the craft passing over the hills, a rainbow astride of it, which gave it an almost spiritual appearance with the statue of Christ in the foreground. To her relief, there were no reports of any casualties, at least not in Rio anyway. A huge number of traffic accidents had occurred on London roads. Hospitals had been inundated by people suffering from stress, anxiety and heart attacks. Several people were reported as missing near, or within the landing sites. It was being debated if they might be trapped alive somehow, underneath the ships. There followed a recap of the earlier news, involving the downing of the Prime Minister's plane in Paris. One hundred and thirty-seven people on board had been killed, including the PM's children and his wife. It was being described as a despicable, heartless act of cruelty and she could not disagree, it was barbaric. French Police were actively pursuing a number of leads, and had killed one man in the hunt for the terrorists. Then she saw him again. Ryan on television. The only man she really cared about showing another side to him that she had never seen before. It was a clip of a speech he had given earlier that day. He was very statesmanlike and delivered it with real conviction. She knew straight away, the words were not his own. But he read them aloud as though he truly believed in them. It was also a little scary. He was now the most powerful man in the United Kingdom, potentially at least, and she wasn't sure what that meant for her. His phone call had made it obvious what it meant for their relationship. She knew that ending things probably hadn't been his decision, but why didn't he stand up for her? Did he have a choice? Probably not, but she was angry with him all the same. Having seen his speech, she was really proud of him and wanted to tell him so. She knew Ryan, of all people, would not want this level of responsibility placed upon him. Hell, all he did was complain about his job. Yet, there he was, on a podium, telling the world to remain calm. She had decided she was going to go and see Pearl. Pearl was someone else she cared about. It would be better to wait this thing out in good company, than be alone. She could do a couple of deliveries on the way, but the rest would have to wait until later. If she did more than a couple with the same driver, a stranger, he might get suspicious. It didn't pay to ever carry too much cash around in London. It could be easily stolen by pickpockets, or lost through sheer stupidity and she specialised in the latter.

Her phone vibrated. Her driver was here. She had to look for a white Toyota Yaris. She made sure to take her Oyster travel pass. If her driver gave her any shit, she would just get out and take the tube or the bus, even though the very thought of travel on public transport appalled her. On that basis, she decided to keep her heels in her bag for now. It was dark outside, and her road was oddly quiet, but a few streets away she heard the sound of breaking glass and people shouting mixed with the sound of police sirens. She saw the car, checked the number plate and then opened the door to the back and got inside.

"Wharf Road, Old Street?" Asked the driver.

"Yes," Candice replied, determined to keep conversation as minimal as possible. The driver sounded Eastern European, though she couldn't tell exactly where he was from and really didn't care to ask. As they turned onto Kentish Town High Road, the majority of the traffic was all heading north and they had to go south, then east. It was after 9pm, normally her time of choice to grace the streets of London with her presence. The coming of the night was always the welcome companion of any transgender. Back in Brazil, she had rarely gone out before dark. Her country had, on the one hand, a very accepting attitude towards the transgender community, but it also had a brutal unforgiving undercurrent that could explode in your face in an instant. Girls were murdered almost daily on the streets back home. The same men who went looking for a blow job were often the same ones who beat up the girls to prove to their mates that they weren't *gay*, the following day.

In her experience, half the men she met in her life swore they weren't gay, but they couldn't get her cock down their throats fast enough. It was a lifestyle of contradictions. It could be a world full of many disconnected, and confused individuals, both among those who would seek out her gender, and those who were of her gender. It was also a world of contrasts. Some of the most interesting, dynamic friends Candice had in her life were others from her community. They were often characters who were born out of extremes.

"People seem to be keen to leave London. I think they want to be with their families." Finally she got his accent. He was Turkish. She had had bad experiences with Turkish men in the past, that had left her with no desire to ever visit that country.

"Yes, I am going to see mine in Walthamstow, just a couple of things to do first," She said, deliberately looking out the window.

"I see. If we go across the middle of London, the traffic will not be so bad. It was bad earlier but not so much now. The roads going out of London are jammed."

"Just go whichever way will get me there fastest." She wasn't really listening as she played with her phone.

"People are saying it is the end of the world. Time to make your last wishes, huh?" the driver said.

In less than twenty minutes she made her first destination. She made her first delivery just round the corner from Old Street Station, telling the driver she would ensure he got an extra tip for waiting. A gay client of hers, Justin, wanted coke for his sex party. He lived up in one of the tower blocks, accommodation that had gone very out of fashion since the fire in Grenfell Tower killed over eighty people in 2017. She pressed the buzzer and he answered, dance music playing in the background.

"You know where to come!"

"Fuck that honey, you come down. I'm in a rush this evening."

"I'm off my tits!" he protested.

"So is half the world. You want your Charlie or not?"

"Okay, okay... give me five minutes."

"You've got two and then I'm gone."

You had to be strict with clients. Give them an inch and they'd take a mile; give them a mile and they'd rob you blind. She'd heard every excuse there was: the old "I'll go to a cash machine later" being the most common one. She always told them they would go right away, or they could get their supplies from somewhere else. The lift rang, announcing it had arrived on the ground floor and a man stepped out. It wasn't Justin. This man was older, and clearly didn't care who saw him, as he only wore a red jock and some leather chaps embossed with red. He had a skinhead haircut. He looked gaunt and unhealthy, his eyes wide pools of darkness. He carried had a wad of cash in his hands. She took it from him as soon as he came to the door. It was all there. Their exchange was brief. The man looked at her with a sincere sadness.

"Don't spend tonight alone, love. Come and be with us. Justin said you'd be welcome."

"Thank you, but no." She about-faced and headed back to the Uber. The driver was smoking a cigarette out of the window. She gave him the post-code for her next delivery. If she set up the transaction, there was no need for her to change vehicles.

"Do you mind if I smoke? Why worry about cancer now, huh? It's the end of the world," he asked, lighting up another one in the front seat.

"Go ahead."

Perhaps it was the end of the world, but it hadn't happened yet. For all everyone knew these things, whatever they were, had just come to do a little shopping. She saw on the news reports that one had landed just north of Milan – the perfect parking spot for any alien vessel as far as she was concerned. Handy for shopping and daily excursions to both Venice and Lake Como. If they were here just to purchase some designer labels, those intentions were not immediately apparent at the moment. Such thoughts reminded her of the last time she'd gone to Italy. A client had taken her. Marco was an Italian entrepreneur of high social standing. He was the ideal client, though somewhat hairy for her tastes. He was in good shape for his age, which he claimed was fifty-eight but a sneaky look at his passport confirmed that he was nearer sixty-four. He took her to Milan for a long weekend, where he had a rather spacious penthouse apartment over-looking one of the city's canals. Roof gardens dripping with leafy plants seemed to be all the rage in Italy, and his was grand by any standards. It had a small fountain surrounded with vines, and a lovely decked veranda that caught the sun in the late afternoon. They had sipped on a fantastic glass of Pinot and eaten incredible food, which he had brought to the door by some sort of gourmet home delivery service. Like many of her older clientele, his thing was to get fucked really hard on all fours while feeling the touch of her breasts upon his back. Predictable and boring, but it was her favourite position where exchanges of money were concerned. She could invariably just get herself inside the client and then thrust strokes that were slow enough to allow her to multitask and use her phone at the same time. Marco however, had mirrors all over the bedroom, in front of him and on the ceiling. It was a room that had been designed with sex in mind, so she had to commit to the role the entire time. It was tiresome. Marco had incredible stamina for his age. This presented a challenge. He could book her for hours but she was exhausted after spending a single evening in his company, and she still had another three nights to go. It was hard to complain when he was paying her £1500 a night plus expenses. He wasn't shy with the liberal use of his credit card on their daily shopping trips, either. She tried every trick in the book to tire him out but nothing seemed to work. He wasn't interested in drugs and he could handle his wine, which he consumed at a rate of three bottles a night without becoming the slightest bit woozy. How his member performed was not really important, because of course he did not wish to use it. When he was finally ready to sleep after considerable physical exertions on her part, he would fall into a deep slumber, emitting a sound akin to that of a foghorn on a ship finding its way through mist at sea. Each tremendous toot from his nostrils would be followed by a long slow wheeze, which made sleeping in the same room an impossibility. The next thing to announce their presence were his bowels. For an hour, a continuous succession of the most fetid seasoned bursts of wind would impose their presence one after the other, forcing her onto the balcony for a much-needed cigarette. Never had the phrase "light a match" been more appropriate. By the second night, she'd managed to convince him to let her sleep in the spare room. Despite these drawbacks, Marco of Milan had been one of her most profitable clients. She would return from Italy with enough outfits and shoes to last her well into next season. He would have been a good second choice to spend her last night on earth with. They could have had one last fantastic meal and drunk a bottle of Italy's finest red. She could never find such good red wine in the UK. Searches for it had proven to be an exercise in futility… Her thoughts were disturbed by someone reaching inside the car; smelly dirt-encrusted nails, hands were pulling at her from outside the vehicle. The Uber had stopped. The side door was opened and before she could react, strong hands had pulled her out from the back seat, dragging her by the neck around to the back of the vehicle. Candice realised that they had parked up under some railway arches somewhere in the vicinity of Limehouse. It was the Uber driver who was the cause of her assault. The man grappling with her was bigger than he had looked when seated in the front of the vehicle. He was not as tall as her but had broad shoulders and a well-built physique. His fingers stank of cigarettes and a type of cooking seasoning that she couldn't place. An odd thing to ponder, even momentarily, when a man was forcibly trying to assault her. She heard her phone drop onto the tarmac below and felt the anger in her body boil over.

"It is all over for us so we should have some fun hey? Don't make me take what I want!" He said, forcibly groping her.

His left hand was already ripping through her blouse. She felt a button pop from the material. His right had slipped inside her jeans and was now cupping her left buttock. His breath reeked of whisky. She realised he must have been drinking before he even picked her up. She cursed herself for not checking his breath before getting in the car. He kissed her neck feverishly. She only had the briefest of windows before he discovered she was not quite the woman he imagined her to be. She had to think fast. There was only one way to deal with such an individual. She had after all been put in this position back in Brazil, and had learnt quickly how resolve such situations.

"Okay honey, slow down. Let's make it nice, huh? Let me get some protection from my purse…" In her purse, she knew she had some pepper spray if she could just get to it.

He pulled her bra away from her breast, fondling her flesh. She knew they felt real, having paid enough for them.

"Why we bother, huh? It is the end of the world for us both so what does it matter?" He manhandled round to the bonnet of the car. She would have to distract him,

"Okay sugar, let's see what you've got for me."

She undid his belt and reached into his jeans, feeling his cock which was already beginning to harden. He certainly wasn't small, but she had seen much bigger a tool on far more passive a man, but this man wasn't passive. Soon he would discover that part of her was very much still male, but even then he might still be determined to continue, or worse. She wasn't going to let that happen.

"Well you're a big boy, aren't you?" She pulled out his testicles and cupped them with her hand. They swung freely from his jeans, which he willingly dropped around his ankles. His first mistake. This was, she knew, his biggest moment of vulnerability. She dropped to her knees, keeping one hand on his balls while slowly stroking his leg with the other, enabling her to work down to the belt around his fallen jeans. He placed both his hands firmly on the back of her head and began aggressively thrusting her towards his groin.

"Oh yeah, swallow it, swallow it all, bitch!"

She stole a quick glance up at him and saw his head was tilted back in expectation of what was to follow. She had to take the end of his member in her mouth for the deception to be complete. It tasted vile, smelled of stale beer and evidently hadn't been washed since yesterday. She made sure her hands were in place, clenching her grip slightly on both his balls and his belt. Then with a single firm motion she pulled hard on the belt of his jeans while twisting his balls as tight as if she were pulling grapes from a vine. The man barely had time to let loose a howl of pain when she stepped back pulling the belt with all her might, pulling him off his feet. He hurtled backwards, his head hitting the car bumper not once but twice on the way down. Candice let him fall to the floor. Then with his head still reeling from the double blow to the back of his skull, she kicked with every ounce of strength straight at his exposed swollen testicles. He let out a second scream followed by a third and a fourth as she kicked him repeatedly, unleashing her anger on this man who had so wrongly abused her.

"You picked the wrong fucking bitch, honey! You're my bitch now!"

On any other day, his screams would have been heard, but this was not a normal day. The streets near the arches were empty, the businesses closed. She took her time with him. He would learn never to do this to another human being, and the lesson would be a painful one.

Candice hated taking the London Underground, but she found herself sitting in one of its carriages some forty minutes later. Being in Limehouse had enabled her to get on the DLR network that would take her closer to her destination. She would not do any more deliveries tonight. She was lucky to catch an eastbound train almost as soon as she arrived at the platform. By now the time was past ten o'clock in the evening. The train was less than a third full and she picked a carriage that had fewer people in than the rest. An unusual sight greeted her. Complete strangers in every carriage were passionately engaged in conversation. Just along from her, a group of twenty-somethings were talking excitedly with an older couple, who looked to be returning from the theatre in the West End, still clutching their programmes. Candice wondered why the show had not been cancelled.

"200 of these things! I'm telling you it's the end of mankind," said a worried youth, who looked as if he was either on the way from or going to a rave. Two women sat either side of him both clutching their handbags tightly, as if somehow this would make them safer from whatever fate awaited them.

"I can't believe we lost our Prime Minister on the same day! Now they've put the Minister of Health in charge," said the middle-aged female theatre patron.

"That bloke's a proper wanker. We're all fucked, either way," muttered the man, his eyes rolling.

"So, where are you going then, young man?" her partner asked.

"End of the world rave in some place in Stratford. I think the police will be too busy to shut it down, somehow," the youth replied.

Candice knew that much had to be true. As the DLR snaked its way above ground through the grand tombstone-like structures of the financial district of Canary Wharf, every few seconds she caught the flash of blue lights hurtling in one direction or another between the buildings. A sign of how preoccupied the authorities were. Lights of another kind, fire, could be seen on the southern side of the river. Something near the O2 building, London's dome of entertainment, was burning and flames were licking their way across clusters of buildings, causing an eerie flickering reflection in the dark, winding waters of the River Thames.

"I'm amazed anyone's shown up for work," said another woman in the carriage.

"Ah well, you see, that Ryan Wallace is not that dumb, he's announced double pay for the next seventy-two hours for everyone who comes in from all essential services," the man said. "I wonder who'll pay for that?"

"Us, I expect..." his wife replied.

"I see the cast turned up for your show," the clubber commented, with a smile.

"Yes, well, the understudies did. I guess they thought it was their big chance. They were very good, weren't they, love?' said the man.

"Oh yes, they really went for it. I wish the audience had been bigger, but we gave them a standing ovation, didn't we? I mean they deserved it just for coming in," his wife said.

"Yes, and it took ages for us to get these seats, really good ones too. Of course, tonight we could have sat pretty much anywhere."

Candice saw she had a signal. She immediately called Pearl. The phone only rang twice before it was answered with a joyous voice.

"Candy, where are you? I can't believe you got through! They say the networks are struggling to cope." It was good to hear the voice of a friend, the voice of someone she cared about. She was spiked with such a mix of emotions that her hands began to tremble.

"Oh babe, I had some trouble on the way. I'm on the DLR," Candice said, suddenly aware that the little group of passengers were at once all trying their own mobile phones, having noted her own success.

"I still can't get through to anyone," said the woman.

"Neither can I! Who you with?" asked the clubber.

"Vodaphone," replied the husband.

"Fuck. No wonder."

Candice heard Joanne in the background. She sounded worried. "Is she okay? Where is she? Can she pick up more ciggy papers on the way?"

"Joanne wants to know if you can pick up some Rizla papers on the way. We're out."

"I'll try. Are the shops near you still open? I might have to get the fucking bus!" Candice hated the bus even more than the tube. At least on the tube out of rush hour you had a decent chance of avoiding sitting next to someone with serious personal hygiene problems, but on the bus you had almost no chance of avoiding them. She could still smell the Uber driver's breath.

"Cand, listen, we're hearing reports on the news of some looting. Apparently there's some riots in Stratford, around the shopping centre, so don't come through there, try coming via…"

And then the signal went. Pearl's voice was gone.

"I had the internet for a bit. It says there's some looting at Westfield!' the clubber announced to the carriage.

"Which Westfield?' one of his female companions asked.

Westfield was a monstrosity of a shopping centre, a singular pool of opulence constructed for the sole purpose of depriving you of every single pound you had in your wallet. Set over three levels, two almost identical versions of the design had been built, one living up to its name was actually built in West London while the second was constructed in time for the London Olympics, next to Stratford station in London's East End, which in turn had caused local house prices to rapidly rise in what once had been a cheaper part of the capital. Candice often wondered why the second location was not called Eastfield to avoid confusion between the two. Overpriced restaurants mingled with overpriced street food, connected by walkways containing every designer label outlet you could want. Despite London being in a constant state of economic depression, Westfield was always rammed. Everything was under one roof, only it would cost you more to buy it here than anywhere else. It was somewhere you could easily spend £1000 in the blink of an eye. If the retail spending didn't empty your wallet then the conveniently located champagne bar by the exit would finish the job. Candice loved it. When she bagged herself a really wealthy client, she would always get them to take her there. Ryan had never liked it however, and simply refused to take her, point blank. He said the place was crude, lacked class and was full of wankers.

"It says they've deployed Riot Police to protect it," the woman said, reading the updates on her phone.

"Of course they have. All those shops are owned by rich people, innit?" The clubber seemed less concerned, though she thought the loss of the Lego store might upset him if his home-made Lego earrings were anything to go by.

Candice's hands had still not stopped shaking from her phone call. She pictured the man who had tried to rape her only an hour ago. Hours before that, the man she loved had told her he could never see her again, and the world was facing a potential global catastrophe. Now, more than ever, she just wanted to reach her friends in East London, and she needed to eat something.

She felt a drop of something wet upon her hand, and only then realised she was crying. Tears had involuntarily rolled down both her cheeks, she had been so consumed in her thoughts. She reached into her handbag to find something to wipe them away with, when they pulled into the next station. The clubber exited with a wave, and a dozen more passengers entered the carriage, settling down the far end where a flood of conversation was still taking place. Their own little group was only joined by one more passenger. Her attempts to find a tissue were unsuccessful. She remembered she had used them all to clean up and re-apply her makeup after the recent encounter with the Uber driver. The new occupant to the carriage sat right opposite her. Candice would not have paid him any attention, but for the fact that he must have seen the tears upon her face and instinctively produced a handkerchief. She looked up into the face of the owner, and said "Thank you."

She was staring straight into the face of a man whose dark, precise features could have only been chiselled from granite by a master angel craftsman. Sitting before her was simply the most beautiful young man, who looked to be in his late twenties. He had a light olive skin tone. She noted how soft and smooth his skin felt as she took the handkerchief from his hand. She let the look linger for a moment too long, her fingers touching his momentarily.

"I am sure it is a day of tears for many people. Perhaps the whole human race is crying today. Do not worry," he said with a warm smile. He had an unusual accent.

What a day of all days to meet such a mesmerising creature.

"Where are you going to?" they asked each other in unison.

DIANA

As soon as Diana had regained consciousness, it became slowly apparent that she was no longer in the car. A cacophony of images came galloping back into her head, each vying for her attention. It took a few moments for her to recall everything that had happened. They had been racing away from under the ship and then there was a crash. Hadn't her children been in the car? Then she had seen a face... Her daughter! She sat up in the army medical cot, only for pain to shoot through her arm and back causing her to scream involuntarily. She quickly took in her surroundings. She was in some kind of medical tent, restrained on the cot by straps. Her other hand was in a cast. Different parts of her body ached and she was covered with a number of small cuts and bruises. She couldn't remember when she had last felt this bad – Perhaps after a night of drinking with her friend, Jackie, some six or seven years ago. She missed drinking sometimes, but she loved her kids more than she loved alcohol. That said, a shot of the good stuff would go down real well right now.

"Please don't move, Mrs Morrow. You suffered a fracture in the accident. Let me have these straps removed. They were for your own safety, we didn't want you falling out of bed with your injuries."

The voice was that of a man, unfamiliar, older than her. It reminded her of her father's. If this was Heaven it was not a good interpretation of the Bible.

"Where are my children? Are they hurt?" she asked, finding her voice dry and desperate for water. It was less of a question more an urgent demand for information. Further taking in her surroundings, she realised she was inside a large dark marquee that appeared to be a makeshift hospi-

239

tal. An air conditioning unit could be heard somewhere pumping cold air into the room. Despite that, she was sweating, it was giving her a chill. There were three people clustered around her. Two were men standing at the end of the cot, and a third, a young female Nurse was checking her pulse. The Nurse removed the restraints and helped her to sit up properly. It must have been dark outside, the only light in the room came from several small portable lamps which were spaced at intervals between the cots.

"Your daughter has been airlifted to Barton Memorial hospital. She took quite a knock but you mustn't worry - her condition is stable. Your son, Jack, is fine. They were lucky they both had their seatbelts on." The man spoke with confidence, which was reassuring, but perhaps that was his intention. She was never more overjoyed at having drilled the importance of putting seatbelts on into her kids, than she was in that moment. She wanted to get up, she wanted to see them, now more than ever. She tried to move again, only then realising that her left hand was bandaged. Underneath the dressings, she became aware of a gash along her arm. The wound did not feel deep, but it burned like nothing else she had ever experienced. She was going to have another scar. Great.

"You were lucky to get out from under the ship when you did. You could have all been killed," the male voice told her.

"Where is he? Where is my son?" she asked, as she struggled to focus. He was tall, extremely tall, well-built and dressed in a dark, snug-fitting suit, oddly inappropriate for the climate in this part of the country. Men wearing hand-tailored suits were not common on Highway 50. At least not that she had seen. Was she even still on Highway 50? He had short, neat grey hair and an American Flag button pinned to his left lapel.

"Where am I?" she pressed. She wanted answers and she wanted them now. The Nurse continued to check Diana's pulse as she spoke to her.

"You're in the F.I.M.A. emergency hospital. We're dealing with the casualties from the Mount Augusta landing."

"Casualties? Where is my son?" Diana asked, her eyes searching the room. It was large and there were several dozen cots, but most of them were empty. Some were occupied by older civilians and looked most likely to have suffered heart attacks or heatstroke. She assumed the ship would have caused total devastation on its impact. There would have been thousands of civilian casualties, but then they had been in a very remote area.

"He's fine, Mrs Morrow. He's next door with a social worker."

Jack was close by. Good. She felt a huge sense of relief.

"A social worker? How long have I been unconscious?"

The Nurse leaned in to answer her question. "Just for a day. You'll be fine to walk after a little rest. Take these painkillers, they'll help to make you feel more comfortable. You have a couple of fractured ribs and you banged your knee up pretty good. I'm going to give you something for that. We're just waiting for more supplies to arrive today," she said, her voice kind and laced with experience. The Nurse presented Diana with three small tablets in a plastic cup, handing her a bottle of water. Diana eyed the tablets with suspicion; two blue and one white. The Nurse waited expectantly for her to swallow them. It appeared she didn't really have much choice. The pain she felt in her back and arm was twinging sharply every few seconds, so there was plenty of incentive. She duly complied and took the largest gulp of water she could. There was nothing worse than getting a fat tablet stuck at the back of your throat. She tried to rationalise and slow down her racing mind. Jack was with a social worker. She needed to see him as soon as possible. A day, did they say? They had a social worker here already, as well as FIMA. The tall man moved over towards the end of the cot and unfolded a canvas chair so he could sit close to her. The second man who accompanied him stood further back, and appeared to be taking notes. Diana couldn't make him out too clearly but he was African-American. Her head still hurt and the lamplights that backlit the figures crowding her bed began to sting her eyes.

"Mrs Morrow, I need to ask you a few questions, then you can be with your son, okay?"

The Nurse frowned at this suggestion. She at least seemed genuinely concerned for her wellbeing. She tucked a foam pillow behind her head and made it easier for her to sit up.

"Only a few. She needs to rest. Mrs Morrow, I will go and check on your son for you. I will let him know you're awake and see if we can bring him in to see you. It's getting late, so he might be sleeping."

"Either you go and get him or I will!" Diana said, feeling the anger in her voice but trying to contain it. Shouting at people generally never got you anywhere. She so wanted to see Jack, but if he was sleeping it was probably best to let him alone. It was just that until she held her babies, her children, that she'd fed and clothed, in her arms, she knew she wouldn't be able to stop thinking about them. She had to see them for herself to know for sure they were okay. She needed to get to the hospital to see her daughter. What had happened to Craig and Owen? The memories of the two men who had saved them from certain death came flooding back to her. The man removed the handcuffs from her left wrist.

"What were they for? Was I under arrest?" She hadn't even noticed them, before.

"No, no. I am very sorry about that," the man said. He didn't look sorry. "We've had some security issues with some of the people we have detained. There have been instances of aggression towards some of the medical personnel. At a time of crisis, we really can't have that but I don't think you're going to cause us that kind of trouble – are you?"

The man let the open question hang in the air. Diana did not reply.

"I'll get you some more water." The Nurse took the cup from her.

She nodded at the Nurse, who smiled at her and left. The man offered a smile of his own, but Diana could see it contained the barest shred of genuine compassion.

"Mrs Morrow, I will try and be as brief as I can. Tomorrow morning we will lay on some transport to take you to the hospital at Lake Tahoe so that you can join your daughter, but I can assure you she is in good hands. I have spoken to the hospital personally. I have two daughters of my own you know, so I can understand how worried you must be."

"Thank you." There was something about this man she instantly mistrusted. His suit was just a little too neat and there was not a speck of dust on it, which meant he must have been flown in here by helicopter.

"We've had to do some tests to make sure you've not been put at risk..."

"You mean infected? Wouldn't it be more prudent for us to have been put in quarantine?" She immediately regretted asking the question. The last thing she wanted was to be separated from her children. The man became a little flustered, losing his composure for a second.

"It would have been but that didn't quite happen. You're in a quarantine of sorts for now, but we have no reason to believe anything is medically wrong with you other than the injuries caused by the car crash."

"Do you work for FIMA too?" she asked, cautiously.

"I'm with a different branch of the Government, but I'm working alongside the various agencies involved here."

"Do I get a name" She knew getting a name was always vital.

"My name is Jackson Bryce. I've been tasked with gathering information from anyone who got to see one of these ships up close. It certainly sounds like you had a close encounter, from what I understand."

"You could say that. We were nearly crushed by it!" The images of just how close they had been had not left her memory.

"Yes, you had a very lucky escape it seems," he added.

Diana flared up at the very suggestion. "Luck had nothing to do with it. If it hadn't been for those two young men that came along, me and my kids would have been trampled to death underneath it."

"You mean Mr Phillips and Mr Connors?" Bryce asked, casually.

"I didn't exactly get around to asking them their surnames. I mean Craig and Owen. My car broke down and then the... the thing, the ship or whatever you want to call it came along, and decided to land right where we were stuck."

"I see. So where were you and the children heading off to?"

"Lake Tahoe, to see my brother. It that illegal? Because last time I looked it wasn't." She was becoming fed up with his questions, and it was obvious he had barely started.

"Did you get to see anything under the ship?"

She had seen something. She was trying to remember... then she remembered. Holding her hand out... If she told him it could delay her from seeing her children. No.

"Like what? Little Green Men?" Her sarcasm was evident, but she was in pain and one of her kids was in hospital. The other was in the company of a stranger. She wasn't in the mood to answer more questions.

"Mrs Morrow..."

"Miss. My divorce just came through last week. I hadn't had time to update my ID yet, if that's where you got the Mrs from,' she said, dryly.

"Miss Morrow then. I am sure you can appreciate that these craft represent a considerable threat to this nation's security and indeed the world, so if you can tell us anything useful I would be very grateful."

What could she tell him? The images were all still so jumbled in her head.

"I didn't see anything, apart from one huge damn ship coming down on top of me and my kids. The lower part of it looked to be drilling down into the ground. That much I do remember, but it was weird...'

"How so?"

"It felt as if more dust or dirt should be coming up, if you were drilling into the ground like that. Nothing like that happened. So I guess you could say that was weird. You know, apart from the twenty-mile-wide spaceship thing!" she added, sarcastically. It occurred to her to ask him something.

"Are we being invaded? I mean, this thing, is it still here?"

"Oh it's still here, and others like it, all across the world. We're in a state of national emergency, Miss Morrow."

Bryce took a moment before he asked his next question. She thought he was trying to gauge if she was being truthful. The reality was that she was too tired to care. Her head was throbbing and her wrist ached. She wanted to see Jack, then get out of here and get to Jules' bedside as soon as possible. The thought of her in a strange place, alone, made her go cold. Though she was certain her daughter, brave though she was, would be even more distressed. Bryce removed a small silver case from the inside his jacket, opening it to reveal his business cards.

"If anything comes back to you Mrs Morrow, sorry, Miss Morrow, please give me a call or drop me an email."

He showed her the card, but rather than giving it to her he placed it down by the side of the cot. She craned her head and noticed her bag was actually right next to her cot on the floor. She would have to wait for him to leave before she searched it for her phone. The Nurse returned, accompanied by an excitable small figure running towards her.

"Mom! Are you okay?" Jack yelled, as he clambered on to the cot.

"I'm fine... Mommy's okay, just a bit shook up is all" She winced in pain as he flung himself over her stomach, his arms clinging on to her for dear life, his face streaked with tears.

"Not so tight, Mom's a bit delicate right now" Her son eased his grip. Bryce watched, smiling. He looked pleased to see her reunited with her son, and backed away from the bed.

"I shall leave you to your family reunion. Nurse, please show me where the other witnesses are located." It was a demand rather than a request. Whoever this Bryce was, he carried a great deal of authority around here. She thought to ask him another question.

"Mr Bryce. Can I ask you something?"

Bryce stopped and turned.

"I stopped at a gas station at a place called Middlegate, east of where my car broke down. The owner there was very kind to me. Do you know if the ship passed it by?"

Bryce dipped his head for a moment, before he gave her an answer.

"It's underneath the circumference of ship. Anyone who worked there would be listed as missing. That's all I can tell you for now." He walked off towards the other cots, guided by the Nurse, with his quiet companion in tow. Diana remembered the woman at the truck stop and the free meal she had given them, the husband in the kitchen she could not quite see, his funny arms flapping around in the kitchen. She hoped they had left in time. She turned back to Jack, holding him as close as was comfortable. She recognised his familiar smell and felt the need to touch his hair. His hands felt cold, but he was free of injury except for a small plaster on his forehead.

"Have you been okay?"

He nodded his head, looking around the room. Then he saw her bandages on her hand, and his face was at once full of worry.

"Are you hurt, Mommy?"

"Just a little knock, but Mommy's fine. I just banged my hand. Have you seen Owen or Craig? The two men who helped us?"

He shook his head. "Your sister?" He shook his head again. She pulled him towards her and gave him as much of a hug as she dared, her body protesting in pain.

"Don't worry about Jules, she's okay. They had to take her somewhere to get fixed. We'll go and see her really soon." Jack seemed unconcerned.

"I've been watching the TV with some other children. They have a room set up for us but you should see outside, Mom!" Jack pointed to the door.

She hoped they hadn't let him watch any horror films. Once he'd managed to start watching *The Thing* when she had fallen asleep next to him on the sofa. She was woken an hour later to him screaming at the scene depicting a man's stomach ripping open, revealing teeth that bit off another man's hands. He'd had nightmares for weeks after that. The Nurse returned to her bedside with some pain medication.

"Take two of these every four hours for the next couple of days. You were lucky Miss Morrow. Nothing was broken but you've been banged around quite a bit."

"Is it okay if I take a walk? I really need the rest room."

The Nurse looked around behind her as if checking to see if she might get in trouble.

"Okay, go on then, but don't take too long. They're just to the right outside the tent. Make sure you get some rest tonight, you need to sleep." The Nurse turned to her other patients. There were perhaps twenty in all, and the capacity of the marquee must have been able to deal with ten times that. Diana was surprised there were so few, even with the remote nature of their location. With the dimensions of the ship, it must have caused some casualties in some of the surrounding towns and farms. It took a few slow, careful movements to get out of the bed and stand up. Everything ached, and she could tell that rest was certainly what her body required right now, but her determination was focused elsewhere. She needed to speak to Jules. She checked her bag, but her phone was gone. Jack pulled at her hand and led her towards the opening that led into the night air. Outside of the FIMA tent, she was amazed at the sight before her, reminding her of the first time she had seen a music festival but somewhat more organised. Row upon row of khaki tents and portable cabins of different shapes and sizes stretched out endlessly in either direction in long rows north and south of the east-west running Highway 50. She was standing about five hundred metres south of it. She judged she was some way west of where her car had broken down. An angry buzz of helicopters came from overhead, while on the ground, groups of men in a variety of uniforms ran back and forth completing urgent tasks. The camp was illuminated by a series of colossal lights mounted on portable cranes. She thought for a moment that she was stepping into daylight. It reminded her of the football games on late, warm summer evenings back at High School. Facing west she could see Highway 50 curving its way in-between the distant hills and mountains, beyond which she knew was Lake Tahoe. The Highway itself was easily distinguishable because of the slow-moving trail of headlights emanating from a continuous stream of road traffic that was arriving beyond the camp. A smaller number of vehicles could be seen departing from the town of Fallon, further out to the west. A clear indication of those who wanted to stay and those who wanted to go. The incoming traffic came to a halt at the first of a series of checkpoints that barred entry to the encampment. Rows of wire fences had been hastily erected across the road, and three checkpoints set up at intervals, each manned by squads of American Marines. Diana could see the intention was to construct a perimeter to keep sightseers away. Soldiers in their hundreds continued to deploy coils of wire across the open desert to deter people from simply driving around the checkpoints in their 4 x 4s and coming closer to the landing site from across country. People were certainly trying, with every type of transport imaginable, arriving from the west and pulling off the road. More than one car was warned away by a low, swooping helicopter and the occasional clatter of distant gunfire was heard. Undeterred, many had begun to pitch up camp in their RVs; she could even see one couple starting up a barbecue. They were going to need a vast amount of wire, she thought, to get it all the way around this thing. She was trying to understand why so many people would want to come so close to see something that represented such potential danger. The trail of cars went back even past the twinkling lights of Fallon, into the west until they faded from view. A collection of satellite trucks from local and national television stations had also pitched up beyond the wire. She was certain she saw one of the reporters from CBS News momentarily lit up by a cameraman, as she filed her story. The press on the ground were not alone. Helicopters had come with them. Dozens appeared, one after another, only to be warned off by patrolling military craft. Warnings were shouted from loudhailers in the air, while instructions were bellowed out from military working in unison with them on the ground. Just another layer to the scene of pandemonium that was unfolding before her eyes. If she had ever seen anything so crazy before in her life, she was struggling to recall it. Immediately around the tent she had emerged from, a wire mesh fence had been erected, similar to that which would surround a tennis court in a park. Beyond it to her left, a number of radar trucks and other military vehicles formed another hub of the encampment just two hundred metres along from where she stood. Between them and her was the block of portaloos, but her need to urinate had all but vanished. The sound of engines revving came from another unfamiliar-looking vehicle that pulled up across from her. It was a portable dual-missile launcher mounted on tank tracks, several of which now began to deploy at intervals, men with lights waving them into place like someone would guide a plane into a terminal at an airport. How on earth was she caught in the middle of all this? Even though this encampment was still taking shape, she sensed the grouping of vehicles to her left was the head-quarters of the operation, judging by the number of dark 4 x 4s arriving there, their blue lights flashing, important-looking men disembarking by the dozen. The man she knew as Bryce emerged from the marquee behind her, with two other companions. They marched purposefully towards this area, going through a gate manned by two armed marines with a salute, before disappearing inside a long dark truck that looked similar to the sort used as a Command Centre by the city police. She assumed this much at least, having only ever seen such things in the movies, not actually having ever seen a Police Command Centre in reality. A collection of portable cabins had been put in place near the vehicle, along with portaloos at regular intervals. Other personnel, who wore long white overalls, ran back and forth from one building to the next. Beyond the command area was a series of makeshift helicopter landing pads, marked out with sandbags and portable rotating yellow lights. Helicopters of all types and sizes were landing, disgorging more personnel and supplies and taking off again barely a minute later. Jack must have been as mesmerised by all the activity going on as she was. He didn't say a thing, but just held her hand and stared in every direction and then looking back at her. Everywhere someone was busy carrying out a task. There was not a stationary soul to be seen anywhere, apart from a small group of civilians who had emerged from another marquee next to their own, but they were looking in the other direction. East! She thought to look east and turned around one hundred and eighty degrees to see for herself once again the cause of all this activity. It was still there, a surreal sight in the dark desert landscape.

The glowing pearl-white edge of the craft was nestled between the hills, with the remote cone-shaped tower rising high in the distance, its presence dominating the night sky. The illumination that came from the object gave ghostly shadows across the landscape. The tower was perhaps a dozen miles away, standing as a beacon that must have been visible all the way back to Lake Tahoe. Several spotlights from more than a dozen helicopters were shining their beams upon it, reminding her of a Christmas tree with its twinkling lights, at this distance. The rim of the saucer part of the ship was at least two or three miles from where they stood. It ran in either direction, both north and south, for as far as she could see, before it began to curve slowly out of sight. With the town of Fallon in the west being within sight of the camp, she must have been on the other side of the foothills from where her car had broken down. That was good. She knew it put her closer to both Jules and Danny. She would need to find out when and where this transport was departing to the hospital at Lake Tahoe. A sign marked *Secondary Quarantine* was attached to one of the fences, but no one had worn any protective clothing when they had visited her. She didn't feel sick, at least not aside from the aching limbs and her pounding head.

"Looks like you made it okay," said a familiar voice. She turned around and was unexpectedly filled with joy to see Owen and Craig standing before her. Owen's hand was in a cast, but Craig appeared to have come through their crash unscathed, aside from a small cut on his forehead. Jack broke free from her hand and ran to hug them both. Diana was always surprised by how affectionate he could be to people he had just met. Not such a good quality in a child where stranger danger was concerned, but endearing nonetheless. These guys had, after all, saved their lives, so her son's enthusiasm was not entirely unwarranted, and it had to be said Craig was very easy on the eye.

"Hey little dude! Glad to see you're okay." Owen ruffled Jack's hair.

"How you feeling?" Craig asked, joining her to gaze at the ship, its soft glow bathing the surrounding hills with light.

"I've got one hell of a headache. How's your van?" she asked. Craig shook his head, indicating it must have been a write-off.

"I think my insurance premiums have probably just gone through the roof! I'm so glad Jack's okay. Your daughter… is she alright?" Craig could have almost been stepping on glass as he said those words, because they sounded so painful.

"They told me she was airlifted out. Do either of you have your phones?" she asked, with vain hope. They both shook their heads.

She could see Craig was holding something. It was her rucksack, the one that contained all the food.

"I managed to get your pack. Don't ask me how, I picked it up after the crash, told them you had urgent medications. In the confusion they let me keep it." Craig handed it to her.

"Yeah but then that Bryce douchebag came along and took all our phones and cameras," Owen said, sounding angry.

"What's a douchebag?" Jack asked. Diane covered his ears in bemused embarrassment.

"Bro, the kid. Mind your language," Craig chastised his brother. Diana and he locked eyes for a moment until they both smiled. She felt herself biting the top of her lower lip. God, did she really just do that? Craig looked away, back at the ship. She could see he felt guilty, it had been their car after all, but she knew the reality was that the crash was probably her fault. She was the one who'd delayed their departure by grabbing their bags and ID. Those few crucial seconds probably made all the difference. Ultimately, they didn't need to rescue her and the kids at all. They could have just beat it out of there and left them to their fate. She went through her bag. She had stuffed their ID and what little money they had into the top zip-up pocket and she was pleased to see it was all still there along with the diamond rock the size of a child's fist. It was darker somehow than she remembered. She wrapped it in some tissue and put it back inside.

"We appear to be prisoners," Craig said, pointing to the makeshift wire fence. The four of them stood there in awe at the complex military operation taking place around them. Their compound around the marquee contained a block of portable toilets and some picnic-style tables, but not a great deal else. It had two exit points, both manned by armed soldiers. Diana had never liked guns around her children. Too much could go wrong too quickly. She found the number of mass shootings in America in the last two decades extremely troubling, praying like everyone else that it would not be something that rudely came calling on her one day. One exit led back towards the highway, and the main entry point to the camp. The second cut through to the collection of command vehicles in front of the helicopter landing pads.

"How the hell did they set all this up so quickly?" Diana said.

"That over there," Craig replied, pointing back westwards behind them towards the lights of the town, "Is the town of Fallon, and that second bunch of lights where you can see the planes coming in and taking off, that is Fallon Naval Air Station. There's actually a second naval base right near where we picked you up, just on the other side of the hills. The ship must have completely enclosed it, so that would partially account for the military being able to deploy so much so quickly. Transport planes have been coming and going non-stop since we've been detained here."

"They probably didn't take to kindly to the ship landing on top of a Naval Station," Diana said.

"No, probably not, but it's there. We saw it on Google Earth. Just past Middlegate, to the south," said Craig.

"This whole area is used by the Navy for training. They've probably been testing ships with alien tech on them for years. That airbase is America's Top Gun now." It was the most intelligent Owen had managed to sound since Diana had met him.

"I thought that was at Miramar?" She remembered that from the movie with Tom Cruise, wondering where the bar was that was so populated with beautiful women hunting for handsome fighter pilots – Somewhere in *Imaginationland*, she expected.

"They moved it back here in 1996. I don't think the actual Top Gun academy exists anymore. They have over twenty radar stations there, so if anyone had an advanced warning of this thing's arrival, it would have been them."

"They have a nice museum too, it's very informative," Craig added, with a grin.

Diana hadn't noticed Fallon Naval Air Station before, but a cluster of red flickering landing beacons indicated its location to the west, just south of Highway 50 before the town. In the night sky above it, a chain of airborne lights could be seen approaching the station and coming in to land. Tonight, the place must have been as busy as LAX. Diana saw that it was from the base that the smaller helicopters were continuously ferrying men back and forth to their camp.

"They must have had plans in place for this sort of event, but this isn't the only ship on American soil. There's three more, well one of them is half in Mexico, the rest north of the border," Craig added.

"I bet the President loves that!" They both laughed. Were they flirting or was he just being nice? She couldn't tell.

Owen broke in. "They had to know they were coming! They had to know when, they had to know where! No way could they set all this up that fast, even with the navy on the doorstep!" The blaring of car horns drew their attention towards the ever-increasing number of headlights pulling up around the outer perimeter, west of the encampment. More and more civilian vehicles were pulling off the side of the road and forming a camp of their own. More people were lighting up gas stoves and barbecues. People had come prepared. Someone had planted a big billboard that read *Welcome to Earth*.

"Reminds me of the *Asterix the Gaul* books – all those little Roman Camps surrounding the Gaulish village," Craig said. She wasn't sure what he was talking about. She hadn't read the Asterix books. Graphic novels were not really her thing. French ones from the 1970s even less so. It was apparent however, that anyone who could grab some transport had come to get a look for themselves. There was now a huge build-up of additional arrivals at the outermost checkpoint, which stood about a mile away from where they were standing. The roar of engines belonging to several khaki canvas trucks drew their attention for a moment, their horns blasting angrily by as they stopped at the inner checkpoint, disembarking scores of soldiers who then ran up to reinforce the outer checkpoint in two columns. Someone could be heard shouting on a bullhorn, but the instructions were not audible from this distance. The build-up of traffic from the west was continually increasing. People were parking their cars either side of the road, and on the plain scrubland that ran along either side of the highway, making room for more vehicles coming up behind them. Some were content to just sit and look at the ship from where they stood. An almost carnival atmosphere had begun to form in places. Diana could see several blinks of light that must have been flash photography. The sea of lights reminded her of a crowd at a Michael Bolton concert only somewhat less congenial. Angry protests could be heard. People were determined to get closer and the military was not going to let them. How they could contain an area as large as this was anyone's guess. She could not see this ending well. If there were more of these things, one of which spanned the border of another country, what was going to happen? Oh dear. What a dilemma.

"I'd like to see the government try and blame this on a crashed weather balloon," Owen laughed. "but I'm sure they're going to try. Did you guys meet The Spook?"

"Spock?" Diana repeated, mistakenly thinking Owen was making a Star Trek reference. She didn't know much about Sci-Fi but she knew who Spock was.

"Spook, not Spock. Lady, you really did bang your head. No one's seen any aliens yet. I mean the guy from the Government. Bryce or whatever his name was. He didn't work for no FIMA. He was from the Agency, C.I.A all the way, no doubt about it."

"CIA, really? I wonder whose jurisdiction this mess falls under." Diana said. She didn't really wonder, she didn't really care. She just wanted to see her daughter, or to speak to her, at least. The Nurse might have a phone. She could ask her. Her mind raced with questions. She turned away from the distant shouts of chaos and looked back toward the pearl-white ship again, its glow giving the night sky a strange aura, lighting up the few scattered clouds above it.

"Incredible, isn't it? I wish my Jessica could have seen this," Craig murmured, almost to himself. She wondered who Jessica was and considered it might have been his ex.

"What do you think is in there?" she asked, wondering herself.

"Not sure. The good news is they haven't attacked anyone yet," came Craig's reply. "Whoever, or whatever, they are maybe."

He still reminded her of Lance Guest. She wondered did he even have a real job or just run around chasing UFOs for a living? That said, he might have hit a vein of job security for the immediate future.

"She's going to be okay, you know," he said, placing a hand reassuringly on her shoulder, and giving her that warm smile again. But she could see he was holding something back.

"I know. Are you okay?" She wanted to know what he was thinking.

A crack of thunder broke above them as two Air Force jets came roaring by, and shot towards the object before banking and following its circumference to the north.

"Give them time! We may just provoke them into a war yet! I wonder what the President has said about all this?" as Craig spoke, Diana dreaded to think.

"Maybe he's going to build a wall around it?"

"They seem to be trying already – Look at that…" Craig pointed to a chain of raised floodlights that were being switched on at intervals, heading in both directions around the circumference of the ship.

"That's going to be one hell of an electric bill. I mean how wide is that thing? Twenty, thirty miles?' Owen's question echoed what Diana had been wondering herself. It seemed even larger than it had when she'd first laid eyes on it.

"Did you hear, Diana? They've landed all over the world – two hundred of them!" Owen said, still marvelling at the craft in front of them. "They can't deny their existence any longer. Now we just need to find a way to talk to them, but you can bet our government will find a way to screw that up."

Diana didn't doubt he was right. Foreign diplomacy hadn't been America's strong suit, lately. She still couldn't get over the size of the thing. A huge part of it must have buried itself. If there were 200 of these things and they had all done the same thing, could that pull the earth apart?

"Soon no one is going to be able to get a close look at this thing. At least no one like us." Craig's words had a tone of conspiracy that worried her.

"We were nearly crushed by it! How much closer would you like to get?" Diana was not keen to repeat that experience.

"I want to see inside it," Craig stated emphatically.

"The thing nearly landed on top of us and crushed us all to death and now you want to go inside it?" Her words of protest were falling on deaf ears. She knew these guys had to be crazy.

"Sure, don't you want to know why they're here?" Craig pressed.

"I want to get back to see my daughter and make sure she's okay. What if you get into the thing and it decides to head back into space? Don't you have anyone who cares about you?" Diana wasn't sure entirely why she asked the last question.

"I want to go too, Mom. I want to see the aliens!" Diana had been so engrossed in their debate, she had completely forgotten that Jack was still there. She knelt down to him at once, and was going to pick him up but realised her injuries would not let her.

"Honey, you see that thing? We don't know where it's come from, or how long it's going to stay or why it's here. We need to get to the hospital and make sure that Jules is okay. You want to see your sister, don't you?"

"I guess. But I want to see the aliens too, Mom! If we go we might miss them!"

"The kid's right, this is world history happening right here, lady. Don't you want him to see that and be part of it?" Owen said, giving Jack a smile. Craig rolled his eyes. This twenty-something hippy obviously did not have kids or know the meaning of parental responsibility. If he did, he wouldn't have asked her something so stupid. If she had still been in her twenties, and childless then this sort of adventure might have appealed to her, but she wasn't. She was a single mother in her late thirties and she was getting angry and tired.

"He has seen it! It damned near killed him!" she snapped back. "I need to find my daughter, not be part of some foolish escapade, so you guys can be interviewed by the History Channel!"

She felt suddenly weak.

"I need to get out of here. I have to lie down. Craig, can you take Jack back to the social worker for me?"

She began to feel a little light-headed and staggered back to her bunk. Once in the tent, the last thing she remembered was the Nurse telling her off for staying on her feet for too long, before she fell into a deep sleep.

DIAMONDS IN THE SKY - PAROUSIA

PART TWO - THE NEXT SEVENTY-TWO HOURS

CHAPTER I

"Everyone says they knew what they were doing when 9/11 happened. Well, this was like that. Everyone knew what they were doing when they first saw them. For me it was blips on a screen. I was working an early shift at Air Traffic Control at ***censored*** *and everything was normal. There were no bulletins, no warnings, I mean even the weather was good that day. One minute my screen was quiet, just the scheduled traffic, nothing out of the ordinary, the next I've got a wave of blips that just appeared out of nowhere, and reports coming in from aircraft of UFO contacts across the board. Everyone was requesting go-arounds. The whole tower went haywire. It took us the rest of the day to get a handle on the situation and of course soon after that the order was given to ground all air traffic. One thing I never understood was how these things arrived on Earth without being detected. I mean they would have had to travel through our solar system. With all the satellites and other junk we have up there, how is it that no one saw them coming? Someone, somewhere, must have known something. We have all this technology that's pointing out into space. Are you telling me none of that picked these things up? Some of them are fifty miles across for God's sake! How on earth did they arrive completely undetected? That never made any sense to me."*

Anonymous Air Traffic Controller, giving evidence to the Fulton Commission, 6 months after Parousia

OMARI

I n the last hour it had become very evident to Omari that he hadn't yet
passed on to Paradise and was still very much alive and living on the
earth. But he felt he had been chosen by Allah to witness everything he had
discovered in the last few hours, even if he was not yet sure why. The final
leg of his journey home passed without incident. Omari, along with his
three camels, Abu-Sir, Abu-Kir and Abi-Baba arrived in Fada in the early
hours of the morning. He avoided several scattered groups of people who
had come to view the unearthly object, by travelling south first for a short
distance before turning directly east. He would give the impression he had
come from the caravan trail, and not from the landing site. He and his
animals covered the last few miles in record time, his beasts completing the
journey with an unusually energetic effort. His lungs breathed in the cool
morning air and he exhaled like an athlete, feeling the oxygen race around
his body. He could not recall a previous time in his life when he was able to
breathe with such vigour.

Fada was one of the most remote settlements in all of Chad, and if it
hadn't been for the wooded oasis that lay at the foot of the eastern mountains, then it was doubtful anyone would have ever settled there. It was
said to have a population of over twenty thousand people, though to an
outside observer one might wonder where they all lived. Three trails
converged at the central watering hole. The road coming in from the west
on which Omari travelled would take you to the larger town of *Faya-
Largeau*, and then eventually take you back to the capital, a distance of
several hundred miles. North, the trail led to the sparse village of *Ounianga*
on *Lake Yoa*. South led down towards the more fertile farmlands. With no

257

decent roads to speak of, to reach either of these destinations was a journey of several days, even weeks, making Fada an extremely isolated place. Visitors attracted attention easily. Most of its population had never even seen a foreigner apart from the odd teacher that had come. But Omari knew the presence of the incredible gift from Allah would bring many outsiders. He thought about everything he had seen and how different he felt. Normally, upon returning from his trading travels he would be exhausted, but this time he felt refreshed and energised. He would have to be careful what he said to people, and to whom. Once everyone discovered the wonderful properties that lay inside the gift from Allah all would want to partake in its riches, which would only bring the townsfolk of Fada into direct conflict with the Chadian army. Did he have the right to keep such knowledge from his people, though? This amazing place could heal the sick and rid his tribe of the wasting disease that still plagued many of his people. The medications were available but getting them was not always easy and once a person was on them, they had to have them for life to stay alive. If this was truly a gift from Allah for his people then all of them should benefit from it. He would have to meet the clan elders and discuss it with them. They would know what to do. He reached the outskirts of Fada just as the first light of dawn began to seep into the sky from the east. The scattered settlement had, however, not gone to sleep the night before. Its crude mud-constructed compounds that formed its many humble dwellings was awash with candles and small fires. Most of its population were still awake, observing and debating the awesome spectacle that lay west of the town. Omari could smell roasted goat and chicken, the scent of which made him hungry. He passed families clustered around their homes, many with children sleeping alongside them covered in blankets, the parents standing watch over them and all looking to the west. Omari nodded at a few familiar faces but was keen to press on to Attah's house in the northern part of the settlement, where both his brother's and his own homes were located. He reached the dusty crossroads on the south-east corner of the oasis. Omari had missed the smell of the palm trees, that greeted his nostrils in the pre-dawn breeze. Their fronds swayed gently in the air above him bringing back a rush of memories from his childhood, each of which he could recall with incredible clarity: running through the oasis paths playing games with his sisters; how he and his friend, Mustapha had hidden among the trunks of the trees to watch the girls bathe; the beatings they had both endured when they had been caught. He stopped his camels for a moment and his mind was filled with images. So many old memories attached to each place he passed came back to him. The wealthier clans of Fada lived in the area closest to the oasis. The larger compounds of the more affluent villagers and its elders sat next to the town bakery. Its adjacent market happened in a small square once a week. He remembered eating his first sweets at the simple trading post on the corner and buying clothes from Mama Bendi with his father. He steered his three animals slowly between the buildings. The sandy pathways between the houses in Fada were narrow affairs. Above them lay a bundle of wires hastily strung on wooden poles that spread and drooped in every direction, running power from one house to the next.

Here and there, a palm tree nestled between the light brown walls of the compounds. A group of excited children ran up to greet him and his camels. They wanted to know if he had seen "the white ark" on his return. Normally, he would give them sweets and engage them in conversation, but he passed the children with nothing more than a nod of his head, leaving them with looks of disappointment on their faces. As he trotted slowly along the dusty lane, it was even more evident that most of the town had not slept. Scattered clothes and other items to trade were still laid to sell outside people's doorways from the day before. Never losing an opportunity to trade, his people had obviously decided to try and sell a few more things in the process, as everyone was still up. Trade meant survival in this part of the world. Everyone knew and respected that simple equation. Bartering was a way of life.

Directly west of the oasis lay the old fort, covering an area of some 250 square metres. It had an inner and an outer compound, the former sporting a single tower on one corner from where the daily prayers of Adhan would be broadcast over the speakers when there wasn't a power cut. Omari knew he would be hearing that sound shortly. The walls of the fort were thick, and at places had buildings constructed into the sides that had once been stables to house the cavalry. It was still used as a base by the small local garrison. It would have been from here that the trucks would have transported its limited security force and deployed them to examine "the white ark", as the townsfolk of Fada had taken to calling it. The fort encased two of the larger wells that made up the oasis. Dotted around the inner courtyard were a number of palm trees and it was under the shade of one such tree that he had last laid eyes on his eldest daughter, Nya.

"Be good to your husband. Be safe and bring me news of my grandchildren. I am sure you will have many."

Omari recalled these last words to Nya, five years earlier. He could picture the conversation now so clearly, as if they were standing there only yesterday. Nya's beauty was unmatched by anyone in all of Fada, as if Allah had carved her face for himself. At their last meeting she had been leaving with her husband for the capital. Omari was proud of her, for she had married well and he had been given a generous dowry as a result which had allowed him to increase the size of his compound and buy more live stock. Nya had caught the eye of a visiting army Captain, who had been stationed in Fada to complete his training. Their courtship had been the subject of much gossip in the town. The road to their marriage had not been an easy one. In his clan, family was all-important and the bigger clans in Fada had all the power and controlled access to the most important thing, the oasis and its wells. Almost everyone in Fada had been born here. Clans had come and gone as families had risen and died out. Marrying into a powerful clan formed a bond of strength, and for two clans based so far apart to form a marriage was extremely rare. The marriage, it was rumoured, had been opposed by his family back in the capital, whose mother did not approve of their prodigal son marrying some village girl. But the Captain had made up his mind and would not be deterred. When he'd finished his training, Nya travelled with him back to *N'Dajmena*. Her departure had been the second hardest day in Omari's life. There was one thing that Omari always disliked and that was change but change was something that was imposing itself on his life ever more forcefully in recent years. His people had traditionally always lived a nomadic life, but as the world around them changed, this tradition was slowly dying and now many people had settled in Fada permanently as the caravan trade began to diminish.

"Omari, you're back! It is so good to see you! How long were you out for this time?"

Omari turned to see the owner of the town's trading post and his best customer, Pappa Bendi. Bendi was a tall, thin man, adorned in his simple white garments and a *tagiya*, wrapped round his head, sporting a long thin beard that came down almost to his groin. The bags under his eyes hung heavily and his skin was dry and blistered, his voice low and husky. Outside his shop, two other men looked up and nodded at Omari. They were playing backgammon and did not want to be disturbed, not even it appeared by such an unearthly event as the one taking place to the east of Fada. Pappa Bendi was older than Omari, though he wasn't sure quite how old. Both men were widowers and as such, a strong bond had formed between them. Everyone called him Pappa because he had fathered many children, and, it was rumoured, not all from the same woman. His shop was the best-stocked and everyone came to him for their cooking spices, the rarer ones of which Omari had always procured for him. Omari leapt down to hug the man he considered almost family. Pappa greeted him with a cry of joy then studied him hard, before breaking into a wide smile.

"You look good, my friend! Younger! I barely recognise you! What has happened? You even feel stronger!" he cried, as he squeezed Omari's arms. "Where are the rest of your camels?"

Omari gestured to the three creatures standing behind him.

"These three are all that is left. I think my trading days may have come to an end, brother. I was only able to fulfil half your order," Omari said, detaching the saddlebags from Abu-Sir and placing them next to the door.

"Everything is there. I can come back for the bags later." Pappa Bendi saw his sadness. Bendi had always been a very kind man. He recalled his father bringing him here in his youth for honey drops and tasting his first and only piece of chewing gum, some vile American invention. Omari recollected the horrid taste with utter clarity. He could even picture the pink wrapper of the gum and the money his father had used to buy it with. His ability to recall such memories as if selecting a book from a shelf, was incredible to him. He thought all such poignant memories were long gone. Pappa Bendi shuffled past him.

"So what do you think of our visitor? Did you get close to it?" Pappa stood aside from his shop and pointed west where the white tower was beginning to catch the first rays of sunlight, emerging from the eastern horizon. It looked taller than it had last night. Omari didn't like lying but he wasn't yet ready to tell the truth, even too his oldest friend. He took a swig of water to clear his throat.

"No. Not yet. I saw it landing yesterday as I returned. How are you?" he asked, trying to change the subject.

"What do you think it is? Where has it come from?" Pappa Bendi asked, nodding towards Allah's gift.

"I have no idea my friend, but if it has chosen to land here, close to our town, then it must be because Allah has willed it!"

Pappa Bendi nodded his head in agreement, and resumed his seat in front of the shop. Omari pulled another seat up and sat opposite him. He was keen to get home, but it would be good to know what people in the town were thinking and to refuse hospitality would cause not only offence but also suspicion. Pappa Bendi poured Omari a cup of hot, sweet tea and they both drank as they talked.

"The clans think the same. We hear on the television the President is saying it landed here because our town was his birthplace. They say people are travelling from all over Chad to come and see it, because it's the closest one. The Elders are holding a clan meeting today to discuss it."

Omari's mind stumbled for a moment. What did he say? The closest one?

"Pappa, are there more of these things in Chad?" he asked.

"Not just Chad, more of them all over the world Omari! There is another one in Sudan, another in Lake Victoria. Many have landed in Africa, more than any other continent!"

Omari's face betrayed a look of confusion. He thought this gift was something unique for his people alone. He felt disappointment that such a thing would be shared worldwide, thinking about what the consequences might be of such power being in the hands of others. He could not imagine westerners treating the place with the same reverence and respect as he had. Why would Allah do such a thing? But he reasoned with himself, was it not the will of Allah to bring peace? Yes, he could see the global potential of Allah's will. It could heal the sick and the needy all across the world, but he could also foresee the conflict this could cause. Omari's heart sank steadily the more the thought about it. Once the military, the wealthy and politicians knew of its potential power, his people would not be allowed anywhere near it. The powerful would want it for themselves. His people would be deprived of all it had to offer them. No, he could not allow this to happen. He would have to act fast.

"Are you okay, Omari?" Pappa Bendi asked. Abruptly, their attention was drawn skywards. The whirling sound of propellers drew them towards an approaching aircraft coming in from the south-west. The other locals, Omari, Pappa Bendi and all three camels looked up to see the small plane with Chad Airforce markings pass low above them and then bank west towards the vessel. They watched it bank and turn again around the structure of the tower before coming into land. Omari knew if Chad didn't send their army here, someone else certainly would. Their country had plenty of angry neighbours to choose from. It was good to know Sudan had their own object to contend with.

"He must be landing at the old strip. They say this thing landed just a mile west of there. The pilot would have had a good view, for sure. I never thought I would live to see such a thing, at my age!" Pappa Bendi took a small sip from the tea, sounding refreshed.

"Has anyone else come from the capital, yet?" Omari asked, as he drank deeply. The tea tasted sweet, better than he could ever recall. It was as though his taste buds were more sensitive than before. Sharper, even. He took a second sip, which was even more delicious than the first.

"No, just some of the caravans have come in, but no one else. Do you think they will send more people?" Bendi asked.

"I am sure they will. The army will come in force for certain. Probably the people from the television too, with their cameras." Omari had seen a camera crew once before, when the fighting had broken out in the capital when he had been there with his father. He had forgotten that before, but he could remember it now, as though it happened just yesterday. His mind turned to the Elders and what he might say to them.

"When are the Elders meeting?"

"After morning prayers, in the compound of the fort. I think most of the town will be present."

Omari knew that a meeting with the Elders of all the local clans would be a very rare thing for Fada. Such occurrences would always be much smaller affairs, normally to resolve local disputes between clans. Several heads of other families would come and sit, listen, debate and mediate until a resolution was found. Once a decision was made, it was almost never broken. For one to break the will of the clans would incur the wrath of them all, and a family's name would be forever tarnished. It was a system of local law that had served the region for many generations. The region's plots and wells were all owned by the local clans. Access to these meagre resources by outsiders was not welcome without payment. The clan with the most influence in Fada, were the brothers Aziz. Both had fathered many children and the younger brother had taken many wives. Polygamy was uncommon in Fada but it was acceptable, though Omari always marvelled at the men who did so. One woman was more than enough as far as he was concerned. Even the most respected of clan Elders never made a decision without first consulting his wife in secret for guidance.

"Some people in the town are talking about leaving. You know Little Ubba? One of the children from the orphanage school run by the Limey..."

Little Ubba, one of the orphans of Limey Dennis. Dennis was the only citizen in Fada with an English-sounding name and also the biggest supporter of Arsenal in Fada, he was one of the few outsiders who had lived in the city, left and then returned. Dennis must have been a similar age to Omari, when he had first appeared in Fada to teach children a few years back. He then left, only to return to run and teach at the orphanage school a year later. He had personally taken in many of the orphans in the town, and was highly respected by many of the villagers for doing so. Little Ubba was one such child and the craftiest of all the orphans in Fada. He knew every street, and every place where he could scrounge food to eat. That boy was a bundle of curiosity, and always wanted to know about everything and everyone. People weren't sure of his age. Perhaps he was eight, perhaps ten. His height was one thing that was not in debate. He was extremely small, but never lacking in energy. As with many of the street children, Dennis had taken him under his wing. Pappa leaned in close to whisper to Omari, for the jungle drums could travel fast, even in the desert.

"Little Ubba claims he went out onto 'the white ark' last night. He said he got inside but I don't think anyone believed him. How would he have got all the way there with no camel or no car and then back here in time for morning?"

Little Ubba had a reputation for telling fantastic stories, few of which were true but Omari knew the boy could have done it. He would need to speak to him.

"When did he return?" Omari asked.

"I think an hour ago. The Elders have asked to see him. That boy has such an imagination. Do you know he said that there is water surrounding the object now? What a story!"

Pappa Bendi laughed so hard, he almost fell off his chair. Omari feigned a smile in response, but now he knew the boy was not lying. This was no longer a secret that could be contained. He would need to see the Elders as soon as possible.

"Do you know what some of the children are calling it? The coconut! They say it looks like one that has been skinned!" Bendi laughed again. "I like the white ark better I think."

Omari admitted he was not sure what to call it himself. Ship? Vessel? He wasn't sure what was most befitting. Perhaps once others had been inside, they would all come to call it what it was to him - Paradise. They drank the rest of their tea in silence, as they marvelled at the pre-dawn light changing the colours of the sky before them. They watched in reverence as the upper portion of the tower of the coconut shone with an incredible brilliance. Its height making it privy to the first rays of the dawn, several minutes before the land beneath it.

"You must be tired. Will you not stay and eat at my bar?"

Pappa Bendi's bar was nothing more than two fridges and a big TV set, where the men sat and watched the football games played by their favourite teams. People referred to it locally as *The Bendy Bar*, which Pappa himself was not too fond of. The sign above it read *Pappa's*.

'I must go, I need to get back and see my daughter. Thank you for the tea." He rose to leave, but at the mere mention of his daughter there was at once a change in the face of his friend.

"Do not go home, go straight to your brother's. Do not warn him you are coming. Approach his home quietly. Make no sound," Bendi said, his face now serious.

"What are you saying, Pappa?" Omari did not like his cryptic words. They were weighted with a meaning, one which had been nagging at the back of his mind.

"I'm just saying that I think it would be good if your brother did not know you were coming."

"He is only my half-brother," Omari said, feeling a need to verbally distance himself from the man. He had never really been that close to him.

"Yes, you and he are not alike, my friend. Not alike in any way at all. Come by later and we shall eat together."

He nodded and returned to his animals with a single purpose in his mind. The camels appeared to be in tune with their master and obliged him with an urgent pace. Fada was now fully awake. While some people had gone back to sleep, others were beginning their daily tasks undeterred by the continual presence of the white structure on the horizon. People congregated in small groups, talking and pointing, uncertain of what it was they were looking at. He saw several fearful faces, with many talking of leaving. He knew if his people abandoned Fada it would be a mistake.

"Do not leave, my friends. I travelled very close to it and it did not harm me, it is a gift from Allah." He repeated the words again to several more groups of people, but refused to be drawn into further conversation. Omari continued up the main road passing the imposing sandy walls of the ancient fort on his left. He could see that the gates to the eastern entrance were open, but he saw no soldiers. He suspected the local commander had probably taken every able-bodied man with him to investigate the landing site. He went on past, to where the main track of the town split in two, with one fork to the right heading north-east and through the oasis, while the other headed north-west, where several of the more desirable dwellings lined the road. Omari took the left-hand fork, heading north-east, passing the two compounds belonging to the tribal leaders, each containing more than a dozen trees behind their high walls. The houses were modest, not much larger than his own, but to have a space where your own palm trees grew freely was worth its weight in water in Fada. Attah's compound was located further along the track, another ten minutes of travel away. Here, beyond the oasis, the dwellings of Fada became more sparse and spread out. Date palms still sprouted at intervals between the houses which had been constructed at random intervals with no thought to the design or layout of the town. Families had built where they liked when they first began to settle here, but now clan consent would have to be given for any new building work to take place. Not many people requested such permission. Fada was not a growing settlement. Up ahead he saw the walls of Attah's compound. Attah was Omari's half-brother by a marriage his Father had entered into when he was very young. His first wife had died in childbirth and his Father never spoke of her, until Attah turned up on the family doorstep in his twenties, resulting in a family meeting where his father was forced to explain who he was. Omari remembered now, with more clarity than ever before, how his father would never look Attah in the eye when he spoke to him. Attah had lived with them for a while, but he never wanted to embrace the nomadic way of life. Back then the family moved around with the caravans and everyone would travel together. Attah would dip in and out of their life at different intervals, until one day after an argument over something Omari wasn't privy to, Attah had left and his father promptly announced he was no longer welcome.

Attah's compound was on the corner where the track split again at another junction. His compound was a good size for a man of his means, though Omari was never really quite sure how he made his living. He always seemed to have an abundance of money one week and nothing the next. He had asked to borrow money from Omari once, but Omari didn't have anything to lend him, even if he had wished to do so. He had been to Attah's house before and he knew the layout well. High mud walls enclosed an area of about one hundred square metres. Inside, there were two compounds split by a second central wall, which formed one side of the main house. The gated entrance was located on the south-east corner, directly facing him as he came up the road. Attah had, last year, rather boastfully, installed a heavy iron gate with spikes along the top which contained a lockable smaller door through which one could step. Theft in Fada was extremely rare. The price was very heavy for anyone who was unlucky enough to be caught, so Omari had always thought the gate to be a totally unnecessary expense. He knew that Attah had once employed a gateman, who slept in a small hut located just inside. He wasn't even sure if the man still worked there, but he decided upon entering via a different way. The dispersing clouds of night were already becoming lamps of purple and red as the dawn fully emerged in the sky above Fada. Soon it would be day. Omari steered Ali-Baba over towards the southern wall of the compound. He stood upright on Ali-Baba and reached upwards to the top of the wall. "Steady my friend, please do not move." A day earlier, he never would have had the strength to perform such a task but this morning he felt extremely agile and able-bodied. Placing one foot softly on the top of Ali-Baba's hump, he quickly pulled himself up and over, dropping into the other side of the compound. In one corner a goat sat up, tethered by rope to the ground. His presence made the chickens in the nearby coop, cluck in concern for their eggs. Omari crouched and waited to see if he aroused any attention, but there was no movement anywhere. He glanced back at the gateman's hut. A simple one-room affair containing a raised box constructed from wooden pallets on which to sleep. It looked unused for sometime, its occupant had obviously long departed. Attah probably had been unable to pay him, such was his reputation. The courtyard was littered with the debris of unfinished projects. A collection of white plastic water containers was piled up against one wall, while a stack of car tyres propped open the door that led further inside. Omari thought them strange, as he knew Attah could not drive. Over by to his right next to the chicken coop, Omari noticed something odd. There was a pile of broken beer bottles on the ground, which, upon closer inspection Omari realised had been used for target practice. Clusters of bullets were embedded in the wall. Owning a weapon in Fada was not unusual. Many people prized Russian assault rifles, especially if they were Deza, the more warrior-like clan of the Toubou people. Such weapons were durable, easy to clean and handled well in the desert, (and were probably the only rifle that Omari knew could claim that achievement). All of their variants used the same calibre ammunition, which made them very popular with clans and bandits alike. The only rifle he had ever owned, given to him by his late Father, was long since lost and he had never wished to replace it. He had never killed a man, and he didn't wish to add it to his small list of life achievements.

Omari craned his head around the door, looking across at the doorway that led inside the home. Attah's main house was a simple three-room affair, with a kitchen, living room and a bedroom at the back. As he stepped through to the inner compound, a pervading stench of excrement hit his nostrils, originating from the outhouse that was located in the far corner. A line of washing hung from the house to the one tree that grew inside the inner compound, holding both male and female garments. Two fraying armchairs sat outside like the abandoned thrones of a forgotten kingdom. People of Fada took pride in their houses, but there was little evidence of that here. The walls of the house were more modern in construction, but poorly tended to, littered with cracks in which lizards would sleep during the day. The ground was strewn with rubbish and covered with further broken beer bottles. Children could not run freely here. His daughter, Joy, was a very petite girl, extremely slim and looked young for her age. When Omari had last seen her, she still looked like his little girl and had been dressed in her bright orange burka. That burka was hanging from the washing line. As he touched it he heard something, a noise, from somewhere inside the house. Voices, two perhaps, sounds, but not a conversation. He entered the dimly lit living area. A small table sat in front of several cushions scattered across the floor and a large television was in one corner. Omari had not seen many people with a television so large, nor so flat in Fada. He wondered where and how Attah had acquired it. A few books and magazines were strewn about the floor. Flies buzzed around the open area of the kitchen, which contained a single chair covered in dirty towels and a solitary wooden table. Unwashed pots and pans were stacked up in one corner, while in another sat the fridge. Cupboards were open and bare, but a basket of fresh fruit and vegetables sat on the work-top. A bucket full of peeled potato skins along with a stool was tucked into one corner. Omari stepped through the kitchen and into the short corridor that led to the bedroom. Ahead of him a dark cloth had been pinned to hang above the doorway to the bedroom, creating a curtain, beyond which he could hear the whispered voices. Omari instinctively stood back and reached back around into the kitchen, grabbing a beer bottle from the table, then stood behind the cloth. His hearing had been quite poor of late but now was acutely sensitive to even the smallest of sounds. He could hear hands gripping clothing and removing them from flesh. The rapid heart-beat of a young woman and her nervous protest in whispered words.

"No, not again, please uncle!" The heavy breathing of a man and his words. "Just give me what I want, then you can make us breakfast..." Flesh upon flesh. Tearing. Pain. "Oh yeah, that's it, just like your uncle taught you... be good for your uncle now!"

Omari pulled back the dark curtain, just enough to reveal the bedroom beyond. There were no windows but Omari could see the naked shape of his half-brother standing at the end of the bed. Omari had never seen him undressed. He was more portly than stocky. He had more hair on his arms and back than on his head and was shorter than Omari at only five-foot-four. His bulk towered above the waif-like body of his daughter. Joy was on all fours at the end of the bed with rolled blankets placed underneath her stomach, her legs protruding from either side of where he stood behind her. Omari could smell his breath and sweat from here. "Please Uncle, it always hurts so much…"

"Come now, my little flower, you ought to know how to do it by now…" Attah barely had time to react to the sound of the bottle being smashed, before the glass was being plunged forcefully into his throat. Omari with bottle in hand came into the room with such strength, he even surprised himself. He charged into his half-sibling, carrying him of his feet and throwing him against the wall. Attah's eyes widened as he searched for the identity of his surprise assailant. Joy curled up on the bed, watching as Omari took the bottle out from Attah's neck and plunged it straight into his half-brother's still erect penis. He stabbed Attah several times in the groin before bringing the bottle back to his face again. All this happened in barely a few heartbeats. Attah tried to scream but all that came was a gargle from his torn throat. Blood sprayed across Omari's face and onto the wall. Omari pulled the bottle out again and plunged it back into the neck wound, sending it right through the man's throat and embedding it into wall. Attah's eyes bulged from their sockets staring back at him. The sounds of his last gasp for air was something Omari knew would haunt him. He let the fat carcass of the man stay pinned to the wall in front of him, his adrenaline still pumping through his veins. Joy burst into tears. Omari stepped back from the lifeless body, his face and hands covered in blood, shaking. He turned to see his daughter sobbing on the bed, her face buried into the covers in shame, pulling them around her to protect her modesty. Omari searched the room for her discarded clothing. He caught a brief glimpse of blood from between her legs as he began to cover her. The sound of her raw sobbing was more than he could bare. A sound that no parent would ever wish to hear. Omari knew that this kind of abuse was common in his part of the world. No one ever liked to talk about it, but he couldn't believe it would ever happen to someone he cared about, especially not a member of his own family.

"Father, I am sorry, I have brought such shame upon you… he forced me…" Her words were barely audible as she pressed her face even further into the bedding. Omari immediately cradled his daughter in his arms and forced her face up to look at his. It was the first time he had locked eyes with Joy in many months. Her face was streaked with tears, her cheeks bruised from a beating.

"He did this? He beat you?"

"Many times. It started soon after you left. He asked me to do things, things I knew were wrong. When I tried to stop him, he hit me so I did as he asked but sometimes he would hit me anyway."

"Why didn't you run away?"

He was angry. His daughter could have left. She could have told someone. Pappa Bendi, even. They were not without friends.

"Because of Tabitha. He said if I did not do the things he wanted he would do them to Tabitha and that would be my fault. I'm sorry, I have brought so much shame upon you." She buried her head in her hands and a second wave of crying and tears came. Omari lifted her chin and forced her once again to look him in the eye.

"Listen to me, precious daughter. It is I, who has brought shame upon you. Do you understand? This is my fault, not yours. I never should have left you with your Uncle. I had my doubts about him but I never thought he would do anything like…" He held her tight and let her cry out the last of her tears as he hid his own from her. After some minutes had passed where neither of them spoke, he took her firmly by the shoulders.

"Joy, you are never to speak of this to anyone. You understand? He will not hurt you again." Joy's eyes flittered towards the body, but Omari held his daughter tightly and brought her back to him. "Focus on me, don't look at him. He is gone. You, you were not here today, do you understand? Now we need to leave." Omari stopped. Who had she been talking about?

"Who is Tabitha?"

Joy pointed back towards the compound outside.

JOY

J oy dressed quickly and beckoned her father to follow her outside. She
felt light-headed and hungry. She wanted to wash, but such thoughts
were abated by the reunion with her father and other more immediate
concerns. She could still smell her uncle's foul breath and taste his saliva on
her lips; a taste which would linger long past any immediate washing.
Now there was another in greater need than herself. Joy had always put
others' needs before her own. Her father had said many times that her
generosity one day would be her undoing. When she had asked if this
meant she should change, he had replied, "I wouldn't have you change for
all the gold in the world." This had always seemed a silly thing to say. She
wondered if she could just change something small, and then they could
have just a little of the gold instead. That was a conversation that happened
two years ago. Now change had come to her anyway. After the events of
the last few weeks, she knew she would never be the same again. Her
Uncle had warned her to do whatever he asked, or there would be consequences, so she acquiesced to his every physical command. When her
father had left almost three months ago, her plans were to stay with her
uncle on the occasional day, do his cooking and his cleaning. Attah had told
her he would give her more money if she stayed with him during the week
and cooked every meal. With little else to occupy her time, she agreed. For
the first few days everything had been fine. She saw the way he lived, and
knew it could not be good for him nor for the few animals he had. Joy set
herself the task of putting his home in order. She immediately cleaned out
the chicken coop and made sure the goats were fed properly. She brought
fresh oils, vegetables, fruit and meat from the market and made sure he had

two decent meals a day. He was one of the few men in Fada who was fat. Joy wondered how he had got so large when he had no wife to feed him. Such questions were not for her to ask. Before his departure, her father had talked of another local trader who had been looking to marry and was, like himself, planning on settling in Fada for his retirement. Joy had never met the man, but she knew he was old. She prayed he was not a large man like her Uncle. His body odour was something that was present in the house even when he was not; personal hygiene not being one of his inherent skills. Attah started drinking alcohol early in the afternoons, and would be slurring his words by dinner. It was then that his gaze would fix upon her, and his lingering stares began to make her feel uncomfortable. She began to make sure her body was always fully covered, even when she thought he was out. His closeness to her in the kitchen as she prepared his meals began to make her feel more and more uneasy. She had always slept on the floor in the kitchen when she stayed, but once his interest in her turned physical, whenever she could she would sleep in the gateman's house, spending her nights talking to Tabitha. The abuse did not start straight away. It only started after the arrival of Tabitha. She was his leverage, making Joy agree to his demands in order to protect her. Once Attah had revealed his secret leverage to her, he would rape her twice a day. First when he awoke in the morning, and again before he went to sleep. The morning was always the worst and would last longer. She would close her eyes, her mind taking her elsewhere to happy memories of her mother, her sister and her father, until the pain would stop, indicating he had finished. She had been praying daily for her father's safe return. Today her prayers had been answered. Her face still wet with tears, Joy guided her father towards the small hut by the gate. She would not leave Tabitha to her fate. She must intervene. Inside the cramped space lay a long wooden box that had been constructed to act as a bed. Upon it lay an old tattered mattress which had given Joy a place to hide away from her uncle on many an occasion. She gestured to her father to help her remove it. He did so, despite looking apprehensive and wanting to leave. They pushed the mattress off and propped it against the wall. Attached at one end of the long piece of wood that formed the base of the bed was an iron hoop through which a large peg had been placed. Joy removed the peg and began to push the base off the frame, struggling with its weight. Her father stepped in to assist her in its removal but his patience was wearing thin.

"What is it, Joy? We do not have time to take any pets with us! We really must go now. No one must see us here! Your Uncle was a very bad man, but he was not without influential friends who might want to hurt us!" Joy remembered her father had that small torch, a gift from her mother.

"Father please pass me your torch." Her father reluctantly produced it from his belt and passed it to her. Joy shone the torch inside the small box.

"Father please look." Joy shone the light inside the framework of the box directing it at the floor space, where a dirty old rug lay. Joy climbed over and removed it. Sand and dirt fell away from it as her father tossed it to one side. "Look Father!"

Joy shone the light upon the floor at a small wooden hatch that had been concealed by the rug. Four small planks of wood had been nailed together to form a small cover. Joy climbed out from the space and gave the torch back to her Father, pointing back at the cover. She knew the hatch was heavy and she didn't want to risk it falling into the well below. Her father looked at her, still with a disbelieving face. "Whatever your Uncle has hidden in here Joy, we can come back for it later when..." The whimper of a child's cry brought his words to an abrupt halt. Joy had only seen her father move this fast once before, and that was a few minutes ago when he attacked her Uncle. He was normally a slow and meticulous man. He had a saying that went he would only cross a room if the pencil he needed to write with was located on the other side, otherwise he would say "Why cross the room?"

He climbed into the space and dropped to his knees, handing her the torch. "Hold this and shine it above my head." He pulled away the wooden hatch and put it aside, staring down into the hole below.

"Give me the torch," he said. He called into the well, "Hello. I am with Joy, she is my daughter. What is your name?"

Joy craned her head in as close as she could get but her father blocked her view. "Tabitha I am here," she cried. "He is my father! Reach up to him, he is going to pull you out!"

"Joy, hold my legs!" Omari said. Her Father lay flat and began to shift his body over the well's edge. Joy dropped the torch at once and grabbed on to his feet. She could see he was leaning into the hole as far as he dared. He felt heavy, and Joy felt weak. She grabbed his ankles when one of her father's sandals came away from his feet. In that brief moment, she couldn't help but notice how clean and washed the sole of his foot was. His skin appeared smoother. She knew her father's smell and something about it was different. There was a scent of honey. In her surprise, she nearly let him fall as the sandal came away in her hand. His feet kicked as he pulled himself up. His right foot caught Joy hard in the mouth, causing her to reel backwards from the small compartment. A second bang to her head came as she caught herself on the frame of the bed. She tumbled back into the small gatehouse but quickly regained her stance, determined not to disappoint her father twice in the same day. Omari wriggled back into the room empty-handed, and he sat catching his breath for a moment. For the first time since his return, she now took a moment to really look at him. His face was dripping with sweat and black with dust, but she could see something in him had changed. Normally upon his return, he looked so tired and a little older, the desert stripping him of his youth a little bit more with every journey. Not this time. He looked clean and refreshed, the normal dirt under his fingernails was nowhere to be seen. The bags under his eyes had vanished along with the furrows and scars upon his face. Her Father made her focus on their task. She would ask him about it later.

"How did Uncle Attah get down to her? Did he climb down? He would never fit in that hole," he said, pressing her for an answer. She shook her head.

"No, Father, he used a sheet. I can get it." On the few occasions she had seen Tabitha, Uncle Attah always pulled the child up to them. Sometimes Tabitha would be allowed to join them for dinner, but most of the time Joy was instructed to place the food in a plastic dog bowl and lower it down to her. Joy snuck her extra food whenever she could. Joy could have escaped herself at any time, but she couldn't have taken Tabitha with her. Alone, she couldn't move the bed, nor could she pull the girl to safety. Uncle Attah said if she left he would do the same things to Tabitha, that he did to her, only harder.

Until today, Joy had never seen her father get violent. He had given her and her sister Nya many a beating as kids when they were naughty, but Joy knew this was something her father never took pleasure in. The act of violence she had witnesses replayed in her mind as she ran from the gatehouse and back through to the inner courtyard, where the washing was hanging and removed two of the larger bedsheets. Her father had followed her. He removed the others, and together they set about tying the knots together, only stopping for a beat when they heard Tabitha cry out, redoubling their efforts soon after. The moment two pieces were tied together, her father took one end and passed her the other. "Hold it as tight as you can and I will pull to make sure it is safe."

She did as he instructed, and they tested all the knots in this way. Her father looked at her as they tied the bedding together. It was still hard for her to look back at him.

"I thought you would be so angry with me."

"Why would I be angry with you?"

"Because of what Uncle Attah made me do. I have dishonoured you and shamed our clan."

"You did not dishonour me. You are my daughter. You will always be my daughter. The only person who brought dishonour to our family is lying dead in the house behind us. It was not your fault. You're still a child. My child. I failed to protect you. The shame is mine to bear alone."

Joy could not stop more tears from coming. "He made me a woman... before I was ready..." Her father immediately left his task and pulled her to his chest. His clothes were still stained with Attah's blood as he wrapped his arms around her. Joy felt his hand stroke her head. He gently lifted her face up to look into his.

"You haven't shamed me," he kept repeating. She needed to hear that and her father clearly needed to say it.

"We will never speak of this again. Not because you did anything wrong. I do not want people to look at you differently. You will be a woman soon enough, and one day you will marry a man who will protect you long after I am gone."

He tested the knots a final time.

"You want me to marry that trader from the north?" she asked.

"Ah yes, Amar from Kebir."

"Father, he is so old. Older than you, even!" She knew she risked disappointing him further, but if there was a time to speak about such things it had to be now.

"I do not want another old man like that to touch me. Please do not leave us alone again," she pleaded

"I will not. I will never leave you again. I promise." He smiled at her, the first time she had seen him do so, since his return. A second cry came from the hole in the floor.

"Go and speak to your friend. Tell her we are going to lower the sheets in a loop, and she must sit in the loop." Her father instructed. "She must hold on and not let go. You understand?" Joy nodded and climbed back inside the cramped space, leaning her head over the entrance to the well. She shone the torch directly down, illuminating the hole. She could see Tabitha at the bottom. The girl's frame was slight because she had not been fed well. Around her were scattered refuse, and gnawed chicken bones. The smell coming from the well was repulsive almost causing Joy to gag. The girl was curled up in a ball, her head facing the wall. Joy could hear her sobbing softly. She wasn't sure if the child had heard them, but she reacted to the torchlight and slowly pulled herself to her feet, looking up. Joy waved at her and the frail girl weakly waved back, her hands looking so small and delicate. "Tabitha soon you will eat like a Princess!" Joy called to her.

Tabitha jumped with excitement, but soon coughed and had to sit down. The child was weak and looked to have a fever. Her father came back inside.

"Father, we must take her to Doctor Aziz."

Her Father nodded, pulling over the knotted sheets to the hole and together they began to lower them down with Joy repeating her father's instructions to Tabitha several times as they did so. Joy kept the torch shining down as the sheets were lowered gently to the bottom of the well. Tabitha sat upon them and Joy watched as her father slowly pulled the loop of sheets back up using both his hands.

'Father stop! She's going to fall!' Joy could see Tabitha was too weak to hold on. Her father lowered the sheets again, but the child released her grip before her feet touched the bottom. She fell the last two feet onto the soft mud below. Tabitha began to sob. Joy knew they would never get the girl out this way. Joy moved back from the hole and gave her father the torch, and looked at the opening. The hole was about three feet across and around twenty feet deep.

"Tabitha I am coming, don't worry. We will not leave you." Her father gave her a look of incredulity. "Father you must lower me into the well and then pull us both up."

"No, I cannot risk losing you. If I have to call for help then your Uncle will be found. You cannot do this."

"Father, a very kind man said to me once that I should always care about others as much as I care about myself. He said I should always treat them as I would like to be treated."

"Who was this very kind man?" he asked her, doubtfully.

"You. You told me that when I was eight."

Her Father paused as if searching for the actual memory in his head, then his eyes abruptly widened as if he had recalled the very conversation, letting out a sigh.

"Yes, you're right. I did say that. We... we could come back for her and bring her food."

"Father she is sick. She has been here almost as long as you have been away. We must help her. Lower me down, please!" Joy had never commanded her father to do anything before. She braced herself for a beating. He hadn't done that in a long time but she knew it was certainly not beyond him. She stepped either side of the sheets and pulled them up into her groin. It would be uncomfortable, especially as she was still feeling tender, but it could work. Her father relented and looped the other end of the sheets around his body, sitting opposite one side of the well with his legs out in front of him so that his right leg could brace his weight on the wall, then he lowered Joy slowly into the hole. Joy ran her fingers down the dank walls of the well, which felt clammy and there was a pervading smell of damp in the air. She felt a loss of balance and soon locked her hands together so that even if she did fall she should be able to hold onto the sheet. The sounds of Tabitha's sobbing grew louder just a few feet below her. She had not been able to carry the torch with her so it was incredibly dark, and the stench was overpowering. Her feet finally touched the soft ground below. "Tabitha, I am here. It is me, Joy. Come to me. Listen to my voice. I am going to take you out of here and you're going to come and live with us!"

She felt tiny fingers reach out from the darkness and touch her outstretched hand. Tabitha's skin felt hot, the child was burning with a fever. She was shivering and her clothes were sodden. Joy scooped the child up in her arms and held her tightly. "Hold on to me and I will do the same to you and we will not fall, okay?"

"Okay." Tabitha's answer was barely a whisper. Joy could tell the child would have perished in a matter of hours. They could not have delayed her recovery any longer.

"Father! Pull!" Joy shouted.

The sheet began to move up, a few feet at a time. Joy could hear her father screaming at the top of his lungs from above as he strained to pull their combined weight. Gradually the light grew from above, causing Tabitha to squint. Joy covered the girl's eyes with part of her headscarf. She knew the child couldn't have seen proper daylight for several weeks and thought it must be painful for her. The two of them were soon near the top. Joy could have reached and pulled herself out there and then, but if she let Tabitha go the child might release her grip and fall back down. She had to wait. She saw the pain on her father's face, and strain upon his hands as he pulled the sheet again and again, with one hand at a time until finally they both were in the room above. The three of them collapsed, catching their breath for several minutes.

"It is time to leave this place. Gather anything you have here. I want no sign to remain of your visit." Her father began checking Tabitha over and gave her some dried meat to eat. Joy immediately stopped him.

"Father, you cannot give her this to eat. It will be too hard. She will need some millet, with a sauce!" Her Father took the meat back from Tabitha, who looked profoundly disappointed at its sudden removal. Joy remembered she still had some honey sticks and gave her one of those to chew on instead. Tabitha ate it greedily. Omari produced his water bottle and told Tabitha to drink from it. She consumed almost the entire bottle before Omari took some more himself. Tabitha perked up slightly and let out a little giggle. Joy had never heard her laugh before. Happy memories in her life had been few in recent months, but the moment her Father made Tabitha laugh was something she knew would stay with her forever.

Joy went back into the house for the last time to seek out her belongings, leaving her sandals outside as was the custom. There was little time for such niceties, but that one had been instilled in her. She had a small backpack which she had acquired at the market, that contained a few personal items; several dresses, fresh wraps and underwear but it was located in the bedroom. She could have asked her Father to get it but she did not wish to trouble him further. Passing through the kitchen and the corridor, she pulled back the black cloth that hung from the doorway and stepped inside. Feeding flies danced around the room, disturbed by her entrance. They were gorging on the body of her dead uncle. She averted her eyes from the body still pinned to the wall. Her feet touched the sticky floor. It felt warm and wet. As she moved through the room, her steps made an uneasy squelching noise. By the side of the bed, were her discarded clothes and underwear. They needed washing. She didn't want to lose them because that would mean asking her father to pay to replace them. A further search revealed a suitcase that Joy did not remember seeing in the room before, possibly because it was partially concealed down one side of the bed. She glanced quickly at her Uncle, the glass bottle still protruding from his neck. His eyes were wide open, motionless, staring back at her. Even in death, he was able to instil fear in her. Inside the suitcase were several items of female clothing, and a large wad of American dollars. It was a huge sum of foreign currency for a man of Attah's means. The clothing looked brand new and would have fitted a girl of her age. Joy remembered when she had first arrived, her Uncle had given her two new dresses as presents. This was clearly where he'd stored his remaining gifts. She removed everything she could and stuffed it into her backpack. She thought about taking the case but it was too big, very distinctive and would attract attention. She soon found some clean clothes suitable for a child, and returned immediately to help change Tabitha. As both girls changed, her Father crossed the compound dragging her uncle's body towards the gateman's hut. The two girls held each other's gaze for a instant, as they heard the dull thud of the body hitting the bottom of the well. The child said nothing. She simply stood still holding her arms aloft as Joy washed away the dirt and grime from her body, and dressed her in fresh clothes. Tabitha was not much to look at. Her ribs were poking through her skin more than they should have been, and her size was small for a girl her age. Joy wasn't sure exactly how old she was, but she thought about six. Joy had found a pink dress that was clean, but was far too large for Tabitha. She took down several of the clothes pegs from the washing line, and pinned the dress back so that it would not billow behind her.

"Tabitha, once we leave here, we're never going to come back, nor talk to anyone about this place or the bad man, okay?"

"Has the bad man gone?" the child asked.

Joy's Father leaned down to the child. "Yes, yes he has."

"Will you be my sister?" Tabitha asked Joy. Joy felt the child's words with such affection. She missed her older sister Nya so desperately. She had only seen her once on a webcam at Pappa Bendi's in the last year. Another sister would be so welcome. They could be a family. She looked at her Father with pleading eyes. He drew in a breath and shook his head as if he was going to say no, but his words brought a smile to Joy's face.

"You will live with us like you're family, if this will make you happy."

Tabitha nodded, and sucked her thumb.

"We must take you to the doctor first."

Tabitha pointed at the water bottle. Joy's Father tipped it up to reveal it was empty.

"Don't worry. I have two more of them outside. Now remember, we were never here."

Tabitha surprised Joy with her energy. As she was pulled from the well she looked to be on the edge of death, but a little food and water had worked wonders. Now she was walking upright on her own and almost looked ready to run. Her father produced some dark glasses from his pouch and placed them on Tabitha's face. They looked ridiculous and were far too big for her head, but were a simple solution to the child's constant squinting. The sunlight, which she had seen so little of in the last few months would take some getting used to again. Joy found a small wrap to protect the girl's head from the sun. The child's scalp was covered in scabs, but it was shaven, which Joy hoped would mean no lice. She thought they had some soap for that back home. She would have to check. Her father looked up and down outside the compound to make sure no one was passing, but this part of Fada was empty. He led her and Tabitha outside and placed both of the girls on his camels. Joy thought the trio of beasts looked pleased to see her, but she wondered what had happened to the rest.

"Let us get home. Have you not seen the white ark?" her Father said, pointing to the white tower in the sky to the west.

RYAN

Despite the myriad of dilemmas pressing on his mind, Ryan still found time to admire the sight of Miss Brewster-Smith's rear view as she ascended the steps into the plane. Her rear body shape was not dissimilar to that of Candice and Candice's rear was indeed a sight to behold. One that Ryan suspected he would not see again in quite some time. Possibly never. His conscience had put in a rare appearance, he felt troubled by their last conversation. He had to find a way to call her. He knew her number by heart, didn't he? He had to think to try and recall it. The consumption of too many illegal chemicals had made his short-term memory somewhat lacking of late. But as he took his seat on the aircraft, it came to him and he put it in his new phone under *notes*. This new phone had been supplied to him earlier today, and would no doubt be tracked and logged by internal security. Spears probably had the means to monitor it. Either way, he couldn't risk using it to contact her. He had to get a message to her some-how, to explain. He couldn't leave things the way they were. She was the only person he had cared about in a very long time, and he never really cared about anyone. General Spears was already in the plane ahead of him, still relentless with energy. Ryan hadn't seen him sleep yet, but the man had to rest sometime. At least he wouldn't have to worry about Darren Fine. He had elected to take a first class train back to London and work on press releases *en route*, rather than take to the air again today. That should give him at least half a day's breathing room away from the horrible little man.

As the plane began to taxi for take-off he thought about the more pressing matter of his Grandmother. How on earth had Agatha Davey-

Wallace ended up on a bus with a Nigerian immigrant, two students pilling their nuts off and a bus driver who was a part time Elvis Karaoke act, on top of the ship? The footage of the group trying to evade the British military alongside Scottish Hell's Angels had been playing on every news bulletin possible, and had now gone viral. In China, it was apparently the comedy news story of the day. Word hadn't yet leaked that his Grandmother was the elderly passenger, but it would and soon he would have to deal with that on top of everything else. Then there was the more immediate concern over the question of her whereabouts. Elvis was certain she had gone inside the object, yet no one could find any sign of a door. Inside... Was that really possible? Had she been kidnapped by aliens? What on earth were the odds that his Grandmother could be kidnapped by aliens on the day that he should become Prime Minister of the UK? He knew his Grandmother was in relatively good health, even if he hadn't physically seen her for a couple of years, not counting two skype calls. He did speak to her on the phone every month. Even he had to confess she was a kind and caring woman, if somewhat irritating to his own sensibilities. Annoyingly, she always knew when he was lying. All she ever wanted to know was who he was seeing, and if he was going to get married. God, how he wished he could just turn time back to the other night, he could make a run for it with Candice to the Maldives. Ryan barely noticed the plane taking off as he was running it all through his mind. Jennifer fastened his seatbelt for him. He had forgotten to do it. He managed a weak smile by way of thanks, before he returned to pondering the complex issues facing him. The burdens of being a leader it appeared were many, yet few of the problems he currently faced were of his own making; at least that made a change. They were soon airborne and the pilot banked past the landing site once more, before turning south back to London. Ryan managed a brief glimpse of the tower from his window. It glowed brightly in the dark, as if lit from within by a single source. Small chains of lights could be seen on the surface from the south and east, leading towards the centre. He had been down there at the east camp only minutes earlier, conversing with the Doctor. Jacobs? Was that her name? He couldn't quite recall. She had been very helpful; factual and to the point, but the total sum of what she knew for certain was very little. What to say to the nation would be the next thing on the agenda. People wanted answers. Why couldn't he have been on that holiday in the Seychelles when these things arrived? It didn't have to be the Seychelles. Any island would have sufficed as long as it was far away from here. Then they could have watched the whole thing play out on television without the burden of any responsibility.

"Sorry to trouble you, Prime Minister..."

It was General Spears. Could the man not leave him alone for a moment to gather his thoughts? Apparently not.

"Yes General. Have any more disasters unfolded in the time it took us to get back to the plane?" Spears sat down opposite him in the vacant seat next to Jennifer. Jennifer was so much more pleasing to the eye, with her perfectly applied makeup and light grey suit. She had changed again, and still managed to smell fresh, which reminded Ryan that his armpits were positively rank. He hadn't showered in over twenty-four hours. How was it that she looked so clean, pristine even? The General, on the other hand, had the more immediate effect of making him really need a wee. The military man placed his iPad on the table. BBC News 24 was constantly running. Spears offered him headphones. Not the small type you had for your iPod, but the large sort with the cushions on the earpieces some people seemed to love wearing on the tube. God, he hadn't taken the tube for years. He put them on. The words of a reporter pounded into his eardrums. The General had neglected, probably deliberately, to turn the sound down to a more reasonable level. Ryan placed them around his neck, watching footage of the biker group on the surface of the ship play out.

"It would seem that the biker gang have now been identified. That's one of them being interviewed now. He claims to be the group's leader. Have a listen. Not much of a security threat to the nation."

Focusing his attentions to the young man being interviewed on the screen, Ryan saw a group of individuals who looked more like they had just been plucked from a Comic-Con than some Hell's Angels gang. Their leader couldn't have been more than twenty-eight and looked like the sort of college student who paid for his courses by selling weed to other students.

"We didn't do anything illegal, we just went to have a look. What people need to understand is that these are ships from another world, another universe and we, the common people, have as much right to go and see them and say hello as anyone else does."

The group certainly had the leather jackets with the denim cut-offs, but these were not Sons of Anarchy. Their spokesman was identified by an on-screen graphic as *Khai Kirk* – What sort of name was that? He didn't have a Scottish accent. Then Ryan saw the emblem on his breast and read it out loud.

"The Star Trek UK Society of Bikers." He removed the headphones. "Are you fucking serious?"

Jennifer looked up and took the iPad from him. She wanted to see what he was talking about.

"Apparently some Science Fiction Biker Club, yes. We've already traced them all from their Facebook group and identified every single member of the club who was present on the surface of the ship. I've arranged for all of them to be detained."

The General's stony face did not seem the least bit amused by the fact that the government had been outwitted by a bunch of nerds on bikes.

"Oh well that's good. What are we going to do? Put them in prison? For what? You heard what the kid said. Did we publicly state that the ships were government property before Motley Crüe here decided to go on their little jolly on top of the thing?"

"We didn't. We advised the public to stay inside. That was all," Jennifer said, interrupting. Did she have his back or was she just stating the facts? Ryan couldn't tell. If she had his back, a threesome with her one day was an absolute must. If she was up for it. Would she be up for it? Of course she would. She was a minx.

"We should question them, at the very least," the General said.

"What for? We already detained the group who got furthest on the surface and what were they able to tell us? Fuck all, that's what," Ryan didn't see the point of wasting manpower and resources.

"They told us about your Grandmother. At least we know that much. She's inside it somewhere," Spears replied.

"Yes…" Ryan removed his tie. "With aliens doing God knows what to her, and we still have no apparent way to rescue her!"

"We're still trying. We're having drilling equipment brought in from one of the rigs off the coast. They're designed to drill through the hardest rock on the planet. If anything can get through the surface, it will be that but…"

"But…" *Here it comes*, thought Ryan.

"American news networks are reporting that they already tried something similar with the ship that landed halfway between the United States and Mexico. It was a failure. Nothing would penetrate the surface. China is talking about using a nuclear weapon against one of theirs. An option that we could also employ if it became aggressive."

"Oh yes, brilliant. Let's turn Scotland into a nuclear wasteland! That would be just wonderful, General…" Jennifer cut in. She had put down the iPad. Unusual for someone in her position to interrupt them, but it was a very unusual day.

"I am talking with the Prime Minister, Miss Brewster-Smith. You're his personal assistant, no one is asking for your opinion on the matter." It was hard to detect emotion in Spears' voice usually, but this time he did not hide his anger. Ryan wasn't having it.

"Her opinion matters to me. Miss Brewster-Smith, you may speak freely at any time if you feel the need to in my presence. In fact, I would prefer it that way." She did have his back, so he had to have hers, it was only fair. Oh that threesome with her was so on.

"Prime Minister, I might remind you that you hold this post because of, well, shall we say extraordinary circumstances and you have few friends in cabinet, of which I am one..."

Fuck this, Ryan thought. He had nothing to lose. He cut him off.

"General Spears, your friendship and support mean a great deal to me. We are facing the worst crisis this country has ever seen, as you are not short on reminding me. I will do everything in my power to get us through it, but one thing we are not going to do is even consider the use of nuclear weapons..."

Ryan stood up, addressing the entire plane. "There are so many things we do not know. Where these things came from, why they're here, who or what is inside, what their intentions are. Those intentions, whatever they may be, might be entirely peaceful, for all we know. What we do know is that we cannot gain access. Nothing that has been employed so far by any other country has enabled them to gain entry. Nuclear weapons are not a last resort. They are not a resort at all. There's two hundred of these things on the Earth! What if everyone else decides to follow suit and we have that many nuclear detonations worldwide to contend with? We won't have to worry about why these things have landed, because we will have annihilated the human race ourselves. So, if anyone wants to argue a strong case as to why we should use them, please do so now."

Ryan realised he should have saved this rant for when he got back to London. He could have done it in front of the Cabinet, or even Parliament, instead of a plane full of security personnel and a couple of minor ministers. Dilks and Willis, his two personal security guards, sitting in the row behind him, were transfixed. No one in the plane made a sound. The only noise came from the aircraft's engines and headphone crackle from numerous electronic devices.

"You," Ryan pointed at Dilks. "Do you think we should use nuclear weapons? Speak up, you're a security guard, not a mute in a monastery. You can have an opinion."

"Prime Minister, my job is to protect you, not involve myself in your decisions," Dilks replied, plainly.

"Do you have a family? Children? Mr Dilks, is it?" Ryan could see the man didn't want to answer, but could also tell Ryan was not going to give up.

"Yes, Prime Minister. One of each. I am not married..."

"I see. Divorced?" Ryan asked the question to get clarity before making his point, but a moment later wished he hadn't.

"Well, she... That is, my wife passed away last year. Cancer."

"Mr Dilks, I am very sorry." Ryan felt like a complete cunt. "Please accept my condolences, but may I ask, would you want nuclear weapons used in an offensive role knowing that the consequences of that action is going to directly impact on your children and their children and so on, for generations to come?"

Dilks didn't say anything.

Spears cut in. "Mr Prime Minister, I think you're very tired and need some sleep."

The General offered a hand to him, but Ryan flinched away and kept his eyes locked on the security man.

"No… that is to say, no Prime Minister. I would not want someone to have to make that choice," Dilks said.

"Thank you. We won't be making that choice, will we General? Is that understood?"

"Perfectly clear, Prime Minister. I do suggest you get some rest, though. You clearly need it." Spears turned away and headed back towards the cockpit.

"Oh and General Spears, does my personal protection fall under your jurisdiction at any time?"

"No sir, that's the responsibility of the Police and MI5.'

"Well just in case it should, at any time, this man is never to be reassigned from my personal detail under any circumstances. Is that clear?"

"It wouldn't be my prerogative to do that, Prime Minister. Now I am going to get some sleep. I suggest you do the same, sir. The Cabinet will be meeting again two hours after we land."

Ryan sat back down. Everyone continued with their tasks, people descending into low murmured chats. Willis turned to Dilks, within earshot of Ryan.

"You're in the boss's good books."

"I'm starting to like him. He's a dick, but not as big a dick as I thought."

"Mr Wallace, you're becoming quite the tenacious politician," Jennifer said. She sounded pleased, but he knew everything he had said was a bluff. If the world decided to blow itself up well, that would be the end of his life of sex and drugs. He planned to get that life back as soon as possible. Besides, someone else in another country could well make the decision to use a nuclear weapon before he did.

"Miss Brewster-Smith, you can call me Ryan."

"That still would not be appropriate, Prime Minister." She crossed her legs and focused on her iPad.

"Fine. I will settle for Mr Wallace when we're alone then."

"In which case I am certain the opportunities to address you as such will be extremely limited," she said, cleaning her glasses. God, this girl was hard work. Still, good at her job though, that was the main thing. She produced a second phone from her bag. It was red and had been personalized with her initials, JBS. Evidently not her work phone then. She began texting.

"Can you get a signal on that while we're airborne?" he asked, unsure of the tech the plane actually possessed to send and receive calls.

"We're flying relatively low, so we'll pick up reception from time to time. Not sufficient enough to make a call, but the odd text will get sent. If not it will just go as soon as we're back on the ground at London City Airport. I won't have time to call my family, or my partner once we land or…"

She was a lesbian. He knew it. A girl this well-groomed, working in government circles, well, she had to be, of course. Could make the three-some easier to arrange, though ultimately it would be a more voyeuristic experience for him.

"… once we're back on the road, so I might as well update everyone now, let them know I'm okay. Nothing about the trip of course. They won't even know I was in Scotland. Not an issue I hope, Prime Minister?"

Ryan leaned in, checking around the plane as he did so to see who was within earshot. Willis and Dilks were both already sleeping, taking advantage of their one chance to do so. Ryan couldn't blame them but it wasn't very reassuring if someone tried to hijack the plane.

"I need to send someone a message. Can I please borrow that phone? Only, Miss Brewster-Smith, no one can know about this. No one."

"I really wouldn't feel comfortable letting you…'

'Look, I'll even say at the start I'm using a friend's phone, so in the event your partner… what's her name?"

"His name is Jermaine," she said, icily.

Jermaine. Okay, wrong about the lesbian thing. Jermaine. He sounded black. Big and black. Could be an even more interesting threesome. Best not press her for personal details now.

"Miss Brewster-Smith, there is someone, very important to me too and I haven't been able to speak to them since, well since this all started. If you would please just let me do this, I would be most grateful. I cannot use my work phone. Please."

Ryan wasn't often sincere, but evidently this was a tone of voice that Jennifer had not heard before, because she offered the phone to him. Ryan took it. At once he began typing the message, checking every few moments on Spears, who, he noted was indeed asleep on a seat just before the cockpit. He couldn't take any chances. The General was a man of some influence and probably had spies everywhere. He was certainly very well informed about Ryan, which was surprising when it was obvious to anyone who knew him that he was not interested in the leadership of the party. People in his business did due diligence in their line of work of course. He typed faster.

"Using a friend's phone, don't reply to this message. I was forced to say what I did. As soon as this is over I will resign from my job. I want us to be together. I don't care what anyone thinks about it – R."

He hadn't even actually had a conversation yet about entering into an actual relationship with Candice but he might as well put it out there. He had to let her know he just wanted things to go back to normal. Who knew when that would be? Where the hell had that emotional outburst come from? Unless… oh balls. Did he just lecture the most senior man in the British Armed Forces because he was having his come-down? Shit. No wonder he was all over the place. He had been properly "on it" until two days ago. It was the beginning of the grumpy Tuesdays. Party on the week-end, do nothing on Monday and snap at people on Tuesday and Wednes-day. Oh well, Jennifer was impressed, so it wasn't all bad. Signing the message with as many kisses as he could, he pressed *send*, and handed the phone back to Jennifer.

"Thank you," he said, with a sincere smile. He knew he needed to rest but he couldn't. His mind was racing and there was just no way to turn it off.

"I don't think I will be able to sleep. Let me ask you something? How come you manage to always look so good? I mean, that's a different suit, your hair is slightly different, your makeup is all in place. How on earth did you find the time?" At first Jennifer looked as though she didn't want to respond but then she replied.

"At the camp we went to. When you were questioning the people who were being detained, I took advantage of the moment to take a shower and change. There's over two hundred personnel at the eastern camp, they all have to shower somewhere."

He promptly tried really hard to visualise her in the shower… She stood naked under the water when she was joined by a tall, muscular black man with long dreads, who stared at him, as if to say "Why you looking at my lady, bro – get the fuck out of here." Yeah, that must have been Jermaine.

"Prime Minister…" Her voice disintegrated the image.

"Hmm?"

"Your mind's wandering, I think."

"Well of course it is, I have a great deal to think about right now." This wasn't a complete lie. He did indeed have a great deal of stressful dilemmas to think about, but where possible he always preferred to think about other things instead. The steward was bustling past, Jennifer stopped him.

"Can I have a diet coke please? Do you want one, sir?"

Sir now, was it? Not Mr Wallace or Prime Minister. So now there were three name options. It all sounded a bit S and M, something he wasn't into. All that Slave/Master business, he couldn't be doing with it. Now people were dressing up as dogs for kicks – what the fuck was that about? Still, each to their own.

'"Prime Minister… can I get you a drink?"

"Oh yes. A coke please, the full-fat version. Could do with a sugar rush I think."

"Coming up right away, Prime Minister." The steward hurried and returned quickly with the drinks. Ryan dispensed with the cup and napkin placed before him, and cracked open the can. The fizzing bubbles on his tongue and the sweetness of the caffeinated drink had never tasted so good.

"You did it again just now," Jennifer said, downing her own drink.

"Did what?" He was tired, not sure what she was getting at.

"Tuned me out. You do it all the time. I've noticed it."

"I'm just tired and like I said, I have a lot on my mind."

"Like your Grandmother? I would have never guessed that you had such a sweet-looking relative. Her name's in the press already, though no one seems to have made the connection to you yet. It must be her surname. Davey-Wallace, what's that about?'

It was nice that she was taking an interest. She would have to, if she was going to help him handle the press later.

'My Grandfather was Scottish, my Grandmother is English, from London actually. I think they met just after the war, there. I forget the exact details. They were the only parental figures I had. You probably know about my parents and the boating accident…'

"Yes, I'm very sorry. You were quite young, weren't you?"

"Yes, just eleven, an only child. I went to live with my Grandparents after that. My Grandfather had been involved with the local Conservative party for a long time. Not in Scotland, but they had a home there, just outside Kilmarnock. My grandmother said she preferred it to the south. She didn't like London anymore, said it had changed too much. If I can be honest, I always thought she was a little bit racist. Don't get me wrong, she wasn't going to burn crosses or anything like that. She just didn't like change much. Anyway Grandpa had various businesses, so there was always money. He had some good connections so I got in to Cambridge and sort of fell into politics. That's where I met David Jackson, our former PM. We were roommates for a while, as I am sure you know. He was always the clever one. I was always fucking up. He looked out for me, covered my arse more than once back then. I don't know why. I was never worth saving really."

Looking back to those simpler days, Ryan could picture David as he spoke. The two of them in the student union bar sipping on cheap cider, and checking out which of the girls they were going to invite to some posh party or other.

"Maybe he saw something in you that you never saw in yourself."

"Really – what do you think was, then?" Ryan never did fully understand why David had looked out for him. Perhaps it was just out of friendship. David always said that true friendships were priceless, and they would only get harder to find as their careers went forward. It was a political dog eat dog world they were entering, after all. Ryan found himself welling up. It could have been part of his come-down, but with everything that had been happening he really hadn't had much time to think about his friend, his wife, their children and the others he knew who had all been killed in the terrorist strike. Admittedly, most of them he didn't give two shits about, but David and his family had always been close friends. Even his wife, Joan, had been kind to him and was always trying to set him up with some eligible woman or other. She had probably been more responsible than any other single individual in providing him with the most boring sexual encounters he had ever had in his life. That Baroness from France aside, they were all awful. She, on the other hand had been positively filthy, and even taught him a thing or two, but outside the bedroom she was a pompous, self-entitled bore. You could never have it all.

"It was worthiness that he saw in you. Worthiness. Ryan, do you understand? You didn't want this job, I know that, but now you have it. Make him proud."

"Did you just call me Ryan?"

"No." Jennifer averted her eyes and looked out the window.

"Yes, you did, you just called me Ryan. I thought you just said that would be inappropriate?" he teased.

"You looked as if you were going to cry. I reserve the right to use it then and only then, when such emergencies present themselves."

She put her glasses back on and started to text. If he had not met Candice, this beautiful exotic, intelligent creature sitting opposite him would be wife material, unless she was boring in the bedroom.

"So how long have you and Jermaine been married?" he asked, trying to make the question sound casual.

"I didn't say we were married."

Worth noting, Ryan thought. Jermaine was getting bigger and more rugged every time she mentioned his name. In any event, if it came down to a competition of who had the biggest cock, he knew Candice would win hands-down, though imagining an event where such a comparison occurred seemed rather unlikely. Still, spaceships were landing, Grandmothers disappearing, who knew what tomorrow might bring?

"Prime Minister, I had the foresight to pack you a fresh pressed shirt, some clean underwear, socks and a choice of ties. They're hanging in the back near the last seat by the toilets. You'll bound to have to face the press soon after we land."

Ryan wondered if she ironed Jemaine's shirts before he went to work.

"Thank you, that was very thoughtful of you."

"Just doing my job." she was back on her phone again.

The plane soon landed at London City Airport where a convoy of cars waited on the runway tarmac. Ryan had been expecting to take a helicopter straight to Westminster but the one allocated to them was having technical problems so they were going to have to drive. It was getting on for 4am when they made their way into central London. The city, however, hadn't really gone to sleep. Trails of cars choked the roads heading away from the capital. Apparently, anyone who owned a home in the south-west of England was on their way to Cornwall, so the decision not to land at Heathrow had been a wise one. Congestion on the motorways around that airport was said to be at a standstill. Their police escort made short work of what hold-ups there were but once they were into the financial district of East London it was largely deserted. Normally at this time of the morning, which Ryan would freely admit he was not too familiar with, there would at the very least be an army of cleaners and dustmen present on the streets. He had on occasion been known to Uber it in the early hours from Candice's apartment back to his own in Canary Wharf when those couple of hours before dawn held a certain magic quiet. On this particular drive back through the streets however, the business district of the capital was positively ghostly. Even the lights of the small cafés getting ready for the day's business were not seen flickering between the grey office buildings. There were no cleaners visible, no drunken revellers passed out at bus stops, no last stragglers trying to find their way home from the previous evening's party. It was deathly quiet.

The convoy of four cars weaved quickly through the narrow streets and was soon nearing St. Paul's Cathedral. Turning a corner, an extraordinary sight greeted them. Crowds of people filled the street ahead. For a brief vain moment Ryan thought they had come to greet his arrival back to the capital, but soon he realised from their defeated demeanour these were people devoid of all hope, heading towards a known religious landmark. They were shuffling towards the Cathedral, hoping that one last prayer to an unknown entity might somehow save them from impending calamity. Ryan found zealous religious types comical, at best. There were so many different religions all over the world. They couldn't all be true, but trying to prove who was right was like watching two children argue over whose imaginary friend was the best. The streets became increasingly choked with humanity, that for a while the convoy slowed to a crawl as their escorts cleared a way through. Queues of people were crowding every path and concourse that led to the steps of the mighty dome of St. Paul's Cathedral. The grand structure designed by Sir Christopher Wren had represented a symbol of hope to Britain, when it somehow managed to remain undamaged by the German Luftwaffe during the Blitz of World War Two. Clearly people were looking to that symbol to save them once again.

Ryan sat in the back of the spacious 4 x 4 with Jennifer. On a small seat facing them was Dilks in his neatly pressed dark suit. Willis was in the passenger seat up front. Neither of the two security men had said a word during the journey. Ryan thought to ask the man for his opinion on the use of nuclear weapons again while they were in a more intimate setting, but decided against it. Fortunately, the size of the convoy had meant that General Spears had to travel in a separate vehicle with his aide, much to Ryan's relief. He said he had some matters to check on and might be late to the Cabinet meeting. Ryan didn't really care, he just wanted the man out of his face. He wasn't entirely sure what the nuclear weapons protocol was, now that he was Prime Minister, but he wanted to make damn sure that Morris Spears, General or not, couldn't get anywhere near the means to fire one. He wrote down a note on his phone to remind him to investigate it. Jennifer's phone beeped, she showed the screen to Ryan.

Update from Parliament. An emergency meeting of the house has been called for later today by the speaker and opposing parties.

"Of course they bloody have. I'd like to know what else they think we should be doing that we're not already." He tutted, thinking this would have been an appropriate time to suck on his teeth. Jennifer then checked her other phone, reminding Ryan about the message he sent.

"Can you check to see if my text went?" He whispered.

"It did, as soon as we landed and before you ask, no, no reply yet. I'll check it for you from time to time, if you want?"

Yes he did want, even though he had told Candice not to reply.

"Thank you, that would be most kind. You won't read it, of course?"

"Of course not. I'm not you."

She was correct of course. Not only would he have read it, had the shoe been on the other foot, he might have sent a funny reply just for comedy value.

"So what are all these people doing here, do you think?" she asked, as they passed the last of the crowds around St. Paul's.

"The last refuge of the desperate," Ryan replied, curtly, "When people have no hope left, they often turn to God for answers and then convince themselves everything else from that moment on in life is God's will. Of course, if they're right and there is a God, well then he created these ships too, didn't he? In which case if they destroy us all, well, that will have been God's will too."

"Remind me not to introduce you to my sister, she is a major Hillsong fanatic." Jennifer had a sister?

"We're you planning on introducing me to her?" Ryan asked, already knowing the answer. He certainly wasn't going to attend a Hillsong event any time soon. It was a Christian rock concert gathering on a Sunday and was a living definition of a cult if he ever saw one.

"No." Jennifer crossed her legs and looked out of the window. The silence only lasted another minute before her phone rang again.

"Yes, yes, let me see if he's available. Hold on please." Ryan knew it could only be for him. That was after all Jennifer's job, to act as a mobile secretary while they were on the move, among other things. He hadn't had time to read her full job description yet. This could only be more bad news.

"Who is it?" he asked.

"The leader of the Labour Party."

Unexpected! Should he take the call? His previous colleagues almost certainly wouldn't have. Ryan knew there could be a fierce debate coming up and it was better that it should be as cordial as possible, or perhaps…

"I'll take it, put it on speaker, I want you listening in." With a barely concealed look of surprise, Jennifer handed him the work phone and taking the call off hold. Ryan took a deep breath in.

"Ryan Wallace." There was a beat before he heard the Leader of the Opposition.

"Prime Minister – I guess this is a crash course at being in at the deep end of political leadership for you. One hell of a first day in office."

Bastard, but entirely true.

"You'd be correct, but I'm quickly learning to swim," Ryan said. He was going to be polite but certainly wasn't going to let the man score any points. Jennifer smiled. It was a good comeback.

"I wanted to offer you my personal condolences on the passing of our former Prime Minister, David Jackson. I know you'd been friends for a very long time."

"Since we were teenagers," Ryan replied, reinforcing the point.

"Well yes, quite. He was my rival but we enjoyed many a good drink in the bar at the Commons. He'll be missed," the Leader replied sincerely.

"I appreciate your sentiments, though I'm sure I'd be right in saying that this is not the only reason you called me," Ryan said, leaving the floor open.

"You would be correct. As you know there will be a meeting of Parliament in the House of Commons this afternoon. I am told several members of my party will be absent. No doubt you will be missing a few of your own."

Ryan had no idea. He gestured to Jennifer for an answer but she clearly didn't have one. Ryan thought for a few seconds before he replied.

"I would imagine that some of our members feel this could be the end of humanity, so it's possible they're choosing to stay with their families. So, yes, I expect we'll be missing a few from the back benches. My Cabinet however will be there in full, at least they will if they value their jobs," Ryan added. They had damn well better be.

"As will the Shadow Cabinet. I think it's important that we should stay united at this time. Any squabbles on other matters should be put to one side. I heard a rumour that some inside your party are not happy with the way you assumed your leadership…"

Ryan was going to respond to this, but Jennifer put her fingers to her lips, urging him to keep quiet. He duly complied, allowing the Labour leader to continue.

"You will be well aware that the tradition in British Politics is to be critical of one another in public debate, to never find common ground. One party tries to make the other look inferior or distasteful to the voters and they respond in kind. Right now, I am not interested in scoring election points, only in our nation's survival, both physically and financially. You don't have to give me the details, but can you assure me that the necessary steps are being taken by our Armed Forces in order to protect the population against any threat, wherever it may come from?"

Jennifer nodded, but Ryan already knew what to say.

"I can. Forces are being redeployed from the Middle East and Germany. The Territorial Army reserves have been called in and are ready. All serving soldiers have had leave cancelled, the same goes for all medical services, the Fire Services and the Police Forces of course."

"Good. I know to some extent that went without saying, but I still wanted to hear it from you. Are you personally proposing we take military action against these ships?" The question hung heavily and Ryan couldn't tell what the man wanted to hear. He knew at heart the Leader of the Opposition was a pacifist. But being a pacifist was one thing, an alien invasion was quite something else.

"I am not. In fact I argued very strongly against such action only a few hours ago. I can tell you that I went to see the ship in Scotland personally and spoke to people who had walked upon it, civilians in fact. Nothing that they or the scientific personnel we have in place currently examining the phenomenon gave me any information which would lead me to the conclusion that these landings, well, let me clarify that, to say the one that landed in the United Kingdom at least, has hostile intentions at this time." Ryan waited, there was a long pause before the man responded and for a moment it felt as if the line had been cut.

"I see. Do you know anything else that you can share with me?"

"I'm afraid not. We're none the wiser at the moment. I haven't kept up with everything else from around the world in the last hour or so. Has anyone else reached a different conclusion?"

"If they did it's certainly not in the press. Prime Minister, I want us to reach a mutual understanding on the current crisis. Our country is in the middle of a national panic. I am sure you've heard but the shelves of super-markets have been emptied overnight by panic buying. There's still queues of people outside the twenty-four hour stores, even now.'

Jennifer confirmed the news by showing Ryan the screen of her other phone. Facebook live displayed a near-riot taking place outside the twenty-four hour super-Tesco's in Finchley, North London.

"If we are to calm the nation, then we must appear united in Government. I do not intend to challenge your position as Prime Minister. Your speech yesterday was, well, frankly a surprise from someone who previously has only ever defended health cuts. It showed a moral courage that I did not expect to see from you. Now, that's not to say that I'm completely sold on you being the man to lead us through this crisis, but for now, I will keep my party's focus on matters at hand. The question of your leadership can be kept for another day."

A wave of relief swept over Ryan. It was not what he was expecting. People had said this man was someone who had integrity. He certainly couldn't question that right now.

"I am most grateful to you for your support."

"But..." the Leader added.

Ryan knew there had to be a catch. What if he knew about his Grandmother already? What if he knew about Candice? If General Spears knew about her, then someone else in the intelligence community must have told him. How many people must have had that piece of information before it got to Spears?

"I must insist that you keep me personally updated on any developments regarding these vessels. If there is communication from them, I want to know about it. Not read about it online, or in the paper the same time as everyone else. I expect to be kept fully informed directly by you, as and when it happens. If we can agree upon that, then we'll be united in the Commons later today."

Not what Ryan was expecting, but considerably easier to agree to.

"I will have my PA email you personally a daily summary of the information I receive from our teams in the field. We don't know much but what we do you'll have by the end of every working day, including today. Anything more immediate, I will call you personally. Will that be satisfactory?"

"Completely. Thank you, Prime Minister. I shall not take up any more of your time. Until this afternoon then."

"Until then. Goodbye." The relief on Ryan's face as he hung up the phone must have been palpable. Jennifer did this cute thing with her eyes where she rolled them to one side. Ryan had noticed it before.

"I thought that went rather well,' she said. Ryan was still shaking with surprise, he had not normally known political rivals to be so cordial, but the British people did have a habit of uniting when their backs were against the wall.

"For a first conversation with a rival party leader, I think I would have to agree," he replied.

"Maybe this signals a new era of co-operation between us and the opposition?" Was she being sarcastic? He couldn't tell.

"I wouldn't go quite that far." He doubted it would remain that way for long.

Jennifer's work phone rang again. He was glad most of his calls would come through her.

"Yes. I don't think he is available, let me check." She put the phone on mute. "It's the leader of UKIP calling to offer his support." Her voice this time was most certainly laced with sarcasm.

"I'm not available." Ryan liked the way that sounded.

"Sorry, he's not available right now, but I will personally pass on your message of support." She hung up promptly, not waiting for a reply.

"I've had some thoughts about how to deal with the situation regarding your Grandmother," she said, coldly.

"Oh yes?"

"I think you should lead with it at the press conference."

Was she serious? How was that going to help? Didn't he have to appear to be concerned with the safety of the nation rather than the safety of one person?

"I was hoping we could keep that under wraps, for now."

"It's only a matter of time before someone talks. She has nurses who look after her, right?" Jennifer asked.

"Yes, two." A lovely young gay oriental nurse whose exact origin he could not recall, and an Australian female nurse whose name he couldn't remember.

"One of them is bound to talk. I am sure she will have spoken to them about her son's occupation. With them having worked in healthcare you would have come up in conversation, at least once. It's just a matter of time before one of them talks to the media." She had a point, he hadn't thought of that but…

"The thing is, I never really told my Grandmother I worked in the government."

"Oh? What does she think you do then?" Jennifer sounded surprised.

"I told her I was an accountant for the NHS. She never watches the news. Says it always bad and just depresses her."

"Right. She's got photographs of you though? Probably has one next to her bed."

Shit. Yeah, that was true. Jennifer pressed on with her idea. "Look, if you come out with it immediately at your next conference, or even in

Parliament, you will gain nothing but public sympathy. Your own Grand-mother, personally affected by the arrival of these things. Possibly kidnapped…"

"It did appear she went rather willingly." From the little information that Ryan had, it appeared she had instigated the whole thing. This was entirely possible, knowing her as he did.

"We can let the press decide how to spin that. The point is that you have been directly affected by what's happening. You will be seen as a leader with human qualities." Jennifer's argument was convincing. Unless she was setting him up for a big fall. For all he knew, she could even be working for Darren Fine. That was probably paranoia on his part. Long-term cocaine use was known to induce that.

"Couldn't I also be perceived as a man who might act indecisively because of the concern I have for Granny? They might see it as a reason to question my ability to run the country." It was a valid point.

"I don't think you have a choice. If the press gets hold of this before you make it public, then you'll be seen as deliberately deceitful by both them and the media. Not something you want."

An equally valid point.

"Very well. Arrange for me to speak to the press as soon as possible after we get back. I'll make it public, tackle it head on as you suggest. I hope you're right.'

She was right. He knew he didn't have a choice.

CHAPTER II

"If you want to make a rich man go crazy, take away his wealth. That was the joke going around Wall Street that week, among those of us who decided to stick it out. Even at the end of the world, a good stockbroker can always find a way to make money. That first week though, even for someone as savvy as myself, it was just impossible. You have to understand, this wasn't just the bottom falling out of one part of the market - this was the entire world going into a financial meltdown. You couldn't sell shares in anything because no one wanted to buy anything. On the other hand, you had people who just wanted me to sell everything. My clients didn't make much money that week, but I sure as hell did. I figured if we were all going to die anyway, I might as well bet on the shortest odds of surviving. Having made that decision, I used every penny of my savings to buy up the most valuable stocks I could and, yeah, I made a killing. Of course, the markets never went completely back to normal, but within a month they'd settled sufficiently for us to be able to claim that it was 'business as usual'. We all knew that was a lie. By then we knew that the world's social order was going to change dramatically, and the markets along with it. I could have quit my job then. I'd made over sixty million dollars, I had a nice house, three actually, but I was a broker through and through. The job was in my blood, flowing through my veins every day, never more so than when I stuck it out to make the biggest financial killing of my life. Those were the glory days. Who knew it was all going to end anyway? These drinks are going on your tab, right? Can I get another double bourbon?"

Extract from a recorded interview with an anonymous Wall Street Broker.
Date unknown.

OMARI

O mari watched his daughter's eyes widen with surprise and fascination at the magnificent sight, soaring into the sky, west of the town. Wherever they walked through the small sandy streets of Fada with its simple dwellings and clusters of small compounds, the white tower of the object could be seen ascending into the clouds.

"It reminds me of a temple, Father. Is it a place of worship sent to us by Allah?" his daughter asked, innocently, sitting on Abu-Kir.

Omari pulled his animals by the reins as he walked quickly, carrying Tabitha with the other, giving neighbours the occasional hurried nod and greeting. On any other day, people would have noticed a change in him: the fast pace of his walk, his youthful appearance. They might have questioned him over the identity of the young girl he was carrying. But the people of Fada had more pressing matters on their minds, the apex of which loomed above them. Tabitha pulled her scarf firmly over her face to shield her eyes from the stinging sunlight. Omari did his best to keep her head pressed into his neck, away from the sun. She had lost the sunglasses he had given her. The town's scattered population had gathered in larger groups and were talking feverishly about the gift from Jannah that had landed on their doorstep. Evidently, Omari was not the only one to have reached the edge of the vessel and seen the change in the landscape around it. The water, the fish within it, the palm trees, the vegetation. People were speaking of nothing else. Although there was a palpable tension, there was also a pervading mood of positivity. Such circumstances would present the chance for advancement for local people, of profit and prosperity. The reasons for jubilation however, were already being met with equal pessimism from people voicing concerns over the disposition of the Chad military. They were already trying to bar people from approaching the object.

Omari avoided all attempts to be dragged into any such conversation and soon arrived at the fort, where inside the main parade ground, a chorus of raised voices were already reaching a crescendo. He tied up his animals and went inside. holding Tabitha in his arms and with Joy following from behind. A huge number of people from the town had gathered in the compound, along with all the clan Elders. They were in the middle of a heated debate. Pappa Bendi gave him a wave, which he acknowledged. But Omari sought the attention of someone else and soon found him. Doctor Aziz was the local dentist, but had some years ago managed to find work at the army barracks as their go-to physician. Omari had no doubt that some financial incentive had probably been agreed upon for this arrangement. Although Omari doubted Aziz's medical qualifications, his main job was to treat the VD that was rife among the soldiers, who were known to frequent the few local prostitutes. His half-brother Attah had found cause to visit the doctor on a number of occasions. Omari was certain that the reason was not toothache. The crowd was angry and on the verge of physical confrontation. Captain Daskar, the commander of the small militia at the fort, had informed all present that an entire battalion of the soldiers was on its way from the capital. The first of them were due to arrive that evening. Until then, no one else from the town was to approach the ship on the orders of the President himself. Arguments raged back and forth among the crowd on this very issue.

"It is clear that this thing is a gift to the people of Fada from Allah and we all should be able to enjoy in its riches!" shouted one man.

"You have no right to deny us! If the President says we cannot stand upon it, let him come here and tell us this himself!" cried another, causing many to nod in agreement.

"It has come to bring the desert back to life and give it to the people of Fada!" cried another, and so the argument raged on. Omari found the Doctor watching proceedings by the gate to the inner compound, where he now had a surgery in the old officers' quarters. Omari deftly moved around the rear of the crowd, going almost entirely unnoticed. The white tower still dominated the skyline above the walls of the fort and was the focus of any eyes that wandered away from the debate. Doctor Aziz was middle-aged, perhaps old compared to some of the men in Fada, but he was in good health, dressed in the same traditional robes as the others. His beard was more pointed than the rest, and Omari imagined him as quite handsome when he was younger. A diet of luxury foods presumably provided by his connections to the army had caused him to become fatter in recent years. Aziz noticed Omari and opened his arms to him in greeting.

"Omari, I had no idea you were back! It is good to see you! Who would have thought brother, that we should live to see such a day as this? Can you believe it?" his eyes turned at once to Joy and the girl Omari held in his arms, whose face was now buried into his chest. Aziz then studied his friend's face and could not disguise his shock at Omari's healthy appearance.

"You look so well. Travelling clearly agrees with you. How long were you gone?"

"Several months!" Omari replied, already steering him towards the inner compound.

"Incredible. You seem not to have aged a day! In fact you look younger than when you left! How are you, Joy? And who is this young girl?"

Tabitha shrank away from the stranger. Omari was keen to quickly change the subject. "Doctor, I must speak with you privately. Both my daughter and this girl require your assistance, and your confidence."

Aziz could see he was serious, and gestured for them to follow him through the arch into the inner compound leaving the village to continue its arguments. Dennis Chorely, the fifty something, rather portly built South-African teacher followed Omari with his beady sunken eyes until he lost sight of him. He was the one European-looking man in attendance at the meeting. His presence had gone unnoticed by Omari, so eager was he to speak to Aziz.

Doctor Aziz's surgery comprised two large rooms, one of which he used as his office and surgery, and the second contained his personal sleeping quarters. Patients would normally wait under the shade of several large palm trees, which were clustered in a small knot in the middle of the inner courtyard, but today it was quiet. People were all too pre-occupied with the arrival of the object. This suited Omari. Women in Fada had been known to listen in at the door of the Doctor's and spread gossip round the town. Today the gossip merchants had other things to talk about, enough to last their flapping tongues several weeks.

They went inside and sat on the floor. The room was spartan, containing a desk and chair next to which there was a stack of files and notebooks. The Doctor had a small collection of medical books and a large, locked, metal, medicine cabinet where the more expensive treatments were kept. Other medications and bandages were stacked in crates and boxes around the room. Thankfully, he looked to be recently supplied. Omari put Tabitha down upon some cushions on the floor. He and Joy sat upon the others.

"What is it that I can do for you?" Aziz asked, trying to add a tone of warmth to his question. His doctor-patient manner had always been quite good for a dentist, Omari thought. His hands began to shake as he spoke.

"My daughter has been defiled against her will... This atrocity occurred over many months. I... I am concerned the man who did this to her could have destroyed much more than just her honour..."

It was hard to say out loud. He felt his voice breaking, but the hand of the Doctor was at once upon his shoulder. A tear fell from Joy's cheek.

"Say no more, my friend. Nothing of this conversation will leave this room."

"Thank you. Is there something you can do to, to check? The man who did this was someone... someone who was known to lay with whores."

Doctor Aziz retrieved a small box.

"If you will permit me, I will carry out a physical examination. I have recently taken delivery of some kits from the Red Cross, that can provide instant results. They will tell you what you want to know," the doctor said He turned to Joy, speaking softly.

"Joy, I am going to have to place you on my examination table just to check if you're hurt. Then I will need to give you just a little scratch with a needle."

Omari saw his daughter wince at the suggestion of the needle, her hand gripping his arm. She feared this more than the examination.

"Joy, you must do this. Please let the Doctor do what he must. I will be right outside. You must show little Tabitha here how it is done, so that she will be equally brave. Do you understand?"

Joy nodded solemnly. Tabitha sat quietly, her eyes peering through her shawl. She had not said a word since they had left Attah's. Omari left the room and waited outside, momentarily drawn to the sight of the shining white spire that reflected the sun everywhere. He overheard the doctor saying kind words to the girls, asking them to be brave, with the promise of honey cakes afterwards. For the first time since his reunion with Joy, he had a moment to himself, to evaluate everything that had happened. His experience on the ship, the healing of his scars, his new-found strength and energy, all of which he attributed to his immersion in the pool of water, that he'd found in his room. Was it his room? Would it even be there when he went back? If he could get back. What about the army? Soon there would be dozens, if not hundreds of militia around the ship. But it was so vast in size, they couldn't possibly guard it all. He debated how to tell the Elders what he had seen and experienced, but knew now that he could not. It was all too complicated. Such gifts would cause conflict, even just among his own people. His mind turned to Attah and the act of his murder. He had taken another man's life. Even though he knew he had been justified in doing so, the violence with which he'd carried it out had horrified him. Aziz joined him outside.

"Your daughter is getting dressed. I examined her and the little one... Tabitha?"

"Yes, Tabitha."

"May I ask where you found her?" Aziz said.

Omari thought carefully before answering, "Somewhere she should not have been. I thought it best to bring her to you."

"I see. She is in poor health, has a temperature and is malnourished but she should recover if you can continue to care for her. She needs to eat properly. I have seen her before, but not for over a year. She is the younger sister of Little Ubba... I remember him saying on the street that the devils had taken his sister..."

Little Ubba, the same street child he and Pappi Bendi had talked of only hours earlier. He was one of a small collection of orphans in the town, most of whom were looked after at the school run by Dennis, the white teacher from South Africa whom Omari recalled worked for some charity or other. Omari was weary of these charities that claimed to raise so much money for the poorest people of the Earth. By the time such things filtered through the middlemen, there would be very little left for the people who really needed it. The supply lines were always rife with corruption and he never trusted the people who worked for them. He was not aware that the boy had an actual sister by birth. But he certainly had his own clan of children who followed him everywhere.

"I tested both of the girls. They were brave and no trouble. Tabitha is fine, but..."

Omari felt his world stop.

"Joy, your daughter, I am afraid her result has come back as positive. I can of course check again but these disposable kits from the Red Cross have been proven to be very reliable."

"There is no need. I am certain the results are correct. Thank you, Doctor."

"I am sorry, my friend. I will of course keep these results confidential."

Omari knew now that his next choice had already been made for him.

"I must say Omari, you're handling this the right way," the Doctor said with pride. Omari wasn't certain what he meant. The Doctor was from the capital, where they handled things differently, no doubt. Out of the corner of his eye he could see Joy looking at them from the doorway, as she helped Tabitha get dressed.

"Other people have come to me with similar problems and their daughters have been held responsible. I can assume what took place was not consensual." He made it a statement rather than a question. Omari knew Aziz was a good man, but he had never really had cause to trust him until now.

"You can, yes," Omari said. He would not allow himself to cry, not yet and not here.

"You should tell someone, Omari. There have been stories while you have been away. Rumours..."

"What rumours?" Omari wondered who else his brother might have shamed. There were already two victims. He could have been doing this for years in the town. Hiding in plain sight the entire time.

"Children disappearing. Orphans mostly. I've heard stories of cars leaving late at night, taking children away. If this has anything to do with that…"

"It doesn't," Omari cut him off. He knew it could be connected. His brother could have been involved in anything, but he couldn't get into a discussion about that now, he needed to leave.

"Thank you Doctor. You have been most kind. I must go and tend to my daughter's needs." He waved to the girls to come to him.

"I have medications to deal with this affliction. Things are not what they once were. People live long and normal lives with this condition as long as they take the tablets. She can still marry and have children, my friend. She has bruising but she will heal. I haven't said anything to her and I would recommend for now that you do not either."

"Such medications are expensive, no?"

"To guarantee getting the real thing, an exchange of money is sometimes required, but the Red Cross send me some from time to time. The soldiers normally take them all but I could try and procure you some when they next arrive…"

"No thank you, Doctor. We must go. I will see Tabitha is well fed and looked after." Omari shook the man's hand and offered him the one currency he knew was worth something, an old American ten-dollar bill. The Doctor shook his head. "Please Omari, you offend me. Use that money to feed the girl and buy her new clothes. Joy will need the medication. Without it she will… Two years is the average life span…"

"Thank you Doctor, I will take everything you have said to me under consideration. Girls, let's go."

The men exchanged a firm handshake. Omari carried Tabitha, holding Joy's hand. He wanted to leave this place as soon as possible. He looked to the white tower to the east. He knew what he had to do.

JOY

The Doctor had been kind and delicate in his examination of her, but she still could not wait to leave the fort. It was a place of men and Joy did not like to be in the presence of so many. Her Father scooped up Tabitha who buried her face once again into his chest, averting her eyes from the light of the sun. Joy was pleased that the child had taken to their Father as a protector, and that she had not seen him as a threat. Joy exchanged a smile of mutual assurance with the young girl whenever she could. Sometimes she received a weak one in return, other times Tabitha stared blankly as if her mind was somewhere else. The girl's childhood had been a world of evil and darkness. Joy knew her Father was going to have to cross men of influence in the town to confront the people responsible, Attah had not acted alone. She had seen men come and go from his house, men who Joy knew belonged to the most powerful clans in Fada. It would be no simple matter to resolve this. There was a time when her Father's name carried great weight among the clan leaders and he was well respected. Times had changed however, and his trips away had become longer and longer and to most people in Fada he was but a distant memory. Joy had not known it was possible to hate someone to the point that you wished them real harm, but she was glad her Uncle was dead. She could still smell the tobacco on his fingers, the taste of him on her lips, the marks of his grip upon her skin, the smell of him, which even now had not left her clothing. She tried to push the memories from her mind but they would seep back in whenever she found her thoughts beginning to wander. Joy had few memories of her Mother, but one that had always remained vivid was of the time she talked with her and Nya about men and their role in the world.

"The purpose of the Toubou women is to serve their husbands in all things," she had told them. Her Mother had paused as she said those words with her two daughters listening, "But..." she continued, "a good husband will see more than this in his wife, he will know she is in fact his equal, his best friend, the pillar of his strength. The power of the relationship is always in the hands of the woman."

It was the only conversation she could remember with any clarity. Her Father led them quickly back into the outer compound, leaving Doctor Aziz behind them. The Doctor, true to his word, had given them a small brown paper bag containing four honey cakes. Joy knew Tabitha needed food desperately. The little girl ate all four of them before they even had a chance to get on the move. The crowd in the parade ground had grown larger in number and the debate continued to rage. Many of the clan leaders had not come alone. Each clan was present with a show of strength in numbers. Joy could see weapons among many in the crowd. She knew people could be quick to use them in anger. Her Father rushed them towards the gates, muttering to both of them, "Don't worry, both of you, I am going to take you somewhere safe, where no one will ever hurt us."

She saw him look up towards the distant tower, ever present yet somehow aloof. The angry shouts grew louder. The frustration on the Captain Daskar's face, the local commander, was clear for all to see. Joyful he was not. As they weaved past the edges of the crowd towards the exit gate Joy noticed a set of eyes following them. They belonged to the one white man in the crowd. Dennis had been listening to the argument go back and forth when Joy heard his voice: "We'll need to keep the children indoors. It might not be safe for them here. Who knows why these things are here or what their intentions are?" She recognised it at once. She had heard him before, talking with her Uncle but she had never seen the man until now. His accent was South African and he stood out at once in the crowd, with a wide-brimmed hat and his partial western clothing. She turned away from his gaze. Had he seen her or recognised her? She wasn't sure. As they went through the gates, Tabitha looked over her Father's shoulder and pointed at the white tower in the sky.

"Is that Paradise?" the young girl asked.

Joy was surprised by her Father's answer.

"Yes, it is and we're going to go there."

They rushed back to the family home, leaving the three camels tethered outside the gate. As they entered the compound, she found herself being glad that her father was fully aware of the reasons behind her absence from their family home. It was evident nothing had been cleaned recently. The chickens had not been properly fed, with two lying dead in the courtyard, flies feasting on their rotting corpses which were almost bone. The stench of dead meat was everywhere. They all were forced to cover their noses from the smell. The house was a simple dwelling. It had four rooms in all. One had been for her Mother and Father, that now only he occupied. As her Father was away so often, he had given up the bed for his daughter's comfort. She had previously lived in the second bedroom, which had only rugs and cushions on the floor. It had been Joy's alone ever since Nya had married the man from the army and moved to the capital. The third room was a kitchen with a small stove and several urns for storing water plus others for storing grain and spices. The fourth, which connected them all had a small table and a very old, light brown leather sofa the sides of which were peeling like a lizard shedding its skin. It was not traditional to have such furniture. Joy could not remember where it had come from, it had just appeared in the house one day, many years ago. A stray dog ran out of the house as soon they opened the door. For a moment the rabid mongrel looked as though it was going to stand it's ground and lay claim to its new home but her Father didn't give it a chance. He swiftly kicking the ragged creature, which let out a yelp and ran back into town. Her Father wasted no time. He put Tabitha on the sofa and told her to rest, giving further instructions to Joy to collect as many clothes and useful things as possible from the house, for they would be travelling tonight. They would not be returning for a while.

"I will need to go back into town, to get some food and other things. You must wait here."

Fearful of being alone, Joy at once grabbed his hand.

"Father, do not leave me again. Please! Let us all stay together!"

He hugged her in his arms and lifted her up, something she recalled he had not been able to do in many years. He held her close to his face and put his cheek next to hers. He smiled at her, a smile she had not seen in a long time. She saw again how he was markedly different. His scars, bags and lines were really all gone; she thought she might have imagined it before when she was still upset. His smile was that of the man she knew when she was not much older than Tabitha.

"I want you to know, you have not shamed me"' he said. His words were meant to reassure her but Joy knew in anyone else's eyes she had brought terrible shame to his name.

"Oh Father I have…"

"No, I will not hear of it and you must banish all such thoughts from your mind and cast them out forever, do you understand me? You're my daughter, you're all I care about in this world…"

"What about Nya? Don't you care about her too?"

"Yes of course I do but… she is married now and has a man to protect her. Protecting you was my responsibility. Your dishonour was my failure, it was not yours, do you understand me, child?'

"I am no longer a child, Father." She knew that part of her life was well and truly over. It was time to grow up and face the evil that dwelled within men.

"You will always be my daughter. Nothing will ever change that."

Joy nodded in reply. She had rarely heard her Father speak with such emotion or such strength. Remembering her Mother's words, she impulsively found herself saying, "I will be your strength, Father."

His face lit up with pride at hearing the words. Perhaps he also connected them with her late Mother. She did not wish to ask. He sat her down next to Tabitha, and held them together before she heard him whisper into her ear, "I am going to take care of you both. I promise." His embrace was all too brief and his tone now became more serious.

"Pack only your most treasured possessions. We will travel light. I will be back before nightfall, probably sooner. You must lock the gate to our compound and do not answer it to anyone but me."

Her father always did a certain knock to announce he had returned home. Joy recalled how it had brought such happiness to her Mother's face when she heard the knock. This was apparently how she came to be given her name, because of this joy.

Omari brought the camels inside the compound to offer them a greater degree of shade. The midday sun became incredibly unforgiving. He left them some feed, and departed. Her Father hadn't yet explained what had happened to the rest, other than to say that Abu-Sir, Abu-Kir and Ali-Baba were all that remained. Joy carried the already sleepy Tabitha into the bedroom, pulled a blanket over her and then went to seek out what to take with them on their journey. The most valuable possessions to Joy were her books, a collection given to her by her Uncle Joseph on her Mother's side, before he died. One was called *Emma* by a writer called Jane Austen. It was long and had been difficult to understand at first but Joy enjoyed it more whenever she read it, even if she still struggled with many of the words. Her Mother had always told her it was important to learn the English language, and the best way to do this was to read. The teachers at the school were normally from other countries and would teach whichever children were willing, as extra lessons. Joy had been one of the first to volunteer, and it had been at these lessons where she had come to know many of the orphans of Fada, who would also attend. Each child was told to choose their own book. There was a small selection of English books in the school, but her favourite was a birthday present given to her. It was called *The Lion, The Witch and The Wardrobe*. It was the first book she had ever been given by her Uncle Joseph. Joseph had told her that one of his customer's children no longer had any use for it so he had asked if he could have it, knowing that she would enjoy it, as worn around the edges as it was. It was about children who went to live with an eccentric professor, and found a door through a closet to a fantastical world full of mythical creatures that Joy often had trouble trying to visualise. During the months of her virtual imprisonment, she had dreamed of such a place, hoping that such wonders were real so she could offer those in need a place of safety. Away from the clutches of evil men. Nothing in this world that she had seen had convinced her that such a place could really exist, but that was before the white diamond tower from Jannah had arrived in Fada. To her it offered something – hope. Now they were going to see it. She packed both books along with a third called *Wonders of the World*, that her father had brought back for her on his last trip. Its pages were filled with pictures of incredible things and places that Joy knew she would probably never get to see. She would stay up at night with a candle and look at the pictures long and hard. She studied every line of the Egyptian Pyramids and the wonders of the never-ending water that fell from *Niagara Falls*. She stared in awe at *The Great Wall of China* that snaked up and around the hills in the photograph, seeming to go on forever, while somewhere called *The Hanging Gardens of Babylon* were only depicted in a painting. They were said to have been destroyed by man long ago. The last photo she always looked at before she went to sleep was that of something called the *Northern Lights*. The picture had been taken in some place called Norway. The ground was covered in white powder that she had seen in other photographs, atop the peaks of mountains. He father had called it snow, and explained it fell from the sky and was very cold. To her it looked so beautiful. In the photograph, magic streaks of light in red and green were painted across the night sky above fields of white. Joy wondered what power on earth could create such a thing. She had never seen anything like it in her country. Playing as a child in Fada, the mud adobe walls and dusty roads were her playground. She and the other children would play at the oasis, which back then had a stream of water, compared to the small choking pools that lay among the reeds today. Fada was not a large town, but to her it was the whole world. The hours of her youth had been spent getting to know every house, every alley, every gap between the walls and most importantly every trader who would give away sweets to children. The town had a hierarchy of children that was clan-dependent. The more affluent came from the families who were connected to someone in the Chad Government or military, but Fada was not a posting that affluent people sought and the visible divide between rich and poor in Fada was an extremely slim line. The orphan children were firmly on the bottom rung of the ladder. Joy knew she was lucky to be in a position where she had a family home and relatives to care for her, until her Uncle Attah had changed all that. The children from the largest clans always claimed the best places to play, and always produced the best toys in front of the other children. Joy often received presents from her sister Nya, gifts sent from the capital, each unique to this part of the world, but she would not brag about them to those less fortunate than her. Her sister had sent her colouring books, candy, an English dictionary, a watch and even something called a Gameboy, that it had taken a while for Joy to fully grasp the use of. Nya knew of her sister's love for reading and would send her old magazines, mostly beauty magazines which displayed pictures of the most exotic women, each of whom had hair and makeup that was so elaborate, she could not comprehend how they would achieve such a look. The older children would often congregate around the single internet café in town. On the rare occasions Joy would be lucky enough to tag along, she would gain a small insight into the world that existed beyond the desert wastes that surrounded Fada. Visits to the computers were rare and they were often hogged by adults talking to relatives in faraway places. It was not the same as a book that you could call your own. Joy always loved being able to take a book with her to bed. She could conjure the images of the stories and characters in her head. So her life had been as it was for most women in this part of the world; a relatively simple, if not always easy one. Fada was her home and it felt far away from the social calamities of the larger world. News in Fada was always concerned with food and water. If there was a shortage of either it would be all anyone ever talked about. Missing goats were the highlight of weekly conversations among the town Elders. Life here had been simple. As Joy became a teenager, she found herself in demand to babysit the younger children, while learning to cook and clean with the older women became the normal daily routine. Joy was quick to observe that it was better to keep your mouth shut if you wanted something to stay secret, because when the women congregated they liked to talk, and talk, and talk. Although the older ladies from the town would converse about absolutely anything, the three most frequent topics seemed to be: who was sleeping with whom, who had died and who was next expecting a baby. Joy was asked about her Father from time to time, and when he was expected to return home next. The women talked of him warmly and the eyes of those Joy knew to be widows would light up whenever his name was mentioned, but she never had anything new to tell them so the conversation would quickly change. Things had begun to alter in Fada about a year earlier. Until now, she had not made the connection of that coinciding with the time that the new teacher, Dennis, had arrived back in Fada from South Africa. Joy knew all the street children in the town, most of whom would sleep at the orphanage. Dennis replaced the Danish teacher who had been in the town for the last two years, and had ended up marrying the daughter of one of the local clan leaders. He was an extremely kind man and Joy was profoundly sad when he left with his new wife to return to Denmark. It was not uncommon for several of the orphans to be absent from the school for days at a time. Joy had heard stories about groups of boys staying out all night in nearby caves in the hills, but children often made fantastical boasts when there was little else with which they could impress each other. Twelve months ago however, children had started to disappear. The orphans first, perhaps because no one would miss them. Joy noticed and so did the other children, as well. There were rumours of children running away, but the town was so remote going anywhere was impossible without a vehicle, a camel or an adult. Acquiring any of those three would be beyond a child's means, without attracting attention. There were rumours of children being sold off to unknown parties but such talk was the gossip only of the orphan children who would meet regularly at the oasis. Recently, a mixed group of orphan and clan children had been called to discuss the topic. This was the first time she had heard Little Ubba speak on the subject. How she wished they all had heeded the warnings he gave back then. He told tales of men taking children in cars in the middle of the night from the orphanage, with the full consent of the new South African teacher. He claimed other key figures in the town were also involved, including someone from the army. The older children laughed at him and thought his story nonsense. Teachers could be trusted couldn't they? Why would anyone want to steal an orphan? They had nothing of value, after all. The boys from the clans accused him of lying but Joy, even back then, was not so sure. Little Ubba was the most inquisitive and cunning of all the orphans. He was a boy of undetermined age, small in height, but his local knowledge had no such limitations. Joy had come to realise that Ubba was as cheeky as he was crafty, and knew every inch of Fada even better than she did. Joy was fond of many of the orphans and knew most of them by name, but Ubba always remained a little more elusive than the rest. He was, Joy noted, an intense observer of things. If she caught him watching or studying something then she knew he was doing so for a reason. Many of the traders did not want him near their shops. Even the normally kind Pappa Bendi, the most generous of all the people in the town towards children had exchanged harsh words with him on more than one occasion. Ubba had earned the reputation of being a food thief. Joy was certain that if he was ever caught he might find his hands chopped off, but he was quick and such laws were rarely enforced on Fada's streets. There were few Elders willing to chop the hands off from a starving child. Joy knew when the boy was older, it would be a different matter.

When the White Coconut (as the children of Fada had taken to calling it) had arrived in the early hours, less than forty-eight hours ago, Joy was certain every animal in Fada knew of its presence before the town's people did. Chickens began to fret in their coops, dogs both tamed and wild began to bark wildly towards the west. This noise roused Joy from her sleep.

Camels and goats were heard bleating in their pens. The bells around their necks tinkled all across the compounds of the town. It took a while for people to wake but Joy was one of the first. Her Uncle had forced her to stay with him the night before. He had been drinking heavily and tried to get Joy to do the same. She hated the taste of alcohol and was not interested. After he had forced himself on her, which thankfully had been a relatively short experience, he had fallen asleep, snoring loudly as always. She had woken, and walked into the courtyard only to see the huge white disk passing overhead, blocking out the entire sky above. She had rushed back inside, gone back to bed and thought the whole thing a dream the following day. When her Uncle finally awoke from his drunken slumber and went outside, he saw the white tower and thought it to be the end of the world.

If the world was indeed ending, then he decided he was going to have his fun with her again, and again and again. It was then that her father had appeared and saved her. It was getting on for the evening by the time she had gathered all the possessions she assumed they would need. She packed some cooking utensils and a selection of spice, spare clothes that were worth taking and some more for Tabitha. They wouldn't fit her but they would keep her warm at night. Any food that she could find, sugar beets and a few dried fruits and vegetables along with her books were all packed and ready to go. Tabitha still lay sleeping in the bed and Joy thought it best not to wake her until they had to travel. As she came out of the house and back into the courtyard, she thought to leave out plenty of feed for the chickens. She had just finished cleaning the courtyard when the door on the gate opened and a man stepped through the opening. He had on the uniform of the Chad Army. Her Father followed him.

"Colonel Malloum, this is my other daughter, Joy,' her Father said. Joy immediately bowed her head, as was the tradition. Out of the corner of her eye, she saw Tabitha duck back into the house to hide.

"Ah yes, Joy, of course. She was just a child when I was last here. How you have grown!" the Colonel bellowed, surveying the compound. "This will do just fine, Omari. It will only be for a few nights." The Colonel took note of the chicken coop. "Roasted chicken will suffice for dinner tonight."

Her Father had a defeated expression on his face.

"Colonel Malloum is your sister's husband. He has just arrived from the capital, he's going to be staying with us a while."

Joy bowed again and went immediately inside the house. She had to hide Tabitha and keep her quiet, or there would be questions.

BLESSING

GARGOLIE, 10 KILOMETRES WEST OF ABERDEEN,
SCOTLAND, APPROXIMATELY 10AM, APRIL 3RD

I t was some hours later when the trio were been given the all-clear by the Doctor. Blessing knew it was a good sign when the woman had entered their bubble without wearing any protective clothing. All three of them were then interviewed separately by a team from the government. The focus of their questions were the events leading up to the disappearance of Mrs Agatha Davey. Had they touched anything before the opening had appeared in the depression of the ship? Had she seen anyone else touch anything? Had she seen the opening? What did it look like? What did Mrs Davey do before she went inside? Did she say anything? What was inside the object? Was there a noise when the opening had closed and so on and so on. Blessing was beginning to regret her part in the whole escapade. There had been four people present the entire time, a man and a woman, both in army uniform, and two male detectives. Blessing had thought to ask for a lawyer to be present, just as she had seen in the movies but ultimately decided against it for fear of delaying her departure further. She was aware she had missed her cleaning rounds that morning, that should have started at 5am. She was worried about losing her job. She mentioned as much during the interview, but the first man told her she had more important things to worry about. It would serve her best by answering their questions as quickly and as truthfully as possible. She was so stressed by it all she even forgot to check which of the men wore wedding rings.

Finally her possessions were returned to her, including her bag and purse with the little money that she had inside it. She received a plastic bag with her clothes and was escorted outside of the khaki green tent, where she had been questioned. She was concerned that she was still dressed in her prison issue bright orange jumpsuit, which made her look somewhat masculine. It was also rather tight around certain parts of her body and felt a little uncomfortable, but they weren't going to give her time to change. The woman escorting her was the same one from the army who had stood quietly in the interview room. It was only when they exited the tent that she realised it was the following morning. She had thought she might awake to find the whole thing had been a dream, because it was known that her medications would from time to time give her extremely vivid nightmares, but it had not been a dream. Just behind the collection of tents, from the low rolling hills it stretched up into the morning sky like a bright white icicle. The tower they had failed to reach. She was only some five hundred yards or so from the edge of the ship, the vast body of which spanned each direction to the north and south as far as she could see.

The woman led her out of the field and across a metal stepladder that had been constructed to bridge the stone wall to the courtyard of the farm beyond. Blessing found herself ushered through the farm, and back onto the main road. Military Police were stopping incoming military vehicles, and organising parking just beyond a coiled low wire fence that had been laid across the road. Men and women in both civilian and military clothes were heading busily in all directions, reminding Blessing of the rush hour in the London Underground. Everyone was rushing somewhere different with a sense of purpose. Blessing had seen the Nigerian military on the move before, but never anything on a scale such as this. In the direction of the ship, groups of people donning similar suits worn by those who had spoken to them the previous evening were heading to and coming back from the edge of the ship. The road heading east towards Aberdeen was lined with armed soldiers and dark green armoured vehicles that Blessing assumed were tanks. She had never seen such a vehicle up close before and they carried an unpleasant smell of metal and oils, making her keen to leave as soon as possible. She was put in a group with several other civilians and led towards a waiting coach, parked up outside a small country pub just past the checkpoint. Waiting in line to board was a collection of elderly people, women and children, some of whom had sustained minor injuries. Blessing hoped they had occurred as a result of the ship landing and not from when they were being questioned. She was the only person of a different ethnicity in the group. Everyone else was white and sounded local. Stories were being exchanged about who saw the ship and when, with tales of escape being reiterated for all to hear. These were people who had lived inside the perimeter of the landing site and were now effectively refugees, their homes and farms presumed destroyed. They were distressed and complaints were frequent.

"When can we come back, like?" shouted one.

'Mah wee cat is still missing, noo. I cannae find her!" yelled another woman, as she was all but manhandled onto the waiting coach.

Lined up with her were four other people in the orange jumpsuits. Blessing wondered if they too had managed to get on the surface of the ship, but she didn't want to ask. As she was corralled towards the waiting coach, she stole a final glance back at the ship, the white tower glowing back at her in the warmth of the morning sun. It was a beautiful day and the structure reflected the light of the sun down on the surrounding landscape, projecting a warmth across the fields. The uppermost part of the tower sat above the white clouds that dotted the cool blue sky. *Why are you here?* She asked the question over and over in her head. For now, there was no answer. She let out a huge yawn. She hadn't slept well, and it was normal for her to feel exhausted even before she started work on an average day, such were the side effects of her medication. Last night, she had grabbed three or four hours at best and should have felt terrible, yet she did not. She had a spring in her step that she could not recall having in years. A familiar voice called out from behind her, causing her to turn and lock eyes with a friendly face.

"Hey beautiful. So they let you go too, huh?" it was Rain, her Californian accent purring through every word. Though still dressed in her orange jumpsuit, Rain appeared to have customised by shortening the sleeves and legs to make it appear more interesting which she thought must have made her very cold. The two of them together, Blessing with her dark skin and Rain with her dyed pink hair and caramel skin tone would have stood out in any crowd. There was no sign of Elvis. Rain pushed forward in the queue to be next to Blessing as they were herded onto the coach. Someone chastised her for pushing in.

"She's my sister, alright?" Rain shouted. "Did they question you?" she asked Blessing.

"Yes. The same questions again and again. They wanted to know how the door opened," Blessing replied.

"Yeah, they asked me the same thing."

A soldier stepped forward. "Okay everyone, take your seats."

Rain went on first and went straight for the back of the bus. Rain offered to let Blessing sit down first, giving her the window seat. Blessing was not used to people being so polite. Perhaps they were becoming friends now. She hoped so, it would be nice to have some friends in Scotland. At the moment she didn't have any.

"What did you tell them?" Blessing asked.

"Nothing. What could I tell them? One moment the old lady was there, then she wasn't. Then I asked them if they were actually going to charge me with anything, and demanded a lawyer be present. After that they left me alone. They said my bike would be returned to me, didn't say when though! Bastards."

Now Blessing felt foolish for not asking for a lawyer for herself. Rain leaned in, muttering quietly. Her breath was scented with something sweet, a huge improvement on Elvis who reeked of cigarettes whenever he spoke too close to her. Maybe it was just a new brand of gum.

"I don't know about you, but I feel like I'm buzzing. I mean when I woke up this morning, I felt like I had slept for ten days. I feel really..."

"Refreshed?" Blessing finished the sentence for her. It was the first time she had ever done that, with anyone.

"Yes. Exactly that. I feel like I could run all the way back to Aberdeen."

Their conversation was halted by the arrival of a woman at the front of the bus. She stood in the aisle, about to address all the passengers. The bus was only just over half-full.

"Ladies and Gentleman. I know some of you have had a very rough time these last 48 hours and that you have friends, family and loved ones waiting for news. Two emergency centres have been set up on the eastern outskirts of Aberdeen for those of you whose houses have fallen inside the militarised area. We will be stopping at both of these before taking the coach to Aberdeen Central bus station. Your evacuation from this area is entirely for your own safety and you will be updated as to when it is safe to return as soon as possible."

A woman sitting in the middle of the bus interrupted her.

"I didn't manage to retrieve my purse. I have nae money or credit cards! Where am I supposed to live and eat in the meantime?"

"Emergency accommodation will have been arranged for all those who have been directly affected by the event," the woman countered, trying to control the situation, but others wanted to speak.

"My medication is in my house. I didn't have time to get it..."

"Those of you with pressing medical concerns will have them addressed at the centre! Look, our priority right now is to get you to a place of safety!"

"The only thing unsafe is you army lot running around with your guns. You gonnae blow that thing up now are ye? Start a war with aliens? Typical fookin' English!" yelled a man from down the front.

"Aye, wait until Mel Gibson hears about this!" said another.

The woman gave up and got off the coach, the doors promptly closing behind her. Blessing could see their driver was a civilian, but the coach was being escorted front and back by military jeeps.

"Did you see Elvis?" Blessing asked.

"No. He might have left on another coach. Someone said two more left before this one. Ours is the last." Rain replied.

Blessing felt a pang of guilt towards the man. He had given her the chance to see something truly unique and wonderful that she might never see again, and he had probably lost his job as a result. The expected alien invasion as yet, had failed to materialise.

"Did you get your phone back?" Rain asked, producing her own and scanning through the pictures.

Blessing nodded, getting her own out, noticing her battery was at ten percent.

"All my pictures have gone. Everything's been deleted. Even before we got to the ship. Shit… God knows who's looking at that stuff! Fuck! Perverts!" Rain moaned, clearly upset.

"Did you lose anything important?' Blessing asked. Photographs could be replaced, couldn't they? Then she remembered she only had one photo of her Mother, a very old picture in black and white, fixed to the wall back at her bedsit. That was priceless.

"It was more kinda personal stuff, you know. Me and an ex of mine, we were having some fun. Anyway, some scientist will be getting their rocks off to that, no doubt."

"Oh…" Blessing wasn't entirely sure what she meant by "getting their rocks off". The photos she had on her own phone were just a few of Aberdeen, that she had sent back to her friend in Birmingham. She was on Facebook, but didn't use it much on account of not having anything exciting to post to her massive following of seventeen friends. Rain began furiously texting one message after the next. "I can't get into Facebook. What's that about? Nor Twitter!"

The coach rolled slowly down the road, going through two more check-points, each manned with over a dozen military personnel. More vehicles of every size and type passed by, heading back towards the ship. Blessing even saw a cement mixer, though she couldn't contemplate why on earth it would be needed in the current situation. The coach continued winding its way along the B road, leaving the low rolling hills behind them, making its way eastwards back towards Aberdeen. There was a noticeable lack of civilian traffic, but they did pass a number of abandoned vehicles. Many had raised bonnets. Blessing thought they must have broken down during their owners' escape. Spirals of smoke could be seen in the east as though fires had been left to burn. Blessing couldn't see their origin, but they were coming from somewhere within the centre of Aberdeen, just coming into view on the horizon. They reached the turn-off for Aberdeen International Airport, which was under heavy military guard. Two police cars pulled back to allow the coach to move through the western exit, surrounded by large-tracked military transport vehicles that had been arranged to block off the traffic travelling west, and with good reason. Rain sat up and pointed towards the oncoming lane.

"Would you look at all that?" They both stared at the scene on the other side of the road. The road was choked with vehicles, bumper to bumper, extending all the way back towards the city. People were outside their cars, standing and taking pictures of the distant alien tower, which Blessing could see still dominated the horizon behind them. Police were arguing with the owners of those of the first few cars, forcing them to turn around and create space for others to leave. Ambulance sirens filled the air. The coach was forced to momentarily pull over but then a policeman waved the coach onward. Blessing could see now that they had been lucky to get as close as they did. It was clear the army intended to keep any other unwanted visitors as far away from the landing site as possible.

It wasn't long before the coach reached the first Evacuation Centre. They had turned into the north-west suburbs of the city and arrived at Sheddocksley Playing Fields, a large expanse of flat green soccer fields upon which a sea of Khaki tents were in the process of hastily being erected. Other coaches arrived, disgorging groups of displaced and bewildered-looking people who were greeted by volunteers and led inside. A young man in army fatigues boarded the coach and after conferring with the driver, addressed everyone on board.

"Anyone who does not have alternative accommodation, or relatives waiting for them in central Aberdeen, please alight here and make your way inside the sports hall."

His announcement was greeted with silence and total lack of movement on the part of the passengers.

"Inside you will find hot tea, coffee and food awaiting you. Our staff will then see to those of you who have non-urgent medical needs and your accommodation for the night."

That did the trick. Gradually, people began to get off in ones and twos, until only just over twenty people remained on board. Blessing's stomach growled, reminding her she hadn't eaten properly in some time but before she even considered moving, Rain grabbed her arm.

"You're not getting off here. We're going to eat somewhere else, honey."

"What if nowhere in the city is open? Who would come in to work today?" she said. After all, she had missed work herself.

"Let's wait and see. I'm not putting my fate in the hands of the Territorial Army and a bunch of Boy Scouts."

Rain evidently was not enthused, even though the army preparations to deal with the current situation appeared impressive. As the coach headed for the exit, khaki trucks were continuing to arrive disgorging soldiers, while large marquees and tents continued to be erected over all the football pitches. This operation, combined with the camp they had been detained in would have required a great deal of planning in such a short time. It was a testimonial to the skills of the British army unless...

Rain was thinking the same thing. "They must have known. I mean, look at all this. They must have had some idea that something was going to happen to put all this together so fast. I mean how many rehearsals can they have done to deal with an alien invasion? I remember seeing anti-terrorist drills being carried out on the River Thames and at train stations, but I don't remember seeing anything in the media about the emergency services preparing for this sort of event!"

Rain was sharp, and Blessing wondered at her age. She had incredibly good skin, very smooth. Obviously that of someone who had been moisturising regularly for years. She wanted to ask her about her heritage but didn't want to appear nosey. Rain caught her staring.

"What you looking at, Baby Jane?" she said, holding her gaze.

Blessing was embarrassed. She had been staring at the girl and she wasn't even sure why. Why did she call her Baby Jane?

"My name is Blessing," she said for no reason other than to clarify it. Had the girl misheard her before?

"I know, hun. It's just a turn of phrase. Like a nickname, like your bus driver, Elvis."

Blessing hadn't had a nickname before, but decided there and then it would be nice to have one. Rain smiled and turned to look out the window as the coach turned back on the main road. The voice of the driver came over the intercom.

"I'll be stopping at Mastrick Community Centre next, in case this is more convenient for anyone living in east Aberdeen. After that it's the city centre."

The coach turned onto Greenfern Road. Their attention was drawn to the scores of people gathered outside the small Romanian Orthodox Church. Crowds stood on the grass outside and a queue was coming of out the doors. Some portable speakers had been erected on the pavement, so the service could be heard on the street.

"I expect the churches are doing very well out of this. They'll be counting their coffers all the way to the bank," Rain snorted, as she turned her head away from the scene. Blessing did not like her tone.

"The churches do a great deal of good work. Do you not have faith in God?" she asked, immediately regretting the question.

"I only have faith in one person," Rain shot back.

"Who is that?" Blessing asked.

"Me. You can only depend on yourself in this world. I don't believe in things I can't see. I didn't even believe in UFOs until yesterday. Everyone in my club is a science fiction geek, right?" Rain spoke as though Blessing should understand what she was talking about. She didn't. What was a UFO?

"You do know what an Unidentified Flying Object is, right?"

Blessing shook her head, feeling stupid.

"Unidentified Flying Object, UFO," Rain said.

"I had never seen one before," was all she could think to say, by way of reply.

"Don't worry. Most of the world's population hadn't seen a UFO before this week. After this, I think you would be hard pushed to find someone who hasn't seen one."

Blessing had completely forgotten about the rest of the ships that Donny had said were landing all over the world. How many had there been again? Dozens? She wondered as to the fate of the two students.

"Look at this." Rain passed Blessing her iPhone, showing her the news-feed online. It was filled with stories about the ships and their landings. Europe, Asia, Australia, Africa, the Americas... they were everywhere. A total of two hundred landing sites had been confirmed by a variety of sources.

"You're gonna need to stock up on food." Rain's statement was perfectly timed, as they witnessed a sea of humanity surrounding the local Lidl supermarket. The tills were heaving with huge queues of people buying an abundance of goods. Fights were breaking out as a group of soldiers arrived to take control of the scene. As the supermarket fell out of sight, Blessing thought she heard a gunshot. No one on the coach said anything. Rain shook her head and sat back. Further into the city, much of Aberdeen appeared deserted. Fewer cars than normal were parked on the streets, and nearly all the other shops they saw were closed. Blessing heard snatches of other passengers talking to friends and loved ones on their mobiles.

"Why did you go down to Edinburgh without me? No, well obviously I am not dead, otherwise I wouldn't be calling you..." moaned one man.

"Cannae you meet me at the bus station? Aye, the one on Guild Street! I'll be there in an hour," an elderly woman asked, sounding concerned she might be stranded.

'No, no I wasnae squashed by the thing. No, I told ye. Aye, it was amazing. You should've seen it. It was incredible. You can see it from Dundee? Really?"

This nugget of information surprised Blessing. Dundee was over 70 kilometres to the south, with some low-lying country in-between. Could someone really see the tower from so far away?

"How tall do they say it is, Rain?" As the girl took her phone back to find the answer, their fingers touched. There was an instant feeling of heat, as if Blessing had touched a hot oven, yet without being burned. Blessing felt the warm blood underneath the girls skin. She felt acutely sensitive to contact with another human being - more than she could ever previously recall. The last time someone had touched her hands, it had not been pleasant. She immediately removed the image of her idiot local pastor from her mind. Something inside her felt warm. It was as if something had lit a fire under the endorphins in her body. She was confused. Rain looked back at her. The two of them sat back in their seats, letting the feeling wash over them.

"Girl, what did you just do to me then?" Rain asked softly, letting out a low hushed sigh.

"I… I don't know," Blessing whispered. She could not rationalise the surge of emotion she was feeling from her brief touch with the girl.

"Will you let me try something, hun?" Rain asked, holding her hand out beckoning Blessing to take it. Unsure, Blessing found herself looking round the bus to see who was watching them. Most of the remaining passengers had taken seats down towards the front, apart from one middle-aged woman sitting by the emergency exit, just two seats ahead of them. Blessing nodded and Rain took her hand, wrapping her fingers around her own. A surging wave of electricity filled Blessing's body. Her muscles in her feet began to tighten. She found her eyes closing while her mind filled with a blinding white light…

Oh my God! This is amazing, she heard Rain say inside her head. Something was different.

What is happening? I feel like we're connected. Wait. I'm not speaking out loud, am I just thinking? Blessing heard her own thoughts as if she was shouting them inside a cave.

I can hear you. Can you hear me? Rain's voice asked inside her head.

Yes. I can hear you! Blessing did not understand what was happening.

Wait. Try opening your eyes and looking at me. Rain said.

Blessing had to focus to bring her vision back in the real world. She became aware of the two of them, their hands still locked tight together. Rain slowly opened her eyes, smiling back at her.

Fuck, this is wild. Can you still hear me? I can see you. Blessing could hear the girl's voice, but her lips remained closed.

How is this happening? How can we talk like this? My lips are not moving. Your lips are not moving. Is this the work of the Devil? Blessing heard herself say.

Unless the Devil is an alien. Hun, I do not think so. I think something must have happened to us when we walked on the ship. Did you touch the surface with your hands?

Blessing shut her eyes again, seeing images her brain had stored, playing out before her as though someone was playing back a video of her moments on the ship. There they were walking down the depression, looking for a way in, helping Agatha. Blessing felt the cool surface of the blank wall. She had touched it and saw Rain had done the same. The connection between the two of them intensified as the girl gripped her hand ever tighter. She felt Rain's emotions, the very essence of who she was, overlapping with her own mind, as if their every inch of their personalities were in two glass jars of water placed side by side, both completely transparent, able to see everything about the other. Rain's fingers gripped hers tighter still.

God I feel so wet! It was Rain's voice, but Blessing became conscious in that moment that her underwear was completely soaked. Something was causing her to become sexually aroused. She felt her breathing quicken. She began to lose control of herself. She didn't understand what was happening. Because she didn't understand, she thought it had to be wrong. Somehow the Devil had taken hold of her from her encounter with that ship.

No, this is wrong. I need to stop, she thought, knowing Rain could hear her thoughts. Their minds were linked. She began to try and unlace her fingers from Rain's hand but the girl's grip only intensified.

Oh my God, Oh my God! Fuckkkkkkkkkkkkkkkkkkkkkkkkkkkkkkkkkkkkk!

Blessing and Rain's hands were still interlaced as Rain pushed herself up into the back corner of her seat, her left leg kicking on the seat in front, her right leg stretched out over Blessing's lap. The girl's legs flinched and tightened then relaxed. Blessing felt a wave of joy wash over her, as she lost control of her own body, hit by a wave of orgasms. In that moment she had become detached from everything around her. She lost track of where they were. The woman sitting ahead of them was engaged in a conversation on her phone. Blessing overheard the woman say, "Some people are having sex on the coach. Can you believe it? I guess they think it's the end of the world."

Who was having sex? She couldn't hear anything apart from Rain's diminishing squeal. She turned to see her new friend catching her breath, their hands still locked together. Blessing wanted to pull away but something stopped her.

"Fuck. That was one hell of an orgasm, Baby Jane! How the hell did you do that just by holding my hand? Normally, there's more work involved!"

Blessing didn't know what she meant. She hadn't done anything. She had never had an orgasm, at least not as far as she knew. She had never really had a sexual relationship, at least nothing she would want to remember. God had a plan for her. The right man was coming from somewhere surely? Her heart was racing and her fingers trembling.

"Girl, seriously, what the hell? Nothing ever happened to me like that, not even with my ex and definitely not on set!" Rain said.

On set? What did she mean? Was she a movie star? Blessing noticed a pungent scent filling the air at the back of the bus. It wasn't unpleasant, but she wasn't familiar with it. She felt sticky and dirty. She could feel her underwear needed to be removed. She wanted to get home and change, yet she couldn't stop looking at Rain. As they continued to hold hands, a dozen images, memories of this girl's life came flooding into her head. Pictures from her past… She could see Rain's parents. Her Mother, a beautiful Scottish redhead, slender, pretty with a warm smile. Her Father carving the Christmas roast. He was a Caribbean man with long dreadlocks and a cheeky laugh. She was seeing a memory of a Christmas gone by. Was this last Christmas? Then palm trees, the warmth of the California sun, its wide freeways, parties, lines of white powder, Rain was snorting them off the table. She was naked, next to a swimming pool, with two other girls, there were cameras and lights and they all began to… Oh. Blessing turned off the thoughts and the images were gone. At least she could control what she saw.

"Your Father's name is Bob, named after the singer Bob Marley…"

Rain looked back at her, bemused. "Yes!"

"Your Mother's name is Heather…" Blessing stated, recalling the redheaded woman.

"Yes. This is incredible. You saw my memories!" Rain's eyes widened with surprise.

"You're an Adult Film star. Oh my God. You work in Porn?" Blessing was as shocked as she sounded. She wrenched her hand free.

"Yes, I do. Well, I did. I stopped three months ago and came home, to take stock, great timing huh?" Rain turned her head to the side, saying the words as she looked away out of the window. It wasn't in embarrassment or shame, but Blessing could tell it was something she would have rather told her in her own time. Blessing's first reaction would have been to ask her why she did such an unholy thing, but she already had all the answers. Glimpses into her childhood, which was a happy one. Her first forays into modelling, past relationships, with boyfriends and girlfriends, some happy, some not, good times and bad times. No one had talked her into it, it was a decision she had made on her own. There were moments when Rain had cried alone and sat at a window, singing to herself that things would change. There were others when she went to bed happy and content. A few minutes ago, Blessing would have never understood why another woman would ever choose such a career, yet somehow now she could understand. Her mind felt clearer, somehow more accessible. She found herself able to see memories from long ago. Her childhood in Nigeria… Not everything was clear. It was as if she could see every memory her brain had stored, but couldn't quite open all the different segments yet. With Rain's memories, she saw a similar snapshot of everything, like photographs whirling on a merry-go-round. She only had to make it to stop to view that part of her life. But if she could see so much about this girl she had just met, then was it true the other way? Had this girl just seen everything in her life? Did that mean… Oh no.

Blessing looked into Rain's eyes. The beautiful mixed-race woman staring back at her was completely captivated, processing her own thoughts. The coach reached the outskirts of the city centre, causing the woman sitting just ahead of them to get up, tutting and move towards the front of the vehicle, keen to get off. Rain glared at the woman then turned back to her. Blessing felt a single tear roll down her cheek. Rain touched her own face with her fingers then reached her hand out to Blessing and gently stroked the side of her face.

"Your name is Blessing Amoya and you lived in Nigeria until you were twenty." Rain was shaking as she spoke. Blessing was praying that she knew no more.

"Yes," she said, trembling.

"You were sexually assaulted just before you came to the UK. It was the first time you had ever had sex…"

"Yes." She had seen it. God, she had seen it all.

"Your parents are both dead and your sister brought you to the UK seven years ago, but she died three years after you arrived."

"Yes." Oh God. She had to know. No. No. She didn't want that. She had just made a friend and now she was going to lose her.

"You were diagnosed with HIV just after you arrived in the UK."

She knew. Blessing said nothing, the tears rolling down her cheeks. Rain did not move a muscle. She said nothing and the two young women simply sat there staring at each other, unaware that the coach was beginning to pull into the station. It was packed with people waiting to leave Aberdeen. Rain's hand gingerly stroked Blessing's face and began to wipe her tears away.

"You're worried that because of this, no one will ever love you."

Blessing managed a weak nod. Rain threw her arms around her and hugged her tightly. Blessing could feel Rain's breath on her neck as she spoke.

"You will always be loved while I live and breathe," Rain whispered, holding her tight. In that moment, Blessing felt something she had never felt in her life before. Safe. They didn't move until the driver shouted for everyone to get off the coach. Rain broke away from her, wiping tears away from her own eyes.

"Well shit, this is a lot to process! What say we find a bar that's open and I buy you a drink?"

Rain drew a large breath in and stood up. It sounded like a good idea only…

"I… I don't really drink alcohol," Blessing stuttered.

"Honey, let me tell you something. It's been a week of firsts for me too. One drink isn't going to kill you."

She had to admit, it sounded like a good idea. She did not want to go home.

"Okay then," she said, following her new friend off the bus.

"Great. Somewhere in this town still has to be serving!"

CHAPTER III

"It's true to say that in those first few days when there was so much uncertainty, the world really didn't know how to react. In the U S military we were given plans for attack and plans for defence before finally being more or less regulated to the role of watchdogs. There was a great deal of speculation and rumour of a united global offensive. One might have expected a certain level of unification across the globe, with people putting old conflicts aside to unite against the common enemy. The fact that beyond landing they, by 'they', I mean 'the ships', didn't show any signs of hostility at all, actually caused us bigger problems because several nations were undecided on what their course of action should be and of course everyone had their own theories as to their true intentions. If they had attacked straight away I suspect you would have seen a world united against a common enemy. But that wasn't what happened and in the long run, that caused us even bigger problems and the origins of those problems were predominantly human in nature."

Extract from an interview with an anonymous United States Marine. Date unknown.

TARIQ

He had abandoned the bike, but his journey to Charleville had not been an easy one. He was feeling weaker and was sure he wouldn't make it to Namur that evening. Fortunately, he had planned for every type of contingency, nothing had been left to chance. He knew the area well. He knew the train times and the bus routes. Public transport was reasonably reliable in Belgium, unless there was a strike then all bets were off. How it was going to fare on the day of an alien invasion was another matter. Tariq had waited until he saw a bus ahead of him destined for the town of Charleville-Mezieres, a place he knew well. The town occupied both sides of the curving river Meuse that snaked through the middle of it, looping around and back on itself twice before continuing into the forested hills of the Ardennes. The town was not short on hotels and late night cafés around the main square. He could rest there and catch a train or bus back to Namur in the morning. It was the best course of action. Having got ahead of the bus by three stops, Tariq pulled the motorbike up and parked it in a side road, in a legal space, placed the helmet in the rear container and padlocked it up. He knew if he dumped the vehicle elsewhere or attempted to conceal it, someone would eventually report it. Better to leave it where it was entitled to be, then hopefully it would be days, perhaps even weeks, before it was discovered. It was registered under a false name that could be traced back to Southern France; another deliberate false lead which would waste weeks of police time. Tariq removed anything useful from the side panniers and walked quickly back towards the main road. His rucksack felt heavy. He still had his handgun. He debated ditching it, eventually deciding he would better off keeping it.

"Bonsoir. Lumiere. S'il vous plaît?"

The man had come out of nowhere and he almost bumped into him. His accent was French, rather than Flemish. Tariq did have a lighter in his jacket pocket. He reached for it, wincing as pain shot up his arm. The old man was out walking his dog, the small animal fussing around him, sniffing at his feet. He wasn't sure of the breed but the creature was curious and friendly, causing Tariq to smile and the man to apologise. It appeared the local was up for a friendly chat. He mentioned the arrival of the spaceships.

"Even with aliens arriving, I still have to walk my dog!" he laughed. Tariq quickly wished him good night and headed for the bus stop. The bus came hurtling down the road only moments later, but the driver didn't look like he wanted to stop. Tariq had to step out into the road to force it to a halt. He boarded the vehicle, using a pre-paid pass that everyone on the team had been issued with. The driver didn't want to hang around, shooting off down the road before Tariq had a chance to take a seat near the back. The bus driver was smoking; normally a disciplinary offence but today he didn't give a shit about the rules. The single-decker bus was about half-full, alive with chatter. Everyone was talking to each other about the alien vessels. Who had seen them first and when, how many had landed. Speculation was rife about why they were here. No one seemed to have any concrete answers, but people certainly weren't short on theories.

"I think they have come to take us all away!" said a middle-aged woman wrapped up in a large woollen coat.

"If they have come to do that, then they had better get on with it then!" responded a man of similar age.

"It's an invasion!" cried an excited young man.

"If it's an invasion, then where are the invaders? Tell me that?" the middle-aged man responded.

"Maybe they just came to refuel? They could be getting it from the ground somehow before moving on!" a younger woman suggested.

"Yes, we saw it drilling into the ground, like it was mining or something!" her male companion added. Of all the suggestions, this one seemed to make the most sense to Tariq. People were showing each other this photograph and that video taken at one place or another, on their phones.

"I heard from my cousin that the ground around the thing north of Paris has changed!" an elderly man said, turning round to address everyone.

"Changed how?" asked another passenger.

"They say there's trees growing around it, blossoming with fruit and a ring of fresh water, like a moat round a castle!"

Everyone on the bus looked at him in disbelief. Tariq thought his information was being dismissed too quickly. Two hundred alien vessels arriving on earth was itself something that was hard to believe in the first place. Why should some fruit growing somewhere it shouldn't, be so hard to digest after that?

"Maybe your cousin has been smoking something he shouldn't!" A youth fired back sarcastically.

"My cousin is eighty-nine and he doesn't smoke any of that crap!"

"Eighty-nine? Maybe he has bad eyesight!" the young man scoffed. The elderly man was less than amused.

"There is nothing wrong with my cousin's eyesight, he is as fit as a fiddle, fitter than you I daresay! He said everything around the ship has changed. He should know. It landed right on his farmland! The French army moved him out a couple of hours ago, said it wasn't safe. They put him in some hotel. He said he found valuable rocks in the earth. He said the government is trying to steal them from him, keep them all to themselves."

Tariq listened to the conversation with interest. An African woman who had said nothing perked up, and became attentive to the pensioner's every word.

"My parents didn't fight in the war so we could be ordered off our own property by the government. We should be allowed to go and see the thing if we want. My cousin should, at any rate. It's on his land after all!" the old man said.

"Your cousin must be rich already if he already owns ten square kilometres of land north of Paris!" a young girl said, doubtfully. Her male companion nodded.

"I didn't say he owned it all. I said he owned some of it!"

"You should speak more respectfully to your elders! If you spoke like that in my country to your seniors you would be beaten!" the African woman said, abruptly. The young couple were shocked at the interruption. There was a silence. The young man then stood up and leaned in towards the woman. Tariq guessed he was in his early twenties and from the look of his clothes, not in steady employment.

"If you like how things are done in your country why don't you fucking go back there, you fucking monkey!" he shouted.

The girl laughed at her boyfriend's bullying behaviour. The African woman shrank back into her seat. Tariq watched the old man, expecting him to say something in her defence, but he just looked out of the window. Gutless. The other people on the bus said nothing. That was all the license the young man needed. He sat down next to the woman, who looked away out of the window in an attempt to ignore him.

"Why don't you try and beat me then? Hey? You fucking wog!"

Perhaps the young man was always this hateful. Perhaps it was world events that had somehow ignited his behaviour. Tariq remembered how things were in France after the majority of the British people voted to leave the European Union. There had been a wave of racial attacks against people of ethnicity all over Paris. There was much talk among the working-class whites that France should do the same. Tariq had thought then that the man from the United Kingdom, Nigel Mirage or whatever his name was, would have made a tempting target for their operation. He had seen him once at the airport, travelling with just one other companion and no other escort. Killing him would have been all too easy, but why make such a foolish and unimportant man a martyr? It would only shed light on his demented racist views and bring credence to his cause. Better to let him face the music of his calamitous lies. In the Brexit vote he had played on people's xenophobia and racial insecurities to maximum effect. This resulted in the United Kingdom becoming more isolated from Europe than ever, its political clout severely diminished. It was in many ways a victory for terrorists everywhere, leaving Europe more divided than ever. When countries felt divided it meant international co-operation on every level was always more difficult, and that included their work to counter terrorism. Divide and conquer; one of the oldest rules to the art of warfare. So it was that such divides had trickled down to the social morality of the man on the street. It was harder for people to conceal their racist feelings and easier for them to lash out. Tariq was witnessing the effects of that here and now, on the bus, right in front of him. When sitting at home in his comfortable apartment in Brussels, it was easy to digest such things in purely strategic terms. But to witness such things in person was more difficult. Tariq did not like bullies. It had been part of his motivation for learning how to box when he was younger. The more he saw this young man intimidate the woman, perhaps even a woman of Muslim origin, the more difficult it was for him to remain passive. The last thing he wanted to do was attract attention to himself, but now it would seem he might have to intervene.

"Maybe the aliens have come to rid of us all the monkeys!" the youth said.

"Go back to your seat!" Tariq said, without raising his voice.

All eyes on the bus were immediately upon him as he spoke. His tone left no room for ambiguity. The man turned towards Tariq, who was sitting in the central seat on the back row, directly opposite where the racist stood. The youth wasn't even that tall, perhaps five-foot-eight, short for a man. Now Tariq got a good look at him, he could see he had a skinny physique, bad skin and was no older than twenty. Tariq caught sight of a tattoo on his left arm. He couldn't be certain but he thought it depicted a swastika, an emblem that had been embraced by racist ideologies worldwide. His girlfriend turned round to look at him. She was a couple of years younger than him, pasty-looking with dirty blonde hair. She had on some kind of hoodie with the logo of a rock band that Tariq was not familiar with. Judging from their name *Absurd*, it was appropriately worn. Tariq wondered if the band members themselves could have seen the irony. The girlfriend was laughing. Tariq's stern expression remained. He simply sat there staring straight at the youth, without so much as a flicker of his eyelids. Everyone else on the bus watched in anticipation, except for the old man, who stared in shame out the window. The youth took another step towards him, his stupid grin splitting his face.

"Fuck! Look, here's another one, a fucking half-breed. I bet you're some kind of Arab wog, aren't you?" The youth impressed his female companion, who laughed.

"A French Foreign Legion half-breed, and if you take another step towards me it will be your last," Tariq said, his face remaining neutral, the words hanging in the air. The old man turned, his eyes lighting up, upon hearing Tariq's words. Perhaps he was ex-military himself and it was a hint of kinship towards a fellow soldier. One of the older women sat back and smiled, folding her arms, pleased that the youth had been challenged. Now Tariq could see the young man was uncertain about what to do next. The girl's grin faded. She looked at her boyfriend, then back at Tariq and then at the boyfriend again.

"What the fuck are you going to do?" the youth said, trying to laugh it off, but his voice was trembling, and his hands shaking.

"Why don't you take another step and find out?" Tariq said, with total sincerity. Only the most cowardly of men would pick on a woman. The man took a step back, his girlfriend said nothing. Tariq now realising from her jerky movements and blank look in her eyes that she was high on something. It was no excuse.

"Apologise to the lady," Tariq said, gesturing towards the African. She had been staring out of the window the entire time, but now turned to look at her saviour. Tariq could see she had been crying. Tears were still falling across her face.

"I'm not apologising to a fucking coon!" The man sat down next to his girlfriend. They both stared straight ahead. She immediately put her arm around him, briefly glaring back at Tariq. Tariq stood. He said nothing. He walked, making sure they could hear his footsteps in the aisle behind them.

"Apologise now or I will throw you and your little whore off the bus, and I won't ask the driver to stop."

Tariq saw that one of the middle-aged women had taken her phone out and was about to record the unfolding events. Tariq was quick to shake his head in her direction. She instantly returned the phone to her purse. The young man did not look back round at him but simply said the word "Sorry."

He stood up and rang the bell. The driver stopped the bus, not even waiting for the next stop, and let them off onto the darkened street. He closed the doors and immediately sped off again. Tariq didn't bother looking round at the couple, both of whom were giving him the finger. The African woman smiled at him and mouthed the words, "Thank you." He nodded to her, nothing more. The other passengers returned to their conversations. They started in low, hushed whispers, but soon returned to the same level as before. Tariq saw the African woman produce a small black book from her purse. It was torn and fraying around the edges and it took a moment before he realised it was a bible. He rolled his eyes at the irony. He had just defended a Christian woman. She was not even of the same faith. Still, his personal war was not with Christians but with Western business interests; Corporations and banks, giants of industry, quangos and oil companies, arms manufactures and construction firms – these institutions and their leaders, were his true enemy. Everyone else in the world were pawns. They were just consumers. He understood this. Tariq could see the bus had three cameras, one up by the bus driver, a second above his head, and a third by the central doors. He had replaced his motorcycle helmet with a baseball cap. He wore a grey hoodie underneath his jacket, that he would pull up over his head when he left. It should make him as obscure as possible, but the incident would have been recorded.

It was well after midnight when the bus pulled into Charleville-Mezieres, the driver announcing he would be going no further. He pulled up opposite the railway station, opened the doors and was the first off the bus himself. Everyone quickly disembarked, the African woman loitering so that she would be the last person to get off, before Tariq. Tariq hung back, waiting for everyone, including her, to leave the vehicle. The driver walked briskly across the small piazza opposite the station, which contained several benches, a cluster of trees and a bandstand. Tariq had yet to see a band play on such a stage, but bandstands in parks were not a common sight among the slums of Paris. Tariq could feel his medication was wearing off as he stood up. Pain shot through the right side of his body. His only choice was to rest here tonight and reach Namur tomorrow. The night-time streets were empty in the area around the railway station. The station itself was a typical grand, grey, stone affair with the traditional Belgian sloping grey-toned roof, littered with small attic windows. The doors and window-frames of the building were painted blue, illuminated by the surrounding street lighting. Theirs was not the only bus parked up here. Tariq counted another seven that sat empty. He took out his personal phone, sat down by the benches on the bandstand and made a call.

"Hello. I was wondering when you were going to call. Where are you?" The male voice asked.

"I'm in Belgium on business. I need you to do me a favour. Find me a hotel, near the railway station in Charleville-Mezieres. Book me a room.

Just explain it's for your brother who has had his wallet and ID stolen, so you're booking a room for him."

"I don't think many people came into work today because of what is happening, but I will try my best. Save your battery and I will text you back when it's done."

Malik hung up. It was good to hear his voice.

"Excuse me, Monsieur!" Tariq turned and saw the African woman standing before him. Judging from her appearance and accent, he guessed she was Congolese. If there was ever a country in Africa that was most manipulated by Western business interests it was the Congo. Tariq had studied its history well in his youth. The Belgian Congo had been ruled by Prince Leopold of Belgium, only to finally gain its independence in 1960 with native politician Patrice Lumumba being its first democratically elected President. Lumumba was soon betrayed when it became clear he was not going to be a puppet for Western business interests. The Congo had many valuable resources and the mining contracts there alone were worth millions. Europe and America needed a man in power who would bow to their will, but Lumumba had dreams of an independent and powerful Congolese nation that would create its own destiny. He was mistaken in thinking that the West would simply let that happen. Belgium and the CIA conspired to have him arrested and murdered by more co-operative elements within his own government. It was a sad chapter in Africa's history and one that filled Tariq with rage when he read about it, not least because Lumumba asked the United Nations to help him quell the political unrest. Instead they stood idly by and did nothing while more pro-western elements in this country seized power. Lumumba had paid the ultimate price of self-sacrifice, but had left a legacy of hope and a vision of the future for the Congolese people.

"I wanted to thank you, for what you did on the bus. I cannot believe the way some people behave today. The man I defended, he said nothing! Next time I will just keep quiet," the woman said. She spoke in French with a heavy Congolese accent, but Tariq could tell she was an intelligent woman, probably in her late forties, probably a mother. Tariq did not want to get into a conversation with the woman. He just smiled and nodded.

"You're running from something or someone. I've lived long enough to know. I guess everyone is on the move now that these things have arrived. Don't worry, I won't tell anyone. I am no friend to the Belgian Police myself. Here, let me give you a card, in case you ever need anything. Perhaps I can give you a home-cooked meal to say thank you, some time."

Tariq looked at the card which read *Josephine Mobotu – African Arts & Crafts*. He put it in his pocket, wondering if the woman was a distant relative of the late military dictator, Joseph Mobotu, who had been one of the people responsible for the execution of Patrice Lumumba. He'd ruled as a despot before he too was eventually overthrown. The woman smiled as she gave it to him. She was wearing a heavy coat, and carried two bags. She could be a useful contact or a potential witness. He had to decide which, right now. Scenarios raced through his head as he tried quickly to process his options. If he asked her to cook for him right now, which frankly would be most welcome, she would want to get to know him. Even if he just told her a cover story, his identity would become public eventually. She would be able to give the authorities some information about him, or they would get it out of her. He could go with her and kill her, but her body would be discovered eventually. He didn't have time to properly dispose of the body, and there were numerous witnesses to the incident on the bus. Also, she didn't deserve to die. She was actually showing him some kindness. Such acts of humanity were rare, in his experience. He put the card in his pocket.

"Thank you. Never know when I might need a gift for someone. I might take you up on that meal another time, but I have to meet my brother now, so I must go."

"Thank you again," the woman said, sounding a little disappointed.

"It was nothing. Some people in this world must always be stopped. They have to learn their actions come with consequences." Tariq stood up.

"I can see your mother brought you up well..." she let the sentence hang and held out her hand, clearly expecting a name.

"Aris," he said. It was the name of a friend of his from the projects in Paris. He shook the woman's hand, not having the heart to tell her she was dead wrong about his upbringing.

"Well I wish you a safe and pleasant evening, Aris. God be with you."

"And Allah be with you," he replied, and headed off into the town.

The streets of Charleville-Mezieres were deserted but the blue lights of television sets could be seen glowing in almost every house. People were glued to the news, wanting to know what was happening, what they should do, where they should go. The odd café had stayed open here and there. Each one rammed with people huddling together, watching the news in comfort, actively debating what course of action they should take. Tariq was tempted to try and order some food in one when his phone vibrated, He looked to see a text from Malik.

Hotel booked under your name. I called them. Be well brother.

Tariq arrived at the hotel and there were no issues. It was a typical French three-star establishment, slightly dated. The young man at reception was watching a twenty-four hour news channel on an I-Pad with the sound turned right up. He apologised that no one would be able to help Tariq with his bags. He was the only member of staff who had turned up today, apart from one of the cleaners, so he couldn't promise any breakfast either. "Incredible isn't it? Just sign here, please," he satiated, as he passed him the key to room eleven, barely taking his eyes away from the screen.

"Yes. Are there any more developments?" Tariq asked.

"They say some people in Mexico found a way inside one, but it's not been confirmed."

There was a shot of the ship in Mexico. Tariq noticed the heavy American military presence both on and around the vessel. The news report cut to shots of the ship, presumably taken from a helicopter flying above it. The aerial view was impressive, the white disk below stretching for several miles in each direction.

"Are those not American military?" Tariq was curious to know how they had come to be on Mexican soil.

"That ship has landed half-way across the border. The American President claimed it's a threat to their national security, so they sent in the Marines and surrounded the whole thing. I don't think the Mexicans are very happy."

Tariq could imagine they weren't. What an opportunity! If only he was based in America… He knew there would be cells in the United States, plotting their own actions, but no one would have any way of contacting them. It was the safest way to function and made them impossible to penetrate by Western Intelligence. Each cell was entirely responsible for their own missions. The newsreader went on to talk about other cross-border landings worldwide, that were causing tension between countries. A vessel had landed in the waters between North and South Korea and both were claiming it was their responsibility to secure it, leading to tensions between the two countries. That sounded like a major step backwards for the two countries which had been making slow steps towards a potential reunification in recent years. Another in South America had landed where the borders of three countries met, but Tariq didn't catch the names. His exhaustion was kicking in and he needed to get to his room.

"Can I have the password for the Wifi?" he asked.

The receptionist passed him a small strip of white paper with some numbers printed on it, and turned his attention back to the news. As Tariq climbed the stairs, each step sent a separate jolt of pain up his arm. His exhaustion began to overtake him. His body felt weak and he knew his wound would need cleaning and soon, otherwise he risked infection. He reached the first floor and found his room. The hotel seemed fairly quiet, though further down the corridor, Tariq could hear the sounds of passionate love-making. No doubt they thought the world was about to end and were making the most of their time together. Tariq unlocked the door and quickly closed it behind him. The room contained a large double bed, a desk, a chair and a small en-suite bathroom. A television was mounted on the wall. He flicked on the news channel and threw his rucksack on the bed before stepping into the bathroom. He heard several commentators discussing the day's events and what it meant to the world, as he turned on the shower and slowly began to undress, careful of his wounds.

"And all this on the day of probably the worst terrorist atrocity since 9/11…"

Finally! His bringing down the British Prime Minister's plane would have been the lead news story for days, had it not been for these ships arriving. This global event had hijacked what should have been their moment of glory, their triumph. It was good to know their success had not been completely forgotten already. Tariq tuned out the voices from the other room as he stood under the streaming hot water, grateful for the sense of relief that it brought him. The water felt amazing against his skin, but he had to angle his body to keep the bandage dry and partly wrapped himself in a towel in order to do so. The debate as to the true intentions of the visitors continued to rage back and forth on the news, as each studio guest advanced their own theories. Tariq came and sat on the end of the bed. It appeared as if a dividing line was forming between those who thought the intentions of the aliens were hostile, while others thought the opposite was true. After all, where was the attack?

"So if they're not here to harm us, then why do you think they're here?' asked the host of the news programme.

"Perhaps they've come to help us in some way," a female guest replied.

He made a mental note of this, it might be useful later on. He logged onto the email account using his phone, and sent a message to himself which said, *Contact me directly.*

He then lay down on the bed, leaving the television on, and was asleep within minutes. When he was awoken by the sound of his personal phone ringing, daylight was filtering through the gaps in the curtains. Tariq reached out for it, seeing he had already slept through two other missed calls, all from the same number. He tapped the answer button.

"Hello?"

"It's me. I got your message. We can talk, this is a new phone," a woman said, immediately causing him to sit up. "Where are you?" she asked.

"I'm in a hotel in Charleville-Mezieres, not far from the station. Hotel Le Cleves. Room eleven on the first floor." Tariq made a note of the time, it was nine-thirty in the morning.

"I can be there within the hour." The woman's response made him smile.

"I've been wounded. I think I've controlled the bleeding but I'm not sure how much blood I've lost. Bring your kit." Tariq looked at the bedsheets. The towel he had laid below him had a huge red bloodstain on it, but the sheets themselves only had a few flecks of blood.

"Understood. Just rest. Let reception know your wife is coming to collect you. Arrange for a late check-out in case I am delayed. Things are a little crazy. Even in Namur people are trying to move somewhere else."

"Okay I will. It will be good to see you." Tariq tried not to sound too personal, but it was becoming harder to hide his feelings towards her recently.

"You too." She hung up. Tariq called down to reception and left them instructions. He wasn't sure if the next thing he heard were the sounds of a dream or sounds of reality. He remembered a knock at the door and getting up. A woman with dark hair, her voice reassuring him, holding him, laying him back on the bed. An injection, stitches, some pain, drinking water, feeling drowsy, lying back, sleeping, waking, walking, entering a car, it being night, entering a familiar place, another bed, bandages being changed, a smile, a soft touch, drinking water, taking tablets, a pillow and then once again it was dark. He was finally home.

CANDICE

The events of the previous night were something akin to watching a fireworks display. She had enjoyed it but couldn't recall all of it in detail. She rose from the bed that morning in a mood of reflection. Candice slipped on the soft white bathrobe that hung on the back of the bedroom door. Leaving her lover to sleep, she wandered through the open plan living area to retrieve her cigarettes before sitting out on the balcony. The name of the man of who got on, and subsequently off, the underground carriage with her was Alphonse. He was half-Dutch, half-Italian and worked for an advertising company, which in light of the current crisis had given all its staff the rest of the week off. Alphonse rented a small flat in one of the new modern high-rises just over the road from Stratford Station in East London. Candice knew she could get a bus from Stratford to Walthamstow. With the bus station being conveniently located right next to the railway station, she expected to catch one fairly quickly. Alphonse offered to call her an Uber, but Candice declined, so he insisted on waiting with her until she caught her bus. Her plan was that they were going to swap numbers, just to ensure that she could text him to let him know that she had got home safely. She didn't want him to worry, after all. Things hadn't quite worked out like that. A scene of total chaos greeted them as they'd exited the station. People were being filtered away quickly from the exit by lines of police dressed in riot gear. When Candice looked behind her, she could see why. The Westfield Shopping Centre was being ransacked by looters. A combination of disenfranchised youth, and chancers wanting to get in on the action. People were running off with everything, from bags of clothes to television sets. She even saw a kid

343

dodging Police, struggling to carry an unwieldy box containing *The Lego Death Star*. The steps that connected the outside of the station to Westfield had been cordoned off. Several squad cars and vans were parked up in the bus station concourse, and officers were directing people away from the area. There was no sign of any buses. If any were running at all, they had been re-routed. A crowd had gathered across the road by the entrance to the older, smaller high street shopping centre. Tatty and unappreciated, Westfield had diminished its outdated rival to a tacky market, second-hand trade-in stores and pound shops. Lucky for the store owners, because no one was interested in looting it. The two centres were divided by an extremely busy ring road that curved through central Stratford. She still was not taken with the area, no matter how much money had been spent on it because of the London Olympics. The police were not letting any traffic through on the ring road at all. Getting to Pearl's place was becoming more problematic by the minute. Candice looked at her phone, saw the battery was low and realised she hadn't brought her charger. She decided to turn it off and save what little power she had left for emergencies, even though it already felt like she was right in the middle of one.

Alphonse had been quick to suggest that she could come to his place and wait until things calmed down a little. That had been yesterday evening. Now it was morning, and she was relieved that her latest conquest did not snore but instead made little wheezing noises, which were quite adorable. Candice didn't get picked up by men, she picked them up, sometimes literally. His high-rise apartment was a modern new-build, all spotlights in the ceiling, white finish cabinets and granite worktops in the kitchen. Matching monochrome furniture filled the open plan living and dining area. His bedroom had an en-suite shower, and toilet that Candice had urgent need of as soon as they'd arrived. He was a clean tidy man. Everything was neat and in its proper place. Organised. She liked that. He had fresh white Egyptian cotton sheets on the bed that were cool to touch. Something she appreciated when she finally dipped under the covers after their Olympic sexual exchange.

Last night had been wonderful. It was the first time she had made love to someone without an exchange of money taking place in quite a while. It felt good. Even though her recent times with Ryan had not felt like work, he still put the little brown envelope in her purse before he left. Candice wasn't sure if Alphonse had guessed her gender when they first met, but he made no comment on it. When they'd arrived, he made her a drink and put on the television while making some calls to his relatives back home. His parents were divorced and his mother was now living in her home town of Gouda, back in Holland. Candice hadn't heard of the town but she had heard of the cheese with the same name. His father was still in Rome and was seeing a young girl half his age. Alphonse said he was glad. His mother was happier and it was better for them to be apart. Why be together when they just made each other miserable? He had excused himself, making a Skype call on his laptop in his bedroom. Candice then tried calling Pearl on her mobile, but found there was no service. She took her Jack Daniels and coke onto the balcony. Every flat in the block had a small outside terrace sculpted into the side of the modern building. The high-rise extended up from the ground like a slanted finger. She had a bird's-eye view of the train station and Westfield, as well as the Olympic Park and its stadiums. Blue flashing lights littered the concourse on the other side of the road. Scores of men in black uniforms and riot gear were running into the Westfield building. She witnessed other people fleeing from the place via other exits, carrying bundles of clothes under each arm. BBC News 24 carried the story in its hourly bulletin, and there was mention of the possibility that the Territorial Army would be called in to protect life and property. Candice didn't know who the Territorials were, but if they were anything like the Brazilian Army, she knew there would be casualties. It would be too dangerous to try and get to Pearl's tonight. If everyone did indeed think the world was ending, people were capable of anything. At least for the moment, she felt safe. The night air was filled with a smell of burning fires, along with the never-ending sounds of sirens, nearby and in the distance. People were stupid, she thought. The world hadn't ended yet. These aliens haven't attacked us. In fact no one seemed to have seen any aliens yet, but everyone was taking the arrival of the ships alone as a license to go crazy.

Alphonse called her back inside. Candice had studied him carefully; his mannerisms, the way he spoke to her, the tone of his voice. She thought he must have had a good mother who had instilled good manners in him. He spoke kindly to her, and offered to cook her something. She was so hungry that she agreed without even thinking about it, and in no time at all a creamy pasta dish was sitting before her, fragrant steam from the white tagliatelle wafting into her nostrils.

"The key is not to use too many ingredients. The English always overdo it, too many different spices and herbs. Keep it simple and rich in flavour," he commented. He evidently knew what he was talking about as the food tasted wonderful. Normally, Candice tried to avoid carbohydrates to keep her diet in check. Like every Italian man she had ever met, he also knew about his wine and had a variety of bottles stocked in the kitchen. He cracked open a bottle of white Malvira, explaining that the Malvira grape was notoriously difficult to grow. The fragility of the grape gave the wine a particularly delicious finish. She couldn't disagree. It went incredibly well with the pasta dish. He went on to explain that if they were eating red meat then they would have had red wine. Alphonse sat opposite her while they ate. He looked relieved at being able to speak briefly to both his parents.

His mother seemed unconcerned by the arrival of the alien vessels. Alphonse had to point out that one had not actually landed in the Netherlands, though she had been able to see the spire of the ship that had landed in northern France as she flew into Amsterdam airport from the south of France. Alphonse then explained that his mother had a second home just near Nice. Candice wished she was there right now.

"I can tell you're from Brazil. I've never been there but it's on my list of places to visit." Alphonse said.

He then asked her about her own family. She kept the details as short as she could, without sounding too evasive. As they talked, and ate the delicious meal he had prepared, she forgot all about Ryan. Cooking was not Ryan's forte. His attempts to cook for Candice one night had led to a culinary disaster, resulting in them ordering an Indian takeaway. This too turned out to be a mistake as both had forgotten to ask the restaurant to go mild on the chilli. Terrible wind kicked in about an hour afterwards. Sex was off the menu that night. Last night however, Alphonse made it clear everything was up for grabs. Any doubts about how he would react once Candice had got her clothes off, were soon put firmly aside when Alphonse instigated a discussion: "What would you do on your last night if it was the end of the world?" Her reply was as honest as it could have been: That she "would spend it, if I had the choice, in the company of people I loved." Which ironically was in fact what she was trying to do when she had met him. His response to his own question, rather unashamedly, was that he would try and tick off as many of his sexual fantasies as he could in a single night. They were on the second bottle of wine when she realised Alphonse must have known her gender all along, because he just came out with it.

"I have always wanted to sleep with a transsexual." The words hung in the air, as he swirled the last remaining drop of wine around in his glass before tipping it into his mouth. Candice was contemplating if she should be offended by his use of the word transexual to describe her gender when a loud bang from outside made the window to the balcony shake.

"Maybe the invasion has started…" he said, getting up and going for a look. Candice followed him to the balcony, and once again they found themselves looking at the activity below. Somewhere on the other side of the main Westfield building there was a fire. The glow could be seen from behind the silhouettes of the buildings of Stratford Industrial Park. She wondered, in that moment, what kind of chaos might also be happening back in Rio? How were people handling it at all back home? She needed to find a way to speak to her Mother, somehow. She took the chance on the balcony to light up a cigarette, asking Alphonse if he minded. He did not, and asked if he could have one. If he was going to start smoking, now seemed as good a time as any. Soon they witnessed a pair of fire engines racing up the street, turning off towards the source of the flames. She had to ask him.

"I need to call my Mother."

Alphonse kindly offered his laptop and let her sign in on both her Facebook and Skype accounts, but to no avail. There was still no contact from her, or any sign of her having used her social media. She tried to call her, Alphonse even offering her the use of his own mobile but the network was not working.

"All the networks must be overloaded, with everything that's happening. Tonight was the first time I managed to speak to my parents since this thing started. I heard in some countries Facebook and Twitter are completely offline," he said, sympathetically.

They sat on his leather sofa and watched BBC News 24, which still carried the arrival of the ships as its main story. Those that landed across the national borders of several countries, were causing all sorts of problems over who exactly had responsibility for the security of the craft. There still wasn't any news as to their exact intentions, but the newly appointed British Prime Minister, Ryan Wallace, had been up to Scotland to see that one for himself, an act which had seemed to gain him considerable favour with the British press. Candice caught a glimpse of Ryan getting in a car, some caramel-coloured girl close behind him. Was she his Personal Assistant? He was bound to find her attractive, that was for sure. When it came to females, Candice knew his type. Ryan looked tired, but more serious than she could ever remember. Maybe the new job would force him to grow up, though his reckless sense of fun had always been part of his appeal. She laughed inside at the irony of him running the country. She bet he hated it. It was while she was lost in that particular thought that Alphonse had leaned in for a kiss. It caught her a little by surprise but she decided not to rebuff him. It could have been the wine, or the fact that the entire world was descending into madness that made her drop her guard and just go for it. He was a good kisser, which was just as well, otherwise things would not have gone any further and a massively awkward moment would have soon followed. He wasted no time in quickly disrobing and was, to her surprise, quite well hung. No competition with her, but he certainly wouldn't be embarrassed by the comparison.

"Would you like to do a line with me?" he said, opening a small box under the coffee table, and producing a bag of the white powder that Candice was all too familiar with.

"If it's the end of the world, we might as well party in style," he said.

"Honey, I bet mine is bigger than yours," came her reply. She produced a generous ten-gram packet from her bag, dwarfing his own amount on the coffee table.

"It would be rude of me not to contribute," she said, smiling.

"Now we can really have a party, huh?" Alphonse said, looking at the bag with a grin.

Candice had for the most part always followed her own self-imposed rule – Don't get high on your own supply, and she hadn't, not for a long time. But today was an exception. After all, how often did you get dumped on the day of an alien invasion, with the man you love then becoming Prime Minister of the country? Yeah, fuck Ryan, she thought. Alphonse chopped lines with a gym membership card, which explained why he was in such good shape. There was something slightly effeminate about the man. She wouldn't be at all surprised if he turned out to be more gay than bisexual. She produced her own metal straw from her purse, an item purchased purely for purpose of ingesting cocaine. Alphonse cut four generous lines for them on the glass coffee table, Candice would hear her friend Pearl refer to such bumps as "tampon lines" when they used to do them together back in the day. Life seemed simpler then. It was hard for her mind not to wander to thoughts about her Mother, but there was little she could do at present. She would try her again later. She took her line right after Alphonse, taking only from her own coke. She had learnt never to take recreational drugs from people she didn't know. No matter how pretty this Italian man was, she wasn't going to make an exception for him. She knew people cut cocaine up with anything from washing detergent to sugar to increase their profit. The more it burned your nose when it went up, the more it had been cut. At least, so the theory went. Bending down, she hoovered up the two lines with the grace of experience and sat back on the sofa, feeling the powder's effects at once. It raced up her nostrils, making its way to the receptors in her brain.

She could still remember the first time she had taken drugs in Brazil. She had run away from home and stayed out all night with friends. Someone had offered it to her, and for a while she was a regular user, but as with any drug you can only party on the edge for so long. She saw what it did to the people she hung out with. They had always appeared so confident and fun but Candice realised, once she got to know them, that it was the drug that gave them such confidence and made them so animated. Take that away from them and they became shells of their former selves. Behaviour was something you could never predict when someone had taken cocaine. People could turn nasty very quickly. The euphoric high rapidly turning into rocket fuel for an aggressive state of mind. So now, she just supplied it and only took it if she needed to stay awake with a client, or when she was with Ryan. That cunt. So he got the biggest job in the country. So fucking what? He could have been the first ever President... ah, wait, Prime Minister – wasn't that what he was? Yes. Prime Minister of the UK, with a transgender wife. They could have made world history. Throw an alien invasion in there and you're really cooking. Now he was going to pretend as though she never even existed. Bastard.

"Wow, you're a pro at this, huh?" Alphonse remarked, as he bent down and snorted his line. He sat back on the sofa and pulled her in for a deep kiss. Candice responded in kind, their hearts both beating at an accelerated rate. She pulled away and lit another cigarette.

"I would say more a seasoned veteran that you temporarily brought out of retirement."

"Do you mind?" Alphonse gestured towards the pack politely.

"Not at all." She pulled out a cigarette and lit it for him.

"I could not wish for better company," he said, with a smile, looking her body up and down, his expression full of expectation.

"Me too." It was a lie. She knew she would have rather been with Ryan or her Mother, or Pearl and Joanne. It was always nice to spend time in the company of a beautiful man, but it would have been better to do so on a night of her choosing and preferably not at the twilight of the end of humanity. Alphonse leaned in for another kiss and slid one hand beneath her top, seeking out her breasts. She pulled away.

"Is anything the matter? Did I do something wrong? You find me attractive, no? Because I find you very attractive!" he said. His accent was, she had to admit, extremely sexy. Fuck it. She deserved to have a good time. Why did she even have to justify it to herself? Ryan could go and live in Big fucking Ben for all she cared. He had hurt her and she couldn't just let that stand. No. No other client of hers would get away with such behaviour without paying a price, so why should he? It was time to pay the ferryman, Ryan Wallace. She reached for her phone.

"Honey, you're beautiful. I just want to text my Mum okay? Then I am all yours."

"Sure, I understand. Family is important. I know most people would want to be with the people they love, on a day like today. What with everything happening in the world…"

She logged into her Twitter account, her mind swirling with the effects of the alcohol and cocaine. It was under a different name – Brandy Dior, from her amateur modelling days. She had amassed something of a cult following when Twitter was all the rage. In most of her pictures associated with that account she looked very different. Her older photographs were over-styled, many of them in black and white. She took another sizeable gulp of wine. Shit, that tasted good. Then looked for the picture on her phone. Her mind was racing. If he was going to hurt her, she was going to hurt him. It was that simple. No one fucks with Candice Alvares, honey. No way, no how. She found it, typed some words and hit send.

"All done…"

She extinguished her cigarette and turned her attention back to the eager young man in front of her. Ryan could deal with the consequences himself. Alphonse turned out to be capable of a great many things between the sheets. He had barely reacted when she revealed her own considerable endowment. In fact he wasted no time in gobbling it for all he was worth. Clearly not his first time sucking cock. He must have known, or at least, suspected she was indeed a transsexual because he was something of an expert. Candice had to admit it was always more fun pulling men in straight clubs, getting them home and then seeing their reaction. She had to be careful though, there were those who could react violently to such a discovery, not taking the news well at all. Judging from his reaction however, Alphonse thought it was Christmas. But try though she might, she couldn't completely eradicate Ryan from her mind, despite the best efforts of the lovely young Italian man in the bedroom. Now he was fast asleep, worn out by his Herculean efforts to impress her, which had taken them into the early hours.

Last night had been fun at least, but as she surveyed the sprawling sight of London she could see the world had not ended. She switched her phone on. She could see the battery was down to less than 15%. Alphonse's charger had not been compatible with her phone, so she would have to wait until she got to Pearl's to sort that out. Why couldn't bloody mobile providers make them all the same? That would be far too logical, and no doubt, unprofitable. The balcony faced west back towards central London, but she could see the creeping light of dawn approaching from the east. It felt like it was going to be a nice day, but the weather in London could betray you in April. Stunning sunshine at nine in the morning would often be followed by grey clouds and rain by eleven. She sat down on one of the two silver metal chairs on the terrace, noting that the time was a quarter past five. She knew she wouldn't sleep until she had properly come down. That would take a few hours yet. A number of police cars were still outside Stratford Station. A plume of black smoke drifted skyward from the warehouses, just beyond the shopping centre. Candice caught the scent of burnt plastic in the air and grimaced. The London skyline seemed different somehow this morning, smaller perhaps, but it was, more importantly, all still standing. If the aliens were coming to attack, they were certainly taking their time about it. The tall towers of the city's finance district ascended skyward, silver fingers built proudly as monuments to wealth and industry. It was not a world she knew or understood, but had spent many a week-night in the bars and clubs that inhabited the nooks and crannies of the narrow streets below. Further west she could see the iconic landmarks associated with central London's West End. The tall Shard stood proudly on the south bank of the River Thames near London Bridge, signalling the beginning of the city, which carried on up to the plush riverside apartments of Chelsea. Between these two points, were the Houses of Parliament and the iconic clock tower of Big Ben, not quite visible from this distance. But somewhere out there, she knew Ryan would be dealing with the myriad problems the country was facing. She wanted to call and say she was proud of him, because she was. He was doing something real, something that mattered, perhaps not quite saving the world but he was certainly trying his best to save his country. Maybe one day the world would be a place where the leader of a nation could be gay or have a transgender partner, perhaps even a transgender leader, but that day had not yet arrived. Wasn't there a gay Prime Minister in Scandinavia somewhere? She couldn't remember. She inhaled a long slow drag and let out a cloud of smoke. She needed to quit smoking, but that wouldn't happen today nor would it happen this week. She scrolled through her phone. There were several frantic texts from Pearl demanding information on her whereabouts. Oh God. She forgot. She quickly sent a reply.

Sorry hun, couldn't get to Walthamstow, ended up staying in Stratford, hoping to get to you today – will you still be there? Battery low. Text only.

Less than a minute later came Pearl's response.

We were worried. Public transport is all fucked up. Supposed to be better today. You with someone?

Yeah, a friend.

A friend? Oh. Ohhhhh. Candice! Only you could get a hook-up when we're all facing the end of the world! – We saw your twitter! It's gone viral!

The last text was followed by a series of emojis expressing jaws dropping to the floor and mouths agape in general shock and surprise. What was she talking about? Oh, wait. Shit. Had she really done that? She quickly pulled up her Twitter account. Yup. There it was. A picture of her flaccid cock placed tactfully across Ryan's sleeping face, with the caption *Not as straight as he appears! The new leader of Great Britain!*

It had already been shared over nine thousand times and people had come up with plenty of captions of their own.

The world's biggest slug invades face of PM!

Cock of the morning! Ryan Wallace knows what he likes!

Is it an alien attack on the PM?

Cocktastic!

Good to know the new PM bats for our team…

And on they went. Oh God! What on earth was she thinking? Ah, she wasn't thinking. Cocaine was doing the thinking for her. Just say no. Fucking drugs. Fuck. Delete. The horse had well and truly bolted. This would have serious consequences. She had to think for a second. She hurriedly lit another cigarette. She was almost out. Maybe no one important had seen it yet… What with everything else going on. They must have more pressing matters to attend to. Her phone buzzed again. It was Pearl.

I think you should delete it. Probably not a good idea.

Yeah no shit. Her fingers furiously typed back her response.

Already done it. Heavy night. Wasn't thinking straight. Got dumped.

Sorry hun. Not surprising considering his new job! Her reply was followed by a sad face and several more with the jaw dropping to the floor.

Candice's reaction had been stupid, selfish, thoughtless and above all made under the influence of chemicals. Not a good combination for making a sensible decision. She began typing again.

Want to get to you as soon as I can. Are you guys going into work today?

No, we will be here. Pick up ciggies & some papers if you can. XXXXX – P

Okay on my way.

She was way ahead on the first item, having another forty in her bag, care of her Uber driver from last night. He smoked her brand so she decided to liberate him of his. It was the least he could do. She decided to have one more before getting herself together to go. She hadn't slept in forty-eight hours now, and was beginning to feel it. She debated taking a line from the bits of coke left on the table to keep her going. There was a time when youth and energy enabled her to power on through, but today she had neither. She remembered there had been Red Bull in the fridge. She went back inside and took three, placing two in her bag, bringing the third back out onto the balcony. She'd been pretty generous with her coke last night so the least the guy could do was spot her a couple of energy drinks. Standing back on the balcony, feeling the morning breeze wash over her face, she lit up one more time and made a mental checklist of everything she had to do. Should she close her Twitter account? Was she being paranoid? Think rationally, Candice. The account was set up in Brazil on an ex-boyfriends ISPN number. She hadn't tweeted much in the last few months but when she had, she had done so from this phone. The pictures were mostly old. She could get them back from elsewhere if she had to. Couldn't you reactivate accounts just like you could on Facebook? Fuck it. She went into her settings and turned the Twitter account off before turning off her phone and breathing a sigh of relief. Her phone was down to less than ten percent battery, making her wish she still had her old Nokia. Now, that would stay charged for a week. She missed playing *Snake* on it.

It was getting lighter. The dim pre-dawn grey was slowly being eradicated by the ever-growing light from the east. Distant sirens belonging to the emergency services could still be heard, but that morning an uneasy calm seemed to have settled over the city. Perhaps those who wanted to seek refuge elsewhere had done so. As she took the last drags of her cigarette, the sound of several car doors being opened below drew her attention downwards. Two cars had pulled up outside the front of the block and three men got out from each one. Something about them struck her as odd straight away. The similar dark clothing worn by them all - a uniform in all but name. Not unlike the undercover squads that operated in and around the favelas back home. The way they moved, the way they communicated said military to her. Why would undercover military be coming into this block unless... Shit! She instantly ducked her head back in and went inside. She knew she only had seconds to react. They would take the lift and probably cover the stairs too. They could be here for someone else, but she wasn't going to wait and find out. She was near the top of the block, which would give her perhaps half a minute, maybe even less. She grabbed her bag, swiped the small amount of coke left off the coffee table and collected her things. Glancing quickly towards the bedroom, she saw Alphonse was still out cold. Holding her shoes, she ran for the front door. Opening it slowly, she could hear the lift ascending. She darted out and shut the door to the apartment softly behind her. Glancing down the corridor, she saw the lift was just to her left and stairs were at either end of the passageway. The lights on the lift were already moving up the floors towards her floor – six, seven, eight... She ran at full pelt to the end of the corridor. She opened the door and slipped through carefully, closing it quietly behind her. Still clinging onto her shoes she ran down two flights of stairs, before she became aware that several flights below her two men were coming up. She ducked into the doorway leading to level seven, sliding in behind it but making sure it did not close completely, thus avoiding clicking the lock, attracting attention. A metallic squawk indicated the men were on a radio network. She strained to listen to their conversation.

"Unit 3, where are you?"

"We're just on floor six, four below you," came the reply, from a man sounding a little short of breath.

"Hurry up, will you? We're just down from the target address now."

"Hurry up he says. It's all right for him, taking the fucking lift," came the sarcastic response from the first man.

"Don't complain. It'll keep you fit." The second voice sounded younger, fitter, and less likely to complain.

"Cover the stairs, he says. It's not like they know we're coming, do they?"

"Standard operating procedure, mate. Cover all exits before you go in."

"Yeah, I said the same thing when I was young. Trust me, when you get to my age your standards start to slip a bit."

The voices were closer now, passing her door. Her mind began to race. Who the fuck were these guys and how had they found her so quickly? Unless... her phone! But how was that even possible? Wasn't that something that just happened in the movies? Why would they bother with her, anyway? She was just a harmless... She stopped. She knew. She had after all just threatened the career of the most powerful man in the country. But she hadn't meant it. She was angry and high for

God's sake! Now the lovely stranger who had helped her out when she was a damsel in distress was going to get his flat turned over and a night or two in the cells in exchange for his kindness. She was pretty sure he had used all his drugs and she had what remained of hers in her bag, so he should be okay in that respect at least. She took a deep breath and held it.

"Fuck me, how many more flights is it?" the older voice complained.

"Two," replied the younger one.

She crouched motionless, observing the two shadows pass the door and continue up the stairs.

"As long as they don't ask me to be involved in the clean-up after. I'm a professional but that job is beneath me."

"Act professional, and shut the fuck up, then."

"They'll be sleeping. They won't even hear us coming."

"They will if you don't shut your bloody pie-hole."

"Some pie would be bloody nice about now."

Who hired these people? Wait. Did he say "Clean up"?! She heard a door being opened and then closed with a gentle click. Candice opened the door, closing it quietly behind her running barefoot down the concrete stairs as softly as she could. Reaching the ground floor, she realised the stairs continued to a lower level where there was a car park. She contemplated hiding there, but for all she knew they could have people covering that too. No, she had to get out of here, and fast. She entered the corridor on ground level. Through a glass panel in the door she saw a man standing in workman's clothes by the two lifts near the front entrance. He was talking on a radio with one hand and holding a clipboard in the other. He could have been there working, or he could have been with the men who just came in. Prudence told her she had to assume the latter. She slid down her dark sunglasses, and took a breath before re-applying her lipstick and putting on her shoes. Candice had a face that was naturally feminine but it couldn't fool everyone. She could try for the back, but she wasn't even sure where that led. She took a deep breath, thinking *if you can enter Miss Trans Brazil 2019*, you can do this, and casually strolled into the lobby, doing her best American accent.

"Hi there, sugar. Is there something wrong with the lifts today? Only I just came down from the second floor and they didn't seem to be running properly."

The man was taken aback by her appearance.

"Sorry Miss, where did you say you came from?"

This was no workman. He wasn't even wearing workmen's boots. She remembered the number of Alphonso's flat, realising the first number referred to the floor. His flat was 904.

"I'm from 205. Is it going to be working later? Only I'll be doing my weekly food shop tonight, and when I come back from that I really won't want to take the stairs, honey."

"Oh yeah, it should be working by then, Miss..." He scanned his clipboard, looking for a name, when the door to the opposite stairwell opened and an elderly man with a walking stick came struggling through, the heavy weight of the fire door working against him. Candice saw her chance.

"Age before beauty! Excuse me..." Candice strolled with confidence across the lobby, almost leaping to hold the door open for the man.

"Thanks love, not as young as I used to be!" Candice saw the man in the overalls speak into his radio.

"Remind of your name again, babe..." she whispered to the old man.

"George, but I'm quite happy for you to call me babe," he said, looking Candice up and down with a twinkle in his eye.

"George, let me get the other door for you. I know how you like to go out and get your tobacco every morning. Have you run out again?" Candice could smell it on his clothes.

"Yeah. How did you guess?" he responded dryly, happily taking her arm.

"I hope the lifts will be working later," she called to the workman. "George hates taking the stairs!"

With that, she whisked the two of them out of the front door and turned right, heading towards the crossing for Stratford Station. They passed the two dark Range Rovers that had pulled up outside. Both were occupied by a driver in the front seat, one of whom gave her a cursory glance, then went back to reading his paper. Candice caught the front page headline which read, *Don't Panic!* She rushed on, almost dragging George along with her. She knew she had to get to where there were people as fast as possible. Fortunately, London was waking up and several commuters were already making their way to the train station. Many were returning to work for the first time, following advice given on the television that it was vital to keep infrastructures intact. The area around Stratford Station, and the crossings leading over the main road to it were already a hive of activity. Cafés were already beginning to open. The first wave of people were heading out to their jobs. It wasn't as busy as it could have been, but it was busy enough. George was clearly enjoying being seen on the arm of a beautiful woman and said "hello" with a proud smile, to a neighbour who was out walking his dog.

"He probably thinks you're my daughter," the elderly man said, giving her hand a squeeze. "I think the last time I was seen out with a woman as beautiful as you was when I got back from the war!"

"You fought against the Germans?" Candice asked.

"Germans? Bloody Falklands, love. The Argies... You American?"

Ah, The Falklands War. She hadn't been born when the conflict had occurred between the United Kingdom and Argentina, who Brazil supported at the time. Her Mother had talked about it once, after the former British leader Margaret Thatcher had died. A shameful waste of lives over seaweed, penguins and sheep, she had called it.

"Sure am, honey. Los Angeles," she lied. Her accent wasn't bad, though.

"Come round for a cup of tea some time. I'm in 202."

"I'll be sure to do that," she said, giving George a quick peck on the cheek. He grinned.

"See you again, my lovely!" George shouted after her, as she dashed across the road towards the station. Just as she reached the other side, a piercing scream caused her to stop and turn. Something about the sound was unnatural, and filled her with dread. A blurred shape fell down from the ninth floor, accompanied by the chilling howl of a man. Shouts and cries followed, as people clustered around the mangled body which now lay in front of the tower block. She froze on the other side of the road, mesmerised by the horror of the scene before her. It was as if a mannequin had been dumped on the pavement from a shop window display. A dark pool of blood formed round the body. The body had fallen quite far out from the building itself, landing on the curb. The left arm and hand of the man lay outstretched as if to communicate a warning to Candice. Pointing away from the scene. Telling her to run. The man in the overalls with the clipboard and the radio appeared, ignoring the blood-splattered corpse and the crowd of onlookers. He stared across the road and straight into her horrified eyes. Candice broke into a run. He sprinted through the crowd towards the crossing. She fumbled in her purse for her Oyster travel pass, makeup spilling out onto the concourse of the station as she ran. It was quieter than normal but the station was filling up with early risers, keen to beat London's packed rush hour. A group of twenty or so people were gathered around the television screen mounted on the wall of one of the smaller cafés inside the station. The images of the alien ships were playing on the news, continually cutting from one landing site to another from round the world. She merged with the group of captivated commuters, crouching inside the café while frantically searching for her pass. She didn't want to jump the ticket barrier, knowing it would only attract more attention. Animated conversation between the strangers around her filled the air.

"Have there been aliens yet?"

"No. No one has come out and no one has gone in!"

"I saw a video on YouTube taken by an American kid from inside one of the ships, but now it's been taken down!"

"Yeah. I saw that too. Didn't the American government say it was fake?"

"Do you trust the American government?"

"No - They probably knew they were coming for years!"

"God, this coffee is awful. First alien invasion and now bad coffee – what is the world coming too?"

Candice didn't know what it was coming to, nor did she like where it was going. That had to have been Alphonse lying there broken on the pavement. God, he was dead! Dead because of her. Why? How? She felt dizzy. She wanted to smoke but couldn't. What had she done to make this happen? It had to be the picture. Ryan. Oh God. Did he order this? She felt sick. Breathe. Just breathe. A quick glance up and she saw the overalls man enter the station. He was joined by two more men. The three of them split up, each heading to a different part of the building. Stratford Station was large and could be confusing to strangers. It had overground trains leaving via one concourse, connections to the Central and Jubilee lines on London Underground, The Docklands Light Railway and you could get connections to Europe. Her passport. She had it on her. Did Eurostar trains stop here? She had to get away. She could go to France, wait the whole thing out. No, Brazil would be safer but air travel was on hiatus. How would she get back home? Some people were rumoured to be paying thousands for tickets on cruises just to ensure they got back to both the north and south American continent. She didn't want to waste her hard-earned savings on such extravagances. She decided on the London DLR, the best option available to her without being spotted. Her stomach was still churning at the horror she had witnessed. How could they do that to such a beautiful boy? He hadn't even done anything. Those motherfuckers! They were going to pay for this! But that would have to be for another day. Every minute that ticked by, the station filled up with more and more people making their way back to work. Numbers were on her side. The atmosphere was not the insular London norm where each person was so concerned about getting to their destination as quickly as possible, that they plugged in their headphones and ignored everyone around them. No, people were talking to strangers today, bound by what they perceived as a common threat to their way of life. Everyone wanted to talk to someone. So that morning, the corridors of the east London transport hub was filled with not just the noise of footfall, but of conversations between strangers. It worked to her advantage. Dipping behind the group still glued to the news bulletin on the television, she tied her hair up in a bunch and spotted a coat someone had left over their chair. Candice confidently swooped it up and put it on, as if it were her own. Luckily it turned out to be a good fit and the colour of dark navy, like so much formal business wear, would help her blend into the crowds. She swapped her sunglasses with the spare pair in her bag, having finally realised her travel pass was in fact in the rear pocket of her jeans. She went through the ticket barrier and headed for London's DLR. Up ahead, she spotted one of the drivers from the vehicle outside Alphonso's address walking back towards her. She had only seconds before he would see her. Behind her, two women were talking anxiously about the impact of world events on one of their impending wedding nuptials.

"Everyone is bloody cancelling! Why couldn't they have come next damn weekend? We would have been on our honeymoon by then! I've paid a fortune for that venue just so all his bloody extended family could be accommodated and now we won't even need half the space! It's going to be awful, Denise. No one's going to come!"

Thinking fast, she spun on her heel and reached out, grabbing both women by the shoulders, stopping them in their tracks. They were both late thirties, attractive, peroxide-blonde, dressed in above the knee dark skirts with power jackets. They probably worked in PR or publishing. On any other day such a physical action would have caused both women to recoil in horror. She had but a moment to take control of the situation.

"Babes, can I just say to you…" she said with a cockney accent, the best she could get away with. "That it's your special day on Saturday and you can't let what's going on in the world take anything away from that. You just have to tell everyone it's happening. Make sure they know you're not going to let anything, not even beings from another world, change all that. I can see you've had your hair done already, you can't be letting that go to waste now, can you darling?"

The stunned woman looked back at her. For a beat, neither one said anything, then the bride-to-be threw her arms around Candice and gave her a hug. Candice just held her for a moment, long enough to let the man pass. Their familiarity with each other giving the impression of work colleagues debating the current crisis. The man walked past back towards the ticket hall.

"That is such a nice thing to say! Thank you so much," the bride-to-be said. The three of them walked on together.

"Are you heading to Canary Wharf?" the other woman enquired politely.

"Yes, if I still have a job to go to," she lied. "You should be staying at home, sorting out your wedding plans," she said, to the bride-to-be.

"Oh, I didn't really want to go into work, it's his bloody parents, my soon-to-be-in-laws. They want to cancel the whole thing. They say we should postpone, until we know what's going on. Staying at home was driving me crazy!" she cried.

"Have you heard anything new this morning? I stayed up until two o'clock watching it all, but nothing seems to have happened!" her friend asked.

All she had seen was what was on the news last night.

"No, just the same as you." The three of them took the steps up to the platform, chatting. Candice learned nothing new. Apparently footage had been released on social media of a bus from Aberdeen that had driven out east of the city. The bus driver had decided it would be a good idea to have a drive on the surface of the object. Had he been high? Probably, she decided. There were rumours of people going missing, and talk of possible abductions, but nothing to really substantiate these claims. Candice wished the girls good luck and caught the eastbound train. She still wasn't on the right line to get straight to Walthamstow, but at least some sense of normality was kicking back into London. She decided she would get off in the city and then risk calling another Uber to take her from there to Pearl's. Any ideas she had about travelling to Europe were put in doubt by conversations she heard among other passengers.

"We're supposed to be going to Gran Canaria next week! When are the airports going to open again? That's what I want to know!"

"Are the ferries still working do you think? Marie wants us to take the kids to our place in Bordeaux."

"What makes you think you'll be any safer in France? There's one over there too you know!"

By the time she came out of Canary Wharf Station, the sun was creeping up to impose itself upon the city. A clear April sky had painted the gaps between the tall buildings of London's commercial district with a clean blue. The imposing grey towers had been constructed on the old docks of London's now defunct shipping trade. The whole area had been completely revitalised over the last three decades. A client had told her the local history during a visit to his rather swanky modern apartment nearby. Candice was still shaking. Her stomach was roiling and she paused to take a breather. Canary Wharf would normally be teeming with people at this time in the morning as the area got ready for the day's trade, but today was more like a Sunday. Less people and less restaurants open. The staff that had come in looked distracted. Everyone again still glued to the television sets that hung on the walls inside the few bars and cafés that had opened for breakfast. Taking note of the address, she ordered the Uber noting her phone had less than 5% battery life remaining. Eleven minutes. She shrugged. Considering world events the wait could have been considerably longer. It gave her time for a cigarette. Remembering Pearl's request for water and papers she found a small newsagent stand and purchased two more packets of Marlborough Lights, some gum, rolling papers, two bars of chocolate and two bottles of water. Every paper ran a front page about the ships' arrival. She found an empty bench nearby, facing three old loading cranes on the quayside. They were structures out of time, mechanical beasts. Graceful somehow, but now redundant, standing as monuments to history. Their only purpose now was to be standing works of art. She lit up with trembling fingers, taking in huge drags of nicotine, gathering her thoughts. It was hard to absorb. Alphonse had not fallen by accident from that tower block. He had been pushed. Thrown. Murdered. Because she had compromising pictures of Ryan on her phone. Tears came, and made her makeup run so she took out her compact and repaired it the best she could. She smoked the first cigarette fast, taking out a second one from the packet with her lips. She was searching again for her lighter, when a man sat down next to her on the bench with a zippo lighter in hand, ready and flipped open.

"Allow me," he said politely, holding the lighter just below her cigarette.

"Thank you," she said, leaning in and lighting up. The man was in his mid-thirties with short, cropped hair and a face like a boxer's. His clothes seemed rather drab, but something about him seemed familiar. Very familiar. She kept her hand in her bag, searching for something.

"My name is Lennox." The man said with a strong cockney accent. She really was not in the mood to be picked up. Besides he wasn't really her type, being a little portly for her tastes.

"Sorry honey, I'm taken."

"You've caused us quite a bit of trouble this morning, Ms Alvarez."

Now she remembered. He had been outside the flat that morning, sitting in the car reading the paper in the front seat. How did he get here so fast? It didn't matter for the moment. Two other men crossing the square caught her attention. One on her right stopped by the wall twenty yards away, his hands clasped together in front of him. The second stood just outside the exit of the station, forty yards away, with the same posture.

"I suggest you come with us quietly. Don't make this difficult. We wouldn't want to have to hurt your Mother now, would we?"

Lennox stared ahead blankly as he pocketed his lighter. Threatening her Mother was a mistake but it was also, she realised, a bluff. She knew how Brazil worked. Finding her Mother, let alone sending a hit squad into the slums on the hills of Rio de Janeiro, without word getting back to her? Yeah, good luck with that. She had to play for time. There were still plenty of people around and that gave her a chance, at least.

"Isn't the condemned woman traditionally allowed to smoke her last cigarette?" she said, deadpan despite the sudden rush of adrenaline kicking into her bloodstream.

"It's the last wish of the condemned man, but seeing as you are technically a man, I'll let you finish it."

Now he was just being rude.

"Oh I am a woman, but I suspect where it counts I'm more man than you'll ever be," she said, blowing smoke into his face, almost goading him to hit her. If he did that in front of so many witnesses, somebody was bound to do something. A man striking a woman in public, not very cool. He didn't go for it.

"I suggest you enjoy that cigarette, Ms Alvarez. It's going to be your last."

If it was going to be her last, then she was going to have some fun with this prick.

"So do they make you wear these awful clothes or do you get to pick your own? Because honey, let me tell you, if it's the latter – you have terrible taste."

"Give me that phone."

She reluctantly handed it over.

"Are all the pictures on here?"

'Pictures of what, honey?" She knew what he was asking about but she wasn't going to concede a thing.

Lennox rose to his feet.

"Get up before I make you."

On the other side of the square, a dark-coloured van pulled up and two more men got out. If she was going to run it had to be now. Her right hand found what she sought, grabbing the cylindrical object as firmly as she could, flipping off the lid. She took in a deep breath then stood up abruptly and screamed as loudly as she could.

"How dare you touch my breasts!"

"What? I didn't... oh you fucking..."

Before he finished his sentence, she'd pulled the small can from her bag and coated his eyes with pepper spray sending him reeling from the bench. Pepper spray was hard to find in the UK, but not impossible. The man tried to punch her but she was already backing away and his lunge missed. Her accusation and the man's punch had attracted more than just a few passers-by. People weren't so concerned about getting into work on time that morning. Many ran to her aid.

"What happened Miss, are you all right?" came the caring voice of an older man in a suit.

"That man propositioned me for sex and when I refused, he assaulted me!"

Her assailant still staggered about, clutching his eyes.

"I'm with MI6, she's wanted for terrorism offences!" he retorted.

Someone else began filming the whole episode on their phone.

"That's bullshit!" shouted Candice, attracting more attention. "He's lying! He's a sex trafficker, don't listen to him! And he stole my phone! Take a look at it, it's my phone!"

As Lennox went to speak, she sprayed him a second time, directing the contents into his mouth. He sputtered and coughed, rage spreading across his face. He staggered forward blindly, trying to open his eyes but only causing himself greater discomfort. The rest of his men hesitated as the crowd grew around them. She snatched her phone back from him.

"You bitch, I'm going to fucking kill you!" He took a blind swipe at her.

"See what I mean? And would a terrorist bother travelling around with a bag from Christian Dior and Fat Face Victoria Dora pumps? Baby, please!" Candice held up her Dior bag as she made the point.

"Yeah, she's right! This man's obviously a pervert!" said another woman in the crowd.

"This man's a sex trafficker!" cried another.

"Someone call the police!" shouted another man.

"I did. They're on their way," someone else said but Candice knew she couldn't depend on their arrival. The police probably had other more pressing things to do right now. A crowd of concerned commuters had grown around her. Candice backed away, checking on the whereabouts of the man's colleagues. They were hanging back, confused, uncertain of what to do. Now was her chance. Taking off her shoes, she ran. Candice had a runner's physique. Implants aside, her legs could take her up to a tremendous speed very quickly but she wasn't rested and lacked energy. Her adrenaline had kicked in, but there wasn't too much of it. She broke past the crowd, ignoring their cries. Glancing back, she saw two men escorting their blinded colleague back to the van. A fourth man was tearing after her. She left Montgomery Square and turned towards the north dock. She raced over the bridge and ran up Churchill Way, which led to a roundabout and a second bridge out of the docks, that crossed the Blackwall Basin. Beyond it lay a series of residential blocks, behind which there was a small marina littered with canal boats and private yachts. A London Fire Brigade launch boat was in the basin tending to a fire on one of the canal boats. Apartments here were expensive. The canal boat owners were the trendy artistic lower middle-class whose cramped homes clung to the waterways beneath the flats of millionaires. She sped onto the bridge, becoming breathless now. A quick glance behind showed no sign of her pursuer. She recognised this place; another client, a different night. She recalled that they lived in one of the buildings as she crossed the basin, running over the road. A car blared its horn, narrowly avoiding hitting her. Now she knew she had to leave the UK. It didn't matter where to. A boat or train to Europe, then from there she would find a way to get back to Brazil. She had enough money saved and contacts in France and Italy to help her with that. If she could just…

Something struck her hard in the back with such force that it sent her stumbling towards the railing on the side of the dock. She grasped it with both hands to stay upright but felt herself swaying. Searing pain shot through her body, and she began to feel breathless. Was that blood she tasted on her lips? Had she bitten her tongue? Clutching the rail, she twisted around and looked straight into the face Lennox, his face still red from her pepper spray assault. The van idled on the road nearby.

"I told you not to make this difficult, but you wouldn't listen. You fucking trannies, you're all the same."

The derogatory cunt. Who the fuck was he to talk to her like that? Oh, she was going to make him pay. Bastard. He had something in his hand. Was that a gun? That pain, where was it coming from? She felt round to her back which was wet and sticky. Looking at her hand she could see it was covered in blood. Shit! She had been shot! Oh God.

"Mother! Adrina! Please hear me!" She shouted her Mother's name as loud as her lungs would allow, praying somehow she would hear her. They had always been so close, her Mother always knew when she was in trouble. She heard a muffled thud as a second bullet hit her. Blood spewed into her mouth. Her head began to spin as Lennox ran across the road towards her. Then she fell backwards, losing her grip on the railing, toppling over it. *What a shame she had never learnt to swim*, she thought as she felt her body twist over the barrier and fall down into the dark water below.

RYAN

Yesterday's press conference followed by the meeting in the House of Commons had gone far better than he had expected. Jennifer had risen to the occasion, ensuring he had a clean shirt and tie on hand for both. Handy, as by the end of the conference his armpits were drenched in sweat. Ryan had led the press conference with a personal announcement on the Alien Question, as people were calling it. He had been impacted upon directly by the arrival of these unknown craft. His own Grandmother was now missing, last having been seen on the surface of the ship in Scotland. He referred to the news footage that had been shot inside the bus during its time on the surface of the vessel, where she could clearly be seen on board the vehicle. He had waited until her identity could be verified before making this news public, (and that wasn't bullshit because, you know, all old people do tend to look the same once they hit eighty, so he had wanted to be certain it was her). He then answered a few questions about her: yes, he had spoken to her every week, and yes, last time she was in good health both physically and mentally, and no, he had no idea what would make a woman in her eighties want to go and see such a potentially dangerous thing up close. He added, "She always did have a burning curiosity about everything. Perhaps at her age she thought she had nothing to lose." On this matter both members of The House and of the press had been relatively sympathetic.

Casualties from the Scottish landing site had so far been remarkably light. In fact, the only known fatalities had been from road traffic accidents caused by people looking up instead of where they were going. A number of others were caused by heart attacks. But so far it could not be verified that anyone had actually been killed by the ship's landfall. Not the Scottish one at any rate. Property damage was also minimal. All structures located within the perimeter of the ship were presumed to be destroyed, though of course there was no way to actually verify this beyond common sense. They must have been crushed. Some seventy-six people, including his Grandmother, were unaccounted for, but the majority of those who lived in homes and farms that were now located underneath the vessel had for the most part either escaped unharmed, or were still turning up. Several were unable to actually recall exactly how it was they had escaped. To quell the fears of The House, Ryan stated:

"Right honourable members, if this is an invasion, then it would seem to be one most considerate of human sensitivities."

That was a good line, one of Jennifer's of course. Ryan had already been handed the speech by the time Darren Fine arrived back in Westminster from his rather long return train journey. It was overbooked and he bemoaned that he didn't have a seat, not even in First Class. There were some difficult questions about the Army firing on civilians who had been on the top of the alien object. Ryan said he couldn't comment on ongoing Military operations but stated that the landing site in Scotland was now a matter of national security and the area was completely off-limits to the public. He moved on to announce the Territorial Army was being deployed in all city centres, and at larger supermarkets to protect them against looting, theft and property damage. He advised people to buy only what they needed and to shop sensibly. Sainsbury's and Tesco were already limiting food shops to twenty items per person, per day. Other supermarket chains were expected to follow suit. There had been a huge increase in petty theft. Ryan addressed this in his press conference and in his address to the house, calling for calm and resolve from the British public. He mentioned Dunkirk Spirit and the need for the UK to lead the world. They had to be an example of how to react to a global crisis. To help humanity avoid a catastrophe of its own making, it was vital that social and economic infrastructures remained intact. A limited evacuation of the city of Aberdeen was taking place for the safety of its citizens, but he understood a number of its residents wished to stay. He confirmed that they would not be forcibly removed. As for the rest of the United Kingdom, people would go on paying their bills, and going to work, but should avoid driving where possible, allowing the roads to stay free of traffic. It was vital that train and bus drivers go to work as normal. Hospital services must not postpone important operations and extra manpower would be provided to essential services wherever it was possible to do so. Jennifer had written him a good speech, supplemented at the last minute for him to avoid answering any questions on embarrassing pictures leaked on social media. What embarrassing pictures? he had wanted to ask her but there wasn't time. The opposition had for the most part been supportive, as much as British politics would allow under such circumstances. A minute's silence took place to honour those killed in the plane crash in France, which he now understood included several French civilians on the ground, in addition to half a dozen French police said to have been casualties in the ensuing gun battles with the terrorists. One terrorist was known to be dead. Good. They had killed his friend, one of the few people who had ever been there for him in times of need. Information on who was behind the attack was not forthcoming. The French were taking a frustratingly long time to identify the body, or what was left of it, of the one terrorist they had on a slab in the morgue. He had apparently got cornered on his way to the Belgian border. After a brief but ferocious fire-fight with the French Police, he decided to blow himself up. His arm was recovered half a day later, missed due to the fact that it was hanging from the branch of a nearby apple tree.

Towards the end of the day, Ryan had trouble staying on his feet. Although he had managed to eat properly he still had not had a decent nights sleep since his unexpected promotion. His adrenaline was non-existent. No amount of coffee or even illegal recreational drugs could have kept him going. At the end of Prime Minister's Questions, he informed the house:

"Now if you will all forgive me, like many of you I have gone three days without sleep. If I am to continue to lead this country I had better go and get some rest, no matter how brief it may be."

He was then surprised to find himself promptly being driven to Number Ten Downing Street, without further delay. It appeared his word did carry some weight, after all. Number Ten was of course the expected live-in London address of the British Prime Minister, but Ryan still hadn't got to grips with the realities of his new title yet or indeed the job, nor he did really expect to be moving into Number Ten so soon. As the car drove up, past waiting photographers and press held back at the barrier, he saw removal men leaving the building carrying bundles of bags and possessions that once must have belonged to David Jackson and his wife, possibly even their kids. Did the children also live here? Perhaps not. He couldn't remember ever having seen them during his own visits. The building next door had actually been refurbished to accommodate a large family during the the Blair administration, but such apartments would be far too big for just him alone. The moment they stepped out of the car, the famous door was opened for him. Ryan managed a brief wave back towards the press behind the barrier at the end of the street, before being whisked inside by Willis and Dilks who immediately followed him into the building. Ryan had read somewhere that the door to Number Ten was always manned from the inside, and could not be opened by anyone, even with a key, from the street. He remembered David telling him how the door was blast-proof.

It appeared to be oak, but that apparently was just a façade. The oak covered a series of steel plates, making it as tough as the armour of a light tank. He hoped he wouldn't have to put it to the test. Upon entering it looked different somehow than on his previous visits. It felt far less official for some reason and certainly less homely. The spacious stairs and upper landing were like rush hour in a tube station, with men and women bobbing left and right carrying papers and personal effects either out or into the building, or from one room to the next. As he went up the staircase he noticed that on one wall some Jackson family photographic portraits still hung. His friend David, standing proudly, with his wife and two beautiful children at his side. As Ryan lingered in front of it, a man in overalls reached out and removed it.

"You!" Ryan said. All human traffic in Number Ten came to an abrupt halt as he barked. Had he snapped at the man? Yes, he had.

"Yes? I mean, yes Prime Minister?" The stunned man said.

"That photograph. Give it to me!" Ryan said.

"They're to be returned to the family, Mr Wallace," the man replied, uncertain of what to do next. Ryan snatched the framed picture from his hands.

"He was family to me. Do you understand? Besides, who do you think he has left?" Ryan turned away from him.

"Yes sir. Well you hang on to that one then. He was a good man, David Jackson. I didn't like his politics much, but he treated us all right."

The man went down the stairs, removing the last of the framed photos from the walls. Ryan stopped and turned.

"Yes, well… I will do my best to do the same," Ryan said. Jennifer ushered him upstairs, shouting to the staff as she did so.

"The Prime Minister has had a very busy couple of days and is extremely tired as I am sure you can imagine. Please have all the household staff meet me downstairs in ten minutes. Proper introductions to the Prime Minister can wait until tomorrow morning."

On reaching the landing, someone else stood there waiting for him. It was Darren Fine.

"I'd like a moment with the Prime Minister, if I may."

Ryan could tell from his tone that the meeting was going to be a painful one, probably predominantly for him. Jennifer led them towards a small annexe, holding the door for Ryan, then for Fine who stopped in front of her.

"Alone," he said pointedly, stepping in front of her. She looked at Ryan.

"Anything you say to me, can be said in front of my Private Secretary," Ryan said.

"Very well. As you wish, Prime Minister." Fine gestured for Jennifer to close the door behind them. Ryan hadn't been in this office before. The dark furnishings matched the large oak desk, while the shelves were covered with volume after volume of studious-looking books that Ryan knew he would never read. Fine placed his iPad on the desk, turning it to face them. It showed an image of Ryan sleeping, a large, dark flaccid penis resting across his forehead. He would recognise that cock anywhere. Oh shit.

"This image began circulating on social media yesterday. That is you, isn't it?" Fine asked the question with heavy expectation. If Jennifer was shocked by what she saw, she didn't show it.

"It's amazing what people can do with Photoshop these days," she said, unconcerned.

It was true, people could do amazing things with Photoshop, but it was also true that he was looking at a picture of himself sleeping, with Candice's cock draped over his head. When the fuck had she taken this? After one of their extremely late and long nights, no doubt. He was fucked.

"I ask again, that is you in the picture isn't it, Prime Minister?" Fine said.

"I agree it looks like me," Ryan replied, trying to sound unconvinced.

"A very good likeness, I would say. I have been fending off questions from the press all day. They want a statement on this. No one has run a story on it yet, but they will, I can promise you."

"Fending off questions from the press is your job though, isn't it, Mr Fine?" Jennifer cut in. He really was beginning to warm to this new Secretary of his. His old one would have never had the balls to go head to head with someone of Fine's reputation.

"It is. However, my job would be made considerably easier if I knew the origins of this photograph. Then I would know how best to handle the situation." Fine was enjoying this. What an arse-wipe.

Ryan leaned in across the desk, studying the picture closely. He could kill her for this. This was revenge for him dumping her, no doubt. That had been pretty cold but what was he to do? He had a country to run and people's lives were at stake.

"Hmm," he pondered, somewhat louder than he intended.

"Prime Minister?"

"It's fake, obviously. Like Jennifer said, it's amazing what people can do with Photoshop these days."

Fine glared back at him, as if willing him to change his mind and confess. "Right, so that's our official position is it?" he asked.

"Yes," Ryan said, without blinking.

"Right, it's just things like Photoshop can normally be proved or disproved. Could you perhaps find the original photograph, the one without a…a male member placed on your head?"

"I am sure I could…" Ryan was certain he couldn't.

"Right. I'll prepare a statement to that effect then." Ryan walked Fine to the door.

"Just as well it is fake, it would terribly embarrassing for everyone if more photographs emerged, taken on the same night perhaps. Or even video footage. Because once we go down the path of total denial, there is no going back from it. As long as you understand that," Fine said.

"I do," Ryan said, holding open the door. Fine smiled, leaned in and whispered, "Good to know you bat for my team, Prime Minister. Who would have guessed?"

"I like to think we're all on the same team here, Mr Fine," Ryan replied, evenly. Cheeky bastard, best not to provoke him.

"That we are, sir." Fine left.

Ryan closed the door, turning to see Jennifer leaning on the desk, her arms crossed. It was a shame he felt so exhausted, she looked gorgeous. He guessed that the desk could almost certainly take the weight of both of them.

"Fake?" it was a question. Not a statement.

"That's right. It's not the first time someone's called me a dickhead, metaphorically or otherwise." It was his best comeback. Jennifer was unmoved.

"You looked very peaceful in that picture. Almost happy," She said. Yes, he probably had been.

He was having trouble standing, now. He found himself unable to think of an answer.

"Like you said, I think you need some rest. Just for a few hours," Jennifer said, as she opened the door for him. He could not disagree.

As his principal Private Secretary, Jennifer Brewster-Smith held some weight when it came to household matters. She sorted out who was going to make his bed, clean his toilet and so on. The latter task being something he certainly wouldn't want to wish on his worst enemy, though he did think he might make an exception in the case of the current President of the United States. Which reminded him, he was due to have a video conference with him tomorrow morning. That would be right up there with his parents' funeral for sheer entertainment value, of that much he was certain. Jennifer had informed him on the drive over, that she had been here earlier in the day to tell the staff that Ryan would be moving into Number Ten for the foreseeable future that evening. Removal of the Jackson family personal possessions had already begun in earnest that morning. Up until then, rumour had been rife that Ryan would only hold the office for a couple of days and who would be moving in to take Mr Jackson's place had remained uncertain. Jennifer had put paid to those doubts, and told everyone in no uncertain terms that Prime Minister Wallace, would be retaining that title for now and the house needed to rapidly prepare for his arrival, followed by business as usual. As he headed out to the landing, Jennifer gave a brief overview of the layout of the building, but Ryan wasn't really listening. He could barely walk straight as he negotiated the stairs. He only remembered part of what Jennifer had said to him.

"The Blairs and The Camerons deemed the residence upstairs too small to live in for their family, so they chose to live in Number Eleven, which for your information can be accessed from this landing. However, as you're presently unmarried and won't have children to consider, at least not that we know of, I think you will find the quarters here more than adequate. They were good enough for Margaret Thatcher."

"As long as they don't smell like Margaret Thatcher." Ryan hadn't actually ever met the Iron Lady, of course. By the time he was into politics she was living her last few years out of the London Ritz Hotel and died a lonely death if ever there was one. Radio stations played the song from the Wizard of Oz – *Ding Dong the Witch is Dead* – in celebration of her passing. Falklands victory aside, she was not a well-loved Prime Minister. He did not want a similar epitaph. He knew how he wanted to leave this world. Preferably from a heart attack due to some marathon sex act, not slowly withering from old age and Alzheimer's disease. No, thank you very much. Jennifer led him upstairs, continuing her description of the layout. Number Ten could look deceptively small from the outside, but it occupied not one but three houses on the street. The rooms were able to lie width-ways across, with impressively high ceilings. They'd been extensively redecorated by its various occupants over the years. The building's upper floors had been divided into a series of interlinked staterooms, each unique in design: The Pillared Drawing Room, the Terracotta Drawing Room and the White Drawing Room, all with furnishings that matched their respective names. David had shown Ryan round during one of his first visits to the house shortly after he had taken office a year ago, but Ryan had consumed such vast amounts of recreational drugs since then, that consequently he couldn't recall anything in much detail. He did remember that he and David had occupied the plush cream chairs in the White Room, helping themselves to a bottle of extremely old and rather good Scottish Brandy, which a previous occupant had rather foolishly left behind for their indulgence. A shot of that would be good right now. The staterooms were normally used for entertaining world leaders, and less formal meetings or chats between the President of the United States and the Prime Minister. He hoped he would be long out of office before such a face to face meeting might occur. He would freely admit that they had some complete idiots in their own Cabinet, himself among them but he could not stand that American buffoon. Every British Prime Minister had always vowed not to be the one pushed around by American interests and each in their own way had always capitulated, even Winston Churchill. Fortunately, his smaller failures would always be overshadowed by the great downfall of others, like Tony Blair. Ryan laughed inside as he thought to himself that at least he wasn't faced with the decision of taking the country to war over faulty intelligence to placate American foreign interests. Oh no, his problems: the sudden assassination of the country's leader, coinciding with the arrival of alien intelligence, if not alien life on a global scale, was far less demanding! Jennifer showed Ryan into his personal quarters. He remembered not caring much for the décor, but little else because he had fallen asleep before he even hit the pillow.

It seemed barely minutes later that he was awoken by light spilling into the room, caused by Jennifer pulling back the curtains. He could not even remember taking off his clothes, but was sleeping in a t-shirt and his Star Wars-Rogue One boxer shorts, a birthday present from one of his cousin's children. Jennifer was followed in by a rather dowdy-looking housemaid carrying a breakfast tray. Martine Mccutcheon from *Love Actually* she was not. Fresh orange juice, a steaming cup of coffee, the delightful aroma of which was most welcome, a bowl of strawberries (unusual, but okay, he did like fruit), four slices of warm toast and a selection of jams and butter. Good God, was it already 6.30am? He glanced at his watch which had not been removed, leaving his wrist feeling somewhat sore.

"Forgive me, Prime Minister but Ms Brewster-Smith said we shouldn't wait to bring it in for you," the frumpy-looking woman said as she placed the tray on the rather spacious bed. Ryan wondered if he could choose his own household staff. A quick visit to Peter Stringfellows should bring in ladies a little more pleasing to the eye to wait on him every morning. He reached for a piece of toast.

"Well quite, very good," he said, digging in. Jennifer dismissed the woman, and began telling him his itinerary for the day as Ryan dived in the shower, toast still in hand. He left the door partially open, in order to hear her as he let the all too brief beats of hot water wash through his hair.

"You have the conference with the President of the United States of America in thirty minutes, it will probably only last five minutes..." Bonus! He was hoping it would be less than ten. "Following that, you have the meeting with Cobra. That can be held here in the Cabinet Room which will save you some time, as you then have the full Cabinet Meeting which is due to last an hour."

An hour. Shit. Best let them do all the talking, then. He was in and out of the shower in two minutes. Ryan jumped at the sight of a young man appearing at the door of the bathroom, who stood ready to present him with some clean underwear and socks. Ryan quickly grasped a towel to cover his modesty. Jennifer's voice droned on from the room beyond.

"This will then be followed by another hour of individual intelligence and military briefings, including the Skype meeting with Doctor Jacobs that you requested. You will then brief the Under-Cabinet before going back to the House of Commons and once more addressing Parliament, updating them on the current situation, should there be anything to update of course." Ryan quickly dried himself down while extending his hand through the gap in the door, waving it.

"Toast," he said, snatching another slice, thinking if Candice had received his text and where she might have chosen to wait out the crisis. He wanted to know she was safe and well, and more than anything to apologise and explain his actions. But he also needed to get her to delete that photograph and find out if she'd taken any others. God, he just remembered – she filmed him once. It had been completely non-sexual, they were laughing, joking around. She asked him what his three favourite things were in the world... Oh shit. She wouldn't put that online though, would she? She must have known by now who he was. I mean she did the post on Twitter after all. She must have understood his need to cut all ties with her. It hadn't been what he wanted, but what else could he do? General Spears was right, even with the change in modern attitudes, the British public were all too easily distracted by matters of sexuality. To have them knowing he had a transsexual girl-friend would not help the current nervous public mood, and fragile political situation. Anarchy and complete social unrest was only a stone's throw away.

"Then there'll be meetings with the Joint Intelligence Committee this afternoon," Jennifer said, bringing his mind back to the current situation. He emerged from the bathroom in his pants and socks and quickly finished his breakfast, finding himself accompanied by an additional young man as he continued to get dressed. A third then entered the room with an iPad under one arm and three jackets under the other. How many young men did he need to dress him? Jennifer nodded towards the third member of his young male entourage.

"This is Daniel, he will be your personal dresser from this point on and will purchase all your clothes, toiletries and any other things you may need. He'll also be co-ordinating your new look with your social media advisor."

'Which would be me, Prime Minister. Simon Hall," said the second young man, who was now sitting down at the side of the bed. Ryan was certain he was crunching on one of his strawberries. He eyed him with suspicion as he removed the remaining contents of his breakfast out of the man's reach, and dug into the fruit.

"My social media?" Farcebook, Twatter, Instawank... nothing but a fucking pain in the arse. Just more avenues for him to get into trouble. Daniel presented him with his new wardrobe, which had been expanded overnight. The third youth began measuring him for more clothes, as he got dressed. Were there not more important things they could be doing than measuring him for additional suits? There was a world crisis to deal with, after all! Jennifer introduced the youngest of the three men who held out an array of ties.

"This is Ben, Daniel's assistant. He's going to give you a new look. He's also a qualified makeup artist and hairdresser, which will be handy for when you go before the cameras."

"I'm multi-talented, Prime Minister, there's very little I cannot do," Ben said.

Ryan didn't doubt it but wasn't best pleased. All three of them could not be any more ragingly homosexual if they tried. He snatched a tie being held up by Ben. It was salmon pink. Nope. He changed it quickly for a navy blue one. Safe and very much more appropriate for the Conservative party leader. "Do I really need to be dressed in the morning? I'm not the bloody Queen!"

"Yes, I'm afraid you do. You're the leader of the United Kingdom in a time of crisis, and in a crisis, time is everything. Of course you'll be needing more suits, more of everything in fact." He liked Jennifer far less when she was so serious, which sadly was most of the time.

"Don't worry, love. I'm having one of our team pick up twenty new shirts for you this morning," Ben chimed in with a smile.

Daniel began holding up different jackets to Ryan's body.

"Dark navy, I think for you, sir. We'll need a slogan for you Mr Wallace. I'm sorry, Prime Minister. Still getting used to the changes round here."

No shit. "You're not the only one," Ryan replied, sarcastically.

"You've done very well with your speeches, so something that encapsulates those I think," Simon added. Ryan was certain he saw Jennifer suppress a little smile. Any compliment about his speeches was after all, a compliment for her.

"Simon here is all about branding and sponsorship. He will take care of your overall image and run your official Twitter and Facebook pages."

Daniel began to slip on a light blue shirt over Ryan's shoulders.

"Twitter and Facebook? I can dress myself, you know." Ryan took the shirt from Daniel, and began to do it up. He had to confess it was a very good fit.

"Unassisted will take twice as long, this way you will look the part as soon as you leave the door, plus young Daniel here will make sure you don't walk into a cabinet meeting with loo roll hanging out your arse."

Daniel promptly removed the offending piece of tissue.

"Next you'll be telling me he'll be wiping my arse," Ryan snapped. The three men exchanged raised eyebrows that even the late Roger Moore would have been proud of.

"If it would save two more minutes of your time each day, then he would. You're a leader, dealing with an international crisis and every minute we save you in one place you can spend more efficiently doing something else," Jennifer said. Her response was robust and he couldn't argue with her logic but he hated all this fussing around him. True, there were never enough minutes in a normal day where he was concerned, though he wasn't sure he could remember the last time he had a normal day. He certainly wasn't likely to have too many in the future. A selection of shoes were held out for him by the young spiky-haired blond assistant. Was his name Ben? He had already forgotten. Ah well, far better to be dressed by a gay man than a straight man, they always knew what looked best on anyone, especially other men. Just don't let them choose your trousers. In his experience, gay men always picked something far too tight that would ride right up his arse in no time. So what had he missed while he slept?

"Update me on the salient points of the last six hours. Have there been any other changes with our object in Scotland?"

"No. No changes with any of them worldwide, unless governments aren't talking. The one that's straddling the border of the US and Mexico is causing some real problems. Mexican citizens walked all over the object on their side. At least they did for a while. It has been reported that some of them found a way inside, but nothing has been substantiated yet."

"Interesting. You said they did. What's happening there now?" Ryan asked.

"The US Airforce and military is keeping everyone away, and the President has declared the airspace a restricted US-only fly zone due to the partial incursion into US Territory. The US Army have moved onto the actual ship itself. Now this one is twenty miles across, so you have at least ten miles of it resting in Mexican territory, which is now effectively occupied by US Troops. There's already protests in Mexico City and some unconfirmed reports of fighting near the ship."

Mexico was unlikely to wage war with America over this, but at the same time it was a huge loss of face to do nothing. He didn't envy the Mexican President right now.

"Ouch, that could go wrong very fast," Ryan said. He finished buttoning his shirt.

"Yes it could. Not as fast as the waters around the vessel that have bridged the so-called Northern Limit Line off the coast of Korea, however."

Ryan's knowledge of world geography wasn't great, but he knew the term of reference for this. It was the oceanic borderline used to mark the divide between the territorial waters of North and South Korea. One of the vessels had landed off the coast between the two countries.

"There's been an incident. The South Korean navy was engaged in an exchange of gunfire with the North less than an hour ago. Both sides are claiming the other fired first."

"Of course they are. Tensions rising again between North and South Korea would I am sure please the current American administration no end. "

The landing site in the west of the Sea of Japan was rapidly becoming a source of dispute in what had always been a highly volatile area. Ryan had a vague recollection of a similar incident that had occurred a few years back, without the presence of a UFO.

"One North Korean boat has been sunk and a second badly damaged. South Korea claim three of theirs are dead and another seventeen wounded."

"Christ! There's no alien invasion yet, but we're doing our best to go to war with each other! Any comment from China?"

"Nothing new beyond yesterday. They're still rattling their sabres about dealing forcefully with the alien threat. There's a total of three ships in Chinese territory. Two on land, one at sea. I've had maps drawn up depicting all the worldwide landing sites, as you requested. The MOD have done computerised versions, they're being uploaded to all relevant departments, and you'll have them along with all relevant data for your meetings today."

"Bring forward my Skype conference with Doctor Jacobs, I want to speak with her before, I speak to the delightful American President, not after."

Ryan wanted his scientific update now. If Jacobs had any news for him, no matter how small, best he knew about it before speaking with anyone else.

"You'll be tight for time," Jennifer cautioned.

"You had best see to it right away then!" Ryan's tone was enough to suggest he wasn't going to budge. He downed his coffee in a couple of gulps, doused himself in aftershave then admired his crisp, new, dark blue suit. Did they make it overnight? The Three Stooges were certainly pleased with it. By the time he was dressed, Jennifer had returned.

"I have your Skype call ready with Doctor Jacobs. She's online downstairs in the Cabinet room."

"Very good." Shit, things really could happen fast in this job. Ryan headed downstairs with Simon, Ben and Daniel saying they would return in the evening with some casual wear, suitable for other engagements. Ryan wasn't sure what casual wear he was likely to need any time soon. He certainly wasn't going to be attending any dinner parties, film premieres or charity fundraisers for the foreseeable future. Perhaps they meant appropriate wear for meetings with alien ambassadors, or was there a casual Friday dress code at Number Ten he was not aware of? He hoped the good Doctor Jacobs might have some answers for him. I mean did they really just fly these things halfway across the universe just to land and sit there to enjoy the view of human calamity? Now there was a theory.

It was a sunny April morning. Warm light was already filling the capacious Cabinet Room from four large bay windows, as he entered to take the call. Ryan took the middle seat by the fireplace, sitting down at the long oval-shaped table surrounded by more than two dozen leather-backed, dark oak chairs. The rest of the Cabinet would be here shortly, but he wanted to have this conversation with the doctor by himself. He'd sat in the room before, with its long drab brown curtains and series of small chandelier lights that hung low from the high ceiling but never as its leader. Number Ten was full of paintings of key historical figures; everyone from Queen Victoria to Oliver Cromwell. Hanging on the wall behind where Ryan would sit was a painting of Sir Robert Walpole, the very first British Prime Minister. It was said that he had been key in making relations between the new government and The Crown workable, which reminded Ryan that a meeting at Buckingham Palace would soon be on the cards. An audience with royalty, was, he suspected, going to be of little consequence where two hundred alien vessels were concerned. It was a mere formality. More than anything, he was curious to see the corgi dogs they owned. He always had been a dog lover.

"Doctor Jacobs is online," Jennifer said, adjusting the monitor so that the daylight didn't fall on the screen. Ryan got comfortable in his seat, stifling a yawn before focusing on Jacobs. The Doctor was already sitting in the tent that Ryan assumed was the same he had visited in Scotland. She had bags under her eyes, and she looked as though she'd had very little rest since he last saw her.

"Good morning Doctor. I hope you managed to get some sleep."

"I would have had a little more if we had stuck to the agreed time for this conference call today. I was woken up." Okay, she was clearly upset. His fault.

"Yes. I'm sorry about that but I have a video conference with the President of the United States shortly, and I thought it would be prudent to speak with you first for any updates. I imagine neither of us is getting much sleep at the moment, but please do let me know if I can send you anything else to assist your work."

"I emailed over a list of University professors and specialists yesterday whom I would like to have working under me at the landing site. They're the best in their field, experts in geology and minerals, something that will add a level of knowledge to our team that we're currently lacking." Okay then. Ryan looked at Jennifer. She nodded, which he assumed meant this could happen easily with his approval.

"I will see that everyone you have asked for is assigned to you immediately. I would imagine few will protest, knowing they'll get to see the object up close for themselves. A defining moment in any man's career I would think." At least, he hoped so.

"Or indeed any woman's," Jacobs added, correcting him. "Thank you Prime Minister. It's greatly appreciated. So, I'm afraid we don't know much more since we last spoke…"

The Doctor rubbed her temple and nodded as a cup of coffee was passed to her by someone off-camera. The server had lovely manicured nails. *It was funny what you noticed sometimes*, Ryan thought.

"Please Doctor, anything at all that you think might be useful…"

"I've examined all the video footage from the British military and social media, regarding the bus incident. As a result, we have been able to pinpoint exactly where we believe the entrance was, down to an area of just a few metres square…"

The Doctor took a gulp of coffee.

"This would be where my Grandmother is presumed to have entered the ship?" It was the first time he had thought of her that morning.

"That is correct. I have actually been to the location myself. The surface there now shows no sign of any portal of any kind. It's identical to the rest of the surface of the vessel in every respect. That led us to the assumption that the objects themselves might be somehow organic in composition, so we carried out a number of tests with that in mind."

"Go on." Ryan hadn't considered that the ships themselves could be the aliens, which would make a great deal of sense. Though it would also mean that his Grandmother, if she was still alive, was wandering around the internal organs of an alien life form or even being digested by one. Not such a pleasant thought.

"I cannot say for certain at this time, if that is the case. Most of our tests are meeting with little success. If it is organic, it's not made of anything comparable with life on Earth, so my guess is that it is made of a material which can change shape and mass to suit its purpose, whatever that may be. Having compared the data available on all the other vessels globally, they do all have matching characteristics. The saucer section of the ship, that is to say the disk which remains above ground, is not the same size in every case."

"You said something about that before…" Ryan was trying to recollect their previous conversation.

"Yes, they were all the same size, from what we can tell, when they first entered the Earth's atmosphere, but upon landing, the circumference and diameter of the saucer section of the ships changed. Ours in Scotland is just under ten miles across and perfectly round. But the one in southern Italy, south of Taranto has a circumference of over forty-three miles."

"Forty-three miles! How is that possible? Does that mean its actual body mass has changed?" Ryan was wracking his brains trying to remember the few lessons he had in mathematics back in the day. Yeah, that wasn't happening.

"The Taranto landing is the largest, at least from what we know. The Chinese are not being very forthcoming about their landing sites, so we can't do a complete comparison yet. The Italian Government is having real difficulties keeping the local population away. The reports I have from our contacts on site are that the waters around it are absolutely teeming with fish. There's more data coming in all the time. We're still trying to verify as much of it as we can. I am talking to several of my colleagues around the world later today to compare our findings with theirs. Post-Brexit, many of my European colleagues are less forthcoming than they might have been a few years ago."

That bloody idiot, Nigel Farage. Ryan was relieved to know there were a few people less qualified to run the country than him in the world of politics, and that tosser was certainly one of them. Jacobs looked at her iPad, scrolling through the data.

"Now, the towers, or spires, as some people are calling them, were smaller when the crafts entered our atmosphere. From what we can tell they were all around 2 miles in height at that time. Since the landings, once again they're all identical in height, that is according to the data we have now. They've all got taller. They're just under 6 miles or 9600 metres in height."

"That makes it higher than Mount Everest, right?" Ryan wasn't sure but it certainly sounded like it.

"Yes, that is correct, Prime Minister, in some cases, depending on the height above sea level of the landing site, much higher. Again, these have no openings of any kind. We've been trying to determine their function. I have one theory. I think they might, in some way be controlling the temperature and moisture in the atmosphere around the landing sites, hence the change in height once the landings had taken place. I've sent you some data showing you the change in the landscape and vegetation around the Aberdeen site. Your Personal Secretary was sent them this morning, please play the video file marked S11…"

As if on cue, Jennifer propped up her iPad next to the laptop and clicked on a video recording of what Ryan assumed was the Scientific Team

(The all-in-one blue suits that he had previously worn, being a bit of a give-away) walking around the circumference of the ship in Scotland. The footage had been taken at dawn. It showed lush vegetation, along with an abundance of fruit hanging from vines, bushes and small trees. It sprawled out from the craft in all directions. He saw what appeared to be blackberries, peaches and grapes, oranges and apples. None of which were in season. Was this the Spanish landing site? This couldn't be the one in Scotland.

"I am watching it now. What am I seeing exactly, Doctor?"

"Well, what we have is a massive increase in the fertility of the soil around the vessels, which appears somehow to have been artificially stimulating the extremely rapid growth of some native fruit and vegetables..."

"Do you mean to tell me I'm looking at the site in Scotland? How is that possible?" Ryan was certain blackberries did not grow in April.

"Frankly, Prime Minister it's not possible. I was going to add, if you pay attention to the video footage of the ground you will notice one of my assistants pull something from a plant that's sprouted close to the soil."

Ryan continued watching as the science team waded through what appeared to be a sea of spider plants. Nestled among the leaves at intervals were orange brownish spiky cone-shaped fruits. Ryan couldn't quite tell what they were. The camera zoomed in on one.

"Can you see that, Prime Minister?" Jacobs asked.

"Yes, I can. What am I looking at exactly?" Ryan wasn't sure.

"Is that a pineapple?" Jennifer said with surprise, standing behind him.

"That is correct, it is indeed a pineapple, growing in the ground, in Scotland. We've taken some back to the lab. They're ripe and apparently very tasty." the Doctor seemed to add the last piece of information almost as an afterthought.

"Someone ate one? How did you determine they were safe?" Ryan asked, wondering what tests could have been carried out so quickly.

'Erm, well, it wasn't one of my staff. Actually a soldier patrolling the perimeter found one and apparently he was hungry. We've kept him in isolation but he seems fine. We'll watch him for another twenty-four hours just in case."

"Pineapples, growing in Scotland..." Saying it out loud didn't make it any more believable, but now he remembered – hadn't he tripped on one?

"Not just pineapples, Prime Minister. Bananas and plantains too."

"Bananas?!" Ryan and Jennifer looked at each other.

"Bananas," the Doctor confirmed, sounding almost embarrassed. Jennifer and Ryan were equally dumbfounded. What did this mean? They came, they landed, they planted? What kind of alien invasion was this?

"Tropical fruits of all kinds. Vegetables too. I've sent a team out today to collect samples of everything. I'll be sending a list, but plant life that could not survive here normally is growing, thriving and reproducing at a rapid rate in an environment where normally it would wither and die. Our best guess at the moment, is that the ships carried the seeds with them. They're somehow stimulating the climate conditions themselves to enable the growth of the fruits to occur, in the area around each vessel. The growth is confined to an area within one mile of the edge of the ship. Similar reports have come in from other landing sites in Europe. I'm trying to find out more about those in Africa. I should have a fuller picture later today."

So people weren't going to starve, assuming the fruit was edible and the hungry soldier didn't turn green and explode tomorrow.

"Doctor, what about the drill bit we had sent to you from one of the oil rigs. Any luck?" Ryan was keen for news of his Grandmother. She was one of the few relatives he had left that he actually gave a shit about.

"Nothing that we have tried has given us any access to the ship whatsoever. Nothing will penetrate the surface, and we can't seem to replicate whatever the occupants of the bus did that enabled them to open the portal. I would have liked to take them back up to the ship and have them talk me through what happened in person, but we were both reluctant to hold them against their will any longer. I understand the bikers have a rather powerful Civil Rights lawyer working for them now. He's been on the television this morning. If you want their co-operation again, you'll have to tread carefully.'

Ryan wondered if he had made a mistake letting that group go so soon. General Spears would know their location. He always knew where everyone was. What Civil Rights lawyer?

"Which lawyer is this?" Jennifer asked the question for him.

"Imran Patel." The words had barely left the Doctor's mouth when Ryan felt his stomach drop. He knew Patel. The man had been a doctor before he was a lawyer. They had crossed swords before. He had taken the NHS to court on numerous occasions, and always got his clients a healthy settlement before their cases ever went to trial. He knew the courts and the health system inside out, and that was a dangerous combination. Well, that and the fact that the man was a total publicity-seeking prick. He wasn't short on playing the race card to his advantage, either.

"I can tell from your expression that you know him." The Doctor didn't mince her words. He liked this woman, she was straightforward, honest and someone he didn't remotely find attractive, the perfect combination for keeping him focused on the task at hand.

"By reputation. Is there anything else I should know, Doctor?"

"Yes. The air."

"What about it?" Was something wrong with it? We're they all going to be poisoned now?

"I had a report come in from the World Health Organisation in Atlanta late last night. One of the scientists there, Doctor Jeffries…"

"I don't know him…" Ryan had never heard of the man. He knew who Lionel Jeffries was, but doubted they were related.

"Yes, well, he made an interesting observation about the ship landing sites worldwide, and decided to test the air quality around the ship at the Laredo/Rio Grande site. He recorded a change of percentage in the oxygen levels. Nothing too scary, which is to be expected with the increase in vegetation. It was his examination of pollutants that was more interesting. He's writing a paper on it, which, knowing the attitude of their President I'm not sure will see the light of day, but I had a Skype call with him late last night and what he told me about the level of pollutants in his initial tests was very interesting."

"How so?' Please get to the point. His meeting with the President was due to start any minute. He was not known to be the world's most patient man

"There aren't any." Jacobs brought her hands together and interlaced her fingers. Ryan wasn't sure if he'd heard her correctly.

"What do you mean there aren't any?"

"I'll quote him for you – *The air samples I have taken appear to have no known pollutants compared with samples taken five miles away from the edge of the landing site radius, which have levels that register 35% lower than would be expected. The sample would be comparable with samples taken prior to the industrial age.*"

Ryan still didn't quite understand what he was hearing.

"Laymen's terms, please Doctor," Jennifer said, interceding on his behalf. He gave her a look, as if to say "I could have said that" but it came across more as "Yeah, thanks!" in the most sarcastic way possible.

"The air samples around the Mexico ship have somehow been cleared of all pollution, it's like it was before the 1900s. We're carrying out tests of our own on the Aberdeen site right now. I'll have those for you before the end of the day."

"If you could send me a brief summary that I can pass around The Cabinet, Doctor, that would be very helpful. Just keep it simple though. No speculation. Please stick only to what you know for certain. Ministers tend to get confused and panic easily."

Jennifer gave him a thumbs-up. It was good to know he had said something right.

"I am sending a summary report to be distributed among your various departments, Prime Minister. There is one thing not mentioned in the report that I think I should tell you about personally…"

"Oh?" Ryan wondered what that could be. The Doctor leaned into the camera, lowering her voice confidentially, before she spoke.

The Cabinet arrived and took their seats a few minutes later, as Ryan was still pondering the last piece of information Doctor Jacobs had told him. It was something that could not go public under any circumstances. Not yet at least. He told her to keep the information as secret as possible and she readily agreed to do so. He swore Jennifer to an equal level of secrecy. A larger screen had been arranged, where everyone could view the impending conference call with the United States. General Spears sat immediately opposite Ryan, which he found both unnerving and reassuring at the same time. Darren Fine arrived with two of his assistants, a young man and a woman who looked as though she was from Pakistan or somewhere similar. Ryan didn't have the time or the inclination to enquire further. The well-groomed effeminate young man was clearly Fine's cock puppet of the week. They took their seats on his left, towards the end of the table. Ryan noticed that Spears' eyes followed Fine's every move, as if he were taking mental notes on the short PR man's body language. The new Foreign Secretary, Basil Badgers, shuffled in carrying bundles of notes, his floppy hair clearly having not seen a comb since their last meeting. He did at least greet him "Morning, Prime Minister."

He was one of the few to do so. All he got from Fine was a barely discernible nod. Julie Compston, the equally new Head of MI5, came in wearing a very formal tartan matching jacket and skirt. The Scottish would be pleased with that look, making him wonder if she was trying to show solidarity with the people of Aberdeen. Baroness Childs, who was always easier on the eye, arrived looking a little worse for wear today. As Minister for Media, Culture and Sport she had perhaps less weight on her shoulders, at least in the latter two areas. Technically, Darren Fine worked for her but the two of them seemed to communicate very little, from what he could see. She looked like she had hit the Pinot Grigio for the last two days. Her entrance was less graceful than usual. Everyone had bags under their eyes, but hers were especially pronounced, her makeup rushed, and her movements very delicate as she took her seat. She wore a trouser suit that morning, and sat a couple of seats down to his left. Percy Howells, MP for Wales arrived stinking of brandy, but he was at least on time. Ryan feared for his health. The man was more than a little overweight, and in his late fifties was probably a good candidate for a heart attack. The remaining senior staff from Her Majesty's armed forces all arrived at the same time, taking seats as near to General Spears as possible. The First Sea Lord Admiral Alun Flemyng, with his greying ginger hair peeking out from beneath his cap, came immaculately dressed, as did Air Chief Marshall Henry Davies in his RAF blues. Sir Derrick Winston, the London police commissioner arrived in his neatly pressed black uniform. He wondered how many spares everyone had for such an occasion. No one would have done their own ironing, of course. No doubt they all had their own team of dressers as he did but they probably had to make do with one each and not three.

Chief Whip Horace Saunders handed out the summary reports for each Minister present. There was one from Doctor Jacobs, another from the Police and a third on current Military dispositions. The Cabinet was still several posts short of an entire complement, so a number of Junior Ministers then came in to fill the remaining posts vacated by those killed in France. Youthful and full of hope at their sudden promotions, they also all lacked two other vital qualities: experience and courage. Many of them were trembling when they sat down, with one young woman barely able to pick up the jug of water in front of her, she was shaking so hard. Ryan reached over and poured her a glass, with a smile that caused looks of surprise from around the table. She took a nervous gulp.

"Better?" he enquired.

"Yes, thank you, Prime Minister."

Ryan didn't have time right now to find out her name. She was attractive, in a mousey sort of way. Ryan noted that Steven Wandsworth, the Attorney General was also present. He had been on holiday when the terrorist attack had happened. He wasn't sure how he had managed to get back to the UK, but he was grateful to have him in the room. No doubt all sorts of legalities would be raised on various issues today and they would be needing his advice. Everyone delved into their paperwork and began reading the summary reports. Ryan could tell when people reached Doctor Jacobs' report, as eyes began to universally widen around the table. He would only have a brief moment in which to address them, before the conference call. He took to his feet.

"I think I should point out to everyone, as a matter of order, we are now in contact with the Deputy Prime Minister." it was Darren Fine. His two assistants sitting behind him against the wall making notes.

"Do enlighten us, Mr Fine…" the General cut in. Ryan smiled and sat down again. Score one to Fine.

"He was apparently caught up in some kind of panic in Nairobi on his way to the airport, so he and his party tried to reach the airport on foot. There is a landing site close to the capital as we all know. Local army forces panicked and fired on the crowds, causing some kind of stampede and the Deputy became separated from his escort. He is alive, but has two broken legs and is not likely to be reaching the UK any time soon. At least not while the air travel ban remains enforced."

"Then it seems doubtful he could assume his role, even if he were here, what with two broken legs." Compston said, leaning across the table.

"Yes, that was also his opinion. So it looks like we're stuck with you, Ryan," Fine said, with no attempt to hide his caustic tone.

"When speaking to Mr Wallace, you will refer to him as Prime Minister. If we're going to keep law and order in this country, we'd better damn well start in this Cabinet room. Prime Minister…" Spears handed over the floor to him. Ryan was pleased to have the General's support publicly, at least. God knows what he said about him in private.

"Thank you," he said, standing again. He looked for a moment around the room at a great many uncertain faces. A mix of old and new. Fine was sulking.

"I know I have done nothing to deserve this job, and I did give serious thought to turning it over to someone else, but I am going to stay, for the foreseeable future, at least. If there is to be a leadership challenge, well, let it come and I will deal with it then, but frankly right now we have other things to worry about. I am sure you're all reading the scientific reports in front of you. We will get to those shortly, but first I have to speak to the leader of the free world himself, the President of the United States. I know some of you have just taken up your posts today, and I want to thank you for not shying away from that responsibility. Trust me, when I say I know how tempting that must have been. I haven't had a chance to meet all of you yet, but we'll get to that later. I want everyone in this Cabinet to be crystal clear, when I say that our primary concern must be the welfare of the United Kingdom and its citizens. To that end, we must make sure our social infrastructure and services stay intact during the current crisis. This, above all, is vital. Secondly, we need to have a better understanding of the alien question that faces us, if we're going to know how to deal with it."

The Police Commissioner looked up from his desk, "We can't just continue to tell people to stay in their homes. People want answers. Looting is becoming a big problem, especially in the Midlands and last night Westfields in Stratford was ransacked. My officers only just got that under control this morning."

"I know, I read it in your report, Sir Derrick. The Territorials will provide you with adequate back-up and are being deployed as we speak. General Spears will elaborate on their deployments later today. I will provide as much information as I can later to the House." He certainly wouldn't be telling them the most recent piece of information he had found out. It could complicate things, make security around the vessel impossible and create further unrest. One day, and one problem at a time.

"I am just concerned, as I said before, Prime Minister…" Baroness Childs cut in. "That with so many guns on the streets, we might be inviting the potential for some sort of disaster if things get out of hand. God forbid that the Army should fire on civilians who were pushing in at the meat counter in Sainsbury's, but these things can quickly escalate."

Indeed they could, but what choice did he have? Let the country slip into anarchy?

"I did not agree to this deployment lightly, I can assure you. We already have a country close to breaking point. A mass movement of people, panic buying, looting…" Ryan did not feel the need to labour the point.

"Not to mention the financial markets. They've plummeted," said the Chancellor of the Exchequer, Jack Edwards. "Fortunately, for better or for worse, this is the case worldwide."

"I have no doubt they will stabilise in time," Percy Howells stated.

Jennifer came within his eye line, gesturing at the screen.

"Ah, ladies and gentlemen, I believe we're going to speak to the President of the United States now." Ryan brought the room's focus to the large TV screen.

"Prime Minister, may I suggest that we keep this brief and just let him talk. Then we ask questions..." Fine quickly interjected. Ryan gave him a little nod in response. The curtains were quickly drawn to ensure minimum distraction from the sunlight. A young civil servant operated a mouse on the screen. In an instant, the screen was filled with the image of the President sitting at the head of a small table. He was not in the Oval Office, but a compact meeting room of some kind. Judging from the dark monitors behind them and the enclosed nature of the space, it had to be underground. The President had his team sitting alongside on both flanks. Uniformed men of the Armed Forces were there, as was the Secretary of Defence and a handful of other individuals. There were no women on his team, at least not today. *How boring*, thought Ryan, but then this President was known to be easily distracted by a pretty face, especially those from Eastern Europe. He always thought this President looked not dissimilar to the ex-Foreign Secretary, though with a considerably more square shaped head. Now Ryan thought about it, a number of American Presidents did have these very square, box-shaped heads – Kennedy, Bush (senior and junior), Clinton and now this guy... Obama's was more like a football, so Ryan gave him a pass.

"Prime Minister! May I first offer you my personal condolences on the passing of your Prime Minister, the honourable David Jackson, he was a very good man and a good ally to America." His New York drawl was even more pervasive in person, than on reality television.

"I am hopeful that this special relationship between our countries will continue under your leadership, for however long that may be..."

He added the last part somewhat dryly. The smug bastard. He was putting Ryan on the spot immediately, and he knew it. It occurred to him that having no political ambition or giving a shit about one's legacy in office, was going to be a tremendous advantage to him in dealing with this pompous man.

"Mr President. Thank you on behalf of the entire British nation for your sentiments. Due to the current global situation we have no plans for a change of leadership at the present time, so we will be dealing with each other for the foreseeable future..."

The man tried to speak again, but Ryan decided he would start as he meant this relationship to continue.

"We're living in volatile times Mr President. I'm sure you know of the delicate situation between North and South Korea. War could be imminent and now I understand you have a similar problem with the landing site on the Mexico/US border. That must be quite a challenge, to have one of the ships landing between the border of your country and that of your neighbour. I imagine the international legal ramifications over who is allowed to control the air space must present quite a dilemma for you."

Spears glared at him, but everyone else in his Cabinet just froze, except for Darren Fine who rolled his eyes heavenward at Ryan's last statement. The President moved his arms back from the table, allowing one of his Generals to lean in and whisper.

"There's no dilemma. The ship represents a threat to the United States of America and we have acted accordingly. Congress has backed my decision in this matter, as have the country..."

"That's good news Mr President. How does Mexico feel about it?" Ryan cut in. The President squirmed at the question.

"I am in talks with the Mexican President every day. We're consulting over the issue. I guess the United Kingdom has it pretty easy over there with just one landing site to deal with. Americans are having to deal with three on our soil..."

"Well, two a half to be accurate. Fifty percent of your craft is in Mexico."

At that comment, even General Spears did a facepalm that was impossible to suppress. Ryan thought it best to keep going. Britain always did want the Prime Minister from *Love Actually* and hell, he was going to be that man, at least in his dealings with the American President. Didn't Hugh Grant get caught with a hooker once? That didn't seem to hurt his career any.

"I thought in view of our special relationship, Mr President, I should send over the initial findings on our ship in Scotland. I dare say our scientific resources are more limited that your own, but no less diligent. There might be something in there that would be helpful to you."

One of men around the table nodded to the President to indicate that they had received the report. Ryan had earlier detailed Jacobs to send it over to the WHO in Atlanta as soon as possible, omitting one important detail. He was keen to see if the Americans were going to be equally forthcoming about what they had found out.

"Thank you, Prime Minister. If there's anything in there that we haven't discovered ourselves, I am sure I will be informed about it."

Yes, I am sure you will, Ryan thought. The President wasn't going to offer anything in return.

"Perhaps you could have your colleagues do the same? My team would be grateful for any insights you have yourselves. So we can all compare notes, as it were." Ryan said, blandly.

"I am sure we know as much as you do, but I will certainly have them do that." Ryan was certain it would be a good test to see who would reveal the most interesting details to the other, first. He also felt certain that if the UK landing site was creating edible produce and other valuable resources, those in America and indeed worldwide must be already doing the same. If that were the case, his American counterpart would certainly know by now.

"I understand you're keen to lift the ban on air travel," the American President said. Was he? Oh yes, he was. A question about the issue had been raised in Parliament. The transport secretary had also quizzed him about it. British Airways was panicking and their stock had plummeted. Ryanair and EasyJet weren't faring much better. While many people might not have wished to go away at this precise time, being keen to stay with their families, many were stranded on holiday and there were an equal number who wanted to travel to rejoin families abroad, or in many cases simply go home.

"We have certainly been discussing it. At present, as the alien ships appear to present no threat, we were thinking air travel should resume as soon as possible. France has already begun their national flights again. Germany resumes theirs tomorrow. I expect most of Europe will shortly follow suit."

"My Cabinet and I feel it would be better to limit the movement of people in and out of the US, until such a time as we have a better handle on exactly what we're dealing with."

You mean stop people coming into the USA and keep anyone valuable pertaining to the crisis trapped there, Ryan thought.

"Mr President, we do have a huge number of British citizens currently stranded in the United States, who are desperate to get home. Many are people on holiday, most of whom don't have the resources for an extended stay. Can you assure us they'll be taken care of while your Air Travel Ban is still in effect? We will of course extend the same courtesy to your own citizens."

Ryan watched attentively, as he saw the President confer with his advisors, more than one of whom seemed to want to contribute on this issue.

"We'll take care of them. Once we're sure it's safe for them to travel, we will charter planes to send them home. If it comes to it, I will pay for them to come back on a Cruise ship."

Ryan couldn't quite picture that.

"We're most grateful to you. I'll pass that assurance on to the Foreign Office." it was the best he could hope for, but the President was not done with him yet.

"May I also offer you my best wishes for the safe return of your Grandmother? I understand she was involved in a breach of security at your landing site in Scotland. We saw the footage of the bus online."

There was a ripple of laughter among the President's entourage.

"Thank you for your concern about my relative. She was involved in no such breach. She was, in fact, one of the first people to reach the landing site before we even had a chance to restrict access to the area," Ryan countered.

"I'm surprised it took you British so long to secure it. These things are a clear and present danger to the threat of humanity. We can't have senior citizens wandering all over them."

The President's comment drew laughter from his subordinates again. Ryan wasn't going to take that. He had seen the reports of the Rio Grande landing and how much of a headache it was causing the US Government. People were rumoured to have entered that ship too, though this could not yet be substantiated. Ryan was certain it must be true.

"I saw footage of hundreds of Mexican civilians on the surface of the landing site at Laredo. Some sources say several dozen went inside it."

"Our Laredo cross-border landing site comes with additional complications that yours does not. You should be thankful for that Prime Minister."

"Oh I am, Mr President."

"All three of the American landing sites have ships which measure 20 kilometres in diameter. How large is the Scottish ship?"

Oh so we're doing that now are we? I see... thought Ryan. *Time for a bit of my dick is bigger than yours, is it?*

"Ours is only ten. We've noticed this is the one variation in the ships, worldwide. The vessels have varying diameters, but we're not sure why." Ryan tried to bring the conversation back down to a more scientific level.

"Perhaps ours are larger because they know we're a super-power and so more of a threat to them." As the President spoke, his Cabinet room was a sea of nodding heads. He might be right. "Yours is such a smaller country in comparison, Prime Minister."

"Then they must consider Italy the biggest threat of all, as the one in the bay of Taranto is the largest so far I believe. However I am not yet of the view that these things, whatever they are, wherever they're from, intend us any harm at all."

The American President looked shocked. Ryan almost felt like his hair might stand on end if it were able. His reddening face screwed up and he inhaled deeply, as if his life depended on it.

"What scientific data did you use to come to that conclusion?"

Now he really had put himself on the spot. General Spears raised his eyebrows, as if to say, "Yes, which data, indeed?" Darren Fine was almost biting his nails, no doubt eager to witness his downfall.

"Common sense, Mr President. These ships clearly possess intelligence and technology far in advance of our own. Wouldn't you agree that neither of us needs to have a degree in particle physics to come to that conclusion?"

"I would yes, but…"

Ryan wasn't hanging around, he just cut him off without hesitation.

"So having come to that conclusion, their choice of landing sites must in some way be deliberate. It doesn't seem to me that they're random. Very few land anywhere near the world's capitals. In fact, as far as I can see the landings themselves have tried to avoid loss of life. So if it's an invasion, where are the troops? Where's the destruction of our armed forces? I don't see any beams of light and burning cities."

"Prime Minister, the ship in Nevada landed on an area that included a United States Air Force base! We consider this an act of war on their part…" the President's voice grew louder. His patience with Ryan had run out.

"Did you suffer any casualties?" Ryan was certain he would have seen such stories in the American media, if that were the case. If the alien ships needed to be portrayed as the enemy to stir up national feeling, best to do it as soon as possible.

"We're still trying to ascertain the facts of the situation. A number of our people are still unaccounted for. Who knows what they could do next? For all we know, they're building an army inside these things right now! We're not taking any chances!" His face looked like an inflating radish.

"I'm not saying we shouldn't be prudent in our defence. But as far as we can tell, they haven't been aggressive. Maybe they didn't know your base was there." Ryan knew that argument was weak as soon as he said it.

"Prime Minister, a moment ago you're telling us that they must be supremely intelligent, an assessment I agree with. Now you're telling me they would have missed a US Air Force base? Anyone can see it, it's been on goddamn Google Earth for God knows how long. We spent ages trying to get it removed! In our eyes this is an invasion and the United States will take whatever action it deems necessary in order to protect its citizens! I would expect you to do the same in your country. Now if you will forgive me, I have a very scared country to run. I'm glad I can count on your support…"

The screen went black. Support for what? General Spears took a sip of the glass of water in front of him before carefully placing it back on the table. The silence was deafening.

"That went well…" Darren Fine said, closing the folder in front of him.

Maybe being Prime Minister wasn't such a good idea after all, Ryan thought.

CHAPTER IV

"We had a name for the people who started putting up the recordings on line, claiming to be posting them from inside the ships. We called them 'The Insiders' - The first ones who managed to get inside the vessels before the world's military closed them all off. In those first few days there was just a handful of video clips that made it on line to the Social Media channels - Facebook Live, Twitter, Instagram, Snapchat, all had clips and pictures from someone, somewhere, who claimed to be inside one of the vessels. We knew from the word go that the similarity between them all meant that they could not have been hoaxed. They all looked like they were filmed in the same place but came from all over the world. As soon as the clips were put up, they were either taken down again or heavily debunked. That was when I could see how much a threat they were to those who controlled the World Order. They were scared, because they didn't want anyone to have the answers before they did, because they knew once that started happening their hold on humanity would diminish. They could see even then that a change was coming. It was all about control and even as early as the second day they could already see they were losing it. In those first few days and weeks no one really knew what to believe because it was all so new, so alien and well, so unreal I guess. That was before the avalanche. Before the battle lines in humanity were well and truly drawn."

Owen - The Truth Movement. From a found video blog, exact date of recording after Parousia unknown.

OMARI

FADA, CHAD. AFRICA, TIME? APRIL 3RD

"Omari! I thought that was you. I don't remember you looking so well!"

Having collected what little food and supplies he could, Omari was heading back to the house when he practically walked straight into his son-in-law. Malloum had briefly served as the Commander of the military fort in Fada, a posting which had not been to his liking. Omari's oldest daughter, Nya, had however caught his eye. When Omari next returned from his travels, he found the military officer calling on him, asking for her hand in marriage. Malloum never hid his dislike of Fada. For him, it was a nothing posting, rumoured to be given to officers who had upset the President. Omari did wonder what act he might have committed to have been sent to Fada in the first place. But once he'd left with his oldest as his bride, he hadn't expected to see him again. Yet now he was standing before him accompanied by two other soldiers. His rank had not changed, but his uniform appeared crisp and new. The drab olive-green battledress was neat and well-pressed. It was evident he had arrived by plane. Fada had become a hub of activity in the last twenty-four hours, but the amount of military reinforcements had been restricted by the limitations of the Chadian Air Force. Only one transport plane and a single helicopter had arrived. The garrison had been increased in strength by only by another thirty men. Nowhere near enough men to form any kind of workable security around the landing site. Whispers among the townspeople were that many more were coming overland by convoy, but no one knew when they might arrive. Omari recalled the Chadian Air Force only had one C-130 Hercules transport plane and a small number of helicopters to draw on, but he remembered that several of those were unserviceable. He had overheard a conversation about the state of the nations Air Force over a year earlier, during his last trip to the capital, between two pilots in a bar. They had been complaining about the lack of the spare parts available in order to maintain the helicopters. It was odd that he could recall so much detail about a trivial distant memory, yet there it was in his head, as if he heard it only yesterday. He could even picture the two men quite clearly, and recall what they were drinking (two bottles of Tusker beer). His son-in-law greeted him formally as was the custom, then took a moment to look at him, his expression unable to conceal his surprise at Omari's youthful appearance.

"Fada appears to be agreeing with you better than the capital does with me, Omari! You look incredibly well! I have brought a letter from your daughter, and some presents from her for her sister. How is she and your brother doing? I called on him but there was no one home."

Malloum had, of course, met Attah at the wedding ceremony. Attah was always looking for angles to secure new businesses and he remembered the two of them speaking for some time, away from the rest of the guests.

"Joy is fine. Attah told me he was leaving for Abeche to stay with relatives. He wanted to be as far as he could from the thing!"

Omari knew this lie was plausible enough. He had seen a handful of others preparing to leave Fada, as he purchased supplies that morning.

"I understand. We live in strange times. Let us head to your home. My men will help you with your supplies. Stocking up, I see! You always did think ahead, Omari. I always liked that about you. You are a wise, but uncomplicated man."

He wasn't sure if Malloum meant his last statement as a compliment or an insult. Perhaps it was both. The Colonel's men took his bags and they headed back towards his home. Omari had to think fast. How would he explain the presence of Tabitha at the house? She was too young to be an orphan taken in to be maid or a cleaner, though such a thing was not uncommon for families to do in Fada. Omari always thought such practices were slavery in all but name. Take a child in and treat them as your own kin, or not at all. Malloum talked all the way to the house, and Omari listened to his every word. His mind felt sharper than before, capable of listening to the man speak while multi-tasking his other thoughts simultaneously. Only the pool of Allah could have given him such abilities. He debated all his options while nodding at Malloum and absorbing everything he said.

"I had to offer all the men triple pay to even come up here! In the capital everyone is panicking! The army has had desertions in every unit! I can't blame them really. People think it is the end of the world! You know, we flew over it on the way here? Now all around it an oasis has formed. Can you imagine? Trees and water before where there was only sand. My men say fish swim in the streams! Such a thing must be a gift from Allah!"

On that last point, he could not disagree. He continued to complain, elaborating about his mission. He had been ordered to secure the site until reinforcements from the capital arrived by land, but they would not be here for another week. He was chosen to come because of his previous posting, knowing the area, the fort and the people. Nya had begged him not to leave, but the Colonel had reluctantly left her with his mother. His duty was to their President it was that or treason. Omari doubted he wanted to be faced with charges relating to the latter.

"By taking on such a dangerous mission, I am bound to be promoted. If I had refused and it had turned out to be an invasion, I would probably soon have been dead anyway, so why refuse the order?"

He laughed loudly, but Omari saw nothing funny in such a dilemma. Malloum had always had a horrid laugh. He was tall, in his forties with a thick moustache. He was a widower when he arrived in Fada the first time. His first wife was said to have died in childbirth. Omari had never pressed him for details. Now however, he wanted to ask him for news concerning his daughter. Did they have children? Where were they living? Perhaps the information was in the letter that Malloum carried for him. It was better to ask little of him for now, then the sooner he could be rid of him.

"I need a place to stay. With the reinforcements we have brought to the fort, it has become a little overcrowded. When the rest arrive, I daresay it will become unbearable! So I thought, why not call in on my father-in-law? I could stay with him? We are family after all, and we have much to catch up on! So if you will have me, I think I will be more comfortable staying with you for the present!"

Malloum disrespectfully opened the door to his compound, before Omari had even given him permission to enter. This would have caused offence to any other local, but Omari knew it was Malloum's less than polite way of telling him he had little choice but to comply.

"If you think you will be comfortable, our humble home is yours of course but there is not much space."

Omari hurried in behind his guest. Malloum instructed the men who had accompanied them to return to the fort and bring his personal baggage at once, by jeep. Malloum gave a cursory look around the courtyard and peered inside the main building, giving it a nod of approval.

"You're right. The place could do with a good some additional luxuries could it not?"

Joy emerged from the house, exchanging a look with her father. Omari was relieved that Tabitha was nowhere to be seen. Joy greeted Malloum with a traditional bow, before taking his bags inside.

"Your other daughter looks well. It will soon be time for her to marry, eh? I have a cousin who is looking, though he may of course feel your clan is, well… This will suffice, Omari. I can take this one room and you can sleep in the other with your daughter. I am hungry. Can your daughter cook well?"

"That she can. Please sit. I will bring you some sweet tea. You must be tired from your journey."

So they prepared a meal for their guest in silence, as he relaxed in their home. Malloum received several visitors from the fort while waiting for his meal. Several younger officers came and went, with Malloum instructing one to secure a place nearby where the helicopter could land safely. He could be picked up quickly without having to return to the airstrip. It took some time for Omari to find a moment alone with Joy as she began roasting chicken in the kitchen. Omari noticed his daughter was shaking as she cooked the food.

"We will still leave tonight. Bring the best of what we have to drink and let him have his fill," he whispered to her.

Joy simply nodded.

"Is Tabitha safe?"

Joy nodded again, gesturing towards the bedroom.

"We will talk more after dinner."

Omari sat opposite his guest on the floor, as was the custom. It was the first meal his daughter had cooked for him in a very long time and it tasted better than good. Every mouthful was rich and full of flavour, as if his tastebuds had been cleansed. Malloum observed the tradition of not talking until after they had finished, for which Omari was thankful. Malloum stifled a yawn, having eaten his fill of the food and drunk deeply.

"Your daughter cooks well, my friend. I hope you will not be insulted if I say she cooks better than the one I married.'

"Nya was always more interested in the world, than the kitchen," Omari said, knowing that much was true. She always wanted to know what lay beyond their home, beyond the compound, beyond the houses, beyond the oasis, beyond Fada. He wondered if she had made a good wife and Malloum was satisfied. It worried him.

"Can I be excused, Papa?' Joy asked quietly, her head bowed. He dismissed her with the wave of his hand, as if she was inconsequential. A ruse for the Colonel.

"So how does Nya like life in the capital?" Omari sounded almost apologetic as he posed the question.

"It seems to agree with her. She likes the faster life there."

Omari wasn't sure if that was a good thing or not.

"She is very interested in fashion, my wife. Clothes and shoes especially. We had a second wedding there for my family, you understand. I had relatives who were far too old and sick to have made the journey here."

"Of course. I remember you said you had a big family back in N'Djamena."

"Yes, my mother can be quite the tyrant!" He laughed again, though somehow Omari knew that his statement carried little in the way of jest. He did not think he would like to meet Malloum's mother.

"Here, that reminds me." Malloum reached into his top pocket and produced a small letter.

"From your daughter, for you personally. She apologises for the brevity but there was little time for her to write to you as my deployment to the region was rather rushed."

Omari took the small piece of paper and placed in it in the pouch in his belt. He so wanted to read it now, even if it was short. But it was not the right time. He missed Nya. She had always been the problem child, often scolded or beaten by both him and her mother, but she was his daughter and her happiness was always his first concern. Malloum talked more about his family and gave precious little else away about Nya, apart from that she was happy and enjoyed life in the city. It was not the custom for one to speak in detail about one's wife, even to the Father-in-law. The sound of a vehicle outside the gates made Malloum rise at once to his feet.

"Omari, I thank you for this wonderful meal. Much better than what the cook would have served me at the fort. I will have one of my men drop you off some more supplies so you will have everything you need, but for now I must return to brief my men and ensure the people from the town are not taking advantage of the current situation."

Omari wanted to know more, but did not wish to delay his departure any further. He needed him gone.

"I shall return again this evening when I am done with my duties."

"You will be most welcome, of course," Omari said.

Malloum stepped through the gate to a waiting jeep occupied by two men. As Omari watched them depart, he saw the men exchange words as the jeep trundled back through the dusty streets towards the fort. He discovered he could hear their conversation, at a greater distance than he would have thought possible.

"The locals are becoming angry, Colonel. They do not understand why they cannot go and see this wondrous gift from Allah for themselves," The driver explained.

"Who said it was a gift from Allah? We must not call it such a thing. For now, it is a matter of National Security to the entire Chadian population and we must control access to it until we know more. These are the orders of the President himself," Malloum replied.

"But sir, this will be impossible with the small number of men we have. The circumference of the object alone covers dozens of miles. We're having trouble covering the obvious access points from the town as it is…"

Soon they were out of sight and he could hear no more. Omari closed the gate to the compound with a barely concealed sigh of relief. He did not understand why he had been bestowed such gifts but now that he had his energy back he intended to use it. Joy appeared with Tabitha from the second bedroom. He stared at the two girls. Tabitha was not his kin, but from today he felt he must take care of her as if she was his own.

"Where did you hide her?" Omari saw young girl's face was fearful of visits from evil men.

"In the bedroom." Joy led the girl to sit down near the stove. Tabitha's eyes lit up at the sight of the chicken.

"Wash your hands and eat now, both of you. We have to leave as soon as possible."

Omari rushed around his home, packing whatever else he thought he would need. His possessions were minimal. His time was spent seeking personal mementos of his wife rather than practical things that might be useful. He did, after all, have all those prepared from his previous journey. He did everything in the most sensible order, with a speed and efficiency he he'd never been aware he was capable of. Omari looked at his pocket watch. It was 2pm, late afternoon. A helicopter roared overhead and he watched it buzz towards the distant white tower, becoming no more than a black speck against its colossal presence. A knock came from the compound gates. Joy got up from her meal to answer it, but Omari intervened.

"Let me answer, child."

Omari opened a slot on the door's ironwork that allowed him to see out of the gate, but he could see no one. He closed the slot.

"There is no one there."

Once again there was a knock on the gate. A small rapping sound which Omari realised was coming from further down the door. He opened the slot and still could see no one.

"Stand back from the gate, so I may see you," He asked the unknown visitor.

Little Ubba, the street orphan, stepped out from the shadow of the gate. Omari opened the door and the boy jumped through, his eyes searching for someone. Spotting Tabitha, he ran to her at once. The child screamed in excitement at their reunion. Ubba however, had an urgent reason for calling upon them.

"Miss Joy, you must come. Dennis he is going to take all the children away!" The child told her.

"What are you talking about?" Joy asked.

"I overheard him talking with another man. There's a plane coming to take the children from the orphanage later today."

"But this is a good thing, child," said Omari. "They will be safe. Dennis is the teacher, no? He is probably just getting them out of Fada, away from danger."

"Safe? No! Dennis is the danger!" the boy protested.

"Ubba, do not speak in riddles. Tell us what you mean or we cannot help you," Omari said.

"This man to whom Dennis speaks. He is the same man who has taken the girls and boys from the streets to bad places. I have seen it. The children cannot go with this man!"

"Father, we must help," Joy said, without hesitation.

"How can we help?" Omari's heart sank. What were they supposed to do?

"They have to come with us to the White Coconut, Father!" his daughter pleaded.

Omari knew such a burden would be too much for him. He was already responsible for one new child, he could not take any more.

"No. We cannot risk it. How are we going to get a class-full of children through the town without being spotted? It is daylight. Someone will see us," Omari protested, knowing such a thing was impossible.

"I know a way," Ubba chimed in.

"Father please! If anyone knows a way, it is Ubba. Please Father!"

He looked at his daughter with a sense of pride. He could see she would not be deterred on this, even after everything she had been through.

"Come then, let's go to the school!" he said, relenting. Perhaps he could take a dozen children with him with his daughters help. They all departed at once.

The orphanage and school were two compounds that sat side by side in the southern part of the town. Omari travelled with his three camels and the three children, taking the long way round, along the back of the oasis to the east. Tabitha and Joy rode atop of Abu-Sir, who seemed agreeable enough to the idea. Omari observed that all three of his camels looked extremely refreshed and healthy, trotting along at a brisk pace. Every few moments, he would have them slow down so as to not draw undue attention. Fada was normally quiet in the afternoon when the heat was at its fiercest. However, those few people they saw were also preparing to travel, packing up their baggages and bundles. On the southeast side of town, the palm trees grew thicker. A small area of fertile farmland had been enclosed by a long mud and stone wall that ran along the eastern edge of the oasis. They travelled beside it, heading south before turning back west into town again where the compounds and dwellings once again grew more numerous. The western road that led on towards the fort dissected this part of town before trailing off into the larger cluster of dwellings, ahead of them. All four of them turned their heads up towards the sound of an aircraft taking off to the west. Omari had been to the small airstrip west of town only once, many years ago, yet he could picture it now quite clearly. It was nothing more than a simple runway surrounded by some wire, devoid of any buildings. In its direction, they saw a large grey transport aircraft lumbering into the sky, banking to avoid flying directly over the alien object. The plane then turned south and flew right over them. Omari guessed it would be returning to the capital to pick up more men from the army, assuming they could find any more to volunteer for such an unappealing mission. He did not want to wait around and find out. The school was located among the denser part of the oasis just next to the main east-west track. The school buildings had been here as long as Omari could remember, but the orphanage had come a little later. Built alongside and consisting of no more than three huts filled with bunkbeds and a small cook house, it was typical of such institutions in the region. Being built among the shade of actual trees was a luxury for any property in the town. The school itself was made up of four rectangular buildings, all connected to each other, forming a courtyard in the centre. It was one of two schools in Fada for the younger children, where they learned to read, write and count, but little else. For little else was required of the children in one of the most remote towns of the world.

As they approached the school, Omari saw the children were already getting ready to depart. They had assembled beside the buildings holding a small bag each. Omari counted them in his head and found to his relief they were exactly twelve in number. A mixture of boys and girls which he guessed to be between six and ten years of age. Joy was by far the oldest at fourteen. He knew he would depend on her help to get them all through this. If they agreed to come, he also knew he would have to become a Father to them all. He wasn't sure how he felt about that.

Omari brought his camels to a halt. Joy passed Tabitha down to him. The child flung her arms around him tightly, determined not to let him go. Omari held onto the girl, wanting to reassure her everything would be alright. The closer they had got to the school the more agitated she had become. He could tell this was not a place of safety for her. His camels all sat down, grateful for the break in the shade while they approached the group. The children were mostly dressed in tattered hand-me-downs shorts and t-shirts, a wild mix of colours. Most were barefoot. Some of the girls wore red scarves to protect their heads from the sun, but others had none and their scalps were covered in blisters. The children became excited upon seeing their former classmate hanging around his shoulders.

"Tabitha! Look, it is Tabitha!" one of the older girls cried out and ran towards them, her face full of joy upon seeing the child. Several others followed suit and Omari found himself surrounded by a sea of children with their hands reaching to pat Tabitha. The girl still clung to his neck, but smiled at the sight of her friends. Omari turned to the oldest looking girl. She was tall and thin and had the facial markings of a clan that Omari could not recall being from Fada.

"You all know this child? She was from this school?' Omari asked them all. They looked unsure how to answer, with one of the smaller girls tugging on the arm of the eldest as if looking for permission to respond. The older girl stepped forward, arms outstretched to take Tabitha but Omari took a step back. He didn't want anyone touching the child.

"I would not hurt her. I am her friend!" the girl said, looking wounded by his refusal.

"What is your name?" Omari asked her.

"Jodie," the thin girl replied.

"Jodie, do you know Tabitha? Did she go to this school?"

Jodie nodded. Every child did the same. Flies buzzed between their heads in the shade, it was especially hot today. Omari gestured for Joy to pass around the water from his largest flask. She complied, slowly moving among the group, offering each child a sip.

"You look as if you're preparing to travel," Omari said.

"Yes. We have been told we're leaving, because of the white coconut! Our teacher says it is a bad place," Jodie said, pointing towards the white needle on the horizon.

"Let me ask you, Jodie. Who was the last person you saw Tabitha with?"

The children began to whisper to each other, but Omari could hear them all as if each was speaking in his ear. He kept hearing the name "Dennis" and the words, "The Bad Man."

"She was taken away in the night by our teacher. I did not see this, but others did and they told me," she replied. The other children nodded in agreement.

"I saw it! I was there!" Little Ubba said, but his claim was greeted with a sound of universal derision from the other children. Omari had almost forgotten about him. He had slipped from view as soon as they'd arrived, but then there he was popping up from behind one of the palm trees. The reaction from the other children was not surprising. He was, after all, known to be somewhat imaginative when it came to being a source of information.

"He took her away, to a man's house. A bad man," Ubba protested, determined to be heard. The children did not appear to disagree with him on that point. He began to walk among them.

"There is a better place we can go, where no bad man can come. I have seen it. It is Paradise! I have been there!" the boy said, addressing them all.

"No one wants to go to the eastern caves again, Ubba!' one of the older boys said, with a dismissive wave of his hand.

"Not the caves Martin. There!" Ubba pointed up towards the white tower on the western horizon.

"We cannot go there! The army has forbidden it. Everyone is saying it is dangerous. We should leave with Dennis," said the oldest boy.

"I do not want to go with Dennis," said one child, hanging her head.

"Nor do I," said another. Others said the same.

"Your friend Ubba, is right," Omari said, before he could stop himself. "You're not safe with this teacher. I rescued Tabitha from the evil man he left her with. Joy, my daughter, helped me save her." His words caused silence among all the children and a smile from Little Ubba. Someone sticking up for him was rare.

"Is this true, Tabitha?" Jodie asked the child, making eye contact with her. Tabitha nodded, then buried her face in Omari's chest, her arms gripping him ever tighter. Jodie looked at the group. The children stared back at her, uncertain of what to do. Joy stepped forward.

"We must go, all of us, together. You can trust my Father. He is a good man. He has been gone for a long time from Fada, but now he is back to stay."

To see Joy behave in such a way filled Omari with pride. He knew then just how much of her life he had missed. She had grown in ways he had only just begun to witness.

"Can we all come and live with you?" asked the oldest boy.

Omari gave Tabitha over to Joy. It took some effort for him to get the young girl to release her grip, but she appeared to trust him and his daughter, so she took Joy's hand. Omari looked over the group of young innocent faces, each waiting for him to say something. He knew that something evil had taken root in his home town. Evil against the most vulnerable among them, the children. It had not come from death or disease, wild beasts or drought or famine but from evil men who would do them harm to satisfy their own lusts. The teacher, Dennis, could not have acted alone. Omari's own brother was also to blame. With that blame came eternal shame for him and his family. How could he not have seen this? How could he have let this happen? He felt responsible. He must make this right.

"Father. You must tell us what to do," Joy said, as she held Tabitha in her arms, "Father! Where can we go?" she pressed him.

"As Little Ubba said, we must go there!" He pointed at the tower of brilliant white that shone to the west, beckoning them, glinting in the sun. The children all gasped out loud at once, as if he had asked them to complete an impossible task.

"Father, you have been there?" Joy asked, with a confused look.

"I have. Little Ubba is right. It is Paradise, sent by Allah himself. It healed me of my wounds, made me feel better. Younger. Joy, can you ever remember me looking like this?"

His daughter shook her head.

"But what about the soldiers? They've told everyone in the town not to go there. They said you will be shot!" Jodie said, with a worried look.

"I know a way we can do it," Little Ubba said, standing before Omari. The children looked scared. They did not fully trust him, but they knew Joy. She had come and helped at the school many times in the past. Jodie spoke up for them once more.

"Will you take us all?" she asked.

"Of course," Omari replied. Twelve would not be so hard. If they moved quietly, after dark.

"Come, please." Jodie left the shade of the trees and walked into the school through the main entrance, into the inner courtyard where the four buildings met. Omari eyes widened at the sight that greeted him. In the inner courtyard, shaded from the sun, sat at least another two dozen children, some of them missing eyes and limbs. Others looked frail, making the journey with them would be more than a considerable challenge. Now what could he do? He couldn't take some and not the rest. He had to take all or none. Perhaps with the ship being so vast an area to guard, they could still somehow reach it unnoticed. The garrison at the fort could number no more than what, fifty men? Malloum had brought another thirty, so perhaps with officers and support staff there might be one hundred in total. Nowhere near enough for the job. The edges of the craft spanned all the way to the mountains to the north and south. If they travelled far enough out of the way they could surely avoid the army, but how far could such an impaired group realistically travel without being noticed?

"Will you still take us all?" Jodie asked again as he looked round at the expectant faces staring back at him. Girls and boys with shaved heads in a motley collection of faded, ripped clothes and tattered headscarves. Moving such a cumbersome group covertly would be next to impossible, but they couldn't risk waiting for total darkness, they would have to start out as soon as they were able to travel. He turned and took Jodie's hand firmly.

"I will, but I will need your help."

She smiled back at him and turned to the children.

"Get up everyone, we are leaving with Mr Fakim." The children slowly rose as a group and began to gather their things.

"Take only water, clothes and food. You will not need anything else."

"What about our books?" asked a young girl. Omari had not thought about such things.

"Yes, okay, but only what you can carry comfortably, and no more. We have to walk for about six miles, perhaps even more. It will be hot and then later it will be very cold. You must be prepared for both." He gestured for them to follow him.

Joy had already gathered the rest of the children, as Omari and Jodie led the rest out from the school into the shade of palms by the road. They would need to travel south first, then west. North would take too long. In the south lay two small clusters of rocky hills just outside the town which would provide some cover. He felt someone tugging on his arm.

"Mister Fakim, I know a wadi we can use to move along to go west." It was Little Ubba. Omari clasped him by the shoulders hoping to reinforce the importance to the child of what he said next.

"You Ubba, will be our guide. We need to be like you. Move fast and not be seen. But we are many and will be slow. You understand?"

Ubba nodded. They were ready to depart, but they had to be organised. Omari counted the children: including his Joy and Tabitha they now had numbered thirty-nine. Okay, not as many as he thought, but at least three of them could not walk unassisted, but he still had three camels.

"Right, now we're going to be organised into three groups. My camels will carry the children who cannot walk. Do not worry, these are my camels and they can carry people much heavier than you. Jodie will be in charge of the first group, which will go ahead with the smallest children, followed by Joy who will take all the remaining girls and then you, what is your name?" Omari pointed at the oldest boy. He appeared shy and not exactly leadership material but his height made him stand out.

"Martin." The boy looked as though he had been in a fight recently. His right eye was cut above the brow and slightly swollen.

"Martin, how did you get that cut?"

"Dennis did it."

"Why?"

Martin was about to answer when he looked down at his feet and fell silent. All of the other children did the same. Omari couldn't understand their abrupt change of mood, until a voice spoke in South African-accented English behind him.

"Yes, tell him Martin. Why did I hit you?"

Omari turned to find himself facing a short white man dressed in traditional white robes, his face red and peeling, burnt by the sun. He was shorter than Omari, slightly stocky and perhaps in his mid-fifties. Omari's father had always taught him to be mistrustful of foreigners. This man was holding a silver revolver in his hand that had already marked his cards. Martin and the other children backed away, but Omari stood firm before them all, undaunted by Dennis' presence. The man was shaking and sweating. He couldn't stand still. He fidgeted, nervously.

"I assume you are Dennis." Omari didn't need confirmation.

"It's good to see you're all ready to travel! Thank you for getting everyone ready. I see you found Tabitha!" Dennis said, with a smile.

At the very mention of her name, Tabitha flinched and hid behind Joy. Omari saw his daughter take a step back. His camels began to bleat at the man, unhappy with his aggression. Omari knew they could sense danger better than any human.

"Martin, come here," Dennis said, beckoning the older boy towards him. "Gather the children, we're going to assemble outside the fort."

Martin took a step, but Omari stopped him with a wave of a hand.

"Martin is not your son. You may ask him to come to the fort but you may not demand it of him. Nor may you demand it of any of the children here," Omari stated simply. Dennis' face grew redder with rage. He looked at Joy holding Tabitha, then at Omari. Realisation dawned on the man. He grinned, his tongue licking the sweat from his lips. He pointed the gun at Omari. Two women walking past saw what was going on and hurried on about their business.

"You're Attah's brother. Where is he? Why isn't he here?"

"I haven't seen him. Perhaps you're in a better position to tell me of my brother's affairs while I have been away? The children tell me you were bringing young girls to his house. That's true, is it not?" Omari asked, the question draining the redness from the man's face. Omari could see in his eyes that Dennis knew at once of what he spoke. His guilt was immediately palpable, his composure noticeably changing. His hands shook wildly, his eyes darting around furiously.

"You're all coming with me," he shouted, his voice trembling.

"No one is going anywhere with you." Omari stayed rooted to the spot.

"These are my children!" Dennis shouted, his face flushing red.

"These are children of Fada, children of Chad. They do not belong to you."

Dennis raised the gun and pointed it at Omari's temple, causing all the children to gasp and jump back.

"You need to get out of my way." Dennis pressed the gun into Omari's head.

"No."

The sound of another plane arriving, banking in the sky above them. It must have been coming into land. Dennis looked up expectantly.

"Transport's arrived. Children are valuable commodities. They will be the first ones out of here."

Unseen by both Dennis and Omari, Little Ubba screamed as he ran forward. Dennis only catching sight of him at the last second as the boy threw himself at the man's groin. Dennis screamed, his arms flailing wildly discharging a round from the revolver. It went low and wide of Omari, deafening him. The children screamed as Dennis fell, firing a second round into the trees above. Little Ubba plunged his teeth into the man's groin through the loose fitting cotton trousers he wore, and bit down hard.

"You fucking little cunt!" Dennis screamed in agony.

Omari was already on him. His foot came down on Dennis' arm. He kneeled on his chest and took the weapon. Dennis laughed at him.

"You'll be in so much trouble now. All of you!"

"We shall see." Omari hadn't wanted to hit another man so soon, but he took the pistol and cracked it hard across the white man's face, feeling his nose break under the blow. Omari was again surprised at his new-found strength, but he prayed he wouldn't have to use it in such a way again. Dennis was unconscious. Omari took the gun and pointed it at Dennis, his own hand shaking now. This man had caused pain to many, no doubt far more than he was probably aware of. The world would surely be better off with him sent to the afterlife.

"Father, no!" Joy called out from behind him.

Omari turned to see Joy had fallen to her knees, dropping Tabitha who was crying loudly. Jodie took the tearful girl up in her arms. Joy was holding her chest and it was only then that Omari saw it was awash with blood, seeping between her fingers.

"Father... I can't stop it..." The words had barely left her lips when Joy swayed and collapsed. Omari ran to her side and pulled her to him. She had been shot in the stomach. He knew he had to dress the wound, stop it from bleeding, somehow.

"Jodie. Get me a towel, a clean dress, anything to bind the wound. Quickly girl!" The older girl ran into the school while the other children looked on, frozen in horror. Omari inspected the wound. It was in her side. There was much blood, but if they could get inside the ship, then maybe there was a chance. His hands began to tremble as rage and pain seared through him. He knew what he must do. There could be no delay.

"Everyone, we must go now. Quickly. Gather your things! Abu-Sir! Up!"

The three camels took the lead and were at once on their feet, raising up the weaker children into the air, carrying seven between them. Martin came running back with an improvised stretcher. With his help, Omari carefully placed his daughter upon it. Jodie followed with several clean towels and a dress, that Omari used to apply pressure and form a dressing. He nominated Martin and another older boy to carry her. He took his daughter's hand.

"Joy, can you hear me? Allah, please let her hear me!"

She squeezed his hand, and her eyelids moved a little.

"Don't talk. You're going to be all right. Just hang on for me, my daughter. Please hang on!" He cradled his daughter's head gently. Omari stood, all the children waiting on him. Martin, and Jodie carrying little Tabitha, who was wiping the tears from her eyes.

"Joy. Don't die," Tabitha said.

"Everyone drink some water now, and fill your bottles. We will be moving fast."

Martin looked at Dennis. "What do we do with him?"

"Tie him up in the school and knock him out again."

Little Ubba led a group of children, who dragged the man's body away inside. Ubba ensured the man was given a hard kick to the groin before they left him. Blood seeped through his clothing from his testicles.

"Are we going to the Doctor's for help?" Jodie asked.

Omari looked up at the white tower as the low-hanging sun began to turn the clouds yellow and orange.

"There is only one place that can help her now! Let's go! Quickly!" With Little Ubba as their guide, the group moved quickly out of town and towards the alien structure, its white tower ascending to the heavens, growing ever taller before them.

BLESSING

ABERDEEN, SCOTLAND, TIME APRIL 4TH

"Oh my Lord please forgive me." She repeated the phrase over and over quietly to herself. The first thing she noticed when she awoke was that she was not in her own bed. The second was how much her head hurt. The third was that there was a caramel-coloured arm wrapped around her pulling her close to the warm body that lay alongside her. The fourth was that she was completely naked, a realisation that caused her to immediately pull the bedcovers up to her neck. The fifth was as she looked to the heavens for answers, to her surprise she bore witness to herself, lying in bed with another woman. The ceiling above her held a large mirror. At once, she looked away in shame. How did this happen? She had sinned most grievously, yet she did not want to get up from the bed. The light of day filtered through the red curtains, which moved with the breeze, bringing cold morning air into the room. It stirred the smells of burnt incense and candle wax. As the events of the previous evening all came flooding back to her, they brought with them a tremendous sense of guilt. She lay in a king-size bed, stretched out upon smooth, silk sheets that felt cool beneath her skin. A luxury compared to the tiny bed at her flat. This was a four-poster with carved columns of dark brown wood. It could have accommodated four people comfortably. Her limbs ached but she felt relaxed, despite the thumping headache. She'd had headaches before but not one like this. Was this what people called a hangover? Now she knew why her Mother had always referred to alcohol as *the Demon Drink* – that said, she'd caught her drinking brandy on a number of occasions but this had been explained to her as a medical necessity to help her Mother sleep. She found herself taking a deep breath. Everything she had been taught to believe told her that this was wrong. Yet while the arm lay around her, pulling her close to the body of the woman lying beside her, she felt connected, protected, warm and safe. No one else had ever made her feel such a way before. No, it was wrong. What happened last night... oh... they had kissed... they had touched each other... and so much more. It was already getting light when they finally decided to sleep, falling exhausted into each other's arms. Rain had given her so much last night, not just physically but mentally too. It hadn't just been sexual, they had talked, really talked. Conversations on a whole other level to any that she had ever had before. She had listened to everything Blessing had told her, about her life, the death of her parents, losing her virginity, coming to England, being diagnosed, going on medication, the death of her sister, trying to have a normal life, trying to date, all her insecurities... Blessing had listened too. Rain told her about her adventures in Los Angeles, her life in the pornographic industry and what had followed after. The people who had been good to her, the people who had used her and everyone in between. Stories of ex-boyfriends and girlfriends, break-ups and make-ups, the love and hurt, the good times and the bad had all been shared between them. And physically, well, the girl had opened her eyes to a world of sexual possibility which she knew should have made her feel dirty and disgusted, yet this was not the case. It was completely different from being with a man, last night had been all about her – Rain had taken her to heaven and back, more than once – so how could that be wrong? Was she gay? Her very first experience of sex had left her with a burden which she had to carry every day. In her mind she had justified it as a punishment for sins committed, thought she could not think of any sin for which she would have deserved to have been raped. It had been an event in her life that she tried to remove from her memory but which had come back to her with absolute clarity during that moment of connection between them on the coach. What had occurred between them both last night had been, well... indescribable by comparison. Was this really how sex was supposed to be? Exhilarating, exciting, emotional, unpredictable and so, well, long. She had never seen so many sex toys either, several of which now sat in a bowl like a pile of washing up waiting to be done. They had done so much together, all over the room, not just on the bed and they had used things... things for pleasure... now she felt the need to go to church. She was actually lying in bed with a porn star. She really did need to speak to God, to her Pastor, preferably the less creepy one and ask for guidance and forgiveness. She did not want to incur His wrath a second time. Yet the connection between her and this woman was something she did not desire to ever end. The experience between them on the bus. Something like that couldn't have been normal, could it? They saw everything in each other's past in a single moment. How was that even possible?

She looked around the bedroom. Everything was either red, black or made from dark wood. Posters adorned the black walls depicting characters from the world of Asian cinema. On one wall there were depictions of animated female characters holding swords in power stances, while others were actresses that she recognised from one TV series or another. The other wall had a series of posters for films – The names of the films seemed familiar, yet wrong somehow. Each poster contained a cluster of attractive female models wearing very little, smiling back at her. Each poster was framed and appeared to have signatures written on them. Underneath, atop of a large chest of drawers sat a cluster of award trophies. Some had the appearance of Oscar statuettes but had plaques with the letters *AVN* on the baseplate. She had no idea what that stood for. There were half a dozen or so grouped together, but she couldn't read the inscription on the plaques from here. Mounted on the wall above them was the largest poster of all, depicting a group of four girls clustered around a most striking woman in the centre, all wearing shiny silver outfits and matching boots. Last night, there had not been much time to examine posters. It took a moment to realise the pretty, mixed-race girl with the cropped pink hair standing front and centre, holding what looked like a ray gun, was the girl sleeping next to her. The film was called *Hotties of the Galaxy,* under which was a log line that read *They're coming in your universe to save you…*

Coming. God. This girl had made her have an orgasm, and not just once. Her friends back home had talked about such a thing, as though it were a myth. A reflection perhaps of the abilities of the male company that her friends had chosen to keep. She gingerly removed the hand around her and viscerally felt the moment the physical connection between them was broken. A distinct shiver went through her body, as if someone had walked over her grave. Rain stirred in the bed and turned to one side, stretching out her legs. Blessing could still taste her on her lips from the night before. She slipped out of bed and went to get dressed. Finding her clothes was a challenge, as they were scattered all around the room. She finally found her bra, jeans, socks and jacket, but of her underwear there was no sign. Stepping softly, she gazed at a collection of photographs showing Rain with friends, some of whom she recognised from the myriad images that had flooded her mind when they had connected. One girl she immediately identified as Roxy, a girl who had been for Rain a source of tremendous pain. Last night they had talked about past relationships, while she lay in Rain's arms on the leather beanbag, a soft warm furry throw wrapped around them both as they talked. Blessing's account of her life of love and loss had been relatively short in comparison to that of her new friend. Rain explained there had been seven special people in her life, but Roxy, a girl who had left her for another girl, had hurt her more than any other. It was the only time last night she'd seen Rain getting angry and tearful as they talked. Blessing suggested they changed the subject, but Rain explained it would do her good to talk about it, as she hadn't for some time and felt she needed to unload, if Blessing was willing to listen. She had responded by giving the girl a kiss, the first time she had ever initiated a physical act with anyone. It was not in her nature to be so forward, and certainly not to kiss someone of the same sex. Yet she had, and by then with some degree of confidence. How alien such a feeling was to her! Confidence. The night had been a whirlwind of new senses and experiences. How it had left her feeling was not going to be easily forgotten. As she quietly put on her clothes, she examined the award trophies more closely. One read *For Best Oral Scene,* which made her wonder if that had been on a girl or a boy.

"I never won the big one, sadly... The AVN part stands for Adult Video News." Rain had sat up in the bed and was looking at her with her head resting on one hand.

"The big one?" Blessing could only guess which category Rain was referring to.

"Best Actress or Female Performer of the Year."

"I see you won Best Supporting Actress," Blessing noted, looking at another statuette.

"Yup. I think they gave a few of us ethnic girls that one." Rain's response felt a little dry. Was she implying her industry was racist? How could it be? She had seen interracial sex scenes on the internet before, only by accident of course. She never watched them, well, not all the way through. When she had, she always went to church afterwards and prayed.

"Have any black girls ever won? Girls as dark as me?"

"I don't think so honey, no, but I stopped following it after 2017."

"What about someone mixed, like you?"

"They gave it to some Cherokee Indian once, and a Japanese girl I think, back in the 1990s. I'm so over that industry! Don't get me wrong, I have few regrets, I'm just glad to be out of it. My sex life lost something for a while. I guess it lost its intimacy. I forgot what that really felt like, until last night." Rain's eyes flashed at her.

"It seems a bit racist. You never told me about these last night," Blessing said, reading the inscription on each of the awards. It seemed so alien to her for someone to win a trophy for a sexual act, and on camera too.

'We were talking about more important things. It's an industry predominantly run by old white men, so maybe it is a little racist. Who knows? I'm past caring about it all now. Always look to the future, hun - never behind you, otherwise you can't move forwards in life."

Didn't someone else say that to her once? She couldn't remember right now who or when. Rain got up out of the bed and reached for her sapphire kimono, lying on the back of the black leather chair. Last night had been all dim lights and candles. She gazed at her body, feeling guilty for even looking at her, but that guilt was kept firmly outside the gates of her desires. She watched the girl stand and reach for the garment, her caramel-coloured skin decorated in several places by a series of complex tattoos. Rain had told her the story behind each of them the previous evening – every one relating to a different moment in her personal history. She was fascinating to listen to and equally so to look at. Her skin was so smooth and everything about her looked and felt natural.

"If they had an award for most beautiful actress, you'd have won it."

Rain stopped, turning and staring at Blessing as if scanning her for the sincerity of the comment. She instantly regretted saying it, it was only going to make a complex situation worse.

"You're very sweet to say that. There's lots of beautiful women in the world. I'm looking at one right now."

She blushed. God. She had to go and pray. She turned away, checking she had all her things. She still didn't have her underwear.

"I need to check in with work," she said. It was a feeble excuse to leave.

"So, check in. I charged your phone for you. You had a few texts come in while you were sleeping." She pointed to where her mobile was plugged in.

"You read them?" Blessing hoped she hadn't. Not that there would be anything interesting.

"Of course I didn't! I'm not like that. They're your personal business. I just heard the alert going off."

"Yes, okay. Thank you. Didn't you sleep the same time as me?"

"Soon after. I just watched you sleep for a little bit first."

Blessing turned around to look her in the eye. Rain just sat there, smiling.

"Did you like it, your old job? Sleeping with all those people?" She hadn't wanted to ask her that last night, but for some reason she wanted to know now.

"Sometimes. It was just a job, something I did. It was sex, not love. There's a big difference."

"Men and women?"

"Yup. You know all this. You saw it all. When we connected and again last night."

"Yes, but we didn't actually talk about how you felt about it," Blessing added.

"So, we're talking now. I did guys and girls. I sucked a lot of cock. I ate a lot of pussy. I got fucked a whole bunch of times and I got paid a bunch of money, and I got out. You stay in that industry too long, it will just eat you alive."

"So which did you prefer – guys or girls?" Blessing wasn't even sure why she asked her that question.

Rain laughed a little, and sat back, folding her arms.

"Which did I prefer? Right…"

Blessing needed to go. She grabbed her bag and headed for the door. Rain was up off her feet in an instant, sliding quickly between her and the door. The two of them were face to face. Everyone had their own scent and Blessing found Rain's to be almost overpowering. God, she smelled so good. There was something Asian about her face, the shape of her eyes. Her upper lip was fuller than the lower one. She had a small gold ring piercing through her right nostril.

"Girls." She pulled Blessing to her and kissed her softly on the lips. She wanted to stay, but she couldn't. Not right now.

"I really must go," she blurted out.

Rain removed her hands, and stepped aside opening the door from the bedroom. She walked over to her desk and retrieved a bunch of keys from her purse.

"I'll unlock the front door to let you out."

At the door to the apartment, Rain unlocked and held the door open for her. Blessing didn't know how to say goodbye, she wasn't even sure that she wanted to. Everything was so confusing and she needed clarity; something that she would not be able to obtain if she stayed here. She gave Rain a smile and stepped out onto the landing. Rain grabbed her hand causing her to stop.

"This. You and me. This means something. The connection we had. I don't know what, I mean I'm not sure what it is exactly… I… I will need… just call me, okay? We can talk. This has been intense, I know. For me, too. I know you might think this is all normal for me. It's not, okay? This is very different. You have my number. Just call or text me or whatever. Okay?"

"I will, I just need…? Blessing stammered.

"I know. It's okay." Rain gave her hand a gentle squeeze, biting down on her lower lip as she did so. Blessing just nodded. If she didn't leave now she never would. She dashed down the stairs and Rain shut the door behind her.

The apartment was above the shops on Union Street, the main shopping thoroughfare that cut down the middle of Aberdeen city centre. Checking the time, she saw it was midday. She'd slept in later than she intended. A cold wind coming in from the sea cut into her, as she stepped outside. She did up her coat. As she walked past the collection of Estate Agents, mobile phone providers and charity shops, she noticed two out of every three were closed. They had signs in the window reading, *Sorry not enough staff to open today.* The select few that had opened their doors seemed largely empty, with the staff idle, glued to their phones, laptops or television sets, following the latest news reports. Though devoid of cars, the streets of Aberdeen were not entirely empty. Groups of people were walking steadily past her, turning right through a large pair of iron gates on the other side of the road up ahead. Blessing crossed the road and stopped, taking a breath while trying to process all the events of the last seventy-two hours. She had gone from her regular daily, admittedly boring, routine to witnessing the landing of a ship from another world, to taking a bus and riding on top of it, to being arrested, being released and then drinking with and kissing a girl she had only met three days ago. Actually they did a hell of a lot more than just kiss. What had she done? She prayed the Lord would forgive her. The sound of helicopters could be heard overhead, she glanced up in time to see three, the same in design as the one which she had briefly flown in, heading west towards the white spire on the horizon.

"Come to the midday mass, child. We're praying for a positive outcome."

The man who stood before her couldn't have been much older than forty, and was wrapped up in a bright blue padded jacket. He wore a black beanie on his head, preventing Blessing from assessing his amount of hair loss. She didn't like bald men. She took the flyer from him and read the contents. It was for a church service. Of course. How could she be so dumb? She was standing right outside one of Aberdeen's largest churches, The Kirk of Saint Nicolas Uniting. Though she wasn't sure what the building was uniting exactly. Set back from the road with an ample garden, the building was partly concealed by a number of high stone walls and set between the run of shops on the High Street. Its singular tower was very gothic in nature, with a number of unique carvings that crept along its worn stone corners. Despite her Christian beliefs, Blessing had always found the old-style British churches a little oppressive. Stone bastions of ugly architecture. Give her a Greek or Spanish church any day, not that she had ever visited one, only seen them in pictures. Her mind turned to the fate of the sweet elderly woman, Agatha, who had accompanied them on her adventure. She wondered as to her fate and felt a little responsible for her fate.

"Hey, don't I know you?" the man standing by the gates asked. She certainly didn't know him. Did she have *sinner* written across her forehead? The guilt, there it was again, flooding her feelings as if a dam had been broken.

"No, sorry. I don't think so." She rushed through the gates and joined others heading towards the house of the Lord. A place to pray. A place to think. If Blessing had looked up back at the windows of the flat she had just left, she would have seen Rain sitting at the window, willing the girl to turn around and come back to her. Not today. Blessing had visited Saint Nicolas before, soon after her arrival in Aberdeen. It had been a very pleasant service, also attended by a small number of Ghanaians and Nigerians. That was exactly why she did not go back there. She and other Africans in a small community would always be in each other's business, and her clinic was just up the road. Bumping into a fellow parishioner at an importune moment was almost inevitable. So she chose another church, further out of the city but that hadn't worked out too well either. The Pastor there was more interested in studying her body than he was in studying the Bible. Today however, she needed guidance and this was the nearest place. As she entered, the attendance was an extreme contrast to her previous visit. She had never seen the church so full. It was rammed with people of all types; children, the elderly, teenagers, business men in suits sat next to single mothers with prams, different races and ages. The pews were packed. More people stood at the back. Down the front, the Priest, Father Walters, who had only been its Reverend for a short time, was talking to several other men of the cloth, from various different denominations. While they waited for the service to begin, people were scrolling through their news feeds on their phones or had copies of the local newspapers which all ran dramatic headlines; *Aliens land in Aberdeen.* ran one, while another had a photograph of Agatha with a byline of *Where is the Grandmother of Britain's Prime Minister?* So that was who she was! Agatha had never said anything, but then it was doubtful she even knew her Grandson had been made Prime Minister. Everything had happened so fast the last few days. No wonder the man who visited them had been so keen for information on Agatha's whereabouts. She found a small space on the end of a pew, about half way down the aisle, just as Father Walters took the pulpit. A man in front of her was reading the Aberdeen local paper, The Evening Express. It was yesterday's copy. The front page headline read *Is Aberdeen to be evacuated?* The by-line underneath read, *Exclusion security zone expanded to Westhill and Petercutler.* Security Zone? She wondered how on earth would she ever get back to the ship. She wanted to find Agatha, and she wanted Rain to go with her. She hoped God would give her some answers. Father Walters stood at his lectern and smiled down at his flock.

"Hello everyone. I would like to welcome you all, no matter what your religious conviction or beliefs, to The Kirk of Saint Nicolas Uniting on this rather fresh April day in Aberdeen. It has been a while since I have had to take to this pulpit. Numbers normally being such that people can hear me quite well without using it, but today is a little different. My apologies to those standing at the back! We have put out all the seats we can without risking a breach of the fire regulations."

A small wave of nervous laughter broke out among some of the regulars.

"My predecessor, the good Reverend Stephen Taylor gave me some advice before his departure from this post. He said he had built his congregation upon a belief of openness, making sure all were always welcome here. I see, well, many faces that I have not seen before today. For many of you it might have been some time that you have felt the need in your lives to talk to God. For some today, it may even be the first time. Be that as it may, I can assure you, that all of you are welcome here."

The Priest paused, waiting for a few late arrivals to settle, nodding to them, as they squeezed in at the back.

"I am sure that many a sermon, in many a place of worship around the world today is beginning with the words: we live in uncertain times. I think that in the history of the world, that was never truer than it is today. I have been asked by many of you, is this all a sign from the Lord? Are these ships with their mighty towers; if not worldly, perhaps godly? We all have so many questions we want the answers to, and that is not so different from a few days ago when people would ask me – Father how can I cope with my problems – I don't have enough money, my partner has left me, I feel alone. Our questions today maybe be different but our needs today are much the same. How can we cope in the face of uncertainty?"

His statement caused a sea of nodding heads, in approval. Blessing conceded Reverend Walters was a vast improvement over her local Pastor, who spent most of his sermon talking about himself and how his own experiences had made him such a wonderful person. She hoped she might be able to talk to this Reverend Walters alone later, if time permitted.

"How, indeed? We look to those who run the country for answers, but it appears they know little more about where and why these vessels have come from than you or I do. So we must place our trust and faith in a higher power, we must trust in our Lord Saviour, Jesus Christ... Amen."

"Amen..." the congregation murmured in uncertain agreement.

Blessing couldn't help but wonder where God was at this particular moment in time. The world had faced massive devastation and destruction before, but that was of man's own making. This time it faced a threat that was not of this earth. This time, the entire human race could be destroyed. What would the point be in that? Surely God had better plans for us, didn't he?

"If we are all God's children, then our visitors must be his children too. Perhaps they could even be messengers from God. I know, it is one of the questions we all want an answer to. Whoever they are, wherever they have come from, when we do finally get to meet them, we must greet them not with fear or violence, but with friendship and love. Two words that must have a greater meaning for us all today. Many of us are strangers here, brought together in this holy place by our fear of the unknown. We do not yet know one another. You may have passed each other in the streets, stood next to each other when queuing for your lottery ticket, or in the pub, but we are not all friends. Yet perhaps today, of all days, we should be. We should follow in the footsteps of our Saviour and follow his example, offering our friendship and love to those of us who are afraid, who feel alone, who fear what tomorrow brings."

Damn, this priest was good. She regretted her decision not to come back here.

"Now I want all of you to turn to the person on your left and right, shake their hands and tell them your name, then give them a hug. Tell them everything is going to be okay. Can you do that for me?"

The congregation hesitated, but slowly people began to comply. They turned to the neighbours, nervously chatting. Greetings were exchanged followed by words of shallow reassurance. Blessing's turn came a beat after everyone else, as the only person she was sitting next to turned to their right first, presenting a little delay. The only person she wanted to hug was Rain. The girl had left an indelible impression upon her and one she was finding hard to forget. A feeling of guilt filled her, not this time for what had occurred between them, but for the way she had just left her, while such a dilemma hung over the world. Rain had many friends, sure, so she was unlikely to be alone for long but they had shared something truly wonderful. It was unique and it felt like... like love. Was it love? Blessing stood up before the man next to her had a chance to introduce himself, and headed down the aisle towards the exit.

"You're leaving us so soon, child – why?"

The voice boomed out of the speakers. It took a moment before she realised it was directed at her. As she slowly turned around, she could feel the eyes of the congregation upon her.

"Hey, she's that black girl who was on the bus!" shouted a young woman who evidently felt the need to bring her race into it.

"Aye, it fookin' is her alright - sorry Father!" said another man.

Reverend Walters beckoned her to approach him.

"Please child, come forwards."

She didn't want to. She wanted to run. She wanted to go back to Rain. Coming here was a mistake.

"Please," the Reverend sounded reassuring and truthful. She had to place her trust in God. She nervously began to walk up the aisle towards him, when she spotted her own Pastor sitting with several other Priests in the front pew. What was he doing here?

"Tell us what you know!" shouted a woman.

"Did you get inside? Did you meet the aliens?" cried another.

Father Walters came down from the pulpit and stood in front of the altar, his arms open.

"Don't be afraid, my child. The people just want answers."

Blessing turned to the congregation and saw the sea of faces gazing back at her with expectation. They had expressions of fear and uncertainty, dread and apprehension.

"I... I can't tell you anything. I don't know how Agatha got inside. One moment she was there, the next she was gone. Then the Army took us off and we couldn't get back. We didn't want to leave, not without our friend who had come with us. I came here to pray today like the rest of you... pray for her safe return and pray for myself, for forgiveness."

She could barely get the words out. Public speaking was not her forte and the forgiveness she sought was not from them but from God alone.

"You must have seen something, or found something?" one voice yelled from the back, sounding English and impatient.

"Can ye tell us anything else?" came a very thick female Scottish accent from down the front.

"There really is nothing else I can tell you. I am sure the government knows more than I do."

"What did it feel like? The surface, walking on it?" asked one man.

"Aye, lassie and what did it smell like?" asked another.

More questions fired at her left and right. She looked to the Reverend for protection, but his expression remained passive. She closed her eyes and recalled the moment she walked upon the vessel.

"It felt warm and smooth to walk on and the smell was... it was sweet."

The crowd murmured at this.

"How do we know you're not infected then, eh?" came a more hostile-sounding voice.

"Yeah, shouldn't they have kept you in some kind of quarantine or summat?" fired off another.

Reverend Walters stepped down into the aisle and placed his hands upon her. She felt uneasy. The last time a man of the cloth had laid his hands upon her, it had not ended well, and that was someone she had taken into her confidence. Reverend Walters smiled at her reassuringly, before turning to his congregation.

"This young woman has come into the house of the Lord, and so she should be loved and protected, not hounded and harassed. Did she not walk in a place that descended from the heavens? Who are we to say that she has not been touched by God? It could be by his very will that she stands before us all today. Perhaps her message to us is not to be afraid of that which has come, but to embrace it! Is that your message for us, child?"

"I am not a child and I have no message for you." Blessing stepped away from the man and, for a nanosecond, felt a tinge of anger from him at the rejection.

"But the Lord brought you here to us, today, did he not?" he pressed.

She nodded, knowing she could not disagree with that, but she was confused.

"I came here to pray and ask for his forgiveness, I am not a messenger..."

Another woman stood up.

"Father, how do we know these ships are not vessels from the Devil?" She was in her fifties had the appearance of a regular conservative church-goer; the sort that would always demand to run the cake stall at the summer fête. Blessing could understand the woman's apprehension but she knew she was wrong. Somehow, in her heart, she just knew.

"These things are not of the Devil," she countered.

"How can you be so sure?" the woman challenged her, standing up.

"I know, because I was there. I cannot say that the vessels are of Christ, but they're not evil…"

"You can't be certain of that!" the woman cried, turning to the congregation for support. Many were nodding their heads in agreement.

"Yes, I can! An evil thing would not show me how to love…"

Blessing was trying to articulate the thoughts in her head. It was difficult to clarify the connection she had felt when she had touched the walls of the vessel. She felt the spirit of the ship had somehow transferred to her and Rain, giving them briefly the ability to read each other's thoughts, see each other's past and so much more. Reverend Walters stepped towards her again, his arms open, willing her to come into the fold, yet she sensed a need from the man to dominate and control her. She stepped back.

'How did it show you how to love? Tell us, young lady."

The entire congregation fell silent.

"I… I kissed another person like never before… it showed me the way. I felt love, real love for the first time…"

The Reverend looked upon her with a warm yet somehow artificial smile. "You see, this is God's work. Only a vessel of the Lord could guide you in such a way."

"I kissed another woman," Blessing blurted out. The Reverend tried to maintain his composure, but the summer fête woman, who was still standing aggressively turned to the congregation.

"You see! These things are not of the Lord, they're here to create havoc and chaos, they're here to make us stray from the path!" Her cries drew mutterings of agreement. Another man stood, his accent more southern.

"Anything could have happened to her! She could be an alien for all we know. Hasn't anyone ever seen *Invasion of the Body Snatchers?* Jesus wept! Oh, sorry Father!"

Sounds of scuffling came from the entrance, followed by a familiar dry Scottish voice.

"Leave the lassie alone, why don't youse! She came here to pray, not to be interrogated!"

It was Elvis. Still in his bus uniform, he pushed through the crowds at the back and ran up the aisle towards her.

"This wee lassie needs to rest, she's been through a lot and youse ain't helping none!" he shouted

Blessing couldn't believe he was here. She ran towards him, the two of them almost colliding with a hug in the middle. She was so pleased to see him that she was weeping with happiness.

"He disnae look like much of a lesbian to me," muttered one confused parishioner watching them embrace.

"Child, you're welcome to stay with us and pray," the Reverend said kindly. She didn't want to stay, now people knew who she was. She wanted to go. She turned to the congregation.

"I can't stay here. You people want answers that I don't have. To find them, you'll need to go to the ship yourselves!"

The crowd looked as confused and lost as she was. Elvis promptly took her hand and led her towards the church exit.

"Come on, lassie, let's get oot of here! This could turn nasty, like."

Those standing at the rear were slow to part, but Elvis snarled at them and they soon gave way.

"Come back to us child and your sins will be forgiven! You cannot run from God!" were the last words she heard from the Reverend as they bolted into the cold air outside. They hurried through the grounds to the gate.

"I've been looking for you ever since I got back into town, like," Elvis told her as they ignored stares from people who had been standing listening to the service outside.

"How did you find me?"

"I knew youse were religious. This is the grandest church in all Aberdeen. Not rocket science is it, lassie?" No, she supposed it wasn't. "Looks like I arrived just in time, eh?" He had. She was grateful.

"Someone said they recognised me."

"Aye, we've been all over the press and TV, lassie. Front page! You'd better be getting yourself a pair of dark glasses, noo." Elvis gave her a smile. She noticed his teeth were still completely white.

"I hated being put on the spot like that. Making me speak in front of everyone. It's not who I am!" She sounded angry.

"You did all right, like. Any hoo, I want to get the gang back together. I have a plan."

"The gang? A plan to do what?" They walked through the church gates. Elvis gestured towards a small, strange-looking vehicle that was parked outside. Blessing was embarrassed to get into such a car. For starters, it was a rather gaudy gold colour, and although it was clean, it appeared to only have three wheels. One at the front, two at the back.

"This is yours?" she asked with some hesitation, unsure if she even wanted to know.

"Aye, it'll be the first time I ever parked her on this street without having to worry about a parking ticket. Get in."

He opened the door for her, but she hesitated until she noticed several of the parishioners were in slow pursuit, no doubt wanting to press her further for information. She got in the passenger side and Elvis got in the other.

"I can't believe you drive a huge bus and you own this tiny car."

"There's nowt wrong with this vehicle. Robin Reliants are very, well, reliable, like."

As the car started with a series of grinding noises, he pushed a tape cassette into the antiquated music system. She couldn't remember the last time she had seen a cassette. A song came on at once. Blessing was fairly certain it was the same male American singer she had heard on his bus. A small plastic toy figurine of the male singer dressed in white with black hair wiggled on the dashboard, as the car pulled away. She wondered if it were a toy doll from *America's Got Talent*.

You can shake an apple off an apple tree
Shake-a, shake-sugar
But you'll never shake me
Uh-uh-uh
No-sir-ee, uh, uh
I'm gonna stick like glue
Stick because I'm stuck on you...

Blessing sincerely hoped the lyrics of the song would not turn out to be prophetic. They sped through the deserted northern suburbs of Aberdeen and entered a housing estate where all the houses looked the same. Blessing saw one family tying their possessions to the roof of their car, while on another street there were numerous discarded pieces of furniture on the curb. They parked up outside a modest two-storey house. Elvis took out his keys, checking his face in the rear-view mirror before opening the door. She was glad no one appeared to be around to see her disembark from such an embarrassing car.

"I'm sorry you lost your job!" Blessing said, apologetically.

"Dinnae worry about it, lassie – the world's changed, eh? Nowt will ever be the same from noo on, ye know!"

Blessing noticed that Elvis no longer smelled of smoke, but apart from his teeth looking a bright white he was much the same. He had an odd face. His lips were far larger for his face than you normally saw on a white man and his nose was long, pointing down towards his chin. She couldn't deny it was a relief to be in the company of someone she knew. Three days ago, she didn't have any friends in Aberdeen, now she definitely had one, maybe two. She would have to call Rain and see if that was still the case.

"Did you look in the mirror lately?" she asked him.

"Aye. Ah know. Mah gnashers, like. You know what else? I've not had a fag since I saw youse last!"

"Really? You stopped smoking? Just like that?" Blessing was surprised.

"Aye. I've never felt fitter too. Do youse think it was something to do with being on the ship, like?"

"Maybe... I don't know." Blessing hadn't even thought about it.

"Do youse feel any different?" the Scotsman asked.

Did she? Considering how little sleep she'd had in the last two days, she should have felt completely exhausted. Last night she had displayed a reserve of energy that she was unaware she possessed, but maybe such a physical excursion was simply well overdue.

"I don't know. I probably should feel more tired than I do. I haven't had much sleep," she replied, as they reached his door.

"Aye. That makes two of us, lassie. So, welcome to mah humble abode."

Elvis showed her around his home, which was surprisingly pleasant if a little unusual in some of the décor. Through a double-doored porch, she entered the front lounge with its rear open-plan kitchen on the ground floor. There was a separate toilet, which Elvis pointed to under the stairs. Blessing dashed in to use it. As she sat and had a pee, the poster of a man with a large bouffant hair-do was poised to sing back at her, hanging on the rear of the door. The words *Now or Never!* firmly emblazoned in the middle. She realised she was hungry. Rain had cooked for her last night; a vegetarian meal. The first she had ever eaten. The fried aubergines and courgettes laced with garlic and onions had gone down a treat, but that was over twelve hours ago. As she returned to the kitchen Elvis must have read her mind, because a fruit bowl had been placed on the small divided worktop, where two stools stood. Next to it were three boxes of open cereal, and a bowl and spoon.

"Eat, you must be hungry noo, lassie."

She was, so she ate. Elvis turned on a twenty-four hour news channel but kept the volume low. The story running was about a fire-fight that had taken place between the North and South Korean Navies, around the vessel which had landed in the waters off their coast. Images of the ship partly submerged in the sea with the waves lapping around the edge of the saucer were something Blessing hadn't seen before. Then the newsreader cut to China with a graphic that stated, *China will use a nuclear deterrent against the alien threat.* Huge missiles were being positioned around one of their landing sites. What threat? She hadn't seen any threat. She found herself tuning out at the distressing images. As she munched away on some granola and bananas, her eyes wandered around the room looking at the huge number of framed portraits on the walls. There were coloured photographs, charcoal drawings, and black and white pictures, all of them depicting the same man. He was tall, quite handsome and had the same haircut as her host. In many images, the man was depicted as singing, his hips thrusting forward toward the microphone.

"Is that your Father?" she asked, wondering about the similar styled hair.

"My Paw? Nae lassie! Noo! That's the King!'

"The King? The King of Scotland?" If he was a king where was his crown? Didn't kings wear crowns? Why was there no queen standing along side him in the pictures?

"Of Scotland! Lassie, that is the King of Rock n' Roll! The King! Ye know?"

Blessing stared at him, confused.

"Elvis Presley, love! You've heard of Elvis Presley, right?"

"The name sounds familiar, but I can't say I have," Blessing confessed.

"That's his songs I've been playing! He was a singer!"

So he was some kind of super music fanboy. Her friend Susan from Birmingham had pictures of Arianna Grande all over her wall, but Blessing had never met a man who had pictures of a male pop star all over his house before. The place was like a shrine to the singer. Perhaps Elvis was gay? Best not to go there right now.

"Oh okay... did he have many hits?" she asked.

"Many hits?! Are you shittin' me, lassie? Many hits? He was the King!"

"So did your father name you after him?"

"No lassie, mah dad was a drunken cunt! He pissed off when I was ten! It's mah nickname! I'm a fan! Aren't you a fan of music?"

"Sure, I like Beyoncé." Blessing still listened to her, even now.

"Aye, right. He's like a male Beyoncé, sorta." Elvis didn't sound so sure, but if Elvis was as big as Beyoncé then she could understand why the man had some very big fans. Elvis brought his laptop to the counter.

"Right, I found some of our friends," he announced.

"Which friends?"

"The Star Trek Biker group, I spoke to one of them on Facebook this morning."

These were Rain's friends. Wasn't her ex-boyfriend among them some-where? The two students! What happened to them?

"Our friends Ewen and Donny – are they with them?"

"Aye. I spoke to them too. They weren't too conversational like, said they were coming down with summat – anyways. They all agree."

"On what?" Blessing found herself wishing she had been party to this conversation from the start.

"We have to go back to the ship and find Agatha."

Blessing was so over joyed to hear the proposal she only just managed to stop herself from throwing her arms around the man.

"Great. Count me in. We'll need Rain!" she cried happily.

"Rain? What the fook has the weather got to do... oh, you mean so they cannae see us? I think they have all that heat sensing stuff nowadays, don't they?"

"No, Rain, my friend. Our friend. The one we were detained with. Pink hair."

"Oh Aye, her," Elvis replied, sounding less keen.

"So when do we all meet up?"

"Tomorrow night."

She'd wanted a focus and now she had one. Getting back to the ship and finding Agatha. But she wanted to know more, why the ships were here. She could see from the news that their arrival was causing the world more harm than good. Humanity had never felt more divided. They had to do something. This felt like a good decision. But how were they going to get past the Police and the Army?

"So what was this in Church about kissing a girl, like?" Elvis asked, as he put the kettle on. Not a conversation she wanted to have right now.

RYAN

"Jesus Christ! When did this happen?"

Ryan stared at the image in the Cabinet room, watching the small yellow mushroom slowly grow across the screen. Darren Fine had entered the room only moments earlier, interrupting the Intelligence Briefing from GCHQ Cheltenham with an apology, before switching on the TV to show the breaking news.

"We think in the last hour," Fine replied.

"These images are live though, aren't they?"

"Yes, Prime Minister, I believe so."

"You believe so? Is it nuclear?" Ryan didn't even attempt to hide his frustration.

"We don't know yet, Prime Minister." Even Fine sounded shaken. He ought to be. It was an unnerving turn of events. On the large screen, a huge mushroom cloud expanded across the horizon with a graphic confirming the location was one of the landing sites in China.

"It bloody looks nuclear! Get me the Chinese Ambassador on the phone immediately!"

General Spears was studying the image when his phone buzzed, prompting him to leave the room. Great timing, Ryan thought. He could do with his advice on what he was going to say about this in the Commons later.

"Mr Badgers!' Ryan shouted down the table at the Foreign Secretary making him jump, his buffoonish fringe flopping across his eyes.

"Yes, Prime Minister?"

427

"Can you give us any dynamic insights into why China have done this?"

"Well, they've been continually saying for the last three days that they consider the landings an invasion of their national territory and were preparing a military response. It would seem this is it," Badgers responded, the panic in his voice barely concealed.

Idiot. He could see that for himself. *Tell me something I don't know.*

"Jennifer, we need General Spears back in here!" Ryan shouted.

"Yes, Prime Minister," his Personal Secretary whisked herself gracefully out of the meeting. Still fit. Only she could walk with such poise in a time of crisis.

"So this is happening in Qinghai province – where is that?" he asked noting the location graphic on the screen. Ryan searched his mind for the answer, but realised he wasn't even sure what part of China Beijing was in, so it proved a pointless exercise.

"It's a central eastern province, Prime Minister. Bordered by Tibet in the south, Gansu in the north and Xinjiang in the east. I travelled around China during my backpacking days," Percy Howells added. It surprised Ryan that the secretary for Wales had spent his youth in China. Not Thailand? Ryan had been to Thailand, so much more fun. God, he'd had some good times there. His devious thoughts were interrupted as Jennifer and General Spears re-entered the room.

"We have Admiral Flemyng online. He's been monitoring the latest developments for us, Prime Minister." The General changed the channel of the large monitor. Admiral Flemyng was currently in Southampton, having returned there by helicopter that morning to oversee changes in British Naval dispositions. Still dressed in his finest uniform, it looked to Ryan as though it still didn't have a single crease in the wrong place. How on earth did these military types all do that? Did he have his own two-man team to dress him in the morning as well? Maybe he did – it was the Navy, after all.

Prime Minister..." the articulate voice of the naval officer boomed around the room, from the speakers. The Admiral was seated in some kind of communications room, all low ceilings and scores of men sitting at monitors behind him.

"Admiral Flemyng, have you seen the reports coming in from China?"

"I have, Prime Minister, yes. Early intelligence data suggests this is not a nuclear weapon. Our satellites have not detected the type of nuclear footprint that you would expect to see after such an event. It would appear the Chinese decided to fire the biggest conventional missile in their arsenal at their alien landing site in Qinghai Province. Similar to the MOAB that the Americans possess. Of the three landing sites in China, this is the most remote, so the consensus is this is something of a test before launching a succession of strikes against the two other vessels on Chinese soil."

"The bloody idiots are going to start a war with these things before anyone has had a chance to communicate with them!" Baroness Childs said.

"Did any other events predetermine this response by the Chinese, Admiral?" Perhaps they were provoked... That would not be good news.

"Not as far as we can tell sir. Prime Minister I... I also need to show you these images." His face was replaced by a satellite image of one of the landing sites. From above, looking down the image showed the completely circular nature of the ship with the ascending cone shaped tower at its centre.

"What you're seeing on your screen now is a satellite image taken of the object in the Qinghai Province, taken just over an hour ago. You can see it's one of the largest, forty miles in diameter, but still smaller than the one in southern Italy.'

So it was identical to the one in Scotland in every sense, only bigger. Ryan marvelled at the fact that it just sat right across mountain ranges, hills and rivers with complete impunity. Either it had engulfed them or crushed them. It was impossible to tell. When would Doctor Jacobs have more answers? The scientists she requested were being dragged out of their universities and homes at this very moment, and delivered to her in Scotland. He hoped together they would reach some more helpful conclusions.

"Now, the next picture is just after the missile strike. GCHQ estimated less than two minutes have elapsed since impact."

The image displayed a huge cloud obscuring about ninety percent of the vessel. They had destroyed it. Ryan wasn't sure if he should feel good about it or not.

"It looks like it did the job. I guess I shall have to phone and congratulate the Chinese ambassador," Badgers remarked, clapping his hands.

"Why would you want to congratulate him on an act of such aggression? We don't want to be encouraging this sort of response! Idiot!" Baroness Childs was not one to mince her words. Ryan had to agree. Basil was an idiot. However, Admiral Flemyng was not yet finished.

"Not quite Foreign Secretary. If I could draw your attention to the next image. This one was taken just a few minutes ago of the same area."

The cloud image was replaced by what appeared to be almost exactly the same photograph as the first they had seen, except...

"Isn't this the same photograph from earlier?" Badgers asked, rather irritated.

"No, Foreign Secretary. Note the time stamp. This image that you're seeing now is actually less than seven minutes old."

Ryan stood up and walked over the screen, looking at the ship in detail. There was something different about it but he couldn't quite put his finger on it.

"Admiral, Julie Compston, MI5..." the Intelligence head said. Good, she always had something useful to contribute.

"Yes, Ms Compston, I can see you."

"Yes. Sorry. Could you place images one and two together for us side by side please?"

"I can indeed. I was in fact about to do just that."

The images duly appeared next to each other on the screen, with the Admiral's image reduced to a smaller box in one corner. The comparison drew gasps of astonishment from around the room. Ryan realised what had been bothering him; it was the size of the ship. It seemed to have reduced itself in the second image, by what – ten percent?

"As you can see there is a notable difference in the size of the craft after the missile strike. It had a diameter of forty miles across, in the second image, the ship is just under thirty-five miles across."

Jennifer appeared by his side, leaning to whisper into his ear. God she always smelled so good.

"We have Chinese Ambassador Yen on the video link."

"Can we add him to the other screen on a separate call?" Ryan wasn't finished with the Admiral just yet.

"Yes Prime Minister, we can do that," Horace Saunders cut in. He went to switch on a smaller screen that sat alongside the larger one.

"Admiral we're going to take a call from the Chinese Ambassador. I want you to stay on line and listen, but don't say anything unless I instruct you otherwise."

"Of course, Prime Minister."

General Spears led Ryan back to his seat, muttering "You're getting the hang of this. Good job. Keep it up." The General took a seat next to him, forcing the others to move up. The screen flicked on and Ambassador Yen appeared, seated at his desk in the Chinese Embassy in London. He was a small man, aged close to fifty, who looked exhausted and was doing up his tie when the call started. He was flanked by two crimson Chinese flags mounted on gold poles. Hanging on the wall above him was a rather flattering portrait of the Party General Secretary and President of China.

"Ambassador Yen, I can see you've had a busy morning," Ryan said, in a rather sarcastic tone. Start as you mean to go on.

"Prime Minister. I've not yet had the chance to offer my condolences on the passing of your former Prime Minister..."

"Well, his funeral is in three days. You can do it then. Perhaps for now we should keep our conversation focused on more urgent matters. It's come to my attention that China has fired the first salvo in what could be an international war involving every country of the world. You did so without consulting with us, the United Nations or even your own neighbours!" Yes - that should do for starters.

"My country does not need to consult when its national sovereignty is threatened, Prime Minister. We took what we felt was appropriate action in order to defend ourselves." The ambassador was evidently in the picture, so he had known this was going to happen. Okay then.

"Ambassador Yen, ordinarily that's true. Had some national crisis threatened your country, you would be well within your rights to defend China's sovereignty, but I think you're confusing national and international. The threat to your country and mine are one and the same. China's actions could trigger a response which affects the entire population of this planet..."

"My country has to consider the safety and well-being of its own citizens!" The Ambassador cut in, raising his voice. "We had every right to protect..."

Ryan didn't have the patience for his bullshit. "At the very least, Ambassador, you could have advised us of your intentions, giving us the chance to ready our own armed forces, in case your reckless actions resulted in an international response against the rest of us! Had you even considered that?"

General Spears nudged Ryan at that moment, bringing his attention back to Admiral Flemyng, who was holding up a piece of paper with something written on it. What did it say? – *I have new information!* The General's mobile phone rang.

"We did, we also considered that we are dealing with a threat to our country that is not of this earth..."

"On that much, at least we can agree!" Ryan snapped.

"And that such a threat might have the ability to monitor communication between our nations, thereby undermining our ability for a first strike response!" the Ambassador said.

"You need to speak to Admiral Flemyng immediately," General Spears whispered in Ryan's ear, trying to make sure the Ambassador did not hear him.

"Ambassador, I have to put you on hold for just a second," Ryan said. The Ambassador nodded. The line between them was muted.

"He can still see us, but not hear us, right?" Ryan said.

"Correct," Saunders answered.

"Go ahead Admiral."

"Forgive the interruption, Prime Minister, but considering the nature of your current conversation I thought it essential that you saw this latest image, immediately. It's the same landing site in China, taken only seconds ago. I'll put it up alongside the first image we showed you. As you can see..."

The image appeared on the screen, and for a brief moment everyone in the room was speechless.

"They're identical."

"Are you sure these images are correct, Admiral? They're not being manipulated in any way?" General Spears asked.

"Yes General. Unless someone has hacked our satellite with fake imagery or infected it with a virus... That would be, well, complex if not impossible. I am certain these images are credible."

"How can it have returned to exactly the same size as it was before the missile strike?' asked the Foreign Secretary, voicing everyone's thoughts.

"All I can tell you is that the evidence before me shows that it has, Foreign Secretary. That's all we know for now. Sir, I will let you get back to your call."

"Put the ambassador back on – Ambassador, can you hear me?"

"Yes, I can, Prime Minister. I hope everything is alright in the UK?"

"Yes, we're fine. Just a little update on our own landing site. We have just the one here of course, and another off the coast of Ireland," he said, examining the man's body language. Nothing had changed. Spears leaned in to Ryan.

"I don't think the ambassador knows yet," he whispered.

"Ambassador, are you planning on making similar attacks on your other two landing sites?" Ryan asked.

"It would be most unwise of me to discuss military strategy with you, Prime Minister, especially when I am not privy to such information. My country, as I said, is taking what measures it must to protect itself."

That means yes, Ryan thought.

"It is good that China has not resorted to a nuclear deterrent to protect your nation. I would like to think you would consult with us should you decide you need to take such an action, in the future."

"That is a path that I truly hope neither of our nations ever has to use in defence of our citizens." The Ambassador sounded sincere about that, at least.

Ryan scanned the world map that had been erected in the room at his request, depicting all the landing sites over the world. He didn't know too much about China, but one of the sites was about two hundred kilometres east of Beijing. The other was in the south in Hunan province. Hunan was somewhere that had been mentioned a few times in the numerous Asian films he had watched. He assumed people had to live there. If these idiots were firing their biggest non-nuclear weapons at these things already, then the decision to fire their ultimate weapon would be the next obvious choice. Once they realised their first attack had done completely sweet fuck all.

"Yes, because two of your landing sights are relatively close to large areas of your population. One is just east of Beijing, I see. I can only imagine the problems you would face firing a nuclear weapon. It would have such devastating long-term repercussions on your own citizens."

"That will never happen. Our General Secretary would not be so hasty to use such a weapon," Yen replied, confidently.

"Wouldn't he? He just fired the next best thing without worrying about the consequences for the entire world, so why should I think he's going to think twice about the effects such a decision would have on his own people?" Ryan's sharp tone did not falter. "Your General Secretary has just made a very foolish decision, Ambassador Yen. One that I think you will find has yielded little in the way of results, yet you could have put the rest of the world at risk! Unless China knows something the rest of us don't and just isn't sharing the information? We still don't know why these things are here, where they came from or what their intentions are. They could be entirely peaceful for all we know! God, man, didn't you ever watch Star Trek? We come in peace – shoot to kill is not the way to go here!"

"We do not have corrupt Western television in our country, Prime Minister," the Ambassador replied, unintimidated.

Ryan rose from his seat and walked over to the screen.

"No? Well you might want to watch a few episodes! Please convey my best wishes to your General Secretary. I would like to speak to him, as I am sure many other world leaders will, at his earliest convenience."

"I will tell…"

Ryan ended the call. No one said anything, but everyone drew in a huge breath. The world had taken a step closer to the abyss and they all knew it.

"And I thought the call with the American President went badly," Fine muttered under his breath, just loud enough to be heard.

"I thought Mr Wallace, sorry, our Prime Minister, did rather well, considering he's only been on the job for three days," Julie Compston said. Someone from MI5 was not someone Ryan considered a natural ally. If he was stranded in a bunker and she was the last woman on the earth, would he do her? No, she was a younger Judi Dench, so not his type, even if he did love Judi Dench.

"The Chinese were incredibly reckless to have carried out such an action," Admiral Flemyng cut in, reminding everyone he was still on the other screen. "What they have shown us however, is that these craft are impervious to all forms of conventional attack. We can only hope there isn't some sort of retaliation as a result."

"In view of these events, Prime Minister, I think we need to call an emergency meeting of Cobra again as soon as possible," Compston said.

"The Prime Minister is due to speak in the House of Commons in less than twenty minutes," Horace Saunders, the Chief Whip, reminded everyone.

"Yes, I have to say I think to cancel that would be a mistake," General

Spears said. "Admiral Flemyng, do any of these events give us cause to change our Naval deployment?"

"Not unless there's a strike against the United Kingdom, no, General. We're already taking every precaution we can against a possible invasion. Though I understand the decision has not yet been taken to fully evacuate the city of Aberdeen."

"We don't currently have the resources to oversee such an operation, though many have already travelled south under their own steam," Police Commissioner Winston chimed in.

"I shall leave that decision to others. Such are the privileges of rank," the Admiral said, sitting back in his chair. Everyone looked at Ryan.

"Admiral, I understand you want to be down in Southampton to speak to the troops, as it were, before re-deploying our fleet. Can we have you back for a Cobra meeting this evening at, say, seven?"

"Yes, Prime Minister, I should be done here well before then."

"Very good. Let's schedule Cobra for 7pm this evening then, providing all-out war doesn't break out before then." Ryan thought it best to keep the mood upbeat. There was a general nod of agreement from around the room. People closed folders and iPads, preparing for departure to the House of Commons. Ryan had no idea what the standing protocol was if a war broke out. He hoped he wasn't going to find out any time soon.

"Thank you Admiral Flemyng. Thank you everyone. I think I ought to get over to the House."

Spears placed a reassuring hand on Ryan's shoulder. "Well done, keep it up," he said, then he was on his way out. Everyone else began to leave. It had been a long meeting. The screens flashed back to BBC News 24 which continued to play out the day's stories. Images of the ships world wide still dominated the headlines. He doubted the Media had little of value to tell him. He turned to look at Jennifer, whom he could have sworn was smiling.

Had Ryan watched the screen for another minute he would have seen a short headline about firefighters in Docklands pulling a woman from the Thames. The woman had gunshot wounds and Police were treating it as attempted murder. She was in critical condition and not expected to survive the night.

Ryan was busy thinking about the myriad information he had received in the last twenty-four hours. Among the many facts coming in from all over the world, two vital pieces of information were still lacking. What were these things and why were they here? No one had any answers. There had been some information concerning their arrival. It came from astronomers who had informed him that they had appeared in our solar system, only one day before the landing. They had not been detected at any time before that. This posed more questions than it answered – had they somehow just appeared on the edge of our solar system by other means? And if so, how? Warp drive? A Wormhole? He didn't really understand what such things were, or if they were even possible in reality. They were just things he remembered from watching *Deep Space Nine*. He still needed to find a way to call Candice. Now, of course, she would think he was only calling because of the picture that had come out online. Yes, he was mad about that, but he had wanted to call her anyway, to say he was sincerely sorry about having to end things. Still, such apologies would have to wait. He had more pressing concerns. People were going to want answers. He still didn't know what had happened to his Grandmother. For all he knew, aliens could be experimenting on her right now. Not a delightful image. Hopefully, she was just teaching them how to play Bingo and sampling the best alien tea they had to offer. Shit, he certainly hoped such simple scenarios were indeed the case. He looked up. Everyone had left, it was just him and Jennifer, alone.

"Penny for your thoughts?" she asked, politely.

"I was just thinking we really don't know much more about these things than we did three days ago," he replied, honestly.

"We know they can't be hurt. Not easily at least."

"Somehow, I think the public and opposition are going to want to hear something a little more positive than that!" He could hear the stress in his own voice. Unsurprising. He was bloody stressed. Who the fuck knew he would end up in this mess? He should resign. He could do it right now, in the House, without warning anyone. Just stand up and say it, come clean about Candice and state that he wanted to be with the woman he loved. His career would be over, but so what? Who was he kidding anyway? He wasn't a leader. He was a coward. This new job wasn't his calling, this would be his final folly...

"I thought you just did very well," Jennifer said. "I saw David go up against Ambassador Yen a few months back and he fared considerably worse than you." Was that a compliment? Ryan could never tell.

"I imagine the fate of the world wasn't at stake then!"

"No, it wasn't. You're having to deal with a considerably more complex crisis. We're trying to avoid a war, not bloody start one! What you said to the Ambassador was entirely appropriate." Jennifer was even more attractive when she got all feisty. He found himself getting hard, for the first time in three days. "I shouldn't have to remind you that there's only three people in the world right now more politically influential than you are. The Russian Premiere, the Chinese General Secretary and the President of the United States. I wouldn't bank on any of those three to rein in the crazies. You're going to have to be the voice of sanity for the world!"

"I could give Leonardo DiCaprio a call." Ryan said flippantly. "He's not one for firing missiles and is all about saving the planet. Maybe we could convince him to be the spokesperson for earth. Who's the British equivalent? Tom Hardy? Christ why did these things choose to come now, when the world is already so fucking volatile?" He should have posed that question when the cabinet were still here. Not so much his DiCaprio / Hardy plan.

"Did you ever think that might be the reason why they came here in the first place?" Jennifer said. It was an interesting point. One would have to assume that they had been here before of course, but when? Numerous UFO sightings had occurred in the United Kingdom over the years: Rendelsham in Suffolk, RAF Bentwaters... both had seen a number of unusual phenomena. A flying cross had been seen by numerous policeman in the 1960s, usually the most reliable of witnesses. A retired Policeman had photographed one in 1987. Not all the sightings could have been faked. Ryan remembered his own Grandmother talking about a UFO sighting in Bonnybridge in Scotland. It was only now that Ryan remembered that this area was considered part of the Falkirk Triangle, a notorious UFO-sighting area. Bonnybridge itself getting over three hundred sightings per year. Why? There was fuck all in Bonnybridge, apart from its very bonny bridge! Who would want to come all the way from another universe just to go there, of all places?

"If they came here to fix things, then why aren't they doing it? Hell, the world's about to tear itself to pieces without them even trying!" Saying it out loud made Ryan think that might be their plan after all... watch the human race rip each other apart, while they sustained zero casualties. Jennifer opened the door, gesturing for them to head down to the waiting cars.

"They might be counting on that. That's why we need people like you to make sure that doesn't happen," She said, walking him out onto the landing.

"What can I do? Like you said I'm only the fourth most important man in the world." He smiled. It was a funny way of looking at it. After all, there was nowhere for the fourth person to stand at the Olympics, was there?

"Your car is ready, Prime Minister," Darren Fine said, waiting for him at the bottom of the stairs. "Sir, I've set up a press conference after the meeting in the House of Commons which I can handle for you."

"I want to speak to the press myself," Ryan cut in.

"Prime Minister, I know you're new to this role but as you are aware, sir, it is my job to handle the press. Taking questions from them directly is considered political suicide," Fine said, sounding as if he almost hoped Ryan would still agree to it.

"So be it. Let the wolves come."

That was the beauty of having no long-term political ambition. He simply didn't give a shit.

The House of Commons was a whirlwind of questions and statements from his own side, as well as the opposing parties. There was a surprising sense of unity and universal condemnation of actions by the Chinese. Ryan kept his own comments as short as possible, letting others speak either to him or for him. No one in opposition wanted to be the person to publicly take advantage of a nation in grief and the middle of a global crisis for political gain. To have done so would have been most unseemly and only given one's opponents a great deal of political ammunition to use against the other, later. Ryan didn't really care. He spent most of the session with his eyes glazed over, thinking about Candice. Everything was so relentless and there had been no opportunity for him to be alone to make a private phone call, let alone track her down. She would have to wait. He knew he had hurt her and he didn't like it. Shit, so this was what being in love felt like! Who knew it sucked so badly?

Some questions were put forward by various MPs, but they were much the same, consisting of variations on "Can the Prime Minister assure my constituents that everything that can be done to ensure the safety of citizens, and of those who wish to remain in Aberdeen is being done?"

Which of course it was. There was a general consensus among the parties that over the next forty-eight hours, the priorities would be to try and establish communication with the ships and those who might be inside them, trapped or otherwise, by any means possible. Secondly, points were agreed on having a state funeral for the former Prime Minister, David Jackson, his family and colleagues. Ryan would need to attend them all of course. He hated funerals. He made a mental note to secure a new deputy Prime Minister as soon as possible, so that he could nominate them to attend funerals for the more lowly members of government staff, who had perished in the crash. After the session in Parliament was over, the Press had been assembled in another room and were eagerly waiting to ask their own questions.

"This way, Prime Minister," Fine said, leading them into the room. Ryan could almost swear he was grinning. Jennifer followed, tugging at his arm.

"Prime Minister, are you sure this is a good idea? You have the meeting with the Police Counter-Terrorism Committee later, and Cobra are waiting on you to attend right now."

"People want answers, it's important that I make a statement," Ryan replied. He shook free of her hand.

"Make a statement by all means – but what answers do we have for them?"

"Very few but if we continue to operate behind a veil of secrecy, pretty soon they'll be making up their own answers, anyway."

Ryan was greeted by such a cacophony of camera flashes that he was briefly disorientated. *So this is what it must have been like to be in Take That,* Ryan thought. A sea of voices shouted questions at him, before he even got to the podium. He stood for a moment, looking at the crowd of reporters, faces full of expectation. He held up his hands.

"You make me wish I had brought my Raybans!"

There was uneasy laughter in the room. Someone took the chance to fire off the first question.

"Prime Minister, how can you make a joke at a time like this, when we're a nation under attack and in mourning? Is Britain not facing its darkest hour since World War Two?"

The room fell deathly silent. Everyone was keen to hear his answer. Jennifer stood behind Ryan, alongside Fine who was smirking, waiting for him to fall on his sword.

"How can I make a joke when we face our darkest hour?" Ryan paused and looked at all the faces. They were waiting for the answers that would make tomorrow's headlines. "I'll tell you how… It is because I'm doing the job that no one else wants to do. If any of you in this room think you can do better then, please, do come up now and step into my shoes…"

No one moved or spoke. He glanced at Jennifer, on her face two words – *car crash.* "No takers?" he continued. "Of course not. But keeping our British humour is what gets us through the day. It's certainly got me through the last three days. Do I want to weep at the loss of my friend? Of course I do. I could stand here now and talk about David and what a great man he was and how much I miss him…" He choked a little here, but knew he had best not labour the sentiment. There was sincerity in his words, but only a little. "…But there will be another time to do that. Today we are all seeking answers. The time for secrecy is over and we must share with the world what we know. I will do my best to answer your questions." At once the hands went up and the clamour rose.

"Sarah Dixon – Sky News. Prime Minister, what do you know about the alien threat?"

"About our alien friends I am afraid the answer is very little. You used the word *threat* in your question, I used the word *friend*. We don't know why they've come, or where from, or what their intentions are, but I am still hopeful their intentions are peaceful. I can tell you that the best scientific minds that the UK has are working around the clock to provide us with answers, and they've had even less sleep than I have." He thought for a moment of the haggard Doctor Jacobs, and how exhausted she had looked.

"Prime Minister, Amar Rijiwani, BBC. It has been speculated in some quarters that the governments of the United States and indeed our own government have known about the existence of extra-terrestrial life for some time. Can you confirm if such reports are true? And since you took on your new role as leader of this government, have the British Intelligence services made you aware of any information they already had concerning UFO sightings, or contact with other species that took place prior to you taking office?"

"That's a long question, Amar." Wasn't it just, with a fair few things he'd like to know the answer to himself. He made a mental note to ask later what, if anything, the Intelligence services had known about contact with alien species, and what UFO sightings had credence and were considered viable. There could be some useful information locked away in a cabinet somewhere, gathering dust.

"It's a valid question, Prime Minister," Amar pressed.

"One that I have been asking myself. The President of the United States will have to speak for himself. I have no doubt that Roswell is probably already being mentioned by your colleagues over there. As you know, so much has happened in the last seventy-two hours, that I've not had much time to inquire about what past intelligence we may or may not possess on UFOs. It is a valid line of enquiry, and one I will ensure is followed up after this conference. I am not personally aware of any such contact between our previous governments and species from another world. Until now, such things would have been well below my security clearance. Nor have I been updated on any information on past sightings or occurrences that have taken place inside the United Kingdom, that would in any way assist with our understanding of the alien phenomena we are currently facing. My Press Secretary, Mr Darren Fine, will be giving you a daily press briefing at 4pm from here on in, with any new developments."

"Prime Minister, is there any news on your Grandmother, Mrs Agatha Davey?"

"Sadly, no. She's still missing. Everything that can be done is being done to locate her. It's possible she may be inside the vessel, but the honest answer is that we simply don't know." Not true. Ryan was certain she was inside, but he wasn't going to say that.

"Julie Cox, Daily Mail - How is it that a woman in her eighties can find a way inside the ship when a team of the brightest minds of the United Kingdom cannot?"

"I think you underestimate the brilliance of my Grandmother, Ms Cox, is it? Let me tell you, she's a tough Scottish woman. All we know for sure is that she is still missing."

"Simon Howell, Sunday Times. What would you say to those families who still have people missing from within the perimeter of the Scottish landing site?"

"That we are doing everything we can to find your loved ones and return them safely to you. I would add that several people who were thought to have been missing, or thought crushed, beneath the ship's land-fall, have since been found safe and well at the evacuation centres on the eastern outskirts of Aberdeen. Names are being collected and updated at the present time. This information can be obtained via local police websites and other forms of social media."

A sea of hands still remained raised.

"Prime Minister, families on holidays are stranded at airports all over the world with no way to get back to the UK. When do you think the ban on air travel be lifted?"

"Firstly, I would like to thank the people of those countries and indeed our own citizens, for their generosity by taking people in and giving them a place to sleep, or offering them a meal. That is the true spirit of humanity. We need more of it. I am optimistic that we will be able to lift the ban by the end of the week, assuming there are no further changes in the current status of the ships. Flight exclusion zones are being proposed, and many flights will have to take different routes. We're hopeful that if things stay as they are, we can resume air travel as soon as possible." That was the hope. The reality, Ryan knew, was far more complex.

"Jill Keen, The Sun. What do you personally think of the aggressive action taken in China earlier today, to destroy one of the ships?"

Incredibly stupid was what he thought, but Ryan knew his answer could well determine future diplomacy with China. So be it.

"I think such an action was a most foolish enterprise. I want to make it clear we're in an incredibly fluid situation. We still don't have all the facts yet. That said, to the best of my knowledge since the initial landings, as yet, no aggressive action of any kind has been taken by the alien vessels. I don't think we should be doing anything to provoke an aggressive response from them…"

Voices interrupted him, but he held up his hand for quiet. He had done a little public speaking back in the day, and by that he meant his best man's speech at David Jackson's wedding. He had taken control of the room that day, and he was going to do the same now.

"Please, I am not yet finished. Thank you. Now, I've read all sorts of theories online. Everything from how people think alien armies are being built inside the ships, that will come and attack us any day now. Or that the vessels will combine into some kind of mega-weapon. My thoughts on their presence are this: We're three days in and we haven't seen a weapon or army yet. When I first saw them, I thought the same thing as many of you, the same thing we've seen in countless movies and TV shows: an alien fleet arriving around the globe, unleashing havoc and destruction. Only it didn't happen. So people then said they'll come out and be just like us and deceive us somehow, take over the planet by deception. This also hasn't happened."

"So why do you think they're here, Prime Minister?" interrupted a young female reporter at the front. She was kneeling before him with a microphone, and was rather striking. He must remember to get her name.

"Do you want to stand up for a second? It looks really uncomfortable down there," he said. The reporter promptly stood, looking relieved. Her heels must have been agony in that position. Not the most practical shoes for a reporter.

"Better, Miss…?"

"Sally Shields – The Independent."

"Miss Shields has asked the question on everyone's minds. Why indeed? Not to kidnap Agatha Davey-Wallace, I can promise you that."

The crowd laughed. Good. Careful, Ryan, not too many jokes.

"It seems their very presence, even without showing any direct hostile intentions is already causing conflict within humanity. North and South Korea engaged in limited hostilities over the landing in their international waters earlier today. I understand that the landing between America and Mexico is causing some similar tensions. I think we, as world leaders, need to pause and ask ourselves some serious questions. Is the best way for us to greet intelligent life from another universe, to fire a missile at it? I do not think it is. We're trying to prevent wars on our own planet all the time, let's not start an interstellar one if we can help it. Let's take time to try and understand their intentions before we react so recklessly." Yeah, that should do it.

"Terry Stone, The Guardian - How can we understand their intentions when no one has been able to communicate with the ships?"

They were certainly trying.

"Communication even between the sovereign nations today often takes time. It is possible they're talking to us but we are simply not able to hear them. I hope our scientific team will be able to provide us with answers in due course." What else could Ryan say? The same reporter fired off another question.

"My understanding is that several individuals at different sites across the world have gained access to some of the craft. What do you have to say about that?"

"I'm awaiting confirmation, but I suggest you speak to your colleagues at other networks and find out what they know regarding other sites outside the UK."

"That rather side-steps the question, Prime Minister. The fact remains that at present you cannot communicate with…" The man from The Guardian hesitated. Ryan seized the opportunity.

"With what? Exactly my point. You didn't know what to call them either, did you? We don't know if it's aliens, plural or an alien, singular. These craft could be reconnaissance, or science vessels, or even un-manned probes of some kind? Fortunately, your own pages are not short on specula-tion when it comes to wild theories. This is why I insisted on seeing the ship in Scotland for myself. I wanted to know what we were facing. What we're all…" He took a moment to look around the room, wanting to under-score the word all. "… facing. Right now, I know as much as you do."

"Clive Gordon, The Sunday Sport. Prime Minister, during your time in Scotland, did you discover anything else you can tell us?" Ryan could have told them all there and then about the abundance of fruit and vegetables that had grown around the ship, or the absence of pollutants in the atmosphere, but Doctor Jacobs wasn't ready to release the factual data yet. The last thing he wanted was more members of the public trying to get to the site, especially in light of the one other thing he now knew.

"Our scientific team in Aberdeen is being given every available resource conducive to getting us answers, as fast as possible. All that I was able to ascertain myself were those facts that are already known to you all."

"Which, Prime Minister, I have to say, is precious little." It was the woman from The Mail again, or Hitler's paper as Ryan liked to call it in private. "How long do you think the country will have to wait for answers?"

"We shall have to wait as long as it takes. I have faith in the British people. I ask them not to panic. Do not strip the shelves of food and commodities. Do not add to the burden of the emergency services, because I can assure you that they have their hands full, as it is. I ask you all to remain calm, and can assure you that everyone in the government is working tirelessly to keep all of you, both at home and abroad, safe and well. If our new neighbours are listening to this broadcast, be it those in Scotland or in any of the other ships from around the world, I would like to say we greet you in peace. We are not a perfect people, but we're trying. Do not think that the reckless actions of one nation are representative of humanity. Come and talk to us, we are ready to listen. Thank you very much, ladies and gentlemen."

Ryan left the podium, catching Jennifer smiling for the second time that day. He couldn't tell if he had done well or not, but he seemed to be getting the hang of things. A line of coke still wouldn't go amiss.

"Can someone get me a Red Bull please?"

CHAPTER V

There's been quite a few rumours about what happened at the Mount Augusta landing but I can only tell you what I know. Investigations by other agencies are of course on going, so it would be wrong of me to comment on their findings. Just outside of Carson City there had been a little known survivalist group called 'The Last Legion'. They had never really been any trouble but in recent years, thanks to a well organised social media campaign, their branch now had well over one hundred members. It was nothing short of its own little criminal fraternity. Legally armed to the teeth, they had decided to descend upon the landing site before April 5th. According to statements made to us so far they had it in mind to get to the ship and blow their way inside with explosives they had brought with them. For the last twenty-four hours, they had been moving in small groups into the encampment spreading rumours and misinformation among the waiting crowds. 'The army wants us gone, be ready. They're going to cover all this up again, you wait and see. They don't want us to see what's inside, I'll tell you what's inside, diamonds, thousands of them…' Things of that nature.

Rumour fuelled rumour so by the time they decided to launch their assault and get through to the ship tensions were extremely high. We believe five of their men, armed with hunting rifles, were well positioned to cause as much chaos as possible. As civilians were being escorted back to Carson City Airport they fired a number of shots which led to the events that occurred that day. The shit hit the fan and when it did they did their absolute utmost to make it worse. To repeat, I am certain they were responsible for the first shots that were fired which led to the now infamous

'Salt Wells Massacre' which claimed the lives of three Police Officers, twenty-two men and women of the Armed Forces and one hundred and ninety-eight American civilian lives, including eleven children.

It was my worst day serving on the job.

From the personal notes of Patrolman Jones, Nevada State Police, made on the morning of April 5th.

DIANA

"Okay, she's coming around."

The words were spoken by a woman, but they sounded muffled, as if someone had stuffed cotton wool in her ears. She heard the sound of helicopters and thundering jets, as she slowly tried to work out where she was. She remembered being outside, talking to Owen and Craig. Her son was there but her daughter... Fuck, she had to get up.

"Please don't get up yet, Mrs Morrow..." the Nurse said.

"It's Miiiiiiss..." She sounded different, as though heavily medicated.

"What the fuuuuck did you doo to meeee..." Nothing sounded quite as it should. This Nurse was not familiar to her.

"I'm sorry Mrs... I mean Miss Morrow. We had to sedate you. You caused us quite a ruckus. You hit one of my orderlies."

Hit? She couldn't remember that. She remembered talking to Craig and Owen, then she felt a little light-headed and after that, nothing. What was she talking about? Why on earth would she have hit someone? She became aware of her surroundings, quickly establishing she was inside a large tent. Wait... she had been in here before, resting. Yes.

"Youuu seeedated meeee...?" She tried to pose the sentence as a question but her voice was barely recognisable, even to herself. She sounded like her late father after he'd had his stroke. Outside, shouts could be heard, several hostile voices overlapping. Someone yelled something on a loud-speaker, as if calling to people at a rally. Protesting voices were heard in response. There was something happening outside, and not something good. She felt groggy and her limbs were heavy, as if weighted down. The smallest movement seemed to require vast amounts of energy to achieve

445

the slightest movement in her arms. She was on drugs of some kind, and clearly not the fun sort she had briefly taken in her twenties.

"The General has ordered all civilians out of the camp this morning, she needs to move," said an unfamiliar male voice. She tried to focus on the source but felt the room spin as she turned her head.

"Not until I say she's ready. See to the others. Just relax please, Mrs Morrow. I've given you something to bring you back to us. You should be able to sit up in about another five minutes, but for now I just need you to lie still, okay?"

"Ooookayyy…" She sounded like a child with speech difficulties. Not a very PC thought to have. Walking in a straight line would be a challenge. This would be worse than having a Saturday night out at Cowboys Red River Bar. It took some twenty minutes before she was fully compos mentis, and finally able to swing her legs off the cot. Her back felt stiff and she was thirsty, but more than anything she needed a shower. Her armpits reeked, but she felt Nurse Charming was unlikely to concede to such a request. The Nurse returned with a bottle of water. She quickly drank it all, and asked for another. Diana noticed two needle marks on her arm. There was still a drip next to her bed. Looking around the tent, she could see it had been evacuated of all the other patients. After another ten minutes the Nurse came back to her with another bottle.

"Where's my son?" she asked.

"I understand he's with your brother," the Nurse replied.

Danny? Danny was here? He had found them? How on earth had he got through the cordon? The nurse handed her the bottle and checked her pulse.

"Okay she's good to go but someone will need to watch her," shouted the Nurse. "That's everyone from here."

Two National Guardsman entered and pulled her to her feet but she wasn't done with the Nurse yet. She remembered the friendly Nurse who she'd met before, and this one wasn't her. This woman was older and more like Nurse Ratched from *One Flew Over the Cuckoo's Nest* with equally bad makeup.

"Nurse! Where exactly is my son? Where is Danny?" Finally, her voice was her own again.

"They'll be on the bus. If you want to join them in time, please go with these men Mrs Morrow."

"I told you before, it's Miss!" she snapped at the Nurse. She was now separated from both of her children again. She had to find them.

"Wait a minute. What time is it? How long was I out?"

Her last memory of being conscious was speaking to Craig and Owen. It had been in the evening, just after sundown. It looked like the middle of the day from here. The soldiers waited. Their body language suggesting their patience was wearing thin. The Nurse sighed.

"You slept for over thirty six hours. It's April 5th, Ms Morrow!" The Nurse about-faced and marched away. Further inquiry was out of the question. She shook off the soldiers' hands.

"Take your hands off me. I can find my own way out!"

The men waited for her to grab her ruck-sack, which someone had kindly left next to the cot. She had that much, at least. She knew she looked a sight, wearing a medical gown, socks and trainers. She found her jeans and shirt, putting them on in a hurry. Leaving the tent, she was greeted again by the familiar sight of the military encampment. It had grown in size, as had the number of people camped out beyond the fence around it. The air was warm and she felt sticky. The gentle breeze carried with it the smell of roast meat mingled with jet fuels. Trucks and trailers, vans and jeeps, cars and motorcycles had all come in their thousands to get a look at the ship. The Military was in the process of trying to move them further back from the perimeter. Helicopters buzzed back and forth overhead. A quick glance behind her confirmed the alien structure was still there. The tall white tower dominated the eastern horizon, dwarfing the surrounding hills and mountains, as if it were a beacon for all the trouble it was attracting below. The Guardsmen escorted her towards the inner chain-link fence, where she joined several other civilians awaiting departure. She searched faces for Jack or Danny, seeing no one but strangers. Danny must be here somewhere, otherwise how would the Nurse have known she even had a brother? She had been out for how long? Had the nurse even told her the truth? Oh God – what would poor Jules be thinking? In that hospital all on her own, she had to get back to her – today! Her attention was drawn to angry shouts emanating from the crowd of people just beyond the outer perimeter gate on the highway. Beyond the coils of wire, lines of men in khaki, their rifles held ready, were at a standoff with the frustrated civilians. The onlookers were singing a ragged version of, "We shall not be moved..." Diana thought she had heard it sung before, probably on some drama series depicting a protest against the Vietnam War, or something. This scene certainly was reminiscent of that. Her group was ushered further along towards the highway that bisected the camp. The camp had been greatly expanded. There were more tents, more armoured vehicles, more helicopters, more soldiers and an endless sea of civilians encamped beyond it, their cries of protest becoming louder with every minute.

"You can't keep this one quiet, man!" came the incensed shout of one man, whom Diana thought was a biker.

"No more Roswell. You can't cover it all up, this time!" cried another.

"We have as much right to speak to them as you do!" shouted a woman.

"Yeah, and we're less likely to fuck it up and start a war!" yelled the biker again. The sound of disenchanted voices grew ever louder from the teeming wall of people. A single belt of wire with guard towers at intervals formed the outer wall of the encampment, with a second belt of wire on the inside. Diana strained to see how far it went in both directions.

'Right guys, let's get this last group on the bus," one of the Guardsmen ordered.

The two soldiers steered her group of five towards two waiting school buses that sat either side of the road, just inside the inner gates. They had to weave their way through a large group of tents to get there. "How did this get so bad? They were supposed to put all these people back past Fallon yesterday!" one soldier with a Texan accent moaned to another.

"They went around the checkpoints. I hear it's the same on the east side. People are just coming from all over," his partner replied.

"How on earth are we supposed to contain this thing? More people are arriving every hour. They need to expand the perimeter now or this is all going to get nasty real soon."

"So where are you boys from?" Diana asked, casually.

"We're from the Texas National Guard, ma'am. Sorry about the rough stuff, but that bitch of a Nurse outranked us," the older one replied.

"Yeah, she's a Lieutenant. Had us running up and down for her all day long," added the younger one. She could easily picture him wearing a ten gallon hat, smoking his Marlborough cigarettes while he tied up his horse and offering to take her line dancing.

"Texas? You're a long way from home, aren't you, boys?" she commented, sounding as friendly as possible.

"Here on an executive order, ma'am. California National Guard are here too. This thing is nearly twenty miles across. They wanted it contained, so they called in reinforcements from neighbouring states."

Yeah, these guys weren't Marines, otherwise they wouldn't be so chatty. *Might as well take advantage of that*, she thought.

"I've been kinda out of it. So has there still been no contact from them?"

"No, ma'am," the younger one replied.

"What, nothing at all?"

"No, ma'am," the older man said. "Sorry ma'am, we're not really supposed to talk to you."

"Sure, I understand, I wasn't after any military secrets or anything. It's just that I got separated from my son, and my daughter is in hospital. Be good to know what's been going on while I slept." Might as well play for sympathy, she thought.

"There's been some trouble at the landing site in Mexico," the younger one blurted out, sounding anxious.

"Steve! Don't tell her about that. This woman needs to find her kids!"

"What kind of trouble?" The younger man seemed more amenable to her charm. She could tell he was nervous.

"Hell, she's going to find out anyway. We might be going to war with Mexico!"

"War? Really? Why?" Goddamnit. Had the whole world gone insane? What was the point of going to war with Mexico? This was nonsense.

"I don't know if you heard, but the UFO there came down right on the border between us and Mexico," the older one chipped in.

"Yeah, it was as if the aliens knew and did it deliberately. Some scientist on TV said the ship was spilt over the border line exactly equally. Fifty per cent each side of the border. Our President has declared the landing zone a site of National Security and that US forces would assume responsibility for the entire location, but Mexican civilians got there first. Some say they actually went inside." The younger one was on a roll now.

"That hasn't been confirmed," the older soldier said, doubtfully.

"My cousin said there were videos put up on YouTube from people who had gone inside. Next day, they were taken down!"

"Don't go believing all that conspiracy junk," the older man retorted, taking a tone. The younger pointed back at the ship.

"So I'm imagining that then, huh? You're gonna tell me it's not really there?" he said. The older one didn't respond, herding the group forward.

"So what happened?" Diana wondered on Craig and Owen's fate. They were keen to see inside the ship themselves. She wondered if they had found a way.

"Some people got shot. Their airforce turned up, shot down one of our helicopters. We shot down two of their planes. I think some people on the ground were killed. The Mexican government is calling it an act of war. Our President says we were just defending ourselves. It's all getting a bit ugly, but I don't think Mexico is about to invade or anything."

The older one sneered at his colleague's last comment. "They wouldn't dare! Don't have the balls or the firepower to take us on! Besides, they got two more of these things, same as us. They have their own problems."

It didn't sound good at all to Diana. Three in Mexico? Craig had said something about them landing all over the world. Where were the aliens then? Where was the invasion? What was the point of coming here then doing nothing? Were they on holiday? Ah – who gave a shit? She just needed to get her kids and get the fuck out of Dodge. As they approached the gates, more Guardsmen were in the process of building a third wire barrier. Diana thought she should buy some shares, in military barbed wire, whoever the manufacturer was. To encompass the entire ship with three rings of the stuff, would take a shitload. Wasn't it twenty miles across, or something? How on earth were they going to control access to an area so vast? She could see America had a big problem but all that mattered to her was to find her two children. They reached the first of the two security gates that had been placed across Highway 50; a route she wouldn't be travelling on again if she had the choice. The double gate system had been designed to enable the rear gate to be closed, while the outer one was opened, thus making it harder for people to run inside. They joined a much larger waiting group of civilians; a mixed bunch of the old, the young, and several with minor injuries, probably victims of similar accidents to hers. They formed a queue to board the waiting buses.

"Please wait here with the others, ma'am. These are the last two buses, the rest moved out an hour ago," the older soldier said. He headed back inside the chainlink fence that enclosed the inner area, containing the rows of tents and clusters of trucks. She searched the group of people milling about, waiting impatiently in the dry heat. Like her, she could see they were tired, hungry and wanting to be anywhere but here. It was then that she felt a hand on her shoulder.

"Diana!" The touch made her jump. She turned to see not her younger brother, Danny but Owen's chubby face with his pimply skin and five-dollar haircut.

"It's so good to see you!" he said, pulling her in for a hug. She had to admit that though he smelled as ripe as she did, it was good to see a friendly face.

"Have you seen my son?" she asked, her eyes frantically moving past him, still mentally checking off the faces of the restless crowd that awaited evacuation.

"I have. I met your brother too. He seemed real nice. Kind of flouncy."

Thank God! They were safe and Danny was with them. Only Danny could be described by someone as flouncy. Danny was a little camp, not just in the way he dressed but in his manner. A spiritual gay hippy was something of an unusual combination. He could take a little getting used to.

"But really nice…" Owen added quickly, as if in apology.

"Where are they?" she pressed him.

"They left hours ago, on another bus…" Owen was interrupted by a shouting elderly voice just ahead of them.

"What's the hold-up? Why aren't we leaving?" an old lady vented at one of the two guards standing near the gate. These guards had a different set of camouflage fatigues on compared to those who had just escorted her here. They looked far more serious, and far less willing to engage in chat. Beyond them, past the gate, was a second group of two dozen soldiers wearing gas masks, with an officer standing on a jeep bellowing instructions from a bullhorn at the thickening crowd of civilians that had congregated at the entrance. Thousands more were spread out along the wired perimeter that ran north and south of the gate. Diana couldn't help thinking that the number of soldiers on their side of the wire was painfully few. Small squads of a dozen men were spread at intervals along the fence. In front of the outer gates, units of local and state police were parked up with a dozen or so officers assisting in crowd control, but they were overwhelmed. The crowd edged closer all the time. Among the civilians, there was no shortage of reporters giving live coverage to their camera crews. Local and national television trucks were parked up in abundance, beyond the outer gate. Owen tried to comfort her as she devoured a granola bar from her rucksack.

"Don't worry about your son. I saw him and Danny leave myself. I could have gone with them, but I made an excuse and hid in the toilet. I wanted to find you and Craig. I knew you would be worried about your boy. Danny said to tell you he had been to see Jules, he said she was okay."

Diana had some difficulty processing all this. Jules was doing okay. Danny had seen her. A wash of relieve came over her. Okay. Fantastic. Danny and Jack were already on their way out of here. Also fantastic. They would probably go to the hospital and wait there with Jules.

"Do you still have your phone?" She knew it was unlikely.

"No, they took it. I think they took everyone's. I don't know what the point was. I mean how can you hide this thing – really?" He looked back up at the ship with its smooth white tower now shining brilliantly, as it caught the midday sun. She had to concur. Hiding one of these would have been tough, but two hundred. The secret is out, people!

"Did they say where the buses were going?" she asked him, desperate for news of where Danny and Jack had gone.

"West I think. Some buses were going all the way to California. They've been trying to stop more people from coming out here, but it hasn't worked. Too many videos up online about the truth. It's like a river, they can't stop us this time," Owen said with pride.

"Owen, much as I would love to celebrate the triumph of the conspiracy theorists with you, I'm more concerned about my children right now. Can you tell me anything else about Jack and Danny, please?' She saw he was a bit wounded by her indifference, but she just wasn't on the same ride as this geek. Once she had her kids, she could get excited about the whole UFO thing.

"Sorry… no… I, well I don't know. They kept me pretty much locked up for two days. I only met your brother because Jack came running up and gave me a hug. Then they were ushered on the next bus out of here. Danny didn't want to go without you but they didn't give him any choice. I said I'd find you and tell you…"

Her boy was such an affectionate child. She felt bad how she had spoken to Owen. He could have left, but he'd stayed so she could know both her children were safe.

"Owen... sorry. Thank you!" She wasn't sure if it was the sudden pang of guilt, but she gave him a peck on the cheek.

"Oh..." He was taken aback by her sudden gesture, something which Diana suspected he didn't get too often from women. Maybe he would have more luck with the aliens.

"Thanks. I just wanted to help and I want to find out where Craig is..." Craig, She had forgotten all about him.

"Craig? Where is he? Wait, you were locked up? What happened?" The Guardsmen waiting to open the gates seemed preoccupied, Diana took the chance to pull Owen away from the group, dragging him between two blocks of portable toilets. "Tell me..."

Owen trembled. He was very emotional as he recalled the events that had taken place. The night that Diana had passed out and been sedated and put on a drip, he and Craig had snuck out the back of the tent in the early hours of the morning and made a run for the ship. Owen described how they had got onto the actual surface of the ship itself, all glowing in the night, but they had soon been spotted by the Military while searching for a way inside. As Soldiers closed in, Craig had found a depression in the surface that led to a blank wall, but at that moment the Military caught up with them. Then the strangest thing happened. The wall at the base of the depression was replaced by an opening, leading to a corridor. Owen described how he, his hands raised in surrender, had already been walking back towards the Soldiers when Craig impulsively dived inside the opening, causing them to fire. Owen shook uncontrollably, as he told her what happened next. Owen saw Craig get shot in the chest. As soon as he said the words, Diana felt a terrible chill, making her shiver. That young man had saved her life, and that of her kids. Owen had too, to be fair, though admittedly, he wasn't as attractive. If Craig's life had been taken so needlessly, it would not only be tragic, but an act of murder by the United States Army.

"But like I said, it was strange. It all happened really fast, but I saw him fall back, into the opening, you know, the door, like I said, then the next thing I knew all the Soldiers were standing around were screaming, dropping their rifles."

"Screaming?" Diana was trying to take it all in. Craig had been shot? Where was he? What had happened to him? "How do you mean, screaming? Screaming from what?"

"It was their hands. They were burnt. I took a chance and ran back here."

"Didn't they identify you?" Diana was amazed the chunky twenty-something had managed to escape.

"No. We stole some army uniforms. We even had balaclavas. See..." Owen proudly produced the black balaclava from his pocket before quickly stuffing it back in. He wasn't wearing army fatigues now, though. Diana was still trying to picture what he had just told her.

"How far were you onto the ship?" she asked.

"Not far, maybe half a mile in from the edge. I was sure the depression we found wasn't even there before. I thought we walked right past that exact spot but I guess we missed it, what with the surface looking exactly the same everywhere. I know Craig was wounded. I need to get back there and find him."

"You didn't see what happened to him after he fell through the opening?"

"No, when I looked back, it was just the wall again. No sign of Craig, no door, nothing. There weren't even any buttons, it was so weird. There was one thing though…"

"What was that?" She was curious and feeling a little jealous. They had walked on the thing! Of course, she had seen it from below. The diamond! She just remembered. She put the larger one in her daughters backpack and the smaller stones were scattered around her own. She would have to check for them later.

"Right after the soldiers fired, the whole thing, the ship, it seemed to glow brighter, like it was angry or something. That was when the soldiers all began to scream and dropped their guns. It was like it made their guns too hot to touch. I saw this one guy who went to pick his rifle up to fire at me, when I started running. I guess he just did it on instinct. I heard him scream so loud that you would've thought his balls were being cut off! So I knew then I could make a break for it. Over twenty of them, rolling round in pain. Actually, I didn't run. I just walked back. They had helicopters buzzing around, and I wanted to appear as if I was one of them. Craig is inside that thing, I am sure of it but if he doesn't get help he might die."

"Maybe there's someone inside that thing that can help him?" It sounded stupid as soon as she said it, but she could think of little else to offer Owen in the way of support. Their conversation ended when a platoon of khaki-clad soldiers came rushing over, followed by another platoon of men in black riot gear to reinforce the men outside the gate. Two other men wearing the same uniform as the National Guardsman that had escorted her over, boarded each bus, taking the driver's seat and starting up the engines.

The civilians showed a mixture of elation and relief to be finally leaving but a few wanted to stay. There was talk from some of disembarking via the emergency exit, as soon as they were beyond the outer fence. They wanted to rejoin the other protestors. A Staff Sergeant with an impressively wide physique strode over to the waiting group. He shouted over the continual barrage of protests that could be heard beyond the perimeter, some four hundred meters away.

"Ladies and gentlemen, I am sorry for the delay, we had some issues finding you available drivers. Those of you who have had medical attention will be boarding the first bus. You will be taken to a hospital and checked over to make sure your needs are met, before you travel further. Everyone else please board the second bus. This will drive to Carson City Airport, where other transport has been arranged for you. Those of you who are stranded will find hot food and bed there if you need it."

"Excuse me Staff Sargent, which hospital will people be going to in the first bus?" Diana knew to always address such men by rank, it generally resulted in a better response.

"Medical facilities have been set up at Fallon Air Naval Station, which will see to all your needs. Are you injured, ma'am? Because you don't look so bad..."

"No... I was in a car accident, but I feel okay. Just some cuts and bruises." Diana knew she didn't want to get stuck in Fallon.

"You need the second bus, then. Right everyone, let's get going or the Colonel will have my ass for grass, come sundown!"

People began to shuffle on to the buses. If the second bus was going to Carson City Airport, it would put her just a short ride from Danny's retreat and the hospital in Lake Tahoe; close to Jules, more importantly. With a bit of luck, she would see both her babies tonight. Diana caught a few snatches of conversations from people as they boarded the second bus. One local man saw the ship come in and land right on his farm a few miles north of here. He had lost everything, and didn't want to leave until he knew he was going to be compensated. There was a British guy, some actor who had been in LA and had driven all the way out here to see the vessel. He'd gotten close to walking on the surface, but was forcibly removed. He was explaining that when soldiers recognised him, they were more concerned with taking selfies with him and getting an autograph for their kids, than they were in telling him off. Owen got excited upon seeing him, telling Diana he was in the new Star Trek movies. Diana hadn't seen them. She hadn't even seen the old ones. Was he playing Spock? She knew who Spock was. Apparently he was not Spock. He was none too pleased at being evacuated but was currently on the phone to his agent checking if his audition for Monday with Denzel was still happening. Several people on the bus also recognised him. Lines like "I bet you never thought you'd see a real spaceship in your lifetime!" and "Now you have boldly gone where no one has gone before, buddy!" were bandied about, as the bus slowly trundled through the first gate. Every seat on the school bus was occupied. A couple of people even sat in the gangway, which Diana was pretty sure was illegal, but this was a National Emergency so it seemed none of the usual rules applied. The bus in front of them reached the outer gate. A large group of Soldiers stood ready on either side of the road beyond, ensuring that no one tried to rush the gap once it was opened. As their bus rolled towards the outer gate, the second inner gate was closed behind them, and they were now in the holding area between the two. Further out to the north, Diana spotted groups of engineers constructing additional watchtowers. Two such towers had been erected either side of the outer gate, both of which were manned with two men apiece, their rifles held at the ready. This was a choke-point, a magnet for all those travelling here. Either side of the road heading west, extending all the way back towards Fallon, vehicles were double-parked. Immediately opposite the outer ring of wire, camper vans and motorhomes in their hundreds formed an almost city-like ring of vehicles. 4 x 4s and oversize-wheel trucks had taken advantage of their ability to travel off-road, taking to the rough tracks that split off from the main highway in their attempts to circumnavigate the hastily constructed defences of the Military. Now an uncomfortable standoff was taking place, and Diana didn't like the look of it one bit. Whatever attempts had been made to stop people from coming to the area had evidently failed. Diana could see the Military must have been overstretched just to create a cordon on the west side of the vessel, let alone build any further security measures. It was like a large musical festival surrounding a smaller private one, to which no one had a pass, but which everyone wanted to attend. Why? Because the main event on stage was sitting right in the middle of the private festival. The ship.

The outer gates remained closed while the Officers conferred among themselves. Someone came up to the driver's window of the first bus and said something to the Guardsman at the wheel.

"Doesn't look like they're going to let us out, yet," Owen commented, looking through the windows. The chanting around the perimeter of the camp grew ever louder as the crowd grew. They were becoming more hostile as the minutes went by. Owen produced two bottles of water from his bag, passing one over to her. She was grateful. Geeks always thought of everything.

"I was told there had been some shooting in Mexico. Some people had died or something?" Had Owen heard about it?

"Yeah, it was all over the internet. They said a load of Mexicans got inside the ship there and put some video on YouTube."

"Did you see the videos?" Diana was curious to know what the inside looked like. She doubted she was alone in that respect.

"No. YouTube was down for about twenty-fours yesterday. When it came back up this morning, everything taken inside one of the ships had been removed. National censorship!"

"No shit! I bet that nearly caused a riot!" Diana couldn't imagine people taking that lying down. How did the government think they could actually contain this?

"There's been protestors outside the White House all day. Not just hundreds, but thousands. The Governor of Atlanta called our President a Social Media Nazi!'

"He did? Holy shit! Good on the Governor of Atlanta!" About time someone said something challenging.

"Yeah something kicked off there too. Some kind of envoy came down from Washington and tried to arrest the Governor, but he had a judge with him from Georgia, who called the grounds for the arrest illegal and base-less. I think there was some kind of standoff between local law enforcement and the FBI. The city already had the National Guard present. Bottom line, the Governor wasn't arrested and the President is mighty pissed.'

These were the grand events shaping the world around her that she knew were going to somehow influence the fire of her children yet she felt helpless to change them. There was no alien invasion, but everyone still seemed ready to kill each other. "So, did I miss anything else?"

"Erm, well just that North and South Korea might be about to go to war with each other,' Owen added, somewhat dryly.

"Aren't they always?" That concerned her far less than a war in her own country.

Owen and Diana sat on the right side of the bus, the view of which looked north across the Sand Mountain Recreation Area, the hills of which had been engulfed within the circumference of the ship. Between the cordons of the perimeter to the north was a valley that covered about three miles, wedged between the west low rolling hills and another barren rocky peak known as Rainbow Mountain. Diana had seen all the names on Google when she'd checked their original route. The Military cordon stretched up through this valley, curving around slowly with the circumfer-ence of the ship back east. As with the south, the valley was filling up with visitors coming in trucks, camper vans and even Humvees. Owen pointed to a series of distant clouds kicking up in the valley to the north west.

"See those? That's more people cutting across country coming down from Highway 116 near Stillwater, to get past the checkpoints. I'll bet the Army is having the same problem on the east side with people cutting through Dixie Valley by Mount Augusta, from Highway 50. That's why their calling this the Mount Augusta landing in the media. I can't see how they can contain this thing!" Owen said, victory in his voice.

Diana had to admit he was right. Then she saw the outer gate began to open, giving her a sense of relief. The sooner they left here the sooner, she would be with her children.

"Finally!" said a woman sitting in front of her. As the bus ahead of them began to roll through the gates, a surge of people tried to rush in but the front line of Soldiers and a second line in riot gear were ready for them. The

Guardsmen had formed two lines either side of the road, while the second squad formed a line abreast of the road, between them and the gate. Diana presumed the plan was for them to clear a way for the buses to come through, when they were at the second gate. The people pushed, the soldiers pushed back. Batons were drawn, with men shouting orders. A few brave souls tried to rush the Military, but were met with brutal force. A baton came down hard across one man's head, blood pouring from the wound. Then she saw a policeman draw a gun. No! Shit, now she knew someone was going to die. The Army wouldn't fire unless ordered by a Superior Officer. Police officers were not all of equal calibre as the video footage of one killing a civilian at Fruitville Station had proven. That guy might as well have trained in a Police Academy movie, for all the restraint he had shown. Now right in front of her, four State Patrolmen were waving their guns at the crowd, ordering them to get back. They levelled them ready to shoot. Behind them stood another hundred well-armed men. The crowd shouted and catcalled, but no one else rushed the gates. The people waiting outside had already formulated other plans. Then Diana saw movement. A large tractor she thought, thundering towards the outer perimeter fence, maybe half a mile or so north of the gates. Whoever had been manning the wheel dove off the vehicle, letting it plough towards the two rings of barbed wire fences. Shots were fired to try and stop it, but from this distance Diana couldn't see who was firing. What she did notice was a garbage truck come racing out from behind several of the parked motorhomes, its engine really gunning, following hot on the heels of the tractor.

"Shit look at that, they're going to try and get in!" Owen said. He seemed unable to grasp the danger this would put them in. Someone had just lit the powder keg and this was going to go south very quickly. Diana pulled down her rucksack from the overhead and pulled it on her back. The crowds by the gates began to cheer with cries of, "Go, go!" and, "Get in, breach the fences!" She could see it made the Police even more nervous. They were moving. Slowly they trundled forwards, but the bus ahead of them had yet to clear the outer gate. The garbage truck charged on towards one of the newly constructed guard towers which had been positioned roughly five hundred yards or so apart, smashing into it at great speed, sending the two occupants hurtling to the ground. The tractor ploughed through the two belts of wire, ripping up the stakes from the ground like a harvester shredding wheat, creating a large gap through the perimeter to the north. A flurry of smaller vehicles now emerged from the civilian encampment followed by people on foot, all charging for the gap it had created. The commotion to the north caused the press to run across the road ahead of their two-bus convoy, causing the bus ahead to brake hard just as it cleared the outer gate. Theirs did likewise. Diana could see reporters jostling for the best position, as they got ready to report back live to the studio.

Now the crowd at the gate saw their chance. With the bus stalled part-way through the open outer gate, they surged forwards. Pandemonium erupted before Diana's eyes. Reporters, their cameras rolling, didn't know where to start with their reportage. Immediately behind them, people were pushing and shoving to access the open gate. To the north, a mixture of dune buggies, motorcycles and two dozen other vehicles were dashing for the gap, causing the military elements at the gate to be distracted and lose focus. Helicopters swooped towards the scene, while a number of khaki-coloured Humvee's inside the perimeter began to converge to defend the gap. Loud-hailers could be heard but among all the confusion, Diana couldn't make out the words. Then there were a series of sounds she did recognise – crump, crump, crump! Rounds of tear gas were being fired close by. A heavy white mist was filling the air outside the bus. Someone shouted something to the driver. Their bus lurched forward again, but only managed to get part-way through the outer gates. They stopped as the bus ahead of them again did the same. Owen drew her attention to further movement to the south. Standing in the aisle, he leaned over a middle-aged couple sitting opposite them to get a better look out of the window.

"Do you mind?" The man sounded irritated.

Owen completely ignored him.

"For God's sake, get moving, we can't stop here!" an older man shouted at the driver.

Then there was a gunshot. It sounded like a car back-firing, followed by people screaming. A mass of blurred running figures surged through the white clouds ahead of them. Diana caught a glimpse of a young man lying still on the road. The second line of Troops clad in their black riot gear rushed out to push the civilians back, but they were outnumbered by the crowd. Diana saw blurred scuffles breaking out in the clouds of tear gas ahead of them.

"Everyone close the windows!" the driver shouted over the speaker, sounding panicked. Someone ran out to where the young man had fallen. This sudden movement caused one of the State Troopers to fire his weapon, and that was the straw that broke it all. The state of Nevada had, as it turned out, an *open carry* gun law. This crowd was bristling with firearms and they didn't take too kindly to being shot at. Gun fire crackled around the bus. Diana saw all four of the Police Officers go down very quickly. Metallic thuds clanged as rounds hit the bus. One went through the front window. Bursts of automatic gunfire broke out all around them. There was a sound like heavy rain hitting the roof of the bus.

"Everybody get on the floor, I'm going to try and get us out of here!" the driver shouted over the intercom.

The attack on both sides of the fence had clearly been well coordinated. Now a second group of vehicles rushed the south perimeter. Diana couldn't resist peering momentarily above the seats. Outside, she saw two ranks of uniformed men, their weapons raised. Somewhere, further down the bus she saw someone produce a phone and begin filming, making her wonder how the hell they had managed to hang on to it. The men in riot gear had fanned out into the crowd, most of whom were now fleeing for cover among their vehicles. There weren't just men. Plenty of women and children were running for shelter, coughing, their eyes streaming from the gas. Pensioners had come to watch events unfold, perhaps mindful that it might be the last spectacular thing they would ever see in their lifetimes. Curious locals who had come down with their families were now hurriedly scooping up their crying children and running with them to safety. Tear gas rounds continued to be fired into the air above the crowd. Diana heard a single shot from a rifle and one of the Soldiers fell straight over, the back of his head missing. Then a second wave of gunfire began. This was more brutal than the first; a rapid succession of shots from multiple weapons echoing throughout the valley. People were already fleeing in all directions when it started. Diana saw civilians being mowed down. She should have ducked down for her own safety, but she was captivated, in shock and couldn't draw her eyes away from the unfolding chaos. She saw a woman collapse with a baby in her arms, wounded in the back. Finally the tear gas obscured everything into amorphous shapes. She had seen enough and lay down on the floor next to Owen, who was in the aisle. Shots echoed back and forth around the vehicle as the bus drove blindly through the thick smoke. Diana could smell the gas coming through the broken window and covered her eyes and mouth, gesturing for Owen to do the same. Diana recalled Danny telling her that in Nevada almost anyone could own a gun, even an assault rifle. With the right permit, legally you could carry a weapon openly attached to your person. The mass murder of people at a music festival in Las Vegas in 2017 hadn't changed a thing. Apparently not everyone had come down that day to just have a look, others saw the landing site as a threat and they carried protection and were ready.

Diana was certain she saw men with rifles lying on the top of motorhomes and trucks, firing at the Soldiers. She wanted to warn someone, but their bus was moving on and she had to stay down. Besides, who was she going to tell? The continual sound of bullets hitting the bus made some of occupants hysterical. A girl towards the front could not stop sobbing.

"Who's firing? Goddamnit!" screamed another man, wearing a ten-gallon hat. He could have been on a poster for the NRA. Ironic, Diana thought. The bus struggled on down the road, passing the first bus, which had ground to a halt. Diana looked up and saw why. The driver had taken a bullet to the head. The front windscreen was shattered.

"Christ! Stay down lady or you'll be next. Some lunatic's shooting everybody!" a fellow passenger shouted to her.

More than one lunatic. Diana was grateful in that moment, that she had been separated from her two children. She wouldn't have wanted them with her in the middle of all this. The bus began to accelerate just as a huge eighteen-wheeler turned on the road directly into its path. It looked to be trying to make its own escape from the ensuing chaos, rather than deliberately blocking their exit.

"Jesus Christ! Hang on everyone!" the driver yelled.

The bus swerved hard, turning off Highway 50 to avoid a collision, but in doing so found itself hemmed in. The sides of the road were crammed with other vehicles and tents, that the driver now found impossible to avoid. He braked hard, causing the bus to swerve. Diana thought the vehicle was going to roll, and she wondered how unlucky she had to be to experience such a thing twice in one week. The bus collided with a small camper van, spinning it around, before finally tearing through a family tent where people had been cooking a barbecue before the firing began. The gas canister became disconnected from the valve next to the open flames of the grill, as the vehicle came to a halt, battered but upright and in one piece. Diana and Owen were thrown against the seats, leaving them momentarily concussed.

"Fuck this, I'm getting out of here." Diana didn't see who said those words, but the alarm sounded, announcing that the emergency exit window had been opened at the rear of the bus. She saw Owen had a small superficial cut on his forehead. They could worry about that later. She tried to pull him up from the floor.

"Owen, come on, get up, we have to get out of here!"

Gunshots and screams could still be heard coming from every direction. The scene outside the bus was one of complete pandemonium as people ran back to their vehicles seeking safety, while others had decided to shoot it out with the Police and the Army. She grabbed Owen by the shoulders and gave him a shake. He came to, still shocked by the impact.

"Can you move?' she asked, not wanting to wait for a reply.

"Yeah, yeah I think so," Owen replied, pulling himself up. An explosion abruptly shook the entire bus, knocking them both off their feet again in the aisle. The gas canister had exploded underneath the front wheel of the bus and flames were licking around the driver's seat. Diana's adrenaline kicked in fast. She decided there and then she was going to survive this and find a way to get back to her kids!

"Come on Owen, let's go!" she yelled, pulling the overweight youth to his feet again. The two of them followed other passengers scrambling towards the rear exit. An elderly lady ahead struggled to move, causing the passenger behind her, an obese man of around fifty, to become very frustrated.

"Lady, can you move a bit faster? I really don't want to burn to death!" the fat man wheezed.

"I'm going as fast as I can! I've only just had my hips replaced!" she moaned.

The fat man wasn't going to wait. He practically picked up the little woman, throwing her into a vacant seat then tried to climb out the emergency exit, but his ungainly body wasn't making it easy for him. Diana reached the shaken woman.

"Are you okay?" Diana asked, helping her to her feet.

"I'm all right. People don't respect the elderly these days!"

"He's been too busy eating donuts to have time to respect anyone," Owen said.

"Just be sure you don't turn out like him then!" the old lady said. Owen could certainly do with some exercise. He was about to get his chance.

"Come on, move it!" Another man was pushing Owen from behind, who in turn bumped into Diana as she was helping the elderly woman. Others had realised they couldn't leave the vehicle from the front and were panicking to get out pushing each other over in their haste.

"Come with me. I'll help you. What's your name?" Diana asked the lady.

"Doris, Doris Huntsacker!"

"Well Mrs Huntsacker, hip replacement or not, we're getting you off this bus." Diana and Owen carried her to the exit between them.

"I don't think I can climb through that window, honey. I'm not quite as agile as I used to be!" she replied, still clutching her large sun-hat.

"Would you get a move on there's smoke coming in from the front!" came an anxious voice from behind them. Diana reached the emergency exit, where the obese man had managed to get stuck, trying to get out. No one had waited to help him down and now he was wedged with one leg out the exit window between the bus and the large motorhome it had crashed into, leaving only a narrow space.

"I need to come back inside!" he cried, as he tried unsuccessfully to swing his leg back in the vehicle. Diana had had it with the man.

"There's no other way out and we all need to leave! Move your ass!" her patience was wearing thin, but she could see he wasn't going to move. She didn't have time to debate with him. With all the strength she could muster, she kicked him in the stomach. He lost his grip, falling out the window screaming, with the sides of the motorhome slowing his fall. The man's size saved him an injury, but resulted in him being wedged between the two vehicles on the ground. He was unable to free himself.

"Owen, go in front of me and help the lady down." Owen nodded and climbed through the open window, standing on the man's shoulders beneath, enabling him to reach the ground safely. He reached up with his hands while the obese man unsuccessfully attempted to wriggle his way out between the bus and the motorhome.

"Okay now, Mrs Huntsacker I am going to have to lift you up and pass you down to my friend, Owen, okay?" Diana said as calmly as she could.

"Well it's been a while since I was touched by a young man, but I'm game." Doris appeared up for the challenge, so ignoring the protests coming from behind her, Diana carefully lifted Mrs Huntsacker up and passed her through the window to Owen's waiting hands below.

"Ow! lady, that is my head!" Mrs Huntsacker managed to step on the head of the man wedged in the gap, allowing Owen to lift her down from there. Diana quickly followed, nearly slipping, as impatient people pushed to get out behind her. She found her footing, stepping on the head of the same man in order to escape.

"Goddamnit, lady, help me out of here!" the obese man pleaded. Diana tried to pull the man free but he was truly stuck between the vehicles. Owen appeared at her side, as another person climbed over them all to escape. Together they took his arms and pulled. The man screamed (like a little girl, Diana thought). Extricating him was made all the more difficult by the fact that people were still climbing down over him to get out of the bus. She tried again, when a horrific sight caught her eye. A woman of around her age lay under the bus, having been crushed when it veered off course. Owen, still trembling, had seen her too. The woman was dead. The crack of another gunshot reminded her that the danger had not passed and they still had to get to safety.

"Pull him again!" Diana shouted to Owen to distract him from the woman's corpse. He grabbed the man by his shirt while she pulled his arm, and finally with a loud rip of material he slid out from the gap.

"There's nothing else we can do here, come on!" She ran pulling Owen with her away from the vehicle which was now fully ablaze. A smell of ammonia and burning rubber hung in the air. They fled along with several others looking for a escape route. She did not look back to see what became of the man they had freed. She had also lost sight of Doris. On the road, multiple vehicle collisions had occurred, as people fled the indiscriminate weapons fire. Highway 50 was already bumper to bumper along one lane, with vehicles that had been arriving from out of state for the last forty-eight hours. Drivers honked their horns and screamed from their windows in vain to turn around, while helicopters still roared overhead. Diana felt a stinging sensation in her eyes and realised the wind was blowing the tear gas towards them.

"They're dumping more of it from above." Owen pointed to a *black*

Little Bird AH helicopter that swooped in low over the perimeter gates, discharging some kind of canister into the crowds below. Diana heard distant sirens and hoped they were ambulances coming from Carson City to assist the wounded. Glancing back towards the gates, Diana saw dozens of crumpled bodies lying on the ground motionless, women and children among them. They had managed to get about twenty metres from the bus when an explosion lifted the vehicle off its front wheels, sending Diana and Owen hurtling into the dirt. The bus was engulfed in flames. Screams were heard of those still trapped inside. Two adjacent camper vans caught fire. Diana could feel the heat of the flames against her skin. She felt as though she had been gut-punched as she struggled to get to her feet, her lungs filling with smoke.

Cries and shouts in her ears sounded muffled, as if coming from behind a wall. She and Owen ran blindly with many others away from the encampment, the clatter of gunfire still going on behind them.

"Diana!" she heard her name called out by someone to her right. She stopped for a moment, feeling Owen's fingers break away from her own.

"Diana! Get over here!" The familiar voice shouted again.

A figure from behind the wheel of a motorhome was shouting through an open door, waving her towards the vehicle. Then she saw a beloved face. She had never been so pleased to see her brother, Danny, in all her life. He waved again from the vehicle. Sitting next to him in the passenger seat was a pale skinned woman with long dreadlocks. Danny jumped down from the cabin. He was wearing blue jeans and a faded t-shirt, his shoulder-length blond hair looked dirty, but otherwise he was the same as always.

"What the hell are you doing here?" she cried, as she ran into his arms. Diana was shaking. She looked her brother straight in the face again to check it was really him.

"Dan, the kids! I don't know where they are! They said Jules is in some hospital and... "

"Don't worry, I do! They're okay! Get on board, we have to get out of here!" He pushed her up onto the vehicle, and was soon turning it around and heading back across the valley, speeding off and leaving the chaos to continue to behind them.

"Diana, this is Shirin. She runs the retreat with me."

Diana didn't even hear her name, she just thanked God her kids were safe. She broke down crying there and then. It was another thirty minutes before she realised she had forgotten all about Owen.

JOY

W ith every passing second, Joy felt weaker. Despite the best efforts of some of the children and her Father, she was still losing blood. She slipped in and out of consciousness. Her Father's voice kept pulling her into the present. The crude stretcher was carried by two of the oldest boys at one end, with her Father at the other. Every time they paused he would turn to her with a smile.

"Stay awake my daughter, it is not far now. Just hang on. You must hang on."

Little Ubba had led them out of town along an old dry wadi. Joy thought she saw the same plane that came into land earlier soaring back into the sky, banking around the white tower before heading west. Joy tried to make the sight of their destination her focus. The white tower dominated even the highest cloud in the sky. As the sun began to dip to the west, its rays bathed the structure in a brilliant warm golden glow that was unlike anything she had ever seen. If this was the last thing she would ever see before going to meet Allah, it was indeed a truly beautiful sight, unless she was already dead and what she was looking at was part of her journey to Paradise.

"Get down everyone! Down! Down!" her Father whispered as loud as he dared. She saw their convoy all crouch down in the dry river bed. Little Ubba was scouting up ahead. Joy noticed scars all over his legs. His feet were bruised and blistered. It was not a wise journey to take barefoot, but most of the orphans in Fada had second-hand shoes, if they had shoes at all and this boy had none. It occurred to Joy he could have had hers as she was being carried, but she was too weak to speak. You had weird thoughts when you'd been shot. Her Father clasped her arm.

"It is going to be all right, we just have to get you to the fountain of Allah. It's not much further now. Just hang on!" He whispered.

She wasn't sure what fountain he meant. She still couldn't get over how young and healthy he looked, like the Father she remembered from her youth. Joy was not sure how far out of town they were or how long it had been since they left the school or tied-up Dennis. She could see the eastern sky began to turn a cool blue. Stars were starting to wink in the sky above her, yet in the direction they were travelling the sun seemed reluctant to leave them. She remembered her Father telling her this was his favourite time of day. He would often just sit with them, watching the sun sink into the west, especially after their Mother had died. Father would say to them: "All the beauty you can see before you, all the colours in the sky, the reds, the yellows, the orange, the blues, the light saying farewell at the end of each day' That is your mother saying goodnight to you and letting you know she has been here watching over you today."

The three of them would hold each other, watching the dying of the light before Nya had left. How Joy wished they could do that again. Their three-camel convoy made good progress. The camels had a far calmer than normal temperament that she had not previously witnessed in her father's animals. They had carried those children who could not walk with no fuss and followed Omari's every command instinctively. He put his fingers to his lips, as if to say "Quiet" to all the children. The two oldest, Martin and Jodie, assisted him in getting the other children to lie absolutely still. They lay in silence, while her Father applied more pressure on her wound, with the other children looking on, with fear in their eyes. She would have to be brave for them. The pain was so intense, that Joy could not stop tears from coming but she kept her mouth shut, drowning her own cries through gritted teeth. Little Ubba soon came running back.

"It's okay, they're gone. They're walking around the edge heading north. We're almost there everyone," the small boy said, smiling.

Joy had no idea who *they* were, but soon they were moving again.

"Up, up everybody. Keep it really quiet, we must move quickly, but no talking!" Her Father always spoke in a different tone when he was very serious. The smaller children remounted the camels, who rose compliantly and without a sound. Joy observed the surroundings as the group moved cautiously onwards – something was different. She could see palm trees. Had they somehow come back around into Fada again? There were no other trees anywhere for miles, and certainly none within a couple of hours' walk of the town. Yet there they were, swaying in the sky above her. She smelled something else. Joy heard the gentle splash of water underfoot, and several of the children momentarily broke the order for silence, giggling.

"How is there water here, Papa Omari?" one of them asked.

It was sweet that the children had taken to her Father as a parental figure so quickly, although she was less sure if she wanted so many new brothers and sisters.

"Quiet everyone!" her Father hissed. Joy leaned her arm down to feel the ground, recoiling when her fingers touched cool water. She was struggling to open her eyes now, but managed to look down from the side of her stretcher. She saw clear water, not more than a foot deep covering the ground as far as she could see. The surface was sparkling with the last embers of the sinking sun. Then a short distance ahead of them, she saw a white glow coming from a smooth surface at the water's edge. Little Ubba darted among their caravan assisting her Father with keeping the younger children quiet. They instinctively wanted to play in the water. They had never seen it in such a quantity before. Even during the rainy season, the oasis at Fada did not rise to anywhere near the depth they were standing in now.

"Refill your bottles everyone, quickly now!" She had never heard her Father be so commanding before. Joy felt weak and cold. Parts of her body began to feel numb. She wanted to sleep.

"Father, I am so cold," she muttered.

Her Father rushed her side, holding up a water bottle, pouring some in her mouth.

"Drink a little. Just hang on, my daughter, it is not much further."

"I just want to sleep." She could barely say the words. She knew her strength was leaving her. He gripped her hand tightly, interlacing her fingers with his own, giving her another sip of water. She could feel every drop of it fall into her body, tingling as it did so.

"Now is not the time to sleep. You must stay awake a little longer, my child," he said. His other hand cupped the side of her head and he smiled at her once more. She felt a little strength return to her, and she knew she would try. It was just a little further. She could see the white coconut from here with its mighty tower, beckoning them ever closer. Her Father called softly to Martin and Jodie to come to him. They spoke around her in whispers.

"My daughter is very weak. Moving everyone together, we can only move slowly, but Ubba, if you and Jodie take my best camel with Joy upon her, you can race ahead and get to the object," her Father said.

"What about the soldiers?" Little Ubba asked.

"We will have to take the chance. If we don't, she will surely die. Ubba, you have been inside the ship, have you not?"

Joy could make out Little Ubba nodding. So he wasn't lying.

"Do you know how to get inside?"

"Yes," the orphan replied.

"Did you see a room with the waterfall?"

"Yes. I didn't go into the water though."

"Why not?" asked Martin.

"I didn't want to get wet! I didn't want to be cold when I went back to Fada!" the boy protested.

"Ubba, Jodie, listen to me, when you get inside, you must take Joy to the room with the waterfall, then remove her bandages and place her in the water, no matter how grievous her wounds. Do you understand?"

"What will you do?" Jodie asked.

"Martin and I will bring the rest as soon as we can, but you must race ahead and not look back, do you understand?"

Joy could just make out her friends nodding. Her Father took her in his arms and placed her up on Ali-Baba, the animal readying itself, as though understanding the importance of its mission. Her Father's arms felt strong, lifting her easily. He held her for a brief moment, as if he did not want to let her go. She locked eyes with him. She could tell he was anxious but, as always, reassured her with a smile. His eyes were focused, clear and sharp.

"Know that I am proud of you, child. Where you now go will cleanse you of the sins of your Uncle. You must never speak or think of him again. I want you to promise me."

"I promise…" she whispered, and they exchanged a hug. She tried to smile back at him. Even that small act seemed to require more strength than she could muster.

"Here, one more sip of water." He held the bottle up to her lips and she drank as much as she could, before it spilled, running red from her mouth. Joy tasted the blood on her lips. She coughed, splattering blood onto her clothes. There wasn't much time. With one more reassuring squeeze of her hand, she saw her Father stroke Ali-Baba's head and whisper something into his ear. With that, the camel at once rose to its feet and loped away. Little Ubba sat in front, with Jodie behind, holding onto Joy, ensuring she did not fall. The animal began to trot towards the white coconut that adorned the landscape in all directions ahead of them. To Joy, it looked like a white city, the huge circular disk sprawling endlessly across the western horizon of the Ennedi Desert. Clumps of palm trees, shrubs and reeds had sprouted around the banks of the water, where previously nothing would have been able to grow. The ghostly scattered monoliths of rock loomed, almost protesting at their arrival but themselves bore residence to freshly sprouted vines where before there had been none. Joy thought she saw clusters of lights further north, where the edge of the ship almost bordered the old Fada airfield, which lay just to the north-west of town. She had a difficult time, digesting what she was seeing and wondered if her mind was playing tricks on her. Ali-Baba's trotting hooves splashed water up, occasionally spraying her face. Was that a fish? No. She was surely hallucinating. This was not possible. Not here.

"It is as your Father says, Joy! This object must be a gift to the people of Fada from Allah!" Jodie said, marvelling at the sights around them. The sun had finally sunk behind the mountains, far away in the west but a cool orange light still bled across the sky as twilight came upon them. Everything around kept losing focus. It required the greatest effort just to stay conscious, but she was determined not to let her father down.

"Little Ubba, how much further is it?" she croaked, her words barely audible.

"Not far now, sister. Ali-Baba, we must go faster, towards the white light!"

Joy thought the orphan stupid for trying to communicate with the animal, but at once the camel galloped, the water splashing even higher from its hooves. Camels were not creatures normally associated with great speed but Joy knew they could travel extremely fast in short bursts when they wanted to, as fast as sixty kilometres per hour. Ali-Baba seemed keen to prove the point. Joy felt Jodie hold her tightly, as the animal sped forward with this greater burst of energy than expected. Joy wanted to look behind and see how her Father and the others were doing, but the slightest movement caused her intense pain, so she remained as still as she could. She kept her attention focused on the tower of the white coconut that loomed above them in the darkening sky. A sweet scent that reminded her of honey filled her nostrils. As they approached the edge of the white coconut, the groups of plants and clusters of palm trees began to dwindle, until nothing but a ring of water remained between them and the expanse of glowing surface. Scatters of protruding rocks broke the glittering water, but otherwise the surface was as smooth as glass. Joy realised that the white brilliance of the object emanated from beneath its surface, reminding her of the soft light cast by the moon at night. The apex of the tower reminded her of a needle. She thought if you could go inside and reach the top of it, from there you would be able to see the whole world.

"I think someone has seen us," Jodie said anxiously, looking off to her right. Joy was too weak to turn and just hung on as best she could, as Ali-Baba danced across the water, gaining speed.

"This is where we need to be. Stop here." Ali-Baba did as the boy commanded, grinding to a halt and instinctively kneeling down in the water. Joy thought how, before today, no one would have trusted the orphan boy with an animal of theirs, but now he was their guide to safety. The pain was intensifying and she felt weaker. Everything was becoming harder to see. Little Ubba dismounted.

"Help me get Joy down," he said.

Joy felt herself falling from the animal and sensed the strong glow of light beneath her. Jodie propped her up and pulled an arm around her shoulder, while Little Ubba ran off across the pearl-coloured surface ahead of them. Ali-Baba would go no further and remained at the edge, drinking from the water. If Little Ubba had intended them to walk as far as the tower, Joy knew she would never make it. Jodie was slightly built, already struggling with her weight as they staggered slowly forwards together. Up ahead, Joy thought she could see Ubba waving at them, but she could only see his head and shoulders.

"Come on, I've found it'" he shouted.

Large drops of blood fell onto the surface of the ship, leaving a trail that would be easy to follow. They could do nothing about it. She heard their camel let out a single bleating cry, Ali-Baba turned and trotted back the way they had come. She hoped her Father and the others were making good progress. It had taken them perhaps ten minutes to cover the distance from the edge of the new oasis to the white coconut, but that was with the camel going at full pelt. She knew for the larger group it would be slow going. Several of the children could not walk unassisted and the camels could only carry so many. She prayed they would all be reunited soon. Jodie strained to support her as the two of them staggered across the glowing surface. The ground felt warm beneath her sandals. Joy felt they must be visible from far away, walking under such a light. Far to the north, shouts could be heard, as though someone was yelling orders. She stumbled, and Jodie had to haul her up to keep going. Up ahead, Ubba was no longer visible. Joy wasn't sure if he had vanished, or if her sight was finally failing her.

"Come on, we must keep going!" Jodie's words of encouragement urged her forward, but gave her little strength. She could feel her will to go on was waning with every step.

"Over here!" Little Ubba's head appeared, peering above the ground just a dozen metres ahead of them. Joy felt she was seeing things.

"Help me, child!" Jodie shouted as her own strength gave way. Little Ubba sprang up from a depression in the surface, and ran toward them faster than Joy would have thought the small boy was capable of. He took her other arm, and together they supported her and dragged Joy on. Her whole body felt cold, yet beneath her feet she could feel a warmth coming from the surface, that was somehow soothing. It was as if something from within was urging her to continue.

"Down here!" The boy had brought them to the top of the depression. It formed a natural slope down to an opening, beyond which there was a bright white corridor. She thought she should feel scared about entering such a strange place, yet she did not. The trio staggered down towards the opening. Upon reaching it, Little Ubba broke away and stepped inside, beckoning the two girls to follow. Jodie saw how weak Joy was. Time was vital. Jodie, still taking Joy's weight, stepped through the opening and they were inside. Immediately the opening closed behind them, the walls inverted and the night sky was gone. Joy had trouble comprehending what she was seeing. Little Ubba once again took Joy's other arm, and led the two girls along the smooth white corridor. Joy noticed there were no hard lines or sharp edges anywhere, it was almost like an oval-shaped tube. The corridor was fully lit, from a soft light that came from beneath the surface of the walls, yet no individual light source could be seen. They passed a couple of openings on both sides, before taking the next turning on the right. It glowed brighter than the rest.

"It is reminding me which way to go!" the boy said, as he steered them into the turning. Joy coughed harshly, bringing blood up from her lungs onto her clothes.

"Ubba, she is dying! Take us to this water, please!" Jodie cried. Joy could no longer focus. Her head began to spin. She slumped in their arms and felt herself falling into darkness.

She couldn't remember stepping into the water or even getting into the room, only the sensation of cool water pouring down on to her head from above, and then a feeling of being submerged underwater. She broke the surface with a gasp of air, as if waking from a dream. She was in a state of shock. It took a moment for her to realise she was standing at waist-height in a small pool, that was naturally formed in an arched white cave that opened on one side of what was a larger room. Jodie was standing in the water alongside her, holding her upright. Jodie was naked.

"Praise Allah! He has protected you! It is just as your father said!" her friend cried, breaking into a beatific smile.

Joy became very conscious that her clothes and bandages had been removed. She sank down so only her head and shoulders were above the water. She didn't like being naked in front of anyone, but Jodie had, it appeared, as an act of solidarity, done the same. The two of them sat side by side in the water for a few minutes. Joy's mind came back into focus in a singular flowing rush. It was overwhelming. A flood of memories and images. Every part of her life was available for her to recall, displayed in her mind in chronological order. As she closed her eyes, she saw every moment of her past fly by, all available for her to select if she wished. Times with her Father, her sister Nya and her beautiful Mother who had long passed from this life, appeared in her head with incredible clarity, as if she was replaying the exact scene, moment by moment like a recording. She could hear their words, recall the smells, the sounds and every single detail.

Something surged up from her throat, causing her to convulse as she coughed again and passed an almost solid substance from her mouth. A revolting ball mixed of dirt, dust, bile and blood. Her lungs were purging themselves before her very eyes. Her next breath was unlike any before. It was different, cleaner and pure, filling her body in a way she could not ever recall experiencing before. She sat down again on the small ledge that ran along the inside of the pool, just off to the side of the waterfall. Jodie sat next to her.

"Don't worry the same thing happened to me! I think it is your body, getting rid of all the bad spirits."

It was certainly getting rid of something. She coughed a few more times but soon felt better. Jodie pointed to Joy's stomach, her eyes widening in disbelief.

"Look at your wound!"

Joy had forgotten all about getting shot. The searing pain from before had completely abated. She touched her flesh, bracing herself for pain, but felt nothing but her own healed skin. There was nothing, not even a scar.

"It's gone! But how?" she asked in amazement.

"Is this place not truly Paradise?" the voice of Little Ubba came from somewhere above them, further inside the main room.

"It can't be. They let you in, you're a thief!" Jodie shouted back.

"I only stole what I had to, to live. You would have done the same!" he countered.

"You didn't have to steal, you could have stayed at the school…" Jodie's own voice trailed off. Joy could see she realised the fault within that argument.

"That didn't work out to well for some of the other children, did it?" Ubba said.

Joy peered out of the alcove and could see her clothes had been lain on a seating shelf just outside the pool, where a natural ledge had formed. Little Ubba appeared, coming down the short slope that led to a second landing above them. The ceiling in that part of the room went higher still. Joy leaned out and could see an opening in the side of the wall above enabled the endless source of water to fall into the pool around them, but remembering she was naked, quickly retreated back into the water.

"I don't remember getting into this room," Joy said. She didn't feel the need to cover her modesty for Ubba's sake, but did so more for herself. Jodie opened her mouth and leaning out drank large gulps of the falling water. She giggled with excitement.

"We had to carry you, it wasn't easy, but we did it," Little Ubba boasted, sitting on the bottom of the slope opposite the pool.

"You knew the water would heal me?" Joy asked. Ubba shook his head.

"No. I never went in it before, but your Father, he knew."

Father. The other children. How long had they been separated from them?

"How long have we been in here?" Joy asked. She felt anxious.

"About ten minutes," Jodie replied. Joy immediately stepped out from the pool and reached for her clothes. She was amazed to find they were dry and warm, the bloodstains having completely vanished, though the bullet hole remained. At seeing the girls naked, Little Ubba turned his face away with a groan.

"Did either of you clean these?" Jodie and Ubba shook their heads. Joy would solve that riddle later.

"We must go back and get the others, we must lead them in here!"

The small boy nodded, running up the slope. Joy and Jodie dressed quickly, the two young women assisting each other with their final arrangements. As they slipped on their sandals, Little Ubba looked back at them and laughed.

"You'll find you can run faster in here and on the surface barefoot!"

Joy looked at Jodie, who shrugged. Both girls kicked off their footwear. The ground beneath them felt unusual; cool to the touch, yet somehow there was a feeling of warmth on their skin. The girls quickly followed the boy up the curving slope, and reached the upper room. Joy noticed that it too had a series of small alcoves, each large enough to provide room for someone to sleep. There was a more generous central space where people could sit together that was sunk into the ground. It was bigger and nicer than their house in Fada. She barely had time to take it in. Ubba was already leading them out of the door, running into the corridor beyond. Her strength surprised her. She felt better than ever, full of energy. Joy searched the corridor for a trail of blood leading to the bathing room, but there was none. She felt her stomach again, for fear that she might be dreaming, and the bullet wound would still be there, but there was nothing. Her skin was different somehow, smoother. The scars caused by her life in the desert had left her. Little Ubba was still dressed in his tatty light brown shorts and red short-sleeved shirt that was two sizes too big for him. He was easy to see as he ran ahead, taking them back towards the entrance. Joy noticed that Ubba's legs were free of all the cuts and scars that a lifetime of running through the streets of Fada had given him. They had vanished.

"Jodie. Did Little Ubba also get in the water with us?" Joy asked.

"He fell in when we had to lower you into the water," Jodie replied.

"How do you feel?" Joy asked the girl.

"I feel fine. Good. How do you feel?" Jodie enquired.

"Yes. I feel fine. I feel great. Like I have slept for a week!" Joy realised that as she ran, each breath she took enabled her to run faster and faster. She took in huge, clean gasps, one after the other. Her body felt as though it had been blessed with a new boundless energy. She understood now. Her Father had been here, so this was why he had this same energy. This explained how he looked so youthful, when he came back from his travels. He too must have been to the pool. He must have seen what she had seen, perhaps even more… What other wonders lay ahead for them in this heavenly place? She could not wait to see him! The corridor ended with a blank wall. Little Ubba placed his hand upon it. It peeled back for him, revealing the slope that led up the depression in the surface. They could see the night sky twinkling with stars outside, the last colours of sunset now long since gone.

"Little Ubba, how do we get back inside?" Jodie asked.

"Don't call me that, my name is just Ubba," the small boy scolded her.

"We only call you that because there is a Big Ubba in Fada and you are little, so you're Little Ubba," Jodie said in her defence.

"I'm not going back to Fada, so now you can just call me Ubba."

"Okay Ubba, when we leave, how do we get back inside?" Joy asked.

"Follow me and watch." The boy led them all through the opening. It closed inwards to form a blank wall behind them. Joy had never seen such a strange door. She watched the boy walk up and place his hand against the smooth surface. The area around his fingers glowed brighter for a moment, then once again the wall peeled back upon itself, revealing the opening.

"Now you try." Ubba stepped back. The opening closed as it had before. Jodie stepped forward, Joy watching with interest. The surface seemed to react a little differently. Part of it changed and pushed outwards, forming a small square the size of a human hand. A palm print appeared on the surface. Jodie hesitated, uncertain of what to do next.

"Now touch it," Ubba ordered. Jodie complied, and once again the passage opened before them.

"Now it knows you, it will let you in!" the boy said, smiling.

A clatter of gunfire echoed in the night air, making them all instinctively duck. Ubba crawled on his hands and knees up the slope to the top of the depression. He lay prone, then waved to the two girls to come and lie next to him. Joy and Jodie quickly did so, surprised at their own new nimble agility. He pointed to their left, where at a distance of about two hundred paces, two men in Chadian Military uniforms stood, weapons ready, just off the edge of the saucer. The two men had positioned themselves behind a small outcrop of rock that stuck out just next to the edge of the ship. Beyond them, they could just see the outline of three camels and their riders approaching the far edge of the water. A heated exchange was taking place between the two Soldiers and the approaching group. Joy should not have been able to make out their conversation at this distance, but found as she focused on the two men she could hear their words as if they were speaking right next to her.

"This area is now under the control of the Chadian army! You have no business here and must leave the area!" the Soldier ordered.

Joy heard a second voice reply, fainter and further away but she recognised it immediately as her Father's.

"On whose authority?" he protested.

"The authority of the President of Chad!" shouted back one of the soldiers.

"Where is he then? I don't see him here!" Her Father always did have a sense of humour.

"We are authorised to use deadly force if we have to – please go back!"

Jodie poked Joy in the side and pointed over to their right, towards an area some four hundred paces further south, from where the current confrontation was taking place. Jodie had spotted movement among the clumps of palm trees. Joy followed her gaze until she saw it too. The illumination provided by the surface enabled them to pick out the moving figures that were ducking and weaving among the rocks and newly grown vegetation. It was a large group of children. She could make out Martin leading them, carrying the young boy with the missing foot upon his shoulders. Her father must have split the remaining group in two.

"Look over there, towards the airstrip!" Little Ubba whispered urgently to them both. He was pointing towards a large cluster of torch lights moving rapidly toward the area of confrontation with her Father. Her Father would soon be caught between the two soldiers and this second group approaching from behind him.

"This is bad!" Jodie was right to sound worried. It was going to be impossible for her father to reach them, without confronting the Soldiers and Chadian Soldiers from the capital city were known for being trigger happy. Her Father spoke again.

"My friends and I just want to come and look at this wondrous thing. My camels need to drink the water! How can you deny us that? Let us fill our bottles at least."

"Your camels can take a drink from where they are. You must turn back! Our Colonel is on his way, he will tell you to do the same!"

These men must have arrived on the earlier plane; their accents were not of a local tribe. She could see what her Father was trying to do. Distract them in one direction, while the majority of the children came around from the other side. She knew he had the revolver he had taken from Dennis but doubted her father would use it. The soldiers however, were already pointing theirs at his chest.

"Very well, my camels will drink and then we will go back to Fada!"

Joy could see how the children had split up. With Omari were only those who couldn't walk unassisted. Martin's larger group, moving deftly and slowly among the trees and rocks, were edging ever closer. The gap from the cover to the surface of the ship would still leave them dreadfully exposed, on top of which it was entirely covered with water. Water for all its beauty was not conducive to enabling a group of small children and teenagers to move quietly. Her father took a few steps closer to the Soldiers. There was about one hundred paces between them. One of the smaller girls was with him, holding his hand, while another who had difficulty walking was sitting upon his shoulders. It could have been Tabitha but from here Joy could not tell. His three camels were clustered behind him, standing attentively, each tethered to one another, watching everything with interest. Ali-Baba must have returned straight to him. Joy hadn't known her Father's camels were so instinctive. He bent down to the water and filled his bottles, waving to the Soldiers in appreciation.

"What are we going to do?" Jodie said. Then the dark of night was again disturbed by an angry eruption of gunfire, this time further to the north.

OMARI

The crackle of gunfire took both Omari and the two Soldiers by surprise forcing him to rush towards the nearest rocky outcrop for cover, dragging the limping girl with him, while Tabitha struggled to cling onto his back. His camels let out cries of distress, sensing danger. Each one sat down at the edge of the water, not wanting to desert him. The gunfire came from somewhere behind him and to his right. He turned to see the flashes of a fire-fight between the Soldiers and an unknown group of men off to the north, some of whom were close to the edge of the saucer.

"Bandits!" he heard someone cry. Groups of armed marauders, shunned or cast out by the local clans, were known to roam the wastes of the desert, but in recent years he knew their numbers had dwindled. With the dying of the caravan trade, there simply wasn't enough for them to steal any more. Their survival had always been dependent on preying upon others. Many such groups had since gone into the drugs trade or survived by peddling arms to one clan or another, when local conflicts had arisen. Now, a shining jewel in the desert that could be seen for many miles stood out as a beacon to attract them. It was too tempting a prize for some not to investigate. Who knew what treasures might await them inside? No doubt they thought it better to come here before the army stole anything worth taking. Omari knew such a commotion could only be caused by such a group. He was drawn to a blur of movement, two hundred paces to his left and was relieved to see Martin's group making a run for it while the two Soldiers were distracted by the gunfire in the opposite direction. Twenty-two children dashed across to the surface of the gift from Allah. Omari could almost swear that the glow from the ship began to dim, as if were trying to offer them all a greater cover of darkness in which to succeed in their task. Young Tabitha who was clinging to his back, was becoming restless. He gently put her down next to the second girl.

"It will be fine, my child. You will see," he said with a smile.

Both walked with limps, perhaps from a bout of polio they had caught when they were younger. He didn't want to speculate on other possible causes, but they certainly couldn't run. Tabitha was no more than eight years old, the second infant perhaps four. Omari could see they would one day be pretty young women, despite their disabilities and he was determined to protect them from the likes of Dennis. Omari was certain all the children would benefit from the healing properties of the pool of Allah and if anyone deserved to benefit in such a way it was the young, the innocent. He was committed to seeing all of them safely inside. The exchange of gunfire between the Soldiers and the Bandits intensified. He could see some of the Bandits now, clad in black robes, ducking and weaving between the rocks and newly sprouted palm trees in the water. One Bandit fell back into the water, shot through the head, then a Soldier was wounded, followed by a second one. Orders were shouted, he thought by Colonel Malloum, his son-in-law. The Soldiers began to gain the upper hand. He must not delay, he had to get the children inside. The Bandits swore at the Soldiers, claiming clan rights to the area, demanding that the Soldiers leave. They had come from the north, following the circumference of the vessel round, no doubt looking for a way inside. Omari praised Allah that they had not found one. There could be no place for such violent men in Paradise. Bullets snapped passed his ears as the swaying fronds of a nearby plant were shot off. Omari saw Martin's group had reached the surface, waved on by three other figures who had emerged from a depression a short distance in from the vessel's edge. Joy. One of them was Joy! He was certain it was her. Omari's heart leaped. He smiled with relief, knowing she was safe. She saw him spot her and waved to her. The two Soldiers confronting him had rushed forward to aid their comrades. They crouched behind rocks, firing at the Bandits. He turned to the small group of children behind him, eight in all, crouching by his camels. One of the older boys, Brahim, had stayed with him, bravely volunteering to help Omari move the group of crippled children towards the ship. Three of the children had to be carried by Omari and Brahim, because they were too frail to hold on to the animals themselves. So Brahim carried the youngest, while Omari put Tabitha on his back and carried the other in his arms. His new-found strength meant he could manage this easily.

"Quietly now, we must be brave. Come children, let us move there, towards my daughter. You see? Come now, very quietly."

Carrying the two children, he guided his camels a few paces south to put more distance between them and there solders before turning to cross the water that lay between and the white surface of Allah's gift. Omari kept them within the cover offered by the new vegetation that surrounded the ring of water. The children clung to the animals as best they could, while the creatures stepped deftly between the outcropping rocks and gently swaying palm trees. Omari saw the vegetation had grown extensively both in size and quantity since visit yesterday. There were small green shrubs, which he did not recognise, vying for space around the base of the palm trees. Fish in ever greater numbers could be seen breaking the surface of the water. Even now, Allah was changing the landscape around them, turning this part of the world into a Paradise. Food and crops would soon be plentiful and the town of Fada would become known as a jewel in a desert, no longer simply a dot on a map in a very lonely part of the world. The gunfire grew closer but he didn't look back. He kept the group moving, weaving among the rocks and vegetation, looking over towards the ship, trying to line them up with the spot where the distant figure of Joy was still crouching, her body only partly visible above the surface. He knew they must have indeed found the pool and cured his beloved daughter of her deathly wounds. He felt such great relief. Martin's group soon reached her. The twenty two children with him ran down the slope and out of sight. It was time for his group to move. He turned to his camels. All three animals were tied together with Abu-Kir in the front, Abu-Sir in the middle, followed by this favourite, Ali-Baba at the back. Each carried two children.

"Walk softly my friends, we will follow the others across the water," he told the camels, pointing in the direction where Martin and the others had vanished below the surface. His animals at once trotted forward. There was a loud crack as a stray bullet went past his ear. Omari could see two Bandits making a break for the south, and were fighting their way toward them. The two Soldiers who had confronted him only moments earlier were now locked in a battle with them. So much the better, he thought. These Chadian Soldiers were not battle-hardened. They just wanted to survive the fighting. One made a break for the trees, the water splashing wildly beneath his feet. Both Bandits were armed with old but reliable Russian AK-47 assault rifles. A well-placed shot caught one Soldier in the leg. He fell, screaming. Omari saw the second Soldier in turn gun down one of the Bandits, emptying an entire magazine at the man, until his weapon clicked empty. Sensing his chance, the remaining Bandit charged towards him with a scream. The Soldier tried to reload, but the man was upon him. The two men grappled, each trying to kill the other. Omari knew this was their chance, he instructed the children to hold the camels tightly then he turned to Brahim.

"When we reach the edge, you must run toward Joy. I will follow. Carry the infant! I will take Tabitha and the other child." Brahim nodded and hugged the smallest girl to his chest. He could not have been more than eleven himself, and probably hadn't seen a good meal in days but he showed courage. If only his Parents, whoever they were could see this boy now. Omari patted the camels and urged them onwards to the vessel's edge now only a few dozen paces away. He and Brahim ran across the water behind them but Brahim was tiring. Ahead of them, on the surface, he saw a figure sprint out from the depression towards their group. It was Martin, returning to help them. The camels reached the surface of the vessel and stopped at its edge causing the children they carried to panic and cry but Martin soon reached them and began assisting the young children to dismount. He directed them to run towards Joy and Little Ubba who was waving his arms frantically to guide them toward him. Omari and Brahim followed through the water. Brahim, devoid of Omari's strength, was struggling to carry the little girl.

"Father, hurry!" Joy cried out. He could see her clearly now crouching next to Ubba, a short distance across the surface and he quickened his pace. He soon reached Martin, who had rallied the four other children to run towards his daughter. Upon reaching his camels, Omari tried to calm them as they fretted at the sound of gunfire. He could take them no further, and would have to come back for them later. Omari looked north, seeking out the Soldiers. The gunfire had stopped and was now replaced by the scattered cries of wounded men. A line of swaying torchlights came nearer, emerging from the palm trees where Omari had been standing only moments earlier. The approaching men were tending to their wounded comrades. He had forgotten about Brahim who unknown to him had taken pause behind a rock and obscured himself from view to all. He looked over at Martin, who crouched next to him behind the camels, looking at the two remaining children.

"I'll take her!" Martin cried, scooping the child he had carried in his arms. He turned and ran back towards Little Ubba.

"Hold tight Tabitha, we're almost there," Omari said to the girl on his back, her small arms gripping his neck tightly.

"Okay Pappa Omari." Her reply made him smile. Maybe he could be a Father to all these children. Omari glanced around one final time. The closest group of torches were now at the edge of the water. He turned back and focused on Joy and Little Ubba who was waving at them frantically. His own Father had always taught him that lesson in life – "Always look forwards, never back, Omari" he said to himself, recalling the occasion as if he had said the words to him only yesterday.

"Father, please hurry!" he heard his daughter cry again. Omari broke into a run. He was about halfway to his daughter, when he heard a voice cry out from behind him. It was Brahim with the infant girl. He had just reached the camels and crouched beside them. In all the confusion, Omari had forgotten about the boy.

"Stop where you are. You are trespassing!" a robotic voice shouted from a loudspeaker, echoing around them. A line of torches appeared through the vegetation at intervals, their lights swaying all along his peripheral vision. He heard the sound of weapons cocking. He recognised the voice of his son-in-law shouting.

"Father, come on!" Joy cried, urging him to her.

But against the advice of his late Father, Omari had looked back one last time and seen Brahim. The boy was paralysed with fear at the big open space he had to cross to reach safety. He looked back and saw Martin reached the depression and gave the young girl to Little Ubba who led her down to safety. He saw Joy and the others waving frantically to him. Omari stopped and put Tabitha down. She could walk but not very fast. He shouted to Martin.

"Martin! Help me! You must take her!" The boy had only just reached safety, but again he turned and ran back. Omari waved at Brahim to come to him but he would not move. Omari bent down to Tabitha.

"Now this is a game, you must keep walking towards Martin, as best you can," he said. She nodded and crawled on her hands and knees, almost oblivious to events around her. He saw the rest of the children descend out of sight to enter the ship behind his daughter and knew they were finally out of danger. Joy's eyes pleaded with him to come to her but he knew he could not. He could see she was at her most beautiful in this life. Allah be praised. His daughter's injuries and all her other ills were healed. He knew now only one other thing mattered. He must save the other children. Martin sprinted out towards Tabitha, as Omari turned and ran back towards his camels, who shielded Brahim and the last child from the approaching Soldiers. They were now wading through the water, trying to make sense of what they were seeing. Children, an old man – these were not Bandits. Omari prayed that they would not fire recklessly, then he saw him. Behind one of the sandstone outcrops that protruded from the water, was the last surviving Bandit. He now sought revenge for the rest of his comrades. Omari locked eyes with the Bandit for a moment. The man was perhaps forty, and his face was full of hatred. His group had underestimated the number of Soldiers against them. They probably only expected the garrison from Fada. They had not considered that the President of Chad would ensure more men were quickly flown in. Whatever the reason, the man had seen all his friends die in battle before him. He was now the only one left standing. Omari had seen the same look on the faces of other desperate men: he had nothing left to lose. Omari wanted to call out to him, to beg him not to do what he was about to do but it was too late. With a clan war cry, the man revealed himself to the Soldiers and fired a burst from his weapon, killing the nearest Soldier. This wasn't the charge of a reckless man making a final bid for oblivion. This was a deliberate attempt to pick a target and kill him, followed by the next man and the next and then the next until he had killed them all, or was dead himself.

Omari reached the exhausted Brahim, his arms outstretched.

"Give me the girl! Run towards my daughter!"

He took the crying infant from the boy, and waved him ahead hoping his camels would stay down out of harm's way. A loud clatter of gunfire filled the night air, but he didn't stop to look, focusing only on the entrance and his daughter. Joy and Jodie were crying out to both him and Martin, who now reached Tabitha, picked her up and was running back towards them with her in his arms. Brahim just behind him, running much more slowly. Omari bolted out himself, carrying the young girl whose name he had not yet the time to learn. Martin was a mere ten paces from his daughter when he saw the boy stumble forwards, throwing Tabitha into Jodie's arms. Brahim staggered just behind him.

"Father!" Joy screamed. How beautiful she looked, how young. After today, he knew she would grow up to be an incredible woman. How proud he was of her in that moment. Many thoughts raced through his mind as he ran towards her, cradling the screaming child in his arms. Then he felt as though someone had punched him in the back. The force of the blow sent him sprawling. His legs gave way from under him. He was hit again. He fell sideways and rolled, ending up facing back the way he had come. He heard his daughter screaming, but he could not see her. All around him, bullet rounds were ricocheting off the surface of the saucer. He could just make out the Bandit being hit by gunfire and falling back into the water. Looking back, a more horrifying sight greeted his eyes. Brahim had not made it. The boy lay still on the softly glowing white surface of the ship, his eyes wide with death. Omari tried to move but a pain shot through his body like the electricity he felt as a child when he played with live wires against the advice of his Father. His Father… for a brief instant, he thought he saw him, on the edge of the water, standing among the palm trees; coming towards him across the water. He looked again towards the motionless body of the young boy, who had run with him. Brahim had been his responsibility. Omari saw a round had passed through his head. There was nothing to be done for him. The crackling of gunfire continued unabated, then he heard the dying cries of his animals. The noise was unmistakable.

"No… please!" He tried to put his arms up to stop them, but he had no strength. The shrill cries of Abu-Sir and Abu-Kir echoed through the night air as the creatures were caught in the cross-fire, between the approaching groups of Soldiers. He saw the two animals collapse into the water, but the third, Ali-Baba broke free and fled. Two of his friends were gone, but his family was safe. It took all his strength to turn his head the other way. He saw Joy desperately trying to reach him, but Little Ubba and Jodie were holding her back. It took every ounce of energy he had to shout to her.

"Go my daughter! Go now! Go with Ubba! Get inside where evil cannot harm you!"

His head began to spin. A girl was screaming, two girls. Joy and the young girl he had been carrying, who lay by his side. He saw she was unwounded. She clung to him still. Good. His arms were weak. He looked again at his daughter. He would find the strength for one last act of courage. The surface felt warm beneath him and he thought it glowed a little brighter. He pulled the girl towards him, and stood up.

"Father! No!" Joy's cries were painful for him to hear. He coughed fourth blood upon his lips. The girl was young, but she was heavy because he felt so weak. He took a few steps forwards with her then set her on her feet, pushing her ahead of him before falling to his knees.

"Go to my daughter now! She will take you to Paradise. Behind us are Devils. Do you understand me, child? You must go to her. Joy! Take the girl!"

The child tottered towards Joy and Jodie, who lay flat, just a few paces away at the top of the depression.

"They are all your brothers and sisters now! You understand, my daughter? Go now, to safety. Do not disobey me! Go inside! Go!" he screamed.

The words took the last of his strength. He fell back, hearing the boots of men, Soldiers, thundering onto the surface of the ship. He was sure the surface was brighter somehow… The air was filled with men's shouts, the cries of the wounded and the clatter of weapons falling to the ground.

"What is wrong with you, fools? Fire! Fire! I order you to pick up your weapons!"

It was his son-in-law, Malloum. Omari understood now for the first time all that was happening. It was clear to him. He had been tested and he had failed that test. It had been his fault, he had after all been the person who should have been her protector. She was a small girl, defenceless against any man older than her. He could and should have been there. His way of life had not been profitable for many years. He had only carried on for fear of failure at trying anything else. It had been all he had ever known. No matter. Joy was a good person, kind to all she met. That had been her downfall, but it had also been what had brought her to this place. He had managed to save the best part of her and the price was to be his own life. So be it. He was ready.

"Father, please don't leave me!" he heard her cry, sobbing. Omari focused just long enough to see the little girl reach the waiting arms of Jodie and Little Ubba. He couldn't see Martin, and wondered what had become of him. He hoped they had got him inside to safety. If not he would meet him again soon. He heard the sounds of men approaching. They were cursing, some were in pain. He looked into the eyes of his daughter, one last time and smiled, knowing she would remember him and in far happier times than this one. Jodie and Little Ubba began to pull her down towards the entrance, but still she tried to stay. He sucked in what air he could and cried out his final words.

"Go now, do not let the best part of who you are die because of what you have seen today. Do…"

The rest of the words never came. As the last traces of his breath left his body, Omari's head slumped facing skywards. He gazed upon the stars, no longer wondering where the ship had come from.

He understood why they were here. He had only seen one, but he knew there were many. Everything was going to change. Many more people would die, including Malloum, whose shocked face stared down upon him as all Omari knew and was in this world became forever part of something else.

CHAPTER VI

"I'm going to make a brief statement, I won't be taking any questions at this time. This afternoon at approximately 2pm West Coast Time a deliberate planned assault took place on units of the United States Armed Forces and members of the Nevada State Police protecting the Augusta Landing Site in Nevada. This incident is now being considered a terrorist act. Members of the Nevada and Texas National Guard units and local Law Enforcement Officers came under direct and sustained fire and were forced to defend themselves. In the resulting melee a number of soldiers and civilians were killed and many more were wounded along with several members of Law Enforcement agencies. At this time I can confirm the total number of dead is eighty seven and we do expect this number to rise. This is a dark day for America. Victims families are in the process of being informed. I will say again, these sites, St Augusta, Laredo and Lake Michigan are now under the protection and security of the United States military. They are closed to all civilian traffic, on land, sea and air. I am instructing all civilians to stay away from these areas until further notice. This is not a request, this is a direct order from our Commander-in-Chief, the President of the United States."

Statement read at the Fallon Air Force Base press briefing by General Chester Reno at 9pm, Nevada, April 5th

JOY

T he rest of that night had been something of a blur. She remembered
seeing her father fall, bullets punching through his body, the blood
running out of him, staining the surface of the ship with red. She could see
a wounded Martin being dragged down the slope by Little Ubba and some
of the other children. Then she saw two men she recognized: the Army
Colonel who had married her sister Nya, and Dennis, the South African
teacher. He stood above her Father's body, a smoking rifle in his hand. It
was he who had fired the shot that killed him before running onto the
surface of the ship. She witnessed the soldiers try to turn their weapons
towards them only to watch every man drop them from their hands, as if
they burned like fire. As she cried her final words to her father, Dennis
looked up straight into her eyes. She would never be able to forget the
expression of the man who had robbed her of the most important person in
her life. He was laughing. She remembered being pulled away, down the
slope and through the opening to safety. It had closed behind them, taking
the night sky with it. She remembered hearing screaming, but the cries had
been her own. Looking back now, it felt as if those cries belonged to
someone else. Her Father was gone. He was her protector. He had saved
her from the clutches of her Uncle and even more than that, he had
forgiven her for the shame she had brought on him.

"There is nothing to forgive, child," she kept hearing again and again,
inside her head. Perhaps it was all a dream. Perhaps none of it had really
happened. She heard the shot, she saw him fall. No. It was not a dream. He
was gone and now she had nothing. Exhausted, and in shock, she had

fallen into a deep sleep and many hours had passed. She saw him walking toward her, his arms outstretched, smiling.

"Do not be sad my child. Allah has blessed you with a gift greater than any other."

What gift? She did not understand. "Father!" But he turned away and was gone.

A young girl had woken her, pulling on her arm.

"Joy... Joy, what do we do now?"

Joy awoke to find herself in the upper room she had seen before, listening to the soft beats of the falling water. She sat up. She had been placed in one of the alcoves. It took her a minute to find the strength to get up. In the oval-shaped room sat over a dozen boys and girls. Their faces still held fearful expressions. Some had been crying, some were still in a daze, as she had been. She walked through the arch to the upper balcony and looked down into the lower level. A group of children had carried Martin's body to the pool below, and had bathed him but she could see for him it had been too late, he was already gone, like her father. The pool in the room could heal wounds, but it seemed it could not resurrect the dead. The children had taken care of him as if he were their family, which Joy realised, in many ways, they probably were. The only family most of these orphans had probably ever known, were each other. They had carried his lifeless body and placed him on the flat surface across from the water, crossing his arms over his chest and closing his eyes. He looked very peaceful. A young girl saw her and spoke.

"Joy. What do we do now? Is your Father still coming?"

The little girl, Aisha, was the child her father had sacrificed his life for. A pretty child with black hair. The children who stood around her were an interesting mix. Some were very dark, their skin as black as charcoal, others were very light and could have been almost from India or Pakistan. A mixture of children that no one wanted, discarded to cover up the sins of their Fathers, no doubt, or orphans from Parents who died during the AIDS epidemic. Joy remembered that Aisha had a limp, but now she appeared to be walking around quite normally. Joy walked part of the way down the slope to the pool room and sat, with her legs dangling off the side. The other children from upstairs leaned over the balcony or came and sat alongside her, while those below sat down in front of the pool.

"You can walk now?" she asked Aisha.

Aisha nodded, then proceeded to skip about before her, keen to show off. Little Ubba then did multiple handstands with incredible skill, while the others cheered him on. He finished with a back-flip.

"Ubba! Stop showing off," Jodie chastised him. He fell at once back onto his feet. Jodie sat next to Joy, placing a hand on her shoulder.

"Joy, you must tell us what to do. You're our leader now."

Leader? The only time she had ever led anyone anywhere, was getting the children to the cookhouse from the school building at lunch-time. She felt a single tear fall from her cheek. It could have been a tear for her Father, for Martin or for her childhood, because she knew today she had lost all three of them. The children waited, all looking to her for answers. She wasn't sure how many of them there were, between thirty and forty, she guessed.

"What about Brahim?' she asked, remembering the boy who had been running with her Father. Little Ubba shook his head, confirming what she already suspected. Looking around the room, she realised the few children who were previously missing limbs, now stood before her whole; two arms, two legs, all of them intact. Everyone had, under instructions from Ubba, taken a shower and drunk from the pool during her stupor. The pool had healed them all. They looked remarkably well, clean and refreshed, but all were still in a state of shock.

"How long have we been in this room?"

"I don't know. A long time. We let you rest. You slept," Jodie replied.

"You dreamed too. We all heard it. You were talking," Little Ubba said, as he came and stood just below her.

"Really?" she didn't remember dreaming, she didn't even remember sleeping. "What did I say?"

Aisha came and put her arms around her waist.

"You said you would take care of us. You said you understood what you had to do," the little girl said, holding her tightly. Joy took the child's hands between her own. It felt good to be wanted in this way, to feel useful, needed, loved even.

"Did I? I don't remember," she said, still not recalling any dream, only what had happened the previous night, as her Father fell before her.

"Do you know who I was talking to?" She asked them all.

"To Allah!" Little Ubba replied quickly.

"Allah? Really? How do you know that?" Joy was even more confused. She didn't recall any conversation with Allah, or even praying. She remembered screaming his name when her Father was shot and begging Allah for his help. She tried to focus her mind elsewhere. She recalled when she had first bathed in the pool, she was able to select any past memory. She thought about the day when her sister, Nya, left their home for the last time. Nya - She wondered what she would think of her husband when she found out that he and his men had been complicit in the murder of their Father.

"When you were talking in your sleep, you were speaking to someone… you asked the person if they were God," Jodie said, her face full of expectation. But despite Joy's ability to recollect every memory from her past with precision, it would seem this recent dream was out of her reach.

"What did God say?" she asked, regretting putting such a question to the children, at once.

"Can't you tell us?" Jodie pressed. Joy couldn't.

"Joy, I'm hungry," Aisha said, rubbing her stomach.

"So am I," said a boy, close by.

"Me too," said another, followed by several children nodding in agreement. Joy stood up, carefully unwinding Aisha's arms from her waist. The child would not let go of her hand. Tabitha came and pulled on the other one. The children all looked at her with hope and fear on their faces. Little Ubba standing at the front, Jodie to her side. Joy was the oldest, and now Martin was gone, also the tallest. She was barely three years older than some of them, yet they all looked to her for guidance because there was no one else.

"Joy, are you going to be my mother?" Tabitha said, looking up at her, gripping her hand even tighter. They were in a place that was entirely alien to them, strangers in another country. They couldn't go home. They could only go forward. She looked into the child's eyes and saw them searching for hope in hers. She asked for Allah's guidance and paused for a moment, but none came. The only sound she could hear was the water's eternal splashing into the pool. The sound made her calmer somehow. She walked down the slope and past the pool to Martin's corpse. She stroked his face and closed his eyes then lent down and kissed him softly on the forehead.

"Now you go to Paradise with my Father. Sleep well brother. Brave son of Fada."

She turned to the children, her eyes wet.

"We are all young but we will not forget those who sacrificed everything so that we might live. We will say their names out loud so we will remember them. Say their names... Brahim... "

The children hesitated for a second before they all uttered the fallen boys name in unison.

"Martin..."

"Martin." They all repeated. Joy began to shake and a tear fell from her left eye as she uttered the name above all she wished not to say out loud.

"Omari" Again the children repeated the name.

"Remember their names, for it is because of them that you stand here with me today. Remember their names, not in sadness but in joy at their bravery. Remember their names so we will never, ever, forget what we owe them."

They all nodded in silence. Joy knew for many this was the end of innocence which had come all too soon. She led all the children back upstairs to the main room and each found a place to sit around it's sunken centre. Jodie sat down next to Joy. Soon the children settled and they waited for Joy to speak.

"I cannot be mother to only one child in this room. I can either be a mother to all of you, or none of you…"

They were all so young. Jodie was the next eldest after Joy and she was almost as tall. She leaned close to Joy.

"I will help you," Jodie whispered, squeezing her arm.

It was the final push she needed.

"I will be your mother, and yours and yours and yours… to all of you."

The children all cheered with joy, at once swarming all over her, laughing and crying. Tears of joy, for some the first they had ever shed. For most, Joy would be the first mother they had ever known. For all their predicament, fear now abandoned each of them. Little Ubba did a somer-sault and landed on his feet, laughing.

"Okay… okay… quiet, now," she told them. It felt good to be the cause of such happiness to so many. She could almost hear her Father say it, "that is why I called you Joy, you were put on this earth to make others smile."

"Quiet everyone. Quiet!" Jodie shouted, bringing the energetic group under control. The children gradually simmered down and one or two of them sat down with their legs crossed, as if at school. All the others followed suit. Quietness fell on the room.

"If I am to be your mother, then you must look to Jodie as your Father."

"How can we? She is a girl!" one boy asked.

"I should be Father," Little Ubba proclaimed, standing up with his arms folded.

"Sit down Ubba!" Jodie snapped. He reluctantly sat down, looking sulky.

"If we are to be a family, then the Elders in this family must be respected. Jodie and I are your Elders and we will lead you, but only if this is agreed upon by all of you, here and now. Do we all agree? If we do, raise your hands."

All the hands in the room shot up, except for Little Ubba's. He hesitated briefly before slowly raising his hand.

"If we are to be a family and live here, then all we have is each other. So we must always be there for each other, support one another and look after those who are sick or ill." Joy was making the words up as she went along, trying to remember all the best things her father had taught her.

"I feel fine, we all do," said another girl. The other children murmuring in agreement.

"Yes, we all feel fine today. But what about tomorrow? This is a promise we must all make now as a family. Look around you, look at each other. Each person in this room is your brother and your sister. These are your kin. Our tribesmen in Chad formed clans in the old days, to protect one another. Well, we are a clan now and we must protect one another. The first to be formed from the children of the Bidyat people."

One of the other boys raised his hand. Jodie nodded for him to speak.

"I am not from that tribe... many of us are from different tribes. Some of us are not even from Chad."

"Who you were before is in the past. Now we will all be as one. One tribe, one clan, one family," Joy said, almost with pride. She had never addressed a room full of people before.

"What shall we be called?" Little Ubba asked. Joy was certain he would suggest a name if she didn't, but what indeed?

"Well... I... I am going to have to ask you all to be very brave and strong and loyal to one another, so our tribe should be called something that represents that," Joy explained.

"What is the word for *brave* in your tribe?" a small boy asked.

"It is *Shujae*" Joy replied.

"I think that should be the name of our clan," Jodie said.

"Do you all agree?" Joy asked of the room.

All the children nodded their heads in approval.

"Very well, we are the clan of Shujae – Our motto will be, courage, strength and unity, say it after me. Courage, strength and unity!"

"Courage, strength and unity!' the children chanted, with some considerable hesitation.

"I think our family can do much better than that," Jodie added, looking around the room with a smile. Joy nodded.

"Yes, I think we can. Who are we?" Joy shouted

"Clan Shujae!" the children all shouted in unison.

"What is our motto?"

"Courage, strength and unity!" they shouted even louder.

"Very good. Okay, I want everyone to find a partner, we're going to go exploring and see what we can find to eat. So I need everyone paired up so no one gets lost."

The children at once began to busy themselves with the task, many immediately clasping hands with their best friend, or those closest to them. Joy immediately grabbed Ubba.

"You will be my partner."

Ubba nodded his reluctant approval. Having sorted the others, Jodie sat back down next to Joy, taking in a very deep breath of relief.

"You're very good at this, Joy. You will make a great leader for us!"

"Really?" Joy leaned into her new friend's ear. "I have no idea what I am doing. I'm making this up as I go along."

"Me too. Do you think the men... the evil men, like Dennis, will find a way inside?"

Joy looked around the room, listening to the sound of the water falling into the pool below them. Their new surroundings, all smooth and white, as if made from marble, felt somehow close and comforting. She felt protected. It was as if they were meant to be here, but she did not completely understand why.

"No. I don't think they will, but we must see if we can find some food otherwise we will have to go back outside."

She rose to her feet and clapped her hands, bringing the children once again to attention, each now holding hands with another. Joy had thought she would have to re-organise them to some degree, putting the older ones with the infants, but the children had done it already of their own accord. She wasn't sure if they were growing up faster or if stepping into the pool had made their minds sharper. Her own mind certainly felt different. Her ability to recall the most remote and insignificant little detail from any given moment since she was born, was most unusual. Was it the same for everyone else? Had Jodie had the same experience? It was perhaps a conversation for another time.

"Okay everyone, I'm going to need you to all stay together as a group. No one is to wander off, especially not you Ubba, do you understand?"

"Hey, you called me Ubba!" The young boy was pleased. Joy had singled him out deliberately, knowing if anyone was likely to wander off alone it would be him.

"I will continue to call you by this name as long as you behave," Joy added. She felt her own stomach growl. She hadn't eaten in quite some time. What little food they had brought with them had already been eaten while she slept, leaving them only with water to drink.

"Everyone must go downstairs and drink from the fountain before we move. Fill up your water bottles if you have one and bring it with you. For now water, is the only thing we have so drink it sparingly. Everything else can remain here."

One of the smaller children put their hand up to address her. Good. It was the only way to maintain order. She wasn't sure if she could really be their leader, but she could be their teacher.

"Yes?"

"Mother. I need to pee. Where should I go?" the girl asked.

"Me too!" came another voice.

"And me!" said another child.

"I need to do a doo-doo," Aisha added.

Jodie and Joy looked at each other. Where would they do that? Then she had an idea. Almost another hour had passed, before everyone had gone to the toilet. After exploring the lower level of what everyone now referred to as *the house* Joy noticed that the overspill of the pool flowed along a small shelf, that served as small half-pipe styled conduit, taking the water through a small circular opening in the wall, passing it on elsewhere. Where it went to she had no idea, but the shelf was the most sensible place for anyone to go to the toilet. Waste would flow immediately down and out through the gap in the wall. The water cleared again in an instant. Jodie organised the girls to use it first, while the boys waited upstairs. Joy took account of their group. Including her and Jodie there were thirty-two of them. They had lost Martin and Brahim, the two eldest boys. Several others that had set out with them were also missing. Jodie thought they had run back to Fada, while others were certain they had actually stayed at the school and didn't want to leave for fear of getting in trouble. This may have explained why Dennis had been freed to come after them so soon, but it was impossible to know for certain. Speculating about this now would do them no good. Joy could do nothing for anyone who had been left behind, for now. On inspection, all those who previously had ailments or deformities appeared to be completed cured of them. In fact the group appeared very fit and if she was honest, full of far too much energy. Like them, Joy felt her own stamina was presently limitless. Drinking again from the waterfall instantly made her feel awake and alert. She wondered how on earth how she would ever sleep although of course at present she was not actually walking on the earth any longer, so to speak. While waiting for Jodie and the girls to finish, she took account of the number of boys, nine in all, the oldest of whom was Zura who was twelve. At least she thought he was twelve. He appeared shy and didn't say much, so if a leader was to emerge among the boys it was more likely to be Ubba, who claimed to be eleven. He was getting impatient and wanted to go exploring. Finally, the boys went downstairs after the girls came up. Jodie was unsure of how to get everyone to wash their hands beyond rubbing them in the water when they had no soap. Jodie and she agreed that would suffice for now. Soon they were all ready. Led by Joy, the group moved back out into the corridor, turning right, heading towards what they believed would be the centre of the structure, and away from the entrance. The children's heads turned in every direction, running their hands along the smooth walls. After they had been walking for about ten minutes, a bright glow illuminated the surface on the left wall bringing the curious group to a stop. Joy touched it and felt the wall to be warm, then as if were responding to her touch, a large section of the wall peeled back to reveal a parallel tunnel that ran alongside their own. It was more circular in design and larger. As with the other passageways, the illumination came from within the walls. Faint black lines connecting to each other like a spider-web could be seen under the surface, but at no point were any buttons, levers or other devices to be found. Jodie, who it was agreed would remain at the back of the group, came up to take a look. Together they leaned into the opening.

"Why do you think this opened"' Jodie said, as she looked around at the circular passage, searching for some sign as to its purpose.

"Maybe it wants us to go in." Ubba said, already poking his head between his two newly appointed Parents.

"I don't know. It could be some kind of trap," Jodie replied. Joy examined the space. It was basically a similar corridor to their own, still completely smooth, with no edges. Looking in, she could see it ran back the way they had come and then curved out of sight. Joy thought it was possible when it turned, that it ran along the entire circumference of the saucer, but that was a walk she did not want to take right now. Ahead, it went on for some distance before gradually rising upwards and out of sight.

"Maybe it's a faster way to get to where we want to be," she heard herself say. She wanted to try something.

"Okay, everyone step through this opening... keep in your pairs. Let's go, as quickly as you can now, come on please."

The children did as they were told. Their faces were full of curiosity as they stepped through the opening. Jodie ushered the last of them inside. The opening quickly closed behind them. Startled, the children all bunched together, Joy could see they were afraid.

"Hold hands everyone. That's it." Each took the hand of the other nearest to them, the group formed two rings. Ahead of them the tunnel sealed itself, leaving a blank circular wall. Behind them, it then did the same, sealing them in a tube some forty paces in length.

"I told you, it was a trap! Now something bad is going to happen and we can't get out..." Jodie wailed, pulling one of the younger girls towards her.

"No. It will be all right." Joy was not worried. She waited, smiling at everyone, reassuring them it would be okay. Ubba jumped, breaking the outer circle.

"The walls by the floor! They're moving!" he shouted, pointing to the lower sides of the space which began to form a shelf along their entire length, a small height from the ground on both sides of the passage. Joy understood.

"It wants us to sit. Sit down everyone!" Joy shouted to the group.

"Are you sure, Joy?" Jodie asked, doubtfully.

"As sure as I can be," Joy said, sitting down. Jodie cautiously did the same, sitting opposite her. The children all followed their example, holding each other's hands, their heads glancing in all directions, wondering what was going to happen next. The answer was not long in coming. A sucking sound was followed by the feeling of air rushing through their hair, giving everyone goosebumps on their skin.

"We're moving!" said Zura, his shyness abating. Joy felt he was right. They were moving. The air rushed past them faster and faster. All the children gripped each other's hands tighter and tighter in excitement.

"How fast do you think we're going?" Jodie shouted, her voice trying to rise above the sound of the whooshing air.

"I don't know. Fast!" was all Joy could think of to say.

"Very fast! Woohoo!" added Ubba in delight.

"Everyone, keep holding each other's hands and do not let go until I say. Stay seated!" Joy shouted.

The children happily complied with her request, much to Joy's relief. If they were standing, they would have had an accident and it was a long way back to their house, and the pool with its healing properties. After what felt like an extremely long time, the rushing wind gradually dissipated until it had gone completely. They stopped, and the walls glowed brightly then dimmed again. The walls at either end of the tube abruptly dropped away, revealing once more the circular corridor running in both directions. Ahead of them, it ran further on for a short distance and then curved dramatically upward.

Joy stood up. Aisha and another child following her lead. The other children all stood up from the shelf on their side. At once it receded into the wall. Jodie and the children on her side rose and their shelf did likewise. With everyone standing, the wall along the same side that they had entered peeled back on itself to reveal another large portal to a parallel corridor.

"Hold hands again everyone," Joy said, as they all stepped through.

Joy could see they were in the same corridor they had been walking in before. It still continued in both directions. Ahead, it ran for about one hundred paces, before sloping up at a steep gradient out of sight. As the last of the children stepped through from the tube, the wall immediately closed in on itself, as though it had never been. She wondered how they might find it again, but began to have faith that this strange place would somehow show them how to get to where they needed to be. She wondered where they were in relation to the surface, assuming they must be much nearer to the centre. Possibly under the white tower, or certainly close to it.

"Lead on then, Mother," Jodie said, gesturing to the rising slope. Joy wasn't sure she actually wanted to be called Mother. She knew after today's decision she wasn't going to be having children of her own any time soon. This group was quite enough for now. They walked onwards and reached the bottom of the slope.

"I can hear the sound of rushing water," Joy said. She could smell it too and a cacophony of other scents.

"So can I!" Aisha said, pulling at her hand. Joy led the group upwards. They had only walked a short way when the slope rose steeply towards a vast open space. Beyond it was the most wondrous sight she had ever seen. Any doubts she had about bringing the children to this place were gone the instant she lay eyes on the marvel revealed before her. The children all gasped at once, the entire group stunned into silence by what they saw before them. Still holding each other's hands, they slowly shuffled to the top of the slope, so they could all bear witness to the full spectacle that greeted them.

It was a vast circular space, the dimensions of which Joy could not even to guess. It felt as large as Fada itself. Looking up, she could make out no ceiling, only a brightness, where the interior walls ascended so high that it went beyond her vision. The sound of water she had heard came from powerful waterfalls that opened somewhere high above them and then cascaded down into the vast atrium from four identical waterways, each directly opposite each other as if they were the four points of the compass – North, South, East and West. The waterfalls were far greater than the small one that existed in their house. These were powerful plumes of water, like those that she had seen in books, issuing from great rivers. Each poured down into a small lake beneath, which occupied one of many semi-circular tiers that filled the chamber in every direction; each like large gardens on separate shelves, occupied in abundance by an overflowing wealth of plants, trees and vines. These balconies extended from the walls above and below them, dripping with foliage sprouting with pink blossoms, overburdened with ripe fruits that hung down from the laden branches. One above the next, each curving symmetrically with the white walls they extended out from. Each could be accessed by a number of connecting walkways and sloping ramparts that ran around the walls, ascending upwards to numerous different levels above. Other like pathways descended to the tiers below, some of which were entirely filled with water, while others carried an abundance of plant life, bearing fruit of all kinds or were simple green spaces as if personally manicured to be a park. Joy could see red and black berries shining like jewels. Strawberries grew, alongside pineapples and yams. The humid air was full of different scents. It felt warm and sticky, but not uncomfortable. Joy recalled a painting from her book about the world.

"The gardens of Babylon." She uttered to herself, taking two small steps forwards. The group behind her edged cautiously forwards but none dared to go any further. Almost as if to do so, would be to awaken from the most wondrous of dreams. Some of the gardens grew one type of produce while others held a mixture or were simply filled with a small plain of long grass. Joy looked from one to the next to see what they offered to eat. Maize and corn grew on one level, while on the tier below there were banana and plantain trees sitting side by side. Swaying below them were copses of palm trees bearing coconuts. On another tier there were orange, pear and peach trees, sporting a pink blossoms, each tree rich with fruit. In the soil only a few feet away from her foot, Joy could see potato plants and carrots bursting through neat square patches of earth either side of the white pathway. Joy's knowledge of food was limited, but she had learnt to cook at a young age and was sure that some of these fruits and vegetables could not possibly exist next to one another. A series of white paths eventually connected to the main circular tier that occupied the centre of the spectacular atrium. The children stood upon one such path that led directly ahead gradually sloping down towards the central tier. This central platform that Joy estimated must have been well over a mile wide lay at the heart of the space connected by several other water and pathways, including their own. It contained a flat field of what appeared to be a very long grass, clear of plants and fruit trees. Beyond the grass the ground rose up to a small hillock at its centre and upon the hill were some dark objects which she struggled to make out. Her father had been right, it was Paradise.

"I don't think we're going to go hungry..." Jodie said, rooted in awe at the sight before them.

"No..." Joy replied, barely managing to speak, still trying to take it all in. It was simply incredible.

"What is that?" Aisha said, pointing at a dark shape flying through the air above them. The group looked up and Joy could see the source of the girl's curiosity. A strange winged creature swooped down to the ground around one of the fruit trees on a nearby tier, and with outstretched hands shaped like shovels, it scooped up the fallen and rotting fruit, then promptly flew back up into the endless, bright white structure above. Another identical creature came and did likewise and then another. Their appearance was quite ugly. They had a bulbous head, behind which there was an even larger body, reminding Joy of a wasp. But these things were large, comparable in size to a young goat. Thankfully, they appeared to have no stinger at their rears. They busied themselves with stripping each hanging garden of anything that was rotting, taking it back up where they had come from. They glided downward with a silent precision, their wings making a soft buzzing noise. Joy spotted packs of creatures flying between the cloisters, high up above them. The strange creatures did not react to their presence at all but never ventured near them.

"We must be at the bottom of the white tower," Zura said.

The boys observation made sense to Joy. Where else could they be standing in the white coconut where the ceiling would be so high? The tower interior with its white walls soared up forever. She could not see where it ended. The falling water caused a thin mist that hung at intervals in small clouds far above them. Then, they all saw a rainbow cutting across the air, far up in the heavens of the chamber.

"So beautiful." Jodie remarked. The children looked at the abundance of food with hungry eyes.

"Stay together, don't touch anything yet," Joy ordered them.

"But I can see food. There's things we can eat everywhere!" protested one girl. Everyone's stomachs were growling. The ground was marked, every so often, by smooth white plinths, some of which were circular, and curving in unison with the paths. Almost like marble tree stumps, some were larger and looked to have the function of seats, while others were smaller. Joy thought they could be useful for preparing food on. Jodie reached her hand out to touch the nearest one and realised it was very warm. She touched it again and it grew cooler.

"We could cook on these," she commented. Joy imitated her actions and realised she was right. If they were a continual source of heat, food could be fried or roasted on them. Joy also noticed that from each lake ran thin streams of water along several different half-pipes, similar to those in their house. These larger conduits took the water to the numerous tiers in the chamber, connecting them all. Joy wondered where such a volume of water would be coming from. In the Ennedi Deserts of Chad there was none. The four lakes were connected by white pathways that formed bridges over the streams at various intervals, allowing easy access from one tier to another. Smaller single pools of water, like the one in their house were dotted here and there, some of which bubbled continually. The whole place had something completely symmetrical about its design, with the pathways and hanging gardens matching each other on both sides of the massive atrium from where they stood.

"This water is warm!" Zura shouted, as he dabbled his fingers in the one of the smaller pools that lay next to their path. The group were beginning to get restless, Joy could see the children wanted to explore. It was going to be impossible to contain them any longer, but she wanted to be certain there was no danger. The water in the lakes would certainly be deep. She knew most of the children wouldn't be able to swim, and that included herself.

"You were right, Joy. Your Father was right! Allah be praised! This truly is Paradise itself!" Jodie screamed, unable to contain herself any longer. The children jumped for joy, calling out to each other in excitement. Joy watched the strange flying creatures to see if their attention was drawn towards the group's commotion, but they were not distracted, continuing to collect rotting fruit, clearing the plants and trees as they had before. She noticed they kept their distance, as if they didn't want to disturb the children.

She was pondering the group's next move, when something began to change in the most central part of the space that caught her eye. It was a faint noise that drew her to it. She almost didn't notice the sound at first, it was like nothing she had ever heard before. It was a single tone, which slowly grew louder, expanding to contain other sounds. It sounded like voices. Were they singing? She had heard of choirs, and had listened to music from many cultures, but this was something different, as if Angels were welcoming their arrival to Paradise. The children all held hands again looking for the source of the harmonious sound. Then they all saw it.

Ahead, past the mist of the waterfalls and past the tiers with their dangling vines and trees full of fruit, past the long flowing grass where the small green hill lay in the centre of the space came the source of the sound. Joy could still not quite make out the odd shaped objects, arranged in a circle, that sat on top of the hill. As she tried to focus upon them, from the middle of the circle a singular column of bright blue light shot up, past the cloisters of winged creatures, ever upward, climbing into the tower. The choir of voices grew louder, in unison with this light. If they were singing words to the group, it was in no language Joy had ever heard. The children stood, captivated by the sight of the blue beam.

"What is that?" Jodie asked, with a sense of wonder.

"I think it's a greeting to welcome us," Joy said.

"Is that Allah?" Aisha asked, pointing at the light.

"I don't know, maybe," Joy replied, honestly.

"What do we do now?" Jodie asked, looking to her for leadership.

"Find out if the food is safe, and then…"

"It's safe!" Ubba said, chomping loudly upon an apple, "See? Delicious!"

The children stood, waiting for a signal, like animals in a race at the starting gate. Joy looked at Jodie and shrugged. Everyone was hungry.

"Okay. You will all stay in your pairs and eat only what you know. Then come back here to this exact spot in twenty minutes. Stay close. Don't go in the water. Avoid the lakes. Don't go wandering off to far!" Joy's words had barely left her lips, when the children in their pairs scattered in all directions.

"Joy, what do we call this place?" Jodie asked her.

"Babylon." Joy turned and began to walk towards the central circular tier with its shaft of blue light and its heavenly song.

"Where are you going?" she heard Jodie call after her.

"To talk to Allah," she said, pointing towards the light. The colours of the rainbow above them were reflecting off the beam, bouncing each hue of the spectrum across every surface, through the fruit-laden branches and the trees, finally reflecting in the numerous pools and streams. It was dazzling. Joy followed a straight pearl-white path that cut neatly through the gardens ahead. Joy noted she could have taken any number of paths up to one tier or down to another. As she continued she passed different herbs planted next to the path: mint, coriander, ginger and others, each with their powerful scent. This truly was that place depicted in her book that had been destroyed by man and until now was depicted only in paintings. *The Hanging Gardens of Babylon*. It was said to have been the most beautiful city on earth before mankind destroyed it in its quest for domination. Yet here it was before her and she felt determined it should not share the fate of its past.

The song of the Angels beckoned to her. Joy found her pace quickening, almost breaking into a run. The scents of the flowers ripe fruits and planted herbs washed over her, one after another. At times it was almost overwhelming. The path flowed into an arched bridge that took her over one of the streams. Joy searched the clear water for signs of the fish she had seen in the moat outside, but saw none. At intervals vines tumbled down into the water and drank the liquid, while clumps of moss grew around its banks. Joy felt an unfamiliar sensation underneath her foot which reminded her she was not wearing any shoes. She had momentarily stepped off the smooth path while transfixed by the shaft of light. Her bare feet were on a soft bed of grass for the very first time in her life. The feeling of it between her toes, making her to giggle. She found herself running across it, laughing. She hadn't thought a field full of grass would feel so refreshing. Floating seeds spiralled in the air. White and pink-coloured spores danced before her. She reached the central garden platform, containing the long grass field. The path branched to her left and right curving around the central field, enclosing it completely in a circular white path. The tall grass ahead of her grew to her waist and extended for some way before ending where the ground gradually rose up to form a small hillock, at the summit of which was the base of the column of light. It shone brightly, a continual shaft of blue and white brilliance. The voices that called to her from it sang gloriously. Joy ran through the tall plants, and after ten minutes reached the base of the hill. Finally her boundless energy had reached its limits. She was forced to catch her breath before ascending the gentle green slope toward the top. The grass on the slope was short and looked as if it had been cut to stay that way. At the summit, the sloping ground levelled out into a flat circular green patch of ground that was no more than one hundred paces across. Within it, a number of dark objects formed a ring around the shaft of light. Joy could now see them more clearly. They were a ring of dark rocks, not unlike the sandstone towers in the Ennedi Desert. These were smaller though, and made of an unknown stone that had not come from this region, each twisted and turning to form its own unique shape. The dark brown surface of each rock was bisected with a random number of amber and grey ribbons that rippled through the surface. Each rock appeared to be an equal distance from the other, perhaps six paces or so. The tallest was no more than three metres high, while the smallest was less than one. As Joy moved closer to inspect them, she saw some were wider, others were more slender, but each had a grace and a beauty of their own. The song became more powerful to her ears where she stood, not intrusively so, but she felt she could hear thousands of voices, singing like a choir of spirits. Their voices were singing in perfect unison, as if the light was their beacon, drawing her toward it.

She reached the edge of the stones and touched the nearest one. It was shorter than the others, its form twisted as if it were dancing. As she placed the tips of her fingers upon it and felt a warmth coming from within it. As she ran her hands over the rock's contours, she felt the surface was completely smooth. Though from a distance they appeared to have sharp edges, this turned out not to be so as each edge had a rounded finish. She stepped inside the stone circle and found herself continually drawn towards the blue pillar of light at its centre, edging slowly closer, stretching out her hand towards it. She put out a single trembling finger to touch the edge. The shaft of the light was transparent, enabling her to see the stones on the other side. She wondered what it was. A pure beam, of energy perhaps. Was it dangerous?

"It sings for us," came a voice from behind her. She whirled around to see Ubba, no longer quite so little after all his recent bravery, standing behind her, equally captivated. Only then did she remember she had paired herself with him, so she could hardly chaste him now for his curiosity to follow her.

"Is it Allah?" he asked. He joined her within the stone circle.

"I don't know. It's truly a beautiful thing at the centre of a garden of wonders." She turned her attention back towards the blue beam, uncertain of its intention or purpose but certain in her desire to know more, to reach out and touch it. She extended her finger toward it again.

"What are you doing? It could be dangerous!" Ubba cried with dismay. "We can't lose you! You're the only leader we have!" Ubba looked up at her with pleading eyes. She could see he feared for her life, yet he saw she was not afraid.

"Shall we find out together?" she said, holding a hand out to him. Ubba stared at her, unsure for a moment, then clasped his fingers around her own, gripping them tightly. The child looked nervous but then smiled, placing his total trust in her.

"Let us see where it takes us," Joy whispered, swallowing the lump in her throat. They stepped into the centre of the shaft of blue light. As they passed through the wall it broke around their bodies. Joy expected to feel something as she crossed into the middle of the incredible source of light, but she did not feel even the slightest tingle on her skin. The light dazzled her eyes, and she was forced to close them. Once she stepped into the centre, she was able to open them again with no irritation. She realised the tube of light formed only a thin circular wall around them. Together they stood in its core, like a fish in a water tank, as if they were looking through glass. Ubba never let go of her hand. Then after a few seconds Joy began to feel weightless. Her feet lifted off the floor and she looked down to see they were both floating, their feet were a few inches from the ground. Ubba still gripped her hand tighter. He looked at her and smiled. A bright flash then engulfed them both. It lit up the room with its beautiful hanging gardens and cascading pools of water. Then it was replaced with darkness.

Had Joy not been entirely focused on what she was doing, she would have seen that her actions had been witnessed by the children. Joy and Ubba entered the beam of light hand in hand, and for an instant they appeared frozen before the column shone brighter still, causing every child to look up. Jodie saw them both inside the light, looking at each other, floating, still holding hands. Then in a flash of light they vanished, leaving the light to sing to the remaining children alone.

TARIQ

As soon as he awoke, Tariq felt marginally better. His bandages had been freshly changed and his bloody clothing removed. Opening his eyes fully, he realised he was in bed in his apartment in Namur. He was thirsty and saw there was a pint glass of water next to the bed, which he consumed in seconds. To reach out to the glass caused him pain, but it was minor compared to what he'd experienced when riding his bike back to Belgium. He was also relieved to note his relentless sweats had broken. His body protested with more pain as he slowly sat up. Checking his bandages, he saw his bleeding was under control. He carefully felt the stitches beneath the fabric. She had done a good job.

"You were lucky. The wound wasn't so bad. You lost some blood, but you will fully recover."

It was Anna. She was wearing figure-hugging jeans and a grey hooded top, with her dark hair tied up and covered in a black hijab.

"How long have I been asleep?" he asked, carefully swinging his feet down to the floor.

" Almost two days," Anna said, adjusting something above his head. He saw that he was hooked up to an IV drip as she checked on it. She had been busy. Two days' rest had served his body well. He would be able to travel, but it would be prudent not to exert himself too much. He had lived to fight another day. Soon, he could plan his next operation, but he wondered at the fate of the others. What, if anything, could he do for them?

"I know what you're thinking. Don't. If the stitches come open again, you will start to bleed. The wound will heal but you need more rest. Here, take these. Two every four hours, three times a day. They will help you handle the pain."

She placed two huge white tablets in his palm, passing him a glass of water. He quickly downed the medication, struggling to swallow them because of their size. He hated taking tablets at the best of times.

"Eat some fruit. I have brought you some vitamins and other supplements which will help, but you must eat something solid."

Anna placed a bowl of oranges and black grapes in front of him. She had already peeled two of the oranges. He tore greedily into the segments, enjoying the taste of the sweet juices, quickly devouring them both, before moving onto the grapes. He was unbelievably famished. He had a craving for roasted goat's meat which he knew was not likely to be served anytime soon. Nursing was second nature to Anna, who placed another pillow behind him and refilled the glass of water. She was not supposed to contact him for another six months, but he found it hard to be annoyed with her.

"You should not have come. It is too dangerous," He said.

"After this operation, we knew life would never be the same for any of us. We all knew the risks," She replied.

True enough. He was relieved to see her again. In the short time he had known her, he had come to love her, but he couldn't show it. She had such conviction and determination. He had never met another woman of equal calibre. She was beautiful, it was true. Her big dark eyes were always intense, following you everywhere, but his interest had transcended far beyond merely the physical, during their many late night conversations about their hopes for the new world. He had said nothing about his feelings. He could not afford such distractions. She would have probably just laughed at any suggestion of romance between them. They were fighters for a greater cause than themselves, not Western children seeking a Hollywood ending. When he had taken on this role, he had always known that he could have no expectation of a normal life. Love, marriage, children, a house, a car and a regular job would never be within his grasp. Nor did he want such things. He knew his life in this world had to mean more than such trappings.

She sat down on the end of the bed.

"Mud is dead," she said, her voice devoid of sentiment. "They haven't identified him yet. He took several Police out with him. I think he managed to put his vest on."

Tariq had suspected as much, but thought Salim would have been the one to be caught.

"And Salim?" he asked.

"I haven't heard anything. His phone is off as instructed. I checked the email account and there is nothing from him. He might be okay. There's nothing on the news, not about him anyway."

It was only at the mention of the news that images came flooding back into Tariq's mind of the strange white star in the sky. Huge crystal-shaped objects, landing all over the world. Had he dreamed that? Didn't he see something on the front of newspapers somewhere? Headlines about an invasion? He could see Anna wanted to say something else.

"What is it?" he asked, hoping for no more bad news.

"In the email account. There's several messages from your handler, Abu. He says you should meet at the rendezvous, but this was yesterday and I thought it more important that you rest."

Abu Darus. He had been introduced to Tariq by a third party well over a year ago now. It was Abu who had first suggested that he had the means to provide a mainland European cell to achieve something really big. He had inside information on the movement of government officials in France and the UK, and access to weapons through his own extensive arms network. Abu's weapons dealing domain was much greater than the contacts Tariq had made when working for Executive Armor. It was Abu who had first informed them that the European Anti-Terrorism Conference was going to be held just outside Paris this month. Their original target was to have been the Defence Minister of France. He had only met Abu twice. A devout Muslim, he was said to have originated from Syria, where he had lost most of his family during the war, something which he blamed the Western World. He claimed to have direct contact with the ISIS leadership. It was his intelligence that made their mission possible. Once it was clear that the information on the movements of the French Minister was not forthcoming, Abu revealed he had come into possession of some other information which might provide a more tempting target - the flight details of the British Prime Minister's transport to and from the conference. Tariq's cell had been looking to pull off something spectacular, and this was too tempting a target to turn down. Such an operation would require the right weapons and considerable commitment from everyone involved. Abu had been able to set up a meeting with a Middle Eastern arms dealer, who provided the group with the stinger missile, giving them the means to bring down the plane. Tariq had planned the rest.

"Show me," he said, sitting up a little further as Anna passed him an iPad, with the inbox showing. He knew this account could already be compromised. It was set up only days earlier, especially for the operation. But now that they were on the run, anything was possible.

"Can you also put on the television?" Tariq had a television on top of the chest of drawers. He was keen to see the latest news on world events. Anna went to find the remote. He saw several emails from Abu, the headings of which read *Meet at midday as soon as possible*.

The only two meetings they had ever had with Abu had taken place in a warehouse in Brussels. It had been agreed that it could be used again as a place to return the weapon, should it remain unused. Abu would then buy the device back for half the price. The weapon had been used but he still wanted to meet. Why? Tariq didn't like it. The agreement had been no contact for at least six months unless... Salim? Salim might have been wounded during his escape. He might have reached out to Abu for assistance, but he could have only done so via the email account. Tariq could see there were three messages all with the same heading. One of them had previously been read by someone else logging into the account. He still did not open any of them.

"Did you open any of these emails?" he asked, knowing it unlikely.

"Of course not," Anna said, coming back in with the remote. She turned on the Al-Jazeera news channel, the most impartial of all the Western news stations, which was not saying much. He had not dreamed about the ships. Multiple images filled the screen, as a reporter covered a story from Nevada, America. The rolling text read: *The Mount Augusta Landing Massacre* in a huge red font.

A tearful reporter stood before the cameras with scores of ambulances flooding past her. Behind her, the white tower of the ship could be seen glowing in the night. Between it and her, was a vast army encampment that had barred the road towards the alien object. Beyond where she stood, there was a hive of activity. Medical personnel running in every direction, and voices shouting to be heard above the constant drone of passing helicopters. The reporter herself looked extremely upset.

"Turn the sound down for the moment. Let me think for a second." Anna obliged.

He checked the sent messages. Someone had read the first message that had come in, and sent back a message marked *received*. This was late yesterday, meaning the person would be looking to meet at midday today. Tariq could see the message was blank. Salim! It had to be. He was the only other person who had access to the account, or even knew of its existence, apart from Mud and the people in this room. But why would Abu ask to meet them so soon, when it would be so dangerous? Unless someone had got to him and forced him to turn the group over... Their previous contact had all been done through disposable phones that were long since destroyed. This account was the only means of communication left available between them. Tariq now regretted giving Abu the email address, but there was nothing he could do about that now. It had to be a trap, but Salim might have concluded he had ordered the rendezvous with Abu. Anna interrupted his thoughts.

"The world has changed while you were asleep. Two hundred of these objects have landed. All over the planet, including in the Middle-East. One of them has even landed in Syria. Our strike on the plane is the last item on the news already. America now has the biggest story. Their army fired at civilians at one of their landing sites in Nevada yesterday, that's what you're watching now. Everyone thought this was going to happen at their site straddling the border with Mexico, but it all happened on their own soil."

He was trying to take in what she was saying.

"Is the world being attacked?" he asked.

"There's been bloodshed, but not from the ships. People are missing, I think a few were killed in car accidents. The thing is, there's no aliens. No communication from them. Nothing. They've just landed and not moved. No one's come out to talk to anyone and no one can get in, but people have tried. American soldiers just killed over seventy of their own civilians, some of them children, at their site in Nevada. The Governor of Atlanta's niece was killed in the same incident. He has called for the President of the United States to be arrested for murder."

Murder? Tariq laughed. That idiot should have been arrested years ago. Several people had already tried and failed to get rid of him. He was nothing but a puppet for the military, arms and oil contractors. Still, if they were killing their own people live on television, maybe they would finally tear themselves apart. So much the better.

"Turn the sound up for a moment," he said.

Anna un-muted the television. Immediately sounds of chaos blared into the room, again. Sirens mingled with the shouts of desperate men, women and children. People could be heard sobbing and shouting in anger as the emergency services rushed to and from the scene. The reporter, in tears, looked on at the devastation behind her and back into the camera as she spoke. Tariq couldn't remember reporters being this emotional since 9/11.

"As we understand it, the death toll could now reach one hundred here at Mount Augusta. There's more ambulances arriving now and some belonging to the Military have just left. I heard some more gunshots only moments ago, but the Army have moved us back about another five hundred yards from when we first spoke to you in the studio."

Abruptly a hysterical woman pushed her way in front of the camera, her arms flailing wildly, jostling the reporter aside. She had red hair, and was, Tariq thought, in her late thirties. Her face was drained of colour.

"Are you live? Are you live?" she asked.

"Yes ma'am, we are... can you tell us what happened here earlier?" The reporter tried to get herself back in the shot, but the woman just shoved her aside again, looking straight into the camera.

"They shot my boy... they shot my boy!"

"Who shot your boy, ma'am?" the reporter said.

"Our fucking army, that's who? Are you listening Mr President? Are you? You killed people here today! Killed people who just wanted to see something wonderful! You might not have fired the gun, but you're a murderer, you hear me! You're a murderer!"

The camera re-focused on the reporter as two Police Officers dragged the screaming woman away. She yelled the name of her child but Tariq didn't catch it properly. The reporter tried to regain her composure as she stood back before the camera.

"As you can tell, emotions running extremely high here at Mount Augusta, where just over an hour ago, American Soldiers say they came under fire from a group of civilians who were trying to get closer to the ship. This area around the ship has been called a Zone of National Security. People have been warned to stay away, but as you can see John, that is becoming extremely difficult. This isn't like Roswell where one ship may have crashed, somewhere extremely remote that can easily be cordoned off, away from prying eyes. This is a structure over twenty miles wide, with a tower over six miles high, that can be seen from a considerable distance away. People want answers. Civilians here have been telling us that the soldiers fired first. What is not in doubt is that people are dead. We heard forty, then it was over sixty and now there are seventy-eight confirmed dead, including I believe, three members of the United States Armed Forces and several State Troopers. We're expecting a statement from the local Commander shortly, but people are being advised to stay away from the Mount Augusta landing site. As you can see behind me, this has had little effect and people are still arriving on the perimeter in their thousands…"

The camera panned round. Tariq saw a flood of vehicles sprawling out from either side of the road as if it was an encampment for a music festival.

"Turn it off."

Anna did so. She came and sat next to him. He studied her face. Her headscarf did little to hide her striking features. She was indeed extremely beautiful. If only they had lived in another time... He dismissed such thoughts. Perhaps this news might have something to do with the meeting. World events, it seemed, had superseded their own deeds. There was a new threat to the Western way of life, and it had come from outside the earth. It should not detract them from their goals or aims, in fact, this could be an opportunity. Perhaps Abu and Salim were thinking the same thing. He didn't like it, but he would have to go to the meeting. Best case scenario: Abu might have some more useful information because of world events. Worst case scenario: Salim was in danger. Either way, he could not stay in bed.

Anna had tried to talk him out of it. His name was not in the media yet, but how long would that last? Regardless, he would have to risk it. The meeting would be on the outskirts of central Brussels, an industrial area that had suited their previous exchange of arms well. But Tariq was taking no chances. He was going well armed. Two 9mm Sager pistols; one strapped to his leg and a second on his hip, which also had a silencer. He carried two combat knives, putting on body armour and knee pads, that would give him a greater sense of comfort should the need arise for a fight. He took out a Scorpion CV3 light sub-machine gun, hidden behind the boiler. It was small, easier to conceal than many other weapons, with a stock that folded along the side of the body. He'd always preferred AK-47 variants, but he had practised a great deal with this weapon and knew how to use it well. He had double-taped the thirty-round magazines and had over twenty of them. It was a risk travelling with this much weaponry. If they were stopped and searched, it would all be over, but then going to this meeting carried an equal risk. He knew he might have to fight his way out, so it was best to be prepared. With the weapons slung to his body, he wore a dark heavy overcoat, under which he wore a black suit and tie, with his body armour under the blazer. It was better to be dressed like a business-man, you always were given more respect from the authorities, and gener-ally avoided suspicion from the public. He had a second safe-house property, just north of Brussels city centre known only to him and Anna. If he was being led into a trap he would fight his way out and flee there. He had already stocked it with more supplies and kept its rental paperwork, like the others, separate, making it almost impossible to trace it to him. He was however acutely aware, even with the world facing an alien threat, that no expense would be spared in tracking down the members of his group. Now Mud had been identified, they would be trawling through all his known associates and would soon know they were looking for people who originated from the ghettos of Paris. Retribution would come, it was only a matter of when.

Salim had attended both of his previous meetings with Abu, but Anna had always been kept separate from the other cell members, so Abu wouldn't recognise her. Still, he wasn't about to send her in alone. He stocked up on painkillers and vitamins, almost overdosing on both before they left. He still felt the pain but he could function. In the bathroom, he had taken some industrial gaffer tape and wrapped it round the gauze dressing on top of his stitches. This would help hold his stitches in place while not ripping them out when he took it off. Crude but efficient.

"We will have to look as Westernised as possible. The world might be distracted by other events but we can't take the chance of getting stopped."

Anna let her hair down and did her makeup. Her bone structure was quite sharp and distinctive, making her easy on the eye and able to stand out in any crowd. Normally this was not an advantage, but sometimes it was better to be noticed for the right reasons when one wanted to travel without delay. She was a very light-skinned mixed-race girl and could have easily pass for Turkish or Italian. She had a Turkish passport, so it was just as well. He grabbed his dark glasses and a green baseball cap with *Bulgaria* written on the front. He could not recall how he had come to acquire it, but it was important to hide his face from traffic cameras, even when in the car. Anna wore similar designer glasses. Trendy over-sized frames that also had the advantage of covering much of her face.

"I don't suppose I can convince you not to come?" Tariq asked, knowing the question was pointless. Anna just looked at him, not even dignifying the question with an answer. She grabbed her car keys from the shelf.

"I'll drive," she said.

It took them less than two hours to reach the location. They only passed one police car on the way, and a small convoy of the Belgian Military, but no one was doing any checks. There had been some reports of looting in the city centre, as well as at a nearby Lidl, so Tariq knew the authorities had their hands full. The meeting was set to take place in the industrial area wedged between Anderlecht and Saint-Gilles, both of which had once been small towns in their own right. Now they were engulfed in the sprawling mess of the capital. They made good time, with the roads occasionally filled with traffic but always heading in the other direction, out of the city. Anna talked of a ship that had landed somewhere north east of Brussels. As they drove, they briefly caught sight of the white spire on the horizon.

Tariq could see people were confused. Anna commented on the cars fleeing the city to the south, "At first they thought it was the end of the world, and everyone wanted to run. Now there's rumours that the ground around the ships are changing. There's rumours of things growing in the soil. I don't know what to believe."

"If they contain anything valuable you can bet the Governments will try and keep it from the people."

"Of course they will."

"We shall have to find out more. It could be something we could use to our advantage." Tariq wondered how easy it would be to get onto one of the ships. He would investigate that another day.

The previous meeting had taken place in a small piece of open ground that was an unofficial car park for a small industrial estate, made up of four warehouses and a storage area for two dozen metal shipping containers. It was from one such container that they had taken delivery of the Stinger weapon. The place was just off the main road, among the many industrial units in the area. All the buildings had a uniform grey or white appearance.

The whole area was enclosed by wire mesh fences that lined the nearby roads, and a metal spiked fence that lined the access road into the estate. It was a discreet location with very little foot traffic. Even though their previous meetings had taken place at night on Sundays, there was unlikely to be anyone in at work today. The access road coming into the parking area was via a narrow turn-off from the parallel main two-lane artery road, nearby. Anna's car would not have been known to Abu Darus, but it would have been obvious to anyone waiting that Tariq or his team were likely to be the occupants in any vehicle arriving. They drove past the turn-off. It was 11.15am. They were still early, which was how he wanted it. They passed a flower seller in a nearby lay-by. Nothing unusual, except for the fact that Tariq had not seen them here before, and on a day like today people probably had better things to do than buy flowers, or indeed sell them. They stopped the car further up the road in the next lay-by. Tariq stroked his chin and looked around.

"I don't like it. We've only one way in or out by car. This place was good at night, but in the daytime, it seems like a death trap and that flower seller... Odd place to be selling flowers, especially today don't you think?"

"I see something that will give us an advantage. Drop me off here and give me twenty minutes to get into position," Anna said. He saw what had caught her eye.

He drove around for another twenty minutes, making sure he knew the fastest routes in and out of the city from here. If he had to flee on foot, his best bet would to be to make for the railway yards. There was a small footpath that ran past the back of the industrial estate. It would have been a good way to recon the place ahead of the meeting, but there was no time for that now. If he wanted to escape by car, he knew driving through the city centre was a no-go. He could easily be snarled up in traffic and a gun battle would get very messy. He pulled up on a side road near another warehouse and waited. His phone rang. It was Anna.

"Yes?"

"You're right. Something is wrong. I can see a car, an Audi."

"What colour?" Tariq remembered that Abu Darus' car on their last meeting was a dark blue Audi but he couldn't recall anything else.

"It's dark blue. Someone is in it. I can't tell who it is but he has a large beard. I've been watching him for five minutes. He hasn't moved. He hasn't even used his phone... and something else. He is not alone. I count five Tangos. There's two men in the warehouse behind his car, both armed and with radio headsets, just inside the doorway. There's two more just behind and to the left, from the entrance among the storage containers and a fifth, lying prone with a rifle, on the roof of one of the containers covering the entrance."

"Belgian police or Special Forces?" he asked.

"No. They're professionals but off the books. No uniforms. Weapons are top of the line. There could be more than I can see, but it looks like a small security force or tactical unit. They're wearing mostly light blue overalls, designed to look like workmen."

"Is Abu aware of them?" It was either an ambush, or at least their contact was taking no chances. But why not have your security more visible as a show of force? This sounded more like a welcoming committee.

"If he is, he's not giving anything away. Wait, I see a motorbike coming into the yard. Single rider."

A motorbike? Salim! Allah be praised. He was alive! Alive and… he would have to act now.

"It has to be Salim! Anna, target the one with the rifle first but hold your fire unless someone shoots first. I'm going in."

"We should just leave now…" Anna protested.

"Keep him in your sights. If we get split up we will meet where we agreed. I am dumping this phone." Tariq hung up. He would not leave Salim to such a fate. Tariq threw the phone out of the window and turned Anna's car around, speeding up back towards the roundabout, so he could come back down the dual carriageway to the entrance of the industrial park. He passed the flower stall on the other side, noticing it was now unoccupied. Tariq put his foot down on the accelerator, and went as fast as he dared, not wanting to attract undue attention. He came back around and roared down to the turn-off, kicking up gravel as he turned right into the access road. Instantly, ahead of him he saw two men, both armed, running towards the park. They turned simultaneously at the sound of his car and began firing. Rounds impacted the car body, as he put his foot hard on the accelerator, increasing speed. The man on the left dived off the road into the fence that ran along the side. Tariq went for the one on the right, who was levelling his weapon at his head, putting the car straight into him, dragging him underneath. The car bumped and jounced. The second man fired his weapon, two rounds went into the rear of the Peugeot, miraculously missing the windows.

Tariq pulled into the open industrial forecourt, and saw the motorbike parked up next to the dark blue Audi, the rider already dismounting. It had to be Salim, he knew the model and colour of his bike and it was identical in every respect. Slamming on the brakes, he brought the car to a halt, causing it to turn side on, affording him the best cover. He heard the muffled sounds of bullets hitting the metalwork of the car, as he opened the door. He pulled the pin from a grenade that he tossed high into the air as he stepped out of the car. It went up and behind him. He knew there would be two men there, according to Anna, and they were its intended targets. The two men clad in overalls were already moving to shoot the occupant of the bike, when his unexpected arrival startled them and blocked their line of sight. The men fired a single burst from their weapons at the car, then they both stopped, noticing one of their colleagues pinned under the front of the Peugeot. Neither man fired again, both turning and running in separate directions. The grenade exploded as it came back down, sending shrapnel in all directions, peppering one man in the back and catching the second in the legs. Tariq heard two more rifle shots at the same time, one hitting the ground, close by. Anna had started firing. He focused on the injured two men behind him, and brought his weapon to bear, firing two well-aimed shots at the one wounded in the legs first, putting one in his shoulder and the second in his head. He collapsed and didn't move, his overalls awash with blood. The man with the back wounds reached for his weapon. Tariq put two rounds into his body to make sure he didn't get up, either. Bullets began to tear into the Peugeot from the other side, clanging into the metal-work. Two more men were positioned among the shipping containers opposite the entrance, and firing at him, while the two in the doorway of the main warehouse were firing at the Audi. Tariq could see the rider of the motorcycle had been hit but he was still moving, trying to get under cover behind the Audi. Another gunshot echoed and one of the men in the ware-house doorway dropped to the ground, killed instantly by the unseen sniper. The second retreated inside. Hearing the rifle fire, the men among the containers stepped back into the gaps between them, attempting to conceal themselves, while trying to ascertain the location of the shooter.

Two blocks from the industrial estate stood a single yellow crane on an empty building site. Anna had guessed that positioning herself on the structure would afford her an overview of the entire location. When it came to long-range marksmanship, she was a better shot than anyone Tariq knew. The men hiding between the containers were, however, now out of her line of sight. A second shot fired into the warehouse. Tariq couldn't see from here if she'd hit the target or not, but the weapons fire from the containers intensified around the Audi. The motorcycle rider had crawled round the back of it and was bleeding from a wound to his leg.

"Salim! Stay down! Don't move! I'm coming for you!" Tariq shouted at the rider.

The figure on the ground turned and gave Tariq a thumbs-up. Tariq saw the rifle of one of the men he had killed lying on the ground, a few yards away. The weapons of all of their assailants appeared to be suppressed AK-9s, an assault rifle normally only available to Russian Special Forces. This was a professional, well-equipped hit squad and they were not here to take prisoners. Anna's rifle was not suppressed so it would echo each time it fired. She was being frugal, trying to make every shot count. The explosion from Tariq's grenade would have also attracted attention. One or two rifle shots might be dismissed as a car back-firing, but a grenade going off, not a chance. They were in an underpopulated industrial area, but the noise was bound to be reported. The clock once again was ticking. Darting his head around the car, Tariq snatched a glimpse of the men firing. They had moved apart and were aiming left and right of the Audi from between the containers. He knelt down behind the Peugeot and steadied himself, taking a breath and then rolled out of cover, lying prone as he did so. His wound protested and he felt a sharp jab of pain in his stomach. He was exposed to the man who was 100 yards in front of him, but that man was focused on Salim, not on him. He aimed and fired, the bullet tearing through the man's throat. He fell, clutching at it. Tariq fired twice more, the first tearing through the sole of his army-issue boot, the second in his groin. The man was down.

There was a sound of grinding metal, as the large warehouse door was crashed open by a dirty, white removal van that swerved towards the entrance. Tariq jumped to his feet, forgetting that the second man among the containers would have a clear shot at him. He clicked his weapon to full auto, emptying the rest of his clip into the van windscreen, shattering the glass. The driver turned the wheel furiously. Another crack from Anna's rifle and Tariq caught a man's cranial explosion in his peripheral vision. The remaining man among the containers had stepped out from his cover, to draw a better bead on Tariq and unknowingly exposed himself to Anna's sights. She took him down with a single shot. The van crashed into the metal fence on the corner of the courtyard, by the entrance. Tariq wasn't sure if he had hit the driver or not, but he needed to check on Salim. He ran over to the Audi, stealing a glance into the warehouse on the right. He could clearly see the body of another assailant. He was not moving. He reached the figure at the back of the Audi. He was hit but the wound looked superficial.

"I'm okay," came a muffled voice under the helmet.

Tariq carefully removed it and was greeted by the sight of Salim's thick, black curly hair and handsome face smiling back at him. He had had the wind knocked out of him, but otherwise seemed okay.

"Wow, all those hours I spent playing Call of Duty are really starting to pay off, huh?" he joked. They both laughed for a moment, catching their breaths.

"Where are you hit?" Tariq looked for the source of the wound and saw blood was seeping from a gash on Salim's leg.

"It was a ricochet, off the car. It's nothing. I still have my body armour on. Help me up. We need to get out of here!" Salim said. Tariq pulled his friend to his feet.

"Wait. Abu?" Tariq glanced at their contact who was slumped inside the Audi. He had taken several rounds to his body and one in the side of his head, but then Tariq noticed the knife wound across his throat. The bullet wounds must have happened during the firefight.

"That pig! He betrayed us! He was dead when I got here. Someone got to him first, which means they know about us," Salim said, pointing at the neck injury.

"It is good to see you, brother. Allah is merciful," Tariq said. They hugged but this was no time for celebrations or sharing of stories.

"We will talk later, we need to move. You check the van, I will search Abu and these men. Look for ID, a phone, wallet, anything."

Tariq reloaded his weapon and searched Abu for his ID but the man had nothing on him, not even a phone or money. He must have been killed well before they arrived, because the blood from the neck wound had long since congealed. Tariq doubted they could get any of their attackers to talk. These men were well-trained professionals and wouldn't crack easily. Besides, they didn't have time for that kind of interrogation. Tariq looked over at the two dead men by the containers. In the distance somewhere, Police Sirens could now be heard. He saw the footpath that ran along the back of the industrial complex, with a gate accessing it. They could get the bike along that on foot, and then out if they had to. The Peugeot was drive-able, but it had several rounds in the bodywork and a broken rear wind-screen. That would get them pulled over. He checked on the man who had been pinned under the front of the Peugeot. He was dead. Tariq ran over to the bodies by the containers. Each had a radio headset and spare ammunition in a maintenance belt, but no phones or ID. As he searched their clothing he noted a very distinctive tattoo on the arm of one of the men, depicting a winged skull being pierced by a bayonet. He made a mental note of it, cursing himself for not having a phone with which to take a photograph.

"Tariq – Over here!" Salim shouted. He jumped out of the van holding up a phone.

"Look!" he shouted, pleased with his find, hurrying back over to the bike.

The sirens were getting louder. They could only have a minute or two at most. They had to leave. Then Tariq saw a movement behind Salim, a limping figure coming up the path.

"Salim!" he shouted, but it was too late. Neither of them had seen the gunman approaching up the access road. It was the man Tariq had missed as he was coming in. He was already aiming at Salim when a muffled burst of gunfire came. Salim's smile vanished as he dropped to the ground. Tariq ran back towards the Audi, firing as he did so but he was wide of the target. Salim rolled around on the ground, this time completely exposed, caught between the access gate and the side of the van. He turned and fired at his assailant, but missed, as the man had dropped to one knee, firing again. Tariq saw a round hit his friend's neck snapping Salim's head back, a spray of blood lashed across the dirt behind him. A distant shot rang out and the man's head exploded, dark brain matter evacuating the back of his skull. Tariq knew Anna's shot had found her mark, but his friend would not be getting up. His eyes darted about feverishly, searching for further targets. He knew there could be more men that he hadn't seen, and time was pressing. He had to get away and quickly. Keeping his weapon ready, he ran towards his friend. As he reached his body, he could see blood pouring from his mouth. He had been hit three times, twice on his body armour and once in his neck just above the collar bone. There was little he could do for him without proper medical support. There was no time now for grief.

"Go brother... I will see you in Paradise..." Salim whispered. Life was fading fast from his eyes but Tariq knew he shouldn't feel guilty. They had achieved a great victory. Whatever happened afterwards was Allah's will, yet he did feel as though the life of this teenager had been his responsibility. He had, in his own way, become family to him. Tariq cradled Salim's head and smiled at the boy, whose fingers dug into his arm with dwindling strength.

"Travel well, brother," Tariq said as he slit the boy's windpipe with his knife, and held him tight as his body jerked with the last seconds of life. He closed the boy's eyes and double-checked his body for ID. He took Salim's fake driving license. Scooping up his helmet from the ground, he took a moment to clean his knife and placed it back in its sheath. He wanted to take one of the weapons from the assassination team. Suppressed automatic weapons of this type would be extremely hard to come by and very handy in a confrontation. They would sell for a fortune on the black market, but it was too risky. They would be all too easily traced for one thing, and he couldn't take Anna's car. Concealing large weapons while riding a motorbike was a tricky proposition. He dumped what he didn't need, making sure he left nothing that could be traced to him. He placed his hand under the driving seat of the Peugeot, and found the switch to the explosive device that had been placed there for such an eventuality. He put Salim's body in the car, taking the mobile that he had discovered in the van. He wasn't sure if the unit had employed recorded surveillance of any kind. There could be material in the white van, but there was no time to check it. After moving the motorcycle under cover, he pulled the pin on his last grenade and rolled it into the back of the van before running behind the Audi. There was a tremendous explosion. Tariq felt hot fragments pepper the body of the car. Fire greedily engulfed the vehicle, spewing a spiral of black smoke that began to trail skyward, a secondary explosion from the vehicle was almost inevitable.

The sirens grew louder, it was time to go. He mounted the motorcycle, noting it had nearly a full tank of gas, and fortunately had only superficial damage. Good. He didn't want to be in that situation again. The adrenaline that had been keeping him alert began to leave his body. The pain from his wound was returning, making him wince as he mounted the vehicle. With the roar of the van exploding once more behind him, he made good his escape via the footpath, crossing the railway tracks and disappearing into the back-streets of Brussels.

Tariq's safe-house in Brussels was in the northern suburb of Laken. He also owned properties in Schaerbeek, which had a heavy Muslim population and was known to be sympathetic to anti-Western ideals. It was equally riddled with informants. It was not unheard of for people to betray their own family to stay on the side of the authorities, especially if cash rewards were offered. Tariq did not, however, wait until he got to Laken to check the phone that Salim had retrieved. Phones could be traced, and it would only be a matter of minutes before whoever had sent in the hit squad realised they had failed in their mission. He needed to examine it now, and then get rid of it. He crossed over the canal into Anderlecht and then travelled north, keeping parallel with the canal and found a place to stop. A small retail warehouse complex provided the perfect spot, without attracting attention. It had a car park for several shops, where he could park up and examine the phone without attracting any undue attention. As he lifted his visor he saw the distant black clouds of smoke to the east. He was now over a mile away from the scene of the firefight. Multiple sirens could be heard coming from that direction. He smiled, knowing they would be in for surprise shortly.

The phone was the latest Samsung and had still been left on. Someone must have been about to use it, when they dropped it or were shot. It saved him the trouble of taking it somewhere and having it hacked. Abu Darus had either set them up to be killed, or someone had double-crossed him, hoping to take them out at the same time. But none of these theories made much sense. Abu was an arms dealer with Muslim sympathies and a good reputation, according to the checks that Mud had carried out on him. It was true that he had not known about their intended target, but could have worked that out easily enough, as he'd also provided them with the intelligence information. Stinger missiles were not sold in abundance on the black market, so someone else on Abu's team could have put it all together and betrayed them. The British would know by now that it was a Stinger missile that brought down their plane, so they would have been searching for anyone selling them on the black market. But why kill Abu? That didn't make sense... He would be of far greater value to British Intelligence alive. His contacts alone would be invaluable. How had they got to him? He knew the man to be cautious, and never went anywhere without an armed escort. He had turned up at the meeting alone, which Tariq concluded could have only meant one thing – someone forced him to come against his will and then set the meeting in motion. It was possible he may not have even been killed at the location. His body could have been brought there afterwards, and left in the car. He may not have even sent the emails to arrange the meet in the first place. He was certain of only one thing, whoever was behind this wanted them all dead and had Eastern-European connections. The men had been speaking to each other in Russian, a language he knew well enough to recognise. Only one number had called the phone several times over the last three days, and that number had been withheld. However one number had been dialled out that morning. Tariq knew the code which preceded it meant the call was made to a mobile number in the United Kingdom. That was odd, considering this was a Russian team with Russian hardware. The hit on them had been clandestine in nature. The local Police had not been involved, no one tried to identify themselves or make an arrest. It was Black Ops or something like it. He could call the number and see who answered. Holding onto the phone was risky. He had to get rid of it as soon as possible. He could keep the SIM card after making the call. Yes, that would be prudent. He dialled the number. The phone rang three times before it was answered, Tariq could hear other English voices in the background, several of them talking at once in a meeting.

"I told you not to call me on this number before seven o'clock. Is it done?"

There was a moment of silence. Tariq had heard the voice before, but he wasn't sure when or where. English accent, educated, well-spoken, precise, clearly a man with a military background. He would not be easily rattled, but Tariq felt certain this call was unlikely to be recorded. Tariq was angry. Salim did not need to die, he could have been a greater martyr still. This man was responsible. He said his reply without thinking.

"Your team are all dead. When I find you, you will be next."

He hung up before the man could respond. Tariq removed the SIM card from the phone, and placed it in his pocket. He rode his bike over to the canal and tossed the phone into the water just as a loud *boom* echoed across city. A huge fireball plumed into the sky over to the east. The bomb in Anna's car had exploded, hopefully, he thought, taking more of the Western infidels with it. He put his visor down and raced off, heading north, hoping he would see Anna when he arrived in Leken.

RYAN

"Anything important, General Spears?" Ryan asked, as the General returned to sit down at the table, popping his mobile back in his pocket.

"We might have a new lead on the terror cell who brought down the plane in Paris. I shall have more details in the intelligence briefing for you all tomorrow."

The General sounded confident. Good, Ryan wanted him to be. He wanted to nail those bastards to the wall. All of them. Ryan was pleased to know someone was still on the case with David's murder. He had been so consumed with his new responsibilities, he hadn't been able to give it much thought in the last seventy-two hours.

"It is good to know you're keeping on top of that, General. The French don't seem to be getting anywhere with it. With everything else going on in the world, I don't want everyone here to forget we lost several our own people only three days ago. Those responsible must be brought to justice!" He stood, addressing the whole room.

"Of course, Prime Minister," General Spears replied, while sending a text.

Ryan had been very dissatisfied with the lack of leads, shooting a look at the Metropolitan Police Chief, as well as Julie Compston from MI5. Both looked away, checking their reports. Not only had they failed to find any new leads for him on events in Paris, but there seemed very little background intelligence on the group responsible coming from the French authorities.

"I want some bloody new leads on the group who attacked us in

France, and I want them today! Is that understood, everyone? We might have a global catastrophe looming, but let's not forget those responsible for David's death are still out there."

General Spears stood, putting his hand on Ryan's shoulder as he spoke.

"You can be rest assured I am pursuing every possible course of action, Prime Minister. David was a friend to us all. Nothing would make me happier than to see his killers brought swiftly to justice."

Ryan didn't notice the General's blank expression as he said those reassuring words, but Julie Compston did. It was her job to notice such things.

"Right, well… yes. I know we're all tired. Just keep at it everyone."

Ryan was five days into the job with almost no sleep. He was exhausted. He had taken over running the country in a power vacuum that no one had foreseen, was dealing with both a national and international crisis that was even less foreseeable, he was surrounded by people who wanted his job, he'd given up his lover and hadn't taken a line of cocaine in seventy two hours, or thereabouts. He would need to check the actual time to be sure, but the United Kingdom was still standing, he was still standing, just about. He had never felt more pulled apart in all his life. With the last of those required for Cobra having arrived, General Spears pulled out a seat for him at the head of the table. Everyone waited for him to sit.

"Right, let's get on with it everyone, shall we? We have a country to run and an alien dilemma to solve," Ryan said with a degree of improving confidence. He was actually beginning to warm to this job.

The story continues in Diamonds in the Sky, Book Two coming in 2018…

28410007R00311

Printed in Great Britain
by Amazon